# MAISIE DOBBS

# BIRDS OF
# A FEATHER

# MAISIE DOBBS

# BIRDS OF A FEATHER

## Two Novels

## JACQUELINE WINSPEAR

Quality Paperback Book Club
New York

# MAISIE DOBBS

$\mathcal{T}$his book is dedicated to the memory of
my paternal grandfather and my maternal grandmother

JOHN "JACK" WINSPEAR sustained serious leg wounds during the Battle of the Somme in July 1916. Following convalescence, he returned to his work as a costermonger in southeast London.

CLARA FRANCES CLARK, née Atterbury, was a munitions worker at the Woolwich Arsenal during the First World War. She was partially blinded in an explosion that killed several girls working in the same section alongside her. Clara later married and became the mother of ten children.

Now, he will spend a few sick years in institutes,
And do what things the rules consider wise,
And take whatever pity they may dole.
Tonight he noticed how the women's eyes
Passed from him to the strong men that were whole.
How cold and late it is! Why don't they come
And put him to bed? Why don't they come?

Final verse "Disabled," by Wilfred Owen. It was drafted at Craiglockhart, a hospital for shell-shocked officers, in October 1917. Owen was killed on November 4, 1918, just one week before the armistice.

SPRING 1929

# CHAPTER ONE

ven if she hadn't been the last person to walk through the turnstile at Warren Street tube station, Jack Barker would have noticed the tall, slender woman in the navy blue, thigh-length jacket with a matching pleated skirt short enough to reveal a well-turned ankle. She had what his old mother would have called "bearing." A way of walking, with her shoulders back and head held high, as she pulled on her black gloves while managing to hold on to a somewhat battered black document case.

"Old money," muttered Jack to himself. "Stuck-up piece of nonsense."

Jack expected the woman to pass him by, so he stamped his feet in a vain attempt to banish the sharp needles of cold creeping up through his hobnailed boots. He fanned a half dozen copies of the *Daily Express* over one arm, anticipating a taxi-cab screeching to a halt and a hand reaching out with the requisite coins.

"Oh, stop—may I have an *Express* please, love?" appealed a voice as smooth as spooned treacle.

The newspaper vendor looked up slowly, straight into eyes the color of midnight in summer, an intense shade that seemed to him to be darker than blue. She held out her money.

"O' course, Miss, 'ere you are. Bit nippy this morning, innit?"

She smiled, and as she took the paper from him before turning to walk away, she replied, "Not half. It's brass monkey weather; better get yourself a nice cuppa before too long."

Jack couldn't have told you why he watched the woman walk all the way down Warren Street toward Fitzroy Square. But he did know one thing: She might have bearing, but from the familiar way she spoke to him, she certainly wasn't from old money.

At the end of Warren Street, Maisie Dobbs stopped in front of the black front door of a somewhat rundown Georgian terraced house, tucked the *Daily Express* under her left arm, carefully opened her document case, and took out an envelope containing a letter from her landlord and two keys. The letter instructed her to give the outside door a good shove after turning the key in the lock, to light the gas lamp at the base of the stairs carefully, to mind the top step of the first flight of stairs—which needed to be looked at—and to remember to lock her own door before leaving in the evening. The letter also told her that Billy Beale, the caretaker, would put up her nameplate on the outside door if she liked or, it suggested, perhaps she would prefer to remain anonymous.

Maisie grinned. I need the business, she said to herself. I'm not here to remain anonymous.

Maisie suspected that Mr. Sharp, the landlord, was unlikely to live up to his name, and that he would pose questions with obvious answers each time they met. However, his directions were apt: The door did indeed need a shove, but the gas lamp, once lit, hardly dented the musky darkness of the stairwell. Clearly there were some things that needed to be changed, but all in good time. For the moment Maisie had work to do, even if she had no actual cases to work on.

Minding the top step, Maisie turned right on the landing and headed straight for the brown painted door on the left, the one with a frosted glass window and a To Let sign hanging from the doorknob. She removed the sign, put the key into the lock, opened the door, and took a deep breath before stepping into her new office. It was a single room with a gas fire, a gas lamp on each wall, and one sash window with a view of the building across the street and the rooftops beyond. There was an oak desk with a matching chair of dubious stability, and an old filing cabinet to the right of the window.

Lady Rowan Compton, her patron and former employer, had been correct; Warren Street wasn't a particularly salubrious area. But if she played her cards right, Maisie could afford the rent and have some money left over from the sum she had allowed herself to take from her savings. She didn't want a fancy office, but she didn't want an out-and-out dump either. No, she wanted something in the middle, something for everyone, something central, but then again not in the thick of things. Maisie felt a certain comfort in this small corner of Bloomsbury. They said that you could sit down to tea with just about anyone around Fitzroy Square, and dine with a countess and a carpenter at the same table, with both of them at ease in the company. Yes, Warren Street would be good for now. The tricky thing was going to be the nameplate. She still hadn't solved the problem of the nameplate.

As Lady Rowan had asked, "So, my dear, what will you call yourself? I mean, we all know what you do, but what will be your trade name? You can hardly state the obvious. 'Finds missing people, dead or alive, even when it's themselves they are looking for' really doesn't cut the mustard. We have to think of something succinct, something that draws upon your unique talents."

"I was thinking of 'Discreet Investigations,' Lady Rowan. What do you think?"

"But that doesn't tell anyone about how you use your mind, my dear—what you actually do."

"It's not really my mind I'm using, it's other people's. I just ask the questions."

"Poppycock! What about 'Discreet Cerebral Investigations'?"

Maisie smiled at Lady Rowan, raising an eyebrow in mock dismay at the older woman's suggestion. She was at ease, seated in front of the fireplace in her former employer's library, a fireplace she had once cleaned with the raw, housework-roughened hands of a maid in service.

"No, I'm not a brain surgeon. I'm going to think about it for a bit, Lady Rowan. I want to get it right."

The gray-haired aristocrat leaned over and patted Maisie on the knee. "I'm sure that whatever you choose, you will do very well, my dear. Very well indeed."

So it was that when Billy Beale, the caretaker, knocked on the door one week after Maisie moved into the Warren Street office, asking if there was a nameplate to put up at the front door, Maisie handed him a brass plate bearing the words "M. Dobbs. Trade and Personal Investigations."

"Where do you want it, Miss? Left of the door or right of the door?"

He turned his head very slightly to one side as he addressed her. Billy was about thirty years old, just under six feet tall, muscular and strong, with hair the color of sun-burnished wheat. He seemed agile, but worked hard to disguise a limp that Maisie had noticed immediately.

"Where are the other names situated?"

"On the left, Miss, but I wouldn't put it there if I were you."

"Oh, and why not, Mr. Beale?"

"Billy. You can call me Billy. Well, people don't really look to the left, do they? Not when they're using the doorknob, which is on the right. That's where the eyes immediately go when they walk up them steps, first to that lion's 'ead door knocker, then to the knob, which is on the right. Best 'ave the plate on the right. That's if you want their business."

"Well, Mr. Beale, let's have the plate on the right. Thank you."

"Billy, Miss. You can call me Billy."

Billy Beale went to fit the brass nameplate. Maisie sighed deeply and rubbed her neck at the place where worry always sat when it was making itself at home.

"Miss . . . ."

Billy poked his head around the door, tentatively knocking at the glass as he removed his flat cap.

"What is it, Mr. Beale?"

"Billy, Miss. Miss, can I have a quick word?"

"Yes, come in. What is it?"

"Miss, I wonder if I might ask a question? Personal, like." Billy continued without waiting for an answer. "Was you a nurse? At a casualty clearing station? Outside of Bailleul?"

Maisie felt a strong stab of emotion, and instinctively put her right hand to her chest, but her demeanor and words were calm.

"Yes. Yes, I was."

"I knew it!" said Billy, slapping his cap across his knee. "I just knew it the minute I saw those eyes. That's all I remember, after they brought me in. Them eyes of yours, Miss. Doctor said to concentrate on looking at something while 'e worked on me leg. So I looked at your eyes, Miss. You and 'im saved my leg. Full of shrapnel, but you did it, didn't you? What was 'is name?"

For a moment, Maisie's throat was paralyzed. Then she swallowed hard. "Simon Lynch. Captain Simon Lynch. That must be who you mean."

"I never forgot you, Miss. Never. Saved my life, you did."

Maisie nodded, endeavoring to keep her memories relegated to the place she had assigned them in her heart, to be taken out only when she allowed.

"Well, Miss. Anything you ever want doing, you just 'oller. I'm your man. Stroke of luck, meeting up with you again, innit? Wait till I tell the missus. You want anything done, you call me. Anything."

"Thank you. Thank you very much. I'll holler if I need anything. Oh, and Mr. . . . . Billy, thank you for taking care of the sign."

Billy Beale blushed and nodded, covered his burnished hair with his cap, and left the office.

Lucky, thought Maisie. Except for the war, I've had a lucky life so far. She sat down on the dubious oak chair, slipped off her shoes and rubbed at her feet. Feet that still felt the cold and wet and filth and blood of France. Feet that hadn't felt warm in twelve years, since 1917.

She remembered Simon, in another life, it seemed now, sitting under a tree on the South Downs in Sussex. They had been on leave at the same time, not a miracle of course, but difficult to arrange, unless you had connections where connections counted. It was a warm day, but not one that took them entirely away from the fighting, for they could still hear the deep echo of battlefield cannonade from the other side of the English Channel, a menacing sound not diminished by the intervening expanse of land and sea. Maisie had complained then that the damp of France would never leave her, and Simon, smiling, had pulled off her walking shoes to rub warmth into her feet.

"Goodness, woman, how can anyone be that cold and not be dead?"

They both laughed, and then fell silent. Death, in such times, was not a laughing matter.

# CHAPTER TWO

*T*he small office had changed in the thirty days since Maisie had taken up occupancy. The desk had been moved and was now positioned at an angle to the broad sash window, so that from her chair Maisie could look up and out over the rooftops as she worked. A very sophisticated black telephone sat on top of the desk, at the insistence of Lady Rowan, who maintained that "No one, simply no one, can expect to do business without a telephone. It is essential, positively essential." As far as Maisie was concerned, what was essential was that the trilling of its authoritative ring be heard a bit more often. Billy Beale had also taken to suggesting improvements lately.

"Can't have folk up 'ere for business without offering 'em a cuppa the ol' char, can you, Miss? Let me open up that cupboard, put in a burner, and away you go. Bob's yer uncle, all the facilities for tea. What d'you think, Miss? I can nip down the road to my mate's carpentry shop for the extra wood, and run the gas along 'ere for you. No trouble."

"Lovely, Billy. That would be lovely."

Maisie sighed. It seemed that everyone else knew what would be best for her. Of course their hearts were in the right place, but what she needed most now was some clients.

"Shall I advance you the money for supplies, Billy?"

"No money needed," said Billy, winking and tapping the side of his nose with his forefinger. "Nod's as good as a wink to a blind 'orse, if you know what I mean, Miss."

Maisie raised an eyebrow and allowed herself a grin. "I know exactly what that saying means, Billy: What I don't see, I shouldn't worry about."

"You got it, Miss. Leave it to me. Two shakes of a lamb's tail, and you'll be ready to receive your visitors in style."

Billy replaced his cap, put a forefinger to the peak to gesture his departure, and closed the door behind him. Leaning back in her chair, Maisie rubbed at tired eyes and looked over the late afternoon rooftops. She watched as the sun drifted away to warm the shores of another continent, leaving behind a rose tint to bathe London at the end of a long day.

Looking again at her handwritten notes, Maisie continued rereading a draft of the report she was in the midst of preparing. The case in question was minor, but Maisie had learned the value of detailed note taking from Maurice Blanche. During her apprenticeship with him, he had been insistent that nothing was to be left to memory, no stone to remain unturned, and no small observation uncataloged. Everything, absolutely *everything,* right down to the color of the shoes the subject wore on the day in question, must be noted. The weather must be described, the direction of the wind, the flowers in bloom, the food eaten. Everything must be described and preserved. "You must write it down, absolutely and in its entirety, write it down," instructed her mentor. In fact, Maisie thought that if she had a shilling for every time she heard the words, "absolutely, and in its entirety," she would never have to work again.

Maisie rubbed her neck once more, closed the folder on her desk, and stretched her arms above her head. The doorbell's deep clattering ring broke the silence. At first Maisie thought that someone had pulled the bell handle in error. There had been few rings since Billy installed the new device, which sounded in Maisie's office. Despite the fact that Maisie had worked with Maurice Blanche and had taken over his practice when he retired at the age of seventy-six, establishing her name independent of Maurice was proving to be a challenge indeed. The bell rang again.

Maisie pressed her skirt with her hands, patted her head to tame any stray tendrils of hair, and hurried downstairs to the door.

"Good. . . ." The man hesitated, then consulted a watch that he drew from his waistcoat pocket, as if to ascertain the accurate greeting for the time of day. "Good evening. My name is Davenham, Christopher Davenham. I'm here to see Mr. Dobbs. I have no appointment, but was assured that he would see me."

He was tall, about six feet two inches by Maisie's estimate. Fine tweed suit, hat taken off to greet her at just the right moment, but repositioned quickly. Good leather shoes, probably buffed to a shine by his manservant. *The Times* was rolled up under one arm, but with a sheet or two of writing paper coiled inside and just visible. His own notes, thought Maisie. His jet black hair was swept back and oiled, and his moustache neatly trimmed. Christopher Davenham was about forty-two or forty-three. Only seconds had passed since his introduction, but Maisie had him down. This one had not been a soldier. In a protected profession, she suspected.

"Come this way, Mr. Davenham. There are no appointments set for this evening, so you are in luck."

Maisie led the way up to her office, and invited Christopher Davenham to sit in the new guest chair opposite her own, the chair that had been delivered just last week by Lady Rowan's chauffeur. Another gift to help her business along.

Davenham looked around for a moment, expecting someone else to step out to meet him, but instead the young woman introduced herself.

"Maisie Dobbs. At your service, Mr. Davenham." She waved her hand toward the chair again. "Do please take a seat, Mr. Davenham. Now then, first tell me how you came to have my name."

Christopher Davenham hid his surprise well, taking a linen

handkerchief from his inside pocket and coughing lightly into it. The handkerchief was so freshly laundered and ironed that the folds were still knife sharp. Davenham refolded the handkerchief along the exact lines pressed by the iron, and replaced it in his pocket.

"Miss, er, Dobbs. Well, um, well . . . you have been highly recommended by my solicitor."

"Who is?"

Maisie leaned her head to one side to accentuate the question, and to move the conversation onto more fertile ground.

"Oh, um, Blackstone and Robinson. Joseph Robinson."

Maisie nodded. Lady Rowan again. Joseph Robinson had been her personal legal adviser for forty-odd years. And he didn't suffer fools gladly unless they were paying him—and paying him well.

"Been the family solicitor for years. I'll be frank with you, Miss Dobbs. I'm surprised to see you. Thought you were a chap. But Robinson knows his stuff, so let's continue."

"Yes, let's, Mr. Davenham. Perhaps you would tell me why you are here."

"My wife."

Maisie's stomach churned. Oh, Lord, after all her training, her education, her successes with Maurice Blanche, had it come to this? A love triangle? But she sat up to listen carefully, remembering Blanche's advice: "The extraordinary hides behind the camouflage of the ordinary. Assume nothing, Maisie."

"And what about your wife, Mr. Davenham?"

"I believe . . . I believe her affections are engaged elsewhere. I have suspected it for some time and now, Miss Dobbs, I must know if what I suspect is true."

Maisie leaned back in her chair and regarded Christopher Davenham squarely. "Mr. Davenham, first of all, I must tell you that I will have to ask you some questions. They may not be questions that are easy or comfortable for you to answer. I will have questions about your responses, and even questions about your questions. That is my job. I am unique in what I do. I am also unique in what I charge for my service."

"Money is not a problem, Miss Dobbs."

"Good. The questions may be, though."

"Do continue."

"Mr. Davenham, please tell me what personal evidence you have to suspect that your wife is betraying your marriage in any way?"

"Tuesdays and Thursdays, every week, without fail, she leaves the house immediately after I have departed for my office, and returns just in time to welcome me home."

"Mr. Davenham, time away from the house is no reason for you to suspect that you are being deceived."

"The lies are, though."

"Go on." Maisie wrote in her notebook without taking her eyes off Davenham, a skill that unnerved him.

"She has told me that she has been shopping, visiting friends or her mother—and upon investigation I find that if such visits have occurred, they have taken only an hour or so. Clearly they are a smokescreen."

"There are other possibilities, Mr. Davenham. Could your wife, perhaps, be visiting her physician? Is she undertaking a course of study? What other reasons for her absences have you explored in your investigations, Mr. Davenham? Such absences may have a completely innocent explanation."

"Miss Dobbs. Surely that is for you to find out? Follow her, and you will see that I am right."

"Mr. Davenham. To follow a person is an invasion of the right of that individual to privacy. If I take on this case—and I do have a choice in the matter—I am taking on more than the question of who did what and when. I am taking on a responsibility for both you and your wife in a way that you may not have considered. Tell me, what will you do with the information I provide?"

"Well, I . . . I'll use it. It will be a matter for my solicitor."

Maisie placed her hands together in front of her face, just touching her nose, as if in prayer. "Let me ask you another question. What value do you place on your marriage?"

"What sort of question is that?"

"A question to be answered, if I am to take on this investigation."

"A high value. Vows are meant to be honored."

"And what value do you place on understanding, compassion, forgiveness?"

Davenham was silent. He crossed his legs, smoothed the tweed trousers, and leaned down to rub away a nonexistent scuff on his polished leather shoes, before responding. "Damn and blast!"

"Mr. Davenham—"

"Miss Dobbs, I am not without compassion, but I have my pride. My wife will not divulge the nature of her business on those days when she is absent. I have come here in order to learn the truth."

"Oh yes. The truth. Mr. Davenham, I will ascertain the truth for you, but I must have an agreement from you—that when you have my report, and you know the truth, then we will discuss the future together."

"What do you mean?"

"The information I gather will be presented in a context. It is in light of that context that we must continue our discussion, in order for you and your wife to build a future."

"I'm sure I don't know what you mean."

Maisie stood up, walked to the window, then turned to face her potential client. The bluff of the stiff upper lip, thought Maisie, who keenly felt the man's discomfort, and was immediately attuned to his emotions. Intuition spoke to her. *He talks about pride when it's his heart that's aching.*

"My job is rather more complex than you might have imagined, Mr. Davenham. I am responsible for the safety of all parties. And this is so even when I am dealing with society's more criminal elements."

Davenham did not respond immediately. Maisie, too, was silent, allowing him time to gather his resolve. After some minutes the stillness of the room was broken.

"I trust Robinson, so I will go ahead," said Davenham.

Maisie moved back to the desk, and looked down at her notes, then to the rooftops where pigeons were busy returning to newly built nests, before she brought her attention back to the man in the leather chair before her.

"Yes, Mr. Davenham. I will, too." Maisie allowed her acceptance of the case to be underlined by another moment of silence.

"Now then, let's start with your address, shall we?"

# CHAPTER THREE

aisie rose early on Tuesday, April 9. She dressed carefully in the blue skirt and jacket, pulled a navy blue wool overcoat across her shoulders, placed a cloche on her head, and left her rented room in a large three-story Victorian terraced house in Lambeth, just south of the Thames. It was cold again. Blimey, would spring ever spring up? she wondered, pulling gloves onto already chilled fingers.

As usual Maisie began her morning with a brisk walk, which allowed her time to consider the day ahead and enjoy what her father always called "the best of the morning." She entered Palace Road from Royal Street, and turned right to walk toward Westminster Bridge. She loved to watch the Thames first thing in the morning. Those Londoners who lived just south of the river always said they were "going over the water" when they crossed the Thames, never referring to the river by name unless they were speaking to a stranger. It had been the lifeblood of the city since the Middle Ages, and no people felt the legacy more keenly than those who lived with it and by it. Her maternal grandfather had been a lighterman on the water, and like all of his kind, knew her tides, her every twist and turr

Londoners knew she was a moody creature. Human beings possessed no dominion over the Thames, but care, attention, and respect would see any vessel safely along her meandering way. Maisie's grandfather had all but disowned her mother when she had taken up with Maisie's father, for he was of the land, not that Frankie Dobbs would have called the streets of London "the land." Frankie was a costermonger, a man who sold vegetables from a horse-drawn cart that he drove from Lambeth to Covent Garden market every weekday morning. To Frankie Dobbs the water was a means to an end, bringing fruit and vegetables to market, for him to buy in the early hours of the morning, then sell on his rounds and be home by teatime, if he was lucky.

Maisie stopped at the center of the bridge, waved at the crew of a pilot boat, and went on her way. She was off to see Celia Davenham, but Celia Davenham would not see her.

Once across the bridge, Maisie descended into the depths of Westminster underground railway station and took the District Line to Charing Cross station. The station had changed names back and forth so many times, she wondered what it would be called next. First it was Embankment, then Charing Cross Embankment, and now just Charing Cross, depending upon which line you were traveling. At Charing Cross she changed trains, and took the Northern Line to Goodge Street station, where she left the underground, coming back up into the sharp morning air at Tottenham Court Road. She crossed the road, then set off along Chenies Street toward Russell Square. Once across the square, she entered Guilford Street, where she stopped to look at the mess the powers that be had made of Coram's Fields. The old foundling hospital, built by Sir Thomas Coram almost two hundred years before, had been demolished in 1926, and now it was just an empty space with nothing to speak of happening to it. "Shame," whispered Maisie, as she walked another few yards and entered Mecklenburg Square.

Named in honor of Charlotte of Mecklenburg-Strelitz, who became queen consort upon her marriage to George III of England,

the gracious Georgian houses of the square were set around a garden
protected by a wrought-iron fence secured with a locked gate.
Doubtless a key to the lock was on a designated hook downstairs at
the Davenham residence, in the butler's safekeeping. In common with
many London squares, only residents had access to the garden.

Maisie jotted a few more lines in her notebook, taking care to reflect
that she had been to the square once before, accompanying Maurice
Blanche during a visit to his colleague, Richard Tawney, the political
writer who spoke of social equality in a way that both excited and
embarrassed Maisie. At the time it seemed just as well that he and
Maurice were deep in lively conversation, so that Maisie's lack of ease
could go unnoticed.

While waiting at the corner and surveying the square, Maisie wondered if Davenham had inherited his property. He seemed quite out
of place in Mecklenburg Square, where social reformers lived alongside university professors, poets, and scholars from overseas. She considered his possible discomfort, not only in his marriage but in his
home environment. As Maisie set her gaze on one house in particular, a man emerged from a neighboring house and walked in her
direction. She quickly feigned interest in a window box filled with
crocus buds peeking through moist soil. Their purple shoots seemed
to test the air to see if it was conducive to a full-fledged flowering.
The man passed. Maisie still had her head inclined toward the flowers when she heard another door close with a thud, and looked up.

A woman had emerged from the residence she had been observing, and was now depositing a set of keys in her handbag. She
adjusted her hat and made her way down the steps and onto the
pavement. Christopher Davenham had provided Maisie with an
excellent description of his wife, Celia, a petite, fair-complected
woman with fine features, no taller than five feet two. Celia
Davenham had silky blond hair that tended to unsettle a hat that
already required more than one hatpin to render it secure, and hands
that seemed constantly to fiddle with bag, gloves, hat, and hair as she
walked to the main road.

Even from a distance of several paces, Maisie noted the quality of the woman's deep burgundy gabardine suit, and the soft leather gloves and felt hat chosen to complement the expensive ensemble precisely. Her shoes had clearly been chosen with care as well, for they were of fine burgundy leather with half straps at each side that met in the center and were secured with a grosgrain ribbon tied in a small bow. Maisie was intrigued by the bow, for it suggested a certain girlishness, as if the woman could not quite accommodate the maturity her age suggested.

Celia Davenham made her way toward Heathcote Street and turned into Grays Inn Road, where she hailed a taxi-cab outside the Royal Free Hospital. Fortunately Maisie managed to secure a taxi-cab at once, so that she could travel immediately behind Mrs. Davenham. As she sat in the rear seat of the heavy black motorcar, she hoped that the journey would be a short one. For Maisie travel by any means other than her own two feet was nothing but an indulgence. The journey by underground to Warren Street was a treat she allowed herself in the morning only if she considered that she had worked hard enough to warrant the additional expenditure.

At Charing Cross railway station, Celia Davenham climbed out of the cab, paid the driver, and proceeded to the ticket counter. Maisie followed closely. She stood behind Mrs. Davenham at the ticket counter, and pretended to fumble in her bag for her purse, listening keenly as the childlike woman with the soft blond hair stated her destination.

"Nether Green, please. First-class return, thank you."

What on earth could this woman want at Nether Green, a small town on the outskirts of London, where it met with the county of Kent? Apple orchards giving way to terraced houses, an old station, a few good homes. Now if she had asked for Chislehurst, with its new-money grandeur, Maisie thought she might have understood. But Nether Green? Maisie requested a second-class ticket for the same destination, then proceeded to the correct platform to await the train. She stopped only to buy a newspaper, which she carried under her arm.

The train pulled in with a loud hiss, pumping clouds of smoky steam as the engine reached the buffers and the screeching brakes were applied. The olive green livery of the Southern Railways, painted on each carriage, was tarnished by coal dust and wear. Celia Davenham immediately walked toward the first-class compartments, whereupon a guard hurriedly stepped forward to open the sturdy, iron-framed door, and to extend a steadying hand as she stepped up into the carriage. Maisie passed on the way to the second-class carriages, and just before the door closed, noticed that the collar and cuffs of Mrs. Davenham's burgundy suit were edged with the same ribbon used to form a bow on her shoes. She quickly reestimated the cost of the clothes the woman was wearing that day.

Having ensured that the object of her investigation was aboard the train, Maisie claimed a seat in a second-class carriage, pulled down the window to observe the platform, and waited for the whistle to blow and the train to chug out of one of London's busiest stations. Eventually the guard walked down the platform, instructing Maisie as he passed that it would be better for "yer 'ead, Miss," if she sat down. He checked that the train was clear of all platform onlookers, blew his whistle, and waved the green flag, signaling the engine driver to move out of the station.

As the train chugged and puffed its way through south London and out into the city's border with Kent, Maisie pondered the changes she had seen in the city in her lifetime. London was creeping outward. Where there had been fields, houses now stood. Rows of shops were doing brisk business, and a new commuter class was working to improve itself. By the time the train reached Grove Park, Maisie had brought her notes up to date again, ensuring that each small detail of her journey, from the time she left her rented flat in south London that morning until the present moment, was recorded—along with every penny she had spent along the way.

The next stop was Nether Green. Maisie stood, inspected her reflection in a mirror strategically placed between two dim lights on the carriage bulkhead, adjusted her hat, and took her seat again to wait for the train to slow down, for the hissing of brakes. As the carriages rolled into the station, Maisie stood once more, pulled down the window, and poked her head out to keep an eye on the first-class compartments. When the train came to a halt Maisie put her arm out of the window so she could open the heavy carriage door from the outside and, keeping the first-class compartments in view, she jumped smartly from the train and walked at a brisk pace toward the ticket collector. Celia Davenham was ahead by only a few yards, obscured slightly by other passengers, including a very slow old lady who would not be rushed.

"Now just you wait, young man," said the old woman to the ticket collector. "It's a sorry state of affairs if you can't give your elders and betters a minute or two to find the ticket."

The ticket collector stepped back a pace, as if anticipating a blow to the head from the doughty woman's black umbrella. Maisie waited impatiently, for Celia Davenham had passed through the barrier and was leaving the station. Finally she reached the ticket collector, handed over her ticket, and walked as quickly as she could to the station gate. Glancing both ways, Maisie saw that Celia had paused by a flower stall. Luck indeed. She walked toward the stall, rearranging the newspaper under her arm and consulting her watch, even though she knew the time to the second. She approached it just as Celia Davenham was walking away.

Maisie looked over the bunches of fragrant blooms while addressing the stallholder. "Lovely flowers, the ones you wrapped for that lady."

"Yes, Ma'am, very nice indeed. Always has the irises."

"Always?"

"Yes, twice a week. Never fails."

"Oh well, she must like them," said Maisie, picking up a small bunch of Jersey daffodils. "I think I'll have something a bit different, though."

"Color of mourning, those irises," observed the man. "These daffs are a lot more cheerful by half!"

Maisie looked at her watch and made sure that Celia Davenham was still in sight. She walked slowly, but was not distracted by goods displayed in shopwindows. Keeping her eyes focused on the ground, she seemed to be avoiding any contact with people passing by.

"Well, I think so, too. I'll take the daffs, thank you very much."

"We sell a lot of irises, what with the cemetery up the road. That and chrysanths, always popular."

Maisie took the bunch of daffodils and handed over the exact change in pennies.

"Thank you. Very nice indeed."

She set forth at a steady pace, and was soon just a few steps behind Celia Davenham. They had passed the shops now, and although there were still passersby, the number of pedestrians heading in the same direction was thinning out. Celia Davenham turned right, then left onto the main road. She waited for some motorcars and a horse-drawn cart to pass, looking ahead to the green-painted iron gates of Nether Green Cemetery. Maisie followed, careful to maintain her distance yet still keep the other woman in view.

Celia Davenham walked with purpose, her head lowered but her step firm. Maisie watched her, mentally noting every detail of the other woman's demeanor. Her shoulders were held too square, hunched upward as if on a coat hanger. Maisie copied the woman's posture as she walked, and immediately felt her stomach clutch and a shiver go though her. Then sadness descended, like a dark veil across her eyes. Maisie knew that Celia Davenham was weeping as she walked, and that in her sadness she was searching for strength. With a sense of relief, as she walked along Maisie shook off the other woman's way of holding herself.

She followed Celia Davenham through the open gates, and along a path for about fifty yards. Then, without changing her pace, the object of Maisie's investigation turned in from the path and walked across the grass, pausing by a relatively fresh grave. The large marble angel towering above a neighboring grave caught Maisie's eye, and she made a mental note of this landmark. She knew she'd have to be careful. One grave can seem much like the next one when you are in a cemetery.

The cold seemed to close in around Maisie as she walked past Celia Davenham. A train chugged along the tracks nearby, its sooty vapor lingering for a moment over the headstones before being carried away by a chill breeze.

Maisie stopped by a grave that had clearly received no attention for years. She bowed her head and, carefully, looked sideways between the marble memorials, toward Celia Davenham. The woman was on her knees now, replacing dead flowers with the fresh irises, and talking. Talking to the dead.

Maisie, in turn, looked at the headstone she had unwittingly chosen as her cover. It bore the words: "Donald Holden. Born 1900. Died 1919. Beloved only son of Ernest and Hilda Holden. 'Memory Is A Golden Chain That Binds Us 'Til We Meet Again.'" Maisie looked at the weeds underfoot. They may have met already, she thought, while keeping a keen but inconspicuous watch on Celia Davenham, who remained at the immaculate neighboring grave, her head bowed, still speaking quietly. Maisie began to clear the weeds on Donald Holden's grave.

"Might as well look after you while I'm here," she said quietly, placing daffodils in the vase, which was mercifully full of rainwater. She couldn't afford to trudge all the way across the cemetery to the water tap: Celia might depart while she was gone.

As Maisie stepped to the side of the path to deposit a pile of weeds, she saw Celia Davenham move toward the headstone where she had held her vigil. She kissed the cold, gray marble, brushed away a tear, then turned quickly and walked away. Maisie was in no hurry to follow. Instead she nodded at Donald Holden's headstone, then walked over to the grave that the Davenham woman had just left. It said "Vincent." Just "Vincent." No other name, no date of birth. Then the words, "Taken from all who love you dearly."

❖

*T*he day had warmed by the time Maisie reached the station for the return journey to London. Celia Davenham, already on the platform, glanced at her watch repeatedly. Maisie went into the ladies' toilets, walked across chilly floor tiles that radiated more moisture into the damp air, and ran icy water into the porcelain sink to rinse the dirt from her hands. She looked up into the mirror and regarded the face that looked directly back at her. Yes, the dark blue eyes still held a sparkle, but the small lines around her lips and across her brow betrayed her, told something about her past.

She knew that she would follow Celia Davenham this afternoon until the woman returned to her home in Mecklenburg Square, and believed that nothing else of note would occur that day. Maisie knew that she had found the lover, the man who had caused Christopher Davenham to pay a princely sum for her services. The problem was that the man Christopher Davenham thought was cuckolding him was dead.

# CHAPTER FOUR

*M*aisie sat in the early morning half-light of her office considering her subject. Only one small lamp illuminated the room, but it was angled downward toward Maisie's notes and a clutch of small index cards. Maurice maintained that the mind was at its sharpest before dawn.

In the early days of her pupilage with Maurice, he had told Maisie of his teachers, the wise men who spoke of the veil that was lifted in the early hours, of the all-seeing eye that was open before the day was awake. The hours before dawn were the sacred time, before the intellect rose from slumber. At this time one's inner voice could be heard. Maisie had strained to hear that inner voice for days, since the single word "Vincent" had piqued her curiosity, since the apparent ordinariness of Celia Davenham's grief had given rise to more questions than answers.

Slipping off her shoes and pulling her wool cardigan around her shoulders, Maisie took a cushion from her chair and placed it on the floor. Lifting her skirt above her knees to allow freedom of movement, she sat on the cushion, crossed her legs and placed her hands together on her lap. Maurice had taught her that silencing the mind was a greater task than stilling the body, but it was in those still waters that truth could be mirrored. Now, in the darkness, Maisie sought the guidance of intuition and formed the questions that, in time, would give her answers.

Why only one name? Why no dates etched into the headstone? What was keeping the relationship between Celia and Vincent alive? Was it simply grief, perpetuated by disbelief that a dear one has parted? Or another emotion? Maisie saw the grave in her mind's eye, allowed her eyes to regard all aspects of the place where Vincent was laid to rest. But if he was at rest, why did she feel compelled to seek a path that was not as yet marked?

What is this question I cannot voice? Maisie asked herself. Donald Holden died just a year after the war. His grave bore signs of age. Vincent's seemed fresher, as if the ground had been disturbed only in recent months.

Maisie sat for a while longer, allowing the stillness to calm her natural busyness, until the brighter, grainy light of the waking hours signaled her to move. She stood, stretching her arms high while standing on tiptoe. Today she would follow Celia Davenham to the cemetery again.

Celia was a creature of habit. This day she left the house promptly at nine o'clock in the morning, immaculately dressed in a suit of shamrock green wool, the broad collar of a cream silk blouse flat against her jacket, and pinned with a jade brooch, clearly part of a set that included her jade earrings. Matching shoes and bag with a carefully coordinated hat and umbrella completed the ensemble. This time the shoes were plain in design, but each shoe bore a fashionable clip in the shape of a leaf pressed onto the front. Maisie wore her navy skirt and jacket. Her serious business clothes. The journey to Nether Green was uneventful. Once again Celia Davenham traveled in first class, while Maisie sat in the prickly discomfort of a second-class carriage. Celia bought her customary bouquet of irises, while Maisie decided upon something different for Donald—and for her purse—this morning.

"I'll have a nice bunch of daisies, please," said Maisie to the flower seller.

"Right you are, Miss. Always look cheerful, daisies, don't they, Miss? Last a while too. Newspaper all right, or do you need them wrapped special?"

"Yes, they are cheerful, aren't they? Newspaper will be fine, thank you," she said, holding out the correct change for a bunch of daisies.

Then Maisie quickly walked on, trailing Celia Davenham toward the cemetery. She entered through the green gates, and by the time she walked past Vincent's grave toward Donald Holden's resting place, Celia was standing in front of the marble headstone, tracing Vincent's name with the shamrock-green-gloved fingers of her right hand. Maisie walked past, her head lowered, and stopped in front of Donald's grave. After a respectful silent prayer, she busied herself, emptying water from the vase and pulling a few weeds. Picking up the now-dead daffodils from her previous visit, she walked over to the tap, threw the dead flowers onto the compost pile, and filled the vase with fresh water. Maisie returned to Donald's grave, replaced the vase, and arranged the daisies. As she worked, she looked sideways at Celia, who had removed her gloves and was arranging her bouquet of irises at the base of Vincent's headstone. Having placed them to her satisfaction, she continued to kneel by the stone, staring at the name.

Maisie observed Celia Davenham, and once again moved her body to mirror the woman's position. Her head seemed to sink lower on her long neck, her shoulders rounded, her hands tightened with pain. Such melancholy. Such an unending yearning. Maisie instinctively knew that Celia was dying inside, that each yesterday was being lived anew and that there could be no place for her husband until Vincent was allowed to rest in peace.

Suddenly the woman shuddered and looked straight at Maisie. She did not smile; it was as if she were looking beyond Maisie to another place. Regaining her own natural posture, Maisie nodded acknowledgment, a small movement that brought Celia Davenham back to the present. She nodded in return, brushed at her skirt, stood up, replaced her gloves, and quickly left Vincent's grave.

Maisie was in no hurry. She knew that Celia Davenham would go home now. Home to play the loving wife, the role she would assume as soon as she walked through the door. It was a role that her husband had seen through easily, although his conclusions had been erroneous. Maisie also knew that the second's glance and the deliberate acknowledgment she had initiated between herself and Celia ensured that the other woman would recognize her when they met again.

Maisie lingered for a while at Donald's grave. There was something healing in this ritual of making a comfortable place for the dead. Her thoughts took her back to France, to the dead and dying, to the devastating wounds that were so often beyond her skill, beyond everyone's. But it was the wounds of the mind that touched her, those who still fought their battles again and again each day, though the country was at peace. If only she could make the living as comfortable, thought Maisie, as she tidied a few more stubborn weeds in the shadow of Don's headstone.

"Making a nice job of that one."

Maisie swung around, to see one of the cemetery workers standing behind her, an older man with red, bony hands firmly grasping the handles of a wooden wheelbarrow. His ruddy complexion told of years working outdoors, but his kind eyes spoke of compassion, of respect.

"Why yes. It's sad to see them so uncared for, isn't it?" replied Maisie.

"I'll say, after what those boys gave for us. Poor bastards. Oh, Miss, I am sorry, I forgot—"

"Don't worry. It's as well to voice one's feelings," replied Maisie.

"That's the truth. Too much not said by 'alf."

The man pointed to Donald's grave.

"Haven't seen this one being tended for a few years. His old Mum and Dad used to come over. Only son. Killed them, too, it did, I reckon."

"Did you know them? I would have thought it would be difficult to know all the relatives, with so many graves," said Maisie.

"I'm 'ere every day 'cept Sundays, that is. Been 'ere since just after the war. I get to know people. 'Course, you don't 'ave long talks, no time for that, and folk don't always want to talk, but, there again, there's those that want to 'ave a bit of conversation."

"Yes, yes, I'm sure."

"Not seen you before, not 'ere." The man looked at Maisie.

"No, that's true. I'm a cousin. Just moved to the city," said Maisie, looking at the man directly.

"Nice to see it being taken care of." The man firmed his grip on the wheelbarrow handles, as if to move on.

"Wait a minute. I wonder, could you tell me, are all the graves here, in this part, war graves?" asked Maisie.

"Yes and no. Most of these are our boys, but some lived a long time after their injuries. Your Don, well, you'd know this, but 'e 'ad septicemia. Horrible way to go, 'specially as 'e was brought home. Lot of folk like to bury 'em 'ere because of the railway."

The man set the wheelbarrow down, and pointed to the railway lines running alongside the cemetery.

"You can see the trains from 'ere. Not that these boys can see the trains, but the relatives like it. They're on a journey, you see, it's a— you know, what do they call it, you know—when it means something to them."

"Metaphor?"

"Yeah, well, like I said, it's a journey, innit? And the relatives, if they've come by train, which most of them do, can see the graves as the train pulls out of the station. They can say another good-bye that way."

"So, what about that one there? Strange, isn't it? Just one word, the Christian name?" asked Maisie.

"I'll say. The whole bleedin' thing was strange. Two years ago 'e came, this one. Small family burial. 'e was a captain. Injured at Passchendaele. Terrible show was that one, terrible. Wonder 'e came 'ome at all. 'e'd lived away from the family, apparently, after bein' 'ome for a bit. Wanted to be known only by 'is Christian name. Said it wasn't important anymore, seein' as they were all nobodies who could just be written off like leftovers. Shame to 'is family, accordin' to a couple of 'is mates that came up 'ere for a while after. Now only that woman comes. Think she was 'is mate's sister, known 'er for years, 'e 'ad. Keeps the grave nice, you'd think 'e only went down yesterday."

"Hmm. Very sad indeed. What was his surname, do you know?"

By now the man was well into the telling of stories, and seemed glad of the opportunity, and importance, that a question brought him.

"Weathershaw. Vincent Weathershaw. Came from Chislehurst. Good family, by the looks of them. Mind you, 'e passed away where 'e was living. A farm, I think it was. Yes, 'e lived on a farm, not that far from 'ere—though more in the country, like. Far as I know, quite a few of 'em lived there."

Maisie felt a chill as the stillness of the cemetery seeped through her clothing and touched her skin. Yet the shiver was familiar to Maisie, who had felt that sensation even in warm weather when there was no cooling breeze. She had come to recognize this spark of energy passing across her skin as a warning.

"Quite a few of them?"

"Well, you know." The man rubbed his stubbled jawbone with the flat of his thick, earth-stained hand. "Them who got it in the face. Remember, we're not far from Sidcup 'ere—you know. Queen Mary's, the 'ospital where they did all that special work on faces, trying to 'elp the poor sods. Amazin' when you think of it, what they tried to do there—and what they did do. Miracle workers, they were. Mind you, I wouldn't mind bettin' a few of them boys still weren't fancy-looking enough for their sweethearts, and ended up at that farm."

The old gardener picked up the handles of the wheelbarrow. Maisie saw that he was ready to move on, away from recollections of war.

"Well, I had better be getting on, Mr. . . . ."

"Smith. Tom Smith."

"Yes, I have to catch the two o'clock, Tom. And thank you."

Tom Smith watched as Maisie picked her way past the graves to the path, and as he turned to leave he called to her. "I 'spect I won't see you 'ere again ... but you know, Miss, the funny thing about this 'ere Vincent is that 'e wasn't the only one."

"The only one what?"

"The only one buried with just a Christian name."

Maisie held her head to one side, encouraging Tom to continue.

"There was a few of them, and you know what?

"What?" said Maisie.

"All lost touch with their families. Tragic it was, just tragic. Seeing their parents. You should never 'ave to go through that, never. Bad enough seeing 'em go off to war, let alone losing them when they come back."

"Yes, that is tragic."

Maisie looked at Tom, then asked the question that had been with her since the man had first spoken to her. "Tom ... where is your boy resting?"

Tom Smith looked at Maisie, and tears rimmed his eyes. The lines etched in his face grew deeper, and his shoulders dropped. "Down there." He pointed to the row of headstones nearest the railway line. "Loved trains as a boy. Loved 'em. Came back from France not quite right up 'ere." He tapped the side of his head. "Would scream in the middle of the night, but it was all you could do to get a sound out of the boy in the daytime. One mornin' the missus goes up to take 'im up a cup of tea and there 'e was. Done 'imself in. She was never the same. Never. Broke 'er spirit, it did. Passed away three years ago come December."

Maisie nodded, held out her hand, and laid it upon his arm. They stood in silence.

"Well, this will never do," said Tom Smith. "Must be getting along. Got to look after them, 'aven't I? Good day to you, Miss."

Maisie Dobbs bade the man good-bye but didn't leave the cemetery immediately. Later, while waiting on the platform for the train back to London, she took a small notebook from her handbag and recorded the events of the day. Each detail was noted, including the color of Celia Davenham's shamrock-green gloves.

She had found two more graves whose headstones bore Christian names only, not very far from the final resting place of Vincent Weathershaw. Three young "old soldiers" who had withdrawn from their families. Maisie sat back on the bench and started to compose her questions, the questions to herself that would come as a result of her observations. She would not struggle to answer the questions but would let them do their work.

"Truth walks toward us on the paths of our questions." Maurice's voice once again echoed in her mind. "As soon as you think you have the answer, you have closed the path and may miss vital new information. Wait awhile in the stillness, and do not rush to conclusions, no matter how uncomfortable the unknowing."

And as she allowed her curiosity full rein, Maisie knew what her next move should be.

# CHAPTER FIVE

The Celia Davenham file comprised several pages by now, and included details beyond excursions to Nether Green Cemetery. Celia's birthdate (September 16, 1897), parentage (Algernon and Anne Whipton), place of birth (Sevenoaks, Kent), school (St. Mary's), and miscellaneous other details were recorded. Her husband was ten years older, not such a division in years at thirty-two, but it would have been something of a chasm at the age of nineteen or twenty, especially when the past offered more in the way of excitement than the day-to-day round of life in a maturing marriage.

Maisie knew where Celia shopped for clothes, where she took afternoon tea, even of her interest in needlework. Maisie also observed her comfort in solitude, and wondered how such a solitary soul could build a bridge to another. Did the Davenham marriage endure behind a veil of courtesy? The mundane communication that one would accord an acquaintance met on the street, but the formality of which could stifle the bond of affection between man and wife? It was evident that only one person could answer certain questions, and that was Celia Davenham herself. Maisie carefully replaced the pages in the file, placed it in her desk drawer, pushed back her chair, and made ready to leave her office.

A sharp knock at the door was followed by Billy Beale's freckled face and shock of wheaten hair, topped by a flat cap, poked around the dark wood doorjamb.

"Good afternoon to you, Miss Dobbs. 'Ow's business? Don't seem to 'ave seen much of you lately, though I 'eard that you'd 'elped old Mrs. Scott get something out of that thieving son of 'ers. Thought I'd pop me 'ead in to see if you need anything done in the way of 'andi-work in the office 'ere."

"Billy, yes, Mrs. Scott is a client. But you know better than to expect a comment from me, don't you?"

"Miss Dobbs, you're spot-on right there. But you can't stop folk talking about your business, 'specially when you've 'elped them. People round 'ere don't miss a trick, and we've got memories like ele-phants into the bargain!"

"Have you now, Billy? In that case, perhaps you can tell me if you know someone I think you might have heard of."

"Fire away!"

"Confidential, Billy."

"Nod's as good as a wink . . ." Billy tapped the side of his nose to emphasize the integrity of any information he might receive—he could keep a secret.

"Vincent Weathershaw. Captain. Know him?" asked Maisie.

"Weathershaw. Weathershaw. Now that name rings a bell. Let me think."

Billy took off his cap and scratched at his golden hair.

"You know, 'ere's what it is—I've 'eard about 'im. Never actually took an order from the man, but 'eard about 'im. By reputation, like."

"What sort of reputation?" quizzed Maisie.

"If I remember rightly, a bit devil-may-care. Mind you, you saw it a lot. Some of them got so as they couldn't care less about their own lives. Like they were in it so long that the shelling didn't scare them anymore. Poor sods. Some of them, the officers, that is, came out of their fancy schools and straight into the trenches."

"Was he reckless?"

"If it's the fella I'm thinking of, not reckless with 'is men. No, 'e was reckless with 'imself. Got so as 'e would just climb out of the bunker, no 'elmet, to go up and look around for the Kaiser's boys. Reckon they were more surprised than us when they copped sight of 'im walking around without a care in the world."

"Ever hear about him again, Billy?"

"Miss Dobbs, it's not like I talk about it much. Best left behind. But you know that, don't you? You saw enough, must've done."

"Yes, I saw enough for this lifetime, Billy."

Maisie buttoned her coat, secured her hat in place, and pulled on her gloves.

"But tell you what, Miss. I'll ask around down the Prince of Wales, some of the lads might know something. This Weathershaw, he a client, like?"

"No, Billy. No, he's not. He's dead. Two years ago. See what you can find out, Billy."

"Right you are, Miss," replied Billy. Maisie ushered Billy out of the office and locked the door behind her as she left with him.

"It's confidential, Billy. Just bring it into the conversation," instructed Maisie.

"Yes, Miss. Don't worry. Like I said when you moved in. Anything you want, you just ask Billy Beale."

Maisie decided that a brisk walk to Piccadilly Circus would be just what she needed to clear her head for the next part of her task: information gathering, as Maurice would say.

Fortunately there had been several new clients since she had moved into the office in Warren Street. Christopher Davenham's appearance had represented the beginning of a respectable stream of visitors. There were a couple of referrals from Lady Rowan's solicitors, along with three of Maurice's former clients who finally overcame any reticence they might have had about completely confiding in his former assistant, who happened to be a woman.

The work ranged from simple analysis of correspondence to reveal anomalies in funds paid to a company to a report on a "missing" daughter. As Maisie expected, there had not yet been the requests for assistance from government or from the legal or judicial services that Maurice had enjoyed, but she knew that such business would come in due course. She was qualified to consult on matters far beyond those that had come to her. Maurice had seen to that.

Maisie was now busy, and more to the point, had the money to research matters that presented themselves for investigation without initiation by an actual client. Unless you could call Vincent Weathershaw a client.

The restaurant at Fortnum & Mason's was busy, but as she walked in and feigned interest in the menu, Maisie quickly scanned the room and immediately saw Celia Davenham sitting by a window. She was looking out at the rooftops as if in a dream, with her hands clasped around a cup of tea.

"May I have a seat by the window?" requested Maisie of the tall waiter with slicked-back, brilliantined hair who greeted her.

Taking the table next to Celia, Maisie deliberately sat facing the woman, although she did not look at her as she removed her gloves, placed them on top of her bag, and set the bag on the chair next to her. Maisie opened the menu and read down the list of dishes until she felt the woman's eyes upon her, then she looked up, meeting Celia's gaze. Maisie smiled. Her "planetary" smile, as Simon had once said. She quickly banished all thought of Simon; her concentration had to be on the job in hand.

"Hello," said Maisie in greeting. "Such a lovely day today, isn't it?"

"Yes. Yes it is," responded Celia. She smiled at Maisie. "Forgive me . . . but, have we met?"

"You know, I must say, you look very familiar, but I . . . I can't think where." Maisie smiled again.

"Nether Green. I've seen you at Nether Green." Color flushed Celia Davenham's cheeks as she recognized Maisie.

"Why, yes, yes. Look, would you like to join me?" Maisie moved her bag and gloves from the seat next to her, an invitation to Celia Davenham.

A waiter quickly came to assist Celia, and placed her teacup, saucer, and place mat on Maisie's table. The perfectly dressed woman sat down opposite Maisie, who held out her hand.

"Blanche. Maisie Blanche. How do you do."

"Celia Davenham. I'm very well, thank you."

For a while the two women talked of small matters. The price of flowers at the stall, the late arrival of trains this past winter. Before Celia could ask, Maisie offered the story of her visits to the cemetery.

"Donald was a cousin. Not close, but family all the same. I thought that now I'm here in town, it would be easy to go out to Nether Green. One doesn't like to forget, does one?"

"No. Absolutely. No. Not that I could," replied Celia.

"Did you lose your brother?" asked Maisie.

"Yes, one of them. In the Dardanelles. The other was wounded. Seriously wounded."

"I'm sorry. You were lucky to have your brother come home from the Dardanelles," said Maisie, knowing that often brother fought alongside brother, which led to many a mother grieving the loss of not one child but two or three.

"Oh, no. No. My brother's body was never found. He was listed missing. I visit the grave of my other brother's friend. Vincent." Celia fussed with her handkerchief.

"I see. Is your brother, your other brother, recovered?"

"Um. Yes, yes, in a way."

Maisie held her head to one side in question but added, "Oh, this is such a difficult subject—"

"No, I mean, yes. Yes. But . . . well, he has scars. Vincent had scars too."

"Oh. I see."

"Yes. George, my brother who survived, is like Vincent. His face—"

Celia slowly moved her finely manicured hands and touched her cheek with delicate fingers. She flinched and tears filled her eyes. At that moment Maisie saw her chance for connection. A connection that was deeper than she would admit. She reached out and touched

Celia lightly on the arm until the other woman's eyes met hers. Maisie nodded her understanding.

"I was a nurse," said Maisie, her voice lowered, not to avoid being heard but to draw Celia toward her. "In France. When I returned from France I nursed again in a secure mental hospital. I understand the wounds, Mrs. Davenham. Those of the body—and of the soul."

Celia Davenham took Maisie's hand. And at that moment Maisie knew she was in the woman's confidence, that she was trusted. Maisie had anticipated that it would take no longer than the twenty minutes that the women had sat together at the same table. Such was Celia's hunger for connection to someone who understood. And the depth of Maisie Dobbs's understanding of her situation was greater than Celia Davenham could possibly imagine.

Celia Davenham sat for a moment before speaking again. Wave upon wave of grief seemed to break across her heart with such force that she made a fist with one hand, and gripped Maisie's offered hand of understanding with the other. A waiter coming toward the table to inquire if more tea was required stopped suddenly and moved away, as if repelled by the force of her emotion.

Maisie closed her eyes, concentrating her calming energy on the woman who sat opposite her. The moment passed, and Maisie opened her eyes to observe Celia relax her shoulders, arms, and the tight grasp on her hand. But she did not let go.

"I'm sorry."

"Don't be, Mrs. Davenham. Don't be. Take some tea."

Keeping Maisie's hand in hers, the woman took the cup in her other hand and, shaking, lifted it to her lips to sip the still-hot tea. The two women sat in silence for several more minutes until Maisie spoke again.

"Tell me about Vincent, Mrs. Davenham."

Celia Davenham placed the fine bone china cup in its saucer, took a deep breath, and began to tell her story.

"I fell in love with Vincent—oh, dear me—it must have been when I was about twelve. I was just a girl. He came to the house with my brother George. It was my brother Malcolm who died. George was the oldest. Vincent was one of those people who could make anyone laugh—even my parents, who were very stiff indeed. It was as if the sun shone upon Vincent and everyone felt compelled to look at him, just to warm themselves."

"Yes, I have known such people. I expect he was quite the charmer," said Maisie.

"Oh yes, quite the charmer. But he didn't realize it. He just went through his life bringing out the best in people. So, he was definitely officer caliber. His men would have followed him to death's door."

"And no doubt beyond."

"Yes. And beyond. Apparently when he wrote to the parents or wives of men who had fallen, he always mentioned some small detail about them—a joke they had told, an act of courage, a special effort made. He didn't just say, 'I'm sorry to tell you this, but . . . .' He cared."

Celia took up her cup again, keeping one hand on Maisie's. Maisie, for her part, made no move to withdraw, realizing the strength her touch gave the other woman. She moved only to pour more tea and to bring her own cup to her lips.

Occasionally she would look out of the window, and as dusk drew in saw the reflection of Celia Davenham in the windowpane as she told her story. In this way Maisie observed her as an onlooker might, rather than as a confidante. As Celia spoke, releasing the weight of hoarded memory, she seemed to gain strength. She sat straighter. Celia was an attractive woman, and in the reflected scene, Maisie saw the faces of other people in the tearoom occasionally looking toward them, drawn to a conversation they could not overhear but could not help observe.

Maisie knew well, more than the onlookers, that they were drawn by the power of revelation. They were witnesses to the unfolding of Celia Davenham's story, to the unburdening of her soul, though they might not be aware of it. And she knew that once outside, wrapping a scarf around a neck to shield it from the biting wind, or holding on to a hat, a woman might say to her companion, "Did you see that woman, by the window, the well-dressed one?" and her companion would nod and they would speak for a while of what might have been said by the woman near the window to the woman who allowed her hand to be held so tightly. And the picture of Celia Davenham squaring her shoulders to tell her story would come back to them on occasion, especially when they were sad and looking for the answer to a question of the heart.

Celia Davenham paused, as if to summon the fortitude to continue. Maisie waited, then asked, "Tell me what happened to Vincent."

"It was at Passchendaele."

"Ah yes. I know. . . ."

"Yes, I think we all know now. So many—"

"—and Vincent?"

"Yes, although some might believe him to be lucky. He came home."

Celia stopped again, closed her eyes, then continued. "I try, sometimes, to remember his face before. When it was complete. But I can't. I feel awful, that I can only remember the scars. I try at night to close my eyes and see him, but I can't. I can see George, of course; his injuries weren't so bad. But I can't think of *exactly* how he was before the war either."

"Yes, it must be very hard."

"There was something about Vincent, his enthusiasm for life, that turned into something else, as if it had another side. His company came under intense enemy fire. Vincent was hit in the face by shrapnel. It is a miracle he lived. George lost an ear and has scars on the side of his face, which you would think were unbearable but seem light compared to Vincent's."

Maisie looked at the woman, whose grip had relaxed as she told Vincent's story. Celia was exhausted. Maurice had counseled her, in the early days of her apprenticeship, when she was the silent observer as he listened to a story, gently prodding with a question, a comment, a sigh, or a smile, "The story takes up space as a knot in a piece of wood. If the knot is removed, a hole remains. We must ask ourselves, how will this hole that we have opened be filled? The hole, Maisie, is our responsibility."

"Mrs. Davenham, you must be tired. Shall we meet again another day?" she asked.

"Yes, Miss Blanche, do let's meet."

"Perhaps we might walk in Hyde Park, or St. James's; the lake is so lovely at this time of year."

The women made arrangements to meet the following week, for tea at the Ritz, then a stroll through Green Park to St. James's. But before they parted, Maisie suggested, "Mrs. Davenham, you probably have to rush home soon, but I wonder. Liberty has some lovely new fabrics, just arrived from India. Would you come with me to look at them?"

"Why, I'd love to."

*L*ater, when Celia Davenham reflected upon her day, she was surprised. For though she still felt sadness, the memory she reflected upon most was that of huge bolts of fabric being moved around at her behest by willing assistants who could sense in her the interest that led to a purchase. With an enthusiastic flourish, yards of vibrant purples, yellows, pinks, and reds of Indian silk were pulled out, to be rubbed between finger and thumb, and held against her face in front of the mirror. And she thought of the person she knew as Maisie Blanche, who suddenly but quietly had to take her leave, allowing her to indulge her love of texture and color for far longer than she had intended. Thus a day that had seen so many tears ended in the midst of a rainbow.

## CHAPTER SIX

aisie made her way back to her office. It was dark by now, and although she was gasping for a cup of tea much stronger than the light Darjeeling served at Fortnum & Mason's, she needed to work. She reflected upon the Davenham story, knowing only too well that there was a lot more to elicit. But by leaving much of the story untold, Maisie allowed the door to remain open. Instead of being exhausted by her own revelations and memories, Celia Davenham was being helped to shed her burden gradually, and Maisie was her guide.

Jack Barker greeted Maisie outside Warren Street station, doffed his cap and bid her good evening.

"Miss Dobbs, and a good evenin' to you. My, you are a sight for sore eyes at the end of the day."

"Mr. Barker, thank you, although I am sure I'll be better when I get a cup of tea inside me."

"You should get that Billy to make you a cuppa. Does too much jawing of a working day, that one. Do you know, I 'ave to tell him sometimes that I'm busy and can't keep puttin' the world to rights with 'im."

Maisie grinned, knowing by now that Jack Barker could talk the hind leg off a donkey, and that the same complaint about Jack was likely to come from Billy Beale.

"Well, Billy's a good 'un, isn't he, Mr. Barker?"

"'E is that. Amazing how fast 'e can move with that leg. You should see 'im sometimes, running 'ere and there, 'dot and carry one' with that leg. Poor sod. But at least we got 'im back 'ere, didn't we?"

Maisie agreed. "Indeed, Mr. Barker, at least he came home. I'd best be on my way, so I'll bid you good evening. Any reason to buy the latest edition before I rush off?"

"All bloomin' bad if you ask me. Threadneedle Street and the City in a rare two-an'-eight. They're talking about a slump."

"I'll leave it then, Mr. Barker. Goodnight."

Maisie turned into Warren Street, walking behind two women students from the Slade School of Art, who were making their way back to lodgings nearby. Each carried an artist's portfolio under one arm, and giggled as the other recounted her part of a story about another woman. They stopped to speak to a group of young men who were just about to enter the Prince of Wales pub, then decided to join them. They pushed past a woman dressed in black, who had been standing outside the pub smoking a cigarette. She shouted at them to look out, but her warning was met with more giggles from the students. She was soon joined by a man, who Maisie suspected already had a wife at home, for he betrayed himself by quickly looking up and down the street before taking the woman by the arm and hurrying her inside the pub.

"It takes all sorts," said Maisie in a low voice as she passed, and continued on down Warren Street to her office.

Maisie opened the door that led to the dark stairwell, and as she went to turn on the dim light to see her way up the stairs, the light over the upper stairwell went on and Billy Beale called out.

"'S only me, Miss. See your way up?"

"Billy, you should be knocking off work by now, surely."

"Yeah, but I've got some more news for you. 'Bout that fella you was askin' about. Weathershaw. Thought I'd 'ang about in case I don't see you tomorrow."

"That's kind, Billy. Let's put the kettle on."

Maisie led the way into her office, turned on the light, and went to put the kettle on the small stove.

"And that telephone has been ringing its 'ead off today. What you need is someone to help you out, Miss, to write down messages, like."

"My telephone was ringing?"

"Well, that's what it's there for, innit?"

"Yes, of course. But it doesn't ring very often. I tend to receive messages via the postman or personal messenger. I wonder who it was?"

"Someone with an 'ead of steam, the way it was ringing. I was working on the boiler, making a fair bit of noise meself, and every now and again, there it went again. I came up a couple of times, t'see if I could answer it for you, but it stopped its nagging just as I got outside the door—I c'n use me master key in an emergency, like. I tell ya, I nearly got me kit and put in a line so that I could answer it downstairs meself."

"Pardon?"

"Remember, Miss, I was a sapper. Let me tell you, if I could run a line in the pourin' rain and on me 'ands and knees in the mud—and get the brass talkin' to each other while the 'un's trying to knock me block off as I was about it—I can bloomin' well do a thing or two with your line."

"Is that so, Billy? I'll have to remember that. In the meantime, whoever wants to speak to me will find a way. Now then, what do you have to tell me?"

"Well, I was askin' round some of me old mates, about that Vincent Weathershaw bloke. Turns out one of the fellas knew someone, who knew someone else, you know, who told them that 'e wasn't quite all there after one of the big shows."

Billy Beale tapped the side of his forehead, and Maisie inclined her head for him to continue.

"Lost a lot of men, 'e did. Apparently never forgave 'imself. Took it all upon 'is shoulders, as if 'e was the one that killed them. But what I also 'eard was that some funny stuff went on between 'im and the big brass. Now, this is all very shaky, but . . . ."

"Go on, Billy," Maisie urged.

"Well, Miss, you know, if truth be told, we were all plain scared 'alf the bloomin' time."

"Yes, I know, Billy."

"O' course you do, Miss. You know, don't you? Blimey, when I think of what you nurses must've seen . . . anyway, if the truth be told, we was all scared. You didn't know when you were going to get it. But some of 'em. . . ."

Billy stopped, turned away from Maisie, and took the red kerchief from his neck and wiped his eyes.

"Gawd—sorry, Miss. Don't know what came over me."

"Billy. It can wait. Whatever you have to tell me. It can wait. Let me pour that tea."

Maisie went to the stove, poured boiling water from the kettle onto the tea leaves in the brown earthenware teapot, and allowed it to steep. She took two large tin mugs from the shelf above the stove, stirred the tea in the pot, then poured tea for them both, with plenty of sugar and a splash of milk. Since her time in France, Maisie had preferred an army-issue tin mug for her private teatimes, for the warmth that radiated from the mug to her hands and to the rest of her body.

"There you are, Billy. Now then . . ."

"Well, as you know, Miss, there were a lot of lads 'o enlisted that were too young. Boys tryin' to be men, and blimey, the rest of us weren't much more than boys ourselves. And you'd see 'em, white as sheets when that whistle blew to go over the top. Mind you, we was all as white as sheets. I was barely eighteen meself."

Billy sipped his tea and wiped his mouth with the back of his hand.

"We'd 'ave to get 'em under the arms, shove 'em over, and 'ope that the push would get 'em through. And sometimes one of 'em didn't make it over."

Billy's eyes misted over again, and he wiped them with the red kerchief.

"And when that 'appened, when a boy was paralyzed with fear, like, 'e could be reported for cowardice. If 'e'd been seen afterwards, not 'avin' gone over with the rest of his mates, the brass didn't ask too many questions, did they? No, the poor sod's on a charge and that's it! So we 'ad to look out for each other, didn't we?"

Drawing the red cloth across his brow, the young man continued his story for Maisie.

"Court-martialed, they were. And you know what 'appened to a lot of 'em, don't you? Shot. Even if some of 'em weren't quite so innocent, villains getting up to no good when they should've been on the line, it ain't the way to go, is it? Not shot by their own. Bloody marvelous, ain't it? You pray your 'ead off that the Kaiser's boys don't get you, then it's your own that do!"

Maisie allowed silence to envelop them and held the steaming mug to her lips. This was no new story. Only the storyteller was new to her. Happy-go-lucky Billy Beale.

"Well, this Vincent Weathershaw, as far as the brass were concerned, was a soft one with 'is men. Said it was enough with the trenches and shells killing 'em without their own 'avin' it in for 'em. Apparently they wanted to 'arden this Weathershaw up a bit. I don't know the 'ole story, nowhere near, but from what I've been told, 'e was commanded to do a few things 'e didn't want to. Refused. There was talk of strippin' 'im of 'is commission. The word is that no one quite knows what 'appened, but apparently, it was after these rumors went about, that 'e sort of lost 'is 'ead and started to do all that daft business, walkin' around without the 'elmet on in front of the other lot. Then, o' course, they got 'im—at Wipers—Passchendaele. Not far from where I copped it, really, but it seemed like 'undreds of miles at the time."

Maisie smiled, but it was a sad, reflective smile as she remembered how men made easy work of pronouncing "Ypres," referring to it as "Wipers."

"Mind you, they didn't get me coming out of a trench and over the top. No, it was all that business at Messines, not knowing whether the other lot were in the trench next door, or below us, and not knowin' whether the buggers—pardon 'me language, Miss—but not knowin' where they'd laid mines. Us sappers 'ad our work cut out for us there."

Billy lowered his head, swirled dregs of tea to soak up sugar at the bottom of his mug, and closed his eyes as memories pushed through into the present.

Maisie and Billy Beale sat in silence. Maisie, as she so often did nowadays, remembered Maurice and his teaching:

"Never follow a story with a question, Maisie, not immediately. And remember to acknowledge the storyteller, for in some way even the messenger is affected by the story he brings."

She waited a few more minutes, watching Billy sip his tea, lost in his memories as he looked out over the rooftops.

"Billy, thank you for finding this out for me. You must have worked hard to track the details down."

Billy lifted the mug of tea to his lips.

"Like I said, Miss—you need anything doing, Billy Beale's your man."

Maisie allowed more time to pass, and even wrote some notes in her file, in front of Billy, to underline the importance of his report.

"Well, Billy," said Maisie, closing the file and placing it back on the desk, "I hope you don't mind me changing the subject, but there is one thing. No rush, in your own time."

"You name it, Miss."

"Billy, I really need to have this room painted or wallpapered. It's as drab as yesterday's black pudding and needs a bit of cheering up. I noticed that on the ground floor you did such a nice job with Miss Finch's room—the door was open as I came through one day and I looked in—it was so bright and cheerful. What do you think?"

"I'll jump right to it, Miss. I'll put my mind to the colors on the way 'ome, and tomorrow I'll go by me mate's place—painter and decorator, 'e is—and see what 'e's got in the way of paints."

"That'll be lovely, Billy. And, Billy—thank you very much."

And so another storyteller fell asleep that night thinking not of the telling of the story but of the possibilities inherent in color and texture. But for Maisie, there was a different end to the day. She made notes in her file, simply named "Vincent," and started to sketch a diagram, with names and places linked.

Maisie Dobbs was even more convinced that her instinct had not betrayed her, that Vincent's death was simply one thread in an intricate web that led to no good. She knew that it would not be long before she discovered what connected the bright thread that was Vincent to the other boys who were buried with only one name at Nether Green Cemetery. And it was her intention that the next meeting with Celia Davenham would reveal how Vincent had spent the time since the war, and his exact location at his death.

More important, Maisie wanted an explanation as to why he was simply "Vincent."

# CHAPTER SEVEN

Maisie sat back in the wooden office chair and brought her knees up to her chest so that her heels rested on the edge of the seat. She had slipped off her shoes an hour or so ago, to put on the thick bed socks that she kept in her desk drawer. Maisie leafed through her report to Christopher Davenham and wondered how she might best advise him. It was at times like this that she missed the counsel of Maurice Blanche. The relationship between teacher and pupil was an easy one. She had opened her mind to learning his craft, and he had passed on to her the knowledge gleaned in a lifetime of work in what he referred to as "the forensic science of the whole person." Although he could still be consulted, Maisie knew that now that he had retired, it was his intention for her to make her way in the world alone.

She could hear his voice now: "Remember basics, Maisie, dear. Whenever you are stuck, go back to our earliest conversations. And remember connections, that there are always connections."

Now Maisie had to decide how far she should go in her report to Christopher Davenham. The man simply wanted to know where his wife was going and if another man was involved. Any information over and above what he had requested would not be necessary. Maisie thought for one more moment, put her feet back on the floor, placed the file on the table in front of her, and stood up.

"No, that's enough." She said to the empty room.

*

"*D*o sit down, Mr. Davenham." Maisie's chilled feet were now smartly clad in leather shoes.

"You have a report for me, Miss Dobbs?"

"Yes, of course. But first, Mr. Davenham, I must ask you some questions."

"Haven't you already asked enough? I would have thought my purpose for coming here was clear. I seek information, Miss Dobbs, and if you are half as good as your reputation, you will have that information."

"Yes, I do. But I would like us to discuss openly how you might use this information once you have it."

"I'm not sure I understand, Miss Dobbs."

Maisie opened the file, took out a blank sheet of paper that had previously covered her extensive notes, closed the file, and placed the paper on top. It was a technique learned from Maurice, which had proved to be most useful: The blank sheet of paper represented the future, an empty page that could be filled as the observer chose. Pages of notes brought out during conversation were a distraction, so a written report was given only at the end of meeting. "Mr. Davenham, if there were no other man, no reason for you to suspect that your wife's affections lay elsewhere, what would you do?"

"Well, nothing. If there's no reason for my suspicions, then she's in the clear. There would be no problem to do anything about."

"I see. Mr. Davenham, this is a delicate situation. Before I proceed, I must ask for you to make a commitment to me—"

"Whatever do you mean?"

"A commitment to your marriage, actually. A commitment, perhaps, to your wife's well-being and to your future."

Christopher Davenham stirred uneasily in his chair and folded his arms.

"Mr. Davenham," said Maisie, looking out of the window, "it's a very fine day now, don't you think? Let's walk around Fitzroy Square. We will be at liberty to speak freely and also enjoy something of the day."

Without waiting for an answer, Maisie rose from her chair, took her coat from the stand, and passed it to Christopher Davenham who, being a gentleman, stifled his annoyance, took the coat, and held it out for Maisie. Placing her hat upon her head and securing it with a pearl hatpin, Maisie smiled up at him. "A walk will be lovely."

She strolled with Davenham along Warren Street, then turned left at Conway Street into Fitzroy Square. The sun had broken through the morning's gray clouds, and there was a promise of warmer weather to come. The walk was by no means an idle suggestion. Maisie had learned from Maurice Blanche the importance of keeping the client open to whatever was being reported or suggested. "Sitting in a chair gives too much opportunity to retreat into the self," Blanche had said. "Keep the person moving, in the way that an artist keeps the oil moving when he is painting. Don't give them a chance to dry up; don't allow the client to shut you out."

"Mr. Davenham, I have decided to give you my report and my recommendations. I say 'recommendations' because I believe you are a man of compassion."

Davenham maintained an even pace. Good, thought Maisie. She matched his stride, keenly observing the position of his arms, the way he held his head forward and tilted back slightly, as if sniffing the air for a predator. He's terrified, thought Maisie, feeling fear rise up as she began to imitate his manner of walking and carriage. She closed her eyes for just a few seconds to be clear about the feelings now seeping through her body, and thought: He's afraid to give, for fear of losing.

She had to be quick to banish the fear.

"Mr. Davenham, you are not being deceived. Your wife is faithful."
The tall man breathed an audible sigh of relief.

"But she does need your help."

"In what way, Miss Dobbs?" The tension that ebbed with her revelation had no chance to reclaim him before Maisie spoke again.

"Like many young women, your wife lost someone she loved. In the war. The man was her first love, a puppy love. Had he lived, no doubt such an affection would have died with the onset of maturity. However—"

"Who?"

"A friend of her brother. His name was Vincent. It's in my report. Mr. Davenham, may we slow down just a little, you see, my feet . . . ."

"Of course, yes, I'm sorry."

Christopher Davenham settled into a more relaxed gait, to match Maisie, who had reduced her stride to allow him to consider her words.

"Mr. Davenham, have you ever spoken with your wife about the war, about her brother, about her losses?"

"No, never. I mean, I know the facts. But one just has to get on with it. After all, you can't just give in, can you?"

"And what about you, Mr. Davenham?

"I didn't serve. I have a printing company, Miss Dobbs. I was required by the government to keep the people informed."

"Did you want to serve?'

"Does that matter?"

"Perhaps it does, to your wife. Perhaps it matters to your wife to be able to discuss her past with you, for you to know—"

"Your report will give me the facts, Miss Dobbs."

"Mr. Davenham, you may know the facts, but it isn't a catalog of facts that is causing your wife's melancholy. It is the storage of memories and of feelings. Do you understand?"

The man was silent, as was Maisie. She knew she was out of bounds. But this was not new for her. She had spent much of her life out of bounds, living and speaking where, according to some, she had no business.

"Allow the past to have a voice," Maisie continued. "Then it will be stilled. It's only then that your marriage will have a future, Mr. Davenham. And Mr. Davenham . . ."

"Yes."

"Just in case you were considering such a move, your wife does not need medication, and she does not need a doctor. Your wife needs *you*. When she has you, Vincent will be allowed to rest in peace."

The man took a few more steps in silence, then nodded.

"Shall we go back to the office?" Maisie asked, her head to one side.

Davenham nodded again. Maisie allowed him his thoughts, allowed him the room that he needed in which to take her words to heart. If she persisted, he might become defensive. And this was a door that needed to remain open. For there was something about the experience with Celia Davenham that nagged at Maisie. She didn't yet know what it was, but she was confident that it would speak to her. Maurice Blanche maintained that amid the tales, the smokescreens, and the deceptive mirrors of life's unsolved mysteries, truth resides, waiting for someone to enter its sanctum, then leave, without quite closing the door behind them. That is when truth may make its escape. And Maisie had ensured that the door was left open when she last saw Celia.

It was Maisie's intention that Thursday's meeting would reveal what she needed to know about Vincent's passing, about the mystery of the single name on his headstone, and what had occupied his time between the end of the war and his death. She wanted her next meeting with Celia to reveal Vincent's whereabouts just prior to, and at the time of, his death.

Maisie felt that she understood much about the relationship between Celia and Vincent. Their love had been more of a youthful infatuation—Celia had admitted as much herself—and in going forward with marriage to Christopher Davenham, she had tried to bury her feelings for Vincent at a time when emotions were running high throughout the country. But the ordinary rituals of marriage to the seemingly bland Christopher Davenham could not erase the memory of Vincent, the hero of her imagination, the handsome, fearless knight she might have married. Maisie believed that, to Vincent, Celia had remained simply the younger sister of a dear friend. Yet it was among the friends of one's brothers that so many young women found suitable partners.

Maisie met Celia Davenham at the Ritz for afternoon tea on Thursday, as arranged. As she made her way from the main doors of the Piccadilly entrance to join Celia, Maisie caught her breath when she saw the heavy marble columns at either side of the Winter Garden ahead. She walked toward the steps leading up into the venue for tea, and felt soothed by the warm shafts of light that entered through the windows at either end of the room. For a minute she allowed herself not to consider the expense of the expedition. The opulent grandeur of the Winter Garden, designed to resemble a French pavilion, with decorated cornices and a skylight that allowed soft natural light to bathe the room, almost took Maisie's breath away. With perfect white damask tablecloths, shining silver cutlery, and voluminous swags of fabric hung around the windows, the Winter Garden might not have encouraged intimate conversation between the two women, but the surrounding mirrored panels, and calming presence of water in the golden mermaid sculpture, brought a certan serenity to the room. Instead, with the delicate sound of Royal Doulton china clinking in the background, as cups were replaced on saucers, talk between the two women was light, skimming over the surface of confidence like a fly buzzing over a tranquil millpond.

Maisie touched each side of her lips with her table napkin, and placed it at the side of her plate. "I think it's time for that walk, Mrs. Davenham. Such a lovely day, one feels as if summer is almost here." She reached for her handbag and gloves.

"Oh yes, indeed. Let's walk . . . and please, do call me 'Celia.' I feel as if we know each other so very well now." Celia Cavendish inclined her head in invitation.

"Thank you, Celia. It does seem as if the time for such formality has passed, so I expect you, in turn, to use my Christian name."

With the bill settled, waiters hurried to pull back chairs for the women, their deep bows signaling the exit of a well-satisfied customer, and that the table must be cleared and prepared for the next duo of well-heeled ladies. Maisie and Celia left the Ritz and entered Green Park.

"It's so lovely here—the daffodils are pretty, but they're late this year, aren't they?"

"Indeed they are."

"Maisie, the fabrics at Liberty were simply gorgeous, almost overwhelming, as always. I have to confess, I bought three yards of the most exquisite sheer lilac silk."

"Good for you. How very clever of you to be able to sew."

"I learned from one of our maids who was an absolute whiz with the needle. Mummy insisted upon such drab colors and styles—it was the only way for me to avoid looking like a dowdy schoolmistress. Of course, during the war it wasn't as easy to get fabric, but remember there *was* the passion for all things Indian, wasn't there?"

Maisie nodded, remembering the demand for goods from the Indian subcontinent after the Gurkha regiments joined British forces in France. She remembered Khan, laughing as he told her about the invitations he was suddenly receiving from the very best houses, simply to have the presence of one who seemed, in the eyes of hostesses of the day who were not always clear about the geography of the Indian subcontinent, to be an ambassador for the legion of small, hearty, fearless Nepalese men fighting alongside the regular British soldiers.

There was a comfortable silence as Maisie and Celia made their way along Queen's Walk toward St. James's Park. Strolling alongside St. James's Park lake, they commented that it would have been a good idea to save some pieces of bread to feed the swans, and laughed together at an anxious nanny running in pursuit of a pair of mischievous children toddling on chubby legs toward a pair of mallards. Yet as she brought her step into line with that of her companion, and held her shoulders, arms, and hands as if she were her shadow, Maisie felt once again the melancholy that gripped Celia. But Maisie also knew that Celia would soon confide in her as she had when they last met, for her feelings for Vincent had been dammed inside her, and having been once unleashed, demanded to be heard.

"It was 1917 when Vincent came back to England. He was admitted immediately to hospital, for his wounds were so, so . . . ."

Celia put her hand to her face again, searching for a word to describe Vincent's wounds that would reflect her newfound bravery in telling the tale.

"Utterly devastating, Maisie. I could hardly recognize him when I visited. I had to beg my brother to take me with him—George had arrived home some time before Vincent, as his injuries were not as severe. Vincent wore a linen mask and only removed it when I assured him that I would not flinch."

"Go on," encouraged Maisie.

"But I couldn't contain myself. I burst into tears and rushed from the room. My brother was furious. Yet Vincent wasn't angry with me. But he was angry at everything else."

"Many men were angry when they returned, Celia. Vincent had a right to his anger."

Celia stopped in her walk, shielded her eyes from the sun, which was now late-afternoon low in the sky, then looked again at Maisie.

"That was when he said that he wanted to be just 'Vincent.' He said that as far as Britain was concerned, he was just a piece of meat anyway, he might as well buck the whole system. He said he'd lost his face, so he could be whomever he wanted to be. Except he wasn't quite as polite as that."

"Indeed. Do you know what happened in France? To Vincent?"

"I know, mainly from my brother, that something happened—more than being wounded. I believe there was some . . . discord. With his commanding officers."

"What happened when Vincent was discharged from hospital?"

"Convalescence. By the sea, in Whitstable. The army took over one of the large hotels. Vincent wanted to write about his experiences in France. He was very upset. But each time we sent him a quantity of paper, it was taken away from him. The doctors said that writing distressed him. My brother was furious. He gave Vincent a typewriter, which was confiscated and returned. Vincent maintained he was being silenced, but said he was determined to speak before the war was long gone and no one wanted to know anymore."

"The poor man."

"Then I met Christopher. A very solid man. Of course, he hadn't gone to France. I have to admit I never really found out why. I believe his business protected him from conscription. I seemed to go forward into marriage with a numbness in my mind. But I'd lost one brother, and of course Vincent was deeply, deeply injured. Christopher was a port in the storm. And he is, of course, so very good to me."

"What happened to your friend Vincent after the war, Celia? It seemed that he died some time later."

"Yes, he died only a few years ago. He returned to his parents' home, but as he was terribly disfigured, he became a recluse. Oh, people tried to get him out of the house socially, but he would sit in the drawing room, looking out the window, or reading, or writing in his diary. He worked from home after a while—for a small publishing house, somewhere not far from here, I think."

Celia rubbed her forehead as if pressure would squeeze memories into the present moment.

"He read manuscripts, wrote reports. He had obtained the connection through his uncle's business contacts. Very occasionally he would have someone drive him to the office, to discuss something. He'd had a mask made, of sorts, out of that very fine tin. It was painted in a glaze that matched the color of his skin. And he wore a scarf which he bundled around his neck and lower jaw—well, where his lower jaw used to be. Oh, poor, poor Vincent!"

Celia began to cry. Maisie stopped walking and simply stood next to her, but made no move to console by placing a hand on Celia's shoulder or a comforting arm around her.

"Allow grief room to air itself," Maurice had taught her. "Be judicious in using the body to comfort another, for you may extinguish the freedom that the person feels to be able to share a sadness."

She had learned, with Maurice Blanche as a teacher, respect for the telling of a person's history.

Maisie allowed some time to pass, then took Celia's elbow and gently led her to a park bench, set among a golden display of daffodils nodding sunny heads in the late-afternoon breeze.

"Thank you. Thank you for listening."

"I understand, Celia," replied Maisie.

As Maisie imagined Vincent's brutal disfigurement, she shuddered, recollecting the time she had spent in France, and the images that would remain with her forever, of men who had fought so bravely. She thought, too, of those men who had cheated death, only to struggle with the legacy of their injuries. And, in that moment, she remembered Simon, the gifted doctor who was himself a soldier in the struggle to tear lives free from the bloody clutches of war.

Maisie was brought back from the depths of her own memories by Celia, who was ready to continue her story.

"It was a bit of luck, really, that one of the patients he had been in hospital with remembered him. I wish I could recall his name. He had returned to France for a time after the war and saw that men with facial disfigurement were looked after in a different way. They were brought together for holidays, taken to the country to camps where they could live together for a while without having to worry about people drawing away—after all, they all had wounds. And, I suppose, more importantly, the public didn't have to look at them. Terrible, isn't it? Anyway, this man came back to England and wanted to get the same sort of thing going here."

Celia Davenham looked around her and briefly closed her eyes in the warmth of the waning spring sunshine.

"He bought a farm that was on the market, then got in touch with the men he had met while recovering from his own wounds. According to Vincent, he—heavens, what was his name? Anyway, this man had been deeply affected by the war in a way that made him want to do something for those with disfiguring wounds. Vincent was a strong supporter of the idea. It gave him an energy I certainly hadn't seen since before the war. In fact, the man was rather taken with Vincent's stubborn refusal to be known by anything but his first name. So Vincent went to live at The Retreat."

"Was that what it was called? The Retreat?"

"Yes. I think it was Vincent's idea. The name. There was a connection to 'Beating The Retreat,' I think, in that they were withdrawing from society, which for many of them had become the enemy. Vincent said that it commemorated each man who died in France, and every man brought home to live with injuries. He said that it was for all those who suffered and should have had a place to go back to, when there never was one."

"Did he remain there, at The Retreat?"

"Yes, he did. He became very reclusive. My brother would visit occasionally. Of course, by then I was married to Christopher, so I did not visit. I wanted to, though. In fact, I have considered making the journey, since Vincent died. Just to see where—"

"He died at The Retreat?"

"Yes. I'm not really sure what happened. My brother was told by Vincent's people that he slipped and fell by the stream. Breathing was difficult for him anyway, due to his injuries, but perhaps he hit his head. His parents have passed on now. I think they didn't really ask questions. Everyone agreed that it was a terrible accident, but it might have been a release for him."

"Did The Retreat close?"

"Oh no. It's still very much open. The farmhouse has been converted so that the residents each have a room, and specialist craftsmen were employed to work on the outbuildings, so that they could also be used for accommodation. I understand that new residents are welcomed. They are all men who have suffered injury of some kind during the war, and need a place to go."

"How does this man who set up The Retreat pay for everyone?"

"Oh, *they* pay. Resources are pooled. Christopher thought it was all very odd in that respect. But, you understand, Christopher would think that. He's very careful with money. Vincent gave Adam—that's it, Adam Jenkins, his name is Adam Jenkins—Vincent gave Adam Jenkins control of his finances when he decided to become a resident rather than a short-term visitor. The residents work on the farm as well, so it's still a going concern."

"Well, well, well. Vincent must have had tremendous respect for this man, Adam Jenkins."

The two women had started walking back towards the north entrance of St. James's Park. Celia looked at her watch.

"Oh my goodness! I must hurry. Christopher is taking me to the theater this evening. It's quite amazing, you know. He's always been such a stick-in-the-mud, but now he's planning all sorts of outings. I love the theater. I thought I would never go again when I married Christopher, but he's suddenly become quite agreeable to an evening out."

"How lovely! I must dash too, Celia. But before you go, could you tell me where The Retreat is? I have a friend who may be interested to know about it."

"It's in Kent. Near Sevenoaks, that area. In fact, it's not too far from Nether Green. Good-bye, Maisie—and here's my card. Do call me again for tea. It was so lovely. I feel so very light after spending time with you, you know. Perhaps it's being out here in the fresh air of the park today."

"Yes, perhaps it is. Have a lovely time at the theater, Celia."

The two women parted, but before making her way to the St. James's Park underground station, Maisie walked back into the park to reconsider their conversation. She would probably not see Celia again.

Vincent had died while living in a community of ex-soldiers, all of whom, initially, were facially disfigured in some way, although it seemed that the doors were now open to those who had other injuries. There was nothing untoward about the motives of Adam Jenkins, who seemed to want to help these men. It must cost a pretty penny to arrange care for the residents, but then again, resources were pooled, and they were self-sufficient and working on the farm. A farm called, ambiguously, The Retreat. Maisie considered the meanings of "retreat," and wondered if the soldiers were, in fact, relinquishing their position, seeking a place of shelter from the enemy. For such men perhaps life itself was now the enemy.

Maisie picked up the heavy black telephone and began to dial BEL 4746, the Belgravia home of Lord Julian Compton and his wife, Lady Rowan. There was a short delay, then Maisie heard the telephone ring three times before being answered by Carter, the Compton's long-serving butler. She checked her watch immediately the call was answered.

"Compton residence."

"Hello, Mr. Carter. How are you?"

"Maisie, what a pleasure. We are all well here, thank you, but not looking forward to Cook's retirement, though it's long overdue."

"And what about you, Mr. Carter?"

"Now then, Maisie, as long as I can manage these stairs, I will be at the house. Her ladyship has been very anxious to speak with you, Maisie."

"Yes, I know. That's why I've telephoned."

"Oh, well. . . . I should know better than to ask how you know, Maisie."

"Mr. Carter, that really doesn't take a lot, does it? Lady Rowan is a terrier in disguise."

Carter laughed and connected the call to Lady Rowan, who was in the library reading the late-edition newspapers.

"Maisie, dear girl. Where have you been? I thought you'd gone off somewhere."

"No, Lady Rowan. I've been busy."

"Excellent news. But you really must not be a stranger to us. Are you sure that you wouldn't like to move into the upstairs apartments? I know I keep asking, but this is such a big house now. It never used to seem this big. Perhaps I'm getting smaller. They say that about age."

"No, Lady Rowan. Not you. Shall I come to see you this week?"

"Yes. Definitely. Come tomorrow. And I insist that you have dinner with me, and that you stay. I simply cannot have you traveling on your own after dark, and I know that you will refuse any offer to drive you home."

"Yes, Lady Rowan. I'll stay—but just for one night. Is everything all right?"

There was a silence on the line.

"Lady Rowan, is everything all right?"

"I want to talk to you about James. I thought you might have some advice for a poor misunderstood mother."

"Lady Rowan—"

"Yes, I'm laying it on a bit thick. But I'm worried about him. He's talking about going off to live on a farm in Kent. Sounds very strange to me. In fact, it sounds more than strange. Maisie, I confess, I'm frightened for James. He has been in the depths of melancholy since the war, it seems, and now this!"

"Of course. I'll do anything I can to help," replied Maisie.

"Thank you so much, my dear. What time will you be here?"

"Will six o'clock be all right?"

"Perfect. I'll tell Carter. Mrs. Crawford will be delighted to see you."

"Until then, Lady Rowan."

"Take care, Maisie. And remember, I want to know everything about what you are doing."

"I will leave no story untold, Lady Rowan."

The two women laughed, bade each other good-bye, and replaced their respective telephone receivers. Without a second's delay Maisie checked her watch. She reached into the top drawer of her desk and took out a small ledger with "Telephone" marked on the cover. Inside she made a note that the call to Lady Rowan Compton had taken four minutes. Maisie replaced the ledger and closed the drawer before walking to the window.

Of course she would offer Lady Rowan any assistance in her power, for she was indebted to her for so much. And Maisie knew, too, how difficult the aftermath of the war had been for James—but not, perhaps, as hard as it had been for the likes of Vincent. Yet Maisie was sympathetic to his melancholy, which was as much due to a loss still mourned as to his injuries. Maisie wondered whether Lord Julian had concerns regarding the ability of his only son to take on the family's business interests, and she was aware that Lady Rowan had often been the peacekeeper between the two. Tall, blond, blue-eyed James had always been the apple of his mother's eye. Years ago, when his son was no longer a child, Lord Julian had been heard to say on many an occasion, "You're spoiling that boy, Rowan." And now the once mischievously energetic James seemed hollow and drawn. Lady Rowan had been secretly relieved when James, a flying ace, was injured—not in the air but during an explosion on the ground. She knew his wounds would heal, and that she would have him safe at home at a time when so many of her contemporaries were receiving word that their sons had been lost to war.

Maisie turned from the window, and walked toward the door. Taking her coat and hat from the stand, she looked around the room, extinguished the light, and left her office. As she locked the door behind her, she reflected upon how strange it was that a man who had significant financial resources, time, and a beautiful house in the country would seek the peace and quiet that might dispel his dark mood by going to live on a stranger's farm. Making her way downstairs in the half-light shed by the flickering gas lamp, Maisie felt a chill move through her body. And she knew that the sensation was not caused by the cold or the damp, but by a threat—a threat to the family of the woman she held most dear, the woman who had helped her achieve accomplishments that might otherwise have remained an unrealized dream.

SPRING 1910–SPRING 1917

# CHAPTER EIGHT

*orn in 1863, and growing up in the middle years of Queen Victoria's reign, Lady Rowan had delighted her father, the fourth Earl of Westavon, but had been the source of much frustration for her mother, Lady Westavon, who was known to comment that her daughter was "a lady in name only!" It was clear that, far from being content with pursuits more becoming her position and upbringing, she was happiest with her horses and with her brother, Edwin, when he came home from school in the holidays. From an early age she had questioned her father, disagreed with her mother, and by the time she was on the cusp of womanhood, caused her parents to wonder if a suitable match would ever be found.

Maurice Blanche was ten years Lady Rowan's senior, a school friend of her brother. At first Rowan was fascinated by Maurice during those weekends when Edwin brought Maurice home from Marlborough School.

"His people are in France, so I thought he might like to get out for a bit of a break," said Edwin, introducing the short, stocky boy who seemed to have little to say.

But when Maurice spoke, the young Rowan hung on his every word. His accent, a hybrid that came as a result of his French father and Scottish mother, intrigued her. As she grew older, Lady Rowan realized that Maurice moved with ease among people of any background, often changing his accent slightly to echo the nuances and rhythm of the other person's speech. The listener only vaguely appreciated the distinction, but nevertheless leaned in closer, smiled more easily, and probably shared a confidence to which no other person had been privy. Gradually his influence on the life of Lady Rowan challenged and inspired her, and in turn, his trust in her honest opinion was unfailing.

In the course of his life's work, Maurice Blanche could count among his friends and colleagues: philosophers, scientists, doctors, psychologists, and members of the judiciary. It was a self-designed career that had rendered him invaluable to an extraordinary range of people, whether government ministers, those investigating crime, or simply people who needed information.

In 1898, the year in which Lady Rowan celebrated the tenth anniversary of her marriage to Lord Julian Compton, it was clear to Maurice that Rowan needed to be engaged in more than simply London's social calendar. Her only son, James, had just been sent away to a preparatory school, an inevitable event Lady Rowan had dreaded. During a heated political discussion Maurice dared the very vocal and opinionated Lady Rowan to follow her own challenging words with actions.

"It's not enough to say that you want equality, Ro. What do you intend to do about it?

Lady Rowan swallowed hard. Soon after, she became a fully fledged and active suffragette.

Eleven years later Lady Rowan Compton shocked Belgravia by marching on Westminster, demanding the vote and equality for women, rich and poor. Lord Julian was long suffering, but the truth of the matter was that he adored Rowan and would walk on hot coals rather than cross her. Questioned about his wife's involvement,

Lord Julian would simply reply, "Oh, you know Ro, once she's got the bit between her teeth . . . ." and people would nod sympathetically and leave the subject alone, which was exactly what Lord Julian wanted them to do. However, it was Maurice Blanche who challenged Rowan once again on the depth of her commitment.

"So you march on Westminster, and you have these meetings with your sister suffragettes, but what are you actually doing?"

"Maurice, what do you mean, what am I *doing?* This house is full of women meeting together three times a week—and we're forging ahead, make no mistake!"

Lady Rowan had barely taken a sip from her glass of sherry when Maurice issued an instruction. "We're off. Got something to show you. Go and change. Plain walking skirt and a jacket will do. And good sturdy shoes, Rowan."

Blanche stood up and walked toward the window, a move that suggested she should be quick.

"Maurice, you had better have good reason—"

"Hurry up, Rowan, or I shall leave without you."

Lady Rowan went immediately to her room, and when Nora, her personal maid, came to ask if she was needed, she was turned away.

"No. That's quite all right, Nora. I can help myself, you know."

Lady Rowan dressed quickly, with only a cursory glance in the mirror. She cut a handsome figure, and she knew it. Not that she was quintessentially pretty, but with her height and aquiline profile, she was striking. She was an athletic woman, a keen and competitive tennis player, an accomplished equestrienne, and a notoriously reckless skier on the slopes of Wengen until she was well into her forties. Her once rich chestnut hair had dulled slightly and was peppered with gray, but mercifully her weight had changed little since the day of her marriage. On the day Maurice Blanche demanded she accompany him, Lady Rowan Compton was forty-seven.

Rowan was excited. Maurice was prodding her at a time when life had lost some of the edge it had had in her youth. Yes, she was involved in the suffragette movement, she had her horses at the country

estate, and of course there was the London social calendar, engagements and reciprocal entertainment making up an important part of
her life in town during the season. James had just finished his school-
ing. She had looked forward to his company at home when his school
years were over, but she rarely had it, for no sooner had he returned
from the city than he seemed to vanish again. James was a man now,
if still a very young one.

As she dressed, Lady Rowan tingled with anticipation, Maurice
might provide her with a diversion to fill a gap that seemed to be
widening with the passing years. She returned to the drawing room,
and they left the house quickly. The two old friends walked along the
tree-lined street, conversation unnecessary, although Lady Rowan was
aching to know where they were going.

"*I*'m not saying that you are not busy, Rowan," Maurice broke
their silence. "Not at all. And the cause is a worthy one. For women
to have a place of account in this society, they must have a political
voice. And having had one queen on the throne in the modern age
does not constitute such a voice. But Rowan, with you the voice
always comes from a safe place, does it not?"

"You should have been on the march, Maurice. That wasn't safe at
all."

"I'm sure. But we both know that I'm not talking about marches.
I'm talking about the safe place that we remain in, within the world
we were born to. Swimming forever in the confines of our own pond.
Socially, intellectually—"

"Maurice—"

"Rowan, we will speak again of equality later, for it is equality that
you claim to want. Now then, we must wait here for an omnibus."

"A *what?* Now, I told you, Maurice—we should have called for the
motor."

"No, Rowan. We are stepping out of your pond today. I have the fare for us both."

✦

*It* was dark when they returned to Belgravia in silence. Rowan was deep in thought. She had seen much that troubled her. But nothing troubled her more than her own emotions.

"You'll come in . . ."

"No, Rowan. You are tired from swimming in another pond today. A pond that, though discussed in your meetings and debates, you could not truly imagine. Poverty is something we think we understand from description. It is only when it is close to hand that we have a grasp of what it means to be unequal."

"But what can I do?"

"No need to wear a hair shirt, Rowan. But perhaps opportunities will present themselves. One only has to ask, 'How might I serve?' Goodnight, my dear."

Maurice bowed slightly, then left Rowan in the entrance hall of her grand home.

He had taken her to the East End of London. First to the noisy markets, which thrilled her, although she could not look directly at some of the street urchins. Then into the depths of London's poorest areas. And it seemed that always someone knew him.

"Evenin', Doc, awright then?"

"Well, very well. And how is the youngest?"

"Comin' on a treat, Doc. Thanks to you."

Rowan didn't ask about his relationship to the people who greeted him so readily. Maurice was certainly a doctor, but after attending King's College Medical School in London, he had studied at the University of Edinburgh's Department of Legal Medicine. Rowan was under the impression that he no longer practiced. At least not upon people who were still alive.

"To answer the question that is written all over your face, Rowan—once or twice a week, I attend women and children at a small clinic. There is precious little set aside for the poor, there is a constant need for help, for . . . everything. And, of course, bringing children safely into the world and providing care when they are sick is a refreshing change for me."

Rowan rung the bell in the drawing room. She had dismissed Carter, the butler, as soon as she arrived home, but now she craved inner warmth.

How may I serve? What can I do? What would be sensible? What would Julian say? Well, that was something she would not have to think about. If Maurice was her challenger, Julian was her rock.

"Yes, Your Ladyship?"

"Carter, I'd like some hot soup, please—something simple, nothing too clever, you understand. And a sherry please, Carter."

"Very good, Ma'am. Cook prepared a tasty vegetable soup this afternoon, as soon as the delivery arrived."

"Perfect. Perfect, Carter."

Carter poured sherry into a crystal glass and held it out on a silver salver.

"Oh—and Carter. Before I forget. I would like to speak to you about the dinner next week and our guests. Lord Julian's business associates. Tomorrow morning after breakfast, tell Cook to come to my study as well. Ten o'clock."

"Very good, Your Ladyship. Will that be all?"

Later, as Lady Rowan finished the hot soup that had been brought on a tray to the drawing room, she leaned back in her chair and contemplated what she had seen that day, and about the conversation with Maurice. It is so easy, she thought. All I have to do is snap my fingers and someone runs. Equality. Maurice is right, I can do more.

# Maisie Dobbs

While Lady Rowan readied herself for bed in her grand house in Belgravia on that night in the spring of 1910, a thirteen-year-old girl cried herself to sleep in the small back room of a soot-blackened terraced house in southeast London. Her jet black hair, released from a neat braid and purple ribbon, cascaded over the pillow, and the deep blue eyes that so easily reflected joy were rimmed with dark circles and red with tears. She cried for her loss and cried, too, for her father, whose dreadful, deep breathless sobs echoed from kitchen below.

Maisie had held her tears back for days, believing that if her father did not see or hear her crying, he would not worry about her, and his burden would be lighter. And each day, his heart breaking, he rose in the early hours of the morning, harnessed his horse to the cart, and made his way to Covent Garden Market.

At first, after her mother died, Maisie would pinch herself three times on the right arm before sleeping, assured that this one action would make her rise at three o'clock in the morning, in time to make his tea and spread a thick slice of bread with beef dripping for him eat in front of the coal stove before he set off for the market.

"You don't 'ave to do that, love. I can watch out for meself, Maisie. You go on back to bed. And mind you lock that door after I leave."

"I'm all right, Dad. You'll see. We'll be all right."

But Frankie Dobbs was at a loss. A widower with a thirteen-year-old daughter. She needed more, and Lord knows that the girl and her mother had been close, thought Frankie. No, he had to find something better for the girl than for her to be little woman of the house.

Oh, there was so much that they had wanted for Maisie, the child that had come to them in later life, and who was, they said, the answer to many prayers. She was a bright one, they knew that almost from the beginning. In fact, people would remark on it, that even as a newborn it seemed that Maisie could focus on a person and follow them with her eyes. "That girl can look right through you," people would say, when she was still a babe in arms.

· 73 ·

The Dobbses had been putting money away for Maisie's education, so that she could stay on at school, perhaps even go on to be a teacher. They were so proud of their girl. But the money was gone, long gone to pay for doctors, medicine, and a holiday at the seaside, just in case the fresh salty air worked a miracle. But nothing had worked. Frankie was alone with his girl now, and he was afraid. Afraid that he couldn't do well by her, that he had nothing left to give her. No, it was settled. He had to find a place for Maisie.

It seemed to Frankie that even Persephone, his old mare, had lost pride in her step. Frankie always made sure his horse and cart were well turned out; it made a difference to business. He might be a costermonger, but there was no excuse for looking shabby. With trousers pressed under the mattress each night, a clean white collarless shirt, fresh brightly colored neckerchief, his best woolen waistcoat, and a cloth cap set jauntily on the side of his head, Frankie himself was always well turned out. "Just because I use me 'ands to make a livin' doesn't mean to say I can't do with a bit of spit and polish," Frankie had been heard to say.

And as he climbed up onto the driver's seat of his cart, Frankie was more than proud of his shining horse and the gleaming leather and brass traces. Persephone, a Welsh cob, trotted proudly down the street, lifting her hooves high as if she knew how good she looked. But since the death of Maisie's mother, Frankie's inner malaise was felt keenly by Persephone, who now trotted in a desultory manner, as if the family's grief had added several hundredweight to her load.

In the kitchen of the house in Belgravia, Carter and Lady Rowan's cook, Mrs. Crawford, were deep in conversation about the morning's meeting to discuss the week's dinner plans.

"What time will Mr. Dobbs be here, Cook? You'll need to have a complete list of fresh vegetables for Lady Rowan, and your menu planned for the week."

Cook rolled her eyes. Just what she loved, being told how to do her job.

"Mr. Carter, menu suggestions are in hand. I asked Mr. Dobbs to stop by again today to give me a list of what is best at market this week. He is going out of the way to be at our service, poor man."

"Yes indeed, Cook. Mr. Dobbs certainly has his hands full. I quite agree."

Outside the rear entrance of the house, a horse and cart came to a halt. They could hear Frankie Dobbs talking to Persephone, putting on her nosebag of oats, telling her he wouldn't be long, then setting off down the stairs that led to the back door of the kitchen.

"That'll be him now." Cook wiped her hands on a cloth, and went to answer the door.

"Mr. Dobbs," she said, standing aside so that Frankie Dobbs could enter the large warm room. As he removed his cloth cap, Mrs. Crawford cast a glance at Carter, frowned, and shook her head. Frankie Dobbs looked pale and drawn.

"Good morning, Mr. Dobbs. How are you?"

"Very well, all things considered, Mr. Carter. And you?" It was a thin response, and both cook and Carter glanced at each other again. This was not the jovial, robust Frankie Dobbs they were used to doing business with. "I've brought a list of the best vegetables and fruit this week. If I take the order today, I can deliver tomorrow morning. The broccoli and sprouts are looking very nice indeed, and of course there's some hearty cabbage at the market. I know Her Ladyship is partial to a nice bit of cabbage."

"She certainly is, Mr. Dobbs." Cook took the rough piece of paper from Frankie, and ran a finger down the list of vegetables. "I think we'll need something of everything this week. Full house, you know."

"Right you are." Standing uneasily in the kitchen, Frankie fingered his cap. "I was wondering, Mr. Carter, if there was something I might discuss. With both yourself and Mrs. Crawford here."

"Of course, Mr. Dobbs, sit down at the table. Cook, a cup of tea for Mr. Dobbs. What can we do for you?"

Carter faced Frankie across the heavy pine table.

"Well, it's about my girl. She's a bright lass, very bright . . ." Frankie faltered, looked at his shining boots and twisted his cap. "Since 'er mother died, well, we was going to send 'er on to the big school . . . and she got a scholarship and all . . . but there's the money for the special clothes and books, and what with the doctor's bills . . ."

Cook placed a cup of tea in front of Frankie, leaned toward him, and covered his hand with hers. "You're a good man, Mr. Dobbs. You'll do right by young Maisie."

Frankie shrank at his daughter's name, afraid of what he was about to ask. "I was wonderin' if you had a place for my Maisie 'ere, like. In service. She's a good girl. 'ard worker. Very bright. You won't need to tell 'er anythin' twice. She's well mannered and speaks nicely—'er mother, God rest her soul, saw to that. I thought that after a while, she could go back to night school, you see. Take up where she left off. Loves learnin', does Maisie."

Carter and Cook glanced at each other once again, and Carter spoke quickly. "Mr. Dobbs, it seems you have come at the right time, and in answer to a prayer, hasn't he, Mrs. Crawford?"

Cook looked at Carter and nodded her head in agreement. She had absolutely no idea what he was talking about.

"One of our more junior maids recently left service. Help is needed. Have your girl come to the house at five o'clock today—she can pick up the order for tomorrow's delivery. I think you have to check quantities, don't you, Mrs. Crawford?"

Cook nodded agreement, and looked at the list of vegetables again. They both knew that Frankie Dobbs never had to be told quantities, and always delivered exactly what was needed. Carter continued, "I'll interview her, just to make sure that she is right for the position."

Frankie breathed a sigh of relief.

"Thank you, Mr. Carter, Mrs. Crawford. I'll be getting on now. Maisie will be here at five sharp."

The grieving man left quickly, and before leading his horse away, put his head against the Persephone's soft nose and wept. "It's for the best," he whispered. "It's for the best."

It was the nearest he had come to having "words" with his daughter. As Frankie broke the news to Maisie—that times were difficult, that he was only thinking of her, that he wanted her to be safe, and that the Compton household was a fine place to work—he watched the tears well up in her eyes, her jaw tighten with the effort of not giving in to the pressure to cry, and her fine, long-fingered hands clench into fists held firmly by her sides.

"But Dad, you know you need me here. I can help. I helped when Mum was ill. I can get another job, I can even do this job and come home at night, Dad."

"Maisie, love, we'll still see each other, you know that. Sunday afternoons we can go to the park, take a turn, have a cup of tea. We can go to see yer Nan and Granddad. But at least you'll have a place, a good job. And later on, we can get you into night school, to catch up. I'm all out, love. There's no money, and there's bills to pay. I don't even know if I can keep renting this house. Your mother going . . . ."

Maisie drew away as he reached out to her, turned her back to him, and looked out the window. They hadn't been well off, not by any means, but there used to be enough for a few extras. Now there was nothing, and there was ground to be made up. Then they would be all right. She sighed deeply in resignation.

"Dad, if I work at Lady Rowan's, and if I send you my money, and we make up the bills, then can I come back?"

"Oh, love. Then what would you do? I was thinking you might go on from there. Maybe get out of the Smoke. She's got a place in the country, you know. Down in Kent. She's got contacts, woman like that. You do yer classes at night, you might get yerself a private teaching job at one of them big 'ouses. You don't want to be back 'ere. Yer mother and me wanted so much for you, love."

Her father was tired beyond reckoning. They were both tired beyond reckoning. Too tired for this talk. But she would go to Lady Rowan's to see this Mr. Carter. And so help me, I'll work my way out of that place, thought Maisie. And on my own. I'll work so hard I'll take care of Dad. He won't have to get up at three in the morning by the time I've finished. Maisie bit her lip and looked up at nothing in particular on the wall. You'll see, I'll show him who can take care of herself. Maisie sighed, then reached out and put her arms around her father's waist.

"Dad, I'll go. You're right. Annie Clark down the road is in service now. So's Doreen Watts. Lot of girls are. It'll be all right. I'll see Mr. Carter. I won't let you down, Dad."

"Oh, love. You could never let me down."

Frankie Dobbs hugged his daughter close for a moment longer, then pushed her back. "Now then, this is where you go."

Maisie Dobbs watched her father as he took a short pencil from his waistcoat pocket, licked the lead, and began to scribble directions on the back of a scrap of paper.

# CHAPTER NINE

*D*ays after securing the position of in-between maid, Maisie returned to the white four-story mansion in London's Belgravia, at the southern end of Ebury Place. Before reporting for work, Maisie stood in front of the building and looked up, wondering what it might be like to enter such a house through the front door. Transferring the canvas bag containing her clothes, hairbrushes, and several books from her right hand to her left, Maisie took a handkerchief from her coat pocket and wiped her eyes, hoping that no tell-tale marks were left from the tears shed on the bus from Lambeth. She sighed and, making her way to the left of the house, braced her shoulders and held on to the wrought iron banister to steady herself as she walked down the stone steps that led to the kitchen.

Once welcomed by Carter and Mrs. Crawford, Maisie took her belongings to the top floor of the house. The very top floor, the attic reached by "back stairs" from the kitchen. She shared the room with Enid.

Enid was a worldly sixteen-year-old, with pressed rouge on her cheeks and a hint of color on her lips, who had now reached such a high position of authority that she would be called upon to serve in the breakfast room come tomorrow morning. A thin, gangly girl, Enid was friendly enough to Maisie, who felt that circumstances would never give her cause to laugh again.

"That's your bed over there," was Enid's welcome to the shared bedroom. "Make yourself at home. We're up early in the morning. Half past four, five at the latest, so I hope you don't snore and keep me awake."

She grinned at Maisie, her freckled nose crinkling over the teasing remark. Enid was concentrating on her pronunciation, convinced that if she was to get anywhere in the world, she had to work quickly to introduce aitches into her spoken language. Thus every word beginning with the letter *h* was overpronounced, with a breathy start and a rapid completion. *Huh-ome, huh-ouse, huh-ope.* In fact, Enid's rather zealous pursuit of something better resulted in the occasional *h* where *h* had no place.

"H-ave you bin in s-h-ervice before, or is this your first pos-hishun?" asked Enid.

"No, this is my first. My mother passed on and my father thought it better . . . ."

Enid nodded. She never did know what to say when confronted by loss.

"Well, I reckon you'll do all right. You're tall, not as tall as me, mind, but taller than some of them short girls. They reckon the tall ones always do all right, get promoted quickly to serving, being as we look better in the uniform, more, you know, suited to the h-occasion. And you won't find them upstairs doin' any little tests to see if you're an h-onest sort—like puttin' a farthin' under the carpet to see if you take it or leave it on the side. Anyway, come on, Dobbsie, I'll show you where the facilities are. Come along with me."

Enid put her hand on Maisie's shoulder and led her along a dimly lit hallway to the "fac-hilities."

Carter had chosen to introduce her at breakfast. Maisie knew that in some houses the staff weren't introduced until they had reached a higher position, if at all. The practice changed at the Compton residence when Lord Julian had asked a maid to inform Lady Rowan that he would take tea with her in the drawing room, to which the maid had answered, "Yes, Sir. And who shall I say is calling?" Lady Rowan was appalled, and since that time had insisted upon meeting whoever was under her roof, even if the meeting was a short one.

"Your Lordship, Your Ladyship, may I introduce our new downstairs member of staff, Miss Maisie Dobbs." Carter held his hand out toward Maisie, who took one step forward, curtsied, and stepped back to her place alongside Carter.

Lord and Lady Compton were cordial, welcoming Maisie to the household, saying they were absolutely sure that she would be happy there. After a brief encounter, she left the dining room with Carter, to go down to the kitchens and receive her instructions for the day.

"My word, Julian, what a striking girl."

Lord Compton looked over a folded edge of *The Times* toward his wife. "Striking? Yes. Yes, I suppose so. Very young."

"Yes, very young. Very . . . there was something about her, wasn't there?"

"Mmm? About whom?" Lord Julian continued to read the newspaper.

"About Miss Dobbs. Something quite different about her, don't you think? Julian, are you listening?"

"Hmm? Oh, Rowan. Yes. Miss Dobb, Dobbins . . . what was her name? Dobbs?" Lord Julian looked out of the window to recall the conversation. "You know, Rowan, I think you are right. Could be those eyes. Very deep blue. Don't see that very often."

"Julian. I don't think it was the color of her eyes. It was nothing I could put my finger on."

Lady Rowan spread a thin slice of toast with butter and marmalade as Lord Julian turned to the next page of the morning paper. "Yes, Darling, probably nothing."

Within a few days, most people agreed that Maisie Dobbs had indeed settled in well to life at the Compton residence. Her day started at half past four, when she rose and poured cold water from the pitcher on the washstand into a large china bowl. She splashed her face and moistened a cloth to wash her body before hurriedly dressing, then tiptoeing down to the lowest level of the house to fill the coal scuttles.

Her first job was to take heavy coal scuttles to the breakfast room, the drawing room, His Lordship's study, the morning room, and to the hall. Kneeling by each fireplace, she pulled back the black iron grate cover, swept out yesterday's ashes, and placed them in an old empty scuttle. She rolled sheets of yesterday's newspaper, placed them in the grate, then carefully positioned dry kindling on top and lit the newspaper with a match.

As flames licked up and caught on the wood, Maisie leaned forward and balanced bricks of coal, one by one, on the spitting wood. Sitting back, she watched for just a few seconds as the fire crackled and flared into life. Satisfied that the wood and coal had taken the flames, she brushed splinters, coal dust, and ash under the grate, replaced the cover, and put a few more pieces of coal onto the mound before giving the fireplace a quick dust. She was ready to move on to another room.

When she had finished lighting fires in each of the rooms, it was time to fill the scuttles again and feed the fires so that the rooms were ready to warm those who had time to sit by a fire—people who had the time to be warmed by something other than hard work.

Throughout the day Maisie cleaned, ran errands for Cook, and generally served at the bidding of anyone above her in the pecking order, which was almost everyone in the household. But the duties of her waking hours brought a calm to Maisie's life that she had not known since before her mother became ill. She had only to follow the direction of others, and in the rhythm of her daily round, whether blacking the fireplaces, sweeping the stairs, or polishing furniture, there was room for thought—thought of what might be.

Maisie's "day off" was Sunday afternoon. As soon as the heavy clock on the mantelpiece over the kitchen stove struck a single chime at half past eleven, Maisie waited for Cook to look up at her and nod toward the door.

"All right, lass, off you go. And mind you're back by a decent hour!"

It was a feigned warning, because Maisie had nowhere to be at an indecent hour.

Untying her pinafore as she hurried from the kitchen and up the back stairs toward the servants' quarters, Maisie thought that her legs would never carry her as fast as her mind wanted to travel. She quickly changed into a long black skirt that had belonged to her mother, and a clean cotton blouse. She checked her reflection in the mirror just once, pushed her hat onto her head, and reached for her coat and coin purse before rushing through the bedroom door again. She was off to see her father, knowing that at twelve noon he would pull the fob watch from his waistcoat pocket and smile to himself. Frankie Dobbs couldn't wait for his girl to come home so they could spend a few hours together, a precious respite from a work-weary week.

On Sundays, Frankie was always to be found at the stable where he kept his mare, under the dry arches that were part of the Southern construction of Waterloo Bridge. Sunday was the day to clean the horse from head to hoof, to oil the leather traces, polish the brasses, and make sure the cart was ready for another week's work. It was an easy morning, a morning made sweeter by the knowledge that soon Maisie's footsteps would clatter against the cobblestone street leading to the stables.

"Love, you are a sight for sore eyes. How are you, my girl?"

"Well enough, Dad. I'm well enough."

"Let me just finish this, then we'll go home for a cuppa."

Together they worked in the stable, finally leaving the horse to the remainder of her day at rest. After a cup of tea, Frankie would dress in his Sunday best, and father and daughter would catch a bus to Brockwell Park, where they walked together before stopping to eat a packed lunch.

"You should see the library, Dad! I've never seen so many books. Walls of them. About everything."

"You and your books, girl. You keeping up with your reading?"

"Yes, Dad. I go to the public library every week on a Wednesday afternoon. Mrs. Crawford sends me with a list for her and Mr. Carter, and I get books for myself as well. Mind you, Enid says she can't sleep with the light on, so I can't read for long."

"You watch your eyes, my girl, you only get one pair, you know."

"Dad!"

"I know, I'm naggin'. So, what about the other folk downstairs, what're they like, then?"

Father and daughter sat down on a wooden bench overlooking a flowerbed. "Well, you know Mr. Carter and Mrs. Crawford."

"That I do. Good people, both of them."

"Well, anyway, Mrs. Crawford is called 'Cook' and 'Mrs. Crawford' without any—well, without any method to it."

"What do you mean, love?"

"I mean that sometimes she's called 'Cook' or sometimes 'Mrs. Crawford' and there's no rule—sometimes it's both names in one sentence."

Frankie chewed on a sandwich, and nodded his head for Maisie to continue.

"There's two footmen, Arthur and Cedric, and there's Her Ladyship's maid, Nora—she's a bit quiet. Apparently, at the big house, in Kent, there's more staff and a housekeeper, Mrs. Johnson. There's some scullery maids—Dossie, Emily, and Sadie—who help Mrs. Crawford in the kitchen, and of course there's Enid."

"What's she like, then?"

"She's got hair the color of a blazing fire, Dad. Really red, it is. And when she brushes it out at night, it goes right up like this."

Maisie held out her hands to indicate a distance away from the sides of her head, which made Frankie laugh. Something he couldn't understand—how she could look like a child one minute, and like a mature woman the next.

"She nice to you, love?"

"She's all right, Dad. Blows hot and cold, though. One minute she seems full of the joys of spring, and the next, well, I just keep out of her way."

"I might've guessed. Your carrottops are always the same. Remember, love, the more you're yourself, the more it's like you've just put iron shoes on yer feet—they'll 'old you to the ground when that 'ot and cold air comes rushing from 'er direction. That's the key with that sort."

Maisie nodded, as if to take in this important advice, and continued with her story. "The other thing about Enid is that I think she's sweet on Master James."

Frankie laughed again. "Oh! I see it didn't take you long to get wind of the goings-on! What's 'e like, then, this James? Bit old to be called 'Master,' in' 'e?"

"Well, apparently, so I heard Cook saying, His Lordship gave instructions that Master James should be called Master until he proved his worth. Or something like that. He comes into the kitchen sometimes, you know, of an evening, after dinner. I've watched him. He comes in to see Cook, and as he walks by Enid, he always winks at her. She goes all red in the face and looks the other way, but I know she likes him. And Cook pretends to tell him off for coming into her kitchen, as if he was still a little boy, but then she brings out a big plate of ginger biscuits—which he gets stuck into while he's standing there in the kitchen! Drives Mr. Carter mad, it does."

"I should think it does! Likes order, does Mr. Carter. Now then, tell me about the 'ouse itself."

And Maisie smiled, glad to be in the easy company of her father, a man who was given to remark that a person could take him as they found him, there were no airs around Frankie Dobbs. And Frankie was more at peace now. Life itself was easier—easier now that the man knew his daughter to be in good hands. Easier now that the bills were being paid. Yes, thought Frankie Dobbs as he walked with his daughter in the park, it was all getting easier.

⁂

*M*aisie was fascinated by the library. It was well used, for both Lord and Lady Compton enjoyed literature, politics, and keeping up with the fancies of intellectual London. But when Maisie opened the door and brought in the coal scuttle at five in the morning, it was a quiet room. The lush velvet curtains kept drafts at bay and allowed warmth to seep into every corner after Maisie had lit the fire ready for whoever would use the room that morning.

Each day she lingered just a little longer before kneeling down to the fireplace, before her hands were blackened by the lighting of fires. Each day she learned a little more about the depth and breadth of knowledge housed in the Comptons' library, and each day her hunger grew. Gradually she became braver, first tentatively touching the leather binding as she read the title on the spine of a book, then taking the text from its place on the shelf and opening the fine onion-skin pages at the front of the book.

The library seized Maisie's imagination, rendering the small public library with which she was familiar a very poor runner-up in her estimation. Of all the rooms in the house, she loved this the most. One morning, as she replaced a book to attend to the fireplace, a thought occurred to Maisie.

After her mother's death, she had been used to rising at three in the morning to make her father his tea. It had never hurt her then. In fact, she considered getting up at half past four to be "lying in." So, what if she got up at three in the morning and came down to the library? No one would know. Enid could sleep through the roof falling in over her head, and she had started coming up to bed late over the past week anyway. Lord knows where she had been, but it certainly wasn't out, because Carter locked up the house as if it were the Bank of England every night. She dreaded that Enid might be with Master James. Just two weeks ago, as she was leaving Lady Rowan's sitting room, where she had been sent to collect a tray one

evening, Maisie saw Enid and James together on the first-floor landing. Without being observed by them, she watched as James ran his
fingers through his fair hair and continued speaking with Enid, his
gray eyes intent upon her response to his question. Was it a question?
Surely it was, because she saw Enid shake her head and look at the
carpet, while brushing her right shoe back and forth across the fibers.

And now Enid was never in bed before midnight—which meant
that, thankfully, she would be deep in slumber by three o'clock.
Maisie resolved to come to the library when the house was asleep.
That night, before pulling up the covers and extinguishing the small
lamp beside her bed, Maisie pinched the skin on her right arm
sharply three times to ensure that she would awake in time to put her
plan into action.

The next morning Maisie awakened easily by three o'clock. A chill
in the attic room tempted her to forget her plan, but she sat up, determined to go through with it. She washed and dressed with hardly a
sound, crept out of the room carrying her shoes and a cardigan, and
felt her way downstairs in the dark. In the silent distance, the kitchen
clock struck the single chime of a quarter past the hour. She had
almost two hours before the coal scuttles had to be filled.

The library was silent and pitch black as Maisie entered. Quickly
closing the door behind her, she lit the lamps and made her way to
the section that held philosophy books. This was where she would
start. She wasn't quite sure which text to start with, but felt that if she
just started somewhere, a plan would develop as she went along. The
feeling inside that she experienced when she saw the books was akin
to the hunger she felt as food was put on the table at the end of the
working day. And she knew that she needed this sustenance as surely
as her body needed its fuel.

Maisie's fingers tapped along the spines of books until she could
bear the electric tingle of excitement no longer. Within minutes, she
was seated at the table, opening *The Philosophical Works of David Hume,*
and drawing the desk lamp closer to illuminate the pages. Maisie took
a small notebook and pencil from her apron pocket, set it down on

the desk and wrote the title of the book and the author's name. And she read. For an hour and a half, Maisie read. She read with understanding on a subject she had barely even heard of.

As the library clock chimed a quarter to five, Maisie turned to her notebook and wrote a precis of what she had read, what she understood, and her questions. The clock struck five, Maisie put the notebook and pencil away in her apron pocket, closed the book, replaced it ever so carefully on the shelf, extinguished the desk light, and left the room. She closed the door quietly behind her and went quickly downstairs to fill the coal scuttles. Just a short while later she opened the library door again. Without looking at the shelves, as if eye contact with the spines of the beloved books would give her game away, she set the coal scuttle down and knelt by the grate to build and light the fire.

Each weekday morning Maisie rose at three to visit the library. Sometimes a party at the house would keep the Comptons up until the small hours, and the change in routine made the library expeditions a risk she could not afford. She was liked in the house, though she had been spoken to by Lord and Lady Compton only once, when she had first arrived.

✦

*H*alf past two. Maisie crept out of bed. It was earlier than usual, but she couldn't sleep. She had gone to bed early, so it would be just as well to get up now. Enid slept soundly, which hardly surprised Maisie as the girl hadn't been in bed long. She was becoming a late one, that Enid. As late as Maisie was early. One of these days we'll meet in the doorway, thought Maisie. Then we'll have to do some talking.

The house was silent; only the ticking of clocks accompanied her to the library. Now when she entered the room it was as if she were falling into the arms of an old friend. Even the tentacles of cold receded as she turned on the light, placed her notebook and pencil on the desk, and went to the bookshelves. She took down the book she had been reading for the past three days, sat at the desk, found her place, and commenced.

Frankie Dobbs always said that when she was reading Maisie had "cloth ears." She always seemed instinctively to know the time and when she would need to stop reading to run an errand or complete a chore, but as far as Frankie was concerned, "Those ears don't even work when you've yer nose in a book!" And he loved her all the more for it.

*Lord* and Lady Compton were caught up in the midst of the London season, which Lady Rowan loved for its energy, even if she did have to tolerate some people she considered to be "light." Fortunately late nights usually fell on weekends, but this invitation, in the middle of the week, was not to be missed: an intimate yet sumptuous dinner with one of London's most outspoken hostesses.

"Thank God there's someone with a bigger mouth than mine," Lady Rowan confided to her husband.

Guests were to include some of the leading literary lights of Europe. It was an opportunity for sparkling conversation, definitely not to be missed. Maurice Blanche would accompany them, a rare event, as he was known to shun society gatherings.

After-dinner conversation drifted past midnight. It was only as Maisie Dobbs crept downstairs to the library that Lord and Lady Compton, along with Maurice Blanche, bade their hostess adieu, thanking her profusely for a wonderful evening. They arrived home at three in the morning. Carter had been instructed not to wait up, but an evening supper tray had been left for them in the drawing room. Lady Rowan was still in fine argumentative fettle as Lord Julian led the way.

"I tell you, Maurice, this time you are mistaken. Only last week I was reading—where was I reading—oh yes, that new book. You know, Julian, what was it called? Anyway, I was reading about a new hypothesis that utterly controverts your position."

"Rowan, could we please—" interrupted Lord Julian.

"Julian, no, we couldn't. Pour Maurice a drink. I'll find the book, then you'll see!"

"As you will, Rowan. I am very much looking forward to seeing what you have read. One always welcomes the opportunity to learn," said Maurice Blanche.

While the men settled by the embers of the drawing-room fire, Lady Rowan stormed upstairs to the library. Maisie Dobbs was deep in her book. She heard neither footsteps on the stairs nor the approach of Lady Rowan. She heard nothing until Lady Rowan spoke. And she did not speak until she had watched Maisie for some minutes, watched as the girl sucked on the end of her single braid of thick, black hair, deep in concentration. Occasionally she would turn a page back, reread a sentence, nod her head, then read on.

"Excuse me. Miss Dobbs."

Maisie sat up and closed her eyes tightly, not quite believing that a voice had addressed her.

"Miss Dobbs!"

Maisie shot up from the chair, turned to face Lady Rowan, and quickly bobbed a curtsy. "Sorry, Your Ladyship. Begging your pardon, Ma'am. I've not harmed anything."

"What are you doing, girl?" asked Lady Rowan.

"Reading, Ma'am."

"Well, I can see that. Let me see that book."

Maisie turned, took the book she had been reading, and handed it to Lady Rowan. She stepped back, feet together, hands at her sides. Bloody hell, she was in trouble now.

"Latin? Latin! What on earth are you reading Latin for?"

Lady Rowan's surprise stemmed questions that another employer might have put to the young maid.

"Um . . . well. Um . . . I needed to learn it," replied Maisie.

"You needed to learn it? Why do you need to learn Latin?"

"The other books had Latin in them, so I needed to understand it. To understand the other books, that is."

Maisie shifted her weight from one foot to the other. Now she needed to pee. For her part Lady Rowan was regarding Maisie sternly, yet she felt a strange curiosity to know more about the girl she had already thought unusual.

"Which other books? Show me," demanded Lady Rowan.

One by one Maisie took down the books, her hands shaking, her legs turning to jelly as she moved the library steps from one shelf to another. Whatever happened next, it was sure to be bad. Very bad. And she had let down her dad. How would she tell him she had been sacked? What would she say?

Maisie was so scared that she did not notice that, in her curiosity, Lady Rowan had forgotten the formality with which she would ordinarily address a servant. She asked Maisie about her choice of books, and Maisie, taking up her notebook, recounted what she had learned in her reading, and what questions had led her to each text in turn.

"My, my, young lady. You *have* been busy. All I can remember of Latin is the end of that verse: 'First it killed the Romans, and now it's killing me!' "

Maisie looked at Lady Rowan and smiled. She wasn't sure if it was a joke, but she couldn't stop the grin from forming. It was the first time she had truly smiled since coming to the house. The expression was not lost on Lady Rowan, who felt herself torn between regard for the girl and the appropriate response in such a situation.

"Maisie—Miss Dobbs. There is still time for you to enjoy a short rest before your duties commence. Go back to your room now. I shall need to discuss this incident. In the meantime, do not use the library until you hear from Carter, who will instruct you as to how we will deal with this . . . situation." Lady Rowan felt the requirements of her position pressing upon her, just as it had when she had been taken by Maurice to the East End of London. How could she do what was right, without compromising—how had Maurice described it? Yes, without compromising "the safety of her own pond"?

"Yes, Your Ladyship." Maisie put her notebook into in her pocket, and with tears of fear visibly pricking the inner corners of her eyes, bobbed another curtsy.

Lady Rowan waited until Maisie had left the room before extinguishing the lights. It was only as she walked slowly down the staircase that she remembered that she had gone to the library for a book.

"Bloody fool," she said to herself, and walked toward the drawing room to speak with her husband and Maurice Blanche on a new topic of conversation.

# CHAPTER TEN

aisie had hardly been able to concentrate on anything since being discovered. She felt sure that
notice to leave the employ of Lord and Lady
Compton would soon follow, and was surprised that one week had
gone by without any word. Then Carter summoned Maisie to his
"office," the term he sometimes used—especially in grave situations
where a reprimand was to be meted out—to describe the butler's
pantry, a small room adjacent to the kitchen, where he kept meticu-
lous records regarding the running of the house.

Maisie was in a miserable state. The embarrassment of being
caught, together with the pain of anticipating her father's dismay at
her behavior, was almost too much to bear. And of course, she no
longer had access to the Comptons' library. Wringing her already
work-reddened hands, Maisie knocked on the door of Mr. Carter's
office. Her nails were bitten down to the quick, and she had picked
at her cuticles until her fingers were raw. It had been a nerve-
wracking week.

"Enter," said Carter, with a tone that was neither soft and welcoming nor overtly displeased. It was a tone that gave nothing away.

"Good morning, Mr. Carter." Maisie bobbed a curtsy as she walked into the small room. "You wanted to see me, Sir?"

"Yes, Maisie. You know why I have summoned you. Lady Compton wishes to meet with you at twelve noon today. Sharp. In the library. I shall myself be in attendance, as will a colleague of both Lord and Lady Compton.

"Yes, Mr. Carter."

Maisie could bear the wait no longer, and although fear was nipping at her throat and chest, she had to know her fate.

"Mr. Carter, Sir?"

"Yes, Maisie?" Carter regarded her over half-moon spectacles.

"Mr. Carter. Can't you just get on with it? Give me the sack now, so that I don't have to—"

"Maisie. No one has said anything about the sack. I am instructed only to accompany you to a meeting with Lady Rowan and Dr. Blanche. I have also been requested to take your notebooks to the library this morning at half past ten. Please bring them to me directly so that I can take them to Lady Rowan."

"But . . ." Maisie did not understand, and although she thought that Carter did not understand either, she suspected he might have an inkling. "Mr. Carter, Sir. What's this all about?"

Carter adjusted his tie and swept an imaginary hair from the cuff of his crisp white shirt. "Maisie, it is most unusual. However, I do not believe your employment here is at an end. In fact, rather the contrary. Now then. The notebooks. Then I believe the sideboard in the dining room is to be waxed and polished this morning, so you had better get on."

Maisie bobbed another curtsy and turned to leave the office.

"And Maisie," said Carter, sweeping back his well-combed gray-at-the-temples hair. "Although respect should always be accorded our employers and their guests, there's no need to keep bobbing up and down like a sewing-machine needle when you are downstairs."

Maisie absentmindedly bobbed again and quickly left the office. She returned fifteen minutes later with her collection of small notebooks for Carter. She was terrified of the meeting that was to take place at twelve noon, and was sure that she would spend half the time until then in the lavatory.

Carter was waiting at the foot of the first-floor stairs at five min-utes to twelve when Maisie walked toward him from the landing that led to the lower stairs and the kitchen. He drew his pocket watch from his waistcoat pocket, determined to be not a moment too soon or a second too late.

"Ah, Maisie," he said as she approached, hands clasped together in front of her white pinafore.

Carter looked the girl up and down to check for marks on the pinafore and scuffs on her shoes, for stray tendrils of hair escaping from her white cap.

"Nicely turned out. Good. Let us proceed."

Carter checked his watch once more, turned, and led the way to the library. Maisie had a horrible taste in her mouth. What would her father say when she came home with her small canvas bag and no job? Well, perhaps it was for the best. She missed him something rotten, so perhaps it would be a very good thing. Carter knocked briskly at the door. A voice could be heard within.

"Come in."

Maisie closed her eyes for a second, put her hands behind her back, and crossed her fingers.

"Ah, Carter. Miss Dobbs. Maisie. Do come in."

"Thank you, Ma'am," said Carter. Maisie bobbed her curtsy and looked sideways at Carter. Lady Rowan beckoned Maisie to her.

"Maurice, this is the girl of whom we have been speaking." Then, inclining her head slightly toward Maisie, she said, "I would like to introduce Dr. Maurice Blanche. He knows of our meeting in the library, and I have consulted with him regarding the situation."

Maisie was now utterly confused. What situation? And who was this man? What was going on? Maisie nodded and curtsied to the man standing alongside Lady Rowan.

"Sir," she said in acknowledgment.

She didn't know what to make of this small man. He wasn't as tall as Lady Rowan, and while he looked well fed, there was a wiriness to him. Solid, as her dad would have said. Solid. She couldn't even guess his age, but thought he was older than her dad, but not as old as Grandad. Over fifty, perhaps sixty. He had blue-gray eyes that looked as if they were floating in water, they were that clear. And his hands—they had long fingers with wide nails. Hands that could play the piano, very exact hands that made precise movements. She saw that when he took up her notebooks from a walnut side table and flicked a page or two.

He was a plain dresser, not done up like two penn'orth of hambone like some of them that she'd seen at the house. No, this was a plain man. And he looked right through her. And because she thought that she had nothing to lose and because her dad had told her always to "stand tall," Maisie stiffened her spine, pulled her shoulders back, and looked him straight in the eye as he had looked at her. Then he smiled.

"Miss Dobbs, Maisie. Lady Rowan has spoken with me about your encounter in the library last week."

Here it comes, thought Maisie. She clenched her teeth.

"Now then, come with me."

Maurice Blanche walked to the library table and sat down, then invited Maisie to sit next to him, with her notebooks in front of them.

Lady Rowan nodded at Carter, who remained by the door, as she walked to stand by the window. They watched as Blanche spoke with Maisie.

Gradually he broke down Maisie's shyness and the formalities that separated housemaid and houseguest. Within fifteen minutes the two were in animated conversation. Maurice Blanche asked questions, Maisie answered, often with another question. Clever, thought Carter, very clever. The way that Dr. Blanche drew Maisie out, with his voice, his eyes, a finger tapped upon the page, a question punctuated by a hand placed on the chin to listen. Lady Rowan was equally riveted by the discourse, but her interest was of a more personal nature. Maisie

Dobbs's future was part of her own quest to challenge herself, and what was considered correct in a household such as hers and for a woman of her titled position.

An hour passed. An hour during which Carter was sent to bring tea for Dr. Blanche. Nothing was requested for Maisie. It would never do for a man of Carter's position to be at the service of a maid. Yet Carter sensed that something important was happening, that this was an hour during which the established structure of life in the house was changing. And he foresaw that changes that came as a result of whatever came to pass in this room this morning would affect them all. And these were strange-enough times already, what with old King Edward just dead and King George V's coronation around the corner.

Finally Maurice Blanche asked Maisie to close and collect her books. She did as instructed and drew away from the table to stand next to Carter, while Lady Rowan joined Maurice Blanche at the table.

"Rowan, I am more than satisfied," said Dr. Blanche. "You may reveal our plan to Miss Dobbs and Mr. Carter. Then we shall see if Mr. Carter agrees and how we may begin."

Lady Rowan spoke, first looking at Carter, then at Maisie. "Last week when I came upon Miss Dobbs in the library, I was struck by the breadth of her reading. We know that anyone can take down a book and read, but when I briefly looked at her notebooks I realized that there was also a depth of understanding. You are a very bright girl, Miss Dobbs."

Lady Rowan glanced at Maurice Blanche, who nodded to her to continue.

"I know that this is most unusual. Carter has already been given an indication of my thoughts, and has concurred with my decision. Now I can be more specific. Lord Compton and I are believers in education and opportunity. However, opportunities to contribute directly are rare. Miss Dobbs, we have a proposal for you."

Maisie blushed and looked at her shoes as Lady Rowan continued.

"Under the direction of Dr. Blanche you will continue your

studies here. Dr. Blanche is a busy man, but he will meet with you once every fortnight in the library. Your studies, and the tutorials with Dr. Blanche, must, however, be on your own time and must not interfere in any way with your work in the house. What do you say to that, Maisie?"

Maisie was shocked, but after taking a moment to consider, she flashed the smile that seemed to be working its way back into her life. "Thank you, Ma'am. Sir—Dr. Blanche—thank you."

"Miss Dobbs," said Maurice Blanche, "hold your thanks for the time being. You may not take kindly to me when you have seen my plans for your education."

That night, when Maisie was in bed, she was hardly able to sleep for wondering about the events of the day. Carter had been accommodating, but then he was kind. And the other staff, when they had learned about it later—because that Mrs. Crawford was a right old chatterbox—seemed to be all right with it all, as long as she pulled her weight in the house. There hadn't been any snide comments, or jealousy. But when Enid finally came to bed in the early hours, she wasted no time in voicing a thought that had been at the back of Maisie's mind.

"You'd've thought they would've just sent you to one of those fancy schools, on the QT, like. Or even paid for your uniform and all that, for the school where you won the scholarship. They're not short of a few bob, are they?"

Maisie nodded.

"But you know what I reckon, Mais? To be perf-hectly honest with you. I reckon they knew you would 'ave a rotten time there. What with all them toffs. It would get you down, it would. Reckon that's what it is."

Without waiting for a response, and using her hairbrush as a pointer for emphasis, Enid continued. "And what you've got to remember,

Dobbsie, is that there's them upstairs, and there's us downstairs. There's no middle, never was. So the likes of you and me can't just move up a bit, if that's what you think. We've got to jump, Dobbsie, and bloody 'igh to boot!"

Maisie knew that there was more than a grain of truth in her words. But if Her Ladyship wanted a cause, someone with whom to play 'Lady Bountiful,' she didn't mind being on the receiving end if it meant getting on with her education.

Maisie changed the subject. "So, where were you tonight, Enid?" she asked.

"Never you mind. You can keep that there clever mind of yours on your own business now, and don't you be thinking about mine."

Maisie closed her eyes, then quickly fell asleep. She dreamt of long corridors of books, of Dr. Blanche at the library table, and of Enid. And even with the excitement of her lessons with Dr. Blanche, it was the dream about Enid that remained with her throughout the next day, and for some days to come. And she tried not to think about the dream and Enid, because every time she did, she shivered along the full length of her spine.

# CHAPTER ELEVEN

*L*ord Julian Compton knew of his wife's "project" and gave the education of Maisie Dobbs his blessing, although secretly he believed that the exercise would soon falter and any ambitions shown by young Miss Dobbs would be extinguished under the strain of trying to be two very different people, to say nothing of being a girl on the cusp of womanhood. He was intrigued by Maurice Blanche and his interest in Maisie's education, and it was this involvement, rather than his wife's philanthropic gestures, that led him to allow that the project might, in fact, have some merit. He held Maurice Blanche in high esteem, and was even in some awe of the man.

Maisie, for her part, felt no fatigue at the end of a long day. She began her chores in the household at her usual early hour, starting with the lighting of fires, the cleaning of rooms, and the polishing of heavy mahogany furniture. The job of cleaning cutlery fell to the junior footman, though when she handled the solid silver knives and forks, perhaps when cleaning the dining room after dinner guests had departed to the drawing room, she looked with care at the inscription. Each piece of fine cutlery bore the Compton crest, a great hunting dog and a stag together with the words "Let There Be No Ill Will." Maisie pondered the crest as she collected the soiled silverware. The hunter and the hunted, the suggestion of forgiveness between the victor and the victim, and the fact that both stood tall and proud. In fact, Maisie had taken to pondering just about everything that happened in the course of a day, seeing coincidences and patterns in the life around her.

Mrs. Crawford put Maisie's behavior down to her work with Maurice Blanche, an assumption that was, of course, correct.

"I dunno, when I was a girl learning meant your reading, your writing, and your 'rithmetic. None of this lark, this philosophy nonsense."

Mrs. Crawford pointed a floury finger at Maisie, who had just returned from the weekly visit to the library. She was placing books, those for Mrs. Crawford and Mr. Carter, as well as her own, carefully in a kitchen cupboard, so they would not become soiled by the business of the kitchen. Later she would take her selection to her room for more late-night reading. Cook had immediately noted the girth of Maisie's books, and could not resist comment—to which Carter felt bound to respond.

"I am sure that Mr. Blanche knows more about the education of a young person for today's world than either you or I, Cook. But I must say, Maisie, that is rather a large tome, is it not?"

Carter, decanting a fine port, did not stop his task to wait for an answer, but cast his eyes over his spectacles in Maisie's direction.

"Maisie—are you listening to Mr. Carter?"

Carter exchanged glances with Mrs. Crawford, and both rolled their eyes in a compact that hid their true feelings. They were very proud of Maisie Dobbs, and laid some claim in their hearts to the discovery of her intellectual gifts.

"Sorry, Mr. Carter. Were you speaking to me?" She had to remove her little finger from her mouth to speak. Maisie had hurried back from the library to allow an extra few moments to dip into one of her books.

"Yes, Mr. Carter was speaking to you, Maisie—and if I see that finger in your mouth again, I swear I'll paint your nails with carbolic. It's a wonder you've got hands left, they way you chew on those fingers."

"Sorry, Mrs. Crawford. Begging your pardon, Mr. Carter? I'll get going again now. I just thought I'd take a quick peek."

Carter studied the kitchen clock. "You can have five minutes. Cook and I were commenting on the width of that book. It's a fair size. Is Dr. Blanche working you too hard, Maisie?"

"It's Kierkegaard. Mr. Blanche says I should read this because he— Kierkegaard—has had a considerable influence on modern thought. And no, don't worry, I can keep up with everything."

Cook and Carter exchanged glances once again, neither wanting to show ignorance about some newfangled thing that sounded to both of them like "kick the guard."

In the meantime Maisie took a notebook from her apron pocket and began to write down her questions and observations for Maurice Blanche. As Carter had suspected, she had already started reading the book on her way back from the library, and was sufficiently into it to be completely absorbed. Once finished, she replaced the notebook in her pocket, glanced at the heavy oak clock with the pearl white face and bold black numbers that was visible from any angle in the kitchen, and stood up from the table.

"I just need to put my book away, then I'll get on with making up the stove before I do the polishing."

Maisie moved quickly from the room, remembering the house rule that those from "below stairs" never ever ran, but when speed was of the essence, a brisk walk was permissible.

"I don't know how she still manages to see her poor father, what with her work down here, and all that book learning. I will say this for her, she's got some spirit, has that girl." Mrs. Crawford swept her forearm across her brow and continued with the pastry making. Carter had completed the task of decanting the port and was now uncorking brandy, to be carefully poured into a fine cut-crystal decanter. He made no reply to Mrs. Crawford's comments, which rather annoyed the woman, as she was given to strong opinions and the need to defend and discuss them.

"I wonder, Mr. Carter, what will happen when Maisie has a young man. I wonder, you know, what will happen to her. Fish can't survive long out of water, you know."

Mrs. Crawford stopped rolling the pastry and looked at Carter, who remained silent. "I said, Mr. Carter—"

"Cook—Mrs. Crawford—I know what you said. I would suggest that the education of Miss Dobbs is in good hands. I would also suggest that Miss Dobbs is a very determined young woman who will be more successful than most when it comes to surviving outside her established boundaries. Now then, it is not for us to question the decisions of our employers. We can do only what is required of us in the circumstances, don't you think?"

Mrs. Crawford, who had been filling a pastry-lined dish with fresh-sliced apple, added cinnamon and clove with rather more than her usual flourish, replied with a certain asperity, "Right you are, Mr. Carter," before turning her back on him to check the oven.

Maisie's education was indeed going well. Maurice Blanche had encouraged an easy camaraderie while maintaining the certain distance required by his position, and by Maisie's. Within eighteen months of embarking upon the demanding timetable set by Blanche, Maisie was studying at a level of which a master at one of the prestigious private schools of the day would have been proud.

For her part Maisie knew only that the work challenged and excited her. When Maurice handed her a new text, she felt a thrill of anticipation. Would the book be brand new, unread, with pages untouched by another? If so, then Maurice would request a précis of the content, and her assessment of the text.

"Four pages of quarto, if you please. And a word of advice. This man has opinions. Opinions, as we have discussed, are not fact. But of course, as we know, Maisie, they may be the source of truth. I will be speaking with you about the truth demonstrated in this thesis, Maisie, so be prepared!"

Of course, the text may have already been read and in that case, each page would bear penciled notation in Maurice Blanche's small, fine handwriting with its slight slant to the right. A single page of questions would be tucked inside, between the back page and the cover. Maisie knew that each question must be answered.

"I never want to learn that you 'don't know,' Maisie, I want to know what you *think* the answer is to the question. And once more, a word of advice: Stay with the question. The more it troubles you, the more it has to teach you. In time, Maisie, you will find that the larger questions in life share such behavior."

It had been almost two years since Maisie's mother passed away, and still Frankie Dobbs grieved. He swore that it was Maisie who kept him going, for Frankie Dobbs lived for Sundays, and always the ritual was the same.

Although it was not a market day, Frankie would be at the stable with Persephone from an early hour, not as early as on a weekday, but early all the same. He talked softly to his mare, brushing her coat until she shone, caring for mane and tail, and checking hooves that had to pull a heavy load over a considerable distance each day. There was a warm, oaty sweetness to the stable, and here Frankie, often so ungainly when walking down the street or in company, was completely at ease. It was usually as Frankie was halfway through the Sunday morning round of chores that Maisie could be heard walking up the cobblestones toward the stable.

"Dad, I'm here," Maisie called out to him before looking over the half-door and waving. Always she brought something for Frankie from Mrs. Crawford, perhaps a pork pie wrapped in fine white muslin and brown paper, freshly baked bread still warm to the touch, or a steamed apple pudding that needed only "A bit o' warming up over the stove," according to the cook.

Maisie quickly pulled off her coat and rolled up her sleeves. Father and daughter worked together to finish the morning's labor, their talk made easier by their movement. They shared confidences easily as their hands were busy with job of work.

"So, your learning's coming along, is it, Girl?"

"Yes, Dad. Dr. Blanche is looking ahead, he says. Reckons I could be ready for scholarship and entrance exams next year."

"Entrance for what?" asked Frankie, as he moved toward the pump to refill his bucket with water to rinse Persephone's leather reins and traces, which he had just lathered with saddle soap.

"Well, um, university. Dr. Blanche says I can do it. Her ladyship is very keen for me to apply to Cambridge, to Girton College. Says it's the place for an individualist."

"Did she now? Cambridge. Well, there's posh for you, my girl!" Frankie laughed but then looked seriously at Maisie. "As long as you don't push yourself, Love. And Cambridge is a long way off, isn't it? Where would you live? And what about mixing with the type of folk at a place like that"

"I dunno, Dad. I have to live at the college, I think. There are all sorts of rules about that, you know. And I will meet people. I'll be just fine, Dad. Girton is a women's college away in a village, after all."

"Yes, but those other young women have more money than you do, and they've got more, you know, connections, like."

Maisie looked up from brushing Persephone. Even though Frankie had already brushed the horse from head to tail, Maisie loved to feel the warm animal close to her, and knew the horse appreciated her efforts.

"Dad, I'm not a child any more. I'm fifteen now. And I've seen more than a lot of girls my age. Dr. Blanche knows what he is doing."

"Yes, love, I'm sure he does. Clever man, that one. I just worry about you."

Frankie rubbed the cleaned leather with a dry cloth, and hung reins and traces from a hook on the low ceiling. Later, after Maisie's return to Belgravia, Frankie would come back to the stable to feed Persephone, then take down the dry reins, bridle, and traces, and rub warmed neatsfoot oil into the leather.

"Don't worry about me, Dad. I'm doing very well, you know. Now then, where shall we go for our walk? I've got some nice sandwiches and a couple of bottles of ginger beer for us."

Three days after her visit with Frankie, Maisie walked briskly toward the library for her early-evening lesson. She saw Maurice Blanche on alternate Wednesday evenings, meeting promptly at half past five in the library, for three hours, until Dr. Blanche left to join the Comptons for an informal supper in the dining room. She studied alone until he had finished supper, when both he and Lady Rowan joined Maisie in the library to review her work. Lady Rowan was well pleased with the education of Maisie Dobbs, asking questions and suggesting new areas of study. But this evening a new possibility was discussed.

"Maisie, I think it is time for us to embark on some fieldwork."

Maisie looked first at Blanche, then at Lady Rowan. Botany. It had to be botany.

"Lady Rowan has spoken with Mr. Carter, and next week, on Wednesday, we will be taking an excursion. In fact, I have several such outings planned, and on those afternoons we must meet a little earlier than usual."

"What sort of outings? Where are we going?"

"Various places," said Blanche, "Of historical, social, or economic interest."

Little more was said, but in the following weeks Maisie was taken by Blanche to meet people with whom she would spend time alone in conversation. At first Maurice would remain with her, but as time went on, he would quietly leave the room to allow for conversation between Maisie and his friend, for each person who met with Maisie was considered a "friend" by Maurice Blanche. As far as Maisie was concerned, some of them were a strange lot altogether, and she wasn't sure what Frankie Dobbs would have to say about it all.

"Today we will be meeting with my dear friend Dr. Basil Khan," Maurice Blanche informed Maisie as they journeyed to Hampstead by taxi-cab. "An extraordinary scholar, born in Ceylon, into a very-high-caste family. His first name was given as a mark of respect to one of his father's former colleagues, an Englishman. Khan, as he prefers to be known, is completely blind. He lost his sight in an unfortunate accident, but as these things do, it became the foundation for his life's work."

"What's his life's work?"

"Khan, as you will see, is a man of great wisdom, of insight. His work uses that insight. He grants audiences to politicians, people of commerce, men of the cloth. He came to England as a young man, sent by his parents to see ophthalmic specialists, to no avail. While in England he gained his doctorate in philosophy at Oxford. Then he returned to Ceylon, and later traveled throughout the Indian subcontinent, himself seeking the counsel of wise men. To do this he had to give up the life he had once enjoyed in London and Oxford, which he had ceased to enjoy. Now he resides in Hampstead."

"So why am I to see him?"

"Maisie, we are visiting for him to see *you*. And for you to learn that seeing is not necessarily something one does with the eyes."

The visit to Khan was illuminating for Maisie. His apartments in a grand house were furnished in a simple manner: plain wooden furniture, curtains without pattern or texture, candlelight, and a strange smell that made her cough at first.

"You will get used to it, Maisie. Khan uses incense to bring a fragrant atmosphere to the house."

At first Maisie was timid when led into a large room with only cushions on the floor and an old man sitting with legs crossed. He was positioned by the long French window as if contemplating the view, so that as Maisie and Maurice Blanche walked toward him, Khan was framed by shafts of light, and appeared to have been borne into the room by some mystical means of transportation. Without turning, Khan gestured toward Maisie with his hand.

"Come, child, come sit with me. We have much to speak of."

To her surprise Maurice Blanche motioned Maisie to step forward, and moved toward Khan himself. He leaned down toward Khan, took the old man's bony brown hands in his own, and kissed his lined and furrowed forehead. Khan smiled and nodded, then turned to Maisie.

"Tell me what it is you know, child."

"Um . . ."

Both Khan and Maurice laughed, and the old man with long gray hair and almost colorless eyes smiled kindly at Maisie.

"Yes, a good start. A very good start. Let us talk of knowing."

So Maisie Dobbs—daughter of a costermonger from Lambeth, just south of the water that divided London's rich and poor—began to learn in the way that Maurice had intended, from the centuries of wisdom accumulated by Khan.

With Khan she learned to sit in deliberate silence, and learned too that the stilled mind would give insight beyond the teaching of books and hours of instruction, and that such counsel would support all other learning. When she first sat with Khan, she asked what it was she was to do as she sat with legs crossed on the cushion in front of him. The old man lifted his face to the window, then turned his clear white eyes toward her and said simply, "Pay attention."

Maisie took the practice of sitting with Khan seriously and to heart, with an instinctive knowledge that this work would serve her well. In just a few short years, the lessons learned in the hours with Khan would bring her calm amid the shellfire, the terrible injuries, and the cries of wounded men. But for now, Maurice Blanche told Maisie, it was no small coincidence that she often knew what a person was going to say before he or she spoke, or that she seemed to intuit an event before it had occurred.

# CHAPTER TWELVE

*M*aisie, you'll ruin your eyes if you read by that good-for-nothing light in the corner—and look at that time, you've to be up in three hours!"

"So have you, Enid, and you aren't anywhere near asleep yet."

"Don't you be worrying about me. I've told you that."

Maisie slipped a page of notes into the book to mark the place, closed the book, and placed it to one side on her small table. She looked directly at Enid.

"And don't you look at me with those eyes either, young Maisie Dobbs. Gives me the willies, it does."

"You are being careful, aren't you, Enid?"

"'Course I am. I told you not to worry."

Khan might be teaching her many things about the human mind, but as far as Maisie was concerned, it didn't take much in the way of foresight to see that Enid was going to get into some trouble before long. In truth it was a surprise that the older girl was not only still as slim as a whip but was still employed at the house in Belgravia at all. But Enid, who was now almost eighteen, was loved by everyone downstairs. Her efforts at correct enunciation still fell short, and sometimes Maisie thought she sounded more like a music hall act than a maid in service. But she, too, had come to love Enid, for her laughter, for the unsought advice she gave so freely, and most of all for her unselfish support of Maisie.

Enid slipped a thick cotton nightdress over her head, pulled on woolen socks, and proceeded carefully to fold her clothes into the chest of drawers by the wall. Shadows cast by the oil lamp flickered on the sloping ceiling of the top-floor bedroom as Enid brushed out her thick hair with a hardy bristle brush.

"One hundred strokes for a good thick head of hair—have I told you that, Mais?"

"Yes, many a time."

Maisie ensured that her books and papers were carefully put away, and clambered into bed.

"Brrrr. It's cold in here."

Enid took an old silk scarf that had been hanging over the cast-iron bedpost, wrapped it around the head of her brush, and began brushing the silk over her hair to bring it to a lustrous shine.

"No, and it ain't getting any warmer. I tell you, Maisie, a chill wind blows through 'ere sometimes, a chill wind."

Maisie turned to face Enid.

"Enid, why don't you like it here?"

Enid stopped brushing, held the brush in her lap, and fingered the scarf. Her shoulders drooped, and when she looked up at Maisie, it was with tears in her eyes.

"Enid, what is it? Is it James? Or that Arthur?"

Maisie had guessed that the reason for Enid's absences over the past year resided in rooms on the third floor. Though it might have been Arthur, the young footman who had come to work at the house a month before Maisie. His position had been elevated since then. He had been given the task of ensuring the good health of the Comptons' Lanchester motorcar, keeping it polished, oiled, and spick and span. She thought that he had taken a shine to Enid, too.

"No, it's not 'im. That one's full of the old bluster, all mouth and trousers, that's Arthur. No, it's not 'im." Enid picked at the hairbrush, taking out long hairs and rolling them between her fingers.

"Come on, Enid. Something makes you sad."

The older girl sighed, the familiar defiance ebbing as Maisie's eyes sought her confidence.

"You know, Maisie, they're all very nice here until you overstep the line. Now you, you'll land on your feet; after all, 'avin' brains is like 'avin' money, even I know that. But me, all I've got is 'oo I am, and 'oo I am i'n't good enough."

"What do you mean?"

"Oh, come on, Maisie, you must've heard talk—they love to talk in the kitchen of this place, 'specially that old Mrs. Crawford." Enid put down the brush, pulled back her bedsheets, and climbed into bed. She turned to face Maisie. "I don't know what it is about them eyes of yours, Mais, but I tell you, the way you look at me makes me want to spill my insides out to you."

Maisie inclined her head for Enid to continue.

"It's James. Master James. That's why His Lordship is talking about sending him away. To Canada. As far away from the likes of me as they can get 'im. It's a wonder they don't send me off too, to look for another job, but 'er Ladyship isn't a bad old bird, really. At least she can keep an eye on me if I'm 'ere—otherwise, who knows? I might just go to Canada meself!"

"Do you love James, Enid?"

Enid rolled to face the ceiling, and in the half-light, Maisie saw a single tear run from the corner of her eye onto the pillow.

"Love 'im? Gawd, Maisie, what business 'ave I got, going in for all that nonsense?"

Enid paused, dabbing at her eyes with a corner of the sheet. "Love don't put food on the table, does it?" She looked at her crumpled handkerchief, dabbed her eyes, and nodded. "I suppose I do, love him, that is. I do love James, but—"

"But what? If you love him, Enid, you can—"

"Can what, Maisie? Can what? No, there's no 'buts' in the matter.

He's going, and when he's gone, I've got my life to get on with. And in some way or another, I've got to get out of this 'ere job. I've got to get on, like you're getting on. But I've not got your cleverness."

"Dr. Blanche says that having a mental picture works. He said once that it's good to have a vision of what the future may hold. He says it's important to keep that in mind."

"Oh, he does, does he? Well, then, I'll start seeing myself all dolled up like a lady, with a nice husband, and a nice house. How about that for a picture?"

"I'll picture that for you too, Enid!"

Enid laughed and rolled over. "I tell you, Maisie Dobbs, you're one of a kind! Now then, you just turn off that thinking and imagining mind of yours, and let's get some kip."

Maisie did as she was told, but as she settled into the quiet of the night, she was sorry that the conversation had ended. It was always like that with Enid, as soon as you got a little closer to her, she moved away. Yet Maisie knew that at this very moment Enid was thinking of James Compton, hoping that if she held on to a picture of them together, it would come to pass. And Maisie thought of them together, too. Of seeing them on the landing, not long after she had come to work at 15 Ebury Place. She had seen them since, once in Brockwell Park when she was walking with her father. They must have thought that no one would recognize James on the south side of the river— his sort rarely ventured across the water. Enid was in her Sunday best: her long deep-lavender coat, which she kept hanging in the wardrobe covered in a white sheet and protected by mothballs. Her black woolen skirt poked out underneath, and you could just about see her laced-up boots, polished to a shine. She wore a white blouse with a high neck and a little sprig of lavender pinned to the front of the collar, right where a brooch might have been, if Enid had owned one. She wore black gloves and an old black hat that Maisie had seen her hold over a steaming pot of water in the kitchen, then work with her hands to mold it into shape, before making it look just like new with a band of purple velvet ribbon. Oh, she did look lovely, with her red hair tied in a loose knot so that you could see it beneath her hat. And James, she remembered him laughing when he was with Enid, and just before she managed to steer her father in another direction, so that Enid and James wouldn't see her, she watched as he took the glove off Enid's right hand and lean over to press his lips to her thin knuckles, then turn it over to the palm and kiss it again. And as he stood up, Enid reached up and flicked back his fair hair, which had flopped into his eyes.

And though she was now snuggled down into the bedclothes and blankets, a hot-water bottle at her feet, Maisie shivered and was frightened. Perhaps she should speak to Dr. Blanche about it, this strange feeling she had at times, as if the future had flashed a picture into her mind, like being at the picture house and seeing only a few seconds' worth of the show.

*J*ust one week after Enid had taken Maisie into her confidence, James Compton departed on a ship bound for Canada. As a result Enid had become less than affable.

"I do wish you would turn out that bloomin' light so that I can get some shut-eye. I'm sick of it, I am. 'Alfway through the night and all I can hear is you turnin' those bloomin' pages over and over."

Maisie looked up from her book, over to the lump that was Enid in the adjoining bed. She could not see Enid's face, for she was curled sideways with her back to Maisie, and the blankets over her head.

"I'm sorry, Enid, I didn't realize—"

Suddenly one arm came over the blankets as Enid pulled herself up into a sitting position, her face furiously red. "Well, you *wouldn't* bloomin' realize, *would* you, Miss Brainy? Always got yer 'ead in a book round 'ere when everyone else is workin'."

"But Enid, I pull my weight. No one else has to do my work for me. I can manage my jobs."

"Oh yes? You can manage your jobs, can you? Well, next time you go over to that mirror to do 'yer 'air, take a look at the sacks of coal under yer eyes. Your idea of pullin' weight is just a bit different from mine. And what with all that other stuff you 'ave to think about, it's a wonder you can get up in the morning. Now then. I'm off t'sleep, and it'd be a good idea if you did the same thing."

Maisie quickly marked her place in the book Maurice had given her earlier in the week, and extinguished the lamp at her bedside. Pulling the covers up to her shoulders and pressing her hands to her sore, watering eyes, she sought refuge from Enid's words. It seemed to Maisie that since Enid confided in her, she had become standoffish and unpleasant, as if her frustrated aspirations to become a lady had caused an unbearable resentment to grow. Maisie had begun to avoid her when Enid lost her temper at being asked to replenish coal in one of the upstairs rooms, and was reprimanded by Carter. But something must have sparked in Carter, for he called Maisie into the butler's pantry next to the kitchen.

"Maisie, I am worried about your ability to manage both your routine in the house and the schedule set by Dr. Blanche."

"Oh, Mr. Carter, I am managing."

"I want you to know that I will be watching, Maisie. I must obviously support Her Ladyship's wishes, but I must also bring it to her attention if changes should be made."

"No, you don't have to do that. I'll manage, sir. I promise."

"Right you are, Maisie. You may continue with your duties. But do make sure, doubly sure, that your work is complete at the end of the day."

"Yes, Mr. Carter."

It was with a heavy heart that Maisie visited Frankie Dobbs on the following Sunday. More than at any other time since she had started lessons with Dr. Blanche, Maisie couldn't wait to leave the house and immerse herself in the warmth of the stable and her father's love.

"There you are. Bit late today, young Maisie, aren't you?"

"Yes, Dad. I was late getting up, then had to stay to finish some jobs, and missed the bus. I had to wait for the next one."

"Oh, so you couldn't get up in time on the one day you come to see your poor old dad?"

"That's not it, honestly, Dad," responded Maisie defensively.

She took off her hat and coat, folded them and put them on top of her basket, which she left just outside the stable door. She walked over to Persephone and rubbed the soft spot behind her ears.

"I was just a bit late, that's all, Dad."

"You doin' too much of that readin'?"

"No, Dad. No, I'm not."

"So how about your week then, Love? What've you been doing?"

"Oh, we had a to-do in the kitchen this week. Mrs. Crawford was experimenting with pouring brandy over the cooked meat and then adding a flame to it. Some new French idea that Lady Compton had asked Carter about. The whole kitchen nearly caught alight. You should have seen it, Dad. It was hilarious!"

Frankie Dobbs stopped work and looked at Maisie.

"What is it, Dad?" The smile seemed to evaporate from her face.

"'Ilarious, was it? I like that. 'ilarious. Can't use ordinary words anymore. Got to use big ones now, 'aven't you?"

"But Dad . . . I thought . . . ."

"That's the trouble with you. Too much of that thinking. I dunno . . . ."

Frankie turned his back on Maisie, the set of his shoulders revealing a seldom-seen anger. "I dunno. I thought this was all very well and all, you gettin' an education. Now I dunno. Next thing you know, you won't want to talk to the likes of me."

"Now that's silly, Dad."

"Silly, am I?" Frankie looked up again, his eyes blazing.

"I didn't mean it like that. What I meant was . . ." Maisie was exhausted. She let her arm drop to her side. Persephone nuzzled her to continue the ear rubbing, but there was no response. Father and daughter stood in stony silence.

How had this happened? How was it that one minute it seemed that everyone was on her side, and the next everyone was against her? What had she done wrong? Maisie went over to an upended box in the corner and slumped down. Her furrowed brow belied her youth as she tried to come to terms with the discord between her beloved father and herself.

"I'm sorry, Dad."

"I'm sorry, too. Sorry that I ever talked to that Mr. Carter in the first place."

"You did right, Dad. I would never have had this opportunity. . . ."

Frankie was also tired. Tired of worrying about Maisie, tired of fearing that she would move into circles above her station and never come back. Tired of feeling not good enough for his daughter. "I know, love. I know. Let's 'ave an end to the words. Just make sure you come back and see your old dad of a Sunday."

Maisie leaned over to Frankie, who had upended another wooden box to sit next to her, put her arms around his neck, and sobbed.

"Come on, love. Let's put the words behind us."

"I miss you, Dad."

"And I miss you, Love."

Father and daughter held on to each other a moment longer, before Frankie announced that they should be getting along to the park if they were to enjoy the best of the day. They worked together to finish jobs in the stable and, leaving Persephone to her day of rest, went to the park for a walk and to eat the sandwiches that Mrs. Crawford had made for Maisie.

As she traveled back to Belgravia that evening, Maisie couldn't help but remember Frankie's outburst, and wondered how she would ever balance her responsibilities. As if that were not enough, Enid's tongue was as sharp as a knife again when Maisie entered the room they shared on the top floor of the house.

"It's a wonder you can bring yourself to see that costermonger father of yours. Isn't he a bit lower class for you now, Maisie?"

Maisie was stunned and hurt by Enid's words. Slights against herself she could handle, but those against her father she would not tolerate. "My father, Enid, is one of the best."

"Hmmph. Thought he wouldn't be good enough, what with you bein' 'er Ladyship's pet."

"Enid, I'm not anyone's pet or favorite. I'm still here, and working hard."

Enid was lying on her back on the bed, pillows plumped up behind her head. She was reading an old copy of *The Lady* magazine while speaking to Maisie.

"Hmmph. Maisie Dobbs, all you've done is give 'er Ladyship a cause. They like causes, do these 'ere toffs. Makes 'er feel like she's doin' something for the lower classes. Right old do-gooder she is, too. And as for that funny old geezer, Blanche, I'd worry about 'im if I was you. D'you really think you can become a lady with all this book lark?"

"I've told you before, Enid—I don't want to be a lady."

Maisie folded her day clothes and put them away in the heavy chest of drawers, then took up her hairbrush and began to unbraid her glossy black hair.

"Then you're as stupid as you are silly lookin'."

Maisie swung around to look directly at Enid.

"What is *wrong* with you? I can't do a thing right!"

"Let me tell you what's wrong with me, young Maisie. What's wrong with me is that I might not be able to do the learning from books that you can, but mark my words, I'll be out of here before you, 'er Ladyship or not."

"But I'm not stopping you—"

In frustration Enid flounced to her feet, pulled back the bedclothes, and threw herself into bed. Without saying goodnight, she turned her back on Maisie, as had become her habit.

Maisie said nothing more, but climbed into her heavy brass bed to lie upon the hard horsehair mattress between cold white muslin sheets. Without attempting to read her book or work on the assignment Maurice Blanche had given her, she turned out the light.

Jealousy. Now she was beginning to understand jealousy. Together with the exchanges of the past few weeks, and the heated conversation with her father, Maisie was also beginning to feel fully the challenge of following her dream. And she was disturbed, not for the first time, by Enid's words about Lady Rowan. Was she just a temporary diversion for Lady Rowan, a sop to her conscience so she could feel as if she was doing something for society? Maisie couldn't believe this, for time and time again she had seen genuine interest and concern on her employer's face.

"So, Maisie. Let me see your work. How are you progressing with Jung?"

Maisie walked into the library for her meeting with Maurice Blanche and stood before him.

"Sit down, sit down. Let us begin. We have much work to do."

Maisie silently placed her books in front of him.

"What is it, Maisie?"

"I don't think, Dr. Blanche, that I can have lessons with you anymore."

Maurice Blanche said nothing but nodded his head and studied Maisie's countenance. Silence seeped into the space between them, and Maurice immediately noticed the single tear that emerged from Maisie's right eye and drizzled down her face.

"Ah, yes, the challenge of position and place, I think."

Maisie sniffed and met Blanche's look. She nodded.

"Yes. It has been long overdue. We have been fortunate thus far, have we not, Maisie?"

Once again Maisie nodded She expected to be dismissed, as she would in turn dismiss her ambitions and the dream she had nurtured since first planning to visit the Comptons' library at three o'clock in the morning so long ago.

Instead Maurice took up the book he had assigned at their last meeting, along with her notes, and the lessons she had completed in the subjects of English, mathematics, and geography.

Looking through her work, Maurice inclined his head here, and raised his eyebrows there. Maisie said nothing, but inspected her hands and pulled at a loose thread in her white pinafore.

"Maisie. Please complete these two final chapters while I speak with Lady Rowan."

Once again Maisie was left, if only for a short time, to wonder at her fate, and whether all would be well. As Maurice Blanche left the room, Maisie took up the book and turned to the chapters he had indicated. But try as she might, she could not read past the first paragraph of her assignment and retain what she had read. Instead she put her right hand to her mouth and with her teeth worried a hangnail on her little finger. By the time Maurice Blanche returned with Lady Rowan and Carter, Maisie had to plunge her right hand into her pinafore pocket so that the blood now oozing from the cuticle would not be seen.

Clearly much discussion had taken place in the interim. It fell to Carter, as head of the domestic staff, to stand at Lady Rowan's side as she told Maisie of a plan that had been incubating and had just hatched, inspired by her genuine need. It was a plan that would in turn help Maisie. And not a moment too soon.'

"Maisie, the Dowager Lady Compton lives in the dower house at Chelstone·Manor, in Kent. My mother-in-law is in command of her faculties but has some difficulty in movement, and she does sleep long hours now that she is of advanced age. Her personal maid gave notice some weeks ago, due to impending marriage."

Lady Rowan glanced at Maurice Blanche and at Carter before continuing. "Maisie, I would like to offer you the position."

Maisie said nothing, but looked intently at Lady Rowan, then at

Carter, who simply nodded, then raised an eyebrow, and focused his gaze quickly on her hand in the pinafore pocket.

Maisie stood up straighter, twisted a handkerchief around the sore finger, and brought her hand to her side.

"The Dowager Lady Compton has only a small staff," said Lady Rowan, "as befits her needs. Aside from her personal maid and a nurse, household staff do not live at the dower house but at the manor. When we are in residence, as you know, Carter and Mrs. Crawford travel to Chelstone to join the staff. However, Mrs. Johnson, the housekeeper, is in sole charge of the household at Chelstone while we are in London."

Lady Rowan paused for a moment, walked to the window, and crossed her arms. She took a moment to look out at the garden before turning back into the room to continue.

"Employment with my mother-in-law will allow you some—let us say 'leeway'—to continue your work with Dr. Blanche. In addition you will not be subject to some of the scrutiny that you have experienced in recent weeks, although you *will* report to Mrs. Johnson."

Maisie looked at her feet, then at Carter, Lady Rowan, and Dr. Blanche, all of whom seemed to have grown several inches while Lady Rowan was speaking.

Maisie felt very small. And she was worried about her father.

As she remained silent, Carter raised an eyebrow, indicating that she should speak.

"Is there a bus so I can get back to London to see my father on Sundays?"

"There is a train service from the village, on the branch line via Tonbridge. But you may wish to make the visits to Mr. Dobbs farther apart, since the distance requires several hours of travel," replied Maurice Blanche.

Then he suggested that Maisie be given a day to consider the offer.

"You will see Mr. Carter with your decision tomorrow at five o'clock in the afternoon, Maisie?"

"Yes, sir. Thank you, sir—and thank you, Your Ladyship, Mr. Carter."

"Right you are. I will bid you goodnight."

Carter bowed to Lady Rowan, as did Dr. Blanche, while Maisie bobbed a curtsy, and put her hand back in her pocket, lest the company see her handkerchief bloodied from the bitten hangnail.

"I think, Mr. Carter, that Maisie should continue with her household responsibilities this evening, rather than her assignments from me. Such endeavors will be a useful accompaniment to the process of coming to a decision.'

"Right you are, sir. Maisie?"

Maisie curtsied again, then left the room to return to her duties.

Blanche walked over to the window and looked out at the gardens. He had anticipated young Maisie's challenges, which had come later than he might have expected. How he despised wasted talent! He knew that the move to Kent would be a good one for her, but the decision to pursue her opportunity was one Maisie alone would have to make. He left the house, wending his way to familiar streets south of the Thames.

*It* surprised the staff when Frankie Dobbs came unsummoned to the back door of the kitchen the next morning, to report that some very nice lettuces and tomatoes had just been brought in from Jersey, and would Mrs. Crawford be needing some for the dinner party on Friday night?

Usually Frankie would not see Maisie when he came to the house to deliver fruit and vegetables each week, but on this occasion Mrs. Crawford took no time at all to summon Maisie to see her father, for she knew that the motive for Frankie Dobbs's appearance extended beyond urgent notification of what was best at Covent Garden market.

"Dad, . . . Dad!" cried Maisie as she went to her father, put her arms around his waist, and held him to her.

"Now then, now then. What's all this? What will Mr. Carter say?"

"Oh Dad, I'm *so* glad you came to the house. What a coincidence!"

Maisie looked at her father inquisitively, then followed him up the outside stairs to the street, where Persephone waited, contentedly eating from the nosebag of oats attached to her bridle. Maisie told Frankie about the new position she had been offered with the Dowager Lady Compton.

"Just as well I 'appened by, then, innit, Love? Sounds like just what you need. Your mother and me always wanted to live in the country, thought it would be better for you than the Smoke. Go on. You go, love. You'll still see me."

"So you don't mind then, Dad?"

"No, I don't mind at all. I reckon bein' down there in the country will be a real treat for you. Hard work, mind, but a treat all the same."

Maisie gave Carter her answer that evening. It was agreed with Lady Rowan that she should leave at the end of the month. Yet even though he wanted her to see and learn all there was to see and learn, Frankie often felt as if fine sand were slipping through his fingers whenever he thought of his girl, Maisie.

# CHAPTER THIRTEEN

aisie first came to Chelstone Manor in the autumn of 1913. She had traveled by train to Tonbridge, where she changed for Chelstone, on a small branch line. She'd brought one bag with her, containing clothes and personal belongings, and a small trunk in which she carried books, paper, and a clutch of assignments written in Maurice Blanche's compact almost indecipherable hand. And in her mind's eye Maisie carried a vision. During their last lesson before she left for Chelstone, he had asked Maisie what she might do with this education, this opportunity.

"Um, I don't really know, Dr. Blanche. I always thought I could teach. My mum wanted me to be a teacher. It's a good job for me, teaching."

"But?"

Maisie looked at Maurice Blanche, at the bright eyes that looked into the soul of a person so that they naturally revealed to him in words what he could silently observe.

"But. But I think I want to do something like what you do, Dr. Blanche."

Maurice Blanche made a church and steeple with his hands, and rested his upper lip on his forefingers. Two minutes passed before he looked up at Maisie.

"And what do I do, Maisie?"

"You heal people. That is, I *think* you heal people. In all sorts of ways. That's what I think."

Blanche nodded, leaned back in his chair, and looked out of the library window to the walled gardens of 15 Ebury Place.

"Yes, I think you could say that, Maisie."

"And I think you find out the truth. I think you look at what is right and wrong. And I think you have had lots of different . . . educations."

"Yes, Maisie, that is all correct. But what about that vision?"

"I want to go to Cambridge. To Girton College. Like you said, it's possible for an ordinary person like me to go, you know, as long as I can work and pass the exams."

"I don't think I ever used the word 'ordinary' to describe you, Maisie."

Maisie blushed, and Maurice continued with his questions. "And what will you study, Maisie?"

"I'm not sure. I am interested in the moral sciences, sir. When you told me about the different subjects—psychology, ethics, philosophy, logic—that's what I most wanted to study. I've already done lots of assignments in those subjects, and I like the work. It's not so—well—definite, is it? Sometimes it's like a maze, with no answers, only more questions. I like that, you know. I like the search. And it's what you want, isn't it, Dr. Blanche?"

Maisie looked at Maurice, and waited for his response.

"It is not what I want that is pertinent here, Maisie, but what you are drawn to. I will, however, concur that you have a certain gift for understanding and appreciating the constituent subjects of the moral sciences curriculum. Now then, you are young yet, Maisie. We have plenty of time for more discussion of this subject. Perhaps we should look at your assignments—but remember to keep those hallowed halls of Girton College uppermost in your mind."

The old lady was not too demanding, and there was the nurse to take a good deal of the responsibility for her care. Maisie ensured that the dowager's rooms were always warm, that her clothes were freshly laundered and laid out each day. She brushed her fine gray hair and twisted it into a bun which the dowager wore under a lace cap. She read to the dowager, and brought meals to her from the main house. For much of the time, the old lady slept in her rooms, or sat by the window with her eyes closed. Occasionally, on a fine day, Maisie would take her outside in a wheelchair, or support her as she stood in the garden, insisting that she was quite well enough to attend to a dead rose, or reach up to inhale the scent of fresh apple blossom. Then she tired and leaned on Maisie as she was assisted to her chair once again. But for much of the time Maisie was lonely.

There was little conversation with staff up at the manor, and despite everything, Maisie missed Enid and her wicked sense of humor. The other members of staff at Chelstone would not speak with her readily, or joke with her, or treat her as one of their own. Yet though she missed the people she had come to love, she did enjoy having solitude for her studies. Each Saturday, Maisie walked into the village to post a brown-paper-wrapped package to Dr. Blanche, and each Saturday she picked up a new envelope with her latest assignment, and his comments on her work of the week before. In January 1914 Maurice decided that Maisie was ready to take the Girton College entrance examinations.

In March, Maurice accompanied Maisie to Cambridge for the examinations, meeting her early at Liverpool Street Station for the journey to Cambridge, then on to the small village of Girton, home of the famous ladies' college of Cambridge University. She remembered watching from the train window as the streets of London gave way to farmland that was soft in the way that Kent was soft, but instead of the green undulating hills of the Weald of Kent, with hedges dividing a patchwork quilt of farms, woodland, and small villages, the Cambridgeshire fens were flat, so that a person could see for miles and miles into the distance.

The grand buildings of Cambridge, the wonderful gardens of Girton College two miles north of the town, the large lecture hall, being taken to a desk, the papers put in front of her, the hours and hours of questions and answers, the nib of her pen cutting into the joint at the top of the second finger of her right hand as she quickly filled page after page with her fine, bold script, were unforgettable. Thirst had suddenly gripped at her throat until she felt faint for lack of breath as she left the hall, whose ceiling now seemed to be moving down toward her. Her head was spinning as she leaned on Maurice, who had been waiting for her. He steadied her, instructing her to breathe deeply, as they walked slowly to the village teashop.

While hot tea was poured and fresh scones placed in front of them, Maurice allowed Maisie to rest before asking for her account of each question on the examination papers, and her responses to them. He nodded as she described her answers, occasionally sipping tea or wiping a crumb from the corner of his mouth.

"I believe, Maisie, that you have done very well."

"I don't know, Dr. Blanche, sir. But I did my best."

"Of course. Of course."

"Dr. Blanche. You went to Oxford, didn't you?"

"Yes, indeed, Maisie—and I was only a little younger than you at the time. Of course, as I am male, a degree could be conferred upon me. But there will be a time, I hope before too long, when women will also earn degrees for their advanced academic studies."

Maisie flicked the long braid of jet black hair from her shoulder and felt its weight along her spine as she sat back in her chair to listen to Maurice.

"And I was also fortunate to study in Paris at the Sorbonne, and in Edinburgh."

"Scotland."

"I'm glad to see that you have a grasp of geography, Maisie." Maurice looked over his spectacles at Maisie and smiled at her. "Yes, the Department of Legal Medicine."

"What did you do there, Dr. Blanche?"

"Learned to read the story told by a dead body. Especially when the person did not die of natural causes."

"Oh . . ." said Maisie, temporarily bereft of speech. She pushed away the crumbly scone and took a long sip of the soothing tea. Maisie slowly regained energy after the ordeal of the past few hours, which she had endured along with several dozen other hopeful students. "Dr. Blanche. May I ask you a question?"

"Of course."

"Why did you want to learn about the dead?"

"Ah. A good question, Maisie. Suffice it to say that sometimes one's calling finds one first. When I first came to Oxford it was to study economics and politics; then I went to the Sorbonne to study philosophy—so you see we have similar interests there—but it was as I traveled, seeing so much suffering, that medicine found me."

"And legal medicine? The dead bodies?"

Maurice looked at his watch. "That is a story for another time. Let us now walk over to the college again, where no doubt you will be studying later this very year. The gardens really are quite lovely."

The Comptons had gathered a coterie of important and influential guests, not only to sample the delights of a July weekend in the country but for animated discussion and conjecture upon the discord that had been festering in Europe since June, when the Austrian archduke was assassinated in Serbia. It was predicted that the conflict, which had started two years earlier, in 1912, in the Balkans, would become general war, and as the Kaiser's armies reportedly moved into position along the Belgian border, fear of its escalation grew. Dread stalked Europe, snaking its way from the corridors of government to the households of ordinary people.

Carter was in full battle mode for the onslaught of visitors, while Mrs. Crawford held her territory in the kitchen, blasting out orders to any maid or footman who came within range of her verbal fire. Lady Rowan swore she could hear Cook's voice reverberating through every wooden beam in the medieval manor house, though even she declined to intervene at such a time.

"Rowan, we have the very best cook in London and Kent, but I fear we also have the one with the loudest voice."

"Don't worry, Julian, you know she'll pipe down when everything's in its place and the guests start to arrive."

"Indeed, indeed. In the meantime, I wonder if I should tell the War Office about her, in advance. She could put a seasoned general to shame—have you seen how she marshals her troops? I should have every new subaltern serve in Cook Crawford's battalion for a month. We could overcome the Hun by launching meat pies clear across France and into the Kaiser's palace!"

"Julian, don't be absurd—and don't be so full of certainty that Britain will be at war," said Lady Rowan. "By the way, I understand that our Miss Dobbs received a letter from Girton this morning."

"Did she, by Jove? Well, not before time, my dear. I don't think I could bear to look at those nail-bitten fingers holding onto the tea tray any longer."

"She's had a hard life, Julian." Lady Rowan looked out of the windows and over the land surrounding Chelstone Manor. "We can't presume to imagine how difficult it has been for her. She's such a bright girl."

"And for each Maisie Dobbs, there are probably ten more that you can't save. Remember, we may not have done her any favors, Rowan. Life can be very difficult for someone of her class at Cambridge."

"Yes, I know, Julian. But times are changing. I am glad that we were able to contribute in some way."

She turned from the window to look at her husband. "Now then, shall we go downstairs to see what news the letter from Girton has brought? I don't know if you've noticed, but it has gone awfully quiet in the house."

Lord and Lady Compton went together to the large drawing room, where Lord Julian rang the bell for Carter. The impeccably turned-out and always punctual butler answered the call within a minute.

"Your Lordship, Your Ladyship."

"Carter, what news does Miss Dobbs have from Cambridge?"

"Very, very good news, M'Lord. Miss Dobbs has been accepted. We are all terribly proud of her."

"Oh, that's wonderful, wonderful!" Lady Rowan clapped her hands. "We must get word to Maurice, Julian. Carter, send Miss Dobbs to see us immediately."

aisie could not wait to tell Frankie Dobbs her news in person, and as soon as she could, traveled by train to Charing Cross Station, and from there to the small soot-blackened terraced house that had once been her home.

"Well, what do you know? Our little Maisie all grown up and going away to the university. Blow me down, your mum would have been chuffed."

Frankie Dobbs held his daughter by the shoulders and looked into her eyes, his own smarting with tears of pride—and of concern.

"Do you think you're ready for this, love?"

Frankie pulled out a chair and beckoned Maisie to sit with him by the coal stove in the small kitchen. "It's a big step, isn't it?"

"I'll do all right, Dad. I've won a place, and next year if I do well, I might get a college scholarship. That's what I'm aiming for. Lord and Lady Compton will be my sponsors, for the first year, anyway, and I've been putting a bit by as well. Lady Rowan is going to give me some of her day clothes that she doesn't want, and Mrs.

Crawford said she'll help me with tailoring them to fit me, although there are strict rules about what I can wear. Not much different from a maid's uniform, but without the pinny, from what I can make out."

Maisie rubbed her father's hands, which seemed strangely cold.

"I told you, I'll be all right, Dad. And at Christmas, Easter, and summer, I can come back to the house to earn some more money."

Frankie Dobbs could barely meet his daughter's eyes, knowing only too well that it would be nigh on impossible for Maisie to return to the Comptons' employ once she had left. He knew how it was in those houses, and once she had moved beyond her station, she could never go back. She'd been lucky so far, but after she left, she wouldn't be so easily accepted. The gap between Maisie and the other staff would become a chasm. And what worried Frankie more than anything was that Maisie might not ever fit in to *any* station, that she would forever be betwixt and between.

"So when will you be leaving?"

"I'll start in the autumn. They call it the Michaelmas term, you know, like those mauve Michaelmas daisies that bloom in September, the ones Mum used to love. I had to get special permission because I'm not quite eighteen."

Frankie got up from his seat and rubbed at his back. He wanted to get the conversation back to a point at which he could voice his offer.

"Well, talking about 'avin' a bit more, like we were before we started talking about the daisies, I've got something for you, love." Frankie reached up and took down a large earthenware flour jar from the shelf above the stove.

"Here you are, Love. After I paid off the debts, you know, after your mother . . . I started putting a bit by each week meself. For you. Knowing that you'd be doing something important one day, where a bit extra might come in 'andy."

Maisie took the jar, her hands shaking. She lifted the lid and looked into the earthenware depths. There were pound notes, some brand new ten-shilling notes, florins, half-crowns, and shillings. The jar was full of Frankie Dobbs's savings for Maisie.

"Oh, Dad . . ." Maisie stood up and, clutching the jar of money with one hand and her father with the other, held him to her.

*In* August 1914 people still went about their business, and war seemed to be something that had nothing to do with ordinary life. But then a boy she knew in the village was in uniform, and certain foods were just a little more difficult to find. A footman at the Belgravia house enlisted, and so did the grooms and young gardeners at Chelstone. Then one weekend Maisie was called to Lady Rowan's sitting room at Chelstone.

"Maisie, I am beside myself. The grooms have all enlisted, and I am fearfully worried about my hunters. I have spoken to all sorts of people, but the young men are going into the services. Look, I know this is unusual, but I wonder, do you think your father might consider the position?"

"Well, M'Lady, I don't really know. There's Persephone, and his business."

"There is a cottage in the grounds for him if he wants it. You'll be able to see him when you are not at Girton, of course, and his mare can be stabled here. They will both be well looked after."

The next day Maisie traveled by train to London to see her father. To her complete surprise, Frankie Dobbs said he would "think about it" when she told him of the offer from Lady Rowan. "After all, I'm not getting any younger, and neither is Persephone. She could do with a bit o' the old fresh country air. And 'er Ladyship's been very good to you, so come to think of it, if I 'elped 'er out, it'd be only right. It's not as if I'm a stranger to Kent, 'aving been down there picking the old 'ops every year when I was a bit of a nipper meself."

Frankie Dobbs and Persephone moved from Lambeth on a misty, unseasonably cold morning in late August 1914, to take up residence in the groom's cottage and stables, respectively, at Chelstone Manor. Instead of rising at three o'clock to take Persephone to Covent Garden market and then setting out on his rounds, Frankie now enjoyed a lie-in before rising at five o'clock to feed Lady Rowan's hunters and Persephone, who seemed to be relishing her own retirement. In a short time Frankie Dobbs was being feted by Lady Rowan as the man who knew everything there was to know about the grooming, feeding, and well-being of horses. But it was a deeper knowledge that would endear him to her for the rest of her life.

*Only* days remained before Maisie was to leave for Cambridge, so time spent in each other's company was of prime importance to Maisie and her father. They had resumed the ritual of working together in making a fuss of Persephone as often as possible. It was on such an occasion, while they were working and talking about the latest war news, that Lady Rowan paid a surprise visit.

"I say, anybody there?"

Maisie snapped to attention, but Frankie Dobbs, while respectful, simply replied, "In 'ere with Persephone, Your Ladyship."

"Mr. Dobbs. Thank goodness. I am beside myself."

Maisie immediately went to Lady Rowan, who always claimed to be "beside herself" in a crisis, despite a demeanor that suggested otherwise.

"Mr. Dobbs, they are coming to take my hunters—and possibly even your mare. Lord Compton has received word from the War Office that our horses are to be inspected for service this week. They are coming on Tuesday to take them. I *cannot* let them go. I don't want to be unpatriotic, but they are my hunters."

"And they ain't taking my Persephone either, Your Ladyship."

Frankie Dobbs walked toward his faithful old horse, who nuzzled at his jacket for the treat she knew would be forthcoming. He took sweet apple pieces from his pocket and held them out to Persephone, feeling the comforting warmth of her velvety nose in his hand, before turning back to Lady Rowan.

"Tuesday, eh? You leave it to me."

"Oh, Mr. Dobbs—everything depends upon you. What will you do? Take them somewhere and hide them?"

Frankie laughed. "Oh no. I think I might be seen running away with this little lot, Your Ladyship. No, I won't have to run anywhere. But here's one thing—" Frankie Dobbs looked at Maisie and at Lady Rowan. "I don't want anyone coming in these stables until I say so. And, Your Ladyship, I'll come to the 'ouse on Tuesday mornin' and tell you what to say. But the main thing is, whatever you see or 'ear, you're not to mind or to say anything else, other than what I tell you. You've got to trust me."

Lady Rowan stood taller, regained her composure, and looked directly at Frankie Dobbs. "I trust you implicitly."

Maisie's father nodded, tipped his cap toward Lady Rowan, and then smiled at Maisie. The stately woman walked toward the stable door, then turned around. "Mr. Dobbs. One thing we spoke about only briefly when you first came to Chelstone. I seem to remember that you were at a racing yard as a boy."

"Newmarket, Your Ladyship. From the time I was twelve to the time I came back to 'elp my father with the business at nineteen. Bit big for a jockey, I was."

"I expect you learned quite a thing or two about horses, didn't you?"

"Oh yes, Your Ladyship. Quite a thing or two. Saw a lot, good and bad."

The men from the War Office came to Chelstone at lunchtime on Tuesday. Lady Rowan led them to the stables apologizing profusely and explaining, as she had been instructed by Frankie Dobbs, that she feared her horses might not be suitable for service as they had contracted a sickness that even her groom could not cure. They were met by Frankie Dobbs, who stood in tears by Sultan, her jet black hunter.

The once-noble horse hung his head low as foam dropped from his open mouth. His eyes rolled back in his head as he struggled for breath. Lady Rowan gasped and looked at Frankie, who would not meet her alarmed eyes with his own.

"By God, what is wrong with the beast?" asked the tall man in uniform, who held a baton under his arm. He stepped carefully toward Sultan, avoiding any soiled straw that might compromise the shine on his highly polished boots.

"Not anything I've seen for years. Caused by worm. Bacteria," Frankie Dobbs replied, and spoke to Lady Rowan directly. "I'm sorry, Your Ladyship. We'll probably lose them all by tomorrow. That old cart 'orse will be first. On account of 'er age."

The men stopped briefly to glance into Persephone's stall, where Frankie Dobbs's faithful horse lay on the ground.

"Lady Compton. Our sympathies. The country needs one hundred and sixty-five thousand horses, but we need them to be fit, strong, and able to be of service on the battlefield."

Lady Rowan's tears were genuine. She had been primed by Frankie as to what she should say, but had not been prepared for what she would see. "Yes . . . yes . . . indeed. I wish you luck, gentlemen."

The two men were soon gone. After seeing them off, Lady Rowan ran immediately to the stables once again, where Frankie Dobbs was working furiously to pour a chalky liquid down Sultan's throat. Maisie was in another stall, feeding the liquid to Ralph. Persephone and Hamlet were on their feet.

Lady Rowan said nothing, but walked over to Hamlet, and touched the pale, drawn skin around his eyes. As she brought her hand away she noticed the white powder on her gloves and smiled.

"Mr. Dobbs, I shall never ask what you did today. But I will remember this forever. I know what I asked of you was wrong, but I just couldn't bear to lose them."

"And I couldn't bear to lose Persephone, Your Ladyship. But I 'ave to warn you. This war is far from over. You keep these 'ere horses on your land. Don't let anyone outside see them, just them as works 'ere. Times like these changes folk. Keep the animals close to 'ome."

Lady Rowan nodded and gave a carrot to each horse in turn.

"Oh, and by the way, Your Ladyship. I wonder if Mrs. Crawford could use two and a half dozen egg yolks? Terrible waste if she can't."

Ten household staff sat down to dinner at the big table in the kitchen at Chelstone Manor on Maisie's last night before leaving for Cambridge. She was on the cusp of her new life. The Comptons were in residence, so the servants whom Maisie loved from the Belgravia house were there to see her off.

Carter sat at the head of the table in the carver's chair, and Mrs. Crawford sat at the opposite end within easy striking distance of the big cast-iron coal-fired stove. Maisie sat next to her father and opposite Enid. Even Enid, who had been summoned from the London house to assist with late-summer entertaining at Chelstone, joined in the fun and looked happy: She had brightened up considerably since Mr. James had returned from Canada.

"Gaw lummy, I think the world's spinnin' even faster these days. What with the war, Master James coming home, Maisie goin' to Cambridge—Cambridge, our Maisie Dobbs! Then there's all the important people coming tomorrow to meet with Lord Compton," said Cook, as she took her seat after a final check on the apple pie.

"All arrangements are in order, Mrs. Crawford. We will make a final round of inspection after our little celebration here. Now then . . ."

Standing up, Carter cleared his throat and smiled. "I'll ask you to join me in a toast."

Chairs scraped backward, people coughed as they stood up and nudged one another. The entire complement of household staff turned to face Maisie, who blushed as all eyes were upon her.

"To our own Maisie Dobbs! Congratulations, Maisie. We've all seen you work hard, and we know you will be a credit to Lord and Lady Compton, to your father—and to us all. So we've got a small token of our affection. For you to use at the university."

Mrs. Crawford reached under the table and took out a large flat box, which she passed down the table to Carter with one hand, while the other rubbed at her now tearful eyes with a large white handkerchief.

"From all the staff at Chelstone Manor and the Compton residence in London—Maisie, we're proud of you."

Maisie blushed, and reached for the plain brown cardboard box. "Oh, my goodness. Oh, dear. Oh—"

"Just open it, Mais, for Gawd's sake!" said Enid, inspiring a scowl from Mrs. Crawford.

Maisie pulled at the string, took off the lid, and drew back the fine tissue paper to reveal a butter-soft yet sturdy black leather document case with a silver clasp.

"Oh . . . oh . . . it's . . . it's . . . beautiful! Thank you, thank you. All of you."

Carter wasted no time in taking his glass and continuing with the toast. "To our own Maisie Dobbs . . ."

Voices echoed around the table.

"To Maisie Dobbs."

"Well done, Mais."

"You show 'em for us, Maisie!"

"Maisie Dobbs!"

Maisie nodded, whispering, "Thank you . . . thank you . . . thank you."

"And before we sit down," said Carter, as the assembled group were bending halfway down to their seats again. "To our country, to our boys who are going over to France. Godspeed and God save the King!"

"God save the King."

The following day Maisie stood on the station platform, this time with an even larger trunk of books that far outweighed her case of personal belongings. She clutched her black document case tightly, afraid that she would lose this most wonderful gift. Carter and Mrs. Crawford had chosen it, maintaining that Maisie Dobbs should not have to go to university without a smart case for her papers.

On her journey up to Cambridge, when Maisie changed trains at Tonbridge for the main service to London, she was taken aback by the multitude of uniformed men lining up on the platform. Freshly posted handbills gave a hint of things to come:

LONDON, BRIGHTON & SOUTH COAST RAILWAYS
MOBILIZATION OF TROOPS
PASSENGERS ARE HEREBY NOTIFIED THAT IT MAY BE NECESSARY
TO SUSPEND OR ALTER TRAINS WITHOUT PREVIOUS NOTICE

It was clear that the journey to Cambridge would be a long one. Sweethearts and the newly married held tightly to each other amid the crush of bodies on the platform. Mothers cried into sodden handkerchiefs; sons assured them, "I'll be back before you know it," and fathers stood stoically silent.

Maisie passed a father and son standing uncomfortably together in the grip of unspoken emotion. As she brushed by, she saw the older man clap his son on the shoulder. He pursed his lips together, firmly clamping his grief in place, while the son looked down at his feet. A small Border collie sat still between them, secure on a leash held by the son. The panting dog looked between father and son as they began to speak quietly.

"You mind and do your best, son. Your mother would have been proud of you."

"I know, Dad," said the son, moving his gaze to his father's lapels.

"And you mind you keep your head out of the way of the Kaiser's boys, lad. We don't want you messing up that uniform, do we?"

The boy laughed, for he was a boy and not yet a man.

"All right, Dad, I'll keep my boots shined, and you look after Patch."

"Safe as houses, me and Patch. We'll be waiting for you when you come home, son."

Maisie watched as the man pressed his hand down even harder on the young man's shoulder. "Listen to that. Your train is coming in. This is it, time to be off. You mind and do your best."

The son nodded, bent down to stroke the dog, who playfully wagged her tail and jumped up to lick the boy's face. He met his father's eyes only briefly, and after passing the leash to the older man, was suddenly swallowed up in a sea of moving khaki. A guard with a megaphone ordered, "Civilians to keep back from the train" as the older man stood on tiptoe, trying to catch one last glimpse of his departing son.

Maisie moved away to allow the soldiers to board their train, and watched the man bend down, pick up the dog, and bury his face in the animal's thick coat. And as his shoulders shook with the grief he dared not show, the dog twisted her head to lick comfort into his neck.

# CHAPTER FIFTEEN

*U*pon arrival at Girton College, Maisie registered with the Porter's Lodge and was directed to the room that had been assigned to her for the academic year. Assured that the trunk of books would be brought up to her room in due course, clutching her bag, she began to leave the lodge, following the directions given by the porter, who suddenly called her back. "Oh, Miss! A parcel arrived today for you. Urgent delivery, to be given to you immediately."

Maisie took the brown paper parcel and immediately recognized the small slanted writing. It was from Maurice Blanche.

Few women were already in residence when Maisie arrived, and the hallways were quiet as she made her way to her room. She was anxious to unwrap the parcel, and paid hardly any attention to her new surroundings after opening the door to her room. Instead she quickly put her belongings down by the wardrobe and, taking a seat in the small armchair, began to open the package. Under the brown paper, a layer of tissue covered a letter from Maurice, and a leather-bound book with blank pages. Inside the cover of the book, Maurice had copied the words of Søren Kierkegaard, words that he had quoted to her from memory in their last meeting before her journey to Cambridge. It was as if Maurice were in the room with her, so strong was his voice in her mind as she read the words: "There is nothing of which every man is so afraid, as getting to know how enormously much he is capable of doing and becoming." She closed the book, continuing to hold it as she read the letter in which Maurice spoke of the gift:

> In seeking to fill your mind, I omitted to instruct you in the opposite exercise. This small book is for your daily writings, when the day is newborn and before you embark upon the richness of study and intellectual encounter. My instruction, Maisie, is to simply write a page each day. There is no set subject, save that which the waking mind has held close in sleep.

Suddenly the loud crash of a door swinging back on its hinges, followed by the double thump of two large leather suitcases landing one after the other on the floor of the room next door, heralded the arrival of her neighbor. Amplified by the empty corridor, she heard a deep sigh followed by the sound of a foot kicking one of the cases.

"What I wouldn't give for a gin and tonic!"

A second later, with wrapping paper still between her fingers and her head raised to follow the audible wake of her neighbor, Maisie heard footsteps coming toward her room. In her hurry to open the parcel from Maurice, she had left her door ajar, allowing the young woman immediate access.

A fashionably dressed girl with dark chestnut hair stood in front of her, and held out her finely manicured hand. "Priscilla Evernden. Delighted to meet you—Maisie Dobbs, isn't it? Wouldn't happen to have a cigarette, would you?"

It seemed to Maisie that she lived two lives at Cambridge. There were her days of study and learning, which began in her room before dawn, and ended after her lectures and tutorials with more study in the evening. She spent Saturday afternoons and Sunday mornings in the college chapel, rolling bandages and knitting socks, gloves, and scarves for men at the front. It was a cold winter in the trenches, and no sooner had word gone out that men needed warm clothes than every woman suddenly seemed to be knitting.

At least Maisie felt that she was doing something for the war, but it was her studies that were always at the forefront of her mind. If anything, the endless talk of war seemed to her a distraction, something that she just wanted to be over, so that she could get on with her life at Cambridge—and whatever might come after.

There were times when Maisie was thankful that a very bright spark was resident in the next room. Priscilla seemed to gravitate toward Maisie and, surprising Maisie herself, appeared to enjoy her company.

"My dear girl, how many pairs of these infernal socks must one knit? I am sure I have kitted out an entire battalion."

Another sharp observation from Priscilla Evernden. In truth Maisie loved Priscilla's theatrical tone as much as she had loved Enid's down-to-earth wit, and she was only too aware that, though miles apart in their upbringing, the two girls shared a ready exuberance that Maisie envied. Despite her early fumblings with the language of the aristocracy, Enid was sure of who she was and sure of what she wanted to be. Priscilla was equally sure of herself, and Maisie loved the sweep and flourish of her language, punctuated as it was by exaggerated movements of her hands and arms.

"You seem to be doing quite well, really," said Maisie.

"Oh, sod it!" said Priscilla as she fumbled with her knitting needles, "I fear, dear Maisie, that you are clearly made of knitting stock, one only has to look at that plait hanging down your back. Good Lord, girl, that plait could be a loaf at Harvest Festival! Obviously you have been bred for knitting."

Maisie blushed. Over the years the edges had been knocked away from her London accent. She might not pass for the aristocracy, but she could certainly be taken for a clergyman's daughter. And not one bred for knitting.

"I hardly think so, Pris."

"Well, I suppose not. One only has to look at your academic work, and those books that you read. Anyone who can read those turgid tomes can make short work of a sock. Dear God, give me a drink that bites back and good tale of love and lust any day of the week."

Maisie dropped a stitch, and looked up at Priscilla. "Now, don't tell me that, Pris. Why did you come up to Cambridge?"

Priscilla was tall, giving the impression of strength, though she carried no extra weight. Her chestnut hair hung loose around her shoulders, and she wore a man's shirt with a pair of man's trousers, "borrowed" from her brother before he left for France. She claimed that they wouldn't be in fashion by the time he returned anyway, and swore that she would only wear them indoors.

"Dear girl, I came to Cambridge because I could, and because my dear mother and father were ready to fling themselves burning into the lake rather than have me roll in through the window at two in the morning again. Out of sight, out of mind, darling. . . . Oh my dear Lord, look at this sock! I don't know what I am doing wrong here, but it's like knitting into a funnel."

Maisie looked up from her work.

"Let me see."

"Whoopee! M. Dobbs to the rescue."

Priscilla got up from her place on the old armchair, where she had been sitting sideways with her legs dangling over the arm, while Maisie sat on the floor on a cushion.

"I'm going out now, and to hell with Miss What's-Her-Name downstairs' curfew."

"Priscilla, what if you get caught? You're not supposed to be out late. You could be sent down for this."

"Dear Maisie, I will not get caught, because I will not be coming in late. If anyone asks, I know you will say that I've taken to my bed. And of course, when I come in at the crack of dawn tomorrow—

well—I needed the early morning fresh air to clear the mind after my indisposition."

Minutes later Priscilla reappeared, dressed from head to toe in evening wear, and carrying a small bag.

"One thing you have to admit about war, darling—there's nothing quite like a man in uniform. See you at breakfast—and for heaven's sake do stop fretting!"

"*Good* Lord, Maisie Dobbs, where do you think you are going with those books?"

Priscilla Evernden was leaning out of the window of Maisie's room, and turned back to draw upon the cigarette she gamely smoked through a long ivory holder. It was the end of her second term at Girton, and Maisie was packing to go back to Chelstone for Easter.

"Well, Pris, I don't want to fall behind in my work, so I thought wouldn't hurt—"

"Tell me, Maisie, when do you ever have fun, girl?"

Maisie reddened and began to fold a cotton blouse. The intensity of her movements as she ran the side of her hand along the creases and patted down the collar revealed her discomfort.

"I enjoy reading, Priscilla. I enjoy my studies here."

"Hmmm. You'd probably enjoy it a lot more if you went out a bit. You were only away for a few days at Christmas."

Maisie smarted, remembering her return to a depressed household at the end of her first term. The war had not ended by Christmas—as predicted—and, though nothing was said, Maisie felt that others found her studies frivolous at a time when so many women were volunteering for jobs previously held by men who had enlisted to serve their country.

Holding a woolen cardigan by the shoulders, Maisie folded it and placed it in her case before looking up at Priscilla. "You know,

Priscilla, life is different for some people. I don't go back to my horses, cars, and parties. You know that."

Priscilla walked toward the armchair and sat down, folding her legs to one side. Once again she drew heavily on the cigarette, leaned her head back, and blew smoke rings toward the ceiling. Then, holding her cigarette to one side, she looked at Maisie directly. "For all my strange, peculiar privileged ways, Maisie, I am quite acute. You wear your sackcloth and ashes a little too proudly at times. We both know that you will do terribly well here. Academically. But I tell you this, Maisie—we are all a long time dead when we go, if you know what I mean. This is our only ride on the merry-go-round."

She drew again on the cigarette and continued. "I have three brothers in France now. Do you think I'm going to sit here and mourn? Hell, no! I'm going to have fun enough for all of us. Enough fun for this time on earth. And just because it took a tremendous leap for you to be here doesn't mean that you can't enjoy life along with all this—this—studying." She waved a hand toward the books.

Maisie looked up from her packing. "You don't understand."

"Well, perhaps I don't. But here's what I do know. You don't have to rush back to wherever it is you are rushing back to. Not this evening, anyway. Why not go tomorrow? Come out with me tonight. We may not have a chance again."

"What do you mean?"

"Oh, look at me, Maisie. I really am not cut out for all this. I received a severe reprimand when I arrived back here after my last evening out, and was reminded that when I took up my place, I had denied another, more deserving young woman the opportunity to study. Which is true, no getting away from it. So, I'm leaving—and quite frankly, I'm sick of sitting on the sidelines either listening to crusty old dons or knitting socks when I can do something far more useful. And who knows, I might even have an adventure!"

"What are you going to do?"

Maisie walked over to the chair and sat on the arm, next to Priscilla.

"Got to find yourself a new person to share rooms with, Maisie. I'm off to France."

Maisie drew breath sharply. Priscilla was the last person she thought would enlist for service. "Will you nurse?"

"Good Lord, no! Did you see my church hall bandages? If there's one thing I cannot do, it's walk around playing Florence Nightingale in a long frock—although I will have to get a First Aid Nursing Certificate. No, I have other arrows to my bow."·

Maisie laughed. The thought of the dilettante Priscilla having skills that could be used in France was worthy of mirth.

"You may laugh, Maisie. But you've never seen me drive. I'm off to be a Fannie!"

"A what?"

"Fannie. F-A-N-Y. First Aid Nursing Yeomanry. An all-women ambulance corps. Actually they are not in France yet—although from what I understand, it might not be long, as Mrs. McDougal—she's the head of FANY—is planning to ask the War Office to consider using women drivers for motor ambulances. Apparently you have to be twenty-three to go to France, so I am extending the truth a little— and don't ask me how, Maisie, please."

"When did you learn to drive?"

"Three brothers, Maisie." Priscilla leaned forward to take the cigarette stub from the holder, and to press in a fresh cigarette, which she took from an engraved silver case drawn from her pocket. "When you grow up with three brothers you forget your cuts, scrapes, and bruises, and concentrate on your bowling arm, on coming back in one piece from the hunting field, and on not being run over by the lugworms when they come to the table. And unless you show that you are as good at everything as they are, you find that you spend virtually all your time running behind them screaming like a banshee, 'Me too, me too!'"

Priscilla looked over her shoulder to the gardens beyond the window and bit her bottom lip. She turned and continued telling her story.

"The chauffeur taught us all to drive. At first it was only going to be the boys, but I threatened to tell all if I was not included. And now the fact is, my dear, I simply cannot have them in France without me. It's 'Me too, me too!'"

Priscilla wiped the hint of a tear from the inner corner of her left eye and smiled.

"So, what do you say to a party this evening? Despite my dismal record, I have permission to go out—probably because they will soon see the back of me, and also the hostess this evening is a benefactor. How about it, Maisie? You can go back to wherever it is you go to wash the ashes from your sackcloth tomorrow."

Maisie smiled and looked at Priscilla, sparkling in defiance of what was considered good behavior for young women at Girton. There was something about her friend that reminded her of Lady Rowan.

"Whose party?"

Priscilla blew another smoke ring.

"Given by family friends, the Lynches, for their son, Simon. Royal Army Medical Corps. Brilliant doctor. Always the one who remained at the bottom of the tree just in case anyone fell from the top branches, when we were children. He leaves for France in a day or two."

"Will they mind?"

"Maisie, I could turn up with a tribe and no one would turn a hair. The Lynch family are like that. Oh, do come. Simon will adore it. The more the merrier for his send-off."

Maisie smiled at Priscilla. Perhaps it *would* do her good. And Priscilla was leaving.

"What about permission?"

"Don't worry, I'll take care of that—and I promise, all above board. I'll telephone Margaret Lynch to make the necessary arrangements."

Maisie bit her lip for just a second longer.

"Yes. I'll come. Though I've nothing to wear, Pris."

"No excuse, Maisie darling, absolutely no excuse. Come with me!"

Priscilla took Maisie by the arm and led her to her own adjacent room. Pointing to the chair for Maisie to take a seat, she pulled at least a dozen gowns of various colors, fabrics, and styles from her wardrobe and threw them on the bed, determined to find the perfect dress for Maisie.

"I think this midnight blue is really you, Maisie. Here, let's just pull the belt—oh gosh, you are a skinny thing aren't you? Now let me just pin this here . . ."

"Pris, I look like two penn'orth of hambone trussed up for the butcher's window."

"There. That's just perfect," replied Priscilla, "Now step back, step back. Lovely. Very nice. You shall have that dress. Have your Mrs. Whatever-Her-Name-Is at Chelstone hem it properly for you."

"But, Priscilla—"

"Nonsense. It's yours. And make the most of it—I saw a bill posted yesterday that I memorized just to remind myself to have some fun while I can."

Priscilla stood to attention, mimicked a salute, and affected an authoritarian mode of speech: TO DRESS EXTRAVAGANTLY IN WARTIME IS WORSE THAN BAD FORM. IT IS UNPATRIOTIC!

She began to laugh as she continued adjusting the blue silk dress on Maisie's slender frame.

"I'll have no need of evening dresses in France, and besides, there will be new styles to choose from when I get back."

Maisie nodded and looked down at the dress. "There's another thing, Pris."

Priscilla took up her cigarette, placed her hand on her hip, and raised an eyebrow. "Now what's your excuse, Maisie?"

"Priscilla, I can't dance."

"Oh, good Lord, girl!"

Priscilla stubbed out the cigarette in the overflowing ashtray, walked over to her gramophone near the window, selected a record from the cabinet below, placed it on the turntable, wound it up using the small handle at the side of the machine, and set the arm across the record. As the needle caught the first spiral ridge in the thick black disc, Priscilla danced toward Maisie.

"Keep the dress on. You'll need to practice in what you'll be wearing tonight. Right. Now then, start by watching me."

Priscilla positioned her hands on imaginary shoulders in front of her, as if held in the arms of a young man, and as the music began she continued.

"Feet like so, and forward, side, together; back, side, together; watch me, Maisie. And forward, side, together . . ."

*A* car had been sent to collect Priscilla and Maisie, and as they climbed aboard for the journey to the Lynches' large house in Grantchester, Maisie felt butterflies in her stomach. It was the first time she had ever been to a party that had not been held in a kitchen. There were special Christmas and Easter dinners downstairs at the Belgravia house and at Chelstone, and of course she had been given a wonderful sendoff by the staff. But this was a real party.

Margaret Lynch came to greet Priscilla as soon as her arrival was announced. "Priscilla, darling. So good of you to come. Simon is dying for news of the boys. He can't wait to get over there, you know."

"I have much to tell, Margaret. But let me introduce my friend, Maisie Dobbs."

"How lovely to meet you, my dear. Any friend of Priscilla's is welcome here."

"Thank you, Mrs. Lynch." Maisie started to bob, only to feel a sharp kick from Priscilla.

"Now then, you girls, let's see if we can get a couple of these young gentlemen to escort you in to the dining room. Oh, there's Simon now. Simon!"

Simon. Captain Simon Lynch, RAMC. He had greeted Priscilla as one would greet a tomboy sister, asking for news of her brothers, his childhood friends. And as he turned to Maisie, she felt a shiver that began in her ankles and seemed to end in the pit of her stomach.

"A pleasure to meet you, Miss Dobbs. And will the British Army be at your mercy as you sit behind the wheel of a baker's lorry, converted and pressed into service as an ambulance?"

Priscilla gave Simon a playful thump on the arm as Maisie met his green eyes. She blushed and quickly looked at the ground. "No. I think I would be a terrible driver, Captain Lynch."

"Simon. Oh, do call me Simon. Now then, I think I'd like a Girton lass on each arm. After all, this is my last evening before I leave."

As a string quartet began to play, Simon Lynch crooked an elbow toward each girl and led them into the dining room.

Simon had completely drawn Maisie from her shell of shyness and embarrassment, and had made her laugh until her sides ached. And she had danced. Oh, how Maisie Dobbs had danced that evening, so that when it was time to leave, to return to Girton, Captain Simon Lynch made a gracious sweeping bow before her and kissed her hand.

"Miss Dobbs, you have put my feet to shame this evening. No wonder Priscilla kept you locked up at Girton."

"Don't take my name in vain, Lynchie—you brute! And it's a book of rules that keeps us all locked up, remember."

"Until we meet again, fair maiden."

Simon stepped back and turned toward Priscilla. "And I'll bet my boots that any wounded in your ambulance will go running back to the trenches rather than put up with your driving!"

Simon, Priscilla, and Maisie laughed together. The evening had sparkled.

# CHAPTER SIXTEEN

*T*he young women arrived back at the college in the nick of time before their extended curfew—arranged at the request of The Honorable Mrs. Margaret Lynch—expired. Just six hours later, standing on the station platform waiting for the early train that would take her to London for her connection to Chelstone, Maisie replayed, yet again, the events of the evening. In her excitement she had not slept a wink, and now that same excitement rendered her almost oblivious to the chilly air around her. Maisie held her coat closer to her body and up to her neck, feeling only the memory of sheer silk next to her skin.

As Maisie reflected upon the three of them laughing just before they left the party, she realized that it was laughter that held within it the sadness of a bigger departure. The gaiety of Simon's party had an undercurrent of fear. She had twice looked at Margaret Lynch, only to see the woman watching her son, hand to her mouth, as if any minute she would rush to him and encircle his body in her protective arms.

Her fear was not without cause, for the people of Britain were only just receiving news of the tens of thousands of casualties from the spring offensive of 1915. From a land of quiet farms in the French countryside, the Somme Valley was now a place writ large in newspaper headlines, inspiring angry and opinionated debate. The Somme was indelibly enscribed on the hearts of those who had lost a son, a father, brother, or friend. And for those bidding farewell, there was only fearful anticipation until the son, father, brother, or friend was home once again.

From Liverpool Street, Maisie traveled to Charing Cross for the journey to Kent. The station was a melee of khaki, ambulances, red crosses, and pain. Trains brought wounded to be taken to the London hospitals, nurses scurried back and forth, orderlies led walking wounded to waiting ambulances, and young, new spit-and-polished soldiers looked white-faced at those disembarking.

As she glanced at her ticket and began to walk toward her platform, Maisie was suddenly distracted by a splash of vibrant red hair in the distance. She knew only one person with hair so striking, and that was Enid. Maisie stopped and looked again.

Enid. It was definitely Enid. Enid with her hand on the arm of an officer of the Royal Flying Corps. And the officer in question was the young man who loved ginger biscuits: James Compton. Maisie watched as they stopped in the crowd and stood closer together, whispering. James would be on his way down to Kent, most probably on the same train as Maisie, except that she would not be traveling first class. From there Maisie knew that James would be joining his squadron. He was saying good-bye to Enid, who no longer worked for the Comptons. Mrs. Crawford had informed Maisie in a letter that Enid had left their employ. She was now working in a munitions factory, earning more money than she could ever have dreamed of earning in service.

Though she knew it was intrusive, Maisie felt compelled to stare as the two said good-bye. As she watched, she knew in her heart that Enid and James were truly in love, that this was not infatuation or social climbing on Enid's part. She lowered her head and walked away so that she would not be seen by either of them. Yet even as she walked, Maisie could not help turning to watch the couple once again, magnetized by two young people clearly speaking of love amid the teeming emotion around them. And while she looked, as if bidden by the strength of her gaze, Enid turned her head and met Maisie's eyes.

Enid held her head up defiantly, the vibrant red hair even brighter against her skin tone, which was slightly yellow, a result of exposure to cordite in the munitions factory. Maisie inclined her head and was acknowledged by Enid, who then turned back to James and pressed her lips to his.

Maisie was sitting at a cramped table in the station tea shop when Enid found her.

"You've missed the train to Chelstone, Mais."

"Hello, Enid. Yes, I know, I'll just wait until the next one."

Enid sat down in front of Maisie.

"So you know."

"Yes. But it doesn't make any difference."

"I should bloody 'ope not! I'm away from them all now, and what James does is 'is business."

"Yes. Yes, it is."

"And I'm earning real money now." Enid brushed her hair back from her shoulders. "So, how are you my very clever little friend? Cambridge University treating you well?"

"Enid, please. Let me be." Maisie lifted the cup to her lips. The strong tea was bitter, but its heat was soothing. The sweet joy of meeting Simon Lynch seemed half a world away as she looked once again at Enid.

Suddenly Enid's eyes smarted as if stung, and she began to weep. "I'm sorry. I'm sorry, Mais. I've been so rotten to you. To everyone. I'm just so worried. I lost him once. When 'e went to Canada. When they sent him away because of me. And now 'e's going to France. Up in one of them things—I've 'eard they only last three weeks over there before they cop it, them flyin' boys—and if God 'ad wanted us to leave the ground, I reckon we'd 'ave wings growin' out of our backs by now, don't you?"

"Now then, now then." Maisie moved around to sit next to Enid and put her arms around her. Enid pulled out a handkerchief, wiped her eyes, and blew her nose.

"Least I feel as if I'm doing something. Making shells, like. Least I'm not just sitting on my bum while them boys get shot to bits over there. Oh, James . . . ."

"Come on, Enid. He'll be all right. Remember what Mrs. Crawford says about James—he's got nine lives."

Enid sniffed again. "I'm sorry, Maisie. Really I am. But it just gets me 'ere sometimes." Enid punched at her middle. "They look down their noses at me, think I'm not good enough. And 'ere I am working like a trooper."

Maisie sat with Enid until she became calm, as the ache of farewell gave way to anger, tears, and eventually calm and fatigue.

"Maisie, I never meant anything. Really, I didn't. James will come back, I know he will. And this war is changing everything. 'ave you noticed that? When the likes of me can earn a good living even in wartime, the likes of the better-offs will have to change, won't they?"

"You could be right there, Enid."

"Gaw, lummy . . . look at that time. I've got to get back to the arsenal. I'm not even s'posed to leave the 'ostel without permission. I'm working in a special section now, handling the more volatile—that's what they call it—the more volatile explosives, and we earn more money, specially as we're 'avin' to do double shifts. All the girls get tired, so it gets a bit tricky, tapping the ends of the shells to check 'em, and all that. But I'm careful, like, so they promoted me. Must'a bin workin' for that Carter for all them years. I learned to be careful."

"Good for you, Enid."

The two women left the tea shop and walked together toward the bus stop just outside the station, where Enid would catch a bus to work. As they were bidding farewell, a man shouted behind them. "Make way, move along, make way, please."

A train carrying wounded soldiers had arrived, and the orderlies were hurriedly trying to bring stretchers through to the waiting ambulances. Maisie and Enid stood aside and looked on as the wounded passed by, still in mud-caked and bloody uniforms, often crying out as scurrying stretcher-bearers accidentally jarred shell-blasted arms and legs. Maisie gasped and leaned against Enid when she looked into the eyes of a man who had lost most of the dressings from his face.

After the wounded had passed Enid turned to Maisie to say good-bye. The young women embraced, and as they did so, Maisie felt a shiver of fear that made her tighten her hold on Enid.

"Come on, come on, let's not get maudlin, Mais." Enid loosened her grasp.

"You mind how you go, Enid," said Maisie.

"Like I always said, Maisie Dobbs, don't you worry about me."

"But I do."

"You want to worry about something, Maisie? Let me give you a bit of advice. You worry about what you can do for these boys." She pointed toward the ambulances waiting outside the station entrance. "You worry about whatever it is you can *do*. Must be off now. Give my love to Lady Bountiful for me!"

It seemed to Maisie that one second she was with Enid, and then she was alone. She walked toward the platform for the penultimate part of her journey home to her father's cottage next to the stables at Chelstone. With trains delayed and canceled due to troop movements, it would once again be many hours before she reached her destination.

The journey to Kent was long and arduous. Blackout blinds were pulled down, in compliance with government orders issued in antic-ipation of Zeppelin raids, and the train moved slowly in the darkness. Several times the train pulled into a siding to allow a troop train go by, and each time Maisie closed her eyes and remembered the injured men rushed into waiting ambulances at Charing Cross.

Time and again she fell into a deep yet brief slumber, and in her half waking saw Enid at work in the munitions factory, at the toil that caused her skin to turn yellow and her hair to spark when she brushed it back. Maisie remembered Enid's face in the distance, reflecting the love she felt as she looked at James Compton.

She wondered about love, and how it must feel, and thought back to last night, which seemed so many nights ago, and touched the place on her right hand where Simon Lynch had placed his lips in a farewell kiss.

As the train drew in to Chelstone station late at night, Maisie saw Frankie standing by his horse and cart. Persephone stood proudly, her coat's gloss equaled only by the shine of the leather traces that Maisie could see even in the half-light. Maisie ran to Frankie and was swept up into his arms.

"My Maisie, home from the university. My word, you're a sight for your dad."

"It's grand to be back with you, Dad."

"Come on, let me have that case and let's get going."

As they drove back to the house in darkness, dim lanterns set at the front of the cart swinging to and fro with each of Persephone's heavy footfalls, Maisie told Frankie her news and answered his many questions. Of course she mentioned the meeting with Enid, although Maisie left out all mention of James Compton.

"The arsenal, eh? Blimey, let's 'ope she wasn't there this afternoon."

"What do you mean, Dad?"

"Well, you know 'is Lordship is with the War Office and all that. Well, 'e gets news before even the papers, you know, special messenger, like. He's very well—"

"Dad, what's happened?"

"'is Lordship received a telegram late this afternoon. The special part of the factory went up this afternoon, the place where they 'andle the 'eavy explosives. Just as the new shift came on. Twenty-two of them munitions girls killed outright."

Maisie knew that Enid was dead. She did not need the confirmation that came the next morning, as Lord Compton told Carter that Enid had been among the young women killed and that he should take care of informing the staff in a manner that he saw fit. Not for the first time, Maisie considered how so much in life could change in such a short time. Priscilla enlisting for service, the wonderful evening, meeting Simon Lynch—and Enid. But of the events that had passed in just three days, the picture that remained with Maisie Dobbs was of Enid, swishing back her long red hair and looking straight at Maisie with a challenge. A haunting challenge.

"You worry what you can do for these boys, Maisie. You worry about whatever it is you can *do*."

# CHAPTER SEVENTEEN

aisie caught sight of the London Hospital in the distance and did not take her eyes off its austere eighteenth-century buildings until the bus had shuddered to a halt, allowing her to clamber down the steps from the upper deck to the street below. She looked up at the buildings, then at the visitors filing in, people leaving, many in tears, and the ambulances drawing alongside to allow their wounded and bloody cargo to be taken to the safety of the wards.

Maisie closed her eyes and took a deep breath, as if about to jump from a precipice into the unknown.

"'scuse me, Miss, comin' through. You'll get run over if you stand there, young lady."

Maisie opened her eyes and moved quickly to allow a hospital porter through carrying two large boxes.

"Can I 'elp you, Miss? Look a bit lost to me."

"Yes. Where do I enlist for nursing service?"

"You bloomin' angel, you. You'll be just the medicine some of these poor lads need, and that's a fact!"

Positioning his left foot awkwardly against the inside of his opposite shin, the porter held the boxes steady on his knee with one hand, pushed back his flat cap, and used his free hand to direct Maisie.

"You go through that door there, turn left down the long green-tiled corridor, turn right at the end to the stairs. Up the stairs, to the right, and you'll see the enlisting office. And don't mind them in there, love—they pay them extra to wear a face as long as a week, as if a smile would crack 'em open!"

Maisie thanked the man, who doffed his cap quickly before grabbing the boxes, which were about to fall to the ground, and then went on his way.

The long corridor was busy with people lost in the huge building, and others pointing fingers and waving arms to show them the way to reach a certain ward. Taking her identification papers and letters of recommendation out of her bag, Maisie walked quickly up the disinfectant-cleaned tile staircase and across the landing to the enlisting office for nurses. The woman who took Maisie's papers glanced at her over her wire-rimmed spectacles.

"Age?"

"Twenty-two."

She looked up at Maisie again, and peered over the top of her spectacles.

"Young-looking twenty-two, aren't you?"

"Yes, that's what they said when I went to university."

"Well, if you're old enough for university, you're old enough for this. And doing more good while you're about it."

The woman leafed through the papers again, looking quickly at the letter with the Compton crest that attested to Maisie's competence and age. There would be no questions regarding the authenticity of documents that bore not only an impressive livery but the name of a well-known figure at the War Office, a man quoted in newspapers from the *Daily Sketch* to *The Times*, commenting on dispatches from France.

Maisie had taken the sheets of fine linen paper from the bureau in the library at Chelstone, and written what was needed. Emboldened by Enid's challenge, she had felt only the shallowest wave of guilt. She was going to do her part for the boys, for those who had given of themselves on the fields of France.

"You've done *what?* Are you mad, Maisie? What about your university learning? After all that work, all that . . . ."

Frankie turned his back on Maisie and shook his head. He was silent, staring out of the scullery window of the groom's cottage, out toward the paddocks where three very healthy horses were grazing. Maisie knew better than to interrupt until he had finished.

"After all that fuss and bother . . . ."

"It's only a postponement, Dad. I can go back. I will go back. As soon as the war is over."

Frankie swung around, tears of fear and frustration welling in his eyes.

"That's all very well, but what if you get sent over there? To France. Blimey, if you wanted to do something useful, my girl, I'm sure 'is Lordship could've got a job for a bright one like you. I've a mind to go up to that hospital and shop you for your tales—you must've said you were older than you are. I tell you, I never thought I'd see the day when my daughter told a lie."

"Dad, please understand—"

"Oh, I understand all right. Just like your mother, and I've lost her. I can't lose you, Maisie."

Maisie walked over to her father and put her hand on his shoulder. "You won't lose me Dad. You watch. You'll be proud of me."

Frankie Dobbs dropped his head and leaned into his daughter's embrace. "I've always been proud of you, Maisie. That's not the point."

As a member of the Voluntary Aid Detachment, Maisie's duties seemed to consist of daily round of mopping floors, lining up beds so that not one was out of place, and being at the beck and call of the senior nurses. She had obtained a deferment from Girton, and no sooner had the letter been posted, along with another to Priscilla, than Maisie put her dream behind her and with the same resolve that had taken her to university, she vowed to bring comfort to the men coming home from France.

Maisie became a VAD nurse at the London Hospital in May, amid the never-ending influx of casualties from the spring offensive of 1915. It was a hot summer, and one in which Maisie saw little rest and spent only a few hours at her lodgings in Whitechapel.

Sweeping a stray tendril of hair under her white cap, Maisie immersed her hands into a sinkful of scalding hot water, and scrubbed at an assortment of glass bottles, bowls, and measuring jugs with a bristle brush. It was not the first time in her life that her hands were raw or her legs and back ached. But it could be worse, she thought, as she drained the suds and began to rinse the glassware. For a moment she allowed her hands to remain in the water as it began to cool, and looked straight ahead through the window to the dusk-dusted rooftops beyond.

"Dobbs, I don't think you've got all day to rinse a few bottles, not when there are a dozen other jobs for you to do before you go off duty."

Maisie jumped as her name was spoken, quickly rushing to apologize for her tardiness.

"Don't waste time, Dobbs. Finish this job quickly. Sister wants to see you now."

The nurse who spoke to her was one of the regulars, not a volunteer, and Maisie immediately reverted to the bobbed curtsy of her days in service. The seniority of the regular nurses demanded respect, immediate attention, and complete deference.

Maisie finished her task, made sure that not a bottle or cloth was out of place, then went quickly to see Sister, checking her hair, cap, and apron as she trotted along the green-and-cream-tiled corridor.

"Nurses never run, Dobbs. They walk briskly."

Maisie stopped, bit her bottom lip, and turned around, hands by her sides and balled into fists. Sister, the most senior nurse on the ward. And the most feared, even by the men who joked that she should be sent out to France—that would send the Hun running.

"I'm sorry, Sister."

"My office, Dobbs."

"Yes, Sister."

Sister led the way into her office, with its green-tiled walls, dark wood floor, and equally dark wooden furniture, and walked around to the opposite side of her desk, sweeping her long blue dress and bright white apron aside to avoid their catching on the corner. A silver buckle shone at the front of her apron, and her scarflike cap was starched. Not a hair was out of place.

"I'll get quickly to the point. As you know we are losing many of our staff to join detachments in France. We therefore need to move our nurses and volunteers up through the ranks—and of course we need to keep many of our regular nurses here to keep up standards and direct care of the wounded. Your promotion today to Special Military Probationer means more responsibility in the ward, Dobbs. Along with Rigson, Dornhill, and White, you must be prepared to serve in military hospitals overseas if needed. That will be in one year, at the end of your training. Let me see . . ."

The austere woman shuffled papers in a file on the desk in front of her.

"Yes, you'll be twenty-three at the end of the year, according to your records. Eligible for duty abroad. Good."

Sister looked up at Maisie again, then checked the time on the small watch pinned to her apron. "I have already spoken to the other VADs in question during their duty earlier today. Now then, from tomorrow you will join doctors' rounds each day to observe and assist, in addition to your other duties. Is that understood?"

"Yes, Sister."

"Then you are dismissed, Dobbs."

Maisie left the office and walked slowly toward the kitchen.

Yes, sooner than she had thought, she would be in France. Possibly this time next year. How she longed to see Maurice, how she ached to speak with him. For here was time again, the trickster, changing the circumstances of her life in an instant. Yet she knew that Maurice would ask her if she was not herself the trickster. She had lied about her age unashamedly to do this work, and now she was burdened by doubt. Could she do what was required of her? Could she live up to Enid's memory?

# CHAPTER EIGHTEEN

aisie pulled herself away from the side rail of the
ship. She had never dreamed that seasickness
could be this bad. A salty wind blew around her
head and nipped at her ears as she struggled to keep the heavy woolen
cape drawn across her aching body. Nothing in the world could top
this. Nothing could be this unbearable.

"Here, miss, old merchant navy trick for the indisposition . . ."

She looked sideways from the place she had claimed, holding on to
a handrail that led to a cabin door, then rushed to the side of the boat
again. She felt a strong hand between her shoulder blades and pushed
against the guard rail bring herself to a standing position. A member
of the crew, sensibly wearing foul-weather clothing, with his cap
miraculously still on his head, held out a tin mug of hot cocoa and a
lump of Madeira cake. Maisie put her hand to her mouth in terror.

"What you do is, when you think you're going to lose your insides
again, you take a bite o' this and a quick swig of cocoa. And you do
it every time you feel queasy. Then it'll go away; you'll see."

Maisie looked at the man, shook her head, and leaned over the side rail. Exhausted to the core, she stood up again and held out her hands for the cake and cocoa. It had to be worth a go.

Iris Rigson, Dottie Dornhill, Bess White, and Maisie Dobbs had set sail with a small contingent of nurses on July 20, 1916, bound for service in France. Iris, Dottie, and Bess had not suffered unduly on the requisitioned freighter, now in the service of king and country, ferrying supplies—and in this case nurses, too—between England and France. But Maisie Dobbs, granddaughter of a lighterman on the Thames, was embarrassingly seasick. Whatever the battlefield had to offer, it could not possibly make her feel worse than this, though she had in her pocket a letter from Priscilla, who had been sent to France in January with the first FANY convoy. The censors might be able to take out words, but they could not delete the emotion poured from inkwell to paper. Priscilla was exhausted, if not in body then in mind. Her words seemed to bite through the edges of Maisie's thoughts and expectations. For just a moment, as she fingered the letter in her pocket, she felt as if she were a ghostly presence watching over Priscilla as she worked. Priscilla had written:

> My back is killing me, Maisie. Florrie the Lorry did not want to go to work this morning, so I did double duty with the starting handle. I had only two hours rest last night, after a twenty-hour shift. Maisie, I can only barely remember the last time I slept for more than just a few hours. My clothes are becoming one with my body, and I dread to imagine how I must reek! Mind you, one simply cannot go on about one's aching back and stinging eyes when faced with the good humor of these boys, even as they are suffering the pain of torn limbs and the terror of seeing comrades die. Despite rain that seems to come down in buckets here, there are some days that suddenly get very hot and humid indeed, especially if you are lugging around the added weight of a heavy uniform glued to your body. Many of the boys have taken a knife to

their woolen trousers to get some relief from the chafing of army issue cloth. I suppose it's less for the doctors to cut away, but loaded on to Florrie they look like schoolboys who've taken a wrong turning into hell. I had a boy die on me yesterday. Maisie, his eyes were as deep a blue as that dress you wore to Simon's party, and he could not have been more than seventeen. Poor lad hadn't even begun to shave, just a bit of fluff on his chin. I wanted to just sit there and weep. But you know, you just have to go on. If I stood around in mourning for them, another poor boy would die for want of an ambulance. I don't know what the papers are saying, but here's

Priscilla's letter was abruptly halted by heavy black ink of the censor's pen.

"Here she is. Maisie o' the high seas!" Iris announced as Maisie returned to the cabin.

"Blimey, Maisie, how're you now, then?" Dottie came over to Maisie and put an arm around her shoulder. "Come and sit down. We'll soon be there. Le Havre can't be much longer—can it?" She looked at the other nurses, their heavy capes drawn around them, and settled Maisie into a seat. "You poor little mite, Dobbs. There's nothing of you to start with. Never you mind, we'll soon be in Le Havre. Get us a nice cuppa. That's if the French can make tea."

Iris felt Maisie's forehead and looked at her watch. "You do seem a bit better, though."

Maisie looked at the other girls and leaned against Iris. "Cocoa and cake," she muttered, and promptly fell into a deep sleep.

From Le Havre the train journey to Rouen passed uneventfully. The young women were tired from the journey but managed to keep awake long enough to watch their first few minutes of foreign soil speed past. Arriving at the port of Rouen, the nurses were met by a medical officer, and taken to the Hotel St. Georges, where they expected to stay for two nights while they waited for orders.

"Let's get ourselves a nice wash and have a cup of tea downstairs," suggested Iris as they settled into the room all four women were to share.

Iris was a tall, big-boned girl, whose uniform always looked rather too small for her. She considered this a blessing. The unfashionably long and impractical woolen dress of the uniform was shorter on her than on the other nurses. Not only could she move with greater ease, but soon she would avoid having her hemline drag in the never-ending mud, the bane of a nurse's life in France.

"How are you feeling, Dobbs?" asked the soft-spoken Bess, maintaining the discipline of hospital address.

"Much better, thank you. And a cup of tea would be just lovely."

The women each unpacked their few belongings, washed faces and hands at the large white enameled stone sink, and brushed hair back into place. As usual Maisie struggled to fasten the stray tendrils of jet black hair that crept out from under her hat. When they left the room, the women looked almost as fresh as they had in the early hours of the morning, when they had joined their train at Charing Cross for the journey to Folkestone, their port of departure for France.

"*L*ook at those cakes. My word, never seen a pastry like that before; it's a wonder they can do that in wartime," said Dottie.

"No, and you've never tasted a cup of tea like this before either."

Iris winced at the weak tea and reached out to take one of the delicate pastries from the china plate placed in the center of the table.

Maisie was quiet, looking around her at the rather aged grandeur of the dining room at the Hotel St. Georges. Large mirrors were positioned on each wall, and ornate archways led into the lounge on one side and the marble-floored lobby on the other. Waiters ran back and forth, elegant in black trousers that shone with too much pressing, white shirts, black ties, and long white aprons. They were all older men, for the younger men had gone to war.

The clientele was mainly military personnel, and the hotel was packed with officers going on leave or passing through on their way back to join their regiments. Some were with sweethearts or wives, still others with parents, the fortunate ones whose people could make a journey across the Channel to bid them farewell in France.

Maisie sipped her tea, feeling the warmth, if not the flavor, reach the core of her tired body. She was aware of the conversation at their table, a familiar to-ing and fro-ing of observations and opinions, a giggle here, a raised voice there. But for the most part, as the journey to France ebbed away behind her, Maisie was lost in her own thoughts.

"Excuse me, it's Miss Dobbs, isn't it?"

Maisie was jolted from her daydream back into the dining room. She jumped up and turned to face the person who had spoken to her.

"Oh my goodness!" said Maisie, spilling tea onto the white cloth.

Captain Simon Lynch quickly took her elbow to steady Maisie, and greeted her with a broad smile, which he then extended to her table companions, who had immediately stopped all conversation, indeed all movement, to look at the man who had come to the table to see Maisie.

"Captain Lynch. Well, what a surprise this is!"

Maisie regained her composure and took Simon's offered hand. A waiter quickly and efficiently replaced the tablecloth and offered to bring a chair for Simon, who declined, commenting to her companions that he had just been leaving when he had seen his friend, Miss Dobbs.

Simon turned again to Maisie, and as he did so she noticed that he seemed older. Not just in years, for it was just over a year since they had first met. No, he was older in his soul. His eyes were ringed with gray skin, lines had formed on his fresh young man's face, and already gray hair was showing at his temples. Yet he could be no more than twenty-six.

"Just here for two days' leave. Not enough time for Blighty, I'm afraid. I'd heard from Pris that you'd joined up."

"How is she? Have you seen her?"

"Our paths crossed only once. She brought wounded men to my hospital, but, well, we didn't have time to stand and chat." Simon looked at his hands, then back at Maisie. "So, do you know where you are going yet?"

"No, we get our orders tomorrow morning, perhaps even this evening. Seems a bit chaotic, really."

Simon laughed.

"Chaotic? You haven't seen chaotic until you've been out there."

"I'm sorry." Maisie rubbed her hands together. "What I meant was—"

"No, *I'm* sorry. That was horrible of me. And, yes, it *is* chaotic. The right arm of the British army hardly seems to know what the left arm's doing. Look, I have to dash off now, but, I wonder, is there any chance that you could have dinner with me tomorrow evening? Or do you have to be chaperoned?"

Simon grinned and looked into Maisie's eyes.

"Well, um, well . . ."

Maisie looked sideways at her companions, who were continuing with their tea quietly in order to listen to the conversation. She caught Iris's eye and saw the other woman smile, nod her head and mouth the word "Go." Maisie turned back to Simon.

"Yes, Captain Lynch. Dinner would be lovely. And, yes, actually I do have to be chaperoned, so my friends will be dining nearby."

"Right you are. Let's make it an early one then, I'll meet you in the lobby at six o'clock. In fact, I'll meet you all in the lobby at six o'clock!"

Simon bowed, bade good-bye to the nurses, smiled at Maisie, and moved to go.

"Oh, and by the way—that uniform—it's almost as stunning as the blue silk dress."

And then he was gone.

Maisie took her place once again, amid the giggles of Iris, Dottie, and Bess.

"And what silk dress might that be, Dobbs?"

"You kept that one quiet, didn't you?"

"Sure you want a chaperone?"

Maisie blushed at the teasing, which she knew would continue for some time. She was about to explain that Simon was only a friend of a friend when an RAMC officer approached their table.

"Dobbs, White, Dornhill, and Rigson? Good. Orders are here, and travel warrants. Sorry. You won't be going to the same place. White and Dornhill together at the base hospital. Dobbs and Rigson, you're going to the Fourteenth Casualty Clearing Station— enjoy it here while you can."

And with that he was gone, clutching several large manila envelopes under his arm while negotiating his way through the busy dining room, in search of other nurses on his list.

The four women sat in silence for a few minutes, looking at the brown manila envelopes.

"Well, he's a bundle of joy, isn't he?" said Iris, taking a knife from the table and slicing open the envelope.

"Dobbsie, my girl, we are indeed off to the Fourteenth Casualty Clearing Station, near Bailleul, like Cheerful Charlie over there said. A CCS, that's as near to the battlefield as nurses are allowed, isn't it?"

"And we're at the base hospital here in Rouen, so we won't be going far, will we, Bess?"

"Well, there we are, then. Let's make the most of it, that's what I say. And let's get some sleep."

Iris dabbed at her mouth with her table napkin, and a waiter scurried over to pull out her chair.

"Yes, good idea. At least one of us needs her sleep if she's to be walking out with an officer!"

"Oh, Dottie, he's just—"

Maisie rushed to defend herself as the women left the table, but her protestations were lost amid the teasing and banter.

✦

*R*emembering the events of her dinner with Simon Lynch took Maisie's mind off the journey. First by train, then by field ambulance along mud-filled and rutted roads, Maisie and Iris traveled to the casualty clearing station where they would be based until due for leave in four months' time.

As the train moved slowly along, though it was still light, Maisie had a sense of darkness descending. Gunmetal gray clouds loomed overhead, splashes of rain streaked across the windows, and when the train stopped at a station, the sound of heavy artillery in the distance seemed to echo and reverberate along the tracks. Even the birds had been silenced by the mighty orchestra of battle. With the sights and sounds of war around them, people in the landscape loomed with a stark intensity.

Maisie watched from the train window as lines of people trudged along, and more lines of battered humanity appeared to be strung out into the distance. Whole families were leaving communities close to the battlefields, seeking a place of safety with relatives in other towns and villages. Yet the river of civilian evacuation was a stream compared to the long column of marching soldiers, battle weary in weathered uniforms. Young men with faces prematurely aged, showing fatigue and fear as well as a determined levity.

> What's the use of worrying?
> It never was worthwhile, so
> Pack all your troubles in your old kit-bag,
> And smile, smile, smile.

The marching songs rang out, and as their train passed by, Iris and

Maisie leaned out of the slow-moving carriages, waved to the soldiers, and joined in their songs.

It's a long way to Tipperary, it's a long way to go;
It's a long way to Tipperary, to the sweetest girl I know;
Good-bye Piccadilly, farewell Leicester Square,
It's a long, long way to Tipperary, but my heart's right there.

With a final wave, Iris and Maisie pulled up the window, and tried to make themselves comfortable again on the prickly wool train seating.

"Funny that your young man's not that many miles from us, isn't it, Dobbs?" Iris looked inquiringly at Maisie when they were settled.

"Oh, for goodness sake, he's not my young man. He's just an old friend of a very good friend of mine. It really is a coincidence that I saw him at all."

"That's as may be, Dobbsie, but I saw the way you two were looking at each other, and I'd say that you were a-courting. Right pair of turtle doves, if you ask me."

"Nonsense. And don't you go repeating this silliness either, Iris. Please. I hardly know him—and I could get into trouble!"

"Blue silk dress eh?"

Iris continued to tease Maisie.

Iris, Dottie, and Bess had taken a table next to Maisie and Simon at dinner, lest it be thought that she was dining completely without a chaperone. But surprising even herself, Maisie hardly noticed other people in the hotel dining room. From the time he had greeted her in the lobby, at six o'clock as arranged, and held out his arm to her, Maisie and Simon Lynch had eyes only for each other.

Now Maisie lowered her eyelids and feigned sleep, which effectively silenced Iris. Left in peace, she was able to envision the dining room again, the waiters running to and fro, and the busyness of people enjoying last farewells or a few days respite from the business of war. And there, at the table with her, was Simon.

Simon who made her laugh with his jokes, putting her at ease.

Simon who asked her why she had become a nurse, and when she told the story of Enid, leaned across and took her hand. "She must have meant a lot to you, your friend."

"Yes, yes, she did . . . she made me think about all sorts of things. While I was busy with my head in a book, she would bring me down to earth with a thud. Yes . . . she made me reconsider my opinions on more than one occasion."

Simon did not release Maisie's hand, and for a moment their eyes met again and they were silent. Abashed, Maisie pulled her hand away and took up her fork. She poked at her food.

"I hope I didn't embarrass you. I, I didn't think—"

"Oh no. That's all right." Maisie blushed.

"It's a strange thing, war. Maisie, you must prepare yourself for what you are going to see. This past year . . . the Somme . . . I cannot tell you what injuries the men suffer. As a doctor I was trained to deal with one surgical case at a time: I operated on a leg, or a chest, or an arm. But these men are brought in with multiple gaping wounds, I—"

Simon stopped speaking and reached for his glass of claret, which he gripped but did not pick up. He stared into the wine, at the deep red liquid, and then closed his eyes. As he did so, Maisie saw again the lines that crept from the edges of his eyelids to his temples, the creases on his forehead, and the dark circles above his cheekbones.

"I came here thinking I could save every one of them, but half the time—" Simon hesitated, swallowed deeply, and looked directly at Maisie.

"It's so very good to see you, Maisie. It reminds me of how it was before I left England. How I felt about being a doctor. And how very much I hoped that I would see you again."

Maisie blushed again but smiled at Simon.

"Yes, Simon. I am glad too."

Without thinking she reached for his hand, which he took and gripped tightly. Suddenly aware of the proximity of other diners, Maisie released her hold, and they took up their knives and forks.

"Now then, tell me all about Lady Rowan. I've heard of her, of course. She has quite a reputation as a staunch supporter of the suffragettes. And I've heard that Lord Julian is an absolute saint— although I doubt he has much time to worry about what she's up to, now that he's at the War Office."

Conversation slipped into the exchanging of stories, of opinions and observations, and by the time dinner was over, Maisie noticed that they had spoken of their dreams, of what they would do "when the war's over."

In that moment she remembered Maurice, walking with her in the orchard one day while at Chelstone, as she broke the news that she had requested a deferment of her place at Cambridge, that she had enlisted at the London Hospital.

She remembered him looking into the distance and speaking, very quietly, almost to himself. "Such is the legacy of war . . . the discarded dreams of children . . . the waste. The tragedy."

Simon looked at his watch. "Well, sadly, Maisie, I must go. I have meetings while I'm here, I'm afraid. So much for leave, eh?"

"Yes, I have to go, too. We set off early tomorrow morning."

As Maisie placed her white linen table napkin alongside her plate, Simon watched her intently. "Would you mind very much if I wrote to you? It may take a while, but letters can be sent up the line. I'll work out something."

"Yes, that would be lovely. Please write."

Simon rose to pull out Maisie's chair, and as he did so Maisie noticed her three friends at an adjoining table, all holding coffee cups to their lips and looking at her over the rims of the cups. She had forgotten they were there.

In the lobby Simon once again made a sweeping bow. "You may be clad in that wonderfully practical nursing attire, Miss Dobbs, but in my eyes you will forever be wearing a stunning blue silk dress."

Maisie shook hands with Simon, and bade him good-bye before joining the three nurses standing directly behind her, and doubtless waiting to begin teasing her once again.

❖

*M*aisie and Iris saw the tents in the distance, a musty afternoon cordite-laden fog lingered overhead, and a heavy ground mist was moving up and around them.

"I'm freezing just looking at that lot, and it's nowhere near winter yet," said Iris.

"I know what you mean. Looks bleak, doesn't it?"

Maisie pulled her cape around her body, though the day was not that cold.

The main tents had giant red crosses painted on top, and beyond were bell tents that were home to the nursing contingent of the casualty clearing station. The ambulance moved slowly along the rutted road, and as they came closer to the encampment, it was clear that they were in the midst of receiving wounded.

The ambulance pulled alongside the officers' tent, where records were kept and orders given. All around them people moved quickly, some shouting, others carrying fresh supplies. Iris and Maisie stepped down and had barely taken up their bags when a sister rushed up to them.

"No time to dawdle. We need you now—time for the paperwork and receiving line later! Get your capes off, your aprons on, and report immediately to the main tent. It's the deep end for you two."

Two hours later, as Maisie stood over a young man, cutting heavy uniform cloth away from an arm partially severed by shellfire, Maisie remembered Simon's words: "You must prepare yourself for what you are going to see."

Quickly pushing the still-fresh words to the back of her mind, and brushing the sweat from her forehead with the back of her bloodied hand, Maisie felt as if she were in the eye of the storm. The young soldier lying in front of her was conscious, watching her face all the time, searching for the glimmer of expression that would give away her assessment of his wounds. But the sisters of the London Hospital had taught their nurses well: Never, never ever change your expression at the sight of a wound—they'll be looking into your eyes to see their future. Look straight back at them.

As Maisie worked quickly, taking up disinfectant and swabs, a surgeon accompanied by nurses and medical orderlies moved from one soldier to the next, cutting away skin, bone and muscle, pulling shrapnel from the bodies of boys who had taken on the toil of men.

The soldier continued to stare into Maisie's eyes as she prepared his wounds for the surgeon's knife. Following the trail of blood and flesh, Maisie cut away more uniform, taking her scissors to his trousers, pulling at the bindings around his lower leg. And as she felt her hand sink into the terrible injuries to his thigh, the soldier cleared his throat to speak.

"Rugby player's legs, those."

"I thought so," said Maisie as she continued to work on his leg, "You can always tell the rugby players."

"Nurse, nurse," the soldier reached out toward her with his uninjured hand, "Nurse, could you hold my hand?"

And as Maisie took his hand in hers, the young man smiled.

"Thank you, nurse."

Suddenly Maisie was aware that someone was bending back the soldier's fingers and moving his arm to his side, and she looked up at the nursing sister in charge. An army chaplain placed his hand on her shoulder for barely a second before lifting it to perform last rites over the young soldier's not-yet-cold body, while two stretcher-bearers waited to remove him to allow room for more wounded.

"Oh, I'm sorry—"

"No time for sorry," said the sister. "He's been gone less than a minute anyway. You did all you could. Now then, there's work to do here. No time to stop and think about it. Just got to get on with it. There's plenty more waiting outside that need your helping hand."

Brushing back a stray hair with the back of her hand once again, Maisie prepared the table as best she could for the next soldier.

"'Allo, Nurse. Going to make me all better, are you?" said the man as the stretcher bearers quickly but carefully placed him on the table.

Maisie looked straight into the man's eyes and saw intense pain masked by the attempt at humor. Taking up scissors and swabs, along with the pungent garlic juice used to disinfect wounds, she breathed deeply and smiled.

"Yes. I'm going to make you all better, young man. Now then, hold still."

# CHAPTER NINETEEN

$M$aisie awoke in the tent she shared with Iris. Snuggling under her blankets, she looked over at her friend and, in the half sleep of early morning, thought for a moment that it was Enid, but realized that it was the bump of Iris's behind forming a mound in the bed as she, too, curled herself against the early morning chill.

She took a deep breath. The chill air notwithstanding, Maisie suddenly sat up, pulling the blanket around her shoulders as she did so. She must do everything in her power to keep a calm head, to brace herself for the day, and to prepare herself for the elements. Rain had started to fall again. Rain that soaked into the ground to form a stew of mud and filthy water that seeped up into the cloth of her long woolen dress, making it hang heavily against her ankles as she worked again and again to clean and bandage wounds. By the end of each day the mud had worked its way up to her knees, and time and time again she told herself that she was warm, really, that her feet felt dry, really. Then at night, she and Iris would hang up their dresses to allow the moisture to evaporate, and check each other's bodies for the battlefield lice that seemed to know no defeat.

"You first, Maisie," said Iris, still clutching the bedcovers around her body.

"You just don't want to be the one to crack the ice."

"What ice?"

"I told you, Iris, there was a layer of ice on the top of that water yesterday."

"No!"

Iris turned over in her cot to look at Maisie, who sat cross-legged on her bed.

"I don't know how you can sit like that, Dobbs. Now then, are you telling me there was ice on the water? It's not even proper winter yet."

"Yes. Even though it's not proper winter."

Maisie took another deep breath, which, when exhaled, turned to steamy fog in front of her face. She cast the blanket aside and nimbly ran over to the water pitcher and bowl that stood on top of a wooden chest.

"And the sitting in the morning—it's what helps to keep me from freezing solid all day, Iris. It clears my head. You should try it!"

"Hmmmph!"

Iris turned over in bed and tried to ignore her cold feet.

Maisie poked her finger into the water pitcher. She cracked the thin layer of ice as if tentatively testing a piecrust, then gripped the handle of the pitcher with both hands and poured freezing cold water into the bowl. Reaching over to the side of the chest, Maisie unhooked a flannel cloth, which she steeped in the water. After wringing it out, Maisie unbuttoned the front of her nightgown and washed first her face, then under her arms and up to her neck. Oh, what she would give for a bath! To sit in a deep bathtub filled with piping hot water and soap bubbles coming up to her ears.

Again she plunged the cloth into the cold water, squeezed the excess water back into the bowl, and this time lifted her nightgown and washed between her legs and down to her knees. A nice hot bath. For hours. She wouldn't come out for hours. She'd keep twiddling that hot tap with her big toe, and she wouldn't come out until every last molecule of mud, blood, sweat, and tears had been washed away.

Taking down her still-damp dress, which had been hanging from a wire she and Iris had rigged up inside the tent, Maisie checked every seam and in the hem for lice. It was the morning drill: Check for lice everywhere, and when you've finished checking, check some more, because lice are crafty little beggars. She dressed quickly, finally slipping a white armband with a red cross just above the elbow of her right sleeve, and taking out a fresh apron and attaching a silver watch pin to the left side of the bib. Along with the black leather document case, which now held her writing paper and letters received, the nurse's watch was her talisman from home, a gift from Lady Rowan.

Finally Maisie placed a towel on her cot and leaned over it to brush her hair, looking carefully for lice falling out. She and Iris checked each other's hair every night or, if they were on duty at night, whenever they were both in the tent and awake at the same time. But Maisie always checked again in the morning, brushing her hair over a towel until her head spun. Then she quickly pinned her hair up into a bun, and placed her cap on her head.

"I'm all finished, Iris."

"Right you are, Dobbsie." Iris shivered under her bedclothes. "Lord knows what this will be like in the real winter."

"At least we're not up to our waists in mud in the trenches, Iris. Least we're not piling up bodies to make a wall to protect us. Not like the boys."

"You're right there, as always," said Iris as she leaped from bed and began the morning ritual that Maisie had just finished. "Brrrr . . . I 'spect you're going over to see if there's a letter from your young man."

Maisie rolled her eyes. "I've told you, Iris. He's not—"

"Yes, I know, I know. He's not your young man. Well then, go and get your letter from your special friend of a friend then, and leave me to my delousing, if you don't mind!"

The young women laughed, as Maisie pulled back the tent flap, leaving Iris to her morning ablutions. Picking her way across wooden boards covering mud and puddles, Maisie made her way to the cooks' tent to get tea and bread for breakfast.

"There you are, Sister, get this down you." The orderly on duty held out a large enamel mug along with a slice of bread and dripping for Maisie, addressing her as "sister" in the way that soldiers called all nurses, regardless of rank, "sister."

"And a little something else for you, passed on to me this morning." He reached into his pocket and brought out a simple brown envelope that clearly contained a long letter, such was the thickness of the packet. The envelope was crumpled and bore stains of the four sets of dirty hands it had passed through before reaching its destination.

The letters from Simon Lynch to Maisie Dobbs would never travel through the censor's office, passed as they were from orderly to ambulance driver to stretcher bearer to cook. Her letters in return were passed in the same way, from person to person. And each time a letter changed hands, there would be a comment exchanged, a remark about young love, or that it was all very well for him, Captain Romantic over there.

The writers said nothing of love when the first letter, from Simon to Maisie, was sent and received. But in the way that two people who are of one mind on any subject move closer, as if their heads were drawn together by thoughts that ran parallel toward a future destination, so the letters of Simon and Maisie became more frequent, one hardly waiting for the other to reply before setting pen to paper again. Bearing up under exhaustion that weighed on their backs and pushed like a fist between their shoulder blades, Simon and Maisie, each in a tent several miles apart, and each by the strained light of an oil lamp, would write quickly and urgently of days amid the detritus of war. And though both knew that war, and the ever-present breath of despair might have added urgency to their need to be together again, they began unashamedly to declare their feelings in the letters that were passed from hand to hand. Feelings that, with each shared experience and story, grew deeper. Then Simon wrote:

My Dearest Maisie of the Blue Silk Dress,

I have been on duty for 30 hours without so much as sitting down for five minutes. Wounded started coming in again at eleven yesterday morning. I have bent over so many bodies, so many wounds that I fear I have lost count. I seem to remember only the eyes, and I remember the eyes because in them I see the same shock, the same disbelief, and the same resignation. Today I saw, in quick succession, a man and his son. They had joined up together, I suspect one or both lying about their age. And they had the same eyes. The very same. Perhaps what I see in each man is that no matter what their age (and by golly, some of them shouldn't be out of school), they seem so very old.

I am due for a short leave in three weeks. I will receive orders soon. I plan to go back to Rouen for two days. I remember you said that you would be due for leave soon, too. Would it be too presumptuous for me to ask if we might possibly meet in Rouen? I so long to see you, Maisie, and to be taken from this misery by your wonderful smile and inspiring good sense. Do write to let me know.

Iris had leave at the same time as Maisie, providing Maisie with a female companion. The journey to Rouen seemed long and drawn out, until finally they reached the Hotel St. Georges.

"I swear I cannot wait to get into that bath, Maisie Dobbs."

"Me too, Iris. I wonder if we can get our dresses cleaned. I've another day dress with me that I haven't worn. How about you?"

"Yes, me too. Not supposed to be out of uniform, but for goodness sake, this dress will walk to the laundry if I don't take it."

Maisie and Iris hurried immediately to their assigned room. The ceilings seemed extraordinarily high and there was chipped paint on the walls and doorframe. The room itself was small and simple, containing two single beds and a washstand, but after several months of living with the roof of a leaking tent barely six inches above their heads, they saw only grandeur. Two bathrooms were situated along the red-carpeted corridor, and the ever vigilant Iris immediately checked to see whether either was already occupied.

"One already gone, I'm afraid, and he's singing at the top of his voice."

"Golly, I am just aching for a nice hot bath," said Maisie.

"Tell you what. I'll put on my day dress and see if I can get our laundry done, while you draw a bath. We can top and tail it—check for the dreaded lice at the same time. It'll save waiting. Did you see the officers coming in after us? Bet they'll be bagging the bathrooms a bit sharpish."

"Don't some officers get rooms with bathrooms?"

"Oh, yes. Forgot that. Privilege and all that."

Iris and Maisie had discarded their uniform dresses quickly, and Iris gathered the laundry and walked toward the door.

"Never know, Maisie, p'raps your Captain Lynch will let you use *his* bathroom."

"Iris!"

"Only joking, Dobbsie. Now then, go bag us a bathroom."

The bathtub easily accommodated the two women, who lay back in the steaming water and audibly allowed the tension of the past few months to drain away.

"Bit more hot water, Maisie. Another five minutes and we'll swap ends."

"And about time!"

Maisie turned on the hot tap and pulled the plug to allow some of the cooler water out at the same time. After wallowing for another five minutes, they swapped ends, giggling as they moved, and continued to linger in the soothing steamy heat.

"Maisie," said Iris, as she leaned back, trying to comfortably position her head between the heavy taps, "Maisie, do you think your Captain Lynch will ask you to marry him, then?"

"Iris—"

"No, I'm not kidding you on now. I'm serious. What with the war and all. Makes you a bit more serious, doesn't it? Look at Bess White—gets a letter from her sweetheart, says he's going home on leave, she goes on leave, and boom! There they are—married, and him back at the front."

Maisie leaned forward, dipped her head in the water and sat up, sweeping back the long dark tresses.

"Here's what I do know, Iris. I know that when this is over, when the war is done with, I'm going back to university. That's what I know. Besides, when the war's over, I don't know if I'll be . . . well, Simon comes from a good family."

Iris looked at Maisie, then sat up and took hold of her hand.

"I know exactly what you are just about to say, Maisie, and let me tell you this, in case you haven't noticed. We are living in different times now. This war has made everything different. I've seen the letters from your dad, and from that Carter and Mrs. Whatsername with the pies. Those people, Maisie, are your family, and they are every bit as good as Simon's. And you are every bit as good as anyone Captain Simon Lynch will ever meet."

Maisie held on to Iris's hand, bit her bottom lip, and nodded. "It's just that—I can't explain it, but I have a feeling here," she held her hand to her chest, "that things will change. I know, I know, Iris, what you're going to say, 'It's the war. . . .' But I know this feeling. I know it to be true. And I know that everything will change."

"Come on. This water's going to your head, Maisie Dobbs. You are a grand nurse, Dobbsie, but I tell you, sometimes I wonder about all your wondering."

Iris put her hands on either side of the bath and levered herself up. She stepped out onto the tiled floor, grabbed one of the sturdy white towels, and began to dry herself. Maisie continued to sit in the rapidly cooling water while Iris dressed.

"Come on, dreamer. We'd better get a move on. That's if you want to see young Captain Lynch for dinner this evening. What time did he say to meet him?"

"The note said seven o'clock. By the desk in the main corridor as you come into the hotel."

※

*W*earing a plain gray day dress, her hair up in a bun, and accompanied by Iris, Maisie walked down the wide sweeping staircase of the hotel. She had tried not to anticipate meeting with Simon again, in case she imagined too much, in case the expectation of excited conversation, of hands held, of feelings expressed, was to clash with reality.

Iris was accompanying Maisie, but had already made up her mind to retire early. Not that she should, really. Fraternizing between men and women in uniform was frowned upon. But with a bit of luck, Maisie's young man would have a nice friend for company. Chaperone, my eye! thought Iris. Nothing like being the piggy in the middle.

Maisie and Simon Lynch saw each other at exactly the same time, and moved quickly through the throng of visitors. The thumping of Maisie's heart seemed to radiate to her throat, and stopped the words of greeting she had so carefully planned. Simon simply stood in front of her, took both her hands in his and looked into her eyes.

"I thought I would never see you again, Maisie."

Maisie nodded and looked down at their hands held together.

A deep, throaty "Ahem!" brought Simon and Maisie's attention back into the room. Iris was looking at her feet, inspecting the soles of her shoes, when the man accompanying Simon spoke.

"Think you could introduce us, Lynch? Don't know how you folks do things, but where I'm from, we try to get acquainted."

"Oh, I'm sorry. Please forgive me. Maisie, Iris, may I introduce Captain Charles Hayden. Currently sporting a British uniform, but as you can hear, he's an American. Good man came over here with the Massachusetts General Hospital contingent to do his bit. God bless them all. We've been exchanging notes about dealing with gas poisoning. Charles—Miss Maisie Dobbs and Miss Iris Rigson."

"And delighted to meet you. It was worth coming all this way. And Lynch was becoming a bit of a bore, as you might say. Well, are we going to eat, or stand here all evening? Personally I'm for eating."

"Me too," said Iris.

Charles Hayden provided the group with a much-needed dose of humor at dinner, and as time passed the waves of conversation shifted, so that the voices of Hayden and Iris could be heard above all others, laughing loudly, teasing, and generally exchanging good cheer. Instinctively they had assumed the task of allowing their friends the intimacy that can be had, even in a crowded room, when two people want only to be with each other.

"I have longed to see you, Maisie, and yet now that you are here, I hardly know what to say."

"Yes, I know."

Simon turned his body toward Maisie and reached for her hand.

"Talk to me about anything, Maisie. I want to know everything about you. Even if you've already told me in a letter. I want to hear your voice. Start anywhere, but not with the war. Tell me about London, Kent, about your father, your mother—and what about that funny little man Maurice Blanche? Tell me about it all, Maisie."

Maisie smiled, looked briefly across the table at Iris laughing with her head back.

"I'll tell you about my father. Francis. Known to just about everyone as Frankie. He has three loves in his life. My mother, who died when I was a child, me, and Persephone, his horse."

Maisie and Simon each unfolded tales of their lives that transported them from the memory of more recent experiences. Even after dinner had ended, the two walked close together along a cobblestone street that led to nowhere in particular and back again. For two days Simon and Maisie were almost exclusively with each other, apart only when Simon kissed her hand at the end of each day and watched as she climbed the stairs to the room she shared with Iris.

"Well, we're off tomorrow, Maisie. Back to the delightful Maison Tent."

"Have you enjoyed yourself, Iris?"

"Thank God for Chuck—that's what he calls himself—Hayden. Nice man, good company. We swapped sweetheart stories while you collected stars in your eyes."

"Iris, I'm sorry. I can't thank you enough."

"Oh, Maisie, don't get me wrong. It was a very nice time I had. Seriously, like I said, he was good company. Left his wife and young son behind to come over here with other American doctors and nurses. Misses his family something rotten. I told him all about my Sid. Blimey, I dunno if I would've come over here if I didn't have to."

"You didn't have to come here, Iris."

"I know. But there again I did, because it's my country that's here in this war. They're our boys and I'm a nurse. But they didn't; the Americans didn't have to come here. Though Charles seems to think it won't be long before they're in."

Iris began packing her small bag ready for the journey back to the casualty clearing station. "Made a nice job of the uniforms they did, here in the hotel laundry. And in double-quick time. Enjoy the clean dress, my girl; we'll be in mud up to our knees before long. And fighting off the lice again."

"Oh don't, Iris. . . ."

Simon accompanied Maisie and Iris to the station, and while Iris walked along to the platform for their train, Simon and Maisie stood together. Maisie shivered.

"I'll write as usual."

"That would be lovely, Simon. Gosh, it's cold."

Simon looked at her and without thinking put his arms around her.

"Please," Maisie protested weakly.

"Don't worry. No nasty sisters around to report you for dawdling with an unscrupulous RAMC captain."

Maisie laughed and shivered at the same time, moving her body closer to Simon. He held her to him and kissed her first on her forehead, then, as she looked up at him, Simon leaned down and kissed Maisie again on her cheek, then her lips.

"Simon, I—"

"Oh dear, will I get you into terrible trouble?"

She looked up at him, then around at the other travelers, none of whom seemed to notice the pair, and giggled nervously.

"Well, you might if someone sees us, Simon."

The guard signaled a loud whistle to alert passengers that the train would soon be leaving. Steam from the heavy engine was pushed up and out onto the platform. It was time for Simon and Maisie to part.

"Maisie. Look, I have a leave coming up again in a few months. Back to England. When's your leave? Perhaps it will be at the same time."

"I'll let you know, Simon. I'll let you know. I must run. I'll miss the train."

Simon held Maisie to him, and as the train signaled the "all aboard," she pulled herself away and ran along the platform. Iris was leaning out of the window of their carriage waving to her. She clambered aboard and sat down heavily on the seat just as the train began to move.

"I thought I'd be leaving without you, Dobbs."

"Not to worry, Iris. I'm here."

"Yes. You're here, Dobbsie. But I think you've left your heart behind with a certain young man."

Catching her breath as the train pulled out of the station, Maisie closed her eyes and thought of Simon. And as she saw his face in her mind's eye, the pressure returned to her chest. Rain slanted down across the windows as the fields of France seemed to rumble past with the movement of the train. Maisie looked out at this country she had willingly come to, so close to home, yet so far away from all that she loved. Almost. Simon was near.

## CHAPTER TWENTY

On a cold, wintry morning in February 1917, with the sun barely visible through the morning fog, Maisie pulled the wool cape around her shoulders and walked back to the tent she shared with Iris. Burning a hole in her pocket were two letters. One was from Simon. The other contained her leave papers. Her fingers were crossed.

"So, did you get it?" asked Iris, as Maisie tore at the small buff-colored envelope.

"Wait a minute, wait a minute. Yes! Yes! Yes!"

Maisie jumped up and down. She was going on leave. A real leave. Allowing two days for travel, she would have three days at home. Three days! One whole day more than her last leave, which was— she couldn't even remember. She immediately opened Simon's letter, scanned the lines of fine, right-slanted handwriting and jumped up and down again.

"Yes, Yes! He's got it, he's got leave!"

And the dates, April 15 to 20, were almost the same as hers. They would have two days together. Two whole days.

Iris smiled and shook her head. Oh, how that girl had changed.

Not in her work. No, the skill and compassion she brought to her work were as unquestionable as ever. But this joy, this excitement, was something new.

"Dobbsie, I do believe you are becoming a normal young woman!"

"Nonsense. I've always been normal," said Maisie, continuing to read Simon's letter.

"No, you haven't. I can tell. Taken life far too seriously, you have."

Iris reached for her cape and shivered. "And you can't do that in these times, Maisie. Take your work seriously, yes. But the rest of it, it'll drive you mad."

Iris carefully positioned her cap so that the red cross was in the center of her crown, and the point of the linen square was centered at the back of her head, just grazing the area between her shoulder blades.

"Ready, then?"

"Yes, I'm ready."

"Good. Let's get to work."

The weeks seemed to drag on, yet when Maisie looked back at the time between the arrival of her leave papers and the moment when which she walked onto the boat for the crossing back to Folkestone, it seemed that time had flown. As she stowed her bags, sought out hot cocoa and cake, Maisie almost dreaded the start of her leave, for by this time next week, she would be back in France. It would be over.

The crossing was calmer than last time, and though the sea was not quite like a millpond, the boat did not seem to pitch and toss as violently as before, and the tops of waves did not suddenly rear up and cover the deck. The nausea of her previous journey was not repeated to the same extent, yet a band of pressure around her forehead caused her to lean against the rail, counting off the quarter hours until land came in sight. She breathed in, waiting for sea saltiness to give way to the clear air of the county of Kent.

Oh, how she ached to see her father, to be drawn into the warm, steamy atmosphere of Mrs. Crawford's kitchen. In France she had dreamed of Kent, of apple orchards in full blossom, primroses and bluebells carpeting the woodland, and the soft countryside stretching out before her.

She longed to be home. She could hardly wait to see Simon.

Maisie disembarked, walking down the gangway and toward the port buildings. As she came through into the main waiting area, she saw her father, cap in hand, anxiously searching the sea of faces for her. Pushing her way through people jostling for extra height to see over the heads of others to the line of weary passengers, Maisie pulled at her father's arm.

"Dad! What are you doing here?"

"Darlin' girl. Couldn't wait for you to get to Chelstone, could I? So, I took the day off, like, and came down to meet you off the boat. Gawd, this ain't 'alf a busy old place! Come on, let me get that bag of yours, and let's get out of this lot. Never could stand a crowd, even at the market."

Maisie laughed and, still holding tightly to his arm, followed as he pushed his way through the surging throng making their way to the station.

The journey to Chelstone took another two hours, first by train to Tonbridge, then by the small branch line down to Chelstone. In a field across from the station, Persephone was grazing, her cart resting just inside the gate.

"Just a minute, love. Won't take me long to get old Persephone ready for you. Stationmaster let me leave the old girl here. I know it's not a fancy motorcar, but I thought you'd appreciate a ride home on the old cart with Persephone."

"That I do, Dad."

They rode in silence for a while, Frankie Dobbs with his arm around his daughter's shoulder.

"'Ard to know what to say to you, love. Bet you don't really want to talk about it, do you?"

"No. Not now, Dad. I'm not home for long. I'll be back there soon enough."

"And how long will I see you for?"

Frankie looked sideways at Maisie.

"Well, I'll be seeing a friend while I'm on leave. But we've got all day tomorrow."

"Is that all I get? Blimey, this Captain Lynch must be an interestin' fella."

Maisie swung round to her father.

"How do you know—?"

"Now then, now then. Just you 'old your 'orses, young lady. You're still my girl, and that's a fact."

Frankie grinned at Maisie. "There's a letter waiting indoors for you. Just sent to Miss Dobbs at Chelstone Manor. Got 'is name printed on the back of the envelope. Very posh. Knows your old Dad's the groom, does 'e?"

"Yes. He does, Dad. He knows who you are and who I am."

"Good. That's all right then. Look forward to meeting the man."

"Well, I don't know . . . ."

Frankie put his arm around Maisie again, and in the security of her father's embrace and his love for her, she slept as she had not been able to sleep since she left for France.

✤

"Well, I never. Look at you. All skin and bone, Maisie, all skin and bone."

Mrs. Crawford drew Maisie to her, then pushed away to inspect her from head to toe.

"A good dinner, that's what you need, my girl. Thank heavens we are all down here now, have been ever since her ladyship said it was too dangerous in London, what with the Zeppelin raids. Anyway, at least I can get a good dinner down you. That's what you need—a good dinner."

Maisie had hardly stepped from Frankie Dobbs's cart before the "welcome homes" began. And it seemed that one welcome was followed by another. She had been immediately summoned to the drawing room to meet with Lady Rowan. Already the short leave was turning into a whirlwind, but the next day Maisie spent time only with her father, alone.

Frankie Dobbs and Maisie groomed the horses together, walked across farmland, and speculated on the apple crop that would surely be the result of such fine hearty white blossom. And sitting alone in the gardens at Chelstone, Maisie wondered about the war, and how it was that such blooms could give joy to the soul, when one only had to stand on cliffs overlooking the Channel to hear the boom of cannons on the battlefields of France.

On the second day of her leave, Maisie was to see Simon in London, a meeting arranged in letters passed between their respective medical stations in France. She would meet his parents at the family's London home during their first day together. They both knew better than to have Simon suggest she stay at the house, as an overnight invitation would come only after a more formal luncheon meeting, the invitation for which had arrived from Mrs. Lynch, and along with Simon's letter, had awaited Maisie's return to Chelstone. Simon wrote that he couldn't wait to see her.

Frankie Dobbs took Maisie to the station, and they stood awkwardly on the platform to wait for the local train, which would connect with the London train at Tonbridge.

"Now, you make sure you don't overdo it. That Crawford woman was right. Skin and bone you are. You're like your mother, a tall drink of water in a dress."

"I'll eat them out of house and home, Dad."

"And you mind yourself, Maisie. I've not met this young man, but seeing as you've been invited by his people, I'm sure he's a fine person. And a doctor. But you mind yourself, Maisie."

"Dad, I'll be back on the train this evening—"

"Maisie. It's in 'ere that I'm talking about."

Frankie Dobbs pressed his hand to the place that still held grief for his departed wife.

"I'm talking about your 'eart, Maisie. Mind out for your 'eart."

The sun was shining by the time the engine met the end-of-the-line buffers at Charing Cross station. Maisie checked her face in the shell-shaped mirror on the bulkhead between the carriages. She had never been one to fuss over her appearance, but this was different. This was important.

Once again butterflies were holding court in her stomach, and once again she was filled with the joyous anticipation of seeing Simon Lynch. She opened the heavy wooden door and stepped down onto the platform.

"Maisie!"

"Simon!"

The young officer swept Maisie up into his arms and unashamedly kissed her, much to the delight of people rushing to catch trains, or anxiously waiting for loved ones on the platform. There was usually little cause for humor or delight at a wartime railway station, filled as they often were with war wounded, anxious farewells, and the bittersweet greetings of those who would have such a short time together.

"I have missed you so much. I can hardly believe we are here."

Maisie laughed, laughed until the tears fell down her cheeks. How she would hate to say good-bye.

The time spent at the Lynches' London house could not have been more perfect. Simon's parents welcomed Maisie into their home with great affection, as if she were part of the family. Mrs. Lynch personally showed Maisie to a guest room to "repair after the long journey."

Maisie's fears that she might have to field questions about her father's line of business proved to be unfounded, and she was asked only about her time at Cambridge and whether she might return when the war was over. Simon's parents understood that talk of "intentions" was almost futile at such a time, and the joy of having a dear son home was not to be sullied by questions that might give rise to discord. Time was too short.

Simon and Maisie had one more day together, then Maisie would leave early on Sunday morning for France. After lunch Simon escorted Maisie to Charing Cross Station again, and spoke of what they would do the next day.

"So, I've managed to get the car, lucky, eh? I'll leave early for Chelstone, then we can have a nice day out together—perhaps go on to the Downs."

"That would be lovely."

"What is it, Maisie?"

Maisie looked at her watch, and at the many men and women in uniform at the station.

"Remember to come to the groom's cottage, Simon. Not to the main house."

"Oh, I see. You're worried about me coming to Chelstone, aren't you?"

Maisie looked at her hands, and at Simon. "A little."

"It doesn't matter to me, Maisie. We both know that there are bigger things to worry about. Besides, it's me that has to worry about Chelstone, what with the formidable Mrs. Crawford waiting to render judgment!"

Maisie laughed. "Yes, Simon, you may have a good point there!"

Simon held her hand and escorted her to the platform. The arrival of her train had just been announced.

"Tomorrow will be our last day together." said Simon. "I wish I understood time, Maisie. It vanishes through one's fingers."

He held her hands together in front of his chest, and touched each of her fingertips in turn.

"Maurice says that only when we have a respect for time will we have learned something of the art of living."

"Ah, yes, the wise man Maurice. Perhaps I'll meet him one day."

Maisie looked into Simon's eyes and shivered. "Yes, perhaps. One day."

❖

Simon arrived at Chelstone at half past nine the next morning. Maisie had been up since half past five, first helping Frankie with the horses, then going for a walk, mentally preparing for Simon's arrival. She strolled through the apple orchards, heavy with blossom, then to the paddock beyond.

Half of what was, before the war, grazing for horses, was now a large vegetable garden providing fresh produce not only for Chelstone Manor but also for a wider community. In a time of war, flowers and shrubs were seen to be an extravagance, so every cottage garden in the village was almost bereft of blooms. Even the smallest postage stamp of land was needed for growing vegetables.

Maisie made her way back to the cottage and waited for Simon. Eventually the crackle of tires on gravel heralded his arrival. Frankie drew the curtains aside to look out the window in the small parlor.

"Looks like your young man is here."

Maisie rushed from the room, while Frankie stood in front of the mirror, adjusted his neckerchief and pulled down the hem of his best waistcoat. He rubbed his chin, just to make sure, and took off the flat cap that almost never left his head. Before going to the door to meet Captain Simon Lynch, Frankie took up the cherished sepia photograph of a woman who looked so much like the girl who had run joyously to the door. She was tall and slender, dressed in a dark skirt and a cotton blouse with wide leg-o'-mutton sleeves. Though she had fussed with her hair in anticipation of having the photograph taken with her two-year-old daughter, there were still stray curls creeping onto her forehead.

Frankie ran his finger across the glass, tracing the line of the woman's face. He spoke to the image tenderly, as if she were in the room with him, for Frankie Dobbs had prayed for her spirit to be at his side today.

"I know, I know . . . go easy on 'im. I wish you was 'ere now, Love. I could do with a bit of 'elp with this."

Frankie replaced the photograph, and with one last look in the mirror, just to make sure that he wouldn't let Maisie down, he walked from the cottage to greet the man to whom his daughter had run so eagerly.

For hours Simon and Maisie talked, first on the journey by motor car across to Sussex, then throughout lunch at a small inn. It was only after they had parked the car by a clump of trees and walked high up on the South Downs, seagulls whooping overhead, that they spent time in silence. Their pace aligned as they walked along the rough path on the crest of the hills overlooking the Channel. They moved closer together, hands brushing but not quite touching.

The day was warm, but Maisie still felt cold. It was a cold that had seeped into her bones in France and now seemed never to leave her. Simon sat down on the grass under a tree, and beckoned her to sit next to him. As she sat down he took her hand and grimaced, then playfully reached for one of her walking shoes, untied the laces, and held her foot in his hand.

"Goodness, woman, how can anyone be that cold and not be dead!"

Maisie laughed along with Simon.

"It's that French mud that does it, gets right into your bones."

The laughter subsided, and seconds later they were both silent.

"Will you definitely return to Cambridge after the war?"

"Yes. And you, Simon?"

"Oh, I think I'll be for the quiet life, you know. Country doctor. Delivering babies, dealing with measles, mumps, hunters' accidents, farmworkers' ailments, that sort of thing. I'll grow old in corduroy and tweed, smoke a pipe, and swat my grandchildren on their little behinds when they wake me from my afternoon snooze."

Simon leaned forward, plucked a blade of grass, and twisted it between his long fingers. "What about after Cambridge, Maisie?"

"I'm not sure."

Conversation ebbed as Simon and Maisie looked out over the sea, both daring their imagination to wander tentatively into the future. Maisie sighed deeply, and Simon held her to him. As if reading her thoughts, he spoke.

"It's hard to think about the future when you've seen so many passing through who don't have tomorrow, let alone next year. No future at all."

"Yes."

It was all she could say.

"Maisie. Maisie, I know this is rather soon, possibly even presumptuous, but, Maisie, when this is all over, this war, when we are back here in England . . . would you marry me?"

Maisie inhaled sharply, her skin prickly with emotion. What was that emotion? She wanted to say "Yes" but something stopped her.

"I know, I know, you don't have to say anything. It's the thought of corduroy trousers and tweeds isn't it?"

"No, Simon. No. It was just a surprise."

"Maisie, I love you."

He took her hand and looked deeply into her eyes.

"Yes. And I love you too, Simon. I love you too."

Simon drove Maisie back to Chelstone, and brought the car to a halt on the road at the end of the driveway that led to the manor. He leaned over and took Maisie's left hand.

"You never gave me an answer, Maisie."

"I know. It's just me, Simon. And doing what we have to do. In France. I want to wait until it's over. Until there's no more . . . no more . . . death. I can't say yes to something so important until we're home again. Until we're safe."

Simon nodded, his compassion for her feelings at war with his disappointment.

"But Simon. I do love you. Very much."

Simon did not speak, but cupped Maisie's face in his hands, and kissed her deeply. At first, Maisie began to pull away, afraid that someone from the manor might see, but as Simon's arms enfolded her, she returned his kiss, reaching for his neck to pull him closer. Suddenly Maisie was aware of moisture on her face and, pulling away, she looked into Simon's eyes and touched her cheek where their tears had met.

"God, I wish this war would end," Simon wiped the back of his hand across his eyes, before facing her once again. He kissed her gently on the lips. "I love you, Maisie, and I want you to be my wife. I promise that as soon as this war is over, I will walk across miles of trenches to find you, and I will stand there in my muddy clothes until you say 'Yes!' "

They kissed once more. Then, taking up her bag, Maisie asked Simon to let her walk back to the house alone. She did not want to suffer a difficult farewell, possibly in front of her father and whoever else might be in the gardens to witness their parting. Simon objected, on the grounds that no gentleman would allow a lady to walk unaccompanied to her home, but Maisie was adamant, reminding Simon that she had walked along that lane many a time, and often with a heavy basket.

Simon did not argue her decision. Instead of more words, they held each other close and kissed. She went swiftly from the motorcar and along the driveway, eventually hearing Simon start the engine in the distance and pull away onto the road.

Maisie insisted that she travel alone back to Folkestone, and Frankie, seeing a new maturity and independence in his daughter, agreed to allow Lady Rowan's new chauffeur, an older man passed over for military service, to take her to the station. Maisie said good-bye to her father at home. She had no stomach for more platform farewells.

It was on her journey to Folkestone, and then to France, that she thought back over the events of the days she had spent on leave. She remembered Simon's easy camaraderie with her father, his smile upon introduction, and how he immediately began asking about the horses and allowed himself to be led to the stables so that Frankie Dobbs was relaxed in the domain over which he was the obvious master.

Time and again Maisie replayed Simon's proposal in her head, and, though she would no doubt receive a letter from him soon, consid-ered how she avoided making a commitment. She knew only too well the source of such reticence.

As the train moved through the early morning mist of a Kentish springtime, Maisie breathed deeply, as if to remember the aroma of freedom. Though there had yet to be a victor in this great war that had begun almost three years ago, Maurice had written to her that they had, all of them, on all sides, lost their freedom. The freedom to think hopefully of the future.

It was later, much later, more than ten years after the war, that Maisie remembered every thought that had entered her mind on the journey back to the battlefield hospital.

She remembered praying to see Simon just one more time.

SUMMER 1929

# CHAPTER TWENTY-ONE

aisie took the underground from Warren Street to Charing Cross, then changed to the District Line for Victoria. As the train rocked from side to side, Maisie wondered what the evening's conversation with Lady Rowan might reveal. She suspected that the farm where James intended to take up residence was the same place that Celia had described over tea.

Leaving the train at Victoria, Maisie made her way out of the underground station, and walked along Lower Belgrave Street toward Ebury Place. And as she walked, she thought of Maurice, who had told her so many times that coincidence could simply be what it appeared to be: two events connected to each other by the thoughts and experience of a person. But he also told Maisie to pay attention to coincidence.

Coincidence was a messenger sent by truth.

Carter took Maisie's cloche and jacket, and welcomed her into the entrance hall. "So lovely to see you, Maisie. How are you? Her ladyship is waiting for you in the drawing room—and very anxious to see you she is, too."

"I'm well, thank you, Mr. Carter. I'll just nip down to see Mrs. Crawford first. I don't want her giving me an earful for not coming straight down to see her."

"A very wise decision, Maisie. You know the way."

Carter left to hang Maisie's outer garments in the cloakroom as Maisie made her way through the door to the right of the entrance hall and downstairs into the kitchen. The stone stairwell was as chilly as she remembered, but as soon as she walked through the door to the kitchen, she was enveloped in the welcoming warmth and mingling aromas that sent her back to her girlhood.

Mrs. Crawford had become hard of hearing, and continued to work as Maisie stood at the threshold of her domain. Maisie wondered if she had ever seen the old cook's hands clear of either flour or water. They were rough and work-worn hands, but Maisie knew that before touching any food, Mrs. Crawford would have stood at the big square earthenware sink and scrubbed her hands with a coarse bristle brush and a bar of coal tar soap. And by the time she plunged her hands into pastry dough, her red, sausage-like fingers would be in stark relief to the white flour. Maisie loved Mrs. Crawford's apple pie, and if she was visiting, there would be a pie for the sweet course *and* a pie for her to take home.

"Mrs. Crawford," said Maisie in a raised voice, "I'm here!"

Mrs. Crawford turned quickly, her purposeful frown transformed into a beaming smile.

"Well, look at you now! Don't you go getting those nice clothes all covered with flour."

Mrs. Crawford rubbed her hands on her pinafore and came toward Maisie with her arms open wide. Maisie was only too pleased to relinquish her body to a hug that was warm and close, even though the old woman was careful to keep her hands away from Maisie's clothes, instead embracing Maisie with pressure from her elbows.

"Are you eating, Maisie? There's nothing of you! I always said that a puff of wind would blow you away clear to Clacton!"

"I promise I'm eating, Mrs. Crawford. In fact, what's for dinner?"

"A nice vegetable soup, followed by roast beef with all the trimmings—and it's not even Sunday. Then there's apple pie and the cheese board."

"Oh my goodness. I'll pop!"

"Not all for you, but mind you eat a good bit of it. His Lordship will be home late again this evening and will have dinner in his study. And if that James comes in with his face as long as a week, they'll probably eat together. Otherwise Master James will eat in his rooms, with his misery for company."

"I thought he had his own flat—I didn't know he was back at home."

"When he likes. I know, I know, you feel sorry for the boy and all that, and you know we all love him—have done since he was but a streak of lightning running around. But the fact is, he's not a boy anymore, is he? And there's plenty of men out there what saw everything over there in France that he did, and they did what we all have to do—they just got on with it instead of moping around like a lost, wet gun dog, all soppy eyes and sodden coat."

Maisie knew that it was no good reasoning with Mrs. Crawford, who had firm ideas when it came to coping with life's ups and downs.

"That's the trouble with these boys of privilege. Not that I'm criticizing, far from it, I've been treated very well by them upstairs, very well. But that James has had too much time to think about it all. Too much going on up there." Mrs. Crawford had gone back to her pastry but tapped the side of her head to emphasize the point. Realizing that she had touched her hair, she went over to the sink to scrub her hands again but lost no time in continuing to make her point.

"Look at the boys who came back and had to get straight out in the farms and the factories—they had wives and families to look out for. You don't see them dragging their heels along, do you? No, that James should be at his lordship's side, taking some of the weight so that His Lordship isn't in the City at all hours. Not right for a man of his age. After all, look at James, he's thirty-eight this year."

Mrs. Crawford came back to her pastry, rolling out the dough with more than a little thumping of the rolling pin on the table. "Have you heard from your father lately?" Mrs. Crawford looked up at Maisie, yet continued flouring the pastry and sizing it to the pie dish.

"Yes. Mind you it's difficult, Mrs. Crawford. It's not as if he ever liked to put pen to paper. But he's still busy at the house. Master James goes down quite a lot to ride, so there's always work with the horses. And Her Ladyship likes to know that her own horses are cared for, even though she can't ride anymore."

"And that's another thing. All that time to go down there to 'think,' if you please. It's like I said, too much money and too much time on his hands."

Suddenly one of the bells over the door rang.

"That'll be Her Ladyship now. She probably reckons I've had long enough with you. Now then, don't forget to come down for your pie to take home when you leave in the morning."

Maisie kissed Mrs. Crawford on the cheek and went upstairs to the drawing room.

"Maisie, how lovely to see you. I had to ring or Mrs. Crawford would have hogged you for the whole evening! Come here to sit by the fire. I expect you know what's for dinner already. I told Julian that you would be dining with me, and he said 'Oh, good, we'll get some apple pie.' Come on, over here."

Lady Rowan tapped the place next to her on the sofa. The two women spoke of Maisie's business and her new clients. For Rowan Compton, Maisie was a breath of fresh air, and she lived vicariously through Maisie's stories.

"And Maurice is keen to see you again soon, you know."

"I thought he would be glad to have a break from me, to tell you the truth."

"Now, then, Maisie. You are like a daughter to him. You are his protégée. You are carrying his torch and shining your own light too. But I know he made a promise to himself to give you a little room for you to make your own way. He said to me, 'Rowan, it is past time to let our Maisie Dobbs fly free.'"

"I'll bet he said a bit more than that. I know Maurice too, Lady Rowan."

"Well, yes. He said that you would always look down as you were flying overhead, and if the ground was good for a landing, in you would come—or something like that. You know, that man talks in parables. I swear that sometimes I think he is the most profound person I know, and at others he infuriates me with his obscurity." Lady Rowan shook her head. "Will you visit him soon, Maisie?"

"Yes, I mean to. In fact, I need to consult with him."

"Anything interesting?"

Maisie smiled at Lady Rowan, without speaking.

"I know, you can't divulge a secret."

"Tell me about James," asked Maisie.

Lady Rowan rolled her eyes, took up her glass from the side table, and sipped her sherry. "James. Oh, that James. I am at a loss, Maisie. I knew it when that boy was a child, too sensitive by half. Have you noticed how we always call him a boy? Even now. It wouldn't be so bad if he were gadding about town wining and dining and getting into mischief. But this malaise . . . I wish he would speak to Maurice. But he won't go to see Maurice, and you know that Maurice won't go to him. One of his riddles, that James must open the door and walk along the path to him."

"Maurice is right, Lady Rowan."

"Well, you would say that, wouldn't you? You're a chip off the old block. By the way, he and your father are like two old peas in a pod down there, ever since Maurice bought the dower house."

"Tell me about James," Maisie prodded her.

Lady Rowan took another sip of her sherry. "Frankly, I'm worried. Julian is also worried, but he expresses it in a different way. He seems to think that if we are all patient, then James will come round, and that he won't be so incredibly depressed anymore."

Maisie did not speak, allowing Lady Rowan to gather her thoughts. Sitting still and allowing the silence to grow, Maisie felt the frustration, misunderstanding, and anger that had built up in the house, permeating every room—along with an expectation that James would one day bound in as the happy-go-lucky young man he had once been.

Carter came in to announce that dinner would be served in the dining room, and led the way. Maisie held out her arm to steady Lady Rowan, who now walked with the aid of a silver-capped cane, as they moved into the dining room.

"Wonderful, Carter, wonderful. Compliments to Mrs. Crawford, as always."

The conversation continued lightly as each dish was served, moving once again to the subject of James only after Carter had left the room.

"Some weeks ago, James met with a wartime colleague who had heard of a farm, coincidentally in Kent, where old soldiers could go to live with others who 'understood.' That was the term they used, 'understood.' As if no one else is able to understand. It seems that this farm is quite a revolutionary idea. It was originally set up for those suffering facial wounds, but now it is open—obviously when a room becomes available—to those with other wounds."

Lady Rowan set her knife and fork down on the plate, reached for her wine, and took a sip before continuing. "Of course, James still suffers pain in his leg and arm from the shrapnel, but Maurice has said that his discomfort is a result of melancholy. Yet James has become most interested in this community of wounded. He has visited, met with the founder, and has decided to go to live at this . . . this farm for the foreseeable future!"

"You seem distressed by his decision, Lady Rowan. Is there anything else?"

"Yes. A lot more. The founder, a man called Adam Jenkins, maintains that because everyone on the battlefield should have been equal, officers and enlisted men, because they all faced the same enemy, then there should be no advantage while in residence at this farm. Which is fair enough, but James said something about giving up his surname and title. Whatever next?" Lady Rowan shook her head.

At once Maisie thought of Vincent Weathershaw. Vincent.

Lady Rowan went on, "I wish to heaven James would go back to Canada. He seemed happy there, before the war, and at least he would be working and useful. Certainly his father would be delighted; it would be a weight off his mind. I know Julian wants to slow up a bit and wishes James would begin to take up the reins. And now he's signing over his money. . . ."

Lady Rowan had hardly touched her food. Instead she ran the fingers of her right hand up and down the stem of her wine glass.

"What do you mean?" Maisie asked.

"Apparently it's one of the stipulations for entering this Retreat or whatever it's called. You come with nothing, to be part of the group. So James has transferred his personal funds to this Jenkins fellow—and it's not just him, others have done the same thing. Thank God his father is still alive and there are limits to what James can actually relinquish financially. Julian is taking steps to protect the estate—and James's future—until he gets over this horrible idea. Of course Julian had already done a lot to shore up the estate when he saw the General Strike coming a few years ago. I married a sensible man, Maisie."

"What does Jenkins do with the money?"

"Well, it's a sizable property to run, and I'm sure the upkeep isn't insignificant. Of course, when one leaves one is refunded any monies remaining and given a statement of account. James said that he saw samples of the statements and refund documents, and he was happy with the arrangements. Mind you, he seemed eager to isolate himself on this farm. He said that people would understand him there. As if I don't!"

Lady Rowan reached over and clasped Maisie's hand. Maisie had never seen the usually stoic Lady Rowan so vulnerable.

"Where is James now?"

"Out. Possibly at his club, but he doesn't go there much now. Quite honestly, I don't know where he is. He could be wandering the streets for all I know. Most probably he's spending time with some old comrades. He visits them you know, those that are still institutionalized.

He'll probably be back later. Much later. I told him he could remain at Chelstone; after all, it's in the country, there's peace and quiet, and he could do what he likes and come back when he's ready for the City. Lord knows Julian needs his help. But he's determined to go to this farm. I have never felt so . . . so . . . cut off from my son."

Maisie pushed the food around on her plate. There was a time when mother and son had been almost inseparable, sharing a dry wit and a mischievous sense of humor. She remembered being at the London house soon after she received news that she had been accepted by Girton College. James had just returned from Canada, hoping to join the Royal Flying Corps. There was much joy in the household, and as she walked down the outside stairs toward the kitchen, Maisie saw the tall, fair young man through the window, creeping up behind Mrs. Crawford and putting his arms around her ample waist. And as Maisie watched through the condensation that had built up inside the pane of glass, Mrs. Crawford swung around, clipped the young man around the ear, and, laughing, pretended to admonish him. "You, young James, why no sooner are you back than you'll be the death of me. Look at you, you young lout—and if you are after fresh ginger biscuits, I've baked up a batch 'specially for you, though I'm not sure you deserve them now!"

Maisie had walked in through the back door of the kitchen just as James was taking his first bite of a fresh ginger biscuit.

"And look who else is here," said Mrs. Crawford. "Maisie Dobbs, I do believe you are even thinner! My back only has to be turned for one minute, and you're not eating properly."

With crumbs around his mouth, James swallowed the biscuit, and struggled to greet Maisie politely. "Ah, the clever Miss Maisie Dobbs, passing exams that the rest of us mere mortals have nightmares about!"

Then as Mrs. Crawford turned to the stove, James whispered to Maisie, "Tell Enid I'm home."

Later, as she walked past the drawing room on her way to Lord Julian's study to serve afternoon tea, which he had elected to take alone, she saw James and Lady Rowan through the open door. Lady

Rowan was laughing heartily, having been whisked by her son into an impromptu dance, accompanied only by the sound of his own booming voice:

Oh, he floats through the air with the greatest of ease
The daring young man on the flying trapeze
His actions are graceful, all girls he does please
And my love he has stolen away.

"I won't ask you to see James, Maisie," continued Lady Rowan, bringing Maisie back into the present, "I know your opinion will mirror Maurice's, so I know better than to ask. But I wonder. Would you find out something about this farm, or whatever it is? I have to say that I do feel he would be better in the world rather than trying to escape from it."

"I will certainly look into it, Lady Rowan. I'll go down to Kent next week. I have to go anyway, as I need to speak with Maurice, and I must see my father. I'll find out about James's retreat as well."

"Maisie. Take the MG. I know very well that you can drive, so do please take the car. It's not as if I've used it much since Julian bought it for me to run around in—and George drives Julian to the City in the Lanchester."

"Yes, all right, Lady Rowan. It's very kind of you to offer, and I may need to be flexible, so the car will be handy."

"It's almost new, so the young thing should get you there and back with no trouble at all. And Maisie—don't forget to send me your bill!"

Maisie directed conversation to other matters, and soon Lady Rowan was laughing in her old infectious manner. Carter watched as two maids cleared the table and brought in the delicious apple pie, to be served with a generous helping of fresh clotted cream. After dinner Maisie and Lady Rowan returned to the drawing room, to sit beside the fire until Lady Rowan announced that it was past time for her to be in bed.

Maisie made her way to the guest room that had been prepared for her visit. Nora had already unpacked Maisie's small bag and laid out her nightclothes on the bed. Later, as she snuggled closer to the hot water bottle that warmed the sheets, Maisie remembered, as she always did when she slept at the Compton residence, the nights she'd spent in the servants' quarters at the top of the house.

She left before breakfast the next morning, stopping quickly to drink tea with Carter and Mrs. Crawford, and to collect the apple pie. Billy Beale would love that apple pie, thought Maisie. She might need it when she asked him if he would take on a very delicate task for her. In fact, as the plans began to take shape in her mind, she might need more than apple pie for Billy Beale.

# CHAPTER TWENTY-TWO

*R*ight then. Watch carefully, miss. 'Ere's how you start 'er up."

The young chauffeur walked around to the front of the 1927 MG 14/40 two-seater roadster, and put his hand on the engine cover.

"You've basically got your five steps to starting this little motor, very straightforward when you know what you're about, so watch carefully."

George enjoyed the attention that came as a result of his expertise in the maintenance and operation of the Compton's stable of very fine motor cars.

"First you lift your bonnet, like so."

George waited for Maisie to nod her head in understanding before continuing with his instructions, and as he turned his attention once again to the MG, she grinned with amusement at his preening tutorial.

"Right. See this—you turn on your fuel. Got it?"

"Yes, George."

George closed the engine cover, and indicated for Maisie to move away from the side of the car so that he could sit in the driver's seat.

"You set your ignition, you set your throttle, set your choke—three moves, got it?"

"Got it, George."

"You push the starter button—on the floor, Miss—with your foot and—"

The engine roared into life, perhaps somewhat more aggressively than usual, given the enthusiasm of George's lesson.

"There she goes."

George clambered from the seat, held open the door, and, with a sweep of his hand, invited Maisie to take his place.

"Think you've got all that, Miss?"

"Oh yes, George. You explained everything very clearly. As you say, it's very straightforward. A lovely motor."

"Oh, nice little runner, to be sure. 'Cording to them at Morris Garages, this one can do sixty-five miles an hour—up to fifty in the first twenty-five seconds! 'Er ladyship goes out of 'ere like a shot out of a gun, doesn't know where she's going, but goes like a shot anyway. Comes back all red in the face. Worries me with them gears though. Talk about crunch! Makes me cringe when I 'ear it. Thank 'eavens for us all that she don't get out in it much anymore. Now, then, sure of your way?"

"I'm sure, George. Down the Old Kent Road, and just keep on from there, more or less. I've done that journey many a time when I was younger."

"'Course, you was at Chelstone, wasn't you? Mind you, if I were you, I'd go out onto Grosvenor Place, then along Victoria Street, over Westminster Bridge, St. George's Road, and just the other side of the Elephant and Castle. . . ."

"I think I can remember the way, George, and thank you for the advice."

George walked around to the back of the MG and dropped Maisie's bag into the car's rear luggage compartment, while she made herself comfortable in the rich claret leather seat. He checked once again that her door was closed securely before standing back and giving her a mock salute.

Maisie returned the wave as she eased the smart crimson motor car out into the mews. It wasn't until she was across the Thames and past the Elephant and Castle that Maisie felt she could breathe again. At every turn she sat up straight and peered over the steering wheel, making sure that each part of the vehicle was clear of any possible obstruction. She had learned to drive before returning to Cambridge in 1919, but took extra care as it had been quite some time since she'd had an opportunity—although she did not want to admit as much to George. In fact, she did not change from first gear until she was well out of George's hearing, fearing a dreadful roaring as she reacquainted herself with the intricacies of the double-de-clutch maneuver to change gear.

It was a fine day in early June, a day that seemed to predict a long hot summer for 1929. Maisie drove conservatively, partly to minimize chances of damage to the MG and partly to savor the journey. She felt that she only had to smell the air and, blindfolded, she would know she had arrived in Kent. And no matter how many times she came back to Chelstone, every journey reminded her of her early days and months at the house. As Maisie drove, she relaxed and allowed her mind to wander. Memories of that first journey from the house in Belgravia came flooding back. So much had happened so quickly. So much that was unexpected yet, looking back, seemed so very predictable. Ah, as Maurice would say, the wisdom of hindsight!

Drawing to a halt at the side of the road to pull back the roadster's heavy cloth roof, Maisie stood for a moment to look at the medley of wildflowers that lined the grass verge. Arrowheads of sunny yellow charlock were growing alongside clumps of white field mouse-ear, which in turn were busily taking up space and becoming tangled in honeysuckle growing over the hedge. She leaned down to touch the delicate blue flower of the common speedwell, and remembered how she had loved this county from the moment she first came to work for the dowager. It was a soft patchwork-quilt land in which she found solace from missing her father and the Belgravia house.

Maisie had decided already that the day in Kent should become a two or three day excursion. Lady Rowan had given her permission to keep the car for as long as it was needed, and Maisie had packed a small bag in case she chose to stay. The hedgerows, small villages and apple orchards still full of blossom, were working their magic upon her. She stopped briefly at the post office in Sevenoaks.

"I'm looking for a farm, I think it's called The Retreat. I wonder if you might be able to direct me?"

"Certainly, Miss."

The postmaster took a sheet of paper and began to write down an address with some directions.

"You might want to be careful, Miss."

Maisie put her head to one side to indicate that she was listening to any forthcoming advice. "Yes, Miss. Our postman who does the route says it's run like a cross between a monastery and a barracks. You'd've thought that the blokes in there had seen enough of barracks, wouldn't you? There's a gate and a man on duty—you'll have to tell him your business before he'll let you in. They're nice enough, by all accounts, but I've heard that they don't want just anyone wandering about because of the residents."

"Yes, yes indeed," said Maisie, taking the sheet of paper. "Thank you for your advice."

The sun was high in the sky by the time Maisie came out of the post office, and as she touched the door handle of the MG it was warm enough to cause her to flinch. Pay attention, Maurice had always cautioned her. Pay attention to the reactions of your body. It is the wisdom of the self speaking to you. Be aware of concern, of anticipation, of all the feelings that come from the self. They manifest in the body. What is their counsel?

If those from the outside were questioned, albeit in a nonthreatening manner, when they entered, how might it be for the residents, the men who had been ravaged by war, in their coming and going? Maisie decided to drive on toward Chelstone. The Retreat could wait until she had seen Maurice.

Frankie Dobbs put the MG away in the garage and helped Maisie with her bags. She would stay in the small box room at the groom's cottage, which had once been her bedroom and was now always made up ready for her to visit, even though such visits were few and far between.

"We don't see enough of you, Love."

"I know, Dad. But I've been occupied with the business. It's been hard work since Maurice retired."

"It was 'ard work before 'e retired, wasn't it? Mind you, the old boy looks as if 'e's enjoyin' 'avin' a bit of time to 'imself. He comes in 'ere to 'ave a cup of tea with me now'n again, or I'll go over to see 'is roses. It surprised me, what 'e knows about roses. Clever man, that Maurice."

Maisie laughed.

"I have to go over to see him, Dad. It's important."

"Now then, I'm not stupid. I know that I'm not the only reason for you comin' all this way. Mind you, I 'ope I'm the main reason."

"'Course you are, Dad."

Frankie Dobbs finished brewing tea and placed an old enamel mug in front of Maisie, then winked and went to the cupboard for his own large china cup and saucer. As he brought some apple pie out of the larder, Maisie poured tea for them both.

"Maisie. You are lookin' after yourself, aren't you?"

"Yes, Dad. I can take care of myself."

"Well, I know that this work you do is sometimes, well, tricky like. And you're on your own now. Just as long as you're careful."

"Yes, Dad."

Frankie Dobbs sat down at the table with Maisie, reached into his pocket and pulled out a small package wrapped in brown paper and secured with string. "Anyway, I was in the 'ardware shop last week, talking to old Joe Cooke—you know 'ow that man can jaw—and, well, I saw this little thing. Thought it might come in 'andy, like, for you. Natty, innit?"

Maisie raised an eyebrow at her father, wondering if he was teasing her. With nimble fingers, she pulled away the string and opened the paper to reveal a shining new stainless-steel Victorinox pocket knife.

"Old Joe said it was a bit odd, buying a thing like this for me daughter, like, but I said, 'Joe, let me tell you, a daughter on 'er own can make more use of a thing like this, with them little tools, than any of them lads of yours.' In any case, y'never know when it might be just the thing you need, 'specially if you're runnin' all over in that motor."

"Oh, Dad, you shouldn't go spending money on me." Maisie pulled out each tool in turn, then looked at the closed knife in the palm of her hand. "I'll keep it with me all the time, just in case." Maisie slipped the knife into her bag, leaned across the table to kiss her father on the cheek, then reached for her tea.

Father and daughter laughed together, then sat in companionable silence drinking tea and eating apple pie, comfortable with only the heavy tick-tock of the grandfather clock for company. Maisie was thinking about The Retreat, and how she would present the story to Maurice.

Years of working with Maurice had helped Maisie prepare her answers to some of his questions, like a chess player anticipating the moves in a game. But she knew that the ones likely to be most difficult were those that pertained to her own past.

Frankie Dobbs interrupted Maisie's thoughts.

"So, that MG. Nice little motor, is it? What's she like on the corners?"

After tea Maisie walked though the gardens and down to the dower house. Maurice had been invited to use the house after the dowager's death, in 1916, and he had purchased the black-and-white beamed home in 1919. After the war, like many landowners of the day, the Comptons decided to sell parts of the estate, and were delighted when the much-loved house became the property of a friend. The gardens had suffered during the war as groundsmen left to enlist in the army, and land that had lain fallow was requisitioned to grow more produce. At one time it was feared that Chelstone Manor itself would be requisitioned to house army officers, but thankfully, given Lord Julian's work with the War Office, together with the fact that the fifteenth-century ceilings and winding staircases rendered the building unsuitable for such use, the manor itself was spared.

Though Maurice officially became resident at the dower house in 1916, he was hardly seen throughout the war years, and came to Chelstone for short periods, usually only to rest. The staff speculated that he had been overseas, which led to even more gossip about what, exactly, he was doing "over there." Maurice Blanche had become something of an enigma. Yet anyone watching him tend his roses during the scorching summer of 1929, as Maisie did before opening the latched gate leading to the dower house garden, would think that this old man wielding a pair of secateurs and wearing a white shirt, light khaki trousers, brown sandals, and a Panama hat, was not one for whom the word "enigma" was appropriate.

Maisie hardly made a sound, yet Maurice looked up and stared directly at her immediately she walked through the gate. For a minute his expression was unchanged, then his face softened. He smiled broadly, dropped the secateurs into a trug, and held both hands out to Maisie as he walked toward her.

"Ah, Maisie. It has taken you a long time to come to me, yes?"

"Yes, Maurice. I need to talk to you."

"I know, my dear. I know. Shall we walk? I'll not offer you tea, as your dear father will have had you swimming in the liquid by now."

"Yes. Yes, let's walk."

Together they passed through the second latched gate at the far end of the garden, and then walked toward the apple orchards. Maisie unfolded the story of Christopher Davenham, of his wife, Celia, the poor departed Vincent, and how she had first heard about The Retreat.

"So, you have followed your nose, Maisie. And the only 'client' in the case is this Christopher Davenham?"

"Yes. Well, Lady Rowan is a sort of client now, because of James. But we always took on other cases, didn't we? Where we felt truth was asking for our help."

"Indeed. Yes, indeed. But remember, Maisie, remember, truth also came to us as individuals so that we might have a more intimate encounter with the self. Remember the Frenchwoman, Mireille—we both know that my interest in the case came from the fact that she reminded me of my grandmother. There was something there for me to discover about myself, not simply the task of solving a case that the authorities could not begin to comprehend. Now, you, Maisie, what is there here for you?" Maurice pointed a finger and touched the place where Maisie's heart began to beat quickly. "What is there in your heart that needs to be given light and understanding?"

"I've come to terms with the war, Maurice. I'm a different person now," Maisie protested.

The two walked on through the apple trees. Maisie was dressed for the heat and wore a cream linen skirt, with a long, sailor-collared linen blouse and a cream hat to shield her sensitive skin from the beating sun, yet she was still far too warm.

When they had walked for more than an hour, Maurice led them back to the dower house and into the cool drawing room. The room was furnished tastefully, with chairs covered in soft green floral fabrics of summer weight. Matching curtains seemed to reflect the abundant garden, with foxgloves, hollyhocks, and delphiniums framing the exterior of the dower house windows. As the winter months drew in, the light materials would be changed, with heavy green velvet drapes and chair covers bringing a welcome warmth to the room. For now the room was light and airy, and bore the faint aroma of potpourri.

Some indication of Maurice's travels was present, in the form of artworks and ornaments. And if one went into Maurice's study, adjacent to the drawing room, there were two framed letters on the wall, from the governments of France and Britain, thanking Dr. Maurice Blanche for his special services during the Great War of 1914–18.

"I am expecting a visitor this evening, for sherry and some reminiscences. The Chief Constable of Kent, an old friend. I will ask him about this Retreat, Maisie. I believe and trust your instincts. Go there tomorrow, proceed with the plan you have outlined to me, and let us speak again tomorrow evening after dinner—no doubt you will dine with your dear father—and let us also look again at your notes, to see what else speaks to us from the pages."

Maisie nodded agreement. A feeling of anticipation and joy welled up inside her as she realized how very lonely it had been working without Maurice. Before she left the house, Maurice insisted that Maisie wait for one minute.

"A new book. I thought you might be interested. *All Quiet on the Western Front*. It has just been published. You have no doubt read reviews and commentary about it."

Maisie raised an eyebrow, though she would never ignore a recommendation from Maurice Blanche.

"Remember, Maisie, while there is always a victor and a vanquished, on both sides there are innocents. Few are truly evil, and they do not need a war to be at work among us, although war provides them with a timely mask."

"Yes, I suppose you are right there, Maurice. I'll read it. Thank you. And I'll see you tomorrow when I get back from The Retreat."

As Maisie turned to walk down the path and across the garden to the stables and groom's cottage, Maurice stopped her.

"And Maisie, when you visit The Retreat, consider the nature of a mask. We all have our masks, Maisie."

Maisie Dobbs held the book tightly in her hand, nodded, and waved to Maurice Blanche.

## CHAPTER TWENTY-THREE

O n a bright sunny day The Retreat seemed truly to live up to its name, a place that would afford one sweet respite from the cares of the world. As she drew up to the Gothic cast-iron gate with a pillar of rough stone at either side, Maisie could see through the railings to the sun-drenched farm beyond. The road leading from the entrance to the front of the house was dusty, causing a rippled haze of heat to work its way up toward a blue sky dotted with only a few lintlike clouds.

In the distance she could see a large medieval country farmhouse fronted by apple orchards. A high brick wall restricted further inspection of The Retreat, but as she regarded the subject of her investigation and imagination, she noticed in front of her the pink and red blooms of roses that had grown furiously upward on the other side of the wall, and now seemed to be clambering toward her, to freedom. Each bloom nodded up and down in the breeze, and in that moment the wave of roses reminded Maisie of the men who scrambled from a mud-soaked hell of trenches over the top and into battle. Bleeding from their wounds, millions of young men had died on the sodden ground and barbed wire of no-man's land.

Maisie closed and opened her eyes again quickly, to extinguish the images that presented themselves so readily in her mind's eye and had been haunting her since she had torn at the weeds on Don's grave at Nether Green Cemetery. She reminded herself that she could not afford to be distracted or influenced by her memories.

Maisie was leaning back against the MG's door, looking up at the gates, when a man walked through a smaller pedestrian entrance built into the wall. "Can I help you, Ma'am?"

"Oh yes indeed. Is this The Retreat?"

"Yes it is. And what might your business be here today?"

Maisie smiled at the man and approached him. He was tall and thin, with hair that seemed to be gray before its time. She was about to reply when she saw the long, livid scar running from his forehead across his nose and down to his jaw. There was no left eye where the left eye should have been, not even a glass one. The socket was laid bare, defiantly. And as Maisie looked into the right eye of the disfigured man, she saw that he dared her to turn away. She met the man's gaze directly.

"I have written but have received no reply, so I decided to visit without an appointment. It's about my brother. I understand that he might stay here, at The Retreat, until he is healed."

And remembering how Celia Davenham so delicately touched her own face when speaking of Vincent's wounds, Maisie brought her fingers to her left cheek, mirroring the unseen pain of the wounded man before her. He visibly took a deep breath, and waited a second before replying. "You've come to the right place, Ma'am. Wait here and I'll be back in ten minutes. Mr. . . . er . . . Major Jenkins is who you need to see, and I'll have to get permission."

Maisie nodded, smiled, and said she would be glad to wait. He hurried back through the pedestrian entrance and, taking a bicycle that had been leaning on the other side of the wall, raced along the driveway toward the house. Maisie squinted to watch as the man, now a speck in the distance, stood the bicycle by a door at the side of the house, then ran inside. Five minutes later the speck came running out of the door, took up the bicycle, and grew larger in her vision as he neared the front gate once more.

"You can come in to meet with Major Jenkins, Ma'am. I'll open the gate for you. Drive slowly to the front of the house, and park your motor by the big fallen tree on the gravel there. Major Jenkins is waiting for you."

"Thank you, Mr. . . ."

Maisie held her head to one side, seeking a name.

"Archie, Ma'am."

"Thank you, Mr. Archie. Thank you."

"Actually, it's just Archie, Ma'am. We don't use surnames here."

"Oh, I see. Thank you, Archie. Is 'Jenkins' the major's Christian name?"

The man's face reddened, except for the scar, which became pale as the surrounding skin heated.

"No. 'Jenkins' is the major's surname."

"Ah," said Maisie, "I see."

Maisie started the MG and drove to the gravel by the fallen tree as instructed. As she applied the handbrake, the door of the car was opened by a man who wore beige jodhpurs, a white shirt, and tall leather riding boots, and carried a baton.

"Miss Dobbs, I understand. I'm Major Jenkins."

Maisie took the hand offered to balance her as she got out of the car. Jenkins was of average height and build, with dark brown hair, brown eyes, and pale skin that did not seem to match his hair and eye coloring. His hair was so neatly swept back that ridges left by his comb reminded Maisie of a freshly ploughed field. She quickly regarded his face, looking for the scars of war, but there were none. None that were visible.

"Thank you, Major Jenkins. No doubt Archie told you why I am here. Perhaps you could tell me more about The Retreat."

"Indeed. Do come to my office, and we'll have tea and a talk about what we are trying to do here."

Jenkins sat in the Queen Anne chair opposite Maisie, who was seated in an identical chair. Tea had been brought earlier by Richard, another man who seemed not yet to be thirty, who had worked hard to mouth words of greeting to Maisie, his shell-blasted jawbone moving awkwardly as he made an enormous effort to physically frame the voice that came forth from his throat.

For her part Maisie did not draw back from the men at The Retreat, although she was sure she was not seeing those with the more devastating wounds. She had seen such wounds when freshly shattered bone and skin still clung to the men's faces, and scars were the best outcome to be hoped for.

"I read about it, in fact," said Jenkins, "then went over to France to have a look for myself. It seemed that these French chappies had a cracking good idea—provide a place of refuge for the men whose faces were altered, or taken, by war. It was certainly not the easiest thing to get going especially as, just after the war, many of the men here had such terrible injuries."

"What happened to them?"

"Frankly, for some it was just too much—bad enough having the wounds in the first place, but being young and having the girls turn away, not being able to go out without people staring, that sort of thing. To tell you the truth, we lost some—but of course we were their last chance of a bearable life anyway."

Jenkins leaned forward to offer Maisie a biscuit, which she declined with a wave of her hand. He nodded and set the plate down on the tray again.

"Of course, for most of our guests, being here helps. The men have no fear of sitting out in the sun, enjoying life outside. The physical work is good for them. Makes them feel better about themselves. No sitting around in bath chairs and blankets here. We go into Sevenoaks to the pictures occasionally—it's dark in the picture house, no one can see."

"And how long does a patient stay here?"

"Not 'patient,' Miss Dobbs. 'Guest.' We call them guests."

"What about the first names only, Major Jenkins?"

"Ah yes. Reminds them of better times, before they became pawns in the game of war. Millions of khaki ants clambering over the hill and into oblivion. The familiarity of using Christian names only is in stark contrast to the discipline of the battlefield, of this terrible experience. Relinquishing the surname reminds them of what's really important. Which is who they are inside, here." He held his hand to the place just below his rib cage to indicate the center of his body. "Inside. Who they are inside. The war took so much away."

Maisie nodded accord and sipped her tea. Maurice had always encouraged judicious use of both words and silence.

"Now then. Your brother?"

"Yes, Billy. He wasn't injured facially, Major Jenkins. But he walks with some difficulty, and has been so very . . . very . . . unwell. Yes, unwell, since the war."

"Commission?"

"Commission, Major Jenkins?"

"Yes, is he a captain, a second lieutenant?"

"Oh. Actually, Billy was a soldier, a corporal when he was injured."

"Where?"

"The Battle of Messines."

"Oh God. Poor man."

"Yes. Billy saw more than enough. But then they all saw more than enough, didn't they, Major Jenkins? Major Jenkins, why is Billy's rank important?"

"Oh, it's not important, really. Just enables me get a sense of what he might have experienced."

"And how might that have been different for Billy than for, let's say yourself, Major?"

"It's just that we have found that men have different experiences of recovery."

"Are you a doctor?"

"No, Miss Dobbs. Simply a man who wanted to do some good for the men who gave their identity for the good of the country and returned to a people who would rather see their heroes walking tall or at best limping, than reflecting the scars caused by our leaders' ill-conceived decisions."

Maisie took another sip of tea and nodded. It was a fair comment.

She left The Retreat thirty minutes later after a tour of the premises. She had been escorted to her car by Jenkins, who watched as she made her way to the gate at a very sedate five miles per hour, the gravel crackling under the tires like sporadic gunfire.

Archie waited for her, touched his forehead in a partial salute as she approached, and leaned down toward her open window as she drew alongside him.

"So, what do you think? Will your brother be joining us, Ma'am?"

"Yes. Yes I think so, Archie. I believe it would do him a power of good."

"Righty-o. We'll look forward to seeing him, then. Hold on while I open the gate."

Maisie waved as she pulled out onto the road, the roses once again nodding in the breeze as Archie waved her on her way.

While she hadn't flinched or drawn back from his wounds, Maisie felt the discomfort of Archie's injury. The sun shone through the windshield of the MG, its heat and brightness causing her eyes to smart and a sharp pain to move from the socket of her left eye to a place on her forehead. The body empathizing with another's pain, thought Maisie. The subconscious mind alerting her to Archie's agony, though she had been successful in appearing to ignore the scar and empty eye socket.

Maisie didn't go far. Stopping once again in Westerham, she sat on a bench in the old churchyard, took the notebook out of her handbag, and began to write an account of her visit.

A walk through the grounds of The Retreat accompanied by Major Jenkins had revealed very little to her that she did not already know, only now she was familiar with the extent of the house, where the "guest" rooms were, and how the farm worked.

There were twenty-five guests living in the main house and an old oasthouse, no longer used for drying hops—Kent's most famous harvest. Though converted to living quarters years before, the oast-house still bore the strong peppery aroma of warm hops.

The youngest man she met must have been thirty, which meant that he had been shipped to France at about age seventeen. The eldest was no more than forty years of age. Questioning Jenkins, Maisie had learned that although the guests were free to come and go at will, most remained, comfortable in the freedom from stares The Retreat afforded them.

Though the farm was to a large extent self-sufficient, each guest entrusted his personal savings to The Retreat, to draw upon for expenses beyond those of day-to-day living, and to contribute to the cost of helpers. If the farm's produce was bringing in a tidy sum, and providing much of the food, the pooled savings must have earned interest and amounted to a pretty penny in someone's bank account. The thought troubled Maisie.

The needs of the guests seemed to be few. There was no doctor ôn staff to provide for the physical care of those living with such terrible wounds, and no seasoned professional used to dealing with the emotional needs of those traumatized by war. Some of the men still wore the tin masks that had been provided for them when first recovering from their wounds. But the fine glaze used on tin molded to fit a face ten years younger now provided little respite from the mirror's reflection.

Maisie questioned Jenkins's approach. True, it seemed a benevolent idea, and she knew how successful the "holiday camps" had been in France, providing a resting place for wounded men struggling to return to peacetime life. But if The Retreat had been inspired initially by the success of an idea born of compassion, what fuel drove the engine now? The war was almost eleven years past. Then again, those who lived with its memory were still very much alive.

What about Jenkins? How and where had he served? Clearly the men at The Retreat were troubled as a result of their wounds and their memories. But Jenkins's soul was a troubled in a way that was different. Maisie suspected that his wounds lay deep within.

James would soon be going to The Retreat, so she had to act quickly. It was time to go back to London. Archie thought that The Retreat would do her "brother" a world of good. She wondered how Billy Beale would feel about his newfound siblinghood, and if, in a month, he would feel as if time in the country had done him a power of good.

# CHAPTER TWENTY-FOUR

So what you think is that this Jenkins fella is getting up to no good down there at this Retreat 'e's set up?"

Billy Beale sat in the chair in front of Maisie Dobbs, his hands working around and around the fabric on the perimeter of his cap, which he had taken off when he came to answer Maisie's call. Maisie had lost no time in telling Billy Beale why he had been summoned, and how she needed him to help her.

"Yes, I do, Billy. I would only need you to be there for a week, no, let's say two weeks. To let me know what is happening, what you see."

"Well, you've come to the right person if you want someone what's willing. But I'm not sure I'm your man. Not as if I'm a toff, to mix with the likes of them."

"Billy. You don't need to be a toff. You just need to have some money.—"

"And that's even bloomin' funnier. Money—the likes of me!"

"It's taken care of, Billy. As soon as you are accepted as a guest at The Retreat, a sum will be moved from your bank account to Major Adam Jenkins's account."

Billy Beale looked at Maisie and winked. "And I bet I know who's got me a bank account I never 'ad before in me life."

"Yes. It was arranged today."

Suddenly Billy was quiet. He looked again at his cloth cap, and sat with obvious discomfort in the too-small chair opposite Maisie's desk. It was the end of another humid day in London: The summer of 1929 was breaking records for lack of rain, and for heat.

"I'd do anything for you, Miss. I said that when you moved in 'ere to run yer business. I've seen you work all hours 'ere. And I've seen 'ow you 'elp people."

Billy tapped the side of his nose in his usual conspiratorial fashion.

"What you do isn't what you'd call regular. I can see that. And if this 'elps someone, then I'm your man. Like I said before. You 'elped me Miss, when you weren't more than a girl. I remember."

"It could be risky, Billy. I believe this Jenkins is a troubled man, and possibly a dangerous one."

"No. Don't you worry about me. You've explained it all very well. I understand what's involved, Miss. And it won't take me long to set up a line for us, soon as I get the lay of the land. Now then. Let's look at that map again. Mind you—"

Billy rose to look down at the map that Maisie had spread out on the table.

"Just as well the missus is taking the nippers down to 'er sister's in 'astings. You reckon we leave tomorrow?"

"The sooner the better, Billy. Let's go over the plan again, and the story. We'll leave for Chelstone tomorrow. We'll be meeting with Maurice Blanche in the afternoon. He has been seeking some additional information for us from one of his contacts."

"And who might that be, if I may ask?"

"The Chief Constable of Kent."

"Bloody 'ell . . ."

"Quite, Billy. Now then, William Dobbs, we expect a letter from The Retreat to arrive at Chelstone by Friday, so we can drive over on

Saturday. The other gentleman I told you about, who must not see me or know that I am involved in anything to do with The Retreat, will be taking up residence in just a few weeks. I hope to have this . . . this . . . investigation concluded by that time."

"Right you are, Miss. I'd better be getting 'ome then. Got to pack me ol' kit bag again, for the good of me country."

"Dr. Blanche has arranged for your clothes, Billy."

"It wasn't clothes I was going to pack, Sis," said Billy, with an impish smile, "You don't mind if I call you Sis, get used to it, like? I need to pack the other bits and pieces of kit that I'll be needing for this job."

Maisie looked up at Billy Beale and smiled.

"This is good of you, Billy. You were the only person I could ask. I can't tell you how much I appreciate it. Your help will not go unrewarded."

"It already 'as been rewarded. Been getting a bit bored around 'ere anyway. I need a change."

Maisie lingered for a while in the office before leaving, closing the door behind her, and making her way along the hallway to another unmarked door. Here she took a key from her pocket and entered the room. Home. She had moved a few weeks before, when it was clear that she needed to be closer to her work. The bed–sitting room was small, but all that she required was within the walls of this room. And when she needed some respite from the dour familiarity of such spartan accommodations, there was usually an invitation to stay at Ebury Place, or she would go down to Chelstone, to spend time in the calm and comforting company of her father.

***

"There. Reckon I've got everything."

Billy Beale placed one more bag in the luggage compartment of Lady Rowan's car, and stood to watch Maisie, who was securing her navy blue beret with a long pearl-tipped pin. Her corduroy jacket had been thrown around the shoulders of the driver's seat, giving the impression of a rather stout old man who had just sat down. An observer might have considered the young woman "fast," for today Maisie was wearing a pair of long beige cuffed trousers, with a linen blouse and brown walking shoes.

Maisie looked at her watch and took her place in the driver's seat of the MG.

"Good. Not too late. We'd better get a move on. We need to be at Chelstone by noon."

Billy Beale hesitated.

"What is it, Billy?"

"Nothing really, Miss . . . it's just that . . ." He took the cap from his head and looked up at the sky. "It's just that this is the first time I've left London since I got back from the war. Couldn't face it. O' course the missus 'as been away with the nippers. Been down to Kent with 'er people 'op-picking, and o' course to 'er sister's in 'astings. But not me, Miss."

Maisie said nothing, made no response. She understood the power of reflection well, and as she had done with Celia Davenham just a few short weeks before, she made no move to soothe Billy Beale, allowing him the time he needed to step into the car.

"But you never know, at least I might get a good night's sleep down there in the country." Still he hesitated.

"What do you mean, Billy?"

Maisie shielded her eyes from the morning sun as she looked up at him.

Billy sighed deeply, took a breath, opened the car door, and sat down on the passenger seat. The claret leather of the hardly used seat creaked as Billy moved to make himself comfortable.

"Just can't sleep, Miss. Not for long anyway. 's'bin like that since I got 'ome from France. That many years ago. Soon as I close my eyes, it all comes back."

He looked into the distance as if into the past.

"Blimey, I can almost smell the gas, can 'ardly breathe at times. If I fall asleep straight away, I only wake up fighting for breath. And the pounding in my 'ead. You never forget that pounding, the shells. Mind you, you know that, don't you, Miss?"

And as he spoke, Maisie remembered her homecoming, remembered Maurice taking her again to see Khan, who seemed never to age. In her mind's eye she saw herself sitting with Khan and telling her story, and Maurice sitting with her.

Khan spoke of bearing witness to the pain of another's memories, a ritual as old as time itself, then asked her to tell her story again. And again. And again. She told her story until, exhausted, she had no more story to tell. And Maisie remembered Khan's words, that this nightmare was a dragon that would remain alive, but dormant, waiting insidiously to wake and breathe its fire, until she squarely faced the truth of what had happened to Simon.

"You all right, Miss?"

Billy Beale placed a hand on Maisie's shoulder for just a second.

"Yes, yes, I was just thinking about what you said, Billy. So what do you do when you cannot sleep?"

Billy looked down at his hands and began pulling at the lining of his cap, running the seam between the forefinger and thumb of each hand.

"I get up, so's not to wake the missus. Then I go out. Walking the streets. For hours sometimes. And you know what, Miss? It's not only me, Miss. There's a lot of men I see, 'bout my age, walking the streets. And we all know, Miss, we all know who we are. Old soldiers what keep seeing the battle. That's what we are, Miss. I tell you, sometimes I think we're like the waking dead. Livin' our lives during the day, normal like, then trying to forget something what 'appened years ago. It's like going to the picture 'ouse, only the picture's all in me 'eàd."

Maisie inclined her head to show understanding, her silence respectful of Billy's terrible memories, and of this confidence shared. And once again she was drawn back, to that year in the wards after her return from France, working to comfort the men whose minds were ravaged by war. Small comfort indeed. Yet for every one who could not bring his mind back from the last vision of a smoke-filled hell, there were probably dozens like Billy, living now as good father, good husband, good son, good man, but who feared the curtains drawn against darkness, and the light extinguished at the end of the day.

"Ready, Billy?" Maisie asked when Billy put the cap firmly back on his head.

"Reckon I am, Miss. Yes, I reckon I am. Do me the world of good will this, Miss. Bein' useful like."

They spoke little on the journey to Kent. Occasionally Maisie asked Billy questions as they drove along the winding country roads. She wanted to make doubly sure that he understood everything that was required of him. Information. She needed more information. A feel for the place. How did it work when you were on the inside? Was anything amiss?

She spoke to him of intuition, abbreviating the teaching she had received from Maurice and Khan many years before.

"You must listen to the voice inside, Billy," said Maisie, placing her hand to her middle. "Remember even the smallest sensation of unease, for it could well be significant."

Billy had been quick to learn, quick to understand that his impressions were important, just as relevant as facts on a page. As Maisie knew from their first meeting, Billy Beale was sharp, an acute observer of circumstances and people. He was just what she needed. And he was willing.

But was it fair to draw Billy into her work? If she thought that Vincent's death was questionable, was it right to involve Billy? Then again, he would not be at The Retreat for long. And they would be in daily contact. She had promised Maurice that as soon as she had gathered enough information, she would refer her findings to the authorities—if what she found required it.

Maisie knew that her curiosity was drawing both Billy and herself deeper into the mystery of Vincent. And even as she drove she closed her eyes briefly and prayed for the confidence and courage to face whatever was hidden in the darkness.

## CHAPTER TWENTY-FIVE

*M*aisie parked the motorcar outside the dower house and led Billy into Maurice Blanche's home, to introduce her old teacher to her new assistant, and to have lunch together before she and Billy proceeded to The Retreat.

They talked about The Retreat, and Billy added weight to Maisie's earlier deliberations about the naming of this place where the wounded of a war over ten years past still sought refuge.

"O' course, it might not be just The Retreat, you know, as in gettin' away from it all into shelter. There's 'The Retreat,' in't there? You know, the bugle call at sunset. S'pose you'd 'ave to be an army man to know that, eh? Like 'retreating from a position' as well. That's what we should've done many a time—would've saved a few lives, and that's a fact."

Maisie set down her knife and fork and nodded thoughtfully.

The Retreat, the ultimate play on words to describe a place for the wounded. But what happened if someone wanted to retreat, as it were, from The Retreat?

"Maisie, while you are visiting your father, before you and

Mr. Beale—or perhaps I should say 'Dobbs' to get him used to the name—anyway, before you depart for The Retreat, I will walk with Mr. Beale in the meadow, just beyond the orchard."

Maisie knew that this was not a chance suggestion, and watched the two men walk toward the meadow, heads together in conversation, the younger man ever so slightly ready to steady the older man lest he falter. If only he knew, she thought, how much the old man feared the faltering of the younger.

As soon as they returned, Maisie took Billy to The Retreat, but before entering, she drove around the perimeter of the estate and parked under the shade of a beech tree.

"It's a retreat all right, innit, Miss? Pity they don't allow visitors for the first month. Wonder what they'll say when I tell them I'm out after two weeks? Prob'ly be a bit upset with me, eh, Miss?"

Billy surveyed the landscape, the fencing, the road, and the distances between landmarks.

"Look, 'ere's what I think. No point trying to get all fancy here, rigging up lines to, y'know, communicate. Why don't I just meet you at the same time every evening, by that bit of fence there, and tell you what I know."

"Well, Billy, it seemed as if we had a good plan, for your safety, that is."

"Don't you worry about me. From what you've said, I don't think I'm that important to the likes of them. I'm just your average bread and butter, aren't I? No big legacies being signed over or anything."

Billy smiled at Maisie and pointed toward the fields between the large house in the distance, and the road.

"Tell you the truth, looking at this landscape now, it's best if we don't mess around with telephone lines coming too near the 'ouse. Draw more attention. No one's goin' to question an old soldier what wants to go off by 'imself for a jaunt of an evenin'. But they might question an old sapper fiddling around with a telephone line in the dark. And you know, Miss, I might be good at that sort of thing, but I never did say I was invisible. And I can't run like I used to, not with the leg 'ere." Billy slapped the side of his leg for emphasis. "But 'ere's what I can do now. I can rig up a line to that telephone box we just passed back there, on the corner as you leave the 'amlet back there. I 'ad a quick look as we drove by—not that I 'ad much time, what with the speed and all—"

Maisie grimaced at Billy, who continued. "It's one of them new ones, a Kiosk Number Four, I think. They 'ave em in places where there ain't no post office—did y'see? It's got a stamp machine on the back, and a pillar-box for letters. Sort of all purpose—mind you, me mate what works on the things says that the stamps get soggy when it rains, and then they all stick together and make a right old mess. So, anyway, getting' back to me and the old lines 'ere, if I need to get 'old of you urgent, like, or if I'm in an 'urry to get out of 'ere, I can always jump through this fence—well, sort of jump, what wiv the leg and all—and use the box and line what I rig up to connect with the outside line at that box up the road. D'you see what I mean, Miss? Then I'll run like a nutter, bad leg an' all!"

Maisie laughed nervously. "Right you are, Billy, I think I follow you. It sounds like a good idea."

Billy opened the car door, pulled himself out of the low seat, and walked around to the luggage compartment. He carefully took out two large old canvas kit bags and placed them on the ground. Taking out spools of cable, "small, so's I can work with them on me own," Billy walked over to the ditch at the base of the perimeter fence.

Moving aside grasses and wildflowers growing innocently at the side of the road, Billy began to unwind the cable into the ditch, moving away from Maisie, who remained in the car. It was a quiet thoroughfare, so they had little to fear from passing traffic, but nevertheless, country folk were apt to be inquisitive about two strangers lingering on the road. Especially if one were seen unraveling cable.

Maisie got out of the car and walked over to the fence, looking out over the land belonging to The Retreat. The perimeter fence, six feet tall and topped with barbed wire, would merge into a stone wall just half a mile along in the opposite direction to the line being laid out by Billy.

The main gate was situated another half mile away from the beginning of the wall. Eventually Billy returned.

"Nicely done, and quick too. Managed to save meself some work by using the bottom wire of this 'ere fence." Billy pulled back the grass to point to the wire in question. "I hear that's what they've done over there in America, y'know—used the fences on farms to make connections between places, like." Billy pushed back his cap, and wiped the back of his hand across his forehead. "Stroke of luck it bein' there—the telephone—see more of them in the towns, don't you? S'pose it's used by them what live in the terraced cottages in the 'amlet. I tell you, no one will see that line, mark my words."

Billy caught his breath, and for the first time Maisie heard the wheezing that revealed gas-damaged lungs. "You shouldn't be running like that, Billy."

"I'm awright, Miss. Now to this end." Billy held up a telephone receiver. "The old 'dog and bone,' Miss. We used to say in the trenches that them as is on the end of the line only bloomin' 'ear 'alf of what's said—and then only what they want to 'ear anyway. Personally, meself, I reckon it's a poor old situation when you 'ave to make out a person's intentions from their voice in a tin cup."

Billy worked on as he spoke, wiring the receiver to a metal box he placed in the ditch before leaning in and connecting lines. He picked up the receiver, turned the dial, and listened. The operator responded at his request for a connection, charges to go to the recipient of the call, and put him through to Maurice's telephone number. They spoke briefly before Billy replaced the receiver on its cradle.

"I know it's not perfect, and it takes a bit o' time, but it might come in 'andy, you never know."

After ensuring that their makeshift telephone was hidden and secure, Billy then cut into the wire of the perimeter fence, forming a "door" through which he could escape, should escape become necessary. He secured the door with spare wire to camouflage the fact that the fence had been tampered with.

The first part of their task finished, Maisie and Billy loaded up the motor car again and drove slowly toward the main entrance to The Retreat. They said little, only speaking to confirm the time at which they would meet each evening.

Billy would take a solitary stroll at seven o'clock, which would bring him to the fence by the large beech tree at half past seven. Maisie would be waiting to meet with him for just a few moments, then he would make his way back to the main house. In all other dealings with the residents of The Retreat, there was to be nothing about him that could be remarked upon. He was to be invisible but for the bed he slept in and the food he consumed. But he was to watch, and listen and report back to Maisie.

"Welcome back to The Retreat, Miss Dobbs," said Archie as he opened the gate.

He walked toward the car, leaned down so that his face was alongside the passenger window, and addressed Billy.

"William, isn't it? The major is waiting to welcome you personally to The Retreat."

Billy Beale took the proffered hand and seemed not to see the terrible scars that had changed Archie's countenance forever. Maisie nodded to Archie, and moved the car slowly along the driveway.

"Poor bleedin' bugger—oh, I am sorry, Miss—I forget meself at times. Least I can get about and no one worries about a bit of a limp. Blimey, that poor fella, with that face. Not that I 'aven't seen worse. Just not seen it for a long time, not close up. That's all."

Maisie slowed the car even more. "Billy, if you have any doubts—"

"Not likely," said Billy, straightening his shoulders. "If there's any funny business going on here that can cause any more damage to these blighters, then I want to do my bit to stop it." He paused to look at Maisie. "Can't blame them for wanting to get away, can you?"

"No, you can't. But there's a lot that can be done for them now."

"Not when you've been through what they've been through. Just want to be left alone 'alf the time, I should think, never mind being messed around with by newfangled ideas of skin medicine and what 'ave you."

The car drew alongside the main building as Adam Jenkins, the major, came through the front door and down the steps toward them.

"Ah, William. Welcome to The Retreat. I am sure you will be comfortable here. Come into my study for tea, then we can get you settled later."

Adam Jenkins led the way, his white shirt once again crisply laundered, leather riding boots polished to a blinding shine, and not a hair out of place. He invited Maisie and Billy to take a seat, standing behind Maisie's chair to hold it for her, then indicating, with a nonchalant sweep of his hand, the seat by the window for Billy.

How strange, thought Maisie, that he should direct Billy to a seat that took the full strength of the late-afternoon sun, rays that would cause Billy to become hot and uncomfortable, and to have to shield his eyes with the hand that he would need to reach out for the teacup as it was offered to him. Strange to unsettle a person so.

Billy met Maisie's look and raised an eyebrow. He knows, thought Maisie. He knows that Jenkins has placed him by the window on purpose.

Ten minutes of seemingly purposeless conversation had been exchanged between Jenkins and Maisie. As befitting his character— the tired veteran of a war over ten years past—Billy was silent. And hot. Maisie looked at Billy again. She saw the perspiration on his brow, his discomfort as he ran the forefinger of his right hand along the edge of his shirt collar.

Jenkins suddenly directed his attention away from Maisie, toward Billy. "My dear man. How remiss of me. How utterly stupid. Move over to this other chair and into the cool of the room immediately."

Jenkins put down his cup and used one hand to beckon Billy away from the window seat, and the other to indicate another seat.

Interesting, thought Maisie. A small gesture, but a subtle and significant one. Was it a ploy to begin to inspire Billy's trust? Placing himself immediately in the role of savior, and of one prepared to acknowledge a mistake. Or was Adam Jenkins genuinely admitting an error of judgment? Was this opening of his outstretched arms a move to render Billy more comfortable in another seat, an act of genuine concern? Or was it perhaps a deliberate action to draw Billy into his circle of admirers? Arms spread wide to bring him within the force of his influence.

Maisie watched Jenkins carefully, while attending to the business of afternoon tea. In her work with Maurice, Maisie had learned much about the charm and charisma of the natural leader, which, taken to an extreme, can become dictatorial and vindictive. Was Adam Jenkins such a man? Or an enlightened and concerned soul?

"Well, it's time to get some pawprints on the page, don't you think?" said Jenkins. He glanced at his watch, stood up, and walked over to a large heavily carved desk. The top was covered in rich brown leather, and only one plain manila file sat waiting for attention on top of a wooden board. He opened the file, checked the papers within, took a fountain pen from the inside pocket of his light linen jacket, and returned to the chair next to Maisie.

"We have received the necessary documents—thank you, Miss Dobbs—pertaining to the financial arrangements." He turned to Billy. "And I know you completely understand the commitment we request upon taking up residency at The Retreat, William. Now, perhaps you would be so kind as to sign here."

He placed the papers on the wooden board to provide a stable writing surface, and passed them to Billy, tapping the place for signature with his forefinger.

After Billy carefully wrote "William Dobbs" in the space indicated, Jenkins rang the bell for an assistant to escort Billy to his quarters, and as he did so, Billy winked at Maisie. Yet when Jenkins turned back to the two supposed siblings, he saw only the blank resignation of the man, and the worry etched in the face of his sister. But Maisie's concern was no act. She *was* worried for Billy. She had to ensure that he was at The Retreat not a moment longer than necessary.

# CHAPTER TWENTY-SIX

*M*aisie waited anxiously at Maurice Blanche's cottage. Billy had been at The Retreat for three days, and each evening at seven o'clock, Maisie set off in Lady Rowan's MG, along country lanes filled with the lingering aroma of Queen Anne's Lace and privet, to meet Billy Beale by the perimeter fence, across the road from the ancient beech tree.

Each evening, with summer midges buzzing around her head, she watched as Billy approached. First she would see his head, bobbing up and down in the distance, as he walked across the fallow fields of tall grass. Then as he came closer, his wheaten hair reflected the setting sun, and Maisie wondered why no one noticed Billy Beale taking a walk each evening.

"Evenin', Miss," said Billy as he curled back the fence wire and clambered through.

"Billy, how are you?" As always, Maisie was both relieved and delighted to see Billy. "You've caught the sun, Billy," she remarked.

"Reckon I 'ave at that, Miss." Billy rubbed at his cheeks. "All this working on the land, that's what's done it."

"And how is it, the working on the land?"

"'Not bad at all, Miss. And it seems to do these lads good. You should see some of them. Seems that they were right down in the dumps when they came 'ere. Then slowly, like, the work and the fact that no one looks twice at them starts to give them the, you know, the sort of confidence they need."

"Nothing unusual, Billy?"

"Can't say as there is, Miss. O' course, not that I can go around asking questions, but I keep my eyes open, and it seems like it's all on the up and up. The major is a funny bloke, but 'e's doing 'is bit, i'n'e? And now that there's space 'ere, what with some fellas gone, they're taking other blokes, with other injuries, not just to the face and 'ead, like. But you know that, don't you, otherwise I wouldn't be 'ere, not with this fine lookin' physog."

Billy grinned at Maisie and rubbed his chin.

"Quite, Billy. So is everyone happy there?"

"I should say so, Miss. Not much to dislike, is there? Mind you, there is one bloke, has some terrible scars on his face, just 'ere."

Billy turned his head to the right, and with the forefinger of his left hand indicated a line going from his ear, to his jaw, then to his chest. He grimaced, then continued.

"I think 'e's 'ad enough of being out 'ere—says that he feels good and well enough to get back to the real world."

"And what does the major say to that?"

"I don't know that 'e's said anything, Miss. I think they like 'em to give it some thought, you know, them as wants to leave."

"What makes you say that? What would stop someone from just leaving? It's in the contract that you can leave when you want."

"Well, what I've 'eard is that some blokes get back their confidence and next thing you know, they want to go back out, face the world. Then when they get back out, they find that it ain't all that rosy, that they get the stares an' all. Apparently that's 'appened a few times, and the blokes topped themselves."

"Is that what you've heard, Billy?"

"'ere and there. You 'ear talk. They think that this fella, who's wanting to get back to what 'e calls the 'real world,' is worrying the major. Seems the major has said 'e's . . . what was it 'e was supposed to 'ave said?"

Billy closed his eyes and scratched the back of his head. As he did so, Maisie saw the red sunburn at his neck, the farm laborer's "collar."

"That's it. The major 'as said 'e's suspectible."

"Do you mean susceptible, Billy?"

Billy smiled again. "Yes, reckon that's it, Miss."

"Anything else, Billy?"

"Not really, Miss. The major seems a really good bloke, Miss. I don't know what 'appened to those fellas you found out about. P'raps they left and then was the type what couldn't stand up to bein' on the out-side. But I will say this. There's blokes 'ere what love the major, you know. Think 'e's a lifesaver. And I s'pose 'e is really, when you think about it. Given some boys a way of life since the war, boys who thought they 'ad none."

Maisie noted Billy's comments on index cards and nodded her head. Slipping the cards and the pencil into her work-worn black document case with the silver clasp, she looked directly at Billy.

"Same time tomorrow evening, Billy?"

"Yes, Miss. Although, Miss . . . can we make it a bit earlier? 'bout 'alf past six? Some of the boys are 'aving a snooker tournament. Like to give it a go if I can. Join in with a bit of fun, like."

Maisie was silent for some seconds before replying. "Right you are, Billy. But keep your eyes open, won't you?"

"Don't worry, Miss. If there's anything funny goin' on 'ere I'll find out all about it."

Maisie watched as Billy turned and walked through the field again. She walked back across the road, opened the car door, and sat down in the driver's seat, leaving the door ajar to watch Billy become but a speck in the distance.

Had she made a mistake? Had her gift, her intuition, played tricks on her? Were the deaths of Vincent—and the other boys who used only one name—suicide? Or simply coincidence? She sighed as she started up the MG again.

Maisie spent her days at Chelstone close to the telephone. She would pass a precious hour or two with her father each day, but quickly returned to the dower house in case she was needed. Together she and Maurice went over old cases for clues and inspiration, and speculated over the details of life at The Retreat.

"I would very much have liked to see the postmortem findings on our friend Vincent, and his colleagues."

"I located the inquest proceedings, and it seems that they were all attributed to 'accidental death' in some form or another."

"Indeed, Maisie. But I would like to inspect the details, to observe through the eyes of the examiner, so that hopefully I might see what he did not. Let's go back over the notes. Who conducted Vincent's postmortem?"

Maisie passed Maurice the report.

"Hmmm. Signed by the coroner, and not the attending examiner."

Maurice stood up and walked around the room.

"To solve a problem, walk around," he said, noticing her smile.

How often in the past had they worked together in this way, Maisie sitting on the floor, legs crossed in front of her, Maurice in his leather chair. He would get up, pace the floor with his hands together as if in prayer, while Maisie closed her eyes in meditation and breathed deeply, as she had been instructed years ago by Khan.

Suddenly Maurice stopped walking, and at almost the same moment, so close that neither would have been able to say who was first, Maisie came to her feet.

"What is it that you find so interesting about the reports, Maisie?"

She looked at Maurice. "It is not the actual contents of the report, Maurice. It is the lack of detail. There's nothing to go on, no loose threads. There's not the slightest particle of information for us to work with."

"Correct. It is too clean. Far too clean. Let me see . . ." Maurice flipped the pages back. "Ah, yes. Let me telephone my friend the chief inspector. He should be able to help me." He looked at the time, it was half past nine in the evening. "Indeed, he should be delighted to help me—his interior will have been warmed by his second single malt of the evening."

Maisie took her place on the cushion again and waited for Maurice. She heard his muffled voice coming from the room next door, the rhythm of his speech not quite English yet not quite Continental. The telephone receiver was replaced on the cradle with an audible thump, and Maurice returned.

"Interesting. Extremely interesting. It seems that the attending examiner in the case of Vincent, and likely also in the other cases, was on call in the early hours of the morning, with his duty ending at half past eight—and so was able to go to The Retreat immediately after he was summoned. He returned home after completing his cursory examination and writing a brief report. His name, Maisie, is Jenkins. Armstrong Jenkins. Something of a coincidence, I think. And the examination lists time of death at . . . let me see . . . yes, it was at five o'clock in the morning."

"Dawn," said Maisie.

Maisie leafed through the papers that she had spread across Maurice's desk. Her mentor came to her side.

"Maurice. They died at dawn. The time of death for each of the men buried at Nether Green is dawn."

"An almost mystical hour, don't you think, Maisie?"

Maurice clasped his hands behind his back and walked to the window.

"A time when the light is most likely to deceive the eye, a time between sleep and waking. A time when a man is likely to be at his weakest. Dawn is a time when soft veils are draped across reality, creating illusion and cheating truth. It is said, Maisie, it is darkest just before dawn."

"So there's still nothing much to tell you, Miss."

Billy Beale stood with his hands in the pockets of his light sailcloth summer trousers, and kicked at the dry ground between his feet. He had been at The Retreat for only a week.

"Don't worry, Billy. It wasn't definite that you would find something. You're only going to be here a short time anyway. I just thought that some inside observations might be helpful."

Maisie moved to stand next to Billy, and without his noticing, adopted the same stance. She was wearing trousers again, and a light cotton blouse, so it was easy for her to place her hands in her pockets, emulating Billy's pose exactly.

He's embarrassed about something, thought Maisie. There's something he doesn't want to tell me. As Billy moved in discomfort, so did Maisie. She closed her eyes and felt Billy's dilemma.

"And you think this Adam Jenkins is a good man, do you, Billy?"

Billy kicked at the ground again, and though his face was tanned from working on the land, she saw a deep blush move from his chin to his cheeks.

"Well, yes, reckon I do, Miss. And I feel awful, at times. After what 'e's done for them, 'ere I am sniffin' around for something nasty."

"I can see how that might be difficult for you, Billy. You admire Adam Jenkins."

"Yes. Yes, I admire the man."

"That's good, Billy."

Maisie turned to face Billy and with the intensity of her gaze compelled him to look back at her.

"That's good. That you admire the man. It'll make your time here easier, and what I ask you to do easier."

"'ow do you mean?"

"Just go about your business, Billy. Just go about doing what you have to do here. You don't have to do anything other than be yourself. Although I do request two things: That we keep to our evening meetings, that's one. The other is that you take care to maintain your assumed name. Do not give anything away. Is that clear?"

Billy relaxed as Maisie spoke to him, and nodded his head.

"I just want to know about your days. That's all, Billy. Then next week I'll come and collect you. In fact, I'll come tomorrow if you want."

"No. No, miss. I'll stay on as we agreed. Don't expect I'll find anything, though. These 'ere meetings might get a bit boring."

Maisie nodded her head, and continued to mirror Billy's movements with her own.

"Just one more thing, Billy. About the man who wanted to leave. Remember, you told me about him? What's happened to him?"

"Can't say as I've seen 'im for a day or so. Mind you, that's not unusual, if one of the fellas wants to 'ave a bit of time alone. Like they do."

Billy stopped speaking, kicked his feet at the ground, then looked up at Maisie.

"What is it, Billy?"

"Just a thought, though. So keen to leave, 'e was. End of the month, 'e said. Wouldn't think 'e wanted any time to 'imself, now I come to think about it."

Maisie made no move to agree or disagree. "Like I said, Billy. You don't need to go snooping around. Just meet me here every day."

"Right you are, Miss. Now then. Best be going, before I'm missed."

Maisie waited a second before responding to Billy's movement toward the fence.

"Billy . . ."

"Yes, Miss?"

With his good knee bent, ready to go through the hole in the fence, Billy turned to meet Maisie's direct stare.

"Billy. Don't you think that someone would understand that you just needed some time to yourself—if you're back a bit late, that is?"

"Oh, they might do, Miss," Billy replied thoughtfully. Then with a wink added, "But not when I'm due to defend my snooker title in 'alf an hour."

Maisie smiled as Billy climbed through on to the other side of the fence, and secured the wire. But instead of going back to the car, she remained in the same place to watch Billy Beale once again walk across the fields, back to his temporary life at The Retreat.

❖

"*O*h, please don't worry about the car, my dear. Heavens above, I can't even drive the thing, not with my hip at the moment. Besides, I think your need is greater than mine, and you are working in my interests."

Maisie had been holding the telephone receiver away from her ear while Lady Rowan spoke, but brought the receiver closer to reply.

"Thank you. I was worried. But I should have it back to you by the middle of next week."

"Right you are. Now, tell me. What's happening? James is due to leave for The Retreat in ten days. And heaven knows he won't be spoken to about anything. Not even to his father. I swear he hasn't been the same since that girl—"

"Yes, Lady Rowan. I know."

"And if it weren't for you, I would be absolutely frantic."

"Lady Rowan, may I speak to Lord Julian please?"

"Yes, yes . . . I know, I am just about to become tedious. He's in his study. I'll just nip next door to get him. Won't wait for Carter, it would take all day."

Maisie smiled. It would probably take a while for Lady Rowan to walk next door to the study to get Lord Julian. She hadn't been able to "nip" anywhere for some time.

Eventually, she heard Lord Julian Compton's voice. "Maisie, what can I do for you?"

"Lord Julian. In confidence."

"Of course."

"I wonder if you could help me with some information that I believe you may be able to obtain for me from your former contacts at the War Office."

"I'll do what I can—what do you need, Maisie?"

"Jenkins. Major Adam Jenkins. I need to see his service record, if at all possible."

"I've already obtained it, m'dear. Didn't like the sound of this Retreat business when I heard about it from James. Got the service record in my office now. Didn't know he called himself Major, though. I only heard him called Jenkins by James."

"The men at The Retreat call him Major."

"That's interesting. Jenkins was just a lieutenant."

"Is there anything else there, Lord Julian? Any other anomalies?"

"Of course a service record is limited. He was discharged though, medical discharge."

"Where to?"

"Craiglockhart."

"Oh."

"Yes. Right up your alley I'd say, Maisie. Mind you, he was a mild case, apparently. Of course I don't have a record of his treatment. Just the notes of his commanding officer. Says that he went gaga after a couple of chaps in his command deserted. Seems to have been an innocuous fellow, quite frankly. Got a commission based on need rather than any military talent, I would say, from the record. Officers were dropping like flies, if you remember. Well, of course you remember. Mind you, the chap's obviously got a business head on him, setting up this Retreat."

"The men seem to adore him for what he's done there. Providing a place for them to go," said Maisie.

"Yes, I've got to hand it to him. Now he's opened the doors to those who sustained other injuries. Like James. Bit like a monastery though, if you ask me, wanting people to sign over their assets. Mind you, if the idea is a place of refuge forever . . . ."

"Yes."

"Shame, isn't it? That we only like our heroes out in the street when they are looking their best and their uniforms are 'spit and polished,' and not when they're showing us the wounds they suffered on our behalf. Well, anything else, m'dear?"

"No. I think that's all. Is there any chance that I might see—?"

"I'll have it sent down to Chelstone in the morning."

"Thank you, Lord Julian. You've been most helpful."

Maisie had spent most of that day at the dower house with Maurice, taking only a short break to visit Frankie Dobbs. She declined to sleep in the small bedroom that had always been hers at the groom's cottage, instead electing to remain by Maurice's telephone, just in case Billy needed her. Time and again she ran through the details of events and research information she had accumulated.

Adam Jenkins had lied about his status. But was it a lie, or had a man simply called him "major" and it stuck? She remembered her grandfather, working on the Thames boats. People called him The Commander, but he had never been in the navy, never commanded anything. It was just a nickname, the source of which had been lost over the years. But how did Jenkins, "an innocuous little man," assume such power? Billy had become a believer, and the men seemed to adore him. Was fear a factor? Was there a deeper connection between Vincent and Jenkins? And what about Armstrong Jenkins? Family member, or coincidence?

She had missed something. Something very significant. And as she reexamined, in her mind's eye, each piece of collected evidence that had led her to this place, she considered Maurice's words, and felt as if each day, all day, she was living in the moment before dawn broke. Maisie thought back, to that earlier dawn, more than ten years earlier. The beginning of the end, that was what it had been.

# CHAPTER TWENTY-SEVEN

he time is drawing closer, is it not my dear?" Maurice
asked her now. He looked at the grandfather clock,
patiently tick-tocking the seconds away.

"Yes it is. Maurice, I want to take Billy out of The Retreat."

"Indeed. Yes. Away from Jenkins. It is interesting, Maisie, how a
time of war can give a human being purpose. Especially when that
purpose, that power, so to speak, is derived from something so
essentially evil."

Maurice reached forward from his chair towards the wooden pipe
stand that hung on the chimney breast. He selected a pipe, took
tobacco and matches from the same place, and leaned back, glancing
again at the clock. He watched Maisie as he took a finger-and-
thumb's worth of tobacco from the pouch, and pressed it into the
bowl of the pipe.

"Your thoughts, Maisie?"

Maurice struck a match on the raw brick of the fireplace, and
drawing on the pipe, held the flame to the tobacco. Maisie found the
sweet aroma pungent, yet this ritual of lighting and smoking a pipe

soothed her. She knew Maurice to indulge in a pipe only when the crux of a matter was at hand. And having the truth revealed, no matter how harsh, was always a relief.

"I was thinking of evil. Of war. Of the loss of innocence, really. And innocents."

"Yes. Indeed. Yes. The loss of that which is innocent. One could argue, that if it were not for war, then Jenkins—"

The clock struck the half hour. It was time for Maisie to leave to meet Billy Beale. Maurice stood, reaching out to the mantelpiece to steady himself with his right hand.

"You will be back at what time?"

"By half past eight."

"I will see you then."

Maisie left the cottage quickly, and Maurice moved to the window to watch her leave. They needed to say little to each other. He had been her mentor since she was a young girl, and she had learned well. Yes, he had been right to retire. And right to be ready to support her as she took on the practice in her own name.

"*B*illy. Good timing. How are you?"

"Doin' awright, Miss. Yourself?"

Without responding to his question, Maisie continued with her own.

"Any news?"

"Well, I've been thinking a bit and keeping my eyes open."

"Yes."

"And I've noticed that the fella who wanted to leave ain't around."

"Perhaps he's left, gone home."

"No, no. Not in the book."

"What book?"

"I found out there's a book. By the gatehouse. Records the ins and outs, if you know what I mean. Took a walk over to 'ave a word with old Archie the other day, and it looks like the bread delivery is all that's gone on in a week."

"And Jenkins?"

"Chummy as ever."

"Billy, I think it's time for you to leave."

"No—no, Miss. I'm safe as 'houses. Sort of like it 'ere, really. And no one's looking twice at me."

"You don't know that, Billy."

"One more night, then, anyway. I want to find out where this fella's gone. I tell you, I keep my eyes peeled, like I said, and one minute 'e's there and the next 'e's not. Mind you, there is someone in the sick bay."

"And who tends the sick bay?"

"Well, there's a fella who was a medic in the war, 'e does all your basic stuff, like. Then this other fella came up today. In a car, doctor's bag and all. I was working in the front garden at the time. Dead ringer for Jenkins actually. Bit bigger, mind. But you could see it round 'ere." Billy rubbed his chin and jaw. "'round the chops."

"Yes. I know who that is," Maisie whispered as she wrote notes on an index card.

"What, Miss?"

"No. Nothing. Billy, listen, I know you think that Jenkins is essentially a good man, but I fear that you may now be in some danger. You are an innocent person brought into my work because I needed information. That must change. It's time for you to leave."

Billy Beale turned to Maisie and looked deeply into her eyes. "You know, Miss, when we first met, when I said I'd seen you before, after that shell got me leg. Did you recognize me?"

Maisie closed her eyes briefly, looked at the ground to compose herself and then directly at Billy. "Yes. I recognized you, Billy. Some people you never forget."

"I know. I told you, I would never forget you and that doctor. Could've 'ad my leg off, 'e could. Anyone else would've just chopped the leg and got me out of there. But 'im, that doctor, even in those conditions, like, 'e tried to do more."

Billy gazed out across the land to The Retreat.

"And I know what 'appened. I know what 'appened after I left. 'eard about it. Amazing you weren't killed."

Maisie did not speak but instead slowly began to remove the pins that held her long black hair in a neat chignon. She turned her head to one side and lifted her hair. And as she drew back the tresses, she revealed a purple scar weaving a path from just above her hairline at the nape of her neck, through her hair and into her scalp.

"Long hair, Billy, hides a multitude of sins."

His eyes beginning to smart, Billy looked toward The Retreat again, as if checking to see that everything was still in its place. He said nothing about the scar, but pressed his lips together and shook his head.

"I'll stay 'ere until tomorrow, Miss. I know you need me to be at this place at least another day. I'll meet you 'ere at half past seven tomorrow, and I'll 'ave me kit bag with me. No one will see me, don't you worry."

Billy did not wait for Maisie to respond, but clambered back through the fence. And as she had each evening for more than a week now, Maisie watched Billy limp across the field to The Retreat.

"I'll be here," whispered Maisie. "I'll be here."

Maisie did not go to bed, and was not encouraged to do so by Maurice. She knew that the time of reckoning could come soon. Yes, if Jenkins was to make his move, it would be now. If not, then the investigation would lie dormant; the file would remain open.

She sat on the floor, legs crossed, watching first the night grow darker, then the early hours of the morning edge slowly toward dawn. The clock struck the half hour. Half past four. She breathed in deeply and closed her eyes. Suddenly the telephone rang, its shrill bell piercing the quiet of the night. Maisie opened her eyes and came to her feet quickly. Before it could ring a second time, she answered the call.

"Billy."

"Yes. Miss, something's goin' on down 'ere."

"First, Billy—are you safe?"

"No one's seen me leave. I crept out, kept close to the wall, came straight across the field and through the fence to the old dog 'n' bone 'ere."

"Good. Now—what's happening?"

Billy caught his breath. "I couldn't sleep last night, Miss. Kept thinking about, y'know, what we'd talked about."

"Yes, Billy."

Maisie turned to the door as she spoke and nodded her head to Maurice, who had entered the room dressed as he had been when he had bidden her goodnight. He had not slept either.

"Anyway. 'bout—well, blimey, must 've been over 'alf an hour ago now—I 'eard a bit of a racket outside, sounded like a sack bein' dragged around. So, I goes to the window to see what's what."

"Go on, Billy. And keep looking around you."

"Don't you worry, Miss, I'm keepin' me eyes peeled. Anyway, it was 'im, bein' dragged away down the dirt road."

"Who?"

"The fella that wanted to leave. Could see 'im plain as day, in the light coming from the door."

"Where does the dirt road lead to—the quarry?"

"Yes, Miss. That's right."

Maisie took a deep breath.

"Billy, here's what you are to do. Go into the hamlet. Keep very close to the side of the road. Do not be seen. There may be someone else coming from that direction heading for The Retreat. Do not let him see you. Meet me by the oak tree on the green. Go now."

Maisie replaced the receiver. There was no time to allow Billy Beale another question before ending the call.

Maurice handed Maisie her jacket and hat and took up his own. She opened her mouth to protest, but was silenced by Maurice's raised hand.

"Maisie, I never, ever said that you were too young for the many risks you have taken. Do not now tell me to stay at home because I am too old!"

***

*B*illy clambered out of the ditch and stretched his wounded leg. Kneeling had made him sore, and he rubbed at his cramped muscles. The sound of a breaking twig in the silence of the early morning hours, as leaves rustled in a cool breeze, made him snap to attention. He remained perfectly still.

"Now I'm bleedin' 'earin' things," whispered Billy into the dawn chill that caught his chest and forced his heart to beat faster, so fast he could hear it echo in his ears.

"Like waitin' for that bleedin' whistle to go off for the charge, it is."

Billy took his bag by the handle and slung it over his shoulder. Looking both ways, he began to cross the road to take advantage of the overhanging branches that would shield him as he made his way along the lane into the hamlet. But as he moved, his leg cramped again.

"Blimey, come on, come on, leg! Don't bleedin' let me down now."

Billy tried to straighten his body, but as he moved, his war wounds came to life, shooting pain through him as he tried to take a step.

"I'm afraid you've let yourself down, William," a man's voice intoned.

"Who's that? Who's there?" Billy fell backward, his arms flailing as he tried to regain balance.

Adam Jenkins stepped out of the half-light in front of Billy. Archie stood with him, together with two other longtime residents of The Retreat.

"Desertion is what we call it. When you leave before your time."

"I just, well, I just wanted to 'ave a bit of a walk, Sir," said Billy, nervously running his fingers through his hair.

Maisie Dobbs

"Well, a fine time to be walking, William. Or perhaps you prefer 'Billy?' A fine time for a stroll."

Jenkins signaled to Archie and the other men, who pinioned Billy's hands behind his back and tightly secured a black cloth across his eyes.

"Desertion, Billy. Terrible thing. Nothing worse in a soldier. Nothing worse."

Maisie drew up alongside the oak tree in the hamlet of Hart's Lea. There was no sign of Billy.

"Maurice, he's not here," said Maisie, as she swung the car in the direction of The Retreat, and accelerated. "We've got to find him."

Maisie drove at high speed along the lane to The Retreat, scanning the side of the road as she maneuvered the car. Beside her Maurice was silent. Abruptly she swung the car onto the verge by the beech tree and got out. Kneeling on the verge, she ran her fingers over the rough ground. In the early light of morning, she could see signs of a scuffle.

Yes, they had Billy.

Maurice climbed out of the car, with some difficulty, and joined Maisie.

"I must find him, Maurice. His life is in danger."

"Yes, go, Maisie. But I would advise that this is the time—"

Maisie sighed, "Of course, you're right, Maurice. Over here I think we might be in luck."

Lowering herself into the ditch on the other side of the road, near the perimeter fence of The Retreat, Maisie reached down, and pulled up Billy's makeshift telephone.

"Thank God! They didn't find it—they must have arrived just after he replaced the receiver. I'm not really sure how you—"

"Go now, Maisie. I will see to it. I may be old, but such things are not beyond the scope of my intelligence."

Maisie rushed over to the MG, opened the door, and took out the black jacket that Maurice had handed her when they left the house. Pulling on the jacket, Maisie was about to close the door of the car, when she stopped and instead reached behind the driver's seat for her bag. She hurriedly took out the new Victorinox knife, slipped it into the pocket of her trousers, and closed the car door. Maisie crossed the road, pausing only to touch Maurice's shoulder with her hand, before pulling back the wire and squeezing through the hole in the fence. She ran quickly across the field, aided by the grainy light of sunrise.

At first Maisie took care to step quietly past the farm buildings, but soon realized that they were deserted, a fact that did not surprise her. "He will probably want to set an example to the residents," Maisie had said to Maurice as they left the dower house. "He'll have an audience. An 'innocuous' little man would love an audience."

Maisie squinted at the silver watch pinned to the left breast pocket of her jacket. The watch that to this day was her talisman. Time had survived with her, but now time was marching on. Billy was in grave danger. She must be quick

Within minutes she reached the quarry, and as she ran, the memories cascaded into her mind. She must get to him. Simon had saved him, and so must she. She must get to Billy.

She slowed to a walk and quietly crept into the mouth of the quarry, keeping close to the rough sandstone entrance so that she would not be seen. Maisie gasped as she scanned the tableau before her. A sea of men were seated on chairs, facing a raised platform with a wooden structure placed upon it. With their damaged faces, once so very dear to a mother, father, or sweetheart, they were now reduced to gargoyles by a war that, for them, had never ended. There were men without noses or jaws, men who searched for light with empty eye sockets, men with only half a face where once a full-formed smile had beamed. She choked back tears, her blue eyes searching for Billy Beale.

As the rising sun struggled against the remains of night, Maisie realized that the wooden structure was a rough gallows. Suddenly, the men's faces moved. Maisie followed their gaze. Jenkins walked toward the platform from another direction. He took center stage, and raised his hand. At his signal Archie and another man came toward the platform, half guiding, half dragging a blindfolded man between them. It was Billy. As she watched, Billy—jovial, willing Billy Beale—who surely would have given his life for her, was placed on his knees in front of the gallows, and held captive in the taut hangman's noose. It would need only one sharp tug from the two men working in unison to do its terrible work.

The audience stood unmoved, yet in fear; their eyes, behind the terrible deformities war had dealt them, showing terror. And in that dreadful moment when she thought that the strong, fast legs that had borne her to this place had become paralyzed, Maisie was haunted by the past and present coming together as one. She knew that she must take action, but what could stop this madness immediately, without the men rising up against her—such was Jenkins's control over them—and without risking Billy's immediate death? "Fight like with like," she whispered, remembering one of Maurice's lessons, and as she uttered the words, a picture flashed into her mind, a memory, of being on the train with Iris, of watching the soldiers as they marched off to battle, singing as they beat a path to death's door. There was no secret route along which she could stealthily make her way to Billy's side. She had only one option. For just a second Maisie closed her eyes, pulled her shoulders back, and stood as tall as she could. She breathed deeply, cleared her throat, and began to walk slowly toward the platform. For Billy she must be a fearless warrior. And as the men became aware of her presence, she looked at their faces, smiled kindly, and began to sing.

> There's a rose that grows
> In No-Mans' Land
> And it's wonderful to see

Though it's sprayed with tears
It will live for years
In my garden of memory . . .

As she gained on the platform, now keeping her eyes focused on
Jenkins, Maisie heard a deep resonant voice join her own. Then
another voice echoed alongside her, and another, until her lone voice
had become one with a choir of men singing in unison, their low
voices a dawn chorus that echoed around the quarry.

It's the one red rose
The soldier knows
It's the work of the Master's hand
'Mid the war's great curse,
Stands the Red Cross Nurse
She's the Rose of No-Man's Land . . .

Maisie banished all fear as she stood on the ground below Jenkins.
Dressed in the uniform of an officer who had served in the Great War,
he stood with eyes blazing. She avoided looking at Billy, instead meeting Jenkins's glare while ascending the steps to the platform. The men
continued to sing softly behind her, finding solace in the gentle
rhythm of a much-loved song. Standing in front of Jenkins, she maintained eye contact. Her action had silenced him, but in mirroring his
posture, she knew of his inner confusion, his torment, and his pain.
And in looking into his eyes, she knew that he was mad.

"Major Jenkins . . ." She addressed the officer in front of her, who
seemed to regain a sense of place and time.

"You can't stop this, you know. This man is a disgrace to his country," he pointed his baton towards Billy. "A deserter."

"By what authority, Major Jenkins? Where are your orders?"

Jenkins's eyes flashed in confusion. Maisie heard Billy groan as the
rope cut into his neck.

"Has this man received a court-martial? A fair trial?"

Voices murmured behind her as Jenkins's audience, the wounded "guests" of The Retreat, began to voice dissent. She had to be in control of each moment, for if one word were out of place, the men could easily become an angry mob—dangerous not only to this mind-injured man in front of her but to Billy and herself.

"A trial? Haven't got time for trials, you know. Got to get on with it! Got a job to do, without having to tolerate time wasters like this one." He pointed his baton at Billy again, then brought it to his side and tapped it against his shining leather boots.

"We *do* have time, Major." Maisie held her breath as she took her chance. Billy had begun to choke. She had to make her bravest move.

Though Maurice had cautioned Maisie in the use of touch, he had also stressed the power inherent in physical connection: "When we reach to place a hand on a sore knee or an aching back, we are really reaching into our primordial healing resources. Judicious use of the energy of touch can transform, as the power of our aura soothes the place that is injured."

"Major Jenkins," said Maisie, in a low voice. "It's over. . . the war is over. You can rest now . . . you can rest. . . ." And as she whispered the words, she raised a hand, stepped closer to him, and instinctively held her palm against the place where she felt his heart to be. For a moment there was no movement as Jenkins closed his eyes. He began to tremble, and with her fingertips Maisie could feel him struggle to regain control of his body—and his mind.

The onlookers gasped as Jenkins began to weep. Falling to his knees, he pulled his Webley Mk IV service revolver from its holster and held the barrel to his head.

"No," said Maisie firmly, but softly, and with a move so gentle that Jenkins barely felt the revolver leave his grasp, she took the weapon from his hand.

At that moment, as the audience watched in a stunned silence that paralyzed all movement, she saw lights beginning to illuminate the entrance to the quarry. Uniformed men ran toward the platform, shouting, "Stop, police!" She abandoned Jenkins, who was rocking back and forth, clasping his arms about his body, and moaning with a rasping, guttural cry.

Maisie pushed the revolver into her pocket and moved quickly toward the lifeless body of Billy Beale. Archie and his assistant were nowhere to be seen. Maisie quickly took out her pocket knife and, holding back the flesh on Billy's neck with the fingers of her left hand, she slipped the blade against the rope, and freed Billy from the hangman's noose. As Billy fell toward her, Maisie tried to take his weight, and stumbled. She was aware that Jenkins was now flanked by two policemen, and that all around her the frozen moment had thawed into frenzied activity.

"Billy, look at me, Billy," said Maisie, regaining balance.

She slapped his face on both sides, and felt his wrist for a pulse.

Billy choked, and his eyes rolled up into their sockets as his hands instinctively clamored to free his neck from the constriction that he could still feel at his throat.

"Steady on, Miss, steady on, for Gawd's sake."

Billy choked, his gas-damaged lungs wheezing with the enormous effort of fighting for breath. As he tried to sit up, Maisie supported him with her arms around his shoulders.

"It's awright, Miss. I'm not a goner. Let me get some air. Some air."

"Can you see me, Billy?"

Billy Beale looked at Maisie, who was now on her knees beside him.

"I'm awright now that you're 'ere, even if you are a bit 'eavy 'anded. Mind you . . ." he coughed, wiping away the blood and spittle that came up from his throat, "I thought you'd never get over chattin' wiv that bleedin' lunatic there." Billy pointed toward Jenkins, then brought his hand back to his mouth as he coughed another deep, rasping cough.

"May I have a word, Miss Dobbs?" The man looking down at her beckoned the police doctor to attend to Billy, then held out a hand to Maisie. Grasping his outstretched hand, she drew herself up to a standing position and brushed back the locks of black hair that were hanging around her face. The man held out his right hand again. "Detective Inspector Stratton, Murder Squad. Your colleague is in good hands. Now, if I may have a word."

Maisie quickly appraised the man, who was standing in front of her. Stratton was more than six feet tall, well-built, and confident, without the posturing that she had seen before in men of high rank. His hair, almost as black as her own, except for wisps of gray at the temples, was swept back. He wore corduroy trousers and a tweed jacket with leather at the elbows. He held a brown felt hat with a black grosgrain band in his left hand. Like a country doctor, observed Maisie. "Yes. Yes, of course, Detective Inspector Stratton. I . . . ."

". . . Should have known better, Miss Dobbs? Yes, probably, you should have known better. However, I have been briefed by Dr. Blanche, and I realize that you were in a situation where not a moment could be lost. Suffice it to say that this is not the time for discussion or reprimand. I must ask you, though, to make yourself available for questioning in connection with this case, perhaps tomorrow?"

"Yes, but—"

"Miss Dobbs, I have to attend to the suspect now, but, in the meantime—"

"Yes?" Maisie was flushed, tired, and indignant.

"Good work, Miss Dobbs. A calm head—very good work." Detective Inspector Stratton shook hands with Maisie once again, and was just about to walk away when she called him back.

"Oh, Inspector, just a moment. . . ." Maisie held out the service revolver she had taken from Jenkins. "I think you'll need this for your evidence bag."

Stratton took the revolver, checked the barrel, and removed the ammunition before placing the weapon safely in his own pocket. He inclined his head toward Maisie and smiled, then turned toward Jenkins, who was now flanked by two members of the Kent Constabulary. Maisie watched as Stratton commenced the official caution: "'You are not obliged to say anything unless you wish to do so, but what you say may be put into writing and given in evidence.'"

Maisie looked around at Billy, to satisfy herself that he was safe—he was now on his feet and speaking with the doctor—then surveyed the scene in front of her. She watched as Maurice Blanche walked among the terrified audience of 'old soldiers' who still seemed so very young, his calming presence infectious as he stood with the men, placing a hand on a shoulder for support, or holding a weeping man to him unashamedly. The men seemed to understand his strength, and clustered around to listen to his soothing words. She saw him motion to Stratton, who sent policemen to lead the residents of The Retreat away one by one. They were men for whom the terror of war had been replayed and whose trust had been shattered. First by their country, and now by a single man. They were men who would have to face the world in which there was no retreat. Maurice was right, they were all innocents. Perhaps even Jenkins.

Jenkins was now in handcuffs and being led to a waiting Invicta police car that had been brought into the mouth of the quarry, his unsoiled polished boots and Sam Browne belt shining against a pressed uniform. Not a hair on his head was out of place. He was still the perfectly turned-out officer.

# CHAPTER TWENTY-EIGHT

o, what I want to know," said Billy, sitting in Maurice Blanche's favorite wing chair, next to the fireplace in the dower house, "Is 'ow did you get on to Adam Jenkins in the end. And I tell you, 'e certainly 'ad me there. I was beginnin' t'think 'e was a crackin' bloke."

Maisie sat on a large cushion on the floor sipping tea, while Maurice was comfortable on the sofa opposite Billy. She set down her cup and saucer on the floor and rubbed at her cold feet.

"I had a feeling, here." Maisie touched the place between her ribs, at the base of her breastbone. "There was something wrong from the beginning. Of course you know about Vincent. And the others. That was a mistake on Jenkins's part, suggesting to Vincent's family that he be interred at Nether Green because it's a big cemetery, with lots of soldiers' graves. It was a mistake because he used it several times."

Maisie took a sip of her tea and continued. "I questioned the coincidence of several men buried with only their Christian names to identify them. Then I found out that they were all from the same place. The Retreat."

"And what else?" asked Billy, waving a hand to disperse the smoke from Maurice's pipe.

"A mistrust—on my part—of someone who wields so much power. The inspiration for The Retreat was admirable. Such places have worked well in France. But, for the most part, those places were set up for soldiers with disfiguring wounds to go to on holiday, not to be there forever. And using only Christian names was Jenkins's innovation. Stripping away a person's name is a very basic manner of control. It's done in all sorts of institutions, such as the army—for example, they called you 'corporal,' not 'Billy,' or possibly—rarely—even 'Beale.'"

Billy nodded.

"The irony is, that it was one of the first men to live at The Retreat, Vincent Weathershaw, who gave him the idea for the Christian-names-only mode of address."

Maisie caught her breath and continued.

"More evidence came to hand after you went to The Retreat. Each cause of death was different—there was even a drowning listed—yet each could be attributed to asphyxiation of some sort. To the untrained eye, an accident. The word of the examiner would not be questioned. No police were involved, they were considered to be deaths from 'accidental' or 'natural' causes—and as the men were all seeking relief from torment by coming to The Retreat, the families had no lingering questions. In fact, there was often relief that the loved one would not have to suffer anymore," said Maisie.

"Indeed." Maurice looked at Maisie, who did not return his gaze. He took up the story. "Then there was Jenkins's own history. How could someone who had given his superiors cause to refer to him as "innocuous" have gained such power? Maisie telephoned the doctor who had supervised his care at Craiglockhart—the hospital in Scotland where shell-shocked officers were sent during the war. The poet Siegfried Sassoon was there."

"Well, sir, I ain't never bin much of a one for poetry." Billy waved smoke away from his face once more.

"The doctor, who is now at the Maudsley psychiatric hospital in

London, informed me that Jenkins's mental state was not as serious as
some," said Maisie, "But there was cause for concern."

"I'll bet there was." Billy rubbed at the red weal left by the rope at
his neck.

"You know what happened to deserters, Billy?"

Billy looked at his hands and turned them back and forth, inspecting first the palms, then his knuckles. "Yes. Yes I do, Miss."

"They were taken and shot. At dawn. We talked about it. Some of
them just young boys of seventeen or eighteen—they were scared out
of their wits. It's been rumored that there was even a case of two
being shot for accidentally falling asleep while on duty." Tears came to
Maisie's eyes and she pursed her lips together. "Jenkins was the commanding officer instructed to deal with a desertion. 'Innocuous'
Jenkins. Much against his will—and apparently he did question his
orders—he was instructed to preside over such an execution."

"And . . ."

Billy sat forward in the leather chair.

"He carried out orders. Had he not, then he might well have been
subject to the same fate. To disobey would have been insubordination."

Maisie got up from the floor and walked to the window. Maurice's
eyes followed her, then turned to Billy. "The mind can do strange things,
Billy. Just as we can become used to pain, so we can become used to
experience, and in some cases a distasteful experience is made more
palatable if we embrace it."

"Like putting sugar in the castor oil."

"Something of that order. Jenkins's sugar was the power he
claimed. One might argue that it was the only way for him to stomach the situation. He was not a man strong in spirit. So close was he
to the act of desertion that it made him detest the actual deserter, and
in meting out this terrible, terrible punishment, he maintained control over the part of him that would have run away. He became very
good at dealing with battlefield deserters. Indeed, he enjoyed a level
of success, we understand, that he did not enjoy in other areas of
responsibility."

*Jacqueline Winspear*

Maurice looked again at Maisie, who turned to face Billy. "Jenkins's idea of founding The Retreat was formed in good faith. But once again the need for control emerged. The chain of murders began when one of the men wanted to leave. Jenkins felt the man's decision keenly. He was, in effect, deserting The Retreat. For Jenkins, his mind deeply affected by the war, there was only one course of action. And then one death made the others easier."

"Blimey," whispered Billy.

"Had you been at The Retreat longer, you too would have heard it said that it was difficult to depart with one's life. Obviously he could not shoot a man—it would not be easy for the medical examiner to disguise the truth of such a wound—but he could use a more dramatic method. This gallows in the quarry would not break a man's neck, but would deprive the body of oxygen for just about long enough to take a life. A death that it would be easy to attribute to suicide or accident. And he must have been in a hurry with you, Billy, because with the others, a heavy cloth was wrapped around the noose. The rope marks were not as livid as the necklace you're now wearing."

Billy once again rubbed at his neck. "I reckon it's all bleedin' wrong, this 'ere business of shootin' deserters. I tell you, 'alf of us didn't know what the bloody 'ell we were supposed to be doin' over there anyway. I know the officers, specially the young ones, didn't."

Maurice pointed the stem of his pipe at Billy, ready to comment. "Interesting point, Billy. You may be interested to know that Ernest Thurtle, an American by birth, now the MP for Whitechapel, has worked hard in Parliament to have the practice banned—it wouldn't surprise me if a new law were passed in the next year or so."

"About bloody time, too! And talkin' about deserters, what's the connection with Vincent Weathershaw? Remember me finding out that there was something that went on with 'im?"

"Yes," continued Maisie. "From what we know, Weathershaw was disciplined because he complained about the practice of military execution. He was vocal about it too, upsetting higher-ups. He was injured before he could be stripped of his commission and court-martialed for insubordination."

Billy whistled between his teeth. "This gets worse."

"It did for Weathershaw. He came to The Retreat in good faith, a terribly disfigured man. He had known something of Jenkins while in convalescence, but at The Retreat he found out about his reputation as a battlefield executioner. Vincent had put two and two together, so Jenkins decided he had to go. He'd suffered terrible depression, poor man, so accident or suicide was entirely believable."

"Poor sod. What about this other Jenkins?"

"Cousin. We thought Armstrong Jenkins was a brother, but he's not, he's a cousin. Surprisingly, Adam Jenkins was not in it for the money. His reward was the sensation of control. King of all he surveyed, and with a legion of serfs who listened to his every word, and despite what they heard, adored him. And that is the part of the puzzle that is most intriguing."

"Indeed," said Maurice. "Most intriguing."

"That despite the rumors, such as they were, and the demise of those who 'left' The Retreat, Jenkins was held in very high regard by the men."

Billy blushed.

"An interesting phenomenon," said Maurice. "Such control over a group of people. It is, I fear, something that we shall see again, especially in times such as this, when people are seeking answers to unfathomable questions, for leadership in their uncertainty, and for a connection with others of like experience. Indeed, there is a word to describe such a group, gathered under one all-powerful leader, taken from the practice of seeking answers in the occult. What Jenkins founded could be described as a cult."

"This is givin' me the shivers," said Billy, rubbing his arms.

Maisie took up the story again. "Armstrong Jenkins was the one who persuaded his cousin to have the men sign over their assets. And for a man coming into The Retreat, so desperately unhappy that he would willingly cloister himself, it was not such a huge step.

Armstrong held the purse strings. He came to this area to work as medical examiner when The Retreat opened. Like his cousin, his is a case of power laced with evil."

"I'll say. Gaw blimey, that was close."

"I made three telephone calls before our last meeting in the lane, and what I learned alerted me to the level of your danger. One was to the Maudsley, to speak to Adam Jenkins's doctor; one was to the county coroner, to confirm Armstrong Jenkins's history, and finally one to Maurice's friend, the Chief Constable, to inform him of my suspicions. It was his intention to begin an investigation of The Retreat the following day—but of course events overtook him. Billy, I wanted you to relinquish your task as soon as you told me that another man wished to leave The Retreat. But you were adamant."

Billy met Maisie's eyes with his own. "I told you, Miss, I didn't want to let you down. I wanted to do something for you. Like you and that doctor did for me. You never did it 'alf-'earted because you was all tired out. You had men linin' up all over the place, yet you saved my leg. When I got 'ome, the doc said it was the best bit of battlefield leg saving 'e'd ever seen."

Tears smarted in Maisie's eyes. She thought the pain had ceased. She hated this tide of tears that came in, bidden by truth.

"And I know it's a bit off the subject, like, but I wanted to ask you somethin', and I . . . I dunno . . . I just felt you didn't want to talk about it, and who can blame you? But . . . what 'appened to 'im? What 'appened to that doctor?"

A strained silence fell upon the room. The excited explanation of events at The Retreat gave way to embarrassment. Maurice sighed, his brow furrowed, as he watched Maisie, who sat with her head in her hands.

"Look, I 'ope I ain't said anythin' wrong . . . I'm sorry if it was out of turn. It ain't none of my business, is it? I thought you were a bit sweet on each other, that's all. I remember thinking that. So I thought you'd know. The man saved my leg, probably even my life. But I'm sorry. Shouldn't 'ave said anythin'." Billy picked up his jacket as if to leave the room.

"Billy. Wait. Yes. Yes, I should have told you. About Captain Lynch. It's only fair that you should know. After what you've done for me, it's only fair."

Maurice moved to Maisie's side and took her hand in his. She answered Billy's question.

# CHAPTER TWENTY-NINE

t seemed to Maisie that no sooner had she returned to the casualty clearing station, from her leave at home with Simon, than droves of injured were brought in. As day stretched into night, the few hours' sleep that Maisie managed to claim each night offered only a brief respite from the war.

"Did you remember to tie the scarf, Maisie?" asked Iris, referring to the cloth tied to the tent pole, which would indicate to the orderlies that the nurses inside were on the first shift to be called if wounded came in at night.

"Yes. It's there, Iris. 'Night."

"'Night, Maisie."

Often Maisie would fall into a deep sleep immediately upon climbing into her cot. Time and again her dreaming mind took her back to Chelstone, walking toward her father in the orchard. Yet as she came closer to him, he moved away, reaching up to pick rosy red apples before moving on. She would call out to him, and he would turn and wave, but he did not stop, he did not wait for her. This Frankie Dobbs simply picked the deep red apples, placed them in his wicker basket, and moved through the long grass of late summer. Such was the weight he carried, that rich red juice ran from the bottom of the basket, leaving a trail for her to follow. She tried to run faster, yet her long, heavy woolen dress soaked up the red juice, clung to her legs, and caught in the grass, and as the distance between them extended, Maisie cried out to him. "Dad, Dad, Dad!"

"Bloody hell, whatever is the matter with you?"

Iris sat up in bed and looked across at Maisie who, in her sudden wakefulness, lay on her back staring straight toward the top of the main tent pole, her violet eyes following drops of rainwater as they squeezed through the canvas and ran down to the ground.

"Are you all right?"

Iris leaned over and nudged Maisie.

"Yes. Yes, thanks. Bad dream. It was a bad dream."

"Not even time to get up yet. Brrr. Why doesn't it ever seem to get warm here? Here we are in the third week of May, and I'm freezing!"

Maisie did not answer, but drew the blankets closer to her jaw.

"We've got another half an hour. Then let's get up and go and get ourselves a mug of that strong tea," said Iris, making an attempt to reclaim the comfort of deep sleep.

"Looks like we've got some 'elp coming in today, ladies."

One of the medical officers sat down with Iris and Maisie, ready to gossip as he sipped scalding tea and took a bite out of the thick crust of bread.

"Lord, do we need it! There's never enough doctors, let alone nurses," said Iris, taking her mug and sitting down on a bench next to Maisie.

"What's happened?" asked Maisie.

"Think they're coming in from the hospital up the line. We've been getting so many in each day 'ere, and someone pushing a pencil at a desk finally got wind of it. Some docs are being moved. Down 'ere first."

Maisie and Iris looked at each other. She had written to Simon only yesterday. He had said nothing to her about being moved. Was it possible that he was one of the doctors being sent to the casualty clearing station?

"Mind you, they might not like it much, what with them shells coming in a bit closer lately," added the medical officer.

"I thought the red cross meant that we were safe from the shelling," said Iris, cupping her hands around her mug.

"Well, it's supposed to be safe. Red crosses mark neutral territory."

"When will they arrive . . . from the hospital?" asked Maisie, barely disguising her excitement. Excitement laced with trepidation.

"End of the week, by all accounts."

It was late afternoon when new medical personnel began to appear. Maisie was walking through the ward, with men in various stages of recovery waiting for transportation to a military hospital in beds on either side of her, when she saw the silhouette she knew so well on the other side of the canvas flap that formed a wall between the ward and the medicines area. It was the place where nurses prepared dressings, measured powders, made notes, and stood to weep, just for a moment, when another patient was lost.

He was here. In the same place. They were together.

Without rushing, and continuing to check her patients as she made her way toward Simon, Maisie struggled to control her beating heart. Just before she drew back the flap of canvas, she took a deep breath, closed her eyes, then walked through into the medicines area.

He was on his own, looking through the pile of records, and familiarizing himself with the stocks of medicines and dressings. As Maisie entered, Simon looked up. For a moment neither moved.

Simon broke the silence, holding out his hand and taking hers.

"Why didn't you tell me in your letter?" whispered Maisie, looking around, fearful that someone might see her speaking with Simon.

"I didn't know I'd be sent. Not until yesterday." He smiled. "But now we're together. Couldn't believe my luck, Maisie."

She held his hand tighter. "I am so glad. So glad that you are here. And safe."

"Good omen, don't you think? That we're here in the same place."

In the distance Maisie heard a wounded soldier calling for her, "Sister. In 'ere. Quick."

Simon held onto Maisie's hand for a second before she rushed to attend to her patient.

"I love you, Maisie," he said, and brought her hand to his lips.

She nodded, smiled, and ran to her duties.

❖

Working side by side was easier than either had thought it might be. For three days, wounded were brought in to the hospital and, time and time again, Maisie saw another side of the Simon she loved, the Simon who had stolen her heart as she danced in a blue silk dress. He was a brilliant doctor.

Even under the most intense pressure, Simon Lynch worked not just to save a life but to make that soldier's life bearable when the soldiering was done. With Maisie at his side, ready to pass instruments to him even before he asked—to clear the blood from wounds as he brought shattered bones together and stitched vicious lacerations— Simon used every ounce of knowledge garnered in the hospitals of England and in the operating tents of the battlefield.

"Right, on to the next one," said Simon, as one patient was moved and orderlies pushed forward with another soldier on a stretcher.

"What's waiting for us in the line?"

"Sir, we've got about a dozen legs, four very nasty heads, three chests, three arms, and five feet—and that's only as far as the corner. Ambulances coming in all the time, sir."

"Make sure we get the ones who can travel on the road as soon as possible. We need the room, and they need to be at the base hospital."

"Yes sir."

The orderlies hurried away to bring in the next soldier, while Simon looked down at the wounded man now dependent upon his judgment and skill, a young man with hair the color of sun-drenched wheat, and a leg torn apart by shrapnel. A young man who watched his every move so intently.

"Will you be able to save me leg, sir? Don't want to be an ol' peg-leg, do I?"

"Don't worry. I'll do my best. Can't have you not able to chase the ladies, can we, Corporal?" Simon smiled at the man, despite his exhaustion.

Maisie looked up at Simon, then down at the corporal, and as Simon removed the shrapnel, she cleaned the bleeding wounds so that he could see the extent of the injury. To keep the soldier's spirits up—this man so conscious of everything happening around him—Maisie would look up for a second from her work and smile at him. And as Simon cut skin and brought together flesh, muscle, and bone that had been torn apart, the soldier took heart. For though he could not see Maisie's smile through the white linen mask that shielded part of her face, her warm blue eyes told the soldier what he wanted to hear. That all would be well.

"Right. On your way to Blighty you are, my man. Done the best for you here, and God knows you've done your best for Blighty. The sooner you get home, the sooner they'll get you moving again. Rest assured, Corporal, the leg is staying with its owner."

"Thank you, Captain, sir. Thank you, Sister. Never forget you, ever."

The soldier looked intently at Simon and Maisie, fighting the morphine to remember their faces. A "Blighty," a wound sufficiently severe to warrant being sent back to England—and he would keep his leg. He was a lucky man.

"This one's ready for transport. We're ready for the next one."

Simon called out to the orderlies, and Maisie prepared the table as Corporal William Beale was taken to an ambulance for transfer to a base hospital closer to the port. He would be home within two days.

"*I* feel sorry for the ones who are left," said Maisie.

She and Simon were walking by moonlight along a corridor of ground between the tents, quiet and ready to part quickly should they be seen together. Distant sporadic gunfire punctured their conversation.

"Me too. Though the ones I ache for are the ones who are injured so terribly, so visibly to the face or limbs. And the ones whose injuries can't be seen."

"In the London Hospital, there were many times when a woman cried with relief at the passing of her husband or son. They had wounds that the family couldn't cope with—that people on the street couldn't bear to see."

She moved closer to Simon, who took her hand.

"It'll be over soon. It has to be, Maisie. The war just can't go on like this. Sometimes I feel as if I'm doctoring in a slaughterhouse. One body of raw flesh after another."

Simon stopped and drew Maisie to him and kissed her. "My Maisie of the blue silk dress. I'm still waiting for an answer."

Maisie drew back and looked into Simon's eyes. "Simon, I said to ask again when this is over. When I can see a future."

"That's the trouble," said Simon, beginning to tease her, "Sometimes I think you *can* see the future—and it gives me chills!"

He held her to him again. "I tell you what, Maisie. I promise that I won't ask you again until the war is over. We'll walk together on the South Downs and you can give me your answer then. How about it?"

Maisie smiled and looked into his eyes, bright in the moonlight. Simon, Simon, my love, she thought, how I fear this question. "Yes. Yes, Simon. Ask me again on the South Downs. When the war is over."

And Simon threw back his head and laughed, without thought for who might hear him.

"*God* . . . ."

Simon's lips were drawn across his teeth as he looked at the wound to the soldier's chest, and uttered his plea to the heavens. Maisie immediately began cleaning the hole created by shrapnel, while Simon stanched the flow of blood. Nurses, doctors, anesthetists, orderlies, and stretcher-bearers were everywhere, rushing, running, working to save lives.

Maisie wiped the sweat from Simon's brow and continued to work on the wound. Simon inspected the extent of the injury. Lights flickered, and the tent shuddered.

"God, I can hardly even see in here."

Suddenly it seemed as if the battlefield had come to the hospital. As they worked to save the lives of men being brought in by the dozen, the tent shook again with the impact of a shell at close quarters.

"What the bloody hell . . . ?"

"Sir, sir, I think we're coming under fire," an orderly shouted across to Simon. The operating tent was becoming part of the battlefield itself. Maisie swallowed the sour liquid that had come up from her stomach and into her mouth. She looked at Simon, and to combat her fear, she smiled at him. For one second he returned her smile broadly, then turned again to his patient. They could not stop.

"Well, then. Let's get on with it!"

Let's get on with it.

Those were the last words she heard Simon speak.

*Let's get on with it.*

# CHAPTER THIRTY

*J*t was on a warm afternoon in late September that Maisie stepped out of the MG and looked up at the front of an imposing Georgian building in Richmond. Two Grecian-style columns stood at either side of the steps, which in turn led to the heavy oak doors of the main entrance. The house had once been a grand home with gardens that extended down toward the Thames, where the great river grew broader on its meandering journey from the village of Thame in Oxfordshire, after it emerged as a small stream. From Richmond it would rush on toward London, through the city, and into the sea, fresh and salt water meeting in a swirling mass. Maisie loved to look at the river. There was calm to be found in viewing water. And Maisie wanted to remain calm. She would walk to the water and back, to get her bearings.

The Retreat affair had been brought to its conclusion. Jenkins was now at Broadmoor, incarcerated with those who were considered mentally ill and dangerous. Archie and others involved in Jenkins's wrongdoing at The Retreat were also in institutions where they would find a measure of compassion and solace. They were not being held "at His Majesty's Pleasure" but would be released in time. Other men had returned to families or to their solitary lives, some finding renewed understanding.

Billy Beale found that he did not really enjoy publicity, that it was enough for him to go about his business each day, though if a person needed help, then he, Billy Beale, was the man.

"Of course, the missus don't mind gettin' a bit extra when she goes into that skinflint butcher for a nice bit of lamb, and the attention's brought a bit of a smile to 'er face. But me, I dunno. I'm not your big one for bein' noticed on the street."

Maisie laughed at Billy, who daily told of the latest encounter that came as a result of being the hero of events at The Retreat. He was supervising the placement of her new office furniture, which had just been moved to a larger room on the first floor of a grand building in Fitzroy Square, just around the corner from the Warren Street premises. Finally giving in to Lady Rowan's insistent nagging, Maisie would now be living in her own rooms at the Belgravia house.

"Look, my dear, Julian and I have decided to spend most of our dotage at Chelstone. Of course we'll come up for the Season, and for the theater and so on. But it is so much calmer in Kent, don't you think?"

"Well, Lady Rowan . . . ."

"Oh, no, I suppose it wasn't that calm for you, was it?" Lady Rowan laughed and continued. "Anyway, with James on his way to Canada to take care of our business interests again—thank heavens—the house will be all but empty. We'll have a skeleton staff here, naturally. Maisie, I must insist you take over the third-floor living rooms. In fact, I need you to."

Eventually Maisie concurred. Despite the fact that business was coming in at a respectable clip, Billy was now working for her, and money saved on her own rent would contribute to his wages.

As was Maurice's habit at the closure of a case, Maisie had visited the places of significance in The Retreat affair. During her apprenticeship, she had learned the importance of such a ritual, not only to ensure the integrity of notes that would be kept for reference, but for what Maurice referred to as a "personal accounting," to allow her to begin to work with new energy on the next case.

Maisie had walked once more in Mecklenburg Square, though she did not seek a meeting with Celia Davenham. She had received a letter from Celia after events at The Retreat became headline news. Celia had not referred to the inconsistency with the surname Maisie had given, but instead thanked her for helping to put Vincent's memory to rest.

She took tea at Fortnum & Mason, and at Nether Green Cemetery she placed fresh daisies on the graves of Vincent and his neighbor Donald, and stopped to speak to the groundsman whose son rested in a place overlooked by passing trains.

Maisie drove down to Kent in early September, when the spicy fragrance of dry hops still hung in the warm air of an Indian summer. She passed lorries and open-top buses carrying families back to the East End of London after their annual pilgrimage to harvest the hops, and smiled when she heard the sound of old songs lingering on the breeze. There was nothing like singing together to make a long journey pass quickly.

She drew the car alongside menacing heavy iron gates, and looked up, not at blooms, but this time at blood red rosehips overgrown on the wall. The Retreat was closed. Heavy chains hung on the gates and a sign with the insignia of the Kent Constabulary instructed trespassers to keep out.

*Because* memories had been given new life by her investigation, they too were part of her personal accounting. Maisie wrote letters to Priscilla, now living with her husband and three young sons in the South of France, each boy bearing the middle name of an uncle he would never know; to the famous American surgeon Charles Hayden and his family; and to Iris, who lived in Devon with her mother. Like many young women who came of age in the years 1914–18, Iris had no husband, for her sweetheart had been lost in the war. Maisie's letters did not tell the story of The Retreat, but only reminded the recipients that she thought of them often, and was well.

Now, as Maisie stood in the gardens of the grand house, looking out over the river and reflecting once again upon how much had happened in such a short time, she knew that for her future to spread out in front of her, she must face the past.

She was ready.

The conversation demanded by Billy had untied a knot in her past, one that bound her to the war in France over ten years ago.

Yes, it was time. It was more than time.

"Miss Dobbs, isn't it?"

The woman at the reception desk smiled up at Maisie, her red lipstick accentuating a broad smile that eased the way for visitors to the house. She crossed Maisie's name off the register of expected guests and leaned forward, pointing with her pen.

"Go along the corridor to your left, just over there, then down to the nurses' office. On the right. Can't miss it. They're expecting you. Staff Nurse will take you on from there."

"Thank you."

Maisie followed the directions, walking slowly. Massive flower arrangements on each side of the marble corridor gave forth a fragrance that soothed her, just as the sight of water had calmed her before she entered. Yes, she was glad she had made this decision. For some reason it was not so hard now. She was stronger. The final part of her healing was near.

She tapped on the door of the nurses' office, which was slightly ajar, and looked in.

"I'm Maisie Dobbs, visiting . . . ."

The staff nurse came to her.

"Yes. Good morning. Lovely to have a visitor. We don't see many here."

"Oh?"

"No. Difficult for the families. But you'd be surprised what a difference it makes."

"Yes. I was a nurse."

The staff nurse smiled. "Yes. I know. His mother told us you would be coming. Very pleased, she was. Very happy about it. Told us all . . . well, never mind. Come with me. It's a lovely day, isn't it?"

"Where is he?"

"The conservatory. Lovely and warm in there. The sun shines in. They love the conservatory."

The staff nurse led the way down the corridor, turned left again, and opened a door into the large glass extension to the main building, a huge room filled with exotic plants and trees. Staff Nurse had not stopped talking since they left the nurses' office; they do that to put the new visitors at ease, thought Maisie.

"This was originally called the Winter Gardens, built by the owner so the ladies of the house could take a turn in the winter without going outside into the cold. You can have quite the walk in here. It's a bit too big to call it a conservatory, I suppose. But that's what we call it."

She motioned to Maisie once again. "This way, over to the fountain. Loves the water, he does."

The staff nurse pointed to an open window. "And though it's warm, it doesn't get too warm, if you know what I mean. We open the windows to let the breeze blow through in summer, and it still feels like summer, doesn't it? Ah. Here he is."

Maisie looked in the direction of her outstretched hand, at the man in a wheelchair with his back to them. He was facing the fountain, his head inclined to one side. The staff nurse walked over to the man, stood in front of him, and leaned over to speak. As she did so she gently tapped his hand. Maisie remained still.

"Captain Lynch. Got a visitor, you have. Come to see you. A very beautiful lady."

The man did not move. He remained facing the fountain. The staff nurse smiled at him, tucked in the blanket covering his knees, and then gave Maisie a broad smile before joining her.

"Would you like me to stay for a while?"

"No, no. I'll be fine." Maisie bit her lip.

"Right you are. About twenty minutes? I'll come back for you then. Never find your way out of the jungle alone!"

"Thank you, Staff Nurse."

The woman nodded, checked the time on the watch pinned to her apron, and walked away along the brick path overhung with branches. Maisie went to Simon and sat down in front of him, on the low wall surrounding the fountain. She looked up at this man she had loved so deeply, with all the intensity of a first love, a love forged in the desperate heat of wartime. Maisie looked at the face she had not seen since 1917, a face now so changed.

"Hello, my love," said Maisie.

There was no response. The eyes stared at a place in the distance beyond Maisie, a place that only he could see. The face was scarred, the hair growing in a shock of gray along scars that lay livid across the top of his skull.

Maisie put her hand to his face and, running her fingers along the jagged lines, wondered how it could be that the outcome of wounds was so different. That scars so similar on the outside concealed a different, far deeper injury. In comparison, her own wounds from the same exploding shell had been superficial. Yet Simon's impairment freed him from all sensation of the deeper wound: that of a broken heart.

Simon still did not move. She took his hands in hers and began to speak. "Forgive me, my love. Forgive me for not coming to you. I was so afraid. So afraid of not remembering you as we were together, as you were. . . ."

She rubbed his hands. They were warm to the touch, so warm she could feel the cold in her own.

"At first people asked me why I didn't come, and I said I didn't feel well enough to see you. Then as each month, each year passed, it was as if the memory of you—of us . . . the explosion—were encased in fine tissue-paper."

Maisie bit her lip, constantly kneading Simon's still hands as she spoke her confession. "I felt as if I were looking through a window to my own past, and instead of being transparent, my view was becoming more and more opaque, until eventually the time had passed. The time for coming to see you had passed."

Breathing deeply, Maisie closed her eyes and gathered her thoughts, then continued, her voice less strained as the weight of formerly unspoken words was lightened.

"Dad, Lady Rowan, Priscilla—they all stopped asking after a while. I kept them at arm's length. All except Maurice. Maurice sees through everything. He said that even if people couldn't see my tissue-paper armor, they could feel it, and would not ask again. But he knew, Maurice knew, that I would have to come one day. He said that the truth grows even more powerful when it is suppressed, and that often it takes only one small crack to bring down the wall, to release it. And that's what happened, Simon. The wall I built fell down. And I have been so filled with shame for being unable to face the truth of what happened to you."

Simon sat still in his wheelchair, his hands unmoving, though blood colored his skin.

"Simon, my love. I never did tell you my answer. You see, I knew that something dreadful was going to happen. I couldn't promise you marriage, a future, when I could see no future. Forgive me, dear Simon, forgive me."

Maisie looked around, trying to see what Simon's stare focused upon, and was surprised to see that it was the window, where they were reflected together. She, wearing her blue suit and a blue cloche, her hair in a chignon at the base of her neck. A few tendrils of hair, always the same few tendrils of black hair, had flown free and fallen down around her forehead and cheeks. She could barely see his facial wounds in the reflection. The glass was playing tricks, showing her the old Simon, the young doctor she had fallen in love with so long ago.

Maisie turned to face Simon again. A thin line of saliva had emerged from the side of his mouth and had begun to run down his chin. She took a fresh linen handkerchief from her handbag, wiped the moisture away, and held his hand once again, in silence, until the staff nurse returned.

"How are we, then?" She leaned forward to look at Simon, then turned to smile at Maisie. "And how about you?" she asked.

"Fine. Yes, I'm fine," she swallowed and returned the nurse's smile.

"Good. Bet you've done him the world of good." Staff Nurse looked at Simon again and patted his hand. "Hasn't she, Captain Lynch? Done you a power of good!"

Simon remained perfectly still.

"Let me lead you out of the maze here, Miss Dobbs."

As she walked away, Maisie stopped to look back at Simon, then at his reflection in the windowpane. There he was. Forever the young, dashing Simon Lynch who had stolen her heart.

"Will you come again?"

They had reached the main door of the house. A grand house that was now a home for men stranded in time by the Great War, men trapped in the caverns of their own minds, never to return.

"Yes. Yes I will come again. Thank you."

"Right you are then. Just let us know. Loves a visitor, does Captain Lynch."

$\mathcal{M}$aisie drove back into London, waving to Jack Barker as the MG screeched around the corner into Warren Street, before stopping at her new office in Fitzroy Square. She parked the car in front of the building and watched as Billy positioned a new brass nameplate with tacks, then stood back to appraise the suitability of his placement before securing the plate with screws. He rubbed his chin and moved the plate twice more. Finally he nodded his head, satisfied that he had found exactly the right place for her name, a place that would let callers know that M. Dobbs, Psychologist and Investigator, was open for business.

Maisie continued to watch as Billy worked, polishing the brass to a glowing shine. Then Billy looked up and saw Maisie in the MG. He waved and, rubbing his hands on a cloth, walked down the steps and opened the car door for her to get out.

"Better get weaving, Miss."

"Why, what's happened?"

"That Detective Inspector Stratton from Scotland Yard, the Murder Squad fella. Been on the 'dog and bone' four times already. Urgent, like. Needs to be 'in conference' with you about a case."

"Golly!" said Maisie, grabbing the old black document case from the passenger seat.

"I know. 'ow about that? We'd better get to work, 'adn't we, Miss?"

Maisie raised an eyebrow and walked with Billy to the door. She ran her fingers along the engraving on the brass plate, and turned to her new assistant.

It was time to go to work.

"Well then, Billy—let's get on with it!"

# ACKNOWLEDGMENTS

*F*irst and foremost, I am indebted to Holly Rose, my friend and writing pal who read the initial tentative pages of *Maisie Dobbs* and pressed me to continue. Adair Lara, my writing mentor, was the first to suggest I consider writing fiction, and later, after my "accident horribilis," when *Maisie Dobbs* was barely half written, insisted that convalescence was an ideal time to finish the book—broken arm notwithstanding.

I have been truly blessed in my association with Amy Rennert and Randi Murray of the Amy Rennert Agency, for their wise counsel, wonderful humor, hard work, and most of all, their enthusiastic belief in *Maisie Dobbs*. I am equally blessed in my editor, Laura Hruska, who has the qualities that make her one of the best—including, I believe, psychic powers that enable her to see into my mind.

My godmother, Dorothy Lindqvist, first took me to London's Imperial War Museum when I was a child, an experience that brought a new reality to my grandfather's stories of the Great War of 1914–18. Now, years later, many thanks must go to the museum for its amazing resources, and to the staff who were most helpful during my research visits.

The following people kindly responded to emails and phone calls, providing me with detail that has brought color and texture to the life and experience of Maisie Dobbs: Kate Perry, Senior Archivist at Girton College; Sarah Manser, Director of Press and Public Relations at The Ritz, London; Barbara Griffiths at BT Group Archives, London; John Day, Chairman of the MG Car Club Vintage Register; and Alison Driver of the Press & PR Department of Fortnum & Mason, London. For his dry wit and dogged investigative skills, my utmost gratitude goes to Victor—who knows who he is.

On a personal level thanks must go to my parents, Albert and Joyce Winspear, for their great memories of "old London," and their recollections of my grandfather's postwar experiences; my brother, John, for his encouragement; my friend Kas Salazar, who constantly reminds me of my creative priorities; and last—but certainly not least—my husband and cheerleader, John Morell, for his unfailing support, and for sharing our home with a woman called Maisie Dobbs.

# MAISIE DOBBS

## Jacqueline Winspear

# AN INTRODUCTION TO
## *Maisie Dobbs*

At first glance, Maisie Dobbs's inaugural case as a private investigator looks dreadfully routine: Christopher Davenham, whose wife has been making unexplained weekday excursions from their London home, has employed Maisie to discover whether he is being betrayed. However, Maisie recalls the advice of her enigmatic mentor, Maurice Blanche, that "the extraordinary hides behind the camouflage of the ordinary." Events prove Maurice correct, as the trail of Davenham's wife leads Maisie to a mysterious, carefully guarded home for disabled World War I veterans—and toward a painful confrontation with her own haunting past. Set in England and France in the 1910s and 1920s, *Maisie Dobbs* steps beyond the conventional confines of a mystery novel by telling the story of a brave, brilliant young woman who rises from her working-class origins to study at Cambridge and earn a place as a respected detective. In addition, with astonishing subtlety and sympathy, the novel relives the heroic struggles and devastating losses of those who strove and suffered in the so-called War to End All Wars.

For her re-creation of England in the early decades of the last century, Jacqueline Winspear has drawn upon the experiences and stories of her own family. She has also surrounded her cool but compassionate heroine with a host of meticulously created supporting characters: Simon Lynch, the idealistic young doctor whose sense of humane duty draws him toward an unimaginable fate; Enid, a red-haired servant-girl whose fiery spirit and romantic dreams risk being crushed by class prejudice; Frankie Dobbs, who yearns for his daughter to rise and flourish but fears losing her to a social and intellectual world he cannot comprehend; and Maurice, who shapes Maisie's growing mind in his own image. Above all, however, Winspear recaptures the character of an age—a time when venerable social hierarchies began to totter, when the innocent optimism of youth gave way to the bitter truths of experience, and when shell-shocked veterans wandered the London streets at night, dimly searching for a repose that had been stolen from them forever.

Maisie lives on these pages not only as a detective, but as a subtle master of psychology whose every word and gesture seem calculated to lead to the revelation of truth. But Maisie herself has tried to bury a portion of her past. As the plot of Winspear's mystery unfolds, so, too, does Maisie's personal history, and we discover that the riddles of the visible world may be surpassed by the enigmas of the mind and of the memory.

# A Conversation with Jacqueline Winspear

*1. You write in your novel's acknowledgments about sharing your home with Maisie Dobbs. Do you feel as if she has acquired a reality for you that goes beyond the printed page?*

I'm not sure about a reality that goes beyond the printed page. However, in writing *Maisie Dobbs* I immersed myself in a research process that encompassed not only the Great War, but the late 1920s. When I wasn't writing, I was reading, watching documentaries, or wading through my notes. I wanted Maisie to be a woman of her time, to reflect a certain strength of spirit that was so present with women who had lived through the war, yet I also wanted her to have a uniqueness—in that respect, she took up a lot of space in our home. I think for a time I began every conversation with, "Maisie . . ."

*2. The dedication of your novel gives a brief description of two of your grandparents, whose lives helped to inspire your story. Would you be interested in telling us anything more about them?*

The interesting thing about many people of that Great War generation—especially those who were directly involved in the conflict—is how little they talked about it. People like my grandparents simply "got on with it" so to speak, and certainly it's that same strength of spirit that served the British so well in World War II. There are stories about my grandparents that I find fascinating, but the war stories in particular didn't reach me as oft-told tales, more as something spoken of with quiet gravity. John "Jack" Winspear (my name is in honor of his nickname and my brother is also named John) was a costermonger by trade, a man who sold vegetables from a horse-drawn cart or "barrow." In fact, he was considered quite successful because he had several horses—many costermongers had hand-barrows for their rounds. He had talked about some of his wartime experiences to my father, but only when asked—and probably badgered, if truth be told. I know that at one point he was a stretcher-bearer, with the job of going out into no-man's land to retrieve the dead and dying. Two stories are particularly sad: On one occasion he came across the bodies of a British soldier and a German soldier—each had killed the other with a bayonet and their hands were still on their rifles, their eyes wide open looking at each other in death. The other story is his description of waiting for the sound of the whistle, the signal for the soldiers to go "over the top" and into a hell that they could only hear until the point of scrambling out of the trench, then screaming to keep themselves running. It was after such a battle, when only my grandfather and one other man in his company were left alive, that he was assigned to work as a stretcher-bearer before being sent to join another brigade. My grandfather died at the age of seventy-seven, and to the day he died he was still removing shrapnel from his legs, from wounds received in 1916 at the Battle of the Somme. My maternal grandmother, Clara, worked at the Woolwich Arsenal in London and, apparently, was almost immediately ostracized by many of her neighbors. You see, women who worked in the factories earned good money for that time, and money meant freedom, a freedom of choice and action, which led to assumptions about a young woman's morals. The fact was that the women worked long, exhausting hours in dangerous conditions. Exposure to cordite and other chemicals used in the manufacture of explosives meant that the health of the liver was compromised. Many women suffered from jaundice—the munitions workers were known as "canaries" for the color of their skin—and the chemicals also caused the hair to have coppery streaks with a lot of static that sparked when you brushed your hair. The funny thing is that I didn't actually know she was blind in one eye until a few years ago. I was talking to my mother about Clara—she died when I was eighteen—and had always assumed that she had the family "lazy eye" that myself and several of my cousins inherited from somewhere. Then my mother said, "Oh, no, she was half-blinded at the arsenal," and the story emerged about the explosion, how the girls working alongside her had been killed. That's what I mean about that generation never talking about themselves and their experiences. Part of my research was in having my mother talk to other family members (and Clara had ten children), to see what snippets of stories she had told, then piece them together to understand something of her experiences.

*3. Maisie's first case takes her on an unexpectedly personal journey, and it seems that, for you, writing the book was also a voyage of self-discovery. Are there insights this experience has given you about your family history and about yourself that you would care to share with us?*

Writing *Maisie Dobbs* came to be a personal quest in a way that I would never have imagined. I had written about one third or so of the book, squeezing my writing in between work commitments, etc., and then at one point put it aside as I was so busy. During the time of writing that first part of the story, I'd moved, got married, changed jobs—all big events in the space of a year! Then another life-changing moment occurred: I was out riding my horse and had a horrible accident. As I was flying through the air I immediately knew why it was happening, in the grand scheme of things—I had left my writing behind. I suffered a very badly broken arm and crushed shoulder, which required major surgery and the sort of internal hardware that would look at home in a carpenter's shop. Then came convalescence and a good six months of rehab—I was told that even after physical therapy I would be lucky to get 75 percent of the former use of my arm. A few weeks after surgery I was visiting my friend, Adair Lara, a San Francisco writer—I can still remember this so clearly—and she said, "Convalescence is the ideal time to finish your book!" I pointed to my right arm, which was in a sort of padded sling "structure," and said, "With this?" Adair's response was, "Well you've got a left arm haven't you?" So—to cut a long story short—over half of *Maisie Dobbs* was finished with just one hand on the keyboard, and I was so determined to get the other hand operational that I worked hard at rehab and within three months had the book finished and a good 85 percent of my arm back. The interesting thing is that immediately before my surgery, I was reading *Seabiscuit* by Laura Hillenbrand, and then afterwards read her personal story of overcoming chronic fatigue in order to write. I found that to be so very inspiring. My accident paled into insignificance against such a challenge, so I was determined not to let the accident stop me, and in effect used it to make the dream of writing a novel come true.

*4. Mysteries as a genre offer a rich interaction between fragmentation and completeness; the detective is expected to extract consistency from the scattered clues of a piecemeal reality. Your book seems especially fascinated with fragments, whether they concern the shattered faces of the denizens of The Retreat, the disruption of England's social order, or Maisie's need to come to terms with her own broken past. As you were writing, what were you thinking about all these different kinds of fragments, and how did you see them in relation to one another?*

Looking back, *Maisie Dobbs* came together like a mosaic, blending the stories and images as one would blend fragments of color and texture. I had the separate stories in my mind's eye: Maisie, her life and background; the effects of the Great War on one particular group of veterans; Maisie in 1929 and her quest to discover the truth about The Retreat, and also to establish her reputation now that she was no longer working with Maurice Blanche. Braiding the story with these strands was a very organic process for me.

*5. A writer who tries to re-create a historical period faces some formidable challenges. What research or literary models enabled you to reconstruct the 'teens and 'twenties so convincingly?*

In writing about that time between the start of the Great War and the years leading up to WWII, I was drawing upon the fruits of my own curiosity. In addition, I have been very fortunate in the people I've known and where I grew up. We lived in a small hamlet where, until I was about ten, my brother and I were the only children and my parents were among just a few younger couples. Everyone else was from that older generation of people who came of age in the Great War. It was therefore easy for me to capture the way people interacted, the language, the protocols of communication. I always joked that my early childhood had more in common with that of an Edwardian child than with, say, my cousins who lived in London—I think that has served me well with *Maisie Dobbs*. In addition, I've always loved that time between the wars. I am interested in the history of fashion of that time and used to haunt the Victoria and Albert Museum's costume collection in London. Also, years ago I used to help my friend on her stall in London's Portobello Road market. She dealt mainly in Art Deco jewelry and china, so I used to read a lot about the era—I wanted to sound as if I knew what I was talking about! During the time that I was writing *Maisie Dobbs*, I read only nonfiction in connection with the Great War, the events of the first thirty years of the century, etc. I made several visits to use the archives at London's Imperial War Museum and also walked every street that Maisie walks in London. So many people were helpful in responding to my requests for details, as can be seen in the acknowledgments. I can't say that I had any literary models in writing *Maisie Dobbs*, though.

*6. During the flashback portion at the center of the novel, Maisie is often paired with other young women: Enid, Priscilla Evernden, Iris Rigson. However, in the 1929 segments, she has no female confidante near her own age. What do you think accounts for this difference?*

Maisie's journey from a girl who has tragically lost her mother, to maid, to young woman with her own business, has given her an aura of "aloneness." Enid was her friend, but they were thrown together and in truth were a bit like chalk and cheese. Yet Maisie came to love Enid for her spirit and humor, and recognized that Priscilla also had similar qualities. Again, Maisie and Iris were friends of circumstance rather than choice, but their terrible experiences in France resulted in a different kind of bond. The fact that Maisie has no such friend in 1929 is partly to do with her position and partly due to her commitment to her work. Maisie's "aloneness" comes to a head in *Birds of a Feather*, the second Maisie Dobbs novel.

*7. In her studies with Maurice Blanche, Maisie may have become familiar with the principle of quantum mechanics that holds that one cannot observe something without somehow changing it. She seems particularly aware of the fact that her investigations are bound to change the people involved, and she is admirably careful about wanting to change people only for the better. How were you able to create such a humanly sensitive private investigator?*

Maisie's challenges—both in breaking through the "class ceiling" and as a nurse in France—have provided her with a unique perspective. Later, in her work as an investigator, her experiences have allowed greater insights into what it means to be human. In addition, her studies and curiosity have resulted in an innate understanding of how experience changes a person, that even good change can be challenging, and that her interactions with a person might change the outcome of events, or their thinking or attitude. She takes on this responsibility and, in a way, accompanies the person to a point in their personal journey where they are safe. She is not one to simply put the clues together, sort things out and move on. As far as what enabled me to create such a character, I think my own life experiences together with my training and work as a personal/life coach have helped. I have worked with many people who have made enormous leaps of faith to bring about change in their lives and have seen how such personal journeys can be challenging and, frankly, scary. So some of that has been brought into *Maisie Dobbs*.

*8. Despite all the violence that lies beneath the surface of your story—a world war, a series of unexplained deaths, and so on—you tend to deal with the actual moments of violence with careful restraint. The death of one key character is reported in a telegram. Another chapter cuts away just before a horrible explosion. Is there an authorial philosophy behind this well-mannered delicacy?*

I think it's a case of "less is more." While I certainly did not want to offer a clean and tidy image of a war that was filled with pain, terror, and bloodshed, I feel that a scene of violence can be just as effectively conveyed with less graphic images—and leave the imagination to do its work. Also, apart from the scene at the casualty clearing station, I was dealing very much with the aftermath of war, with words unspoken, with memories buried, and with scars so terrible one can but weep to think of the pain suffered. I didn't want to create graphic, violent scenes that overshadowed the whole book. For me the challenge was in conveying the lingering suffering of an individual and a country.

*9. Maisie's mentor, Maurice Blanche, is a man of remarkably keen perceptions. Have you had a Maurice Blanche in your own life?*

Maurice is really an amalgam of the teachers that have most impacted my life, whether in school or work. However, in his manner, Maurice reflects a teacher and friend who was most dear to me and to whom my second Maisie Dobbs novel is dedicated. Sadly, he died before *Maisie Dobbs* was published—and it had been my dream since childhood to present him with a copy of my first book.

*10. For someone dedicated to tracing through the labyrinths and "mazes" of human psychology and behavior, "Maisie" is a beautifully chosen name. In addition, the initials "M. D." are delightfully apt for someone who approaches detective work as a means toward healing. Are we right in supposing that a lot of thought went into naming her?*

Gosh, I hate to admit this, but the name "Maisie Dobbs" just came to me instantly along with the character. I had never written fiction before, yet had been badgered by one of my mentors to try fiction. I had no idea where to start—my other book-length manuscript was a memoir about my childhood—yet one day as I was stuck in traffic while driving to an appointment, Maisie Dobbs just came to me, just as she does in the first chapter. In my mind's eye I watched her walking through the turnstile at Warren Street tube station. I instantly knew her name and who she was. By the time I had driven another half mile, I knew her story. After work, I rushed home to write the first fifteen or so pages that became Chapter One. I have never wavered regarding her name and never doubted that the novel would bear her name. I am forever grateful that such an inspired moment gave me such a name, as it fits her perfectly.

*11. Do you think the traits of a good private eye also make for a good writer?*

I can only speak for myself here, but I do believe that being a good, detailed, and vigilant observer—of events, people, one's environment, sounds, colors, etc.—is the key to being a good writer. Curiosity is important for me, and asking questions. Like Maurice, I'm a great believer in questions. When I think of my favorite writers, their work reflects a quest, a journey of discovery to the heart of a matter—whether that journey takes the form of an essay, a poem, a short story, or a novel.

*12. As you point out, many of the disabled soldiers at The Retreat develop a deep loyalty to Adam Jenkins because he provides "answers to unfathomable questions" and "leadership in their uncertainty." Do you feel that Jenkins's story is in some ways a parallel to the rise of Hitler?*

I do believe that people such as Jenkins, Hitler—or any such leader—gain power amid fear and uncertainty. At the heart of every cult is a compelling personality, one who exudes a certain charisma. In Jenkins I wanted to explore the wounds that resulted in his terrible acts at The Retreat. The trouble is that such individuals come to power on a tide of support from people desperate for leadership—people who are suffering emotionally, economically— and then such leaders create a mood of fear to maintain control when the people begin to doubt. Thus the people—whether a group or a nation—are powerless. And that fear can be of the leader himself and the consequence of crossing him, or of an external threat to one's safety.

*13. The almost blank period that you have intentionally left between 1917 and 1929 is deeply tantalizing. Do you plan to fill this gap in subsequent Maisie Dobbs novels and, if so, would you like to drop any hints at the moment?*

Yes, that period is extremely tantalizing. There are a couple of possibilities: A case from her days with Maurice that is reopened; and a series of stories from the early days of Maisie's apprenticeship with Maurice.

# QUESTIONS FOR DISCUSSION

1. How does Maisie's brief exchange with the newspaper vendor at the beginning of the novel (pp. 3–4) help to establish her character? Why is her combination of "bearing" and her "familiar way" of speaking such a surprise to Jack? How does this combination of qualities fit in with Maisie's desire for an office that is "something in the middle, something for everyone, something central, but then again not in the thick of things"?

2. Maisie initially has a hard time deciding what trade description to put on her nameplate (p. 5). At the end of the novel, she has firmly decided upon "M. Dobbs, Psychologist and Investigator." In what other ways, during the course of the story, does Maisie arrive at a clearer idea of who she is?

3. Enid, Maisie's roommate at Lord Compton's mansion, is vividly contrasted with Maisie. What implicit comparisons are made between the two young women? Despite her lack of formal education, does Enid possess a kind of wisdom that Maisie is slower to acquire? Does Enid's juxtaposition with Maisie help us to understand Maisie better?

4. When he learns that his wife is still mourning the early death of a former love who was horribly wounded in World War I, Christopher Davenham responds, "[O]ne just has to get on with it. After all, you can't just give in, can you?" (p. 52). Similarly, Mrs. Crawford criticizes James for being different from other ex-soldiers who have "got on with it" (p. 207). You may have noticed that the phrase "Get on with it" becomes an important motif late in the novel (cf. pp. 283 and 292). If getting on with it is such sensible advice, why is it so hard to follow?

5. Throughout most of the novel, the facial disfigurement of the veterans who join the colony at The Retreat generates sympathy for them. However, at a climactic moment in the story, their wounds are used to make them appear monstrous and inhuman: "With their damaged faces, once so very dear to a mother, father, or sweetheart, they were now reduced to gargoyles by a war that, for them, had never ended" (p. 262). In the story, and elsewhere, for that matter, can sympathy and repulsion exist comfortably side by side, or must one eventually triumph?

6. How does the young Maisie of the flashback chapters differ from the mature Maisie?

7. What obstacles does Maisie have to surmount, both personally and professionally, because she is a woman? How does her feminine identity influence her professional demeanor and investigative style? How do the obstacles of gender in the novel contrast with the obstacles of class?

8. Maisie finds herself situated between two powerful father figures: Frankie, her natural father; and Maurice, her intellectual "father." Both of these men represent different parts of Maisie's life and character though they have very little in common. How successful is Maisie in balancing their influences?

9. Despite the sinister nature of The Retreat, Billy Beale initially finds the compound somewhat attractive and feels respect for Adam Jenkins. Why?

10. Is Maisie as skilled at resolving her own inner conflicts as she is at dealing with those of others? Are there any relationships in particular that you think she mismanages? Why?

11. Imagine *Maisie Dobbs* as the basis for a screenplay. Choose a scene and discuss how you, as the director, would want to film it.

12. What is your response to the ending of the novel, particularly the last meeting between Simon and Maisie? Is Maisie more focused on her suffering or Simon's? Is her focus where it ought to be? Does the scene resolve the tensions of the story or heighten them?

For more information about or to order other Penguin Readers Guides, please e-mail the Penguin Marketing Department at reading@us.penguingroup.com or write to us at:

Penguin Books Marketing Dept.
Readers Guides
375 Hudson Street
New York, NY 10014-3657

Please allow 4–6 weeks for delivery.
To access Penguin Readers Guides online, visit the Penguin Group (USA) Web site at www.penguin.com.

# BIRDS OF
# A FEATHER

To Kenneth Leech
1919–2002

During my childhood I was lucky to have Ken Leech as my
teacher. In the years of my growing up and into adulthood,
I was privileged to count him among my friends.

How will you fare, sonny, how will you fare
In the far off winter night
When you sit by the fire in the old man's chair
And your neighbors talk of the fight?
Will you slink away, as it were from a blow,
Your old head shamed and bent?
Or say, "I was not the first to go,
But I went, thank God, I went"?

—from the song "Fall In," by Harold Begbie, 1914

*M*aisie Dobbs shuffled the papers on her desk into a neat pile and placed them in a plain manila folder. She took up green marble-patterned W.H. Smith fountain pen and inscribed the cover with the name of her new clients: Mr. and Mrs. Herbert Johnson, who were concerned that their son's fiancée might have misled them regarding her past. It was the sort of case that was easily attended to, that would provide a useful reference, and that could be closed with presentation of a timely report and accompanying account for her services. But for Maisie the case notes would not be filed away until those whose lives were touched by her investigation had reached a certain peace with her findings, with themselves, and with one another—as far as that might be possible. As she wrote, a tendril of jet black hair tumbled down into her eyes. Sighing, she quickly pushed it back into the chignon at the nape of her neck. Suddenly, Maisie set her pen on the blotting pad, pulled the troublesome wisp of hair free so that it hung down again, and walked to the large mirror hanging on the wall above the fireplace. She unpinned her long hair and tucked it inside the collar of her white silk blouse, pulling out just an inch or so around her chin-line. Would shorter hair suit her?

"Perhaps Lady Rowan is right," said Maisie to her reflection in the mirror. "Perhaps it *would* look better in a bob."

She turned from side to side several times, and lifted her hair just slightly. Shorter hair might save a few minutes of precious time each morning, and it would no longer come free of the chignon and fall into her eyes. But one thing held her back. She lifted her hair and turned her head. Was the scar visible? Would shorter hair fall in such a way as to reveal the purple weal that etched a line from her neck into the sensitive flesh of her scalp? If her hair were cut, would she lean forward over her notes one day and unwittingly allow a client to see the damage inflicted by the German shell that had ripped into the casualty clearing station where she was working, in France, in 1917?

Looking at the room reflected in the mirror, Maisie considered how far she had come—not only from the dark dingy office in Warren Street that was all she had been able to afford just over a year ago, but from that first meeting with Maurice Blanche, her mentor and teacher, when she had been a maid in the household of Lord Julian Compton and his wife, Lady Rowan. It was Maurice and Lady Rowan who had noted Maisie's intellect and ensured that she had every opportunity to pursue her hunger for education. They had made it possible for the former tweeny maid to gain admission to Girton College, Cambridge.

Maisie quickly pulled her hair into a neat chignon again, and as she pinned the twist into place, she glanced out of the floor-to-ceiling window that overlooked Fitzroy Square. Her assistant, Billy Beale, had just turned in to the square and was crossing the rain-damp gray flagstones toward the office. Her scar began to throb. As she watched Billy, Maisie began to assume his posture. She moved toward the window with shoulders dropped, hands thrust into imaginary pockets, and her gait mimicking the awkwardness caused by Billy's still-troublesome war wounds. Her disposition began to change, and she realized that the occasional malaise she had sensed several weeks ago was now a constant in Billy's life.

As she looked down at him from what had once been the drawing room window of the Georgian building, he stretched the cuff of his overcoat over the palm of his hand and polished the brass nameplate informing visitors that the office of M. Dobbs, Psychologist and Investigator, was situated within. Satisfied, Billy straightened, drew back his shoulders, stretched his spine, ran his fingers through his tousled shock of wheaten hair, and took out his key to the main door. Maisie watched as he corrected his posture. *You can't fool me, Billy Beale,* she said to herself. The front door closed with a heavy thud, and the stairs creaked as Billy ascended to the office.

"Morning, Miss. I picked up the records you wanted." Billy placed a plain brown envelope on Maisie's desk. "Oh, and another thing, Miss, I bought a *Daily Express* for you to 'ave a butcher's 'ook at." He took a newspaper from the inside pocket of his overcoat. "That woman what was found murdered in 'er own 'ome a week or two ago down in Surrey—you remember, in Coulsden—well, there's more details 'ere, of who she was, and the state she was in when she was found."

"Thank you, Billy," said Maisie, taking the newspaper.

"She was only your age, Miss. Terrible, innit?"

"It certainly is."

"I wonder if our friend . . . well, your friend, really—Detective Inspector Stratton—is involved?"

"Most likely. Since the murder took place outside London, it's a Murder Squad case."

Billy looked thoughtful. "Fancy 'avin' to say you work for the Murder Squad, eh, Miss? Don't exactly warm folk to you, does it?"

Maisie scanned the article quickly. "Oh, that's a newspaper invention to sell more papers. I think they started to use it when the Crippen case became big news. It used to be called the Reserve Squad, but that didn't sound ominous enough. And Criminal Investigation Department *is* a bit of a mouthful." Maisie looked up at Billy, "And by the way, Billy, what do you mean by my 'friend,' eh?"

"Aw, nuffin' really, Miss. It's just that—"

Billy was interrupted by the ringing of the black telephone on Maisie's desk. He raised his eyebrows and reached for the receiver.

"Fitzroy five six double 0. Good afternoon, Detective Inspector

Stratton. Yes, she's 'ere. I'll put her on." He smiled broadly, covering the receiver with his palm as Maisie, blushing slightly, held out her hand to take it. "Now, Miss, what was it that Doctor Blanche used to say about coincidence being a—what was it? Oh yes, a messenger of truth?"

"That's enough, Billy." Maisie took the receiver and waved him away. "Inspector Stratton, how very nice to hear from you. I expect you're busy with the murder case in Coulsden."

"And how did you know that, Miss Dobbs? No, don't tell me. It's probably best that I don't know."

Maisie laughed. "To what do I owe this call, Inspector?"

"Purely social, Miss Dobbs. I thought I'd ask if you might care to dine with me."

Maisie hesitated, tapped the desk with her pen, and then replied, "Thank you for the invitation, Inspector Stratton. It really is most kind of you . . . but perhaps we can lunch together instead."

There was a pause. "Certainly, Miss Dobbs. Will you be free on Friday?"

"Yes, Friday would be excellent."

"Good. I'll meet you at your office at noon, and we can go from there to Bertorelli's."

Maisie hesitated. "May I meet you *at* Bertorelli's? At noon?"

Again the line was quiet. Why does this have to be so difficult? Maisie thought.

"Of course. Friday, noon at Bertorelli's."

"I'll see you then. Good-bye." She replaced the receiver thoughtfully.

"Aye-oop, 'ere's a nice cuppa for you, Miss." Billy placed the tea tray on his desk, poured milk and tea into a large enamel mug for Maisie, and placed it in front of her.

"Don't mind me askin', Miss—and I know it ain't none of my business, like—but why don't you take 'im up on the offer of a dinner? I mean, gettin' the odd dinner fer nuffin' ain't such a bad thing."

"Lunch and dinner are two entirely different things, and going out for luncheon with a gentleman is definitely not the same as going out to dine in the evening."

"You get more grub at dinner, for a start—"

Billy was interrupted by the doorbell. As he moved to the window to see who might be calling, Maisie noticed him rub his thigh and wince. The war wound, suffered almost thirteen years before, during the Battle of Messines in 1917, was nipping at him again. Billy left to answer the doorbell, and as he did so, Maisie heard him negotiate the stairs with difficulty as he descended to the front door.

"Message for M. Dobbs. Urgent. Sign 'ere, please."

"Thanks, mate." As Billy signed for the envelope he reached into his pocket for some change to hand the messenger. He closed the door and sighed before mounting the stairs again. As he returned to the office he held out the envelope to Maisie.

"That leg giving you trouble?" she asked.

"Just a bit more than usual. Mind you, I'm not as young as I was."

"Have you been back to the doctor?"

"Not lately. There ain't much they can do, is there? I'm a lucky fella—got a nice job when there's 'undreds and 'undreds of blokes linin' up fer work. Can't be feelin' sorry for meself, can I?"

"We're fortunate, Billy. There seems to be more business for us, what with people going missing after losing all their money, and others getting up to no good at all." She turned the envelope in her hands. "Well, well, well . . . ."

"What is it, Miss?"

"Did you notice the return address on the envelope? This letter's from Joseph Waite."

"You mean *the* Joseph Waite? Moneybags Joseph Waite? The one they call the Banker's Butcher?"

"He's requested that I come to his residence—'soonest,' he says—to receive instructions for an investigation."

"I suppose 'e's used to orderin' folk around and getting' 'is own way—" Billy was interrupted once more by the ringing telephone. "Gawd, Miss, there goes the dog-and-bone again!"

Maisie reached for the receiver.

"Fitzroy five six double 0."

"May I speak to Miss Maisie Dobbs, please?"

"Speaking. How may I help you?"

"This is Miss Arthur, secretary to Joseph Waite. Mr. Waite is expecting you."

"Good morning, Miss Arthur. I have only just received his letter via personal messenger."

"Good. Can you come today at three? Mr. Waite will see you then, for half an hour."

The woman's voice trembled slightly. Was Miss Arthur so much in awe of her employer?

"Right you are, Miss Arthur. My assistant and I will arrive at three. Now, may I have directions?"

"Yes, the address is as follows: Do you know Dulwich?"

"Ready when you are, Miss."

Maisie looked at the silver nurse's watch pinned to her jacket as if it were a brooch. The watch had been a gift from Lady Rowan when Maisie took leave from Girton College and became a VAD at the London Hospital, a member of the wartime Voluntary Aid Detachment of nursing staff during the Great War. It had kept perfect time since the very first moment she pinned it to her uniform, serving her well while she tended injured men at a casualty clearing station in France, and again when she nursed shell-shocked patients upon her return. And since completing her studies at Girton the watch had been synchronized many times with the pocket watch belonging to Maurice Blanche, when she worked as his assistant. It would serve her for a few more years yet.

"Just time to complete one more small task, Billy; then we'll be on our way. It's the first week of the month, and I have some accounts to do."

Maisie took a key from her purse, opened the middle drawer on the right-hand side of her large desk, and selected one small ledger from the six bound notebooks in the drawer. The ledger was labeled MOTOR CAR.

Maisie had been given use of the smart MG 14/40 sports roadster belonging to Lady Rowan the year before. Recurring hip pain suffered as the result of a hunting accident rendered driving difficult for

Lady Rowan, and she insisted that Maisie borrow the motor car whenever she wanted. After using the vehicle constantly for some months, Maisie had offered to purchase the MG. Lady Rowan teased that it must have been the only transaction involving a motor car in which the buyer insisted upon paying more than the owner had stipulated. A small percentage for interest had been added at Maisie's insistence. Taking up her pen, Maisie pulled her checkbook from the same drawer and wrote a check, payable to Lady Rowan Compton. The amount paid was entered in a ledger column and the new balance owed underlined in red.

"Right then, Billy, just about done. All secure?"

"Yes, Miss. Case maps are in my desk, and locked. Card file is locked. Tea is locked—"

"Billy!"

"Just pullin' yer leg, Miss!" Billy opened the door for Maisie, and they left the office, making sure that the door was locked behind them.

Maisie looked up at the leaden sky. "Looks like rain again, doesn't it?"

"It does at that. Better get on our way and 'ope it blows over."

The motor car was parked at the edge of Fitzroy Street, its shining paintwork a splash of claret against the gray April afternoon.

Billy held the door for her, then lifted the bonnet to turn on the fuel pump, closing it again with a clatter that made Maisie wince. As he leaned over the engine, Maisie observed the gray smudges below his eyes. Banter was Billy's way of denying pain. He gave the thumbs-up sign, and Maisie set the ignition, throttle, and choke before pressing the starter button on the floor of the motor car. The engine burst into life. He opened the passenger door and took his seat beside her.

"Off we go, then. Sure of your way?"

"Yes, I know Dulwich. The journey shouldn't take more than an hour, depending upon the traffic." Maisie slipped the MG into gear and eased out into Warren Street.

"Let's just go over what we already know about Waite. That Maurice had file cards on him is intriguing in itself."

"Well, according to this first card, Dr. Blanche went to 'im askin' for money for a clinic. What's that about?" Billy glanced at Maisie, then looked ahead at the road. "It's starting to come down."

"I know. London weather, so fabulously predictable you never know what might happen," observed Maisie before answering Billy's question. "Maurice was a doctor, Billy; you know that. Before he specialized in medical jurisprudence, his patients had a bit more life in them."

"I should 'ope so."

"Anyway, years ago, long before I went to work at Ebury Place, Maurice was involved in a case that took him to the East End. While he was there, examining a murder victim, a man came rushing in shouting for help. Maurice followed the man to a neighboring house, where he found a woman in great difficulty in labor with her first child. The short story is that he saved her life and the life of the child, and came away determined to do something about the lack of medical care available to the poor of London, especially women and children. So for one or two days a week, he became a doctor for the living again, working with patients in the East End and then across the water, in Lambeth and Bermondsey."

"Where does Waite come in?"

"Read the card and you'll see. I think it was just before I came to Ebury Place, in 1910, that Maurice took Lady Rowan on one of his rounds. She was appalled and determined to help. She set about tapping all her wealthy friends for money so that Maurice might have a proper clinic."

"I bet they gave her the money just to get her off their backs!"

"She has a reputation for getting what she wants and for not being afraid to ask. I think her example inspired Maurice. He probably met Waite socially and just asked. He knows immediately how to judge a person's mood, and to use that—I suppose you'd call it energy—to his advantage."

"Bit like you, Miss?"

Maisie did not reply but simply smiled. It had been her remarkable intuitive powers, along with a sharp intellect, that had led Maurice

Blanche to accept her as his pupil and later as his assistant in the work he described as the forensic science of the whole person.

Billy continued. "Well, apparently old Dr. Blanche tapped Waite for five 'undred quid."

"Look again, and you'll probably find that the five hundred was the first of several contributions." Maisie used the back of her hand to wipe away condensation accumulating inside the windshield.

"Oh 'ere's another thing," said Billy, suddenly leaning back with his eyes closed.

"What is it?" Maisie looked at her passenger, whose complexion was now rather green.

"I don't know if I should read in the motor, Miss. Makes me go all queasy."

Maisie pulled over to the side of the road and instructed Billy to open the passenger door, put his feet on the ground and his head between his knees. She took the cards and then summed up the notes on Joseph Waite. "Wealthy, self-made man. Started off as a butcher's apprentice in Yorkshire—Harrogate—at age twelve. Quickly demonstrated a business mind. By the time he was twenty he'd bought his first shop. Cultivated the business, then outgrew it inside two years. Started selling fruit and veg as well, dried goods and fancy foods, all high quality and good prices. Opened another shop, then another. Now has several Waite's International Stores in every city, and smaller Waite's Fancy Foods in regional towns. What they all have in common is first-class service, deliveries, good prices, and quality foods. Plus he pays a surprise visit to at least one store each day. He can turn up at any time."

"I bet they love that, them as works for 'im."

"Hmmm, you have a point. Miss Arthur sounded like a rabbit on the run when we spoke on the telephone this morning." Maisie flicked over the card she was holding. "Now this is interesting. . . ." she continued. "He called upon Maurice—yes, I remember this—to consult with him about ten years ago. Oh heavens. . . ."

"What is it? What does it say?" asked Billy, wiping his brow with a handkerchief.

"This is not like Maurice. It says only, 'I could not comply with his request. Discontinued communication.'"

"Charmin'. So where does that put us today?"

"Well, he must still have a high opinion of Maurice to be asking for my help." Maisie looked at Billy to check his pallor. "Oh dear. Your nose is bleeding! Quickly, lean back and press down on the bridge of your nose with this handkerchief." Maisie pulled a clean embroidered handkerchief from her pocket, and placed it on Billy's nose.

"Oh my Gawd, I'm sorry. First I 'ave to lean forward, then back. I dunno . . . I'm getting right in the way today, aren't I?"

"Nonsense, you're a great help to me. How's that nose?"

Billy looked down into the handkerchief, and dabbed at his nose. "I think it's better."

"Now then, we'd better get going."

Maisie parked outside the main gates leading to a red-brick neo-Georgian mansion that stood majestically in the landscaped grounds beyond an ornate wrought iron gate.

"D'you reckon someone'll come to open the gate?" asked Billy.

"Someone's coming now." Maisie pointed to a young man wearing plus fours, a tweed hacking jacket, woolen shirt and spruce green tie. He hurriedly opened an umbrella as he ran toward the entrance, and nodded to Maisie as he unlatched the gates and opened them. Maisie drove the car forward, stopping alongside the man.

"You must be Miss Dobbs, to see Mr. Waite at three o'clock."

"Yes, that's me."

"And your companion is . . . ?" The man bent forward to look at Billy in the passenger seat.

"My assistant, Mr. William Beale."

Billy was still dabbing his nose with Maisie's handkerchief.

"Right you are, M'um. Park in front of the main door please, and make sure you reverse into place, M'um, with the nose of your motor pointing toward the gate."

Maisie raised an eyebrow at the young man, who shrugged.

"It's how Mr. Waite likes it done, M'um."

"Bit picky, if you ask me," said Billy as Maisie drove toward the house. "'Reverse in with nose pointing out'. Perhaps that's 'ow I should walk in there, backwards, wiv me nose turned away! I wonder who 'e thinks 'e is?"

"One of the richest men in Britain, if not Europe." Maisie maneuvered the car as instructed. "And as we know, he needs something from us, otherwise we wouldn't be here. Come on."

They strode quickly from the car toward the main door where a woman waited to greet them. She was about fifty-five, in Maisie's estimation, and wore a plain slate gray mid-calf length dress with white cuffs and a white Peter Pan collar. A cameo was pinned to the center of her collar and her only other adornment was a silver wristwatch on a black leather strap. Her gray hair was drawn back so tightly that it pulled at her temples. Despite her austere appearance, when Maisie and Billy reached the top step she smiled warmly with a welcoming sparkle in her pale blue eyes.

"Come in quickly before you catch your death! What a morning! Mr. Harris, the butler, has been taken poorly with a nasty cold. I'm Mrs. Willis, the housekeeper. Let me take your coats." Mrs. Willis took Maisie's mackintosh and Billy's overcoat, and passed them to a maid. "Hang them on the drier over the fireplace in the laundry room. Mr. Waite's guests will be leaving in—" she looked at her watch "—approximately thirty-five minutes, so get the coats as dry as possible by then."

"Thank you very much, Mrs. Willis," said Maisie.

"Mr. Waite will join you in the library shortly."

Maisie sensed a mood of tension that pervaded the house. Mrs. Willis's pace was hurried, urging them forward. At the library door she checked her watch as she reached for the brass door handle. A door opened behind them and another woman hurried to join the trio.

"Mrs. Willis! Mrs. Willis, I will take over from here and show Mr. Waite's guests in to the library," she panted.

Mrs. Willis relinquished them, frowning with annoyance. "Certainly,

Miss Arthur. Please continue." She turned to Maisie and Billy. "Good
morning," she said as she stepped away without looking at Miss Arthur
again. Unfortunately she was prevented from making a dignified exit as
the door opened once more and a rotund man strode toward them,
consulting his watch as he approached.

"Right then, it's three o'clock. We'd better get on with it." Barely
looking at Maisie and Billy, he strode into the library.

Billy leaned toward Maisie and whispered, "It's like a three-ring-cir-
cus in 'ere!"

She responded with a brief nod.

"Sit down, sit down," Joseph Waite pointed to two chairs on the long
side of a rectangular polished mahogany table and immediately seated
himself in a larger chair at its head. His girth made him seem short,
though he was almost six feet tall and moved deceptively quickly.
According to Maurice's notes, Waite had been born in 1865, which
meant he was now sixty-five. His navy blue pinstripe suit was doubtless constructed at great expense by a Savile Row tailor. It was complemented by a white shirt, light gray silk tie, highly polished black
shoes, and light gray silk socks that Maisie could just see as she glanced
down at the floor. Expensive, very expensive, but then Joseph Waite
reeked of new money and of the large Havana cigar that he moved
from his right hand to his left in order to reach out first to Maisie, then
to Billy.

"Joseph Waite."

Maisie took a breath and opened her mouth to reply but was prevented from doing so.

"I'll get directly to the point, Miss Dobbs. My daughter, Charlotte,
is missing from home. I'm a busy man, so I will tell you straight, I do
not want to involve the police because I don't for one minute think
that this is a police matter. And I don't want them turning this place
upside down while they waste time speculating about this and that, and
drawing every bored press man to my gates while they're about it."

Maisie once again drew breath and opened her mouth to speak, but
Waite held his hand up from the table, his palm facing her. She noticed

a large gold ring on his little finger, and as he placed his hand on the table, she saw that it was encrusted with diamonds. She stole a sideways look at Billy, who raised an eyebrow.

"It's not a police matter because this is not the first time she's left my house. You are to find her, Miss Dobbs, and bring her back before word gets out. A man in my position can't have a daughter running around and turning up in the newspapers. I don't have to tell you that these are difficult times for a man of commerce, but Waite's is trimming its sails accordingly and doing very nicely, thank you. It's got to stay that way. Now then." Waite consulted his watch yet again. "You've got twenty minutes of my time, so ask any questions you want. I won't 'old back."

Maisie perceived that although Waite had worked hard to eliminate a strong Yorkshire accent, the occasional revealing long vowel and the odd dropped *h,* unlike that of the London dialect, broke through.

"I'd like some details about your daughter." Maisie reached for the blank index cards that Billy handed her. "First of all, how old is Charlotte?"

"Thirty-two. About your age."

"Quite."

"And with about half the gumption!"

"I beg your pardon, Mr. Waite?"

"I'll make no bones about it; Charlotte is her mother's daughter. A wilting lily, I call her. A good day's work wouldn't do her any harm at all, but of course the daughter of a man in my position has no need. More's the pity."

"Indeed. Perhaps you could tell us something about what happened on the day Charlotte disappeared. When was she last seen?"

"Two days ago. Saturday. Morning. At breakfast. I was down in the dining room, and Charlotte came in, full of the joys of spring, and sat down at the other end of the table. One minute she seemed as right as rain, eating a bit of toast, drinking a cup of tea, then all of a sudden she starts with the tears, sobs a bit, and runs from the room."

"Did you go after her?"

The man sighed and reached for an ashtray, into which he tapped the smoldering end of his cigar, leaving a circle of pungent ash. He drew deeply on the cigar again and exhaled.

"No, I didn't. I finished my breakfast. Charlotte is a bit of a Sarah Bernhardt, Miss Dobbs. An actress—should've been on the stage, like her mother. Nothing is ever good enough for her. I thought she'd've made a suitable marriage by now, but no, in fact—you should write it down there—" He waved his cigar toward Maisie's index card. "She was jilted by her fiancé a couple of months ago. Even with my money she can't get a husband!"

"Mr. Waite, the behavior you describe suggests that your daughter may have been in a state of despair."

"'Despair'? *'Despair'*? She's always had fine food in her belly, clothes—and very good clothes, I might add—on her back. I've given her a good education, in Switzerland, if you please. And she had a proper coming out ball. You could've fed a family for a year with what I spent on the frock alone. That girl's had the very best, so don't tell me about despair, Miss Dobbs. That girl's got no right to despair."

Maisie met his gaze firmly. *Here it comes,* she thought, *now he's going to tell me about his hard life.*

"Despair, Miss Dobbs, is when your father dies in a pit accident when you're ten years old and you're the eldest of six. That's what despair is. Despair is what gives you a right good kick in the rump and sets you off to provide for your family when you're no' but a child."

Waite, who had slipped into broad Yorkshire, went on. "Despair, Miss Dobbs, is when you lose your mother and her youngest to consumption when you're fourteen. That, Miss Dobbs, is despair. Despair is just when you think you've got everyone taken care of, because you're working night and day to make something of yourself, and you lose another brother down the same pit that killed your father, because he took any job he could get to help out. That, Miss Dobbs, is despair. But you know about that yourself, don't you?" Waite leaned forward and ground his cigar into the ashtray.

Maisie realized that somewhere in his office Joseph Waite had a dossier on her that held as much information as she had acquired about him, if not more.

"Mr. Waite, I am well aware of life's challenges, but if I am to take on this case—and the choice is mine—I have a responsibility for the welfare of all parties. If this type of departure is something of a habit for your daughter and discord in the house is at the heart of her unsettled disposition, then clearly something must be done to alleviate the, let us say, *pressure* on all parties. I must have your commitment to further conversation with respect to the problem when we have found Charlotte."

Joseph Waite's lips became taut. He was not a man used to being challenged. Yet, as Maisie now knew, it was the similarity in their backgrounds that had led him to choose her for this task, and he would not draw back. He was a very intelligent as well as belligerent man and would appreciate that not a moment more could be lost.

"Mr. Waite, even if Charlotte has disappeared of her own volition, news of her disappearance will soon attract the attention of the press, just as you fear. Given your financial situation and these difficult times, there is a risk that you may be subjected to attempts at extortion. And though you seem sure that Charlotte is safe and merely hiding from you, of that we cannot be certain until she is found. You speak of prior disappearances. May I have the details?"

Waite leaned back in his chair shaking his head. "She runs away, to my mind, anytime she can't get what she wants. The first time was after I refused to allow her a motor car." He looked across the lawns and waved the cigar in the direction of what Maisie expected were the garages. "She can be taken by chauffeur anywhere she wants. I don't hold with women driving."

Maisie exchanged glances with Billy.

"So she ran to her mother's house, no doubt to complain about her terrible father. I tell you, where I come from, there's women who'd give their eye teeth to have someone to drive them instead of walking five miles to the shops pushing a pram with a baby inside, a couple of nippers on top, and the shopping bags hanging off the handle!"

"And the second time?"

"Oh, she was engaged to be married and wanted to get out of it. The one before this last one. Just upped and moved into The Ritz, if you please. Nice home here, and she wants to live at The Ritz. I went and got her back myself."

"I see." Maisie imagined the embarrassment of a woman being frog-marched out of The Ritz by her angry father. "So in your opinion Charlotte has a tendency to run away when she is faced with a confrontation."

"Aye, that's about the measure of it," replied Waite. "So what do you think of your little 'further conversation' when Charlotte returns now, eh, Miss Dobbs, considering the girl can't even look her own father in the eye?"

Maisie was quick to respond. "My terms remain, sir. Part of my work in bringing Charlotte home will be to listen to her and to *hear* what she has to say."

Waite scraped back his chair, pushed his hands into his trouser pockets, and walked to the window. He looked up at the sky for just a moment and took out a pocket-watch. "I agree to your terms. Send your contract to me by nine tomorrow morning. Miss Arthur will take care of any deposit required, and will settle your account and expenses upon receipt. If you need me to answer more questions, Miss Arthur will schedule an appointment. Otherwise I expect your progress report by Friday. In person and at the same time—that is, should you fail to have found her by then. I'm a busy man, as I've said, Miss Dobbs." He turned to leave.

"Mr. Waite?"

"Yes?"

"May we see Charlotte's rooms, please?"

"Miss Arthur will call Mrs. Willis to show you the rooms. Good afternoon."

Mrs. Willis was instructed to show Maisie and Billy to Charlotte's suite. They were escorted up the wide staircase to the second floor,

where they turned right along a spacious landing. Mrs. Willis lifted her
hand to knock at the door and then, remembering that there was no
need, took a bunch of keys from her pocket, selected one, and unlocked
the door to reveal a large sitting room with additional doors on either
side that Maisie thought would lead to a bathroom and bedroom
respectively. The sash windows were open to a broad view of the perfect lawns at the front of the house, with stripes of light and dark green
where gardeners had worked with mowers and rollers to give an
immaculate finish.

Mrs. Willis beckoned them into the rooms, which were aired by a
light breeze that seemed to dance with the cabbage-rose-printed curtains, flicking them back and forth. Though appointed with the most
expensive furniture and linens, Maisie felt the rooms to be cold and
spartan. There was none of the ornamentation she had expected: no
photographs in frames, no mementos, no books on the bedside table, no
exotic perfume bottles set on top of the dressing table. Maisie walked
through into the bedroom, and back into the sitting room. Like the
Queen Anne chairs beside the fireplace, the rose-printed curtains were
traditional, but the dressing table and wardrobe were modern, constructed of solid dark wood with geometric lines. The dressing table
mirrors were triangular, a jagged icy triptych that unsettled Maisie. Her
skin prickled as if pierced by tiny needles. The design of the dressing
table itself was matched by that of the wardrobe, with its center mirror
set into the wood. It seemed to Maisie that no rest was to be had in this
room unless one stared out of the window or at the curtains.

"It's a lovely suite, isn't it? We only changed the draperies last
week—she has pale green velvets in winter. Lined with a special
combed cotton, they are, to keep the rooms warmer. The dressing table
suite was made 'specially to Mr. Waite's specifications."

Maisie smiled and nodded. "Thank you, Mrs. Willis. We may need to
ask you some more questions in a while. At the moment we just need
to look around."

Mrs. Willis pursed her lips, hesitating. "Of course. I'll come back in
about twenty minutes, but if you need me in the meantime, just press

this button." She indicated one of three brass buttons on a panel beside the door.

Sensing that Waite had given instructions that they were to be escorted at all times, Maisie smiled and nodded. She suspected that Mrs. Willis had enough on her plate to worry about in the house without chaperoning private investigators.

As the door closed, Billy turned to Maisie. "It looks as if nobody ever set foot in these rooms, dunnit?"

Maisie made no reply, but set her document case down on a chair with coverings that matched the curtains and, in the bedroom, even the counterpane on Charlotte's bed. Maisie's work with Maurice Blanche had taught her that a person speaks not only with the voice but with those objects she chooses to surround herself. That photographs tell a story is well accepted, but the way furniture is positioned in a room tells something about its occupant; the contents of a larder reveal desire and restraint, as most surely does the level of liquid in a decanter.

"What are we lookin' for, Miss?"

"I don't know, Billy, but I will when we find it."

They worked together, carefully and systematically searching through drawers, in the wardrobe, and in every nook and cranny of the room. Maisie asked Billy to search carefully under the bed and behind furniture, to pull out cushions from the chair, and to list all items in the medicine cabinet in the white-tiled bathroom. She, in turn, would investigate the contents of the dressing table, wardrobe and writing desk.

Though she was troubled by the design of the furniture, Maisie was even more intrigued by Charlotte's clothing. Instead of suits, dresses and gowns from the houses of Worth, Schiaparelli or Molyneux, as would befit a woman of Charlotte's station, there were just a few plain gray and brown skirts and jackets bought from Debenham & Freebody. A long black gown protected by a sheet of fine muslin was Charlotte's one concession to evening wear, and there was also a black afternoon dress in a style fashionable several years earlier, with a low waistband and below-the-knee hemline. Charlotte's blouses were equally plain and it seemed as if she had bought several of similar design at the same time. Had she taken more colorful and frivolous clothing with her, leaving behind a life that lacked color in search of something more vibrant?

It was in the writing desk, to the right of the window, that Maisie found an address book. At first, she thought that she would find no other personal papers, no letters, nothing that gave away anything of Charlotte Waite's character or hinted at the cause of her distress, but as she opened the second drawer, underneath a collection of pens and stationery, Maisie found a prayer book along with a copy of *The Monastic Rule of Saint Benedict*, and several pamphlets on the life of a contemplative. Taking up the books, Maisie walked again to the wardrobe and touched the dark, drab fabrics of the clothes Charlotte had left behind.

"Miss, look what I've found." Billy came toward Maisie with a piece of paper in his hand.

"What is it, Billy?"

"Found it shoved down the side of that chair cushion. Could've been put there deliberately or fallen out of a pocket." Billy handed Maisie the small slip of paper.

"Looks like someone's jotted down train departures. See here—" Maisie pointed to the letters and read: "'Ch. X to App. Chg Ash'. Then there's a list of times. Hmmm. I'll keep it with these other things for now and we'll look at them later." She folded the paper and placed it inside the prayer book, then turned to Billy.

"Billy, I'd like to spend some time in here alone."

He was now used to Maisie's way of working and showed no surprise at her request. "Right you are, Miss. Shall I interview Mrs. Willis?"

"Yes, do that. Here's what we need to know: First, Charlotte—her behavior over the past two or three months. Was there any change in her demeanor? Ask about even the slightest change in habits of dress, diet, recreation." Maisie looked around the room. "She doesn't have her own telephone, so find out who has called; the staff always know when a new name comes along. Speak to Miss Arthur about her allowance; how much, when it's paid and how it's paid. Does she have her own accounts—heaven knows, I hope the poor woman has some privacy—and are statements kept by Miss Arthur?"

Maisie paced back and forth, as Billy licked his pencil, ready to continue taking notes.

"Most important: Find out about Charlotte's former fiancé, his name, profession—if he has one—and where he works. I'll need to see him. Speak to the chauffeur, Billy, and find out where she goes, whom she sees. You know the ropes. Oh, and a recent photograph, one that really looks like Charlotte; ask different staff if it's a good resemblance. See what you can get hold of. I want about fifteen minutes here, then I'd like to speak to Charlotte Waite's personal maid. Find out who she is and have her come up to this room."

"Awright, Miss, consider it all done."

"Oh, and Billy, tread very carefully on this one. We don't know where loyalties lie yet, though I must say, I can feel a certain chill when there's any mention of Charlotte."

"You know, I reckon I felt that meself."

"Well, keep it in mind. Leave no stone unturned."

Billy quietly shut the door behind him. Maisie sat in Charlotte's chair and closed her eyes. She took four deep breaths through her nose, as she had been taught so many years ago by Khan, the blind Ceylonese mystic to whom Maurice had introduced her, to learn that seeing is not necessarily a function of the eyes alone. From her days of sitting with Khan, and her instruction in deep meditation, Maisie was attuned to the risks inherent in using such a tool in her work, and knew that even her strong spirit was vulnerable to the auras of the troubled soul. Maisie concentrated on her breathing, stilling both her body and her mind, and she began to feel the strength of emotion that resided in the room. This was Charlotte's refuge while in the house and had become a receptacle for her every thought, feeling, inspiration, reflection and wish. And as she sat in meditation, Maisie felt that Charlotte had been deeply troubled and that her departure had had little to do with a broken engagement. Charlotte Waite had run away, but what was she running from? Or to? What had caused such an intense ache in her heart that even now in her room, Maisie felt Charlotte's lingering sorrow?

Maisie opened her eyes and continued to sit in silence for some moments. Then she began to inspect the books and pamphlets that Charlotte had collected. *The Monastic Rule of Saint Benedict* opened immediately to the place marked with a haphazardly torn envelope fragment. She inspected the scrap of vellum closely, for it seemed heavy, then turned it over. On the reverse side was a thick smudge of red sealing wax, about three-quarters of an inch in diameter, pressed into a rose-shaped seal with a cross in the center. Maisie squinted to see the words etched into the seal above and below the cross. She shook her head, reached down into her document case and took out what initially looked like a powder compact but that, when opened, revealed a magnifying glass. Maisie leaned closer to the seal and, using the glass, read the words "Camden Abbey." *Camden Abbey.* The name sounded familiar.

There was a knock at the door. Maisie quickly placed the books, pamphlets and other items in her case, ensured they were secure, then rose, breathed deeply again, and opened the door. A young woman of about nineteen bobbed a half-curtsey in front of her. Her black dress was shorter than the one Maisie had worn when she was a servant at the home of Lord and Lady Compton; a small bibbed apron to protect her dress and a delicate white lace band on top of her tightly curled hair completed the maid's uniform.

"Miss Dobbs? I was told you wanted to see me, M'um. I'm Perkins, Miss Waite's personal maid."

"Oh, come in, Miss Perkins." Maisie stood to one side to allow the woman to enter the room.

"Would you like to sit down?"

The maid shook her head. "No, M'um."

"Well then, let's stand by the window. It's a blustery day now, but I do like to look out upon garden." Maisie knew that an enclosed area encouraged an enclosed mind. Maurice had taught her: Always take the person to be questioned to a place where there's space, or where they can see few boundaries. Space broadens the mind and gives the voice room to be heard.

Maisie sat on the low, wide windowsill, the toe of one shoe touching the floor for balance. Perkins stood at the opposite end of the windowsill, facing Maisie.

"Tell me, Miss Perkins, how long have you worked for Miss Waite?"

"Mr. Waite. I work for Mr. Waite. Mr. Waite pays my wages, so it's him I work for. Looking after Miss Waite is what I do in his house, and I've been her maid for a year."

"I see." Maisie noticed the speed with which she had been corrected, and thought that with just one question, she had discovered where Perkins' loyalties lay.

"And who was Miss Waite's maid before you?"

"Well, there were lots of them, M'um. Isabel Wright left last year, then six months before her there was Ethel Day—I remember them because I've worked for Mr. Waite since I was twelve, M'um."

"And do you like working here, Miss Perkins?"

"I like working for Mr. Waite. He's very good to us here, M'um"

Maisie nodded, and looked out of the window. She was aware that the maid had leaned forward to see the gardens.

"I'll bet you are too busy to look out of the windows, aren't you?"

"Oh yes, 'specially with the way Miss Waite keeps me running. . . . Oh, begging your pardon, M'um."

Maisie smiled, encouraging Perkins into her confidence. "Tell me—what is it like working for Miss Waite? And I should add that everything you tell me will remain between the two of us." She leaned forward, and though the maid did not consciously discern any alteration in Maisie's speech, she had allowed her accent to change slightly so that she sounded just a little like the young woman in front of her. "I need to ask questions to get a sense of what has been happening in Miss Waite's life in the past two or three months, and especially in more recent weeks."

The young woman gazed into the distance again, chewed her inner lip, then moved closer to Maisie. She began to speak, at first tentatively, then with greater strength. "To tell you the truth, she's not the easiest person to work for. She'd have me running up and downstairs all day. Wash this, press that, cup of tea, not too hot, not too cold, lemon—oh no, changed my mind, cream instead. First she's going out, then she's staying in; then suddenly, just as I'm setting my head on the pillow, the bell rings, and I have to go down and dress her for a late dinner. No thank-you's or anything, no little something extra left on the sideboard for me, and I'm the one that has to clean up when she has a temper!"

"Oh dear."

"It's like being outside, you know: no climate but all weather. Hot and cold she is, never seems to know her own mind. One minute she's all happy, the next, you'd've thought the moon had crashed into the stars and set light to the sky outside her window." Perkins shrugged. "Well, that's what Miss Harding, the cook, says."

"And what about the past few weeks or so? More of the same behavior?"

Perkins watched the clouds for a moment before answering. "I'd say she was quieter. More . . . more *distant*, I think you'd say. I mean, she always went through times like that. Miss Harding said she ought to be taken to see somebody about her moods. But this was different. It sort of went on and on, and she didn't go out much. Didn't seem to dress up as much either. In fact, she got rid of some lovely clothes, you know, from Paris and Bond Street. Very strange for a lady, to want to walk around in them drab clothes all day, and only have one evening dress, 'specially as she used to go to the collections, you know, and have mannequins walk up and down the room for her to pick and choose what she wanted. You should have seen it in here when the boxes arrived!"

"Have you any idea what might have caused her to withdraw?"

"Not really. None of my business. I was just glad there were no bells ringing at midnight."

"Do you think Mr. Waite noticed?"

"Mr. Waite works hard. We all know that. Far as I know, they don't see much of each other."

"Are you aware of discord between Miss Waite and her father?"

Perkins looked at her shoes and stepped away from the window just a little. Maisie noticed immediately. *She's closing her mind. Deliberately.*

"Not my business to pry, M'um. I just do my job. What they think of each other upstairs isn't any of my concern."

"Hmmm. Yes. Your work is demanding enough, Miss Perkins. No reason for you to keep tabs on people. One more question, though: Do you know whom Miss Waite saw, or where she went, in the weeks preceding her departure from this house? Did you notice anything out of the ordinary?"

The maid sighed in a way that indicated that she had said all she wanted to say, but that she would try to answer the question. "She did go up to Town a few times. I'm not sure where she went, but she mainly sees a woman called Lydia Fisher, I think. She lives in Chelsea, somewhere around there. And I reckon she was going somewhere else as well, because she took a pair of walking shoes with her on a couple of occasions. But a lot of her time was spent just sitting up here."

"Doing what?"

"Not sure I know, Miss. Sort of in a daydream, looking out of the window."

"I see." The younger woman began to fidget with her hair, her lace headband, her apron, indicating to Maisie that no more valuable information would be forthcoming. As they moved toward the door, Maisie reached into her bag and took out a calling card.

"Miss Perkins, I am familiar with the workings of a house of this size, and also appreciate that the staff are usually the first to know when something is amiss. Please feel free to telephone me if you think of anything that might be useful. It's clear that you have had some difficulties with Miss Waite, but despite everything, her father—your employer—wants her home."

"Yes, M'um." Perkins took the card, placed it in her pinafore pocket, bobbed another half curtsey, and left the room.

Maisie watched the maid walk along the landing, stopping briefly to curtsey as Billy approached in the company of Mrs. Willis, who was looking at her watch. It was time for them to leave.

"Have you got everything, Billy?"

"Yes, Miss. In fact, Mrs. Willis knew where to find a recent photograph of Miss Waite. 'ere." Billy opened his notebook and took out the photograph, which he handed to Maisie.

Charlotte was sitting on a white filigree cast-iron chair set in front of a rose garden, which Maisie suspected was at the rear of the house. She seemed to be what the gentlemen of the press might have termed a "flapper." Her hair, which framed her face, was waved and drawn back into a low chignon at the nape of her neck. She wore a knee-length dress that appeared rather flimsy; a breeze had caught the hem the moment before the shutter snapped. Charlotte had made no move to press the garment down, and laughed into the camera. Maisie held the photo closer to scrutinize the face. If eyes were windows to the soul, then Charlotte was indeed troubled, for the eyes that looked at the camera seemed to be filled not with joy or amusement as the pose suggested, but with sorrow.

Maisie looked up. "Thank you, Mrs. Willis." She turned to Billy. "If you've completed everything, we can talk back at the office. I'm sure Mrs. Willis has a lot to do."

Mrs. Willis escorted them to the front door, where a maid waited with Maisie's mackintosh and Billy's overcoat. They were about to step outside when Maisie paused. "A quick question for you, Mrs. Willis. I have a sense that Miss Waite commands little respect in the household. Why is that?"

"I'm sure I don't know what you mean, M'um," said Mrs. Willis, who now seemed anxious to see Maisie and Billy inside their motor car, driving away.

"Mrs. Willis, in confidence. Tell me what you think." Maisie inclined her head conspiratorially toward Mrs. Willis.

"Mr. Waite is respected by everyone who works for him. He gives back as much as he asks of those in his employ, and sometimes more. His loyalty to his staff earns loyalty in return. And that's all I can say."

Maisie and Billy thanked Mrs. Willis, left the house, and climbed into the motor car.

"Didn't say much, did she?" said Billy, waving at the gatekeeper as they left.

"On the contrary, she told me a lot. It was an impertinent question, and, within the confines of what she *could* say, Mrs. Willis was quite forthcoming."

Billy opened his notebook and began to speak, but Maisie silenced him with a hand gently placed on his arm and a finger to her lips. "No, not now. Allow the information we've gathered to sit and stew for a while. Just tell me one thing—the name and profession of the former fiancé."

# CHAPTER TWO

*B*illy was already at the office in Fitzroy Square when Maisie arrived at eight o'clock the next morning. The spring rain had at last subsided, and now the early morning sunshine was mirrored in puddles remaining from yesterday's downpour, casting dappled shadows across the square and playing upon fresh green leaves.

"Good morning, Billy." Maisie looked at her assistant as she came into the office. "You look a bit drawn—is everything all right?"

"Yes, Miss. Well, not really. Every day I look out as the bus passes the labor exchange and the line ain't gettin' any shorter. I can count my lucky stars getting this job wiv you. You know, I've got the missus and three nippers to think about—the eldest is in school now—and what wiv this ol' leg of mine—"

"You mustn't worry, Billy. Not only are we fortunate in getting new business, but Maurice's clients now know that they can trust his former assistant. If money's a problem, Billy—"

"Oh, no, no, my wages are better 'ere than they were round the corner with old Sharpie. I just—"

"What, Billy?"

"You're sure you need me?"

"Absolutely sure. Time and again you have proved that you are worth your weight in gold, which I would pay you if I could. If I have any criticism of your work, I will tell you."

Billy gave her a wary grin.

"Is that all that's bothering you, Billy?"

"That's all, Miss."

"Right then. Let's see where we are with the Waite case."

The sound of mail being pushed through the letterbox was a signal to Billy to get up from his desk. "Back in a minute, better see if there's anything for us."

Maisie frowned. She knew that even as he made his way downstairs, Billy was preparing to return to the room demonstrating the old Billy, the court jester with a heart of gold. It was Billy's loyalty to her, and the link between him and Captain Simon Lynch, that had won him the job as her assistant—as well as his willingness to help her by working all hours on some of the more tedious surveillance tasks

In 1917 Corporal William Beale had been brought into the casualty clearing station where Maisie was assisting Captain Simon Lynch, the army doctor she been introduced to by her friend Priscilla, while she was at Girton College. Simon had declared his love for her and proposed marriage, and now they were working alongside each other. Billy Beale never forgot the man who saved his leg—and his life. And he never forgot the young nurse who tended to his wounds, instantly recognizing her years later when Maisie Dobbs became a tenant at the Warren Street premises where he was caretaker. Both she and Simon had been wounded subsequently when the casualty clearing station came under heavy artillery fire. She had recovered; Simon had not.

Maisie sat down at the table by the window, opened the file she had taken from her briefcase, and gestured for Billy to join her. He sat down, taking a plain lead pencil from the jam jar, and a large sheet of paper for them to diagram evidence details, thoughts, possibilities, and projections, a technique that they referred to as their "case map."

"First of all," said Maisie, "Waite will receive our contract and terms"—she consulted the watch pinned to the breast pocket of her new burgundy wool suit, and continued—"in about fifteen minutes."

"And we know 'e's got the money!" said Billy.

"That we do. Let's do three things this morning, then split up. I want to map what our impressions were: of the house, the four people we met, and of Charlotte's room. We'll also look at the items we found while we were there."

"And the grounds, Miss. Don't forget all that 'nose pointing out' nonsense, and them lawns what look like they were clipped by a pair o' nail scissors."

"Good. You're right, mustn't forget that welcome! Anyway, after we've made a start, you can set to work on Charlotte's address book, just checking on who's where, and that it's all current."

"Yes, Miss. Just put some flesh on the bones, no need to knock on any doors yet. Where will you be going, Miss?"

"I am going to a branch of Waite's International Stores. I thought I'd go to the one on Oxford Street, close to Tottenham Court Road. It was his first shop in London, and it's his most important branch, next to the one in Harrogate, of course. The main offices of Waite's are above the premises. With a bit of luck, I'll see the man in his element."

"Why do you think it's called Waite's *International* Stores, Miss?"

"I looked up a file of Maurice's, which expanded on the information noted on the index card. I was actually looking for anything that would add to the comment about the severing of contact, but there was nothing there, so I'll have to speak to Maurice about it. Anyway, when he added fruits and vegetables, other dry goods, and more from abroad to his butchery business, he slipped 'International' in between 'Waite's' and 'Stores' and never looked back."

"It must've been 'ard work for 'im, eh?"

"Most certainly, and of course life wasn't easy at home, either. You heard his little monologue yesterday."

"And who's 'is wife?"

"According to Maurice's file, Charlotte's mother was a music-hall singer and small-time actress from Bradford. He met her there at the opening of his shop. Apparently Waite's shop openings were always big events. Charlotte was born just"—Maisie raised an eyebrow—"seven months after the marriage."

"Miss Arthur said that Mrs. Waite spends most of 'er time up in Leeds, at the 'ouse up there. And I made a note to check on 'er information that Charlotte is not with the mother, even though Miss Arthur said she'd already made sure of that." Billy tapped at the points with his pencil.

"Good. I got the impression that Charlotte and her mother weren't close. What do you think, Billy?"

Billy scratched the top of his ear where his hair was in need of a trim. "Well, what I thought was that Charlotte didn't really fit in anywhere. There she was, living with that dad of 'ers, 'Mr. Lord High and Mighty' running 'er life, and at thirty-two, mind you. Most of 'er friends are married by now, so they ain't got time to go out with the other girls like they used to. She's sort of been left be'ind, ain't she, Miss? Like so many, really. I mean, men they might've married are gone, killed in the war. What's she supposed to do with 'erself all day? That father of 'er's don't think much of 'er, not by the sound of it. She's really a spinster, all on her own."

Maisie winced at Billy's assessment of the situation. She was, after all, a spinster herself in those terms. "Good. Yes, good point," she replied, thought for a moment, then opened her document case and removed the books and pamphlets found in Charlotte Waite's room. She laid them out on the table.

"What do you make of it all, Miss?"

Maisie picked up the seal, then the scrap of paper. "Well, the 'Ch. X' is Charing Cross."

"And 'Ash' could be Ashford, couldn't it, Miss?"

Maisie nodded. "It's all fitting together now, Billy. Let's say this is in connection with the trains that go from Charing Cross to Ashford, where one has to change for the trains to—"

"Gawd, I don't know. Apples?" Billy grinned.

"Appledore!"

"*Appledore?*"

"Yes, I used to go there with my father sometimes. We'd go fishing on the canal near Iden Lock." Maisie reached for the seal. "And that makes sense of this."

"What's that?"

"The seal from an envelope. Charlotte had probably received a letter from Camden Abbey, perhaps sent to her with the books and pamphlets, and as she began to read, she tore the seal from the envelope to mark her place."

"So what do you think, Miss? Can you tell from this little lot where she's gone off to?"

"It tells us that Charlotte was curious about the contemplative life. There's something I need to look into. I may know someone who can help us." Maisie gathered the items together and looked at her watch. "Let's move on. We can't allow one possibility to cloud our vision. Charlotte could have left these things to dupe her father. Or she could have left with such urgency as to forget them." She stood up. "Right then. Charlotte's run away before, but she's always let her father know where she is, in one way or another. He's assumed that she's hiding from him this time. We have to question that assumption and consider other possibilities. Even if we take his account of her departure as truth, she may now be being held against her will, or she may have met with an accident. And of course we cannot rule out the possibility that she may have taken her own life. But let us begin by assuming that she has disappeared voluntarily, has been gone for several days and has deliberately covered her tracks. Why did she leave this time? Where is she? Has she run *from* something or *to* something—or *someone*? I want us to try to have a better feeling for what went on last Saturday, and how far we can believe Waite's version of events. No need to move anything on the table, but just help me shift it over there a bit, so it's in the middle of the room."

Billy took one end of the table, while Maisie took the other, and they placed it where Maisie indicated.

"You can be Waite, so sit at this end." Maisie pointed out the place where Billy should set his chair.

"I'll need to shove me jacket up inside me cardigan, Miss, seeing as I ain't got quite the middle that 'e 'as."

"Pretend, Billy. Seriously, I want you to close your eyes, sit at the table, and truly imagine that you are Joseph Waite. I'll go outside the door, give you a couple of minutes, then I'll come in and sit down as if I'm Charlotte. For the purposes of this experiment, I *am* Charlotte."

"Awright." Billy frowned. "I'll give it a go."

Maisie nodded, and walked toward the door, but before reaching for the handle, she turned to her desk, took the *Times* from her briefcase, and dropped it on the table in front of him.

"You'll probably be reading this."

She left the room as Billy shifted uncomfortably in the seat. He closed his eyes, drew back his shoulders, tucked his legs underneath the chair so that his heels rode up and the balls of his feet supported the imaginary weight of his middle. His war wound nipped at his leg as he moved, but he ignored it. He puffed out his cheeks for just a few seconds, and imagined what it might be like to have built a successful enterprise to become a powerful man of commerce. Slowly he began to feel quite different, and realized he was getting just an inkling of the way in which Maisie used her knowledge of the body to gain an understanding of another person. He reached for the newspaper and snapped it open, feeling richer than he had felt in a good long while. And it surprised him that he felt a glimmer of an emotion that rarely surfaced in his being: anger.

"Good morning, Father," said Maisie, entering the room.

"Good morning, Charlotte." Billy reached for his pocket watch, noted the time, and placed the newspaper on the table between them. "What are you doing with yourself today?" He continued, checking his watch again, and taking a sip of tea.

"I thought I might go shopping and meet a friend for lunch."

"Nothing better to do today, Charlotte?"

There was an edge to Billy's voice that almost caused Maisie to break out of character and look up, but she continued, defiantly. "What do you *want* me to do, Father?"

Billy consulted his watch again without responding, while Maisie—as Charlotte—reached for the newspaper. She turned to the front page, read barely two lines, then suddenly gasped and burst into tears. She threw down the paper, scraped back her chair, and ran from the room with her hand covering her mouth. Billy sighed, wiped his brow, and stretched out his legs, happy to be rid of his assumed character.

Maisie returned. "That was an interesting exercise, wasn't it?"

"It was really strange, Miss. I remembered watching 'im when 'e talked about Charlotte, so I mimicked his posture."

Maisie nodded for Billy to continue.

"And, well, it was right peculiar, it was, 'ow I started to feel different, like another person."

"Explain, Billy. I know this seems difficult, but it is most important and helpful."

"I was right touchy, like a piece of tinder ready to catch fire. I started to think about the father that died down the coal pit, 'is mother and 'ow she must've 'ad to work 'er fingers to the bone, and then all that 'e'd gone through, 'ard graft, and all. Then I thought about the wife up in Yorkshire, sittin' on 'er behind, and by the time you walked in the door, I felt all of what 'e'd felt—well, what I felt 'e'd felt—and, to be quite 'onest with you, I didn't even really 'ave patience with you. I mean Charlotte."

" Do you believe he was in the room when Charlotte ran out?"

"I reckon so, but it was as if I was *making* meself sit there, because I'm determined not to let 'er annoy me. I couldn't do any more reading of the newspaper, I was so . . . so angry! That's why I 'anded it to 'er, I mean you. What about you, Miss?"

"You know, after seeing Charlotte's room yesterday, in taking on her character I wasn't exactly 'full of the joys of spring.' I didn't get that feeling at all when I was in her room. Instead, I had the sense of a troubled soul. But there must have been provocation of some sort to make her leave home. I have to say, I felt other emotions, though

I confess I am now drawing upon the feelings I intuited when we went into her room and when I was alone for a while." Maisie picked up a pencil from the table and began to doodle along the bottom of the paper. She drew an eye with a single tear seeping from the corner.

"What did you 'sense,' then?" asked Billy.

"She was confused. As I acted her part at breakfast, I felt a conflict. I could not hate my father, though I dislike what he is and I am trying desperately not to be intimidated by him. I would like to leave his house, to live elsewhere, anywhere. But I'm stuck." Maisie looked out of the window, allowing her eyelids to close halfway and rest as she considered Charlotte Waite. "I felt defiant when I first picked up the newspaper which, according to Waite, was the last thing Charlotte did before bursting into tears and leaving the room."

Billy nodded as Maisie got up from her chair and walked to the window with her arms crossed.

"What this exercise suggests is that Waite's recounting of his daughter's departure has only a tenuous relationship to the truth. It serves to remind us that the story we heard yesterday was told through *his* eyes. To him, it may be exactly as it happened, but I think if you asked Charlotte, or a fly on the wall, you'd get a different account. One thing, though: We should go through Saturday's *Times* to see if anything in it caused Charlotte Waite's distress."

Maisie flicked a piece of lint from her new burgundy suit, which she was beginning to think had been purchased in error as it seemed to attract any white fiber that happened to be passing.

"I'll get a copy." Billy made a note in the cloth-bound palm-size book he carried with him.

"Let's put the table back and go over the rest of the visit carefully. Then I've some paperwork to do before we go our separate ways at noon. We should meet back here about five, to exchange notes."

"Right you are, Miss."

"By the way, I didn't know you could mimic a northern accent."

Billy looked surprised as he leafed through his notebook, pencil at the ready to work on the case map. "What d'yer mean, Miss? I ain't got no northern accent. I'm an East End of London boy. Shoreditch born and bred, that's me."

<br>

*B*illy left the office first, taking with him the address book found in Charlotte Waite's rooms. There were few names listed, all with London addresses except for a cousin and Charlotte's mother, both in Yorkshire. Billy had already confirmed that Charlotte had not sought refuge with either of them. As Joseph Waite supported both his wife and niece, it was unlikely that they would risk their future financial security by deceit. Billy's next task was to confirm each name listed and also find out more about Charlotte's former fiancé, Gerald Bartrup.

Maisie cast a final glance around the office, then departed after locking up. Once outside, she made her way along Fitzroy Street, then Charlotte Street, taking a route parallel to Tottenham Court Road. As she walked toward her destination—the Waite's International Store on Oxford Street—she turned the contents of Charlotte's address book over in her mind, then mentally walked through Charlotte's rooms once more. Maisie always maintained that first impressions of a room or a person were akin to soup when it was fresh. One can appreciate the flavor, the heat and the ingredients that went into the pot that will merge together to provide sustenance. But it's on the second day that a soup really reveals itself and releases the blending of spices and aromas onto the tastebuds. In the same way, as Maisie walked through the rooms in her mind's eye, she was aware of the rigid control that pervaded the Waite household and must have enveloped Charlotte like a shroud.

In suggesting they recreate the scene at breakfast, when Charlotte Waite hurriedly left the room in a flood of tears, Maisie was using one of Maurice's training techniques that had become a standard part of their investigative procedure. She knew that, as her assistant, Billy had to be constantly aware of every single piece of information and evidence that emerged as their work on a case developed. His senses must be fine-tuned, and he had to think beyond what was seen, heard and read. Useful information might just as likely be derived from intuition. He must learn to question, she thought, not to take any evidence at face value. Maurice often quoted one of his former colleagues, the famous professor of forensic medicine, Alexandre Lacassagne, who had died some years earlier: *As my friend Lacassagne would say, Maisie, 'One must know how to doubt.'*

As Maisie walked purposefully toward the shop, a key question nagged at her: Where would a person who carried such a heavy burden run to? Where could she go to find solace, compassion—and herself? As she considered the possibilities, Maisie cautioned herself not to jump to conclusions.

She walked along Charlotte Street, then crossed into Rathbone Place until she reached Oxford Street. Joseph Waite's conspicuous grocery shop was situated across the road, between Charing Cross Road and Soho Street. For a few moments, Maisie stood looking at the shop. Blue-striped awnings matching the tiled exterior extended over the double doors through which customers entered. To the left of the door, a showcase window held a presentation of fancy tinned foods and fruits and vegetables; to the right, a corresponding window held a display of meats. Whole carcasses were hooked to a brass bar that ran along the top and chickens hung from another brass bar halfway down. A selection of meats was displayed on an angled counter topped with a slab of marble to better exhibit the legs of lamb, pork chops, minced meats, stewing steaks, and other cuts strategically placed and garnished with bunches of parsley, sage, and thyme to tempt the customer.

Above the awnings was a tile mosaic that spelled out the words WAITE'S INTERNATIONAL STORES. In smaller letters underneath, the sign read: A FAMILY BUSINESS. EST. 1885.

As customers went in and out of the shop, a small group of children gathered by the window and held out their cupped hands, hoping for a coin or two from the shoppers. Such booty would not be spent on sweets or trinkets, for these children knew the stab of hunger from an empty belly and the smarting pain of a clip around the ear if they came home without a few precious pennies for the family's keep. Maisie knew that for each child waiting there was a mother who watered down a stew to make it go farther, and a father who had walked all day from one employment line to another. Whatever else Joseph Waite might be, he was not completely without feeling. It had been reported in the newspapers that at the end of each day, any food that might spoil before the shops opened the next morning was delivered to soup kitchens in the poorest areas.

Maisie crossed the road and walked through the elegant doors. Counters ran along the walls on either side, with a third connecting them at the far end of the shop. Each was divided into sections, with one or two shop assistants working each section, dependent upon the number of customers waiting. There was an ornate brass till in each section, to receive cash for the items weighed and purchased. Of course the wealthy had accounts that were settled monthly or weekly, with the maid personally presenting an order that would be filled and delivered to the house by a blue-and-gold Waite's delivery van.

The oak floor was polished to a shine. As she watched, Maisie noticed that a boy swept the floor every quarter of an hour. As soon as he had finished making his way, broom in hand, from one end to the other, it was time for him to start again, rhythmically directing sawdust and any debris into a large dustpan as he worked back and forth, back and forth. White-tiled walls reflected the bright glass lights that hung from cast-iron ceiling fixtures, and along the top of the walls a border of colored tiles formed another mosaic, depicting the very best foods that money could buy. A marble-topped table stood in the center of the floor, groaning with a tableau of vegetables and tinned goods. Maisie wondered if a visitor entering the store would believe that there were people in Britain wanting for a good meal.

She walked around the shop, looking first at the cheese counter, then the fruits and vegetables. Dry goods were displayed in barrels and wooden boxes, and as a customer asked for a half pound of currants or a pound of rice, the assistant, dressed in a blue cotton dress and matching cap decorated with yellow piping, would measure the amount onto the scale, then tip the currants or rice into a blue paper bag, which was then folded at the top and handed, with a smile, to the customer. Money was handed over, and as the assistant pressed the brass keys of the heavy till, the tally popped up in the glass panel. Yes, thought Maisie, listening to the tills ringing and willing assistants advising on the best way to cook this or that, Waite's was weathering the country's economic woes very well. She walked to the other side of the shop and stood alongside the fancy-goods counter. A woman had just pointed to the glass-topped tin of biscuits and asked for "a good half-pound of Sweet Maries, please" when Maisie became aware that the physical energy in the shop had suddenly changed. A deep blue Rolls Royce had drawn up outside the entrance, and a chauffeur was walking around to the front passenger door. As Maisie watched, the man silhouetted inside removed his Homburg and in its place set a flat cap on his head. Ah, she thought: Joseph Waite, the "everyman" of the grocery trade. The man who was so in touch with his origins that he would sit alongside his chauffeur in his grand motor car—at least when he was visiting one of his shops.

Waite dispatched the chauffeur to send the street urchins away from the store with a penny each for their trouble. Then he strode into his store, light of foot despite his extra weight. He stopped to speak to each customer on his way to the first counter, and Maisie felt the force of personality that had made him rich, famous, and loved by working-class folk and the privileged alike. Waite was the common man, in business *for* the people who made him what he had become, or so it seemed as he took over the cheese counter, asking the next customer what he could do for her on this bright day. As the woman gave her order, Waite made much of washing his hands at the sink situated on the wall behind the counter, then turned and took up a half wheel of English cheddar. Positioning the cheese on a marble slab, Waite drew the wire cutter across, placed the wedge of cheddar on a wafer of waxed paper, weighed it, then held the cheese out for her inspection in the palm of his hand. Maisie noticed that while washing his hands he had whispered to the assistant. Now as he said, "A nice half-pound for you *exactly*, Mrs. Johnson," she realized that he had asked the customer's name,

Mrs. Johnson blushed and nodded agreement, uttering a shy "thank-you" to the famous Joseph Waite. As he placed the cheese in a paper bag and twisted the corners to secure the item, she turned to other customers and smiled, eager to be seen basking in these few moments of attention from the man himself.

Waite moved on, working at each counter before reaching the section where he was clearly in his element: the meat counter. It was the most decorated part of the shop, with the stuffed head of an Aberdeen Angus mounted on the wall behind the counter, complete with a ring through its nose and glassy eyes that betrayed the fury the beast must have felt upon being taken to the slaughterhouse. Whole carcasses hung from a horizontal brass rod near the ceiling, which could be lowered by a pulley secured on the left-hand wall. The tills had been ringing at a steady pace until Waite walked into his domain. Now they rang even more briskly.

Waving the assistants to one side, he snapped his fingers. An apprentice appeared bearing a freshly laundered white butcher's apron, which he unfolded and held ready. Taking off his jacket, Waite handed it to another assistant, turned and washed his hands again, drying them on a fresh white towel held at the ready by a young boy. He took the apron and placed the bib over his head, wrapping the strings around his waist, bringing them to the front, and tying a double knot. One of the apprentices had begun to operate the rope pulley, slowly inching the carcasses down to ground level, whereupon two others, wearing butchers' white aprons, white shirts and blue-and-gold bow ties, lifted a pig carcass onto the marble slab.

Swiftly and deftly Waite wielded the cleaver and boning knife, his sausage-like fingers holding the meat steady while he separated legs, ribs, trotters, joints, and muscle. With a flourish he held up a leg of pork, explaining to the customers who had gathered to watch Joseph Waite, the famous butchers' boy who had done so very well, yet knew what it was to be poor—that even the cheapest cuts could be cooked to provide a succulent Sunday dinner, and the leftovers minced together with a few carrots, potatoes and a little bit of onion for a pie on Monday—which would, of course, last until Tuesday or Wednesday.

Waite finished preparing the carcass for display and sale and, as he removed his apron, his customers broke into applause. Waite waved an acknowledgment, then washed his hands once more and turned to the apprentice holding out his jacket. He slipped into it, nodded to his staff, and waved to the customers one last time before leaving by a side door that Maisie assumed led to the upstairs offices. The assistants exchanged glances and exhaled, blowing out their cheeks for added emphasis, relieved that the ritual was over.

Having seen all she had come to see, Maisie turned to leave. She had taken only one step when her eyes were drawn to the wall above the doorway and another mosaic crafted at great expense. It was not its beauty that caused Maisie to catch her breath, but the sad truth inscribed there. Upon each tile was the name of an employee of Waite's International Stores lost in the Great War. There were at least one hundred, each name accompanied by the town in which the man had worked. Above the names a banner of colored tiles formed the words: IN LOVING REMEMBRANCE—LEST WE FORGET.

Maisie's eyes filled with tears as she was taken once again by the grief that still assailed her when she least expected it, when the sharp and dreadful memories came to her unbidden. Maisie knew the recollections were not hers exclusively. A shared grief often seemed to linger in the air, perhaps borne on a soft breeze carrying the name of one who was lost heard in conversation or remembered at a gathering, and the realization that one or two of that group were gone, their laughter never to be heard again. It was as if the sorrow of every single man and woman who had lived with the fear or reality of losing a loved one to war had formed an abyss to be negotiated anew every day.

Composing herself, Maisie approached an assistant at the cheese counter, who had no customers to serve at the moment.

"Excuse me."

"Yes, Madam, how may I help you today?"

"I just wondered about the names on the wall."

"Oh, yes, Miss. Tragic, we lost so many. Joined up as pals, a lot of 'em. The Waite's Boys, they called themselves. Mr. Waite had that memorial started as soon as the first were lost. There's one in every Waite's shop, all the same, all the names in every shop."

"You must all think a lot of him." Maisie inclined her head, seeking a response.

The assistant smiled. "Yes, we all think a lot of him, Madam. And he looks after all the families." He nodded toward the memorial tiles.

"You mean financially?"

"Yes, there's not one of those families wants for anything. They get their groceries every Christmas, and a Christmas box—money, you know—and they get a bit off their groceries if they shop at Waite's. Got special little cards, they have, to get the money back. And if anyone's taken poorly, well, Mr. Waite's office is under orders to look after them."

"I see. Very generous, isn't he?"

"Very." The assistant moved to end the conversation as a customer approached, then continued. "Read through those names, Madam, and you'll see why Mr. Waite has a personal interest in the families."

Maisie looked above the door and read: "Gough, Gould, Gowden, Haines, Jackson, Michaels, Richards"—her eyes focused on the bottom of one column, then rose to the top of the next—"Waite . . . Joseph Charles Waite, Jr., London." She could read no further.

# CHAPTER THREE

*O*n Tuesday afternoon, following her visit to the branch of
Waite's International Stores, Maisie telephoned the offices
of Carstairs & Clifton and requested an immediate
appointment with Mr. Gerald Bartrup, for whom she had received a
personal recommendation. She had no doubt that her request would
be granted, for new customers seeking investment advice were thin
on the ground in such times. Maisie was curious about the relationship between Bartrup and Charlotte. Had theirs been a love match
that had soured with time and deeper familiarity? Or had Charlotte
been pressured by her father to make a suitable marriage? The
engagement had ended, but was there still a connection? If so,
Charlotte might well have appealed to her former fiancé upon flee-
ing her father's house.

She alighted at Bank underground station, and walked to the red-
brick building that housed the offices of Carstairs & Clifton. A door-
man directed her to the reception desk, where her appointment was
confirmed, and she was directed to a staircase, at the top of which she
was met by another clerk who escorted her to Mr. Bartrup's office.

Bartrup, a man of medium height, about thirty-eight years old, with a receding hairline and a rather florid complexion, came from behind a large mahogany desk and extended a hand. "Ah, Miss Dobbs. Delighted to meet you."

"And I you, Mr. Bartrup."

"Do take a seat. Would you like some refreshment? Tea, perhaps?"

"No thank you, Mr. Bartrup."

Bartrup took his place behind the desk, and placed his hands together on the leather blotting pad in front of him.

"Now, then, you wish to discuss investment of a legacy I understand, Miss Dobbs?"

"Mr. Bartrup. I must confess immediately that investment counsel is not my reason for coming to see you today."

"But, I thought . . . ." The flustered man reached for a file on his desk.

"Mr. Bartrup, I wanted to speak to you in confidence about a matter of urgency. I am working on behalf of Mr. Joseph Waite, who is concerned about his daughter. She has recently left her father's home and has not since been in communication with her family."

Bartrup threw back his head and began to laugh. "Another bid for freedom until the old man locks her up again!"

"I beg your pardon?"

"Don't worry, I am speaking figuratively, not literally, Miss Dobbs. As you may have noticed, Mr. Joseph Waite runs a very tight ship, and will not brook any wishes counter to his own." He leaned toward Maisie. "And I suppose I am the wicked man who caused Her Royal Waiteness to leave, am I not?"

"I'm not implying that, Mr. Bartrup, though I had hoped you might be able to shed some light on her mood of late even if you do not know her whereabouts."

"I have no idea where she is. And Charlotte is *always* in a mood, Miss Dobbs. In fact, she was in quite the mood when she broke off our engagement some weeks ago."

"*She* broke off the engagement?"

"Oh yes. Without a 'by your leave' and with no explanation whatsoever. Didn't even look sorry about it. Was curt and to the point: 'I'm sorry, Gerald, we cannot marry. Our engagement is over.' And that was that."

"Do you have any idea—?"

"Why she did it?" Bartrup stood up and walked to the window. He turned to Maisie. "No, Miss Dobbs. No idea at all. But . . ." He looked down at his feet, then back at Maisie. "I can't say I was surprised or completely sorry. Charlotte is an attractive girl and by any standards it was a good match, but our communications had been difficult for some time. It was as if she were receding into herself. She is an unhappy woman, Miss Dobbs."

Maisie looked at Bartrup intently. "Can you tell me anything about Miss Waite's previous disappearances?"

"Not really. All I can tell you is that they occurred before we met, and apparently—I heard this from friends—they never lasted long. Frankly, she knew on which side her bread was buttered. We had been engaged for six months, with no date set for the wedding. Of course we'd come up with possibilities, but a reason was always found to eliminate that date and go back to the drawing board. Sometimes Charlotte discovered the conflicting engagement, sometimes her father. She did not do the disappearing act while we were courting, or after we became engaged, though I had been warned by others about her previous forays into freedom away from the pressures of living in Waite-shire!"

Bartrup smiled, though Maisie suspected that he still felt the sting of being cast aside by Charlotte Waite.

"Mind you," he added, "our engagement ended some two months ago, so that couldn't have made her bolt." Bartrup looked thoughtful, then consulted his watch. "Good Lord! Miss Dobbs, I can manage one last question, then I must proceed to my next appointment."

Maisie sensed that there was no other appointment, but one last question would be sufficient. "Thank you, Mr. Bartrup. It's a simple question: Where do you think Charlotte might be? Where would she run to?"

Bartrup sighed, and leaned his chin on the fist he made with both hands, his elbows on the table in front of him. "I wish I could help you, Miss Dobbs, but I really don't know. She certainly didn't come to me, nor am I someone she would confide in."

"You must have been saddened by your engagement ending, Mr. Bartrup."

"Frankly, at first I was taken aback, but then, well, one has to just get on with it, doesn't one?"

"I have taken a good deal of your time, Mr. Bartrup, and I must thank you." Maisie stood and held out her hand for Bartrup, who returned her handshake.

"If I can be of any help, Miss Dobbs, please do not hesitate to call again, though afternoon is always best, given the vagaries of work in the City."

"Of course. Thank you." Maisie bade him farewell and was escorted out of the offices of Carstairs & Clifton. She emerged into bright mid-afternoon sunshine, and hurried to Bank underground station for the quick journey back to Fitzroy Square. Maisie knew that Billy would not return to the office before five o'clock, so she would have some time to review Maurice's notes again and gather her thoughts. Bartrup had been of almost no help, and recollection of the conversation led her to believe that Charlotte had probably done well to break off the engagement. Marriage to such a man would have provided no comfort except financial, and Charlotte had no urgent need for economic security. Perhaps Charlotte's curiosity about the contemplative life, that the book and pamphlets in her room suggested, stemmed from a desire for a deeper, more intimate connection than that promised by marriage to the men in her circle.

Walking across Fitzroy Square, Maisie felt an ominous chill in the air and looked up to see heavy gray cumulus clouds, which seemed to her like water-filled balloons ready to burst. She picked up her pace, keys at the ready to open the front door. She entered the room just in time to see long needles of rain slanting across the windows where sunlight had filtered in that morning.

Maisie removed her mackintosh, hung it on the hook behind the door, and went to a filing cabinet that contained more extensive information than that in the card file. She was concerned; thus far she had made no progress, had perhaps wasted time. The various elements of information gathered indicated to Maisie that finding Charlotte Waite might be even more urgent than her overbearing, yet in some ways dismissive, father believed. As Maisie unlocked the cabinet, she reflected upon the memorial tiles in Joseph Waite's store and admonished herself: How had she missed the fact that Waite had a son?

Leafing through the manila folders, Maisie found the file she was looking for and took it to her desk. She began to remove notes and letters from it, fanning them out on the desk in front of her. Knowing that at that point Maurice might have cautioned her against anger directed at the self, Maisie quickly sat back in the chair with her eyes closed. She placed her left hand on her solar plexus to become centered, and her right hand across her heart to denote kindness, as she had been taught by Khan. She took several deep breaths, opened her eyes, and looked at the documents in front of her, with the intention of studying carefully every detail of Joseph Waite's background. She read for some time, jotted notes and words on a sheet of paper that she would later add to the case map. The thud of the outer door being closed brought her contemplative silence to an end, followed by the unmistakable "dot-and-carry-one" footfall of Billy Beale climbing the stairs. The door opened and immediately Maisie felt the energy in the room change as Billy entered. Clearly he had news to impart.

"Afternoon, Miss. Nice to see the days starting to get longer, innit? Not that you'd notice this afternoon." Billy shook out his overcoat and hung it on the back of the door, while Maisie looked in dismay at the droplets of rainwater that now speckled the floor. "Didn't it come down, all of a sudden? I thought it'd 'old off, what wiv it clearin' up this mornin'."

"Indeed, Billy. Um, could you get a cloth and wipe up the water on the floor?"

"Aw, sorry, Miss." Billy took a rag from one of the drawers in his desk and slowly bent down to mop up the rainwater, favoring the aching knee.

Having completed the task, Billy took his notebook, Charlotte Waite's address book, and a newspaper from the inside pocket of his overcoat, and sat down beside Maisie at the table by the window.

"Well, I don't know about you, Miss, but I've 'ad a very interestin' day."

"I'm delighted to hear it."

Billy placed the address book in front of Maisie, inclined his head toward it, and grinned. "Notice anything strange about this 'ere book?"

Maisie picked up the black leather-bound book, ran her fingers around the closed gilt-edged pages, and flicked open a page or two.

"Go on."

"Well, I ain't never 'ad an address book meself. I might scratch down somethin' on the back of me *Daily Sketch*, but I've never gone in for addresses all written down in alphabetical order, like."

Maisie nodded.

"But what I reckon is that people like you, what 'ave address books because they know enough people to 'ave to write down all the names and addresses and telephone numbers and all, don't 'ave address books that look like this." Billy reached for the book, flapped it back and forth, and then set it down on the table again for effect. "I bet if we looked through your address book, it'd be full of directions and notes and some telephone numbers, and some people would've moved so many times, you've 'ad to scribble out the address to put the new one in. Then no sooner've you done that, they've either moved again or gone and got themselves married and changed names, so you 'ave to move the 'ole thing."

"You've got a point there, Billy."

"Well, I looked at this book, and I thought to meself that she either don't know many people or this ain't 'er main address book."

"Do you think she deliberately left a bogus address book to fool people who searched for her?" Maisie tested Billy.

"Nah, I don't think she's that sort. 'Specially if she ran off a bit quick. No, 'ere's what I think 'appened: She 'ad a new book for a present or bought 'erself a new book because the old one's got a bit tatty. So she starts to put in the names and—course, I'm speculatin' 'ere, Miss—starts with the people she knows best *now*. They're the ones it's most important to 'ave in the book. But because it's not the most thrillin' job, she puts it off and still goes back to 'er old book, because she's used to it, it's like an old friend in itself."

"Good thinking, Billy."

"Anyway, this is all well and good, because the people who're important *now* in 'er life are all 'ere—and by the way, I saw one of 'em today, I'll tell you about that next—but the ones from a long time ago, what she probably 'asn't seen for ages and only keeps the name in the book so she can send a card at Christmas, ain't 'ere . . . and Charlotte Waite took 'er old book with 'er to wherever she went off to."

"I am very impressed, Billy; you've put a lot of thought into this." Maisie smiled.

Billy sat up straighter and reached for his notebook. "So, I was standin' outside the 'ome of, let me see, 'ere we are—Lydia Fisher. Lives in Cheyne Mews—very nice, I'm sure. So, I was standin' outside, taking a dekko at the premises, when up she comes in 'er car. Very posh, I must say. She was dressed to the nines, bright red lips, and that black stuff on 'er eyes, fur draped over 'er shoulder. Of course, I 'ad to say somethin' to 'er, didn't I?" Billy held out his upturned palms for effect. "Seein' as she'd almost knocked me into the wall with 'er drivin' and that she'd see me again when we do our official inquiry. So I told 'er my name, and that I worked for you, and that what I 'ad to say was in confidence."

"And you had this conversation out in the street?"

"Well, the beginnin' of it, yes. I said that we was workin' for the Waite family, and she says, 'Do come in.' There was a maid who brought us tea in the upstairs drawin' room. Mind you, the lady knocked back a couple of quick ones, poured 'em 'erself from one of them fancy crystal decanters on the sideboard. She's only got a maid and a cook, is my guess. Probably no chauffeur because she seems to like 'avin' the car to 'erself." Billy cleared his throat and continued. "So I says that, it's all confidential, that Charlotte Waite 'ad left 'er father's 'ome, and that we'd been retained to look for 'er."

"Good."

"Well, she rolls 'er eyes, says, 'Again!' all snotty, like, then says, "That's no surprise, she's run so many times, they should put that woman in the Olympics!' I knew what she meant, what wiv what we already know about Miss Waite. Then she says, 'Well, not to worry, she's finally run off to a convent, I expect,' to which, Miss, I said, "Are you serious, Miss Fisher?' She says, all airs and all, '*Mrs*. Fisher, if you please.' Anyway, it turns out that in their last two luncheons, Miss Waite'd talked about the end of her engagement and 'ow she couldn't find someone she really loved, so she might as well go off to live in a nunnery where she could at least be useful."

"Did Fisher think she meant it?"

"The funny thing is, y'know, she said that at first she thought Charlotte was tryin' to shock 'er. Then she said she realized that Charlotte might be serious, and that she'd been down to a place in Kent somewhere. 'Ow about that, then?"

"Well, that's interesting." Maisie understood how the serene image of a nun might appeal to a bored, unhappy young woman. She recalled wartime nurses being photographed in such a way as to evoke the purity and dedication of those in religious orders. Such romantic images subsequently encouraged more young women to enlist. "I wonder what Waite will have to say about that?" she added. "He didn't seem to be a religious man, and there's no references to either his beliefs or Catholicism in Maurice's notes."

"Do you think Charlotte is trying to annoy 'er father?"

"Well, she's not a child, but she's clearly capable of such behavior."

Maisie was thoughtful. "You know, we could be awfully lucky here. I didn't say anything about it this morning because I didn't want to jump to conclusions and close our minds in the process, but I used to know an enclosed nun, Dame Constance Charteris. She was abbess of a community of Benedictines living close to Girton. She met with several students for tutorials on religious philosophy. Because they're an enclosed order, communication with outsiders takes place with a sort of barrier in between. I remember it was rather strange at first, being in tutorial with someone who sat behind a grille."

"And 'ow's that lucky, Miss?"

"I can't remember all the details, but shortly after I left Girton to become a VAD nurse, the nuns had to find a new place to live. I think their abbey in Cambridgeshire was requisitioned for military use, and I could swear they went to Kent. I just need to make a couple of telephone calls to find out, and if that's so, I'll send word to Dame Constance, asking to see her as soon as possible."

"Can't we just go down there, see if Miss Waite is there, and put a tin lid on this case?"

Maisie shook her head. "No, Billy. If Charlotte Waite has sought her out, Dame Constance will be very protective of her *and* what the Benedictines stand for."

"I bet old Waite would just march in, find out if Charlotte was there and—if she was—drag her out."

"He could try." Maisie smiled at her assistant. "But I wouldn't bet on his chances against Dame Constance. No, let's do this with an eye to protocol; it'll serve us well."

Billy nodded, and Maisie reached for her own notes.

She described Joseph Waite, the way in which his forceful personality filled the shop, drawing customers to him with his easy camaraderie while at the same time intimidating his staff. Maisie explained to Billy how such intimidation seemed at odds with the regard the assistants appeared to have for Waite, especially for the way he looked after the families of those fallen in the Great War.

Billy chimed in, "Y'know what my ol' father used to say, don't you?

'e used to say that if you 'ad workers, it wasn't so important to be liked as it was to be respected, and it was possible to respect someone without actually likin' them. P'r'aps Waite doesn't need to be liked."

"I think that's a fairly accurate assessment of the situation." Maisie nodded, and continued, "The other thing, and the most important: Joseph Waite lost a son in the war, a son who worked for him at the shop. He was probably being groomed to inherit the business."

Billy was surprised. "P'r'aps that's why 'es so, y'know, miserable. After all, 'e would be, especially if that girl of 'is is a bit of a drooping flower."

"I think 'wilting lily' was the phrase he used. And yes, it could account for a lot, but might have nothing at all to do with Charlotte's disappearance, which must obviously be our focus."

"What 'appened to 'im, the son?"

"It appears that young Waite was killed along with many men employed by Waite's. They joined up together. Joseph was a product of Waite's first marriage. Waite married, quite literally, the girl next door, when he was twenty-four and she was twenty. Sadly, she died in childbirth a year later. By then Waite was doing quite well, but it must have been yet another heavy loss to add to his list."

"It's a wonder 'e didn't mention it the other day. Y'know, when 'e was going on about despair."

"Yes and no. Extreme emotions are strange forces, Billy. The loss of his son might be kept separate from his other griefs, his alone, shared with no one." Maisie stopped for a moment, then continued speaking: "One of Waite's sisters, who was unmarried at the time, came to live at his house to care for the child. As you can imagine, Waite kept his family employed, so they were well looked after, except the brother he spoke of yesterday, who had gone to work at the pit. The son would have been about six when Waite remarried in haste and, as you know, Charlotte was born seven months later. So Joseph, the son, was seven when his sister was born. By the way, you'll notice young Joseph's middle name was Charles, and the daughter was christened Charlotte. Joseph Waite's father was Charles. Thus he effectively named both children after their late grandfather."

Maisie reached for the colored pencils and drew them toward Billy and herself. "Now then, let's map this out and see what we might have missed." They began working together, and after a few minutes Maisie continued. "I'll visit Lydia Fisher this week, Billy. Tomorrow morning, I think, so don't expect me in until lunchtime-ish. It's going to be a very busy week, I may not be able to keep my Friday luncheon appointment with Inspector Stratton."

"Oh, Miss—" Billy suddenly laid a red pencil down on the desk and hit his forehead smartly, as if to reprimand himself for his forgetfulness. "That reminds me, you mentionin' D. I. Stratton. I spoke to ol' Jack Barker—y'know, who sells the *Express* outside Warren Street station— and 'e spoke to 'is mate what sells the *Times*, who 'ad a copy or two leftover from the weekend."

"What has that got to do with Inspector Stratton?"

"Remember we was talkin' about 'im bein' on that case of the woman who'd been murdered, in Coulsden?"

"Yes."

"I said I'd find out what Charlotte Waite was readin', y'know, when she did a runner out of the room where they 'ad breakfast."

Maisie drew breath sharply.

"Anyway, it turns out that the *Times*—and every other paper this last weekend, for that matter—printed the latest news about that woman who'd been found murdered in Coulsden. 'er name was Philippa Sedgewick. She was married, about your age—remember I remarked on it? And she was a vicar's daughter. The *Times* listed it on the front page, wiv the main story on page two. It was right there wiv all the important news, about the deficit and unemployment, and about Mr. Gandhi's walk to the sea for salt. All the papers 'ad the murder story, wiv all the 'orrible details. Would've turned anyone off their breakfast."

Maisie tapped her pencil on the palm of her hand. Billy said nothing, knowing that Maisie was disengaging her mind from his. She looked out of the window at the evening sky. Perhaps it wasn't such a coincidence that Billy had mentioned Mr. Gandhi. Khan had spoken of the man and his idea of *satyagraha*, which in Sanskrit meant "insistence on truth." Maisie shivered, remembering the emotions she had experienced while sitting in Charlotte Waite's rooms, the most powerful of which was the melancholy that seeped from every nook and cranny in the place where the missing woman had lived. Perhaps fear and not an overbearing father had been the true impetus for Charlotte's flight.

# CHAPTER FOUR

*T*he previous September Lady Rowan had insisted that
Maisie leave the rented bed-sitting room next to her
Warren Street office and live in their Belgravia mansion's
second-floor apartment. At first Maisie declined, for she had been a resident of the house before, when she came to live in the servants' quarters at the age of thirteen. And though the veil of class distinction that
separated Maisie and her employer had been lifted over the years—
especially as Lady Rowan became more involved in sponsoring
Maisie's education—the memory of those early days in their relationship lingered like a faint scent in the air. The offer was well meant, yet
Maisie feared that the change in status might be difficult. Finally, however, she had allowed herself to be persuaded.

One evening just after taking up residence, Maisie had waited until
the downstairs staff were having a cup of nighttime cocoa in the kitchen,
then quietly slipped through the door on the landing that led to the
back stairs. She made her way up to the servants' quarters, to the room
she'd occupied when she first came to 15 Ebury Place. The furniture
was covered in sheets, as the girls who usually slept in this room were
currently at Chelstone, the Comptons' country estate in Kent. Maisie

sat on the cast-iron-framed bed she had once wearily climbed into every night, with work-worn hands and an aching back. It was Enid she thought of, her friend and fellow servant who had left the Compton's employ to seek more lucrative work in a munitions factory in late 1914. Maisie had seen her for the last time in April 1915, just a few hours before she was killed in an explosion at the factory.

Maisie consulted her watch. She had to hurry. She wanted to look her best to gain an audience with the possibly indisposed Mrs. Fisher, and to do that she must appear on a social par with her.

She had purchased several new items of clothing recently, an expenditure that nagged at her, for she was not given to frivolous spending. But as Lady Rowan pointed out, "It's all very well wearing those plain clothes while you're snooping around London or tramping through a field, but you've important clients who will want to know they are dealing with someone successful!"

So Maisie had invested in the burgundy ensemble that subsequently seemed to pick up lint all too quickly, a black dress suitable for day or early-evening wear, and the deep-plum-colored suit she now laid out on the bed. The long-line jacket had a shawl collar that extended down to a single button at just below waist level and set to one side. Maisie chose a plain cream silk blouse with a jewel neckline to wear under the jacket, and a string of pearls with matching earrings. The jacket cuffs bore only one button, and revealed just a half inch of silk at each wrist. The matching knife-pleated skirt fell just below the knee. The cost of her silk stockings made her shudder as she put them on. She took care to lick her fingers quickly before running her hand through each stocking, to prevent a hangnail catching and causing an unsightly pull.

Maisie drew the line at matching shoes for each outfit, instead selecting her best plain black pair with a single strap that extended across her instep and buttoned with a square black button. The heels were a modest one-and-a-half inches.

She collected her black shoulder bag, her document case, an umbrella— just in case—and her new plum-colored hat with a black ribbon band gathered in a simple rosette at the side. The cloche she'd worn for some time now seemed tired, and though perfectly serviceable for an ordinary day's work, would not do today. This hat had a slightly broader, more fashionable brim, and revealed more of her face and midnight blue eyes. Maisie took care to pin back any tendrils of hair that looked as if they might creep out and go astray.

Maisie set off to walk to Cheyne Mews, exercise she enjoyed, for this morning the sky was robin's-egg blue, the sun was shining, and though she passed only a few people, they smiled readily and wished her a good morning. Gradually the number of pedestrians thinned out, until Maisie was the only person making her way along the avenue. A light breeze ran though the trees, causing newly unfolded leaves to rustle, and she was suddenly aware of a chill in the air, a chill so strong that it caused her to stop. She rubbed her arms and shivered. A sensation seemed to run across the back of her neck, as if an icy finger had been drawn from just below one earlobe across to the other, and Maisie was so sure someone was standing behind her that she turned quickly. But there was no one.

She was quite cold by the time she reached 9 Cheyne Mews, a typical mews house in which horses had once been stabled, facing a brick street. Now the only means of transportation evident to Maisie was a sleek new Lagonda parked outside the Fisher residence. She knew from George, the Comptons' chauffeur, who regularly regaled her with news of the latest automobile inventions, that this was an exclusive motor car, capable of more than ninety miles per hour. The Lagonda had been parked without due care; one of the front wheels rested on the narrow pavement. Unlike the neighboring houses, the three-storey house was plain, unadorned by windowboxes. There was just one step up to the front door. Maisie rang the bell and waited for the maid to answer. When no one came, Maisie rang the bell again and then a third time, at which point the door finally opened.

"Sorry M'um. Begging your pardon for keeping you waiting." The young maid was flushed and in tears.

"I'm here to see Mrs. Fisher." Maisie inclined her head. "Are you all right?"

"Yes, M'um." Her bottom lip trembled. "Well, I don't know, I'm sure." She took a handkerchief from the pocket of her lace apron and dabbed her eyes.

"What is it?" Maisie placed a hand on the maid's shoulder, a move that caused the girl to break down completely.

"Let's get you inside, and then tell me what's wrong."

Standing in the narrow hallway, the maid blurted out her fears. "Well, the lady hasn't got up yet, and I'm new here, see, and the cook, who knows her better than me, doesn't get here till half past eleven. The lady told me yesterday afternoon that she didn't want to be disturbed until nine this morning, and look at the time now! I've knocked and knocked, and I know she had a drink or two yesterday afternoon, and I know she would've kept going—I've learned that already—and she's got a temper on her if she's crossed, but she did say—"

"Now then, calm down and show me to her room."

The maid looked doubtful, but when Maisie informed her that she had once been a nurse, the maid nodded, rubbed her swollen eyes, and led Maisie up a flight of stairs to the first floor where the main reception and bedrooms were situated. She stopped outside a carved door that looked as if it might have been brought from an exotic overseas locale. Maisie knocked sharply.

"Mrs. Fisher. Are you awake? Mrs. Fisher!" Her voice was loud and clear, yet there was no answer. She tried opening the door, which was locked. Maisie knew that it was crucial that she gain entrance to the room.

"She may be indisposed, especially if she overindulged. I'll need to get into the room. Go downstairs and prepare a glass of water with liver salts for her."

The maid hurried downstairs. Maisie shook her head: She's so new she hasn't even asked my name.

Opening her document case, Maisie reached for a cloth bag with a drawstring top that contained several implements, similar to fishermen's needles, of varying size. She selected one. *That should do it.* She knelt, inserted the sharp point into the keyhole and manipulated the lock.

*Yes!* Maisie stood up, closed her eyes for just a second to control the images rushing into her mind's eye, and opened the door.

Lydia Fisher's body lay on the floor between an elegant pale blue chaise longue and an overturned side table, the contents of a tea tray strewn across an Aubusson rug. Maisie was never shocked upon encountering a scene of death. Not since the war. She automatically reached under the woman's left ear with her fingertips, feeling for a pulse. Nothing. No sign of life. Mrs. Fisher was dressed for an afternoon out. It appeared that she had not changed her clothes after arriving home yesterday.

The corridor floor creaked as the maid returned. Maisie moved quickly to the door to prevent the high-strung young woman from seeing into the room. She stopped her just in time.

"You must do exactly as I say. Telephone Scotland Yard. Ask to speak with Detective Inspector Stratton and no one else. Say that you are acting on the instructions of Miss Maisie Dobbs and that he is to come to this address immediately."

"Is Mrs. Fisher all right, M'um?"

"Just do as I say—now! When you've done that, come back to the room only if there is to be a delay or if you have not been able to speak personally to Inspector Stratton. When the police arrive, direct them to me straightaway."

Maisie estimated that she would have twenty minutes or so alone in the room. Not as much as she would have liked, but enough. Again she brought out the drawstring bag. She pulled out a folded pair of rubber gloves that were at least one size too small and pulled them onto her hands, pressing down between each finger for a snug fit. She turned to the body of Lydia Fisher.

The woman's clothing had been torn many times, though there was little blood from the multiple knife wounds to her chest. Kneeling, Maisie looked closely at each burnt umber-rimmed wound, taking care not to disturb the fabric of the victim's clothing or the position of her body. Next she turned her attention to the terror-filled dead eyes, then to the purple lips and mouth, and the fingers. *Ten minutes.*

The teapot had been smashed, but some of the dregs were caught in part of its base. Maisie reached into the drawstring bag and took out a small utensil similar to a salt spoon. She dipped it into the liquid and tasted. Then she moved closer and sniffed. Next she turned her attention to the room. Little time remained. Apparently Lydia Fisher had been killed while taking tea with a guest. Maisie suspected that the disarray in the room had been caused by Lydia herself. She walked around the body, noting the position of the chaise and of other furniture that had been disturbed. Ornaments had fallen from another side table, bottles had been knocked from the cocktail cabinet. Maisie nodded: morphine. The narcotic would have caused intense muscle spasms and hallucinations before death. The killer would have watched, perhaps avoiding ever weaker lunges by the victim for fifteen minutes or so before death occurred. And once Fisher was dead, the murderer, who had watched the woman die, had taken another portion of revenge with a knife. *Five minutes.*

Maisie closed her eyes and breathed deeply, trying to get a sense of what energies the events of the last twenty-four hours had left in their wake. Though death had surely accompanied him, Maisie felt that the visitor had been known to Lydia Fisher. Maisie had been to murder scenes on many occasions and had immediately felt the frenzy of attack. Fear, and hatred, the emotions that led to such a terrible outcome lingered and caused a constellation of violent jagged colors to blur her vision temporarily, as they had done this morning when she stood outside Lydia Fisher's carved door. *One more minute.*

Two motor cars screeched to a halt outside. Maisie deftly removed her gloves and returned them to the cloth bag, which she slipped into her case before moving to a position outside the door to wait for Stratton. She took one last look at Lydia Fisher's body and the terrible fear etched in the woman's wide-open eyes.

Maisie heard the maid answer the door, which was quickly followed by an introduction lacking any pleasantries by Stratton, and a terse "Good morning" from his sergeant, Caldwell. The maid informed them that Miss Dobbs was waiting upstairs.

Maisie greeted Stratton and Caldwell and led them into Lydia's drawing room.

"I came to the house hoping to meet with Mrs. Fisher in connection with an assignment. The maid was distressed that Mrs. Fisher had not answered her knock. She's new and I think somewhat intimidated by her employer. I informed her that I had been a nurse, and had her bring me here."

"Hmmm." Stratton, kneeling by the body, turned to Caldwell, who was inspecting the disarray in the room.

"Looks like she fought off the murderer, sir. Probably a big bloke, I'd say, what with all this mess."

Stratton met Maisie's eyes briefly. "I'll need the murder bag, Caldwell. And try to get hold of Sir Bernard Spilsbury. If you can't get him, then call out the duty man. Secure the property and place a cordon around the area."

Caldwell regarded Maisie with a smirk. "Will you be needing me when you question Miss Dobbs here, sir?"

Stratton sighed. "I will question Miss Dobbs later. This woman was murdered yesterday, probably late afternoon—as Miss Dobbs already knows." He glanced at Maisie. "For now I want to ensure that the body is inspected and removed for postmortem before the newspapermen arrive. And I have no doubt they'll arrive soon."

Maisie was asked to wait in the ground-floor reception room, where she was later questioned by Stratton, accompanied by Caldwell. Sir Bernard Spilsbury, the famous pathologist, arrived and Maisie was permitted to leave, though she knew there would be more questioning to come. As she departed the house she heard Caldwell voice his unsolicited opinion: "Well, sir, if you ask me, it's her old man. Nearly always is. Mind you, could be she had one on the side, woman like that, all furs and a big car of her own to gad about in. Who knows what she brought home!"

Maisie knew very well who Lydia Fisher had brought home yesterday afternoon. But who might have visited soon after—perhaps soon enough for the tea still to be warm in the pot? Had she answered the door herself? Billy had said the maid left the house on an errand after bringing tea, so he had seen himself out. Had Lydia poured another cup of tea in an effort to regain sobriety in the face of an unexpected caller? How had the visitor found an opportunity to introduce a narcotic into the tea? Had the caller seen that Lydia was intoxicated and offered to make fresh tea? Tea that could so easily be laced with poison? And could more of the drug have been administered while Lydia's muscles began to spasm after the first few sips? So many questions spun through Maisie's mind and the one person who could answer them was decidedly not available for questioning. Or was she?

Maisie wondered how she might gain access to Lydia Fisher's home once more. She wanted to know how Lydia Fisher lived and what had caused her grief, because of one thing she was sure: Lydia Fisher had grieved.

While she walked, Maisie remembered feeling a prickling of the skin on her neck while she stood in the upstairs hallway of Lydia Fisher's house, outside the room where her body lay. She had not shied away from the sensation but had instead silently asked, *What is it you want me to see?* Never before at the scene of a crime had Maisie had felt such a duality of sensation, like a fabric that on one side is smooth and satinlike but on the other, rough with a raised pile. She knew that the last person who had come to the house came with a terrible burden. A burden that was no lighter for having taken Lydia Fisher's life.

Maisie walked quickly toward Victoria underground station. She planned to return to her office as quickly as possible. She would leave a message for Billy to the effect that she would be back at five o'clock. Not a moment was to be lost in the search for Charlotte Waite. If the Coulsden victim, Philippa Sedgewick, had been Charlotte's friend, as was Lydia Fisher, then Charlotte must be found. One dead friend was a tragedy. Two dead friends . . . a terrifying coincidence.

Just as Maisie reached Victoria, the black car she had already seen once that day drew alongside her. The door opened, and Detective Inspector Richard Stratton emerged and tipped his hat.

"Miss Dobbs, I thought I might find you on your way to the station.

I noticed that you didn't have your little red motor with you today. Look—you've had a horrible time this morning—would you care to join me for a quick cup of tea?"

Maisie looked at her watch. Lunchtime had passed and she had hardly noticed. "Yes, I do have time—just—but I must be back at my office by five."

"I would be delighted to escort you there in the motor car. Let's just nip across the road." Stratton indicated a small teashop, and Maisie inclined her head in agreement.

Stratton took Maisie lightly by the elbow to steer her through the sparse traffic. Maisie knew he would likely be less solicitous when he questioned her again formally.

A waitress directed them to a corner table.

"Miss Dobbs, I'm curious about the fact that you visited Mrs. Fisher today of all days. Is there anything else you can tell me about your presence at the scene?"

"I've told you all I can, I believe. The victim was once a friend of the young woman I am seeking on behalf of a client. I thought she might be able to assist me."

The waitress returned with a tray and proceeded to set a white china teapot on the table, followed by a hot-water jug, sugar bowl, milk jug, and two matching white china teacups and saucers. She bobbed a curtsey and left the table, returning a moment later with a plate containing sliced Hovis bread with butter and jam, several iced fancy-cakes and two Eccles cakes.

"Hmmm. Interesting. Mind you, this woman had lots of friends."

"Perhaps mere acquaintances, Inspector."

"Yes, possibly." Stratton looked thoughtful as Maisie began to pour tea.

"So you put the milk in *after* the tea," said Stratton.

"The old London way, Inspector Stratton: Never put the milk in first because you might waste some. If you put it in last, you can tell exactly how much you really need." Maisie handed the cup of tea to Stratton, pushed the sugar bowl toward him, and filled her own cup.

As Stratton lifted the hot tea to his lips, Maisie pressed ahead with her own question. "I take it you agree that the murder at Cheyne Mews is linked to the Coulsden murder, Inspector?"

Stratton set his cup on the saucer so fiercely, the sound caused several people to look in their direction.

"Inspector, it really doesn't take much in the way of deduction." Maisie spoke softly.

Stratton regarded Maisie before answering. "In confidence . . ."

"Of course."

Stratton continued, "The scene was very much the same as the Coulsden murder, with very little bloodshed given the extent of the attack. Spilsbury suspects ingestion of a narcotic, most likely morphine, prior to an assault with a more violent weapon. The same method was used with the Coulsden victim. The body was cold, and rigor had set in."

"Has Spilsbury indicated the time of death yet?"

"Informally he confirmed it was yesterday, either in the late afternoon or in the evening. I'll have to wait until he submits his detailed report. He's usually more definite even at the scene of the murder. Apparently Lydia Fisher dismissed the maid after being served tea yesterday and neither she or the cook had seen her since. But according to the staff, that wasn't unusual. She was frequently known to go out at night without first requesting the assistance of her maid. And she often took to her rooms for several days on end, demanding not to be disturbed and furious if she was. The murderer could have locked the door to the room behind him, let himself out, and no one the wiser for hours. The cook said that the previous maid wouldn't turn a hair if Mrs. Fisher remained in her rooms for two or three days. If you hadn't arrived at the house and found the young maid in tears, the body could have lain there for a long time. The cook would have come along, told· her not to fuss, and that would have been that."

"Thank heavens I called to see her."

"There's something else. The maid went out after tea on Wednesday, which the victim took with a man of about thirty to thirty-five. By the way, Miss Dobbs, I must underline again the need for absolute confidence." Stratton sipped his tea and looked at Maisie intently.

"Of course, Inspector." Maisie wanted Stratton to continue.

"Anyway, he was of medium build, with a slight limp—possibly an old soldier—and he had hair 'like a stook of hay,' according to the maid. He's our best suspect thus far, so we must identify and find him as soon as possible."

Maisie set her cup on the saucer, wondering whether she should preempt Stratton's discovery that Billy Beale had been an earlier visitor. She quickly decided against it. *Perhaps* there had been another caller whose description was similar.

"Inspector, I know you might find this somewhat irregular, but I wonder, might I revisit the room where the body was found? A woman's insight might be helpful."

"Well, it *is* most irregular, Miss Dobbs."

Stratton looked at his watch. "I will consider it. Now then, I should ensure that you are escorted to your office."

Maisie waited for Stratton to pull back her chair. They were met outside by Stratton's driver, who drove them swiftly across London and, arriving at Fitzroy Square, parked the motor car on the pedestrian area outside Maisie's office.

"Having a police car is handy at times," said Stratton.

The driver opened the door for Stratton and Maisie to alight and, just as Stratton held out his hand to bid Maisie good-bye, Billy Beale came around the corner. He was carrying his cap. At that moment the last ray of afternoon sun caught his unruly blond hair at the same time as a rogue breeze swept across the square, giving the impression of a wayward halo around his head.

"Evenin', Miss; evenin', Detective Inspector Stratton."

Stratton shook hands with Billy, who touched his forehead, nodded to Maisie, and turned toward the front door. His appearance was not lost on Stratton, who watched Billy walk up the steps, pull the sleeve of his coat down over his hand and polish Maisie's nameplate in his customary fashion before taking out his key, unlocking the outer door, and entering the Georgian building. As he closed the door behind him, Stratton turned to face Maisie.

"Miss Dobbs, I think perhaps that there is more to discuss regarding your presence in Cheyne Mews this afternoon. However, we can do so tomorrow. I will be here at nine o'clock to collect you so that we may visit Lydia Fisher's house together. As you said, a woman's perspective might be of use to the police in the investigation of this crime."

Maisie held out her hand to Stratton. "Very well, Inspector. However, I would prefer to meet you at Victoria at, say, a quarter past nine? Then we can go on from there. I have other engagements during the day, so I must be back at my office by half past ten."

"Right you are, Miss Dobbs." Stratton nodded, stepped into the police car, and was driven away.

# CHAPTER FIVE

aisie doubted that Stratton would seriously consider Billy Beale a suspect. They had met before and Stratton seemed both impressed by Billy's devotion to his employer and amused by his enthusiastic approach to his new job. On the other hand, he might suspect that Maisie had gone to the house to cover up Billy's tracks. No, the Inspector was an intelligent man, he would not seriously consider such a thing, though he would want to question Billy to eliminate him from inquiries and to extract any useful observations.

Maisie reached the top step of the first flight of stairs and lingered over a concern: Joseph Waite's demand that the police not be notified of his daughter's disappearance despite the possible relevance of Charlotte's friendship with Lydia Fisher. The pursuit of the murderer might require that this information be disclosed. Maisie worried about the consequences of withholding evidence from Stratton. And she worried about something else: What if Waite was wrong? What if Charlotte had not disappeared of her own free will? What if she knew the murderer? Could she have become another victim? But then again, what if Charlotte had killed her friend—had killed two friends?

Before she could open the door to the office, it swung open and Billy stood waiting, his jacket removed and shirtsleeves rolled up, ready for work. Maisie looked at her watch.

"Billy, let's sit down."

Billy's ready smile evaporated. "What's wrong, Miss?"

"Sit down first, Billy."

Billy became agitated, which accentuated his limp. Maisie understood, knowing that the unease of the moment would strike his leg, a point of physical vulnerability.

Maisie sat opposite him and deliberately relaxed her body to bring calm to the room and to communicate that she was in control of the situation. "Billy, this morning I went to the home of Lydia Fisher in Cheyne Mews and found her—dead."

"Oh my Gawd!" Billy rose from the chair, half stumbling, to stand by the window. "I knew she was drinking too much." Agitated, he ran his fingers repeatedly through his hair. "I should've taken away the bottle, got on the blower to you, got you over there. You would've known what to do. I could've stopped 'er, I knew she was downin' 'em too fast, I should—"

"Billy." Maisie left the table and stood in front of her assistant. "Lydia Fisher was murdered after you left her yesterday. There was nothing you could have done."

"Murdered? Topped by someone?"

"Yes. The exact time of death has yet to be determined, but when I quickly examined the body, I estimated that she had lain there since early yesterday evening."

Maisie recounted her visit to the Fisher home, finding the body, her subsequent initial questioning and the meeting with Stratton later. Billy was fearful of the police interrogation that would doubtless ensue. Maisie asked Billy to describe this meeting with Lydia Fisher again, and his departure from the mews house.

"Billy, you did a good job," she said when he had concluded shakily. "I will explain to Detective Inspector Stratton that you were working on behalf of a concerned father, and so on. The challenge will be to keep the Waite name out of the conversation." Maisie rubbed her neck, thought for a moment, and continued. "But the fact is, apart from the killer, you were possibly the last person to see Lydia Fisher alive."

"And she was pretty well oiled when I left, and that's a fact."

"What was the time again?"

"I got back 'ere at five, didn't I? For our meetin'." As he spoke, Billy reached into his jacket, which was hanging over the back of the chair, and pulled out his notebook. "And I 'ad a couple of other errands to do, so it was about . . . 'ere we go, Miss, it was twenty-five past three in the afternoon."

"Was anyone else in the house at the time, other than the staff?"

"Now, it's funny that you should say that, Miss, because although I didn't see anyone, I thought someone else might be about. In fact, now I come to think of it, I saw a suitcase—one of them big leather ones with the straps—on the landing."

"That's interesting. I don't remember seeing a large suitcase this morning."

"P'r'aps the maid moved it. It could've belonged to Mrs Fisher, couldn't it? Remember, she corrected me, Miss? I noticed she 'ad a wedding ring on, but the 'ouse didn't 'ave that feelin' about it, y'know, like there was a man about."

"Why didn't you say anything about this, Billy?"

"Well, Miss, she wasn't dead then, was she? And I wasn't lookin' out for '*er*. I was only there to find out about Miss Waite, wasn't I?"

Maisie sighed. "Fair enough. But remember—"

"Yeah, I know, 'Everything in its entirety must be written down.' Well, Miss, I did do that, I did write it down in my book, but I just didn't say nothin' because Mrs. Fisher wasn't the one what'd run off, was she?"

Billy sat down awkwardly, though Maisie remained standing and looked out across the square. It was darker now. He had mentioned earlier that he wanted to be home in time to take his children to the recreation ground. It crossed Maisie's mind that he had been optimistic in thinking that he would get home while it was still light enough to play outdoors. She turned back to him.

"Yes, you're right, Billy. Now then, recall one more time what happened when you left."

"When she'd told me about Miss Waite and the nuns, and all, she seemed to be lollin' all over the place, so I said my good-byes and thank-you-very-muches, and off I went."

Maisie sighed. "Oh dear. I do wish one of the household had let you out."

"So do I, come to think of it. But the maid wasn't there. Mind you, I think someone else went in after me."

"Well, I would hope so, Billy."

"Nah, Miss, you know what I mean. *Directly* after me."

"Explain."

"I was on the street, and you know 'ow narrow them mewses are, don't you? Well, it was that funny it was, because I came out of the 'ouse, 'ad to squeeze past that big car of 'ers, the way she'd parked it all over the pavement, then I turned right to go down toward Victoria. I 'adn't gone but a couple of yards when I 'eard steps behind me; then the door slammed. I thought it must've been Mr. Fisher, comin' in from work or somethin' and I just 'adn't seen 'im."

"You're sure it was Number Nine's door that opened and closed?"

"As sure as I can be. It was the sound, Miss. I'm good wiv noises. It's 'avin the nippers what does it—always gotta know where the noise is comin' from, otherwise the little beggars'll be getting' up to no good at all. Anyway, if it'd been the next 'ouse along, it wouldn't 'ave sounded the same, in either direction. No, it was Number Nine." Billy looked at Maisie, his eyes revealing the shock of a sudden unwanted thought. "'ere, Miss, you don't think it was the one what did 'er in, do you?"

"It's a possibility."

Maisie considered another possibility, that Lydia Fisher might have been lying to Billy throughout. The suitcase he noticed could have belonged to Charlotte Waite. It might have been Charlotte who—alone or aided by another—had slain her friend. Waite had referred to his daughter as a "wilting lily" but Maisie was begining to consider her a dark horse.

"This is gettin' interestin', innit, Miss?"

"Intriguing is what it is. Intriguing. I've written to Dame Constance at Camden Abbey in Kent, and expect to hear from her by return. Whether Charlotte has run there for shelter or not, Dame Constance will be able to throw light on the mind of an aspiring nun. I'll visit her as soon as I can. And I want to consult with Dr. Blanche, so I'll stop at the Dower House at Chelstone to see him first."

"Will you see your old dad while you're there?"

"Of course I will. Why do you ask?"

"Wonderful man, your dad. You just don't seem to see much of 'im, that's all, seein' as 'e's your only real family."

Maisie drew back, surprised. The simplicity of Billy's observation stung her, as if she had been attacked by an unseen insect. She knew that it was only the truth that could injure in such a manner, and her face reddened.

"I see my father as much as I can." Maisie leaned toward a pile of papers, which she shuffled before consulting her watch. "Goodness me, Billy! You should be on your way. You won't be home in time to play with your children though, will you?"

"Oh yes I will, Miss. Never miss a play before they go up to bed. Nice to 'ave a bit of a romp around, although the missus moans about it, says it gets 'em all excited so they won't sleep."

"We might as well finish work for the day. I'm meeting Detective Inspector Stratton tomorrow morning to go to Lydia Fisher's house. Be prepared to hold the fort for a couple of days while I am down in Kent."

"You can count on me, Miss." Billy extended his wounded leg and rose from his chair.

"That leg giving you trouble again? You seemed to be in less pain this morning."

"It comes and goes, Miss. Comes and goes. I'll be off then."

"Very well, Billy."

Billy pulled on his overcoat and gave a final wave before clambering down the stairs in an ungainly fashion that could be heard with each receding footfall. The front door opened and closed with a thud. It was six o'clock.

Maisie was in no rush to leave. It had been a long day, and so much had happened. But far from being anxious to return to her rooms, Maisie felt a dragging at her heart as she contemplated the evening ahead. Perhaps she would go down to the kitchen and have a cup of cocoa with Sandra, one of several housemaids who remained at the Comptons' Belgravia mansion while the rest of the household were at Chelstone. Though Sandra, Valerie, and Teresa were all nice girls, they weren't quite sure about Maisie Dobbs, whom they knew had been one of them once upon a time but wasn't anymore. So they were often uneasy about initiating conversation with her, though they were friendly enough.

Gathering up her notes, Maisie placed some outstanding correspondence in her document case, checked that her desk was secure, turned off the gaslights and left the office. Tomorrow was another working day, which, it was to be hoped, would reveal more about the death of Lydia Fisher and, perhaps, about the character, motives, and whereabouts of her client's daughter. She made a mental note to prepare some additional questions for Joseph Waite about his daughter's friends. She had not yet decided whether to ask him about his son.

The square was busy when she closed the outer door behind her. There were people wandering across to visit friends, art students from the Slade returning to their digs, and a few people going in and out of the corner grocery shop where Mrs. Clark and her daughter, Phoebe, would be running back and forth to find even the most obscure items that the eclectic mix of customers in Fitzroy Square requested, despite the fact that the country was in the midst of a depression.

Maisie had turned right into Warren Street, pulling on her gloves as she walked, when she stopped suddenly to look at two men who were standing across the road. They had just exited the Prince of Wales pub and stood for a moment under a streetlamp, then moved into the shadows away from the illumination. Maisie also stepped into the shadows to avoid being seen. They spoke for a few moments, each nervously casting glances up and down the street. One man, the stranger, pulled an envelope from a pocket inside his coat, while the other looked both ways, took the envelope, and placed something in the first man's waiting hand. Maisie suspected that it was several pound notes rolled together, payment for the first item. She continued to watch as the men departed. The one she did not know walked back into the pub, while the fair hair of the other man caught the faint light of the streetlamps burning through an evening smog, as he limped unsteadily on his way toward the Euston Road.

Maisie was deeply troubled as she sat in her rooms at 15 Ebury Place that evening. When Sandra came to inquire whether she would like "a nice cup of cocoa," Maisie declined the offer and continued to stare out of the window into the darkness. What was happening to Billy? One minute he seemed to be in the depths of a debilitating malaise, the next revitalized and energetic. He seemed to ricochet between forgetting the most basic rules of their work together—work that he had taken to so readily—and being so productive in his duties as to cause Maisie to consider an increase in wages at a time when most employers were rendering staff redundant. Billy's war wounds were still troubling him, no matter how strong his protestations. And perhaps she had completely underestimated his ability to cope with memories as they were brought in on the tide of pain that seemed to ebb and flow in such a disturbing manner.

Silence encroached, seeping even into the very fabric of the rich linen furnishings. Maisie gathered her thoughts and sought to banish the sound of nothing at all by reviewing her notes on the Waite case once again. Lydia Fisher had been killed before she could ask her about Charlotte Waite. Had she been murdered to prevent Maisie from seeing her? But what about the Coulsden case? Had it really been the newspaper account of that murder that had caused Charlotte to bolt? Could the two murders be random and simply a coincidence that should have no bearing on Maisie's assignment? Maisie pondered more questions, then finally put her work aside for the night. She felt a lack of composure in her body, a sure sign of the turmoil in her mind, which must be stilled if she was to enjoy a good night's sleep and a fruitful morning.

Taking the pillows from her bed, Maisie placed them on the floor, loosened her dressing gown slightly for greater freedom of movement, and sat down with legs crossed. There was only one way to still her thoughts and racing heart, and that was to secure dominion over her body in meditation. She took four long breaths through her nose, placed her hands on her knees with the thumb and forefinger of each hand touching, and half closed her eyes. Allowing her gaze to rest on a barely discernible stain on the carpet in front of her, Maisie endeavored to banish all thought. Slowly the stillness of the room embraced her being, and the heartbeat that had been so frantic seemed to become one with her breath. As a consideration or worry struggled to enter her mind, Maisie relaxed and refused such thoughts an audience, instead imagining them leaving the range of her inner vision, like clouds that pass in the afternoon sky. She breathed deeply and was calm.

Later, as Maisie opened her eyes fully, she acknowledged the truth that had been revealed to her in the silence—the truth that had caused her to avoid visiting her father, for he would see it immediately. The truth that Maisie had been avoiding for so long was a simple one: She was lonely. And as she remained still for just a moment longer, she wondered if that, too, had been Charlotte Waite's sorrow.

# CHAPTER SIX

*M*aisie awoke as the sun forced its way through the crack where the curtains met, fingering at her leaden eyelids until they opened. She moved her head on the pillow to avoid the blade of light, reached out, and pulled her bedside clock a little closer.

"Oh, lumme, a quarter past eight!"

She leaped from the bed, ran to the bathroom, turned the bath-tub taps, and then pulled the lever to activate the shower that had only recently been installed. In addition to piping-hot water that pumped from the eight-inch-diameter showerhead, a series of sprays on the vertical pipe ensured that water reached not only the head but the whole body.

"Oh no!" said Maisie, as she stood under the streaming water and extended her arm to reach the soap, for she had realized that her long tresses, now completely drenched, would not be dry by the time she left the house. Exiting the shower, complaining aloud about the "new-fangled thing," she dried herself quickly, wrapped a thick white towel around her head and put on a plain cotton robe. Sitting at her dressing table, she applied just a little cold cream to her face, rubbing the residue into her hands. She dabbed her cheeks, removing any excess cream with a corner of the towel. She applied only the smallest amount of rouge to her cheeks and lips, then hurried back into her bedroom, opened the wardrobe door and selected a plain midnight blue day dress with a dropped waistline and sleeves that came to just below the elbow. Maisie had generally chosen dresses and skirts that came to her mid-calf, and was glad that fashion was moving in her direction once again following a flirtation with shorter hemlines. Her trusty dark blue jacket, some years old now, would have to do, as would her old cloche and plain black shoes. In fact the cloche would come in very handy this morning.

She removed the towel from her head and consulted the clock: half past eight. It would take fifteen minutes walking at a brisk clip to reach Victoria, so she had only a quarter of an hour to dry her hair. Grabbing her jacket, hat, gloves and document case, she took six hairpins from a glass bowl on her dressing table and rushed out of her room, along the landing, then through a small disguised door to the left that led to the back stairs of the house.

As Maisie entered the kitchen, the three housemaids, who were talking, seemed to jump as she spoke. "Oh dear, I wonder if you can help, I need to dry my hair ever so quickly!"

Sandra was the first to step forward, followed by Teresa.

"Tess, take Miss Dobbs's things. Come over here, Miss. we won't be able to get it bone dry, but enough so's you can pin it up. Quick, Val, open the fire door."

Maisie noticed that now she was on downstairs territory, the staff called her "Miss" rather than the more formal upstairs "M'um." She toweled her head once more, and was instructed to lean over in front of the fire door of the stove, so that the heat would begin to dry her hair.

"Now then, don't get too close, Miss. You don't want to singe that lovely hair, now, do you?"

"Singe it? I feel like burning the lot off, Sandra."

"I suppose we could always go and get Her Ladyship's new Hawkins

Supreme, you know, that green hair-drying machine thing of hers. She only used it the once. Said it was like having a vacuum cleaner going over her head."

As Valerie flapped the morning newspaper so that heat would move around Maisie's black tresses, she began to giggle. Then Sandra lost the battle to hold back her own laughter, as did Teresa. Maisie looked up through a veil of ringlets of still-damp hair and, for the first time in a long time, she began to laugh, too.

"Oh, don't, don't make me laugh like that!" As tears began to fall from her eyes, Maisie rubbed them away.

"Miss, Miss, I'm sorry, it's just that, well, we suddenly saw the funny side of it, I mean, we've all 'ad to do it, you know, I s'pose we never thought you'd ever rush in 'ere all of a fluster."

Maisie leaned back, took up her brush, and began to sweep her hair into a manageable twist. "I'm only human! You know, Mrs. Crawford would have boxed my ears for brushing my hair in the kitchen, and that's a fact!"

Valerie moved to close the stove door, as Sandra wiped down the long kitchen table with a cloth. "Well, Miss, it's nice to see you laugh, it really is. It's good for a body, laughing. Puts a spring in your step, it does."

Maisie smiled. "I appreciate the help, and the company." Maisie looked at the silver watch pinned to her dress, "I had better get moving or I'll be late for my appointment."

Sandra put down the cloth she was holding. "I'll go to the door with you, Miss."

Maisie was about to insist that she need not be escorted, when it occurred to her that Sandra, the longest-serving housemaid and the oldest at twenty-six, might want to speak with her in confidence. At the top of the stone steps at the side of the mansion Maisie turned to Sandra in silence and smiled, encouraging her to speak.

"Miss, I hope this doesn't sound, you know, out of place." Sandra stood with her hands clasped behind her back and looked at her polished black shoes for a second, as if searching for the best way to deliver her words. She hesitated, and Maisie said nothing but moved just slightly closer. "Well, you work very hard, Miss, anyone can see that. Even late into the night. So, what I wanted to say was, that you're always welcome to come down for a chat if you want. You see—" she picked at loose thread on her pinafore "—we know you can't do that when everyone's in residence, because it's not done, is it? But when you're alone at the house, we just want you to know that you don't have to be." Sandra looked at Maisie as if she had finished, then quickly added, "Mind you, we're probably all a bit boring for you, Miss."

Maisie smiled at Sandra, and said, "Not at all, Sandra. You are most kind. Some of my happiest times were spent downstairs in that kitchen. I'll take you up on the offer." Maisie looked at her watch. "Oh heavens, I must dash now. But Sandra . . ."

"Yes, Miss?"

"Thank you. Thank you for your understanding."

"Yes, Miss." Sandra bobbed a curtsey, nodded, and waved good-bye to Maisie.

*Detective* Inspector Stratton climbed out of the police car as soon as it came to a halt, and opened the rear passenger door for Maisie. He took the seat next to her and, without any niceties of greeting, began immediately to speak of "the Fisher Case."

"I'll get straight to the point, Miss Dobbs: What was your assistant doing at Lydia Fisher's house on the day she was murdered?"

"Inspector Stratton, you have not yet informed me as to whether, in fact, my assistant visited on the actual day of her death, as she was not found until eleven yesterday morning."

"Please do not be obstructive, Miss Dobbs. I am allowing you to revisit the victim's home this morning in the hope that you might be able to assist us."

"Indeed, Inspector, I appreciate your trust, though I am only trying to point out that we do not know yet exactly when the deceased met her fate. Or do we?" Maisie smiled at Stratton with a warmth that remained from the laughter that had embraced her less than an hour before.

Stratton looked mildly put out. "Spilsbury has reported the time of death to have been at about six o'clock in the evening on the day *before* you found her. Now, what about Beale?"

"Mr. Beale did indeed see Mrs. Fisher at her home. However, he left Cheyne Mews before four o'clock to return to the office to meet with me, and I can vouch for him."

"When did he leave you again?"

"Oh, Inspector—"

"Miss Dobbs."

"It was approximately six o'clock. No doubt his wife would be able to confirm his arrival at home by, say, half past six or so. He travels to and from work by either bus or the underground, though I believe he prefers to go home by train as it's a bit quicker—from St. Pancras on the Metropolitan Line to Whitechapel. Depending upon the trains, I suppose he might not get home until seven. I doubt if he'd be out much later, Inspector, as he likes to play with his children before they go to bed." Maisie thought for a moment, then added, "I know that occasionally he stops for a quick half pint at the Prince of Wales, but only at the end of the week."

"I'll have to question him, you know."

"Yes, of course, Inspector." Maisie looked out of the window

The car slowed to make the turn into Cheyne Mews, and drew alongside Number 9. A single police constable stood outside. Stratton made no move to leave the car but turned to Maisie again.

"Tell me again why you were coming to visit Mrs. Fisher, Miss Dobbs?"

Maisie had prepared an answer to this question. "I have been clutching at straws, Inspector, and Mrs. Fisher might have been able to throw light on a case I am working on concerning a daughter who has left the home of her parents. It was a tenuous connection. I believe they were acquainted at one point and I wanted to speak with her to see if she could illuminate aspects of the girl's character. I should add, Inspector, that the 'girl' is in her thirties, and has a very overbearing father."

"And Beale?"

"He had been confirming the names and whereabouts of her acquaintances. Our subject's connection with Mrs. Fisher had been so intermittent that we did not even know whether we had her correct address. He was checking our information when she came along and he took the opportunity to speak to her. They conversed and he left. I've told you the rest."

"And the name of the woman you are looking for?"

"As I said yesterday, I have signed a contract of confidentiality. Should it be absolutely necessary to divulge the name of my client, I will do so in the interests of public safety and justice. At this stage I request your respect for my professional obligation to my client."

Stratton frowned but nodded. "For now, Miss Dobbs, I will not press the point. We are looking for a male suspect, not a woman. However, have you any other information that might be pertinent to this case?"

"Only that Mr. Beale commented upon the alcoholic beverages that Mrs. Fisher enjoyed instead of tea."

Stratton rubbed his chin and looked at Maisie again, "Yes, that is in line with Spilsbury's findings."

Maisie pulled on her gloves and took up her bag in anticipation of leaving the car. "Inspector, did Spilsbury comment upon the poison theory?"

"Oh yes," said Stratton, reaching for the door handle. "She was definitely poisoned first. It was taken in tea—so she probably had a cup or two at some point after Beale left the house. Cuthbert is currently beavering away in his laboratory to identify the exact poison or combination of substances employed, though Sir Bernard Spilsbury has said that he suspects an opiate, probably morphia."

"What about the knife attack?"

"She was dead when the attack took place, hence—as you saw—

there was little blood at the scene. But there are some lingering questions about the knife."

"Oh?"

"It seems that the stab wounds are very much like those inflicted by a bayonet. But you know Sir Bernard. We can expect a very precise description of the weapon soon."

Maisie drew breath quickly and asked one more question as Stratton opened the door for her. "And has he confirmed a connection to the Coulsden case?"

Stratton took her hand as she stepped from the motor car. "The means of murder is identical."

"Spoiled a nice piece of carpet, didn't he?" Stratton was looking out of the drawing room window to the street below.

Flippant comments were not unusual among those whose job it was to investigate the aftermath of violent crime. Maurice had told Maisie long ago that it was part of the unconscious effort to bring some normalcy to that which is far from usual. But it was the first time she had heard an Aubusson rug being referred to as a "nice piece of carpet."

"Inspector, may I have some time alone in the room, please?"

He paused, then shrugged before leaving the room and closing the door behind him. Though he had never liaised professionally with Maurice Blanche, he had heard of his methods from colleagues who had worked with the man, and knew his "strange" ways often led to a quick solution of the crime in question. Blanche's former assistant was indubitably using procedures learned from her employer. The room had been thoroughly investigated, so there was no risk to evidence. And Stratton knew that, had she wanted, Maisie Dobbs could have altered or removed evidence when she first found the corpse.

Maisie walked slowly around the room, touching the personal belongings of Lydia Fisher, and again she was assailed by the sense that this was a lonely woman. That she had yearned for conversation rather than talk; for heartfelt passion, not indulgence; and that she had ached for the intimate connection that came with true friendship rather than from a cadre of society sycophants.

She took careful stock of the contents of the drawing room: Pale blue velvet curtains, the deeper lapis blue chaise with pale blue piping, an oak writing table in the art nouveau style, a set of side tables, now properly nested rather than tipped over, a mirror shaped like a huge butterfly on one wall, and a modernist painting on the other. The drinks cabinet in the corner to the right of the window had been "dusted" by the police, and there was a gramophone in the opposite corner. It had been a pleasing, airy room. But it was the room of a person who lived alone, not a married woman.

She walked over to the chaise, knelt by the umber stain on the rug, and touched the place where Lydia Fisher had fallen. Maisie closed her eyes and breathed deeply, all the time keeping a light touch upon the place where the dead woman's blood had spilled grudgingly onto the carpet. As she did so a cold, clammy air seemed to descend and envelop her. The sensation was not unexpected, and she knew it would come as she reached out to the past in search of a reason, a word, a clue. Anything that would tell her why Lydia Fisher had died. Anything that might tell her why there was something so recognizable in a room she had never entered before coming to visit Mrs. Fisher yesterday.

Seconds passed. Time was suspended. Instead of seeing the room in which she stood, she saw the one Charlotte Waite had left so hurriedly five days earlier. Some emotion was shared by the two women, and though she was quick to consider loneliness, which she would find so easy to understand, Maisie knew a more elusive feeling she was as yet unable to name linked them.

Maisie opened her eyes, and the connection with Lydia Fisher began to ebb. She heard Stratton's voice coming closer. He had obviously thought that she'd had time enough to commune with whatever Lydia Fisher had left behind. Maisie took one last look, but just before she opened the door she felt drawn toward the window where Stratton had stood earlier. Leaning on the sill, she wished she could raise the window for air. A sudden warmth in her hands caused her to look down. Perhaps the radiator underneath had heated the wood. She ran her hands along the sill, then knelt to see if she could turn down the heat. To her surprise the iron pipes were cold. Running her hands down the wall, then along the floorboards, Maisie searched with her fingertips. There was something here for her, something of consequence. Just as she heard Stratton's footfall outside the door, Maisie felt a hint of something both soft and prickly brush against her forefinger. She leaned closer. The item was tiny and white, so small, in fact, that it could have been swept up by the cleaners. It would be of no interest to the police. It might have fallen to the floor at any time, a small, stray wisp.

"Miss Dobbs," Stratton knocked at the door.

"Come in, Inspector."

As Stratton walked into the room, Maisie was folding a linen handkerchief.

"Finished, Miss Dobbs?"

"Yes, Inspector. I was rather saddened; do excuse me." Maisie sniffed as she placed the handkerchief in her pocket.

Stratton and Maisie left the house and continued their conversation in the car.

"Your thoughts?"

"I'd like to know more about Mr. Fisher, wouldn't you, Inspector?"

"Absolutely—in fact, I've got my men on the job now."

"Where is he? What does he do?"

"Ah, well, it's what he does that directly affects where he is. He's some sort of traveler, an explorer if you like. According to the maid, he's rarely home. He spends most of his time going off to some far-flung locale with a group of interested individuals—all wealthy—who pay him handsomely to be dragged off into British East Africa, the Gobi Desert, or some such place to be photographed with animals that you could quite easily see at Regent's Park Zoo!"

"So that explains it."

"What?"

"Her loneliness."

"Hmmm." Stratton looked sideways at Maisie.

"Inspector, I wonder if I could ask a favor?" Maisie smiled.

"Miss Dobbs, I fear that your request may be for something else that will bring me near to losing my job."

"Not if it helps to find the murderer. I wonder if I could see any belongings taken from the Coulsden victim's home?"

"Look, Miss Dobbs, though I am grateful for any interpretations you can give me from your 'woman's perspective,' I am intrigued as to why you are interested in that case. The Fisher woman is understandable, given the 'tenuous' link to one of your own private cases. But there can be no reason for you to examine Mrs. Sedgewick's effects. It would be most irregular."

"I understand perfectly, Inspector."

They sat in silence for a moment.

"I can have my driver take us right to your door, if you wish."

"No, Inspector, that will be quite all right, I have other errands to complete before returning to my office."

The car drew up outside Victoria Station and once again Stratton alighted first to offer Maisie his hand.

"Thank you, Inspector."

"Miss Dobbs. While I am sure that your assistant's meeting with Mrs. Fisher went exactly as you have described, I must question him tomorrow morning. You will appreciate that in normal circumstances the procedure would be more formal. However, in this case I will simply ask you to instruct him to present himself at the Yard for questioning at ten o'clock."

As he departed Stratton wondered what Maisie Dobbs might have gleaned from the minutes spent alone in Lydia Fisher's house. What could a nice young woman like Miss Dobbs possibly know about the life of an inebriate partygoer like Lydia Fisher?

It was eleven o'clock in the morning when Maisie left Stratton. Before making her way to Fitzroy Square, Maisie hurried back to 15 Ebury Place. She used the staff entrance at the side of the mansion, walked quickly through the kitchen, which was late-morning silent, and went directly to her rooms, using the back stairs. Once there, she took off her blue jacket, removed the white linen handkerchief from the pocket and,without looking at the wisp that was now secure within its folds, placed it in the left-hand drawer of her writing table. It would be safe there.

"Not bad for a Friday morning, is it, Miss?" Billy took off his overcoat and set it on the hook behind the door. He rubbed his hands together and smiled at Maisie. "Missed seeing you for our little meeting at five yesterday, though I got your note that you were visiting Miss Waite's hairdresser and her seamstress in the afternoon, after your mornin' with D.I. Stratton. I've been checking on more names in that address book, not that there's much else there to be getting on with."

"I thought that might be the case, but we must leave no stone unturned."

"Too right, Miss. Did the hairdresser say anything interesting?"

"No, not really. Only that Charlotte'd changed in recent weeks. Apparently she used to have her hair set once a week, sometimes more often if she had parties to go to. But she's only been in for one cut in the past six weeks, and she wanted it very plain, so she could draw it back in a bun." Maisie reached for a folder on the desk. "And the seamstress hadn't seen her for some weeks, which was unusual, because apparently she was always having alterations made to her very expensive clothing."

"Well then, as we've got to see Mr. Waite this afternoon, p'r'aps we can get some more information from 'im. Bet you're glad it's the weekend, ain't you?"

"My weekend is going to be taken up with the Waite case, and with driving down to Kent. And your weekend is a long way off, Billy; I hate to tell you this, but you've to be at Scotland Yard at ten sharp."

Billy's countenance changed immediately. "Scotland Yard, Miss?"

"Don't worry, Billy, it's in connection with the Fisher case." Maisie looked up from her desk, where she was removing papers from her document case and setting them on the blotting pad in front of her. "Why? You haven't done anything else they'd be interested in, have you?" She smiled but looked at him intently.

Billy turned toward the tea tray and replied with his back to Maisie, "Nah, not me, Miss. Tea?"

"Yes, that would be lovely, Billy. We both have a busy day, especially as I'll be away early next week and we've to leave at two for our three o'clock appointment with Joseph Waite. I don't want to be late for him."

"Right you are, Miss."

"And before you ask, my lunch has been canceled, so I won't be seeing the Detective Inspector today, which isn't surprising seeing as you will be with him for a couple of hours. We need to make faster progress in our work on the Waite case. Charlotte has absconded before, though we both think she's old enough to be off on her own anyway. But the fact is that our opinions don't count, and what goes on in the relationship between Joseph Waite and his daughter is for them to worry about—at this stage anyway." She held her hand up to silence Billy, who seemed about to comment. "Yes, I know we've gone as quickly as we could, but I'm concerned that Lydia Fisher might have been inadvertently or deliberately misleading you about Charlotte's desire to become a nun. We have to ensure that our client is satisfied, and satisfied as quickly as possible, but there are now more pressing reasons to locate Charlotte Waite quickly. We may be *compelled* to bring in the police."

"Yes, Miss."

"We cannot get away from the fact that we have identified a possible—and I must emphasize *possible*—link between the murders of two women and Charlotte Waite's disappearance."

Billy blew out his cheeks. "Gawd, Miss, when you put it like that . . ."

"Quite."

"Mind you," said Billy, changing position in the chair to stretch out his leg. "Mind you, I looked at the address book again, and that first woman, you know, the murder victim in Coulsden, well, she ain't in there. I checked under the *P*'s for Philippa, and under the *S*'s for Sedgewick. So if Miss Waite knew 'er, she's in the other address book."

"Good point. We need to find out more about Mrs. Sedgewick. Look, if you've got time when you get out of the interview with Stratton and Caldwell, see what else you can dig up on the Sedgewick murder, go through the newspapers again. Oh, that reminds me—don't let Sergeant Caldwell annoy you, Billy. Rise above it, and remember it's his job to goad you a bit." Maisie was thoughtful, "I wish there was a way you could get chatty with Inspector Stratton while you're there."

Billy laughed. "I don't think it's me 'e wants to get chatty wiv, Miss."

Maisie blushed, and stood up to view the case map.

"So you 'aven't 'eard from your Dame Constance yet, Miss?"

"No, not yet. One cannot expect to hear from a cloistered nun by telephone. But I'm keeping my fingers crossed that I'll hear by this afternoon's post. Dame Constance will have replied immediately—if she's half as precise as she used to be. My letter to her would have arrived by yesterday morning, so assuming her reply went by the afternoon post, it should arrive today."

"And you'll be off to Kent on Monday, then?"

"Perhaps earlier. I've spoken to Dr. Blanche and will see him first about Waite."

"You'll remember to say 'ello to Mr. Dobbs for me, won't you?"

Maisie looked at her watch and nodded. "Yes, of course I will, Billy. You should be getting along now, you don't want to keep Inspector Stratton waiting."

Billy scraped his chair back and winced slightly as his foot dragged along the floor.

Maisie pretended not to notice, but as Billy pulled on his overcoat she voiced her concern. "Are you sure I'm not leaving you with too much on your plate? I should only be away for a couple of days, but I'll cut my journey short if you aren't feeling up to it."

"Nah, Miss. I told you last week, I'm much better now. Loads of energy, and the pain ain't as bad as it was. Tell you the truth, I reckon it was the weather rusting the shrapnel they left in me legs."

Maisie smiled. "Very well, Billy."

Maisie began to collect her papers, which she placed under lock and key in her desk drawer. She consulted her watch and had just gathered her mackintosh, hat, and gloves, when the bell above the office door rang out as someone tugged the brass bell-pull by the outer door. Maisie wondered who could be summoning her at this inopportune moment. The thought crossed her mind that Dame Constance might have sent word via telegram. She ran downstairs.

"Why, Mrs. Beale, what a surprise!" Maisie was amazed to see Billy's wife standing on the doorstep, holding one child by the hand and the other on her hip. She had met Doreen Beale only once before, at Christmas when she delivered gifts to the Beale's two-up-two-down terraced home in Whitechapel. Maisie had suspected then that this small, sturdy countrywoman did not quite fit into the close-knit neighborhood, as she came from Sussex and did not share the rough-and-tumble language or raucous humor of the people her Cockney husband had grown up with.

"Oh, I hope you don't mind, Miss Dobbs, me coming here without sending word first, but I wonder if you could spare me a moment. I know Mr. Beale isn't here. I watched him leave. I didn't want him to know I'd come to see you."

"Of course. Do come up to the office." Maisie stood back to allow Doreen Beale to enter the building.

"Will the pram be all right, you know, left out here?"

"I'm sure it will, Mrs. Beale. I confess, I've never seen children in

these parts, but I think it's safe. Come in; let's go up to the office."
Maisie smiled at the toddler, who hid his head in the folds of his
mother's coat, and then at the baby, who copied her brother, turning
her head into the coat's upper sleeve, which, Maisie noticed, was
already damp with dribble.

She pulled out a chair for Billy's wife, and then took some plain
white paper from her desk, which she put on the floor with the jam jar
of colored pencils.

"There you are, you can draw me a train!" Maisie smiled again at
the little boy with an elflike cap of white-blond hair, who looked up
at his mother.

"Go on, Bobby, make a nice train."

With one child occupied and the other beginning to fall asleep in
her mother's arms, Maisie smiled at Doreen Beale. "Now then, Mrs.
Beale, what can I do for you? Is something wrong with Billy?"

The woman's eyes reddened, which accentuated her fair skin. Maisie
noticed that the light blue veins at her temples had become swollen as
she fought back tears.

"Oh, Mrs. Beale, whatever is the matter? What is it?"

Maisie reached out to the woman, then came around the desk to
place an arm around her shoulder. The baby began to whimper, and the
little boy stopped drawing and seemed frozen on the floor with his
thumb in his mouth. Tears began to well in his eyes, as he mirrored his
mother's countenance.

Doreen Beale composed herself, and turned to her son with a smile.

"Come on, young Bobby, draw a nice picture for your daddy." She
stood up from her chair, and with her head indicated for Maisie to walk
to the window with her. "Little ears—" she whispered. "It's Billy, Miss
Dobbs. I thought you might be able to tell me what's wrong with him."

"Whatever I can do—" Maisie began, but was cut off by Doreen
Beale, who clearly needed to shed her burden.

"You see, my Billy used to be your solid sort. No tempers, no ups
and downs. Even just after the war when we first started walking out
together—we were both young then, of course—but even after all he

went through, he was always so, you know, straight as a die. Like I said, no moods or tempers." She moved slightly to reposition the child on her hip. "Well, just lately, in the last few months, all that's changed. Now, I know his leg has been giving him trouble again—it never went away, really—and that got him down, you know. It wears you out, that sort of nagging pain."

Maisie nodded, but did not speak. Doreen Beale took a handkerchief from the pocket of her plain brown coat and rubbed a dewdrop of moisture that had accumulated at the end of her nose. She sniffed and rubbed again.

"One minute he's all over the place, doing jobs around the house, playing with the children, you know. He's like a bumblebee, off to work, home again, going over to our allotment to get some vegetables—hardly makes time even to eat. Then it seems that just as quickly he comes down like a lead balloon, and even his face looks gray. And I know it's his leg that's at the bottom of it all. And the—you know—the memories, I suppose." Doreen Beale sniffed and blew her nose again. "Oh, excuse me, Miss Dobbs, for all this. My mother always said that whatever you do, you should never take on so in front of your children."

Maisie was quiet for a moment, then spoke. "I have to say, Mrs. Beale, that I've noticed changes in Billy's behavior, too. I've also been worried, so I'm glad you felt able to speak to me about it. You must be very concerned."

Doreen Beale nodded. "Billy's a lovely dad to the children, and a good provider, always has been. And he's a diamond to me, you know, a real diamond. Not like some of them I see. But, I just don't know what wrong with him. And the terrible thing is, that I'm afraid to ask again."

"What happened when you asked before?"

"Oh, he says, 'I'm awright, love,' and then goes off and does something. Then, of course, he used to stay after work for a half a pint with his friends of a Friday night. Like I said, he's not like some of them—just one half-pint a week, my Billy. But now he's home late two or three nights a week, sometimes full of beans, and sometimes with a face as long as a week. He was out Tuesday, Wednesday, and Thursday, not back home until long after seven."

Maisie tried not to show alarm. "He was late Tuesday *and* Wednesday?"

"Yes, Miss, though I don't blame you, even though you'd asked him to work late."

Maisie did not reveal her surprise. She waited for a moment before asking, "Mrs. Beale, would you like me to speak to Billy?"

"Oh, Miss Dobbs, I don't know. I mean, yes, I would—but there again, I feel like such a yellow belly. You know, my mother always said that you should never speak of your marriage outside the four walls and two people who are in the marriage, that it wasn't right."

Maisie thought for a moment, knowing how difficult it must have been for Doreen Beale to come to the office. "I believe your mother's advice was well meant, but sometimes speaking to someone else, someone trusted, helps. At the very least your load is lightened knowing that I have noticed the same behavior. I'll have a word with Billy. And don't worry, I won't let on that we've spoken."

Doreen Beale dabbed her eyes with her handkerchief, and nodded. "I'd best be getting on, Miss Dobbs. I've got a wedding dress to finish this week."

"Are you getting much work, Mrs. Beale?" said Maisie, knowing that the income of a dressmaker was directly affected by the amount of money in people's pockets.

"Not as much as I was getting, but the jobs trickle in. And people do still appreciate fine work."

"Good. Now then, would you like to splash some cold water on your cheeks? I'll keep an eye on the children while you nip along the landing to the lavatory. There's a basin in there, and I put a fresh towel on the hook this morning."

When she returned, Bobby was still very deliberately using the pencils to draw a train, and Maisie was standing by the table with the baby's head nestled into the curve of her neck. Doreen Beale collected her children and left the office. Maisie watched as she made her way toward Warren Street, pushing the pram with Lizzie asleep under a blanket and Bobby perched on the end, his stubby fingers clasped around the handlebar. And as she turned away, knowing that she now had to hurry to keep her appointment with Charlotte's milliner, Maisie touched the place on her neck where she could still feel the soft downy head of Lizzie Beale.

# CHAPTER EIGHT

*M*aisie suspected that Billy's interview with Stratton had been draining—especially now that she knew that Billy had not returned home immediately upon leaving the office on the evening that Lydia Fisher had been killed. Though Maisie could not believe that Billy had returned to Cheyne Mews, in light of the underhand transaction she had witnessed between Billy and another man on Wednesday outside the Prince of Wales pub on Warren Street, she was concerned.

The interview with Stratton and Caldwell at Scotland Yard had been a long one, and as soon as Billy arrived back at Fitzroy Square, they set off for the appointment with Joseph Waite at his home in Dulwich. On the way, Maisie hoped to discuss their position regarding the search for Charlotte Waite, and for Billy to recount details of the interview, but Billy seemed to have slipped into an abyss of fatigue. He stared out of the passenger window, offering none of the usual commentary upon the people he saw going about their daily business as the MG sped by, nor did he offer conversation peppered with quips and puns.

"I expect you're a bit tired after this morning's meeting with Stratton, aren't you?"

"Oh, no. Just thinking, Miss, just thinking."

"What about, Billy? Is there a matter of some concern to you?" Maisie was watchful as she spoke, both of the traffic and of Billy's demeanor.

Billy folded his arms, as if against the cold. "I've just been thinking about them two women, you know, Miss Waite and Mrs. Fisher. Like two peas in a pod, they were."

"What do you mean?"

"They both seemed, you know, sort of cut off. I mean, they went out and all—well, at least they did before Miss Waite got all quiet. Right pair of social butterflies they were, but when all's said and done, they weren't, you know . . ." Billy crinkled his eyes as he searched for the right descriptive word. "Connected. That's it, they weren't *connected*. You know, not like, say, me, f'r instance. I mean, I'm connected to me wife and the nippers. People are connected to them they love, and who loves them back. You can feel it when you walk into a room, can't you, Miss?" Billy looked at Maisie for the first time since they had set out. "You know, you see photographs on the dresser, and all sorts of bits and bobs lying around that they've been given. And there's comfort, in't there? O' course, my wife would call it clutter, but you know what I mean."

"Yes, I do, Billy."

"Yeah, that's right. Now, like I said earlier, when I spoke to my mate, you know, the one who works for the *Express*, well, he told me that the word is—and you know they can't print this sort of thing—that the Coulsden woman, Philippa Sedgewick, was seeing a gentleman who was married to someone else."

"Will your friend keep you in mind when he gets some more information?"

Billy gave a half-laugh. "Well, 'e's a bit of a new friend, ain't 'e, Miss. You remember, you said I 'ad to make me own connections wiv them what could give me information? This one only took a pint or two down the Prince of Wales on Wednesday after work, and 'e was singing like a nightingale."

"Wednesday night? Weren't you going to try to get home early before the children went to bed?"

"Got to strike while the iron's 'ot, 'aven't you, Miss? Saw 'im going in for a swift one as I was walkin' past, and thought I'd take advantage of the situation, as you might say. Certainly worked, didn't it?"

"Well, we'll talk about it all a bit more after meeting with Waite. I can't say I'm looking forward to this."

"Me neither, Miss. Now then, mind you point your nose out!"

Harris, Waite's butler, had obviously recovered from his illness and welcomed them into the spacious hallway, whereupon he pulled a pocket watch from his waistcoat pocket.

"Four minutes to three. I will show you into the library, where Mr. Waite will join you at three on the dot."

Harris led the way to the library, ensured that they were seated comfortably, and left the room. Maisie and Billy had been alone for barely a moment when the door swung open. Waite strode into the room, pulled out his chair before Billy could stand respectfully. He sat down with a heavy thud and checked his watch.

"Ten minutes, Miss Dobbs. Now then, it's been four days since I gave you the job of finding my daughter. Where's Charlotte?"

Maisie breathed deeply and spoke in a level tone. "I believe she may be in Kent, Mr. Waite, though I cannot yet positively confirm the location of her refuge."

"*Refuge*? And what does my daughter need with a refuge?"

"May I speak frankly, Mr. Waite?"

The heavy-set man leaned back, folding his arms in front of his chest. Maisie wondered if he knew how quickly he gave himself away. With that one move, he was effectively telling her that her frankness was not welcome.

"I suspect that fear was at the heart of your daughter's departure from your house."

Waite moved forward in his chair. "Fear? What's she got to be—"

Maisie cut him off.

"I'm not sure at this stage, though my assistant and I are pursuing several lines of inquiry. Our first priority is to make contact with Charlotte."

"Well if you know where she is, just go and get her; that's what I'm paying you for."

"Mr. Waite. Your daughter may be secure within the walls of a convent. If that is the case, without attention to certain protocols of communication I will not even be able to speak to Charlotte."

"I don't think I've ever heard such a load of nonsense in my life." Waite stood up and leaned on the table, resting his weight on his knuckles. "If you know where my daughter is, Miss Dobbs, then I want you to bring her back to this this house at once. Is that understood?"

"Perfectly, Mr. Waite." Maisie made no move, except to lean back just slightly. Her hands remained folded in her lap in a relaxed manner. Billy followed her lead.

"Is there something more, Miss Dobbs?"

Maisie consulted her watch. "We have almost five minutes left, Mr. Waite, and I'd like to ask you some questions."

Waite stared at Maisie for a second, as if gauging how much power he would relinquish by reclaiming his seat. He reseated himself and folded his arms again.

"Can you tell me if you have ever met Philippa Sedgewick or Lydia Fisher?"

"Aye, I can. They were both acquaintances of my daughter, years ago. I think she's still in touch with Mrs. Fisher but doesn't see her that often. I doubt if she's seen the other woman in years."

"What about other friends, Mr. Waite? Surely your daughter had more than just two?"

Waite hesitated, frowning. He leaned forward and turned the ring on his little finger. "Aye, there was another friend." He sighed, continuing to twist the sparkling ring. "She's dead now. Killed herself a couple of months ago."

Maisie showed no surprise at Waite's revelation. "And what was her name?"

"Rosamund. Thorpe was her married name. She lived down on the coast somewhere. They were all at school together, years ago in Switzerland."

Maisie leaned forward. "Was Charlotte upset at the news of her friend's death?"

"Well, like I said, they hadn't spoken in years. Charlotte only found out when she saw Mrs. Thorpe's name in the obituary columns, far as I know."

"Mr. Waite, it would seem that Charlotte's engagement to Gerald Bartrup ended at approximately the same time as she learned of her friend's death."

"Oh, Bartrup. So you've seen him, have you?"

"Of course. And according to Bartrup, your daughter broke off their engagement. I have no reason to doubt his word."

Waite closed his eyes for a second and shook his head.

"Mr. Waite. Why did you not tell me that Charlotte was your second child?"

Waite was visibly startled. He pursed his lips, then took a deep breath as if to compose himself before responding curtly to Maisie's question.

"Because it has nothing to do with Charlotte's behavior, that's why. It has nothing to do with her running off. I've taken you on to investigate my daughter's disappearance, Miss Dobbs, not my life. Oh, I know, I know, you're thinking of some explanation based on her grief, or something like that. Well, they weren't close, though Joe was as soft as they come and looked after his sister, but she had all the false airs and graces of her mother."

Waite leaned forward but Maisie remained calm while Billy scribbled notes on an index card.

"He was one of the best, Miss Dobbs, the apple of my eye. Always there to help. I started him off in the shops, at the bottom so he'd earn the respect he'd need as he moved up in the company. Took to it like a duck to water, he did. Never complained that a job was beneath him.

But to answer your question, I didn't tell you because she was no' but a girl when her brother died, and she's a woman now. This nonsense of hers has nothing to do with my Joe!"

Maisie checked her watch. She had one minute. "And when did your son die, Mr. Waite?"

Joseph Waite stared down at the table, and when he looked up, his eyes were filled with tears. "Joe was killed in 1916. In July, Miss Dobbs, during the Battle of the Somme."

Maisie nodded in understanding. There was no need to acknowledge his loss with words: Grief from the war cast a shadow that at times was dense and at others seemed as pale as a length of gauze. But it was never gone.

Joseph Waite looked at his watch and shook hands with Maisie and Billy; then, as he turned to leave, asked, "Miss Dobbs, why the interest in Charlotte's three old friends?"

Maisie picked up her document case. "Because they are all dead, Mr. Waite. I thought you might have seen news of the deaths of Mrs. Sedgewick and Mrs. Fisher in the newspapers. Something of a coincidence, isn't it?"

"I must have read straight past those items. I tend to be more interested in overseas commerce and the business of the country, aspects of current affairs that directly affect Waite's International Stores. Which is what details of my daughter's disappearance will do if she is not brought back to this house soon. That's up to you, Miss Dobbs."

"I hope to communicate with her directly very soon. Of course you realize, Mr. Waite, that while Charlotte might be persuaded to return to your home, she cannot be forced."

Waite said nothing but gave a loud *hmmph!* before opening the door. He turned to claim the last word. "I want her back in this house, Miss Dobbs. If she won't find a suitable husband to share a house with, then she'll live under my roof!" Glaring at Maisie, he gave an ultimatum: "I'm off to visit some of my shops for a few days, back next Tuesday. I expect to see you with my daughter upon my return. Tuesday, Miss Dobbs. You've got until Tuesday."

# THANK YOU FOR YOUR ORDER

We're pleased to bring you the books you want to read.

## A note about our service:

Our goal is to provide you with the best service possible.
To help us, please be sure to:

- Include your account number on all correspondence, payments and returns.
- Allow 4 weeks for processing of payments and returns.

If your statement doesn't reflect a recent payment, don't worry. We've probably just crossed in the mail.

We appreciate your prompt payments to help us serve you better.

## To Contact Customer Service

1) To reach us by phone please call 717-918-2665
2) Or write to:       Customer Service
                      PO Box 6400
                      Camp Hill, PA 17012-6400

## To send a PAYMENT

1) Make sure the PAYMENT address, located on the bottom portion of this statement appears in the window of the envelope provided.
2) Place your payment in the envelope and apply the correct postage.

## RETURN Product

1) Please RETURN the bottom portion of this invoice with your package. Please do not include any payments.
2) **Send to:**

    **Product Return Center**
    **Camp Hill, PA 17012**

3) Have your local post office help you apply the correct postage.

**Moving?** Please notify us 4 weeks in advance by indicating your change of address on the remittance form below.

# INVOICE

## Quality Paperback Bk Clb

| ACCOUNT NUMBER | 662719102 | FEBRUARY 22 2005 | ORDER NUMBER 008 | INVOICE NUMBER 77738166 |
|---|---|---|---|---|

| DESCRIPTION | ITEM NO. | TYPE | ITEM STATUS | PUB PRICE | YOUR PRICE |
|---|---|---|---|---|---|
| WINSPEAR: 2-IN-1 | 15-2245 | Main | Enclosed | 38.95 | 24.99 |

Payments received after 03/24/05 will result in a

$4 late fee being assessed.

- Thank you for your order.
- You saved $13.96 on this shipment.
- In the last 30 days we've received these payment(s):
  $62.34 on 02/07.

| | |
|---|---|
| SUBTOTAL | 24.99 |
| SHIPPING & HANDLING | 4.49 |
| TAX | .00 |
| SHIPMENT TOTAL | 29.4 |
| PREVIOUS CREDIT | -30.6 |
| **CREDIT** | **-$1.** |

To Place an Order:
Call: 1-717-918-6633

Web: www.qpb.com

Payment
Address

Payment Processing Center
PO Box 6401
Camp Hill, PA 17012-6401

I..Ill..Ill...I.I..I.I..I...II.II...II.II...II..II

Change of Address Effective Date __/__/__ Account # _____

Name _____ EMAIL _____

Address _____

City _____ State _____ Zip _____ Phone ( ___ ) ___ - ___

## Quality Paperback Bk Clb     THIS IS NOT A BILL

| ACCOUNT NUMBER 662719102 | | INVOICE NUMBER 77738166 |
| --- | --- | --- |

MS. MARIA D LAARA

| SHIPMENT TOTAL | 29.48 |
| --- | --- |
| PREVIOUS CREDIT | -30.67 |
| **CREDIT** | **-$1.19** |

No payment is due.
Your credit will be applied
to future orders.

0077381660     1002948   3   662719102   1000000721

The door slammed, to be quickly opened by Harris, who escorted Maisie and Billy out. Billy was holding the driver's door of the MG open for Maisie when they were both startled by the sound of furiously flapping wings overhead as a flight of doves rose from an old-fashioned dove-cote in the corner of the gardens.

"Lawd, would you look at that!" said Billy.

"Oh, my, they are beautiful!" said Maisie.

Billy shuddered. "Can't see it meself. Rather look at a mangy old dog."

The doves returned in ones and twos, landing on the dove-cote and entering it through tiny doorways.

"Look at that, 'noses out,' Miss!" said Billy, joking again.

"Come on, we'd better be off."

Neither of them said a word as they drove steadily toward the main gate, which was opened by the young man who had let them in on their first visit. Each breathed a sigh of relief upon leaving the Waite residence behind.

"I tell you, Miss, that Joseph Waite really is a study, i'n't 'e?"

"No doubt about that."

"'ere, do you think 'e was tellin' the truth, y'know, when 'e said that 'e never knew about them two women bein' murdered?"

Maisie accelerated the car confidently and replied, "Not in a million years, Billy. Not in a million years."

As soon as they returned to the office, Maisie and Billy set to work, adding new information to the Charlotte Waite case map as well as reviewing other cases in hand. While Maisie was away from London, Billy would complete reports for two clients, in addition to his other duties. Issuance of a final report also meant submission of an invoice, and with clients tending not to pay "on the button," as Billy observed, timely presentation of a final account was vital.

They worked together until six o'clock, when Maisie sent Billy

home. For her part, Maisie would return to Ebury Place to prepare
for the short visit to Kent. She had planned to leave early Saturday
morning for the drive down to Chelstone. The next few days would
be busy indeed: A letter had arrived from Dame Constance in the
afternoon post, informing Maisie that, despite nursing a heavy cold,
she would be delighted to see her again, and there was time to be
spent with Maurice and with Lady Rowan before leaving for
Camden Abbey. As she made her way back to Belgravia, Maisie added
another task to her trip: Chelstone was only an hour or so from
Hastings on the Sussex coast, and she had ascertained that Rosamund
Thorpe had lived in Hastings.

Traffic was mercifully light as Maisie made her way to Ebury Place.
As rain spattered across her windscreen, compounding the dregs of a
yellowish-green smog, Maisie thought not of the work ahead, but of
her father, Frankie Dobbs. Whenever she visited her him, he assured
her, "Me? Don't you worry about me, love. I'm awright, like a sheep in
clover down 'ere." But Maisie did worry, yet was ashamed that her concern had not led her to visit him more often.

She entered the house by the kitchen door. When the Comptons
arrived back in town she would resume using the front door, which
would once again be opened by Carter, the Comptons' long-serving
butler. And once again Mrs. Crawford, who had put off retirement for
just one more year—to add to last year and the year before's "one more
year"—would be mistress of all she surveyed in the kitchen. Maisie
would straddle two levels of household life and knew only too well that
her good standing both upstairs and downstairs was was terrain to be
negotiated with great care.

She placed her document case on the writing table in her sitting
room and slumped down into the armchair by the fire, which was
already burning brightly. Home. Was this home? Had she been too easily persuaded by Lady Rowan to reside at Ebury Place because she did
not want to refuse the woman who had given her so much? When had
she last felt truly *at home*?

Sighing, Maisie moved to draw back the long curtains and looked out at fog swirling around a streetlight. Soon the days would be longer and, she hoped, warmer. London's smog would dissipate as coal fires were extinguished and hearths cleaned out for the summer. As she looked at the streetlight illuminating the twists and curls of fog in front of her, Maisie remembered the small soot-blackened terraced house in Lambeth where she had lived with her parents. With both parents, that is, until she was thirteen, when her mother died in Frankie Dobbs's arms, her last words instructing him to do right by their girl. Her last true home, she remembered, had been with her father, until he had done his best for her by finding a place in service at the Ebury Place mansion of Lord and Lady Compton.

There was a knock at her door. Maisie called out, "Come in."

Sandra opened the door quietly and smiled. "Good evening, M'um. Would you like supper in your rooms or in the dining room, M'um?"

Maisie smiled. She was M'um again, upstairs. Maisie checked her watch. Seven o'clock. A plan was forming in her mind, inspired by the prospect of an evening alone in her rooms. Though she could not identify a place that was now home, there was a person who was home, and Maisie acknowledged her yearning to be with him.

"Sandra, I wonder if you could pack me up something for me to eat in the car, perhaps a piece of pork pie, or a cheese sandwich—and a bottle of Vimto or something like that?"

"Oh, M'um, you aren't going out in this, are you?" Sandra nodded toward the fog, which seemed to be growing thicker outside.

"I don't think it will be any better first thing in the morning, do you? I'll collect my supper on my way to the motor car. I just have to pack a few things, then I'll come straight down to the kitchen."

"Right you are, M'um. I'll have it all ready when you come down."

"Thank you, Sandra."

Maisie edged the MG out of the mews behind Ebury Place and into the damp London night. She drove through south London carefully, making her way along the Old Kent Road, and on toward Sevenoaks, Tonbridge, and from there along narrow country lanes to Chelstone.

As Maisie left London behind, the smog gradually dispersed, leaving only a light rain to contend with. She uncovered the small wicker basket positioned on the passenger seat beside her, and reached for a sandwich. There was something soothing in this journey through the night, with only the flash of headlights as an occasional car passed. The engine rumbled confidently, and Maisie considered not only aspects of her own life that lately seemed to claim attention when she least expected such interruption, but the lives of Charlotte Waite and her women friends.

Keeping her right hand on the steering wheel and her attention on the road, Maisie reached out with her left hand to the basket again, took out a linen cloth, and wiped her hands and mouth. She reached for the bottle of Vimto and pulled the cork out with her teeth. Sandra had already removed the top and replaced the cork halfway to make it easier for Maisie. She took just a few sips, then set the open bottle carefully in the basket, using one hand to tuck a table napkin around it, to keep the bottle upright and within easy reach. She slowed down as rabbits scurried across the open road, requiring that she swerve around them as they froze in the beam of the headlamps.

At last she reached Chelstone. She drove first through the village, where the lights were still on at the Fox and Hounds, probably for the landlord to see by as he pushed a heavy broom across the flagstone floor, for it was well past last orders. Finally, she turned into the carriage sweep leading to Chelstone Manor, the gravel spitting and crackling under the weight of the MG's tires. A few lights were on at the manor house. The Comptons—especially Lady Rowan—kept late hours. Maisie passed the Dower House, where Maurice lived, and turned left several yards along. The lane narrowed as she parked outside the Groom's Cottage, and quietly took her bags from the car before tiptoeing along the path. And as she looked in through the latticed window, Maisie saw her father, illuminated by the mellow light cast by a single oil lamp, staring into the fire.

As flames reflected on the folds and furrows of his face, Maisie realized there was another reason at the heart of her reticence to visit Frankie as often as she might. Though still vital, he was now an old man, and she did not want to confront the truth of the matter: that the person who was home to her was in his twilight years and might be taken from her at any time.

"Oh, Dad," whispered Maisie, as she ran to the back door and let herself into her father's house.

She awoke the next morning to the smell of bacon cooking on the wood-fired stove in the kitchen below. As splinters of sunlight cast a morning glow across her counterpane, she leap out of bed, took her old woolen dressing gown from behind the door and, ducking her head so as to avoid the low beams, ran downstairs into the kitchen.

"Morning, Dad."

"And a very good mornin' to you, love." Frankie Dobbs stood at the stove and turned two thick rashers of back bacon. "Two eggs or one? Collected them myself this mornin', so they're nice and fresh. None of your shop-bought nonsense, sittin' in a warehouse for days before it gets to your plate."

"One egg'll be lovely, Dad." Maisie poured tea for Frankie and herself from a brown earthenware teapot.

"I expect you'll be off to see Dr. Blanche as soon as you've 'ad your breakfast, eh, love?"

Maisie looked up at Frankie, knowing that he expected her to leave, to go immediately to the house of her teacher and mentor. How many times had she spent a moment with Frankie only to seek Maurice's company and counsel for hours? Though she had little time to spare, Maisie sat back in her chair.

"No, I don't have to hurry, Dad. I thought we could chat until you go out to the horses."

Frankie beamed at his daughter.

"Well, I've already been out once this morning," Frankie looked the clock. "But I'd best go to check on the mare again after I've 'ad a bit of bacon and egg. I don't like to leave 'er for long, not with the littl'un due any minute. I'm a bit tired this mornin', to tell you the truth, love."

"I've missed you, Dad," said Maisie.

Frankie smiled, and slid a slice of bacon and *two* perfect fried eggs onto a warm plate, which he put in front of Maisie. "There you are, get that down you, love. That'll set you up for the day."

Maisie waited for her father to depart before she in turn left the cottage, taking the narrow path that led from the bottom of her father's garden to the Dower House grounds. At the edge of Maurice's garden, where the man who had been feted by the governments of France, Belgium and Britain for his services during the Great War now grew prizewinning roses, another gate led to apple orchards and paddocks beyond.

"Ah, Maisie, so very good to see you." Maurice Blanche, now well into his seventies, clasped Maisie's hands with his own veined and bony ones.

"And you, Maurice, and you." Maisie held his hands tightly.

"Come, child, let us sit, and you can tell me why it is that you have come to see your old teacher." Maurice led Maisie to the drawing room, took a pipe from a stand next to the inglenook fireplace, and pressed tobacco from a leather pouch into the bowl of the pipe. Maisie relaxed into a wing chair, and watched as he held a match next to the rim at just the right angle to the tobacco, and drew several times on the pipe.

"Now then, what is the case?" He threw the extinguished match into the cold fireplace and settled into his favorite leather chair.

Maisie told Maurice about being summoned to see Joseph Waite, and the search for his daughter Charlotte. She referred to the murders of Philippa Sedgewick and Lydia Fisher, and the suicide of Rosamund Thorpe, which she intended to look into. She immediately noticed the almost imperceptible response in Maurice's eyes when Waite's name was mentioned.

"Maurice, I have to ask—"

"You have no doubt seen my notes on Waite from so long ago."

"I have. Can you tell me what happened? What caused you to break off communication? I couldn't help but think that it wasn't like you."

Maurice drew several more times on his pipe, then looked at Maisie intently. "Joseph Waite, as you can probably tell, is a natural and decisive leader. He is essentially a good man but at times a hard man, a difficult man. He is generous with those in straitened circumstances whom he believes genuinely cannot help themselves. He is no stranger to hard work and demands hard work from others, which is then repaid accordingly. He is, in fact, the epitome of the self-made man."

Maisie waited as Maurice drew again on his pipe. A "but" was imminent.

"As you will have seen from the notes, Waite was an interested and generous benefactor of my clinics in the poorer areas of east and southeast London. He gave immediately and unstintingly, but . . ." Maurice drew breath deeply and cupped the pipe in both hands, his elbows resting on the arms of the chair. "But he is a man who likes to be in control, or to at least *believe* that he is in control."

"What happened, Maurice?"

"In short, he began to instruct me in the finer points of doing my job. That may seem harmless enough. However, his instructions revealed deep prejudices. He began to make demands regarding the type of people my staff could or could not serve at the clinics. He tried to stipulate the nature of illnesses or indispositions that we could and could not treat. The people who came to the clinics were human beings, and as a doctor I could not turn away one who was sick, whether a felon or a drunkard, though certainly those who abused their health were subjected to strong words of advice."

Maisie was thoughtful as Maurice carefully composed the next part of his story.

"As with his shops, Waite had the habit of turning up at the clinics unannounced. I had always allowed access to benefactors. After all, seeing the work done on behalf of the poor encouraged further contributions from them. Few came. However, Waite was one of those who wanted to see his money at work. On the occasion in question—I was not there at the time—one of my staff was interviewing a girl. She was very young and with child herself, though at an early stage." Maurice brushed some ash from his sleeve. "Those who helped at the clinic were instructed by me personally that our concern was for the health of the mother and her unborn child. We'd given refuge to young women in similar situations, or placed them where they would be cared for. They were never to be put in a position of having to give up a child." Blanche shook his head. "The clinics are not large affairs, usually just two or three rooms, then a little extra space to store supplies. Though we do all we can to ensure confidentiality, Waite heard part of the conversation, rushed to judgment and gave the nurse and the young girl—already emotionally unstable—a piece of his mind. The girl ran away. I was alerted at the earliest opportunity and left Waite in no doubt that his money was no longer welcome."

Relations between Maurice and Waite at the time must have been incendiary, thought Maisie. "What happened to the girl?"

Maurice sighed. "By the time my staff located her, she had already taken her problem to a back alley. She was rushed to the clinic again. It was too late. I did all I could to save her life, but she died clutching my hand."

"Oh!" Maisie brought her hands to her mouth.

Maurice stood up and tapped tobacco from his pipe against the brick of the fireplace, emptying it into the grate. "Even from Chelstone, I am still very involved in the work of my clinics. All the more reason to ensure that the health of women and children is provided for and protected by those who are qualified for such a task. I also now ensure that no benefactor visits a clinic without my express permission. A gift is unconditional by its very nature. Waite brought his tendency to dominate, along with prejudices rooted in experience, into my clinic and, I believe, killed an innocent child. No—two innocent children. I refused later requests to accept funds from him. A difficult man, Maisie."

They were both silent for several moments. Maurice suggested a walk to the orchard. Fortunately Maisie had dressed with such an excursion in mind, knowing Maurice's maxim: "To solve a problem, take it for a walk." Her dark brown trousers, fashionably wide, were complemented by brown walking shoes, an ivory linen blouse and a light-brown-and-cream Harris tweed jacket with a shawl collar and large square pockets at the hips.

They strolled through still-damp grass and trees laden with blossom buds that gave a promise of summer's bounty, and they spoke of Maisie's work, her challenges, and how she had fared in the year since Maurice formally retired and she had set up in business on her own. Finally, Maisie spoke of her worries about Billy.

"My dear, I believe you already know what is at the root of Mr. Beale's erratic behavior."

"I have my suspicions," she confessed.

"How might you confirm them in such a way as to protect Billy?"

"First of all, I think I should visit All Saints' Convalescent Hospital in Hastings. It's where Billy was sent after being discharged from hospital in London. They should still have his medical records. The problem will be gaining access to them."

"I think I can help, my dear. The physician in charge is known to me: He was one of my students at King's College in London."

"Maurice, I do believe you know everyone!" Maisie moved a low bough aside as they walked through an avenue of trees.

"Not quite, but my contacts are useful. I will telephone him prior to your arrival—when will you go?"

"This afternoon. I know they are open for visitors on a Saturday."

"Good."

"Of course, what I really need to do is find a way to get him to a doctor to do something about the continued pain in his leg."

Maurice stopped. "Maisie, I sense that Billy has had enough of doctors. Sometimes people who have endured a chronic illness cannot face even a discussion with a doctor. And though I am a doctor, I can say that often there is good reason for such a reaction. We don't have all the answers."

"What do you suggest?"

"First, you must find out whether your suspicions are grounded. Then you must confront Billy. You know this already. But a confrontation of this sort is best followed by a plan, an idea, a lens through which the future can be viewed once the secret has been revealed. May I make a suggestion?"

"Oh, please."

"I suggest that you bring Mr. Beale to the Dower House, where I would like him to meet a new acquaintance of mine."

Maisie inclined her head. "He's a German by birth, though he came to this country as a child. While he was interned during the war, he met a very interesting man, also a German. The man had developed a means of exercise and movement that helped maintain health in the camp: Even during the first flu epidemic in 1917, not one of those interned was lost. In fact most of those in the camp were released in a healthier state than before the war, despite being poorly nourished. The physical movements incorporated in the regimen have been used to rehabilitate the severely wounded with great success. My friend is a practitioner of the regimen."

"Who is he?"

"Gideon Brown. After the war he changed his surname from Braun, and his Christian name from Günther to Gideon. It made life a little less difficult for him, given the manner in which those of German extraction were treated at the time. The man whose work he has followed now lives in America. His name is Joseph Pilates."

Maisie smiled. "I'm glad that at least I have the bare bones of a plan now . . . But my first step is All Saints'. In fact, I may be able to kill two birds with one stone, as Rosamund Thorpe lived in the same area." Maisie checked her watch. "Eleven o'clock. If I leave by noon, I should be there by half past one."

"You'd better get along then, hadn't you, Maisie? Remember to ask for Dr. Andrew Dene. I will have spoken with him by telephone before you arrive."

# CHAPTER NINE

aisie reversed the MG out of the narrow lane onto the carriage sweep that led from the main gate to the manor house. As she drove slowly along the gravel road, Lady Rowan waved from the edge of the lawn where she was walking with Nutmeg and Raven, her two black Labradors, and a Welsh Springer Spaniel who answered to the name of Morgan. Though Lady Rowan walked with the aid of a silver-tipped cane, her posture gave the impression of youthfulness. She wore a tweed walking skirt, a brown corduroy jacket and a small fur scarf around her neck. Her ensemble was topped off by a jaunty brown felt hat, a single feather pinned to the band with an amethyst brooch. She waved again at Maisie, who slowed the car to a halt.

Maisie stepped from the MG. "Lady Rowan, how are you?"

"Hallo, Maisie, dear. So lovely to see you. How is the motor car running? Serving you well, I hope."

"Oh, yes, very well indeed." Maisie smiled warmly. "It's never broken down, and goes very smoothly. I'm off to Hastings this afternoon."

"Anything exciting, Maisie?" Before Maisie could respond, Lady

Rowan held her hand up. "I know, I know, you can't divulge the nature of your work. I never learn, do I? It's just that you always seem to be involved with something so very intriguing!" Lady Rowan's eyes crinkled to emphasize not a little envy at Maisie's employment. "Mind you, I've had my day, Maisie, I've had my day."

"No you haven't, Lady Rowan. What's all this I hear about breeding racehorses?"

"It's most thrilling. Your good father and I have pored over breeding records. He is a most knowledgeable man when it comes to horses, so we expect to see the will to win in the eyes of this one! I confess i am beside myself with anticipation, which is why I am pacing back and forth across the lawn. Otherwise I would make a nuisance of myself in the stable."

"Dad's keeping an eye on the mare, but he said it could be a day or two yet."

"When do you leave, Maisie? Will you come to see me before you go back to London?" Lady Rowan refrained from displaying the affection that would embarrass them both, but in truth she viewed Maisie almost as a daughter.

"I am here until tomorrow, Lady Rowan. Aren't you coming back to London at the end of this week?"

"Hmmm. I confess, I'm tempted to stay at Chelstone until after Merriweather foals."

"Shall I call on you when I get back from Hastings?"

"Yes, that would be lovely. Don't let me detain you a moment longer. Come along, Nutmeg. Morgan, come here! Oh dear, it seems I've lost Raven again."

Maisie laughed, took her seat in the MG, and continued down the driveway, then along the country lanes until she joined the main road for Tonbridge. The journey to Hastings was an easy one. She saw few vehicles as she cruised through the Weald of Kent, crossing into Sussex near Bodiam, where she could see parts of the old castle beyond the hop gardens.

She entered Hastings from the east, negotiating the narrow streets of the Old Town, which was still so much like a fishing village, in stark contrast to the development along the promenade toward St. Leonards, built up during Queen Victoria's reign to cater for the town's increase in popularity with day-trippers.

Her first stop would be a visit to All Saints' Convalescent Hospital, a red-brick mansion on the Old Town's East Hill. It commanded sun-filled views over the channel on a good day, only to be battered by wind and rain when the weather turned. It was just after one o'clock, she had estimated the journey exactly. Because it was such a fine day, Maisie decided to park the car along Rock-a-Nore, then take the path that led alongside tall wooden net shops where fishermen hung out their nets to dry. She would make her way to the East Hill via the Old Town's small funicular railway, a carriage that took passengers from sea level to the upper lift station, with its castellated towers that each contained an iron tank filled with more than one thousand gallons of water to operate the water-balance lift. Once outside the station, visitors would set off along the cliffs, where they could enjoy the fresh, if sometimes biting, sea air. At the top Maisie would have just a short walk to All Saints'.

Having made her way past the shacks with counters where day-trippers bought small bowls of tasty jellied eels, whelks, or winkles, or strolled while lunching on fish and chips wrapped in newspaper, Maisie bought her ticket, and found that her companions on the ascent were four women clad in walking skirts, leather boots, and heavy pullovers; they were clearly prepared for a day's hiking. She felt her stomach turn when the funicular began to move. As the carriage made its way up the cliff, Maisie wondered if Billy had used this means of coming down into the town when he had reached a point in his convalescence at which short excursions were allowed. She knew that he had met Doreen in Hastings. Had it been on her day off, perhaps, when each had gone with friends to the pier to listen to the band and drink sarsaparilla? She imagined Billy cracking jokes as Doreen blushed and turned away toward her group, then back again to smile in a way that was just a little coy. The carriage lurched again, and Maisie waited while the four women alighted first, maps flapping in the wind, one pointing toward the Firehills at Fairlight where out-of-work Welsh miners had been brought in to create a series of walking paths along the cliffs.

Seagulls whooped and called below her as she walked along the edge of the East Hill. From her vantage point she could see the rooftops below. The architecture revealed the history of the town, from beamed medieval hall houses with huts and fish smokers in the back, to Regency mansions, and brick two-up-two-down cottages built perhaps only sixty years earlier.

Maisie stopped once to look at All Saints' Convalescent Hospital before setting out along the path lined with low trees and shrubs before it turned toward the broad front doors of the house. The route she had taken was infinitely more enjoyable than driving along the ancient streets that spiraled precariously up the hill. The building was laid out in an exact square and had been constructed of red brick and wood at the turn of the century. Its architecture was of the new style, with clean lines and a shallow roof. Some outbuildings had been added during the war when it was requisitioned for use as a military convalescent home. The owner had eventually sold the property to the local authorities, possibly to preempt compulsory purchase at a reduced price, and it was now used for all manner of convalescent cases though many of the patients were still old soldiers.

The door, constructed from a single substantial piece of wood, moved easily after Maisie turned the brass handle, opening into a large entrance hall with wooden floors and plain white walls. There were arched wooden beams above the staircase before her. A lift had been added to assist those who were unable to move themselves. Rubber strips ran along the floor in strategic places, minimizing slippage for invalids learning to walk again with caliper splints, crutches, or new artificial limbs. Despite vases of flowers and a lingering aroma of lavender furniture polish, if one turned quickly or took a deep breath, there was the unmistakable hospital smell of disinfectant and urine.

Maisie knocked on the frosted glass window of the porter's office and was asked to wait while Dr. Dene was summoned.

"Miss Dobbs, delighted to meet you." Andrew Dene began reaching out his hand when he was still three steps from the bottom of the staircase. "Maurice said to expect you here around one-thirty. Please." They shook hands, and he indicated another door, which led to a long corridor. Though he had been one of the students who attended Maurice's medical school tutorials, Maisie had expected someone far older. He seemed to be only four or five years her senior. If she was right, then he had certainly made his mark early. Dene's light brown hair fell into his eyes repeatedly as they made their way toward his office. Maisie had to walk quickly to keep up with his athletic gait. She noticed with pleasure his ease of manner, as well as his obvious respect for Maurice and, by default, herself.

"You know," said Dene, "I always wondered what it must be like to work with Maurice, at his side. He said something once about his assistant, but you could have knocked me down with a feather when I found out that the accomplished assistant was a woman."

"Really, Dr. Dene?" Maisie's tone caused Dene to rephrase his remark "Oh dear, that's not what I meant." Dene opened the door of his office and allowed Maisie to enter before him. "That's me all over: Open mouth, insert foot. What I meant was . . . well . . . sometimes the work sounded so, you know, so tricky that . . ."

Maisie raised an eyebrow.

"I think I'd better just take it all back and get on with the business at hand before I have to show you out on my hands and knees."

"Indeed, Dr. Dene, I can think of no better punishment at this moment." She removed her gloves, and took the seat indicated. Despite his faux pas, Maisie thought Andrew Dene was rather fun. "Perhaps we can get down to business."

"Oh yes, quite." Dene checked his watch and reached for a manila folder with frayed edges that was already set to the side of the other stacks on his desk. "I have a meeting in twenty minutes. Mind you, I can be late." He smiled at Maisie. "I understand you want to know more about the convalescent history of one William Beale, Corporal."

"Yes, please."

"Well, I've already looked at the file. I had to rescue it from what we refer to as the Dungeon down in the cellars. Unfortunately, the attending doctor has passed on now but the notes are all here. Looks like he's lucky to have kept that leg. Amazing what those doctors were able to do over there, isn't it?"

"I thought you . . ."

"Oh no. I was in medical school when I enlisted, but I was not qualified. They pushed me into the Medical Corps anyway, though not as a surgeon. As an assistant. Not quite a nurse, not quite a doctor. I ended up in Malta finding out more about surgical procedures on the job than I ever learned when I returned to medical school. By that time I had become more interested in what happened to soldiers when they came back, their recuperation, their post-operative care, and how I could best help them."

"I see. So what can you tell me about Mr. Beale's recovery?"

Dene looked through the notes once again, sometimes turning the file to one side the better to see a chart or diagram; then he closed the folder. He looked up at Maisie. "It would be less like finding a needle in a haystack if you were to tell me why you are interested—the medical aspects, that is."

Maisie was taken aback by Dene's manner but understood the need, given the array of procedures and therapies that would have been noted in the file. Maisie described her observations of Billy's behavior, adding that his family life was also disturbed by his mood swings.

"Is this is a recent development?"

"Over the past few months, along with the increased pain in his legs."

"Ah. Yes." Dene reached for the file again. "Miss Dobbs, you were a nurse in France, weren't you?"

"Yes, I—"

"And later, according to what I know, you worked with shell-shocked patients before returning to Cambridge. I understand from Maurice that you spent some time at the Department of Legal Medicine in Edinburgh."

"That's all correct."

"So you don't need me to tell you what's going on, do you?"

Maisie looked at Dene intently, her deep blue eyes sparking. "I thought it best to confer with the attending doctor, or his successor, before jumping to conclusions."

"A wise and very professional decision. Oh, and by the way, I'm *her* successor. Mr. Beale's attending physician here was Dr. *Mrs.* Hilda Benton."

Maisie's cheeks reddened.

Dene leaned back in his chair and made a church-and-steeple with his fingers. It was the same way Maurice sat when considering a problem.

"Here's what I suspect is at the root of Mr. Beale's behavior, and I would add that it is not uncommon, though a terror to address. According to the notes," Dene opened the file and passed two pages to Maisie, "he was initially treated for pain with massive doses of morphine. I would imagine he was hard to medicate, probably one of those who can soak up medication and still feel everything."

Maisie remembered Billy being brought in to the casualty clearing station in June, 1917, his eyes wide even as the surgeon's knife cut into his flesh, and his promise that he would never forget the doctor and nurse who saved him.

"Of course, we didn't know as much about dosage then as we do now. In fact, the military was rather slap-happy with morphine, cocaine, and various other narcotics. You must remember that people could buy heroin kits from the corner chemist's, even from Savoy & Moore, to send to their soldier loved ones in France, just in case. Then everyone cheerfully expected the need for medication to go away along with the pain as soon as the men were out of uniform. Boom-boom, good-bye, soldier, you're on your way! Unfortunately in many cases the pain and the craving lingered. And even when both went away, recurrence of pain naturally re-creates that craving for medication. Doctors are a bit more careful now but there's a healthy black market in cocaine, especially among old soldiers. I don't want to cast aspersions, but to be candid, Miss Dobbs, I believe that Mr. Beale is struggling with a dependence upon narcotics. Though from what you say, I would imagine he's not in too deeply. Yet."

Maisie nodded. "Dr. Dene, I wonder if you could advise me on how I might go about initiating Mr. Beale's withdrawal from the use of such a substance?"

"I think we can assume that increased physical discomfort was at the root of his initial self-medication. Now we have the addiction itself to cure, and I'm afraid that there is precious little to draw upon. I'm sure there are psychiatrists who would speak of their successes, but frankly I take such claims with a pinch of salt."

Dene leaned forward on the desk and looked up at Maisie. "If you want to help Mr. Beale I would suggest the following: Get him away from the source of supply, that's the first step. Then ensure that the pain is acknowledged and experiment with physical therapies. If necessary we can admit him here as an outpatient and I can prescribe controlled doses of painkillers. Finally, fresh air and something to do that he truly feels is of importance while he recovers. I do not hold with cures for such conditions while the mind and body are idle, it only gives the patient time to consider the desirable effects of the substance that is now no longer available."

Dene watched as Maisie nodded her head in agreement.

"Thank you, Dr. Dene, for your advice and your time. You have been most kind."

"Not at all, Miss Dobbs. A summons from our friend Dr. Maurice Blanche is as good as a call to arms."

"Before I leave, Dr. Dene, I wonder if by any slight chance you might have known a Mrs. Rosamund Thorpe? I understand she lived locally before her death in February."

"How extraordinary that you should ask! Mrs. Thorpe was a visitor to the hospital. There's a group of women in the town who visit regularly, to read to the patients, talk with them, you know, make the long stay here a little easier to bear. She was widowed not that long before she died, but she never stopped coming here. Mrs. Thorpe was especially good with the old soldiers. Of course she was the same age as most of them, but we do insist upon calling them old, don't we?" Dene shook his head, and continued. "It was such a shock when we heard. I'd spoken to her many times in the course of my work here, and would never have believed she would take her own life." He looked again at Maisie. "May I ask why you inquire about her?"

"I am engaged in work that has brought me into contact with one of her friends. I can say no more. I want to know about Mrs. Thorpe's life, and her death. Is there anything you can tell me, Dr. Dene?"

Dene seemed to consider whether to voice his observations, then continued. "Of course, she had been very sad at the passing of her husband, but I think the death was not unexpected as he was a good deal older than Mrs. Thorpe and toward the end was heavily medicated. In fact they had moved here because of his health, hoping the sea air would effect a cure." Dene shook his head. "The behavior of the younger Thorpes—her stepchildren, who were closer to her in age— over her late husband's will was reprehensible, but she seemed to evince none of the gloom one might expect to see in one at risk of suicide."

"I see." Maisie hoped that Dene might add more depth and color to the picture he was painting of Rosamund Thorpe. He did not disappoint her.

"I will say, though, that she seemed different from the other volunteers." Dene allowed his gaze to wander to a view of the sea beyond the pile of books and notes on the sill above the cast-iron radiators. "She was very intense in her work here, always wanting to do more. If visiting ended at four, most of the women were on their way home at one minute after the hour, but Mrs. Thorpe would spend extra time, perhaps to complete a letter or read to the end of a chapter for some poor soul who couldn't hold a book. In fact, she once said to me, 'I owe it to them.' But it was the way that she said it that caused me to remember. After all, we all *feel* that we owe so much."

Dene turned to Maisie and looked at his watch. "Crikey! I'd better be on my way." He pushed back his chair, and placed the file to one side, having scribbled on the front: "Return to archives."

"Thank you so much for your time, Dr. Dene. Your advice is sound. I appreciate your counsel."

"Not at all, Miss Dobbs, not at all. One caution, though: I need not remind you that in taking on the responsibility of helping Mr. Beale, you are also becoming involved, technically, in a crime."

"Yes, I am aware of the implication, Dr. Dene. Though I hope—no, *expect*—Mr. Beale to destroy any illicit substances soon after we speak."

Dene raised an eyebrow as he opened the door for Maisie. "Don't underestimate the task. Fortunately, Dr. Blanche can assist you."

As they continued along the corridor, Andrew Dene gave Maisie directions to Rosamund Thorpe's house and the name of her housekeeper. Clearly everyone knew everyone else in the Old Town.

When they reached the door, Maisie had one more question for Andrew Dene. "Dr. Dene, I hope you don't mind me asking, but you seem to know Dr. Blanche very well, more than one might expect from someone who was simply one of many students in a lecture hall or tutorial. And your assessment of the situation with Mr. Beale and your subsequent advice are very much what I might expect to hear from him."

Dene affected an accent he had lost long ago, explaining, "I'm a Bermondsey boy, ain't I?" Then he continued, reverting to his previous Home Counties diction, "My father died when I was young—he was a steeplejack—and then, when I was barely fifteen and out at work at the brewery myself, my mother became ill. There was no money for doctors. I made my way to Dr. Blanche's clinic and begged him to come to the house. He visited each week and instructed me in her care, so I was able to administer medicine and make her comfortable even at the end. I paid him back by helping him. At first he trusted me with errands, then I helped at the clinics—obviously not with patients, as I was just a boy. If it hadn't been for Dr. Blanche, I might never have known what I wanted to be, or what I could be. He helped me to apply to Guys, which I attended on a scholarship. Mind you, I had to work night shifts at the brewery to earn my keep. Then the war broke out, and I think you know the rest."

Maisie smiled. "Yes I do, Dr. Dene. I know the rest very well."

# CHAPTER TEN

aisie parked the MG on the West Hill and looked across toward the East Hill, where she had strolled just thirty-five minutes earlier. She had walked down the 158 steps from the top of the cliffs onto Tackleway Street, then through a narrow alleyway known to locals as a "twitten," one of the many almost-secret paths that crisscrossed the Old Town of Hastings. It led out onto Rock-a-Nore, where she had parked the motor car. No wonder smugglers loved this place, thought Maisie.

It was a fine Spring afternoon. The sun and a light breeze conspired to glance light off whitecaps in such a way that the view across the Channel seemed to be repeatedly punctured by shards of crystal. Maisie shielded her eyes from the prismatic flashes of light as she looked out over the water before making her way to the four-storey Regency house that had been the home of Rosamund Thorpe. She was anxious to interview the housekeeper and be on her way back to Chelstone, to plan the next part of her visit to Kent. She was abundantly aware that the initial meeting with Joseph Waite had taken place almost a week ago, and she was not yet certain she had located her client's daughter.

A short woman answered the door and smiled warmly at Maisie. "You must be Miss Dobbs."

Maisie returned the smile. She thought the housekeeper resembled the quintessential grandmother, with her tight white curls, a plain dress in wool the color of heather, and stout black shoes.

"Young Dr. Dene from the convalescent hospital telephoned me and said to expect you. Very nice man, isn't he? Surprised he's not married, after all, it's not as if there's a shortage of young women. Mind you, he was walking out with that one girl last—Oh, excuse me, Miss Dobbs, I do go on at times! Now then—" Mrs. Hicks showed Maisie into a drawing room with bowed windows that commanded a view across the West Hill. "Dr. Dene said that you were a friend of a friend of Mrs. Thorpe's and wanted to know more about her passing on." The housekeeper regarded Maisie intently. "Normally, I wouldn't be talking to anyone outside the family, but Dr. Dene said it was important."

"Yes it is, Mrs. Hicks, though I can't really say much about it at the moment."

Mrs. Hicks nodded and wrung her hands together in her lap, revealing her discomfort and, Maisie suspected, the fact that she wanted to speak of her employer very much. Maisie would give her that opportunity.

"Tell me, Mrs. Hicks, is the house for sale? Mrs. Thorpe passed on some two months ago now, didn't she?"

"They—Mr. Thorpe's children by his first marriage, that is—have asked me to stay on and keep the place up until it's sold. It has only just gone up for sale, as there was a lot of legal to-ing and fro-ing and paperwork and so on to go through after . . ." Mrs. Hicks's bottom lip wobbled, and she hurriedly pulled an embroidered handkerchief from her pocket. "I'm sorry, Miss, but it was so very hard, finding her there. . . ."

"You found Mrs. Thorpe?"

Mrs. Hicks nodded. "I went up in the morning because she was late rising. Since Mr. Thorpe passed away, the house has been so quiet. Even though he was that much older, they were always laughing together. I tell you, if they saw two raindrops running down the window, they'd bet on which one would reach the bottom first and have a giggle over who'd won." Mrs. Hicks kneaded the handkerchief between her hands. "Anyway, Mrs. Thorpe had trouble sleeping and was an early riser, so it was a change to not to see her up and about."

"Was she in bed when you found her?"

"No, she was . . ." Mrs. Hicks rubbed her eyes with the handkerchief. "She was lying there, on the floor in her sitting room. It's a small area that connects to the bedroom. She liked to sit there to have tea, for the view. The tea tray was still out from the day before, and there she was."

"When had you served tea?"

Mrs. Hicks looked up at Maisie. "Well, she must've made it, because it had been my afternoon off. She often made herself a cup, especially if she thought I was busy with something else. They didn't keep a big staff here, the cleaning's done by Mrs. Singleton and Mrs. Acres who come up from the Old Town every morning, and if they were entertaining, they called in a cook and maids. There was only the two of them for me to keep for."

"Mrs. Hicks, I know this is difficult for you, but did you notice anything that made you think twice when you went into the room, or when you looked at it later?"

"It was all such a shock, but I suppose there was one thing that I thought about, you know, afterwards."

Maisie sat forward to listen.

"The tea tray was set for two: Two pieces of malt loaf, watercress sandwiches for two, two scones and some biscuits. But only one teacup had been used. So I wondered if she was expecting someone who hadn't arrived. Mind you, she hadn't said anything to me in the morning. Apparently she'd taken it, the poison, and washed it down with a cup of tea and a biscuit. But, I don't know . . . ."

"What don't you know, Mrs. Hicks?"

"She was a funny little thing at times. She would spend hours up at All Saints' with the soldiers. I used to tell her that she did too much, but she'd say to me, 'Mrs. Hicks, I have to make things right.' Anybody would have thought she was responsible for their suffering, the way she said it. She was well-liked in the town, would always stop to talk to folk if she was out walking, not one of those uppity types." Mrs. Hicks bit her lip. "I know she was sad, very sad, when Mr. Thorpe passed on, but I never, never knew that she was in such a state as to take her own life."

"Mrs. Hicks, I know this is a strange question, but—do you really think she committed suicide?"

Mrs. Hicks sniffed and dabbed at her nose; then, emboldened by loyalty to her employer, she sat up. "No, Miss Dobbs. I do not."

"Do you know of anyone who might have wanted her gone?"

"The younger Thorpes were jealous of her, no doubt about that, but to do away with her? No, they haven't got it in them. No gumption at the best of times, that pair. Still, they did want the money and property that was left to her by her husband, even though they were very well taken care of. They quite enjoyed all the back-and-forth with solicitors. Made them feel important. Otherwise I don't think she had an enemy. Though she must have, if her life was taken by someone else. I don't think she'd've done it by accident, either. Very careful, she was, very careful. Wouldn't even take a powder if she had a cold. Of course, there were still medicines in the house from when Mr. Thorpe was ill. For the pain. That's what the doctor said she'd taken. An overdose of the painkillers. But I just can't see her doing it." Mrs. Hicks rubbed the handkerchief across her eyelids and dabbed at her nose again.

Maisie reached out and touched the housekeeper's arm. "Would you show me where you found Mrs. Thorpe?"

Maisie stood in the light and airy room, a gentle breeze blowing curtains through sash windows that were half open. She was sorry that the death was so far in the past, for the room had doubtless been cleaned several times since Mrs. Hicks found the body of Rosamund Thorpe, as she had shown Maisie, lying between the small table set for tea and the settee placed at an angle to the window, offering views across the rooftops to the East Hill and out toward the Channel.

"Mrs. Hicks, I know this may sound a little unusual, but would you mind if I spent a few moments in the room alone?"

"Of course, Miss Dobbs. Has a funny feel about it, this room, doesn't it? Can't put a finger on it myself, but it was always there, even before she died." Mrs. Hicks dabbed at her eyes. "I'll just be outside if you need me."

Maisie closed her eyes. She stood perfectly still and allowed her senses to mingle with the aura of Rosamund Thorpe that still lingered in her room. Her skin prickled with sensation, as if someone had stood next to her and touched her lightly on the arm, to share a confidence, to say, "I am here, and this is my confession." She opened her mind to the secrets held within the walls and recognized the familiar presence of a troubled soul, kindred spirit to the veils of emotion left behind by Charlotte Waite and Lydia Fisher. She suspected already that Philippa Sedgewick had been equally troubled. Four unsettled women. But what could be at the heart of their disquiet?

As she breathed deeply and silently, Maisie framed a question in her mind: *What can you tell me?* It was immediately answered with a picture in Maisie's mind's eye, an image that began as a simple outline, gaining form and texture as if it were a photograph set in a tray of developing solution. Yes, she could see it. She hoped Mrs. Hicks might be able to offer an explanation, and summoned the housekeeper.

Mrs. Hicks poked her head around the door before entering. "All done, Miss?"

"Yes, thank you."

The housekeeper led the way downstairs, and opened the front door for Maisie.

"I wonder, Mrs. Hicks, if I might ask one more question."

"Of course, Miss. Anything I can do to help."

"Do you know what medicines Mr. Thorpe was prescribed by his doctor?" asked Maisie.

"Well, I do know that there were different mixtures and tablets. Mrs. Thorpe was most particular to measure them out in the morning, putting them in little saucers. He had pills breakfast, lunch, supper, and bedtime. But at the end, you know, the doctor prescribed morphine. Mrs. Thorpe was very upset about it. She said you know there's no hope when they start giving a patient morphine, because it means there's nothing more they can do to save a life. All they can do is stop the pain."

𝕄aisie loved to drive the motor car, whether weaving in and out of traffic in London—which was always a challenge given the noisy mixture of motor lorries, cars large and small, and horse-drawn delivery vans carrying groceries and beer—or meandering along country roads with only her thoughts for company. She found it easy to think in the car, turning over facts and ideas as she changed gear, or slowed down for a farmer moving sheep from one field to another.

Conversations were replayed, possibilities for action assessed and considered, and all manner of outcomes pictured in her mind's eye. Sometimes another driver might stop alongside the MG in slow traffic, look across at the young woman in the fast car with the cloth top down, and see her speaking to herself, her mouth opening and closing as she asked a question. Then, hearing the words aloud, she would nod.

She was driving across Kent to Romney Marsh. Dame Constance Charteris, Abbess of Camden Abbey, expected her at ten o'clock on the dot. She had left her father's cottage at Chelstone just after eight, allowing more time than was required for the journey because she wanted to think, to run through yesterday evening's conversations with Maurice and Lady Rowan, as well as to recollect the time spent with her father.

Maurice had quickly stepped forward to help Billy Beale, assisted by Dr. Andrew Dene who, it seems, had been busy with his telephone again, speaking to Maurice after his meeting with Maisie to offer support in Billy's recovery. Billy could not be admitted as an in-patient at All Saints' Convalescent Hospital, but Andrew Dene offered to monitor his health along with his progress in overcoming a dependence on narcotics—*if* Billy was agreeable to leaving London. By the time Maisie had arrived back at Chelstone, it seemed that Maurice had already devised a skeleton plan, with the help of Frankie Dobbs. Billy would come to Chelstone, stay at the Groom's Cottage with Frankie, and meet with Maurice each day to "talk."

Maisie knew well the healing power of Maurice's skills as a listener, when he would encourage confession with perhaps just one word, question, or comment. One word that could unlock memories and shine a bright light on a person's soul. Maisie had learned much from Maurice, but she knew that she was too close to Billy for such conversation. In addition to his time with Maurice, Billy would become a "patient" of Gideon Brown, who would instruct Billy in new methods of moving his wounded limbs so that he might free himself of the pain that dragged at his spirit. There was only one obstacle to overcome: Billy had to agree to the plan carefully laid out without his foreknowledge. Billy had to *want* to end his reliance on narcotics.

"Getting Billy to Chelstone is the hardest job, Maisie. And it falls to you," said Maurice as he tapped ash from his pipe into the fireplace.

Maisie repeated his words out loud as she drove through Brenchley and Horsmonden. As she drove on, the sun came from behind a cloud and shone across morning-bright green fields where newborn lambs ran on still-unsteady legs, and she knew that, whatever it took, she would get Billy on the road to Chelstone and recovery.

Clumps of primroses lined the hedgerows as she made her way slowly through Cranbrook and on toward Tenterden, winding through country lanes to the picture-postcard village of Appledore with its medieval cottages, thatched roofs, and climbing roses on trellises and doors. The promise of a perfect Sunday diminished as the hills flattened out and the soft undulating Weald of Kent gave way to land reclaimed from the sea, a jigsaw puzzle of fields for arable farming divided by hedges and stone walls. Maisie followed the Royal Military Canal while under a dark thunderous cloud that threatened to do its worst. She had a panoramic view across marshland where trees had grown leaning away from the wind, and small cottages and churches were dotted forlornly in an unforgiving landscape.

Maisie did not stop to pull up the roof of the MG but instead carefully wound a red woolen scarf around her neck and pulled on her black leather gloves. Frankie had insisted on filling a flask with hot tea "just in case." It seemed to Maisie that the Romney Marshes were living up to the description penned by William Lambarde in the sixteenth century: "Evil in winter, grievous in summer, and never good." But Maisie knew there was something to be found in this forlorn wasteland. She was close to Camden Abbey.

Long before she reached the end of the gravel road leading to the mansion that was now the home of twenty-four Benedictine nuns, Maisie saw the abbey in the distance. The abbey was E-shaped, with a long, two-storey north-south spine and three wings extending out. The center wing held the main entrance. The end of each wing had an unusual bell-shaped face and roofline, inspired by the houses of Holland, where the first owner had grown up. In her letter Dame Constance had written that the nuns had lost their home in Cambridgeshire when it was requisitioned by the War Office for officer accommodation. Sir Edward Welch, owner of Camden House, which was fortunately ill-situated for military use, bequeathed his property to the order upon hearing of their distressing circumstances. He died shortly thereafter, and Camden House became Camden Abbey.

Maisie parked the MG, ensured that its roof was properly secured in case of rain while she was inside, and proceeded through the main door to what had once been a substantial entrance hall. To her left an iron grille at face height covered a small door. Maisie took the brass handle of the bell-pull next to the grille, drew it back and immediately heard the deep resonant clang of a large bell. She shivered in the cold, dark hall and waited.

The small door opened, and a nun nodded at her. Maisie smiled automatically, and as she did so she noticed the corners of the nun's mouth twitch before she looked down piously.

"I am here to see Dame Constance. My name is Maisie Dobbs."

The nun nodded and closed the door. Maisie shivered again, waiting alone. She heard another door open and footsteps grow louder as someone came to meet her. It was the same woman. She wore the habit of a postulant, and as she had not yet taken orders, she could meet Maisie without a barrier between them.

"Please follow me, Miss Dobbs." The postulant seemed to swirl around as if practicing for the day when she would wear a full-length habit instead of a calf-length dress, and a cowl would replace the white collar buttoned tightly at her neck. The end of her veil flapped as she walked, reminding Maisie of the wings of a seagull slowing down for a landing on water. She opened an oak door with pointed iron hinges that stretched out into the center of the wood, and allowed Maisie to enter. The nun left her alone in the room, closing the door behind her with an echoing thud.

It was a small room, with a fireplace at one end and a window to the gardens at the other. Coal and wood crackled and sputtered in the grate, and the red carpet on the floor and heavy red curtains at the window made the room warm and welcoming. The plain wall bore no ornamentation but a crucifix. A comfortable wing chair had been placed in front of the grille that covered a small door situated next to the crucifix. A side table held a tray, and Maisie could see steam rising from the spout of a teapot covered with a plain white cozy. Upon closer inspection she found a plate of homemade oatmeal biscuits next to a milk jug, sugar, and a cup upturned on its saucer. The crockery was plain.

Each week for one term, when she had been at Girton, Maisie had walked to the order's former abbey after lunch on a Wednesday, along with her fellow students. At half past one exactly, the small door leading to Dame Constance's room would open, and she would greet them from behind the grille, ready to fire questions, question assumptions, and prod for opinions. Dame Constance had blended compassion with pragmatism. With the hindsight of the worldly experience she had since acquired, it was clear to Maisie that Dame Constance had suffered fools if not gladly, then with gracious ease.

The door clattered back, and the warm smile she had known so well beamed at her from beyond the iron grille once more.

"Maisie Dobbs! How lovely to see you. No, mind you keep well back, I'm still getting over this wretched cold you know, so do keep your distance from my bars." Her demeanor did not give away her age. The timbre of her voice seemed that of a much younger woman. In fact, it had occurred to Maisie that she didn't know how old Dame Constance actually was.

"Do not let me see a biscuit left on that plate at the end of our talk, Maisie. You young women of today do not know how to eat. Why, in my day, that plate would have been nothing but a few crumbs by now, and I'd be licking my fingers and dabbing at them so as not to miss a thing!"

From her seat next to the grille, Maisie leaned toward the iron bars, the warning of germs notwithstanding. "I can assure you, Dame Constance, I eat very well."

Dame Constance was silent for a few seconds before continuing. "Tell me, dear girl, why have you come to me today? What can an old nun can do for a young sleuth? It must be serious for you to come on a Sunday."

"I know of the guiding mission of the Benedictine order, and your solemn oaths of confidence. However, I believe that a young woman I am searching for may be within the walls of Camden Abbey." She stopped. Dame Constance held Maisie's eyes with her own and did not speak. Maisie continued. "Charlotte Waite is missing from home, and her father is concerned for her safety. I believe she has sought refuge here at the abbey. Can you confirm my suspicions?"

Dame Constance responded with a simple, "I see." Maisie waited.

"You know, Maisie, that in his Rule, Saint Benedict bade his disciples to show special care and compassion toward those seeking refuge, the poor and pilgrims, and he did so because 'in them is Christ more truly welcomed.' There are those who knock at the door daily for food and drink, yet sometimes a hunger is deeper, a yearning for sustenance that cannot be named, but one that is always fed at our table."

Maisie nodded.

"One of our pledges, when souls come to us seeking supersubstantial bread to assuage the poverty of the spirit, is the confidence of the cloister."

Dame Constance paused, as if expecting Maisie to counter her words.

"I seek not to . . . interrupt the sacred path of one making her way to the abbey's table for sustenance. I only seek confirmation that Charlotte Waite is here. That she is safe."

"Ah, *only*. An interesting word, don't you think? *Only*." This was the Dame Constance Maisie had expected.

"Yes, and we use it too easily, I'm sure."

Dame Constance nodded. "Only. *Only*. In the sharing of such information—and please do not take this as a confirmation or denial—I would be breaking a trust, a sacred trust. Where is the 'only' in that, Maisie? Come now, what say you?"

It was Maisie's turn to smile. The Abbess had put on the gloves and was ready to spar.

"In this context the *only* is a request for truth. I am here simply to gain information to put the mind of her father to rest."

"Simply and only, *simply and only*. Everything and nothing are simple, as you know."

Dame Constance reached for a cup of water, sipped, replaced the earthenware vessel, and thought for a moment in silence, her hands tucked together inside the copious sleeves of her habit. She looked up and nodded. "Do you know one of the most common questions I am asked? 'Why is an enclosed nun kept behind bars?' My response is always the same: 'The bars are there to keep you out, not us in!' " There was silence again, and Maisie waited for a final decision. "Your request must be considered by the order, and to do that, Maisie, I must have the whole story. Yes, I know—with this comment I have given you the answer you require. However, we both know that your *only* goes further, doesn't it?"

"Yes, it does. Let me tell you what has happened."

Maisie was served an early lunch alone in the sitting room. She excused herself to use the lavatory and washbasin facilities provided for visitors. Upon her return, her shoes clattering on the flagstone floors, a fresh tray awaited her, bearing a hearty bowl of pearl barley-and-vegetable soup, a flask of cider with an upturned glass on top, and three slices of still-warm, crusty brown bread. She was just scooping up the final spoonful of soup when the small door was drawn back and Dame Constance smiled at her through the grille.

"No, do finish. You can carry on eating."

"It's all right. I'm all but finished." Maisie poured a glass of cider, took one sip, and quickly put down the glass. The beverage was clearly homemade and a strong brew.

"The order has decided that, on this occasion, we can confirm that Miss Waite is within the walls of Camden Abbey. She is tired and needs to rest and recuperate. I cannot allow her to be assailed with questions. Give her time."

"But—"

"There may be another life taken? The order has considered, and we have concluded that we must continue to offer refuge to Miss Waite." Dame Constance looked at Maisie intently. "We will pray, Maisie. We will petition God for His strength and His hand in this matter."

Thank heavens Stratton isn't here, thought Maisie. If he thought the order was offering succor to a murderer, he'd have something to say. Then Dame Constance surprised her.

"If you can return to Camden Abbey next week, you might be able to meet with Miss Waite then. I will have had several conversations with her in the interim, so expect my letter."

"Thank you, Dame Constance."

"And perhaps you can stay longer next time. I sometimes miss the debate my students challenged me with when they stopped being scared of me, and before they were mature enough to realize that those who are older may know something after all." Dame Constance paused. "And perhaps you can tell me something, then, that I am curious about."

Maisie inclined her head to demonstrate her own curiosity.

"I'd like to know, Maisie, where do *you* find refuge? And who offers *you* close counsel and companionship?"

Maisie nodded. "I'll see you next week."

"Very well. Until then, dear child, until then." The small grille door closed with a click.

Maisie pulled up the collar of her jacket against the large raindrops that were beginning their assault on Romney Marsh. She opened the door of the MG and looked once again at the imposing building. Yes, it looked safe. Very safe. Charlotte Waite had found herself a fortress and an army of knights to protect her. The knights were women, and the arms they bore were prayers. But whom were they protecting? A murderer or another potential victim?

# CHAPTER ELEVEN

*L*ady Rowan chose to wait at Chelstone until after the new foal was born. Lord Julian had decided to travel to Lancashire to visit the site of a bankrupt factory he was considering for purchase. The economic slump could not last forever, and he wanted to be well-placed to boost the manufacturing arm of his investment interests when the time was right. Upon her return to London, Maisie would be alone in Belgravia for several more weeks with only the servants for company.

Once again the drive back into London gave Maisie time to consider her next steps in light of the past few days' revelations. The task she had been retained to perform in the Waite case was almost complete. She knew where Charlotte Waite had taken refuge, though it remained for her to persuade the woman to return to her father's home. In the normal course of events Maisie would not consider the case *completely* closed until personal conversations with Charlotte and Joseph Waite had taken place individually and jointly, with commitments from each to fashion a new relationship with the other. But could the completion of her assignment conclude *this* case, when there were the deaths of three other women to be considered? Maisie detoured. Instead of driving directly into London, she made her way west into the county of Surrey, then north to Richmond. It was time for her to make her monthly pilgrimage to visit Simon, the former love who had sustained such serious injuries during the Great War that he was now in a convalescent hospital where he could be cared for along with other men who had suffered profound injury to the mind. Though he would not know that Maisie sat opposite him, taking his hands in hers as she spoke, Maisie would feel the warmth in his fingers, sense the blood coursing through his veins, and she would continue to tell him of her days. She would describe the gardens that lay beyond the windows, the leaves turning to brown, red and gold before falling, then, later, she would tell of snow on branches and Jack Frost leaving icicles where leaves would sprout in spring. Today she would describe the new leaves unfolding, the fresh green shoots of daffodils and crocuses, the sun higher in the sky, and the springtime nip in the air. Above all, as Simon's head nodded along with his breathing, his eyes focusing on a place in the distance only he could see, Maisie would share with him her deepest thoughts and secrets.

She parked the MG and, as was her habit, walked to the lower perimeter of the gardens before approaching the main entrance. Maisie watched the Thames snaking through Richmond, and consciously took four deep breaths placing the fingers of her right hand against the cloth of her aubergine jacket at the point she knew to be the center of her body. She closed her eyes and took one more deep breath. She was ready.

"Good morning, Miss Dobbs, very nice to see you again, but then it is your time, isn't it? First week of the month, right on the nail."

"And good morning to you, Mrs. Holt. Do you know if Captain Lynch is in the Winter Garden, as usual?"

"Yes, I believe he is, but drop in to see Staff Nurse on the way, won't you."

"Oh yes, of course. I'll see you on my way out, Mrs. Holt."

"Right you are, Miss Dobbs, right you are."

Maisie turned left and made her way down the corridor that led from the reception desk to the office where the Staff Nurse would be completing medication reports. Though she had only been visiting Simon regularly for six months, Maisie was known to the nurses.

Staff Nurse welcomed her with a broad smile, and Maisie smiled in turn as an almost identical dialogue to that with Mrs. Holt followed. The Staff Nurse commented that Maisie could probably find her own way to the 'Winter Garden' conservatory, by now.

"He's in there, all wrapped up and looking out at the gardens," said Staff Nurse, as she pulled a heavy chain from her apron pocket, selected a key and locked the medicine cabinet. "Never can be too careful." Ensuring the cabinet was secure, she turned to Maisie, "I'll have one of the nurses pop along in a while, to check on the captain."

Maisie found Simon seated in a wheelchair by a window in the conservatory, shaded by tall tropical trees that would surely die if planted outside in England's ever-changing climate. He was dressed in deep-blue-striped pajamas and a thick blue tartan dressing gown. Matching blue slippers covered his feet, and a blanket had been placed across his knees. Doubtless his mother still shopped for him, ensuring a certain dignity in the clothing carefully chosen for an invalid who would never again consciously distinguish shade, hue, light, or dark. Maisie wondered how Simon's parents must feel, in their twilight years, knowing that their son would likely outlive them, and that the only farewell for them to remember was the one that took place in 1917, when he said good-bye after his last leave.

"Hello, Simon," said Maisie. Pulling up a chair, she sat beside him and took his hands in hers. "It's been an interesting month, Simon. Let me tell you about it."

In speaking aloud to one who could not comprehend, Maisie was aware that she was using this time to reexamine details of the Waite case and that of the murdered women.

The door that led in from the corridor swung open, and a young nurse entered, nodded, and smiled. She quickly checked to ensure that her patient was showing no distress in the presence of his visitor, and then left silently.

And as the nurse departed, Maisie wondered what she was thinking as she observed a woman in her early thirties with the broken man who had once been her true love. Did she see futility—she who would later place food in the man's mouth and watch as muscles moved in physical response to the stimulus, without any obvious recognition of taste or texture? Or did the young nurse, probably a girl at the close of the Great War, see Maisie as one unwilling to open her heart to another, while her beloved was still there in body, if not in mind?

Maisie looked out at the gardens. How to remain loyal, but still open her heart anew? It was as if she was required to be in two places at once, one part of her in the past, one in the future. She sighed deeply and allowed her gaze to wander. She watched as two nurses walked along a path, each pushing a veteran of war in a wheelchair. In the distance, an older woman supported a man who walked in an ungainly fashion, his head lolling to one side. As they came closer, Maisie saw that the man was gazing into space, his mouth open, his tongue rolling back and forth between his lips. They moved toward the patio in front of the glass-paned conservatory.

The woman was as plainly dressed as she had been at their first meeting, when she opened the door to greet Maisie and Billy at Joseph Waite's home in Dulwich. In fact she had been so plainly dressed and pedestrian in manner that Maisie had not thought twice about her. Yet here she was again, with this man whose mind was clearly as lost in the wilderness of his past as Simon's. Who was he? A son? A nephew?

As she steered her charge toward a door to the side of the conservatory, a nurse came to her aid, taking the young man's weight on his other side while Mrs. Willis kept her arm around his waist, her hand clutching his.

Maisie remained for a while longer, then bade Simon a solitary farewell. She stopped at the reception desk on the way out.

"Lovely day to visit, eh, Miss Dobbs?"

"Yes, it has been nice, especially to see the tulips coming up."

"See you in about a month, then?"

"Yes, of course, but I wonder, may I ask you a question about another visitor today?"

The receptionist frowned slightly, and pressed her lips together. "Another visitor? Well, let's see who was in today." She consulted the visitors' book on the desk in front of her and tapped a red finger along the names. "Whom were you interested in?"

"I thought I saw an acquaintance of mine, a Mrs. Willis. Could she have been visiting a family member, perhaps?"

"Oh, Mrs. Willis. Very nice woman. Quiet, doesn't say much, but very nice indeed. She's here to see Will, her son. Will, short for Wilfred, Wilfred Willis."

"Her son? Does she come once a month?"

"Oh my goodness, no! Once or twice a week. Never fails, always on a Sunday and, more likely than not, on a Wednesday or Thursday as well. She comes as often as she can."

"And she's been coming since the war, since he was admitted?"

The receptionist looked at Maisie and frowned again before speaking. "Well, yes, she has. But then, it's not surprising. She's his mother."

"Of course, of course. I'd better be off."

"We'll see you in a month then, Miss Dobbs?"

"Yes. A month. See you then." Maisie turned to leave, but the receptionist spoke again.

"Oh, Miss Dobbs, you might see Mrs. Willis waiting down at the bus stop. I don't know if Dulwich is on your way, but I thought you'd like to know. It's a long journey for her by bus."

"Of course, Mrs. Holt. If she's still there, I'll give her a lift home."

"Blast!" said Maisie, as she exited the main gates of the hospital. Mrs. Willis was not at the bus stop, nor was there a queue waiting.

It was still only two o'clock in the afternoon, so Maisie decided to back-track. She was well aware that her curiosity regarding the murders of two women, and the suspected murder of another, had surpassed her interest in the Charlotte Waite "missing person" case. In truth, she was excited that she had discovered a link and that she had reason to investigate further. Maisie had a sense of who Lydia Fisher was, and how she lived, but she wondered about Philippa Sedgewick, the woman murdered in Coulsden. Detective Inspector Stratton had pronounced Lydia Fisher's murder "identical" to Sedgewick's. Were they unlucky victims of coincidence? Evidence suggested that her killer had been known to Lydia Fisher. Had Philippa Sedgewick known *her* killer? And if *her* death was murder rather than suicide, then Rosamund Thorpe had taken tea with her murderer as well. Yet in her case, there had been no vicious post-mortem knife attack. While steering with one hand, Maisie nibbled at the nail on the little finger of the other. Charlotte was the key.

In the meantime, while Maisie waited for an audience with Charlotte at Camden Abbey, she would see what she could find out about Philippa Sedgewick. Nothing could take the place of collecting information and impressions personally.

Maisie drove toward Kingston-upon-Thames, following a route that took her through Ewell as she made her way to Coulsden. A stop on her way from Kent to Richmond would have been a more judicious use of time and petrol but she hadn't planned to visit Coulsden when she set out this morning. Now she felt more anxiety than she had since the death of Lydia Fisher. The killer might strike again soon. If the deaths were random, with the killer soft-talking his way into victims' homes, then no woman on her own was safe. But if the killer was known to his victims, there might be more links in the chain that connected them.

As she entered Coulsden, Maisie pulled over to the side of the road and reached into her document case. She quickly turned to the second page of last week's *Times* until she found what she was looking for. COULSDEN WOMAN MURDER INVESTIGATION, followed by a subheading POLICE SEARCH FOR KILLER. Her eyes scanned the columns, the work of reporters feeding the story. As the words "merciless," "plunged," and finally "butcher" leapt out at her, Maisie finally found what she was looking for: "The dead woman, Mrs. Philippa Sedgewick of 14 Bluebell Avenue...."

Maisie parked the car in the road opposite Number 14 and shut off the engine. The houses were not old, built perhaps in 1925 for the new commuter class, the men who traveled into the City each day on the train, and the women who waved them goodbye in the morning and greeted them with dinner on the table when they returned. Children would be in pajamas, bathed, and ready for bed as soon as father had placed his hat and coat on the stand by the door, kissed each girl on the head, and squeezed each boy on the arm along with the words, "Good man."

Young sycamores grew on each side of the street, planted with the intention of creating an opulent canopy to shade the family homes. Each house was identical, with a broad bow window at the front, an asymmetrical roof with a cat's-slide sweep on one side, and a small turreted bedroom under the eaves of the other. The front door had a stained-glass window, and the same glass had been used in a border that ran along the upper edge of every other window at the front of the house. But this house was special. This was the house where Philippa Sedgewick had spent her days waiting for her husband to return from his job in the City. This was the house where a woman of thirty-two had been murdered. Maisie took out a small pack of index cards from her document case. She did not alight from the car, but simply described the house on a card, and penciled questions to herself: *Why have I assumed husband worked in the City? Find out about husband. Job for Billy?*

The curtains were closed, as was the mourning custom. The house seemed dark and cold, shadowy against the low sun of a spring afternoon. Yes, thought Maisie, death has passed over this house and will linger until the woman's spirit is at rest. She sighed, allowed her gaze to settle on the house again and slipped into a deliberately relaxed observation of the property. It appeared a very sad house, set in a street of homes for families with children. Already she could imagine them walking home from school, girls with satchels banging against hips, boys holding their caps in one hand, with arms out to balance as they returned a football or ran to tease the girls, pulling hair so that screams drew a mother into the street to admonish every one of them. According to the newspaper, there had been no children in the Sedgewick marriage, though perhaps children were hoped for, otherwise why live in such a place? Yes, a sad house.

The curtain moved almost imperceptibly. At first it was just a sensation at the corner of her eye. Maisie focused on the curved window of the turreted small bedroom to the left. The curtain moved again. She was being watched. Maisie stepped out of the MG and set off briskly across the road, unlatched the waist-high gate, and continued along the path to the front door. Taking up the brass door knocker, she rapped loudly, ensuring that anyone inside the house would hear her summons. She waited. No answer. *Rat-tat-tat* again. She waited, listening.

The door opened.

"Can't you people leave me alone?! Haven't you got enough stories? You're vultures, all of you. Vultures!"

A man of medium height stood before Maisie. His brown hair was in need of a comb, his face sported a rough salt-and-pepper shadow of beard, and he was dressed in baggy tweed trousers, a gray flannel shirt topped with a knitted sleeveless pullover in a pale gray with flecks of green and purple woven into the yarn. He wore neither shoes, socks, nor tie, and looked, thought Maisie, as if he could do with a good meal.

"I do beg your pardon, Mr. Sedgewick—"

"Don't 'pardon, Mr. Sedgewick' me, you nasty little piece of—"

"Mr. Sedgewick, I am not a member of the press!" Maisie stood to her full height, and looked him in the eyes.

The man shuffled his feet, looked down, rubbed his chin, then looked again at Maisie. His shoulders, which had been drawn up tensely, almost touching his earlobes, now drooped, making him look as broken in body as he was in spirit. He was exhausted. "I am sorry. Please forgive me, but I just want to be left alone." He began to close the door.

"But please . . . I need to speak to you." Maisie reminded herself that Philippa Sedgewick's husband might also be her killer. While she doubted that this man was a murderer, she had to proceed with caution.

"Be quick, and tell me what you want, though I doubt I can help anyone. I can't even help myself!" said Sedgewick.

"My name is Maisie Dobbs." Maisie opened the flap of her case and pulled a card from an inner compartment, not breaking eye contact with Sedgewick. "I'm a private investigator, and I think there is a connection between a case I am working on and your wife's murder."

For a few seconds, silent incredulity was visible on the man's face: His lips seemed frozen open, his eyes did not even blink. Then Sedgewick began to laugh almost hysterically. He laughed and laughed and laughed, bending over, his hands on his knees before raising his head as he attempted to speak. The thin line between emotions was being breached. This man, who had so recently lost his wife, was indeed in crisis. Maisie was aware that a neighbor was standing on her front doorstep looking across at the house. Then, as she turned again to Sedgewick, she realized he was crying. She quickly helped him inside his home and closed the door behind her.

Maisie illuminated the hallway with electric light and, still holding Sedgewick's arm, directed him to the back of the house, to the kitchen. Maisie connected a kitchen with warmth, but as she turned on another light, she felt her heart sink at the sight that confronted her. Helping Sedgewick to a chair, Maisie opened the curtains, unlocked and opened the back door to the garden, and looked back at the cups and saucers piled on the draining board, along with dirty saucepans and one or two plates. The dregs of stale brandy and half-smoked cigarettes swirled against one another in crystal glasses, perhaps originally given to celebrate the marriage of the young couple years earlier.

"Oh, I'm sorry, I'm sorry, you must think me—"

"I don't think anything, Mr. Sedgewick. You've been through a horrible time."

"Tell me again who you are and why you are here."

Maisie identified herself again and explained the purpose of her visit to the house of—as far as the authorities knew—the first victim of the "Heartless, Bloodless Killer," named for his use of poison before the knife.

"I can't see how I can help. I've spent hours, literally hours, with the police. I have spent every second of every day since my wife was murdered asking myself why and who. And, as you can imagine, for some time the police thought that I was the 'who.' They probably still do."

"They have to explore all avenues, Mr. Sedgewick."

"Oh yes, the police line, I know it." Sedgewick rubbed his neck and as he did so, Maisie heard bones crack in his shoulder and back.

"Will you help me?" she asked.

Sedgewick sighed. "Yes, yes. If helping you ends up helping me, I'll do what I can to answer your questions."

Maisie smiled and, feeling once more like the nurse she had been so long ago, she reached out and squeezed Sedgewick's hand. "I appreciate it, Mr. Sedgewick."

The man seemed to falter, then continued. "Miss Dobbs, would you mind using my Christian name? I know it's rather a cheek to ask . . . and I perfectly understand if you decline my request, but . . . I have been nothing but Sedgewick or Mr. Sedgewick for weeks now. My neighbors are avoiding me, and I have been given leave from my work until the killer"—he seemed about to double over again—"until the case is closed. My name is John. And I am a man who has lost his wife."

They moved into the drawing room. Maisie watched John Sedgewick as he eased himself into an armchair beside the fireplace. She opened the curtains just enough to allow some natural illumination to enter. Sudden light might startle Sedgewick, who would feel a needle of sunray to be piercing and painful. The room was untidy, with unread newspapers in a pile, cigarette ends mounting in ashtrays, and dust layered on the mantelpiece, the small writing desk, and the side tables. Spent coals in the cold grate made the room even less inviting. As if pressed inward by his discomfort, Sedgewick sat forward on the edge of the chair, hunching his shoulders and gripping his elbows. Maisie shivered, remembering Maurice in the early days of her apprenticeship: "Watch the body, Maisie; see how the posture reflects the state of mind." John Sedgewick was clutching his body as if to save himself from falling apart.

Maisie allowed a silence to envelop them, a time in which she composed her body, cleared her thoughts and saw in her mind's eye a connection forming between herself and the man opposite her. She imagined a stream of light emanating from the center of her forehead just above her nose, a bright thread that flowed toward her subject and bathed him with a luminous glow. Slowly the man who wanted to be addressed informally as John relaxed his shoulders and released his arms. He leaned back.

Maisie knew better than to breach his trust by commencing with a fusillade of questions that must have already been put to him by the police.

"John, would you like to tell me about your wife?" she asked softly.

Sedgewick exhaled and gave a sharp, ironic half laugh. "You know, Miss Dobbs, you are the first person to ask me that question in that manner. The police are more direct."

Maisie inclined her head but did not speak, inviting him to continue.

"She was lovely, Miss Dobbs. A lovely girl. Funny, I always think of her as a girl. She wasn't tall, not like you. No, Pippin—that's what I called her, Pippin." Sedgewick closed his eyes again and wrinkled his face against tears that welled up behind his eyelids. Recovering, he continued, "She was slight, not a big girl. And I know she wasn't a girl anymore, but she was a girl to me. We married in 1920. I met her at my parents' house, would you believe? She was visiting with her widowed mother, who knew my mother through the Women's Institute, or the church Flowers Committee, something of that order."

Sedgewick looked toward the garden, as if imagining that his dead wife would walk along the front path at any moment. Maisie knew that he held a vision of Philippa before him. An image began to form in her mind of a young woman in a plain, pale sea-green summer dress. She was wearing green cotton gloves to protect her fine hands while cutting roses in a myriad of colors, placing the blooms into a basket at her feet before looking up when she heard her husband's footfall as he opened the gate and came toward her.

"I think our meeting was arranged by the mothers, actually." Sedgewick smiled, a narrow smile of remembrance. "And we got on famously. She was shy at first—apparently she had been somewhat dark of mood since the war—but soon became quite buoyant. People said it was having a sweetheart that did it."

Maisie made a mental note to delve a little deeper into the source of Philippa Sedgewick's disquiet, but for now she wanted Sedgewick to be at ease with her as his confidante. She did not interrupt.

"We lived with her mother for a while after the wedding. It was a small affair in the village, nothing grand. Then we rented a flat for a couple of years, and when these houses were built in 1923, we snapped one up straightaway. Philippa had a small legacy from her father and I had my savings and some funds in a trust, so it wasn't a stretch." Sedgewick became silent and breathed deeply before continuing. "Of course, you buy a house like this for a family, but we were not to be blessed with children." He stopped to address Maisie directly. "Heavens above, this must be far from what you want to hear, Miss Dobbs! I'm sorry."

"Please continue Mr. . . . John. Please tell me about your wife."

"Well, she was barren. Not her fault, of course. And the doctors weren't much help, said there was nothing they could do. The first one, a gray-haired doddery old duffer, said that it was nothing that a couple of glasses of sherry each wouldn't cure. The blithering idiot!"

"I am so sorry, John."

"Anyway, we just sort of accepted that we were to remain a family of two. In fact, just before . . . just before the end. . . ." Sedgewick closed his eyes against images that now rushed forth, images that Maisie knew to be of his dead wife. Again he breathed deeply to combat his emotions. "Just before the end, we had planned to buy a puppy. Thought it would be company for her while I was at work. Mind you, she kept busy—reading to children at the local school one afternoon a week, that sort of thing—and she loved her garden. Trouble was, she blamed herself."

"Blamed herself?" Maisie watched him closely.

"Yes. For being barren. Said that you reap what you sow."

"Did she ever say what she meant?"

"Never. I just thought that she had dredged up every bad thing she'd ever done and heaped it on herself." Sedgewick shrugged. "She was a good girl, my Pippin."

Maisie leaned toward Sedgewick, just close enough for him to feel warmer and, subconsciously, more at ease.

"Can you tell me if your wife was troubled about anything else? Had there been any discord between her and any other person?"

"Pippin was not one to gush all over other people, or rush over to natter with the neighbors. But she was kind and thoughtful, knew if someone needed help and always passed the time of day if she saw someone she knew on the street. But . . . did you say 'ever,' Miss Dobbs?"

"I know that might be a tall assignment, John."

"You know, I think she only ever walked out with one man before we met. She was shy with men. It was during the war, and she was quite young really, only seventeen or so, if that. If I remember correctly, she'd met him when she was in Switzerland. He was one of several young men paying attention to Pippin and her group, in fact, he courted all of them at some point. He ended up marrying one of her friends, who, I think, had nothing but trouble with him. Bit of a ladies' man, he was." Suddenly Sedgewick frowned, "You know, funny that should come to mind, because he was back in touch with her, I don't know, must have been toward the end of last year. I'd all but forgotten about it."

"Who was the man, and why had he made contact again? Do you know?"

"I have a terrible memory for names, but his was quite unusual. Not like your average 'John,' you know!" Sedgewick smiled faintly. "Apparently his wife, who, as I said, was an old friend of Pippin's, was drinking heavily. He tracked down Pippin and telephoned to see if she could help at all, speak to the wife, try to get her on the straight and narrow. But they hadn't been in touch for years and I don't think Pippin wanted anything to do with it. She said no, and that was that. At least as far as I know. She told me that her friend probably drank to forget. Didn't think much about it at the time. She said, 'Everyone's got something to help them forget things, haven't they? She's got the bottle, I've got my garden.' Sounds a bit harsh, but I wouldn't have wanted her to get involved with a woman like that."

Maisie did not want to influence Sedgewick with her suspicions. "And you are sure you can't recall his name? What letter did it begin with?"

"Oh dear, Miss Dobbs . . . it was, um . . ." Sedgewick rubbed his brow. "Um . . . I think it was *M*—yes, that's it. *Muh, mih, mah . . . mah . . .* yes, *mah . . . mag . . .* Magnus! Yes, Magnus Fisher. Now I remember."

"And his wife's name was Lydia?"

"Yes, yes! Miss Dobbs, I do believe you knew all the time!"

"John, have you read the newspapers recently?"

"No, I can't stand it! They always point the finger, and while Pippin is still somewhere on the front page, the finger is pointed at me."

Maisie delved further. "The police haven't returned since last week?"

"No. Of course they come to the house to check that I'm still here, and I'm not supposed to leave the area, pending the closure of inquiries, or whatever the official line is."

Maisie was surprised that Stratton had not revisited Sedgewick since Lydia Fisher's body was discovered. "John, Lydia Fisher was found dead—murdered—last week. A subsequent post-mortem examination suggested that there were similarities between your wife's murder and Mrs. Fisher's. I suspect the police have not spoken to you yet, pending further investigation. The press was rather too forthcoming with details of your wife's murder and as there are those who will copy infamy, the police might not want to draw attention to similarities at this very early stage. I have no doubt, though, that the police—and the press—will be on your doorstep again soon."

Sedgewick clutched his shoulders, rocking himself back and forth, then stood up, and began to pace. "They'll think it was me, they'll think it was me. . . ."

"Calm down, John, calm down. They will not think it's you. I suspect that their conclusions will be quite the opposite."

"Oh, that poor woman, that poor woman . . . and my poor Pippin." John Sedgewick began to weep as he sat heavily in the armchair, and Maisie knelt so that he could lean upon her shoulder. All formalities of polite interaction between a woman and a man she did not know fell away as Maisie allowed her strength of spirit to seep into Sedgewick. Once again he fought for composure.

"I don't understand; what does this mean?"

"I don't know yet, but I intend to find out. Can you face more questions, John?"

John Sedgewick took an already soiled handkerchief from his pocket and wiped his eyes and nose. "Yes. Yes, I'll try, Miss Dobbs. And I am so sorry. . . ."

Maisie took her seat and raised her hand. "Don't apologize. Grief should be aired, not buried. Do you know if your wife was also acquainted with a woman called Charlotte Waite?"

Sedgewick looked up at Maisie. "The Waite girl? Why, yes she was. Again, it was a long time ago, long before we met. I say, what is all this about, Miss Dobbs?"

"I'm not sure, John, I am simply picking up loose threads."

"Charlotte and Lydia were part of the same—coterie, I think you'd call them. You know, a group of young girls who spend time together on Saturdays, have tea together, and then spend their allowances on trifles, that sort of thing."

Maisie nodded, though as a young girl there had been no coterie for her, no trifles, only more errands to run and her chores below stairs to perform as efficiently and quickly as possible, leaving her more time to study.

"But they grew apart, you know, as people do. Charlotte was very wealthy, as was Lydia. Pippin was part of a certain social circle that, frankly, she did not choose to belong to as they matured. I think they all had a falling out, but as I said, this was long before Pippin and I began courting."

"Was a woman called Rosamund part of the group?"

Sedgewick sighed, and pressed his hands to his eyes. "The name rings a bell. I might have heard the name 'Rosie'—I don't think I heard 'Rosamund'; . . . no . . . not 'Rosamund.'"

Maisie prepared to ask her next question, when he spoke first. "You know, I have just remembered something odd. Mind you, I don't know if it's of any use to you."

"Go on."

"Well, it's about the Waite girl; her father, really. It must have been before we were married." Sedgewick scratched his head, "I'm as bad with time as I am with names. Yes, it was before we were married, because I remember being in Pippin's mother's parlor. Now it's coming back to me. I arrived at the house on my bicycle just as a rather large motor car was leaving. Too fast if you ask me, I remember the gravel spitting up and hitting me in the face. Anyway, the housekeeper let me in, said that Pippin was in the parlor. As I walked in she was there, drying her eyes: She'd been crying. I pleaded with her to tell me what was the matter, but she would only say that she had had some sort of crossed words with Mr. Waite, Charlotte's father. I threatened to go after him, but she wouldn't allow it and said that if I did, then she would never see me again. That it would never happen again, or something like that."

"And she never revealed the cause of the discord?"

"Never. I suspected it might have to do with Charlotte. I thought perhaps that Pippin had told a lie on her behalf—you know, saying that Charlotte was with her, when she was really somewhere else. Apparently Charlotte was quite rebellious as a young girl. See, my memory's warming up now!"

"Did your wife ever see Joseph Waite again? Or hear from him?"

"No, I don't think she did. She never mentioned it. After we were married, we settled into a very ordinary life, especially here on Bluebell Avenue."

Sedgewick looked drawn, almost overcome with fatigue.

"I will leave you in peace soon, John. But first, I understand that your housekeeper found Mrs. Sedgewick?"

"Yes, Mrs. Noakes. She comes in daily to clean and dust, prepare supper, that sort of thing. She had gone out for a couple of hours, to the shops, and when she came home, she found Pippin in the dining room. It appears she'd had someone to tea, which was unusual, because she hadn't said that she was expecting a visitor or mentioned it to Mrs. Noakes."

"And you were at work?"

"Yes, in the City. I'm a civil engineer, Miss Dobbs, so I was out at a site all afternoon. Plenty of people saw me, but of course, I was also traveling between places, which interests the police enormously. They sit there with their maps and train timetables trying to work out if I could have come home, murdered my wife, and been back on a building site in time for my next alibi."

"I see. Would you show me the dining room?"

In contrast to the untidy kitchen and drawing room, the dining room was immaculate, though evidence of police presence was everywhere throughout the house. It was clear that a thorough investigation had taken place in the room where Philippa Sedgewick had met her death.

"There wasn't any blood to speak of." The tendons in Sedgewicks throat became taut as he spoke of his wife's murder. "Apparently the murderer drugged her with something first, before . . . before using the knife."

"Yes." Maisie walked around the room, observing but not touching. All surfaces were clean, with only a thin layer of dust. She walked to the window and opened the curtains to allow natural light to augment the grainy electric illumination. Fingerprinting was used widely now and Maisie could see residues of powder where police had tested for dabs left by the murderer. Yes, Stratton's men had done a thorough job.

As if reading her mind, Sedgewick spoke. "Inspector Stratton isn't such a bad chap. No, not too bad. It's that sergeant of his that makes my skin crawl, Caldwell. He was a nasty piece of work. Have you met him?"

Maisie was preoccupied with scanning the nooks and crannies of the dining room, but an image of the small, brisk man with a pointed nose and a cold stare came to mind. "Only once or twice."

"Just as well. He all but accused me when they took me in for questioning. Stratton was kinder. Mind you, I've heard that they do that, you know, play nice and nasty so that the suspect either gets unsettled or too relaxed before the other goes for the jugular."

Maisie looked on each surface and under each piece of furniture. Sedgewick, who was now very much at ease in her company, seemed to ramble in conversation. Maisie touched a place on the floor, then brought her fingers close to her nose.

"I heard two of the constables speaking. Apparently Stratton lost his wife in childbirth five years ago. Got a little boy at home and is bringing him up alone. It would make him more understanding, I suppose."

Maisie had been kneeling. She stood so quickly that her head spun.

"I didn't mean to startle you, Miss Dobbs. Yes, he's a widower. Just like me."

Maisie quickly completed her investigation, taking care not to let her desire to be alone, to gather her thoughts, distract her from the job at hand. She might not have another opportunity. But there seemed to be nothing that spoke to her here except John Sedgewick's grief.

"It's time for me to go, John. Will you be all right?"

"Yes, I will. Speaking about Pippin seems to have fortified me. I should *do* something, I suppose. Tidy the house, that sort of thing. Mrs. Noakes has been too upset to come back, though she did write to say that she believes me innocent. Which is heartwarming, considering that my own sister and mother are keeping well away, and Pippin's mother is too full of grief to visit."

"Perhaps if you open the curtains, you'll feel even better. Let the light in, John."

Sedgewick smiled. "I could probably do with getting out into the garden. It was always Pippin's domain, you know, the garden. Since she was a child she loved to grow things."

"Enjoy the garden. After all, she planted it for both of you."

As Maisie turned to leave, she felt a pressure in the middle of her back, as if she was being restrained. She gasped at the sensation, and realized that she had missed something, something she should not have overlooked.

"John, is there someplace here, a part of the garden, perhaps, that your wife particularly liked? Did she have a potting shed or greenhouse, that sort of thing?"

"Yes, at the side of the house here. In fact, Mrs. Noakes said that Pippin was in there when she left to go shopping. She loved the greenhouse. I designed it for her. You'll see, it has three parts: a traditional glass section for bringing on seedlings; a shed with windows so that she would have a shaded area for potting; then the third part is a sort of conservatory, where she had her exotics, and where she would sit in her armchair with a gardening book. I don't think I ever saw her with another type of book. Let me show you."

Sedgewick led the way to the side of the house, where a willow tree obscured Philippa Sedgewick's horticultural sanctuary from street view. Maisie entered, and immediately felt the humid warmth of a well-tended greenhouse, along with the pungent salty aroma of young geraniums growing in terra-cotta pots. She walked slowly along an inner path, to a stable door of wood and glass. Opening top and bottom, Maisie entered the musky potting shed, then walked through to the small conservatory-cum-sitting-room on the other side: the dead woman's own special domain.

It reminded her of the winter garden where Simon sat with his blanket and his secrets. A wicker chair with green and rose cushions was still indented, as if the owner had only just risen. It seemed so warm that a cat would have immediately claimed the place. Once again Maisie paced, and was immediately drawn to a gardening book set on a table beside the chair. She opened the front cover and leafed through until the book seemed to fall open at the point where Philippa Sedgewick had set her bookmark, perhaps when the killer had come to call. She imagined Philippa hearing the sharp rap of the door knocker in the distance, quickly marking her place and jumping up to answer the door. Or had the killer come to look for her when his knock was not answered? If he was an acquaintance, she would have marked her place and offered tea.

Geranium. *Pelargonium.* Maisie ran her finger down the spine of the book, and as she did so, she felt a faint prickle. Looking more closely, she reached in and carefully took out the spiny yet smooth source of the sensation. *Yes, yes, yes.*

Maisie placed her find within a handkerchief while John Sedgewick was looking at a rather large waxy green plant in the corner. "Of course, I couldn't tell one from the other, though Pippin could name every one, and in Latin. I think that's the only reason she studied Latin in school, to learn more about plants."

"I learned Latin once myself, simply to better understand another subject. I'd better be going, John. Thank you so much for your help, you have been most kind."

Sedgewick held out his hand to Maisie. "Well, it was a dodgy start, wasn't it? But I think you have helped me more than I've assisted you."

"Oh, you have helped, John. Enormously. I am sure that you'll be seeing Detective Inspector Stratton soon, and I'd appreciate it if no mention is made of my visit here today."

"Not a word, Miss Dobbs, not a word. But, before you go, what case are you working on, if I may ask?"

"It has to do with a missing person." She left at once, to avoid further questions. She needed to think. Starting the MG as quickly as she could, Maisie pushed the motor car into gear. She turned to look at

Number Fourteen Bluebell Avenue one last time before speeding off, and saw John Sedgewick walk slowly toward his wife's roses, then reach down to pull some weeds. Later, as she moved into traffic to return to London, Maisie thought not of Sedgewick but of Richard Stratton. A man who had lost his wife, too. And she thought of the chance discovery she had made, which she would now take back to her rooms and place with the twin that she had carefully wrapped in another linen handkerchief while standing in Lydia Fisher's drawing room.

# CHAPTER TWELVE

*T*he gas fire was turned off, so the room was cold by the time Maisie arrived back at the office on Sunday evening. On the desk in front of her she saw a single sheet of paper filled with Billy's large, primary school handwriting, along with several unopened envelopes placed separately on the desk so that Maisie could view each one individually before slicing it open. Billy had had a productive Saturday morning.

"Brrr. Let's see: Cantwell bill sent out, good. Lady Rowan telephoned, no message. Andrew Dene ... Andrew Dene? Hmmm." Maisie raised her eyebrows and continued. "Returned folders to solicitors—" The telephone rang.

"Fitzroy five six double O."

"Miss Dobbs?"

"Yes."

"It's John Sedgewick here. Glad I caught you."

"Do you have some news, Mr. Sedgewick?" Maisie deliberately reverted to a more formal address.

"Yes I do. I thought you'd like to know that Detective Inspector

Stratton and the obnoxious Caldwell came to the house after you left. They were asking about that Magnus Fisher."

"Really? What did they want to know?"

"Well, more about his contact with Pippin. I told them what I told you. There wasn't more to tell. Don't worry, I did not breathe a word about your being here. But Stratton gave me something to think about."

"And that is?"

"It turns out that Pippin *did* see Fisher. He'd returned from one of his expeditions about two months ago, and it was during that time that they met. He went off again for a couple of weeks, then came back again. Apparently the dates of his return trips almost mirror the dates of Pippin and Mrs. Fisher's murders, so the police are interested in him."

"Did they say anything about motive?"

"No. Stratton gave me the 'all avenues' line again, and asked if *I* knew Lydia Fisher. They also asked me—again, I might add—the most intimate details about my marital happiness."

"All in the line of duty, Mr. Sedgewick. No doubt they asked you to speculate as to why Mrs. Sedgewick met with Fisher."

"Yes, and I said that I thought she might have been trying to help in some way, given Mrs. Fisher's problems. I thought they were suggesting that there was something, you know, 'going on' between Pippin and Fisher, especially as they had walked out together in earlier years. It really is most distressing, Miss Dobbs."

"Of course it is, and I sympathize, Mr. Sedgewick. However, the police really are just trying to do their job. They want to find the killer before he strikes again."

"It's very difficult for me, yet I know you're right."

"Thank you, Mr. Sedgewick. You were most kind to telephone. Are you feeling better now?"

"Yes. Yes, I am. And you know, this evening one of my neighbors came to the house with some shepherd's pie, said she hadn't wanted to come around while the curtains were closed, and that they were so very sorry about Pippin. Mind you, she did bring her husband with her; she wasn't *that* sure about me."

"It's a start, though. Goodnight, Mr. Sedgewick."

"Yes, goodnight, Miss Dobbs."

Magnus Fisher. Possible, thought Maisie, always possible. He had pursued Philippa and each of her friends. And he'd married Lydia. Had there been other, deeper relationships between Fisher and Rosamund and Charlotte? Had an earlier interest in these women lingered and faded, only to reignite and flare out of control later? She looked down and read on through Billy's notes.

"Lady Rowan again . . . definitely not returning to Ebury Place for another fortnight at least."

Maisie smiled at the next note, which was from Billy.

Dear Miss,

It's nice to have you back here in London. I will be in sharp, nice and early tomorrow morning. Hope you had a nice time in Kent.

Yours sincerely,
Billy Beale

Maisie could almost see Billy Beale as a boy, his wheaten hair disheveled and matted, freckles speckling his nose, his tongue clamped tightly between his teeth as he concentrated on sweeping his dipping pen up and down, up and down, as he constructed a letter. No doubt his teacher had emphasized use of the word *nice*.

Maisie perused each sealed envelope in turn until she came to a hand she knew so well, an unmistakable fine copperplate in blue-black ink. She turned the envelope over, to reveal the Camden Abbey wax seal. Underneath the address were the words "By Hand," so the letter had obviously been delivered by later visitor to the abbey who had returned immediately to London, arriving before Maisie. Taking her

Victorinox knife, Maisie slit the envelope open to reveal a folded sheet of crisp cream linen paper, so heavy it was almost card, upon which Dame Constance had written her letter:

Dear Maisie,

How lovely it was to see you at Camden Abbey. A visit from one of my most memorable students is always an event of great joy, but I confess I would like to see a little more weight on your bones!

I will not fill my communiqué with more pleasantries, dear Maisie, but instead will come straight to the point as I must take advantage of delivery of this letter by a visitor from London who will be leaving shortly. I have counseled Miss Waite to see you, and she has agreed. Her confidence is due to the safety and refuge offered her by the community, so I must request that you honor my trust in you to proceed with integrity. Dame Judith has said that Miss Waite should rest for two or three days as she has caught that terrible cold we've all had. I suggest you come on Thursday morning.

Yours sincerely,
Dame Constance Charteris

"Good." Maisie sat at her desk, leaned back and smiled. She had no doubt that Dame Constance's powers of persuasion had been brought to bear on Charlotte, though she wished they had resulted in a more timely interview. She would have to choose her words carefully when meeting with Joseph Waite on Tuesday.

When she left the office a heavy smog seemed, once again, to be spiraling around the trees on the square, and she could barely see the streetlamps. In the distance, she could hear both the clip-clop of hooves, and the pop and chug of motor cars ferrying people—better-off people—home from a Sunday excursion, or out to supper. Sound was distorted not only by the darkness but by the smog. She wished she were in Kent, to see the stars at night and silent fields illuminated by a full moon.

Had she already met the killer? Had they passed in the street outside Lydia Fisher's home? Was Charlotte Waite involved, or was her flight from her father's house simply the action of a woman who could no longer be treated as a girl? Could she *be* the killer? Or was she afraid of becoming the next victim? What of Magnus Fisher? What motive could he have for killing his wife and two of her acquaintances? Had something happened in Switzerland years ago? Something the women knew about that was so serious that he would kill to ensure their silence? What could Charlotte tell her about Fisher? And what of her tiny shreds of evidence, carefully preserved? Or were they nothing at all, just household detritus?

Once again her thoughts centered on the Waite household, and she examined her feelings toward both Charlotte and her father. She admitted some confusion where Joseph Waite was concerned: She found his arrogance distasteful, his controlling attitude toward his grown daughter appalling. Yet at the same time she respected his accomplishments and recognized his generosity. He was a man of extremes. A man who worked hard, who indulged himself, yet who gave help freely, with kindness, if he approved of the recipient.

Could he be the killer? She remembered the dexterity with which he wielded his array of butcher's knives. Did he have a motive? If he did, then did it explain Charlotte's flight?

What did she really know of Charlotte, except that she was not at peace? Her father's view of her was biased. If *only* she could meet with Charlotte Waite sooner. She needed to form her own opinion of the woman's character. In the meantime, could she interview Fisher?

Maisie started the MG. It was time to return to her rooms at Ebury Place. She had much to consider, to plan. Tomorrow would be a long day, a day that had to begin with a difficult encounter. She must confront Billy regarding his behavior.

The front door of the Belgravia mansion was opened even before she reached the bottom step.

"We heard your motor car turn in to the mews, M'um."

"Oh, lovely. It's a cold evening isn't it, Sandra, and a foggy one."

"It is, M'um, and that old green stuff out there going down into your lungs doesn't help, either. Never mind, soon be summer."

Sandra closed the door behind Maisie, and took her coat, hat, and gloves.

"Will you have supper in the dining room tonight, M'um, or on a tray upstairs?"

Maisie stopped for a moment, then turned to Sandra. "I think I'd like a nice bowl of vegetable soup on a tray. Not too soon—about half past eight."

"Right you are, M'um. Teresa went upstairs the minute she heard your car and she's running you a good hot bath, what with you driving up from Chelstone today."

Maisie went immediately to her rooms, placed her now-full document case on the writing table, and undressed, quickly replacing her day clothes with a dressing gown and slippers. Was it only on Friday night that she had left for Chelstone? She had departed again early this morning, indeed, she had arisen as soon as she heard her father's footfall on the stairs at four o'clock; washed, dressed and quickly joined him for a strong mug of tea before he went to attend to the mare.

"I've added some lavender salts to the bath for you, M'um. Helps you relax before bedtime, does lavender." Teresa had set two large fluffy white towels on the rail by the bathtub, now full of steaming aromatic water.

"Thank you, Teresa."

"Right you are M'um. Will you be needing anything else, M'um?"

"No, thank you."

Teresa bobbed a curtsey and left the bathroom.

Maisie steeped her body, reaching forward with her foot to twist the hot tap whenever it seemed that the water was cooling. How strange to be living in the upstairs part of the Ebury Place mansion, to be addressed as 'M'um' by girls doing the same job that had brought her to this house, and this life. She leaned back to allow the scented steam to rise up into her hair, and remembered the once-a-week bath that was all she had been allowed when she herself had been a tweeny maid. Enid would bang on the door as soon as she thought that Maisie had been in too long. Maisie could hear her now. *Come on, Mais. Let us in. It's brassy out here on the landing.*

And she remembered France, the cold mud that seeped into her bones, a cold that she could feel to this day. "You're a chilly mortal, my girl." Maisie smiled as she saw Mrs. Crawford in her mind's eye, and almost felt the old woman's arms around her, comforting her, as she enveloped Maisie with her warmth when she returned, injured, from France. "Let's be having you, my girl. There, there, you're home now, you're home." And she had held Maisie to her with one hand, and rubbed her back with the other, just as a mother would soothe a baby.

There was a knock on the bathroom door.

"Goodness!" Maisie gasped when she realized how long she had soaked in the bath. "Coming! I'll be in right away!"

She quickly stepped out of the bath, toweled off, and pulled the dressing gown around her. She set her hair free, shook her head, and rushed into her sitting room. A supper tray had been placed on a small table set in front of her chair by the fire, which was glowing as flames curled around fresh coals being heaped on by Sandra.

"Better stoke it up a bit for you, M'um. We don't want you catching cold, do we?"

"Thank you, Sandra. A cold is the last thing I want!"

Sandra replaced the tongs into a brass coal scuttle, stood up, and smiled at Maisie. "Looks like Mr. Carter will be returning next week, to get everything in its place for Her Ladyship coming back."

"Ah, then we'll know all about it, eh, Sandra?" Maisie smiled at the maid, taking her table napkin and setting it on her lap. "Mmm, this soup smells delicious!"

Sandra bobbed and nodded her head. "Thank you M'um ." But instead of leaving, she seemed to waver. "Not as many staff as there used to be, are there?"

"Certainly not as many as before the war, Sandra." Instead of taking up her soup spoon, Maisie leaned back in the chair and looked into the fire. "No, definitely not. And if you asked Mrs. Crawford, she'd tell you that there were even more before His Lordship bought the motor cars, when there were horses in the mews, and grooms."

Sandra pursed her lips and looked at her feet. "S'all changing, isn't it, M'um? I mean, you know, we wonder why they keep this place up, now that they spend more time down at Chelstone."

Maisie thought for a while and replied. "Oh, I think they'll keep Ebury Place for a few years yet, at least until Master James comes back to England. After all, it is part of his inheritance. Are you worried about your job, Sandra?"

"Well, we all are, M'um. I mean, I hope you don't mind me saying this, and all, but things are changing. Not so many girls are going into service these days. But, you know, it's funny, like, when you can see change right before your eyes."

"Yes. Yes, you're right. We've seen a lot of changes since the war."

"I think people are trying to forget the war, don't you, Miss? I mean, who wants to be reminded? My cousin—not the one what died over there, but the one who came home wounded from Loos—he said that it was one thing to be remembered, and quite another to be reminded every day. He didn't mind people remembering what he'd done, you know, over there. But he didn't want to be *reminded* of it. He said that it was hard, because something happened to remind him every day."

Maisie thought of her bath, and how the sheer pleasure of it was a reminder of the past. Even if the reminder was of the opposite sensation, that of cold, of discomfort.

"Well, I'd better be getting along, M'um, let you eat your supper. Goodnight."

"Goodnight, Sandra. And Sandra, don't worry about things changing. It usually turns out for the best."

Maisie finished her soup and leaned into the chair again to watch the hot coals turn to embers. She would make up the fire just a little before going into her bedroom, knowing that as she drifted into slumber, the tray would silently be taken from her rooms in the same way that a breakfast tray would silently appear as she was pinning up her hair in the morning. The conversation with Sandra had sparked her thoughts in another direction. Perhaps *she* was ready for change. Not outwardly, though she knew that exterior transformation was a signal of inner change, but in what she envisioned for her future. Yes, perhaps that was a subject worthy of consideration.

As Maisie settled back into the pillows, she thought of the fine line between remembrance and reminder, and how a constant reminder could drive a person to the edge of sanity. Could drive a person to drugs or drink, to anything that took away the past's sharp edges. But what if the reminder was another human being? Then what might happen?

# CHAPTER THIRTEEN

aisie rose early. She washed quickly and dressed in her blue suit, with the collar and cuffs of a white linen blouse just visible underneath. Anticipating a chilly morning, Maisie remembered her navy blue coat, along with her old cloche and black gloves. She grabbed the black document case and left the room quickly.

She was about to open the disguised landing door that led to the back stairs and down to kitchen, when she thought better of it. The girls downstairs might be embarrassed. She would use the main staircase. Then she could knock at the door in fair warning. Straddling the line of her position in the household required some thought.

Maisie knocked, waited a second or two, then poked her head around the kitchen door without waiting for a reply. "Good morning everyone!"

There was a collective gasp from Sandra, Teresa and Valerie. "Oh, Miss, you gave us a fright!" said Sandra. "I was just about to start your breakfast."

"Sorry to scare you. I thought I'd have breakfast in the kitchen, if that's all right."

"Of course it is, Miss. Of course. At least your hair's nice and dry this morning!"

"Your usual, Miss? Porridge, Hovis and marmalade? You'll need to stoke up the fires this morning, it's cold out there. They reckon we could be in for a wintry Easter this year."

Maisie smiled, noting the change of address again, from "M'um" to "Miss." Maisie felt like a citizen of two countries, neither here nor there, but always somewhere in the middle.

"Easter's still a fortnight away and I need to be quick today. I'll have just a slice of Hovis toasted and a nice cup of tea, thank you."

"Right you are, Miss. Cup of tea coming up, and toast to follow. Are you sure you don't want a nice boiled egg?"

Maisie shook her head. "Tea and toast will be plenty for me this morning, Teresa."

Maisie took some letters from her document case and began to read. She was aware that the girls had exchanged glances, and were mouthing messages to each other. Sandra cleared her throat and came over to the table.

"Miss?"

"Yes, Sandra?"

"Well, we was thinking, you know, and wondered if, you know, you'd like to come to the pictures with us, next Saturday evening. We don't usually go out together, the three of us girls—we like to make sure that one of us is always in the kitchen, even if there's no one upstairs—but it's not as if we're leaving the house unattended, what with the other staff being here."

"What's the picture?"

"It's a talkie, and a bit scary, I've heard. It's got Donald Calthrop in it. Called *Blackmail*. It's about this girl, and she's courting a fella in the police, a detective, and he—"

"I don't think so, Sandra."

"Hmmm, I s'pose anything to do with the police would be like going on a busman's holiday for you, wouldn't it, Miss?"

"It's lovely of you to ask, Sandra. Thank you very much for thinking of me. The funny thing is, I don't really like the scary ones, they keep me awake."

Sandra laughed. "Now that, Miss, *is* funny."

Having barely touched her breakfast, Maisie left the Ebury Place mansion via the stone stairs that led from the back door into the street, then made her way to the mews to collect the motor car. George, the Compton's chauffeur, was in Kent, but a young footman had been assigned to keep the garage spick and span, ready for the return of the Compton's Rolls Royce. The old Lanchester was kept in London, and though now used only occasionally, was cleaned, polished and tended to regularly. Maisie's MG gave the footman a more substantial daily job.

"I could've brought 'er round to the front for you, Miss. Anyway, there she is, all cleaned and polished ready for London. Got 'er in plenty of mud down there, didn't you?"

"The weather has no respect for the motor car, Eric, any more than it has for the horse. Thank you for shining her up again. Did you check my oil?"

"All done, Miss. Everything given the once over. She'd take you from John O'Groats to Land's End if you felt like the drive, and that's a fact. Lovely little runner, lovely."

"Thank you, Eric."

Maisie parked once again in Fitzroy Street, in exactly the same spot as the evening before. Few people had motor vehicles, so Maisie was regarded as a subject of some interest as she climbed from the gleaming crimson vehicle.

She walked slowly toward the office, knowing that this morning would be a difficult one. Her feet were heavy on the stairs and she knew that to have the energy for the next part of her day, she must bring her body into alignment with her intentions, that her sagging shoulders would not support her spirit for the task ahead.

Unlocking the door to the first-floor office, Maisie was surprised to note that Billy had not arrived yet. She looked at her watch. Half-past eight. Despite his message, Billy was late. She walked to the window, rubbing the back of her neck where her scar had begun to throb.

Placing her hands on her chest, with her right hand over the left, Maisie breathed deeply. As her tension eased, she began to envisage the conversation with Billy, concentrating on the closing words of a dialogue that had yet to happen. Pressing her hands even more firmly against her body, Maisie deliberately slowed her breathing to settle her pounding heart, and felt the nagging ache of her scar abate. That's a reminder, she thought, every single day, just as Billy's wounded leg is a reminder. And as she stilled her heart and mind, it occurred to Maisie to question herself: If Lydia Fisher chose alcohol, and Billy narcotics to beat back the tide of daily reminder, then what did *she* do to dull the pain? And as she considered her question, the terrible thought came to her that perhaps she worked hard at her own isolation, along with the demands of her business. Perhaps she worked so hard that she was not only able to ignore physical discomfort, but had rendered herself an island adrift from deeper human connection. She shivered.

" 'Mornin', Miss, and what a nice mornin' it is, too. Thought I'd need me overcoat this mornin', I did, but 'ad to run from the bus stop and ended up carryin' the thing."

Maisie looked at her silver watch, pinned to the lapel of her jacket.

"Sorry I'm a bit late today, Miss, but there was a bit of an 'oldup on the road. I caught the bus this mornin', and 'alfway along the Mile End Road, I wished I 'adn't bothered. Would've been quicker to walk—and me with this leg and all. Big mess, it was. Motor car—and you don't see many of 'em down there—'ad gone right into the back of a dray. Thank Gawd 'e weren't goin' too quick. Mind you, you should've 'eard them drivers goin' at 'im. Thought they'd whop 'im one with the whip, I did. One of 'em was shoutin', 'Put the traces on 'im, and give the bleedin' 'orses a rest, the lunatic!' Oops, sorry, Miss, I was just sayin' what I 'eard them say. It's a poor old state of affairs, when motor cars—" Billy fussed as he spoke, avoiding eye contact, taking time to shake out his coat and cap, placing them on the coat stand, then riffling through the newspaper as if looking for something in particular.

"Now then, saw something 'ere this mornin' I thought you'd—"

"Billy."

"Got to do with that—"

"Billy!" Maisie raised her voice, then spoke more quietly. "There's a matter I would like to discuss with you. Let's sit together by the gas fire here. Pull up a chair."

His face flushed, Billy put the newspaper on his desk, dragged his chair out, and set it next to Maisie's.

"Am I getting the sack, Miss?"

"No, Billy, you are not getting the sack. However, I'd like to see a bit more in the way of timekeeping on your part."

"Yes, Miss. I'm sorry, Miss. Won't 'appen again."

"Billy . . ."

"Yes, Miss?"

"I'll get straight to the point," said Maisie, realizing this was a prevarication, that she was far from getting to the point. She took another deep breath, and began to speak. "I have been concerned for some time about your—let's say moods and—"

"I can exp—"

"Let me finish, Billy. I have been concerned about your moods and, of course, about the obvious pain you have been suffering with your war wounds. I have been worried about you."

Billy rubbed his knees back and forth, back and forth, his eyes on the flickering, hissing flame of the gas fire.

"You know only too well that I was a nurse and that I have some knowledge of the substances administered to the wounded during the war. I saw doctors working in terrible conditions, barely able to practice their profession. When it came to administering morphine and other drugs, they didn't always know what they were giving, in the way of strength of medication." Maisie watched Billy, choosing her words carefully as if she were navigating a minefield, trying to keep his attention yet not ignite a rush to defense or the explosive outburst that she feared. Billy's jaw worked back and forth as he listened and continued to gaze into the fire.

"Billy, I believe you were overdosed on morphine, though you probably didn't know it at the time. Even when we had wounded men being brought into the casualty clearing station by the hundreds, sometimes people stood out and, as you know, I remembered you. You were one of those it was almost impossible to medicate. You were immediately released to the general hospital, where you were given more medication, then to convalescent care, where more morphine was prescribed to assist you with the pain."

Billy nodded, but still he did not speak.

"And when the prescriptions ended, like so many, you found that access to a substance with similar qualities was easy, especially in London. Cocaine, wasn't it? You probably gave it up for years, didn't you? But when the leg started nagging at you again, you had a bit more money coming in and a local source." Maisie paused.

Finally Billy nodded, then spoke, his eyes never leaving the hot gas jets that warmed their feet, but did nothing to dent the cold around their shoulders and heads.

"You amaze me sometimes, Miss." Billy's upper body seemed to give way as he resigned himself to the truth. "Of course you're spot-on right, as usual. No use me sayin' otherwise." His voice was uncharacteristically low, his speech slow. "When I was first out of convalescence, after I'd come back to London and before I went back down there and married Doreen and brought 'er 'ome, it was easy to get 'old of it. The Canadians on leave were the ones to see, called it 'snow,' they did. Good blokes, them Canadians. Lost a lot of their own. Anyway, just like you said, I stopped it. Then, oh, must've been four months ago, round Christmas when it was really nippy, me leg started on at me again, this time badly. There were days I thought I'd never get down the old stairs. And it just wore me out, just wore on me . . ."

Maisie allowed Billy to speak. He stared as if mesmerized, into the fire.

"Then this fella, who I'd known over there, saw me in the Prince of Wales. Just 'aving a swift 'alf one night before going 'ome, I was, when up 'e comes. 'Eh, is that you, Billy-boy?' 'e says, full of it. Next thing you know, 'e was tellin' me where 'e could get some." Billy put his hands over his eyes as if trying to erase the image from his mind, then lowered them once more to his knees and began rubbing his thighs. "And so I said awright. Just a bit would take the edge off. And, Miss, it was like before the war, with all the pain taken away. I felt like a boy again, and let me tell you, I'd been feelin' like an old man."

Billy paused. Maisie reached out to the knob at the side of the fire and turned up the flame. Still she was silent, allowing Billy to tell his story in his own time.

"And to tell you the truth, I wish I'd never seen 'im or 'is stash. But I wish I could feel like that all the time. I just wish . . ."

Billy slumped forward and began to sob. Maisie leaned toward him; then she remembered Mrs. Crawford and simply rubbed his back, calming Billy as if he were a small boy. Eventually, Billy's tears subsided and he sat back. He blew his nose.

"Sound like a bleedin' elephant, don't I, Miss?" Billy folded the handkerchief and blew again. "Look, Miss. I'll go. I've no business workin' for you, and that's a fact. I can look for another job."

"Billy, before you do that, think about the lines of men looking for work. Anyway, business is good and I need you. But I also need you healthy and free of this burden, and I have a plan."

Billy looked up at Maisie, dabbing his nose, which had begun to bleed. He held the handkerchief tightly to his face to stem the flow and leaned back slightly.

"Sorry, Miss."

"I've seen worse, Billy. Now then, here's my plan. It will help you, but it will need an enormous effort on your part."

Maisie began to outline the plan of action that she had designed with Maurice.

"Oh, *Doctor* Andrew Dene, the fella what called 'ere for you," said Billy. "There's me thinking that 'e might be someone you'd met down there."

"Well, he *was* someone I met down there," replied Maisie.

"No, Miss, I meant met, as in, you know, *met*."

"Billy, I met him to see if he could give me some advice. I wanted to see what could be arranged for you."

"Well, it's good of you to take the trouble and all, but I don't think I want to leave London." Billy dabbed at his nose, checked to see that the bleeding had stopped, then replaced the soiled handkerchief in his pocket. "I'd miss me nippers and Doreen. And I can't see me sitting around on me duff all day with nothing to do but wait to do some special moving of me legs, and to see a doctor."

Maisie sighed. She had been warned by Maurice that Billy would probably object initially, either mildly or more firmly. At this stage she should be grateful that he had not shown anger when she revealed knowledge of his dependence upon cocaine. Perhaps another means of helping Billy could be found, one that would keep him closer to London. In the meantime she needed a commitment from him. "Billy, I want you to promise that you will not procure any more of this substance."

"I never did let myself get too much of a likin' for it, Miss, not like some. I tried to take it only when I was in that much pain. Frightened me, to tell you the truth, to know that somethin' you took, y'know, could change you that much. Scared the bloomin' life out of me. But then when I felt bad again, 'avin' a bit didn't seem such an 'orrible thing t'do."

"All right. Let's not talk about it anymore today. But I do insist that you speak to Doreen." She was careful to honor the confidence shared with Billy's wife. "If I have noticed changes in you, then I am sure she has. I urge you to speak to her and see what she says about what I've suggested."

"Aw, blimey, Miss, you don't know my Doreen. She's one of the best, but she can be as tough as old boots."

"Tough with a heart of gold, I suspect, Billy. Speak to her, please."

"Awright, I will, Miss."

Maisie felt a weight lifted from her shoulders. Her first challenge of the day was over.

Remembering Maurice's advice, she knew that Billy should be allowed time to regain his balance, now that his burden of secrecy had been lifted.

Now she had to concentrate on the Waite case. "I've quite a lot to tell you about my visit to Kent," said Maisie. "We'll need to get cracking with the pencils today. Charlotte *is* at Camden Abbey. At least I have performed the most important part of the Waite assigment. She has been located and she is safe."

Maisie wondered if she should show Billy what she had collected from the homes of Lydia Fisher and Philippa Sedgewick. Though she would never have asked him, she was sure that when she was an apprentice, Maurice had kept certain things to himself, as if in sharing a find before he felt that the time for revelation had come, he diminished its power. Maisie did not want to share what she had found until she could be sure of its significance.

"I want to speak to Magnus Fisher," said Maisie. "The police are sniffing around, looking into his past, who he's been seen with, and when. I believe he's a suspect in the murder of his wife, Lydia, so if I am to see him, then it must be soon."

"Won't D. I. Stratton wonder what you're up to? I mean, 'e's bound to find out that you've spoken to Fisher."

"That's true, but he also knows that I have been working on a missing-person case, and that Lydia Fisher may have had relevant information." Maisie was thoughtful. "Yes, I'll telephone Fisher now. Billy, what's the number at the Cheyne Mews house?"

Billy passed his notebook to Maisie, who placed the call.

The maid answered the telephone. "The Fisher residence."

Maisie smiled upon identifying the young maid's voice. "Oh good morning. It's Miss Dobbs here. How are you now?"

The maid warmed. "Oh, M'um. Thank you very much for asking, I'm sure. I'm getting over it all, though there've been a lot of people coming and going."

"I'm sure there have. Now then, may I speak with Mr. Magnus Fisher, please?"

"I'm afraid he is not in residence, M'um. I could take a message."

"Do you know where he is? I haven't had a chance to convey my condolences yet."

"Oh, yes, of course, M'um. Mr. Fisher is at the Savoy."

"The Savoy? Thank you."

"My, My, that was a little too easy," Maisie remarked to Billy as she replaced the receiver. "He's at the The Savoy Hotel, if you please."

"Well, 'e's not wastin' any time, is 'e?"

"It's a strange choice if he wants a measure of privacy, but on the other hand, the staff at the Savoy can keep the press at bay, which they'll need to do if the maid keeps giving out his whereabouts."

Maisie picked up the receiver again and placed a call to the hotel. She was surprised when she was connected.

"Magnus Fisher."

"Oh, Mr. Fisher, I am surprised you were located so promptly."

"I was at the desk. Who is this?"

"My name is Maisie Dobbs. First of all, please accept my condolences for your loss."

"What's this about?"

"Mr. Fisher, I am an investigator. I can say little until we meet in person. However, I am currently working on a case that may involve your late wife. I wonder if you might be able to meet with me this morning?"

"Are you working with the police?"

"No."

"Well, you've piqued my curiosity. However, the police are keeping me very much in their sights. I'm currently unable to travel outside London. Where and when do you want to meet?"

"Let's say"—Maisie consulted her watch—"in about an hour. Meet me on the Embankment, by Cleopatra's Needle. I'll be wearing a navy blue coat and a blue hat. Oh, and I wear spectacles, Mr. Fisher."

"See you in an hour, Miss Dobbs."

"Thank you, Mr. Fisher."

"Putting on the fake specs again, Miss?"

Maisie reached into the top drawer of her desk and brought out a pewter case, which she opened, and then placed a pair of tortoiseshell spectacles on her nose.

"Yes, Billy. I've always found this one small change in appearance to be a useful tool. If a policeman follows Fisher and then makes a note of my description, he will most definitely remember the spectacles. And Stratton knows I do not require help with vision."

"You sure Fisher is safe? I mean, look 'ow the weather's turned again, and if it's miserable, there won't be many people walking along by the water. That man could push you in, and no one would be any the wiser. After all, 'e could be—"

"The killer? Don't worry, Billy. You just continue working on the case map. Here are my index cards from this past two days." Maisie reached for her coat. "I'll take the underground—should be back by twelve."

"Right you are, Miss."

Maisie walked toward Warren Street station, thinking that the time alone in the office, and the task of adding more depth of information to the case map, would allow Billy to compose himself, now that his secret was out in the open. Though he might feel apprehensive, he was also free from the burden of guilt that had dragged at his spirit.

Maisie waved briefly to Jack Barker, the newspaper vendor, before going down to the trains. She traveled on the Northern Line to

Charing Cross Embankment. The air was damp and cold as she exited the station and walked down toward the Thames. A drizzle that was not quite rain, yet more than a mist, dulled the day, forcing some passers-by to use umbrellas. Maisie pulled up her collar, quickly rubbed a handkerchief across the spectacles and turned left to walk along the Embankment toward Cleopatra's Needle. The flagstones beneath her feet were wet and slippery and the Thames was a dirty gray. The river air smelled of smoke and rotting tidal debris.

She reached the meeting place and consulted her watch. It was ten o'clock, exactly forty-five minutes since she had ended her telephone conversation with Fisher.

"Miss Dobbs?"

Maisie swung around. The man before her was about five feet eleven inches tall, broad shouldered and heavyset, though he did not appear to carry excess weight. He wore black trousers, a tan mackintosh and a brown hat with a beige band. She could see that under the mackintosh he wore a shirt and woolen pullover, but no tie. His face was partially obscured by an umbrella.

"Yes. Mr. Fisher?"

Magnus Fisher moved the umbrella slightly to one side. He nodded.

"So where do you suggest we talk? Hardly a day for sitting on a bench on the Embankment and watching a dirty old river go by, is it?"

"Let's walk toward the Temple underground station, Mr. Fisher. We can speak as we go. Were you followed?"

Magnus Fisher looked around. They were quite alone.

"No. I slipped out of the staff entrance and then came down Villiers Street. The police know where I am and that I always come back. It's been like a game of cat and mouse, only we tip hats to each other." He turned to Maisie. "What's this all about?"

Maisie set a pace that was businesslike and deliberate. "I am investigating the case of a missing woman on behalf of her family. I believe she was a friend of your wife."

"And how can I help you? I spend most of my time out of the country, so I am not well acquainted with my wife's associates."

"May I assume we can speak in confidence, Mr. Fisher?"

The man shrugged. "Of course. At least this chat of ours will take my mind off whatever the police are cooking up for me."

"Were you acquainted with Charlotte Waite?"

Fisher began to laugh. "Oh, the Waite woman. Yes, I knew Charlotte years ago, and yes, she and Lydia kept in touch."

"Where and when did you meet?"

"Just before the war broke out I was in Switzerland, mountaineering with some chums. Lydia and Charlotte, being the daughters of poor boys made good, were at a second-tier finishing school there. We met at one of those yodel-odel-odel matinee social events."

"So you knew Lydia, Charlotte, and their other friends as well?"

"Yes. There were four of them in their little group. Lydia, Charlotte, Philippa, and wispy little Rosamund. I expect you know that Philippa is also dead. That's why they think it's me. Because I met with Philippa on a couple of occasions when I was back in the country."

"I see." Maisie would return to Philippa Sedgewick later. First she wanted to learn how well Fisher had known each woman. "Did you see the girls in this group often in those days, Mr. Fisher?"

Fisher held the umbrella between them, but put out his hand to feel the air.

"Might as well put this away." He collapsed the umbrella, and continued. "All right, I confess, my friends and I wooed all of them." Fisher sighed. "Look, Miss Dobbs, we were three young men in Europe, unchaperoned, meeting four young women who, it seemed, managed to lose *their* chaperone at every opportunity. What do you think? I courted every one of them. Charlotte was a bit too spoiled for me, frankly. Too many airs and graces. Rosie—not my type, I'm afraid. She was the one who always feared they'd be caught." Fisher laughed again in a manner that Maisie found distasteful. "Philippa fell in love with me, but she got on my nerves. I was twenty-two with the world at my feet—literally—so the last thing I wanted was a weeping willow at my door. I'm afraid I broke her heart."

Maisie remembered the weeping willow at the side of the Sedgewick house, and Philippa's almost secret haven behind the fronds of yellow leaves.

"And Lydia?"

"Lydia was the most fun. A good time was always had by all when Lydia was around, in those days anyway."

"When did you marry?"

"We met again after the war."

"Had you been in France?"

Fisher laughed. "Oh God, no. I joined an expedition to South America in May 1914. I'd tried to join Shackleton's little joy ride to Antarctica. Just as well I didn't, isn't it? They went through hell in the ice, then when they got back no one wanted to know about them. While they were trying to keep warm, I was poking around in ruined temples and swatting at flies. I returned in 1919 with no money, but I did have some good stories that didn't include trenches."

Maisie checked herself. Though the conversation was necessary, and Fisher was clearly enjoying her attention, she detested his attitude.

"I engineered contact with Lydia again; by that time she had come into her inheritance. We were married within the year." Fisher was silent and suddenly thoughtful. "Look, Miss Dobbs, I'll be honest with you: Having a wife with money was attractive to me. I knew that if we were married, I could travel and enjoy a certain freedom that would be impossible otherwise. But I also thought it would be more fun than it turned out to be."

"What do you mean?"

Fisher kicked at a pebble on the pavement. "By the time I returned, it was clear that Lydia enjoyed a drink. I couldn't remember her touching any more than a half glass of Glühwein in Switzerland, but in the interim she had obviously taken to wine by the bottle. I didn't realize how serious it was at first, but later it was a relief when a new expedition came along. Off I went at a dash. As time went on she acquired a taste for those fashionable new cocktails. Now, I like a drink myself, but this was beyond the pale. I tried to get in contact with her old friends for advice and help, but they'd lost touch. Lydia never said anything definite, but I think they had argued before the end of the war. Probably about Lydia's drinking. I did meet Philippa a couple of times in the weeks before she was murdered, as I said, but, frankly, she wasn't very helpful. I wanted her to speak to Lydia, try to get her to dry out."

"And did they meet?"

"No. Philippa said she would, then bagged out. I have to admit, I all but lost my temper. I mean, to let a silly little row get in the way. Women!" He shook his head. "Anyway, my pleas were met with a very cowardly 'You don't understand.' By that time, of course, our marriage had fallen apart completely. If you must know, I clung to the money, and Lydia clung to the nearest bottle. Apparently, she even invited some Cockney tyke up to the house for a drink on the evening she was killed. I've heard he's off the hook, though. Probably the man I saw when I went in to get my luggage. By the way—I'm not telling you anything I haven't already told the police."

Maisie nodded and continued. "You were at the house on the day your wife died?"

"For about five minutes. Lydia was in her cups, so I left again pretty sharpish, taking my belongings with me. The marriage was over."

"I see." Maisie gave nothing away about Billy's visit, and paused before her next question to Fisher. "And you are sure you never saw Charlotte Waite after Switzerland?"

"No. The others didn't even come to our wedding. Mind you, I don't actually know if they were invited. I just smiled and said 'Thank you' throughout the whole thing."

"And did your wife ever say anything about Charlotte?"

"Oh, I think she might have come to the house, and Lydia mentioned that she was kept on a close rein by her father. Absurd situation, if ever there was one. I cannot wait until they find the murderer and I can get back to Africa—or anywhere else as far away from this freezing miserable place as possible!"

They crossed the road to Temple underground station. "And you're sure there's nothing more you can tell me about Charlotte Waite, Mr. Fisher?"

Magnus Fisher shook his head. "No. Nothing. With Stratton and his bulldog, the slobbering Caldwell, at my heels, my concern is self-preservation at the moment, Miss Dobbs."

"Thank you, Mr. Fisher."

"Mind you, there is one thing."

"Yes, Mr. Fisher?"

"Won't you have supper with me, as soon as the police are off my back?"

Maisie's eyes opened wide, so that even behind her spectacles her indignation was obvious. "Thank you for the invitation, but I think *not*, Mr. Fisher. In fact, some time spent in mourning might not do you any harm at all."

And though he had just given Maisie a considerable amount of information to contemplate, she inclined her head curtly and left Magnus Fisher standing outside Temple underground station.

To cool her temper Maisie walked briskly toward The Strand, where she turned left, making her way to Southam Street and Covent Garden.

"The cheek of it!" she muttered under her breath. "And his wife's body isn't yet cold!" But though she found him to be quite detestable, Fisher had not emanated an air of menace. She doubted if he cared enough about anything, even money, to kill for it.

Walking through the market, which was less frenetic now that the morning's business was done, soothed Maisie. It reminded her of her father, who would sometimes bring her to the market with him early in the morning when she was a child. She would laugh at porters moving to and fro with six, seven, eight, or ten round baskets of fruit and vegetables perched on their heads, and the air was always sweetly salty with the smell of sweating horses pulling heavy carts.

She descended into the depths of Covent Garden underground, taking the Piccadilly Line to Leicester Square, then the Northern Line to Warren Street, where she emerged.

"Morning, Miss Dobbs. In a rush today?" Jack Barker doffed his cap as Maisie walked quickly past him.

"Always busy, Mr. Barker."

Maisie slammed the door behind her, causing Billy to jump.

"Blimey, Miss! Gawd, you scared the daylights out of me."

"I'm sorry, Billy. I just met with Magnus Fisher. Not the most savory person in the world, though he was useful." Maisie removed her coat and walked over to the table where Billy was working. She placed several more index cards on the table.

"I jotted these down while I was on the train."

Billy began to read. "Oh, so—"

A sudden thud on the window made Maisie and Billy start. Maisie gasped and held her hand to her chest.

"What the—"

"Stupid bloomin' pigeon!"

"Pigeon?"

Billy walked over to the window. "Not to worry. 'e didn't top 'imself. Probably flyin' around with a bit of a bump on 'is 'ead though. Stupid bird."

"Was it a pigeon, then, Billy?"

"Certainly was, Miss. They do that sometimes, fly into windows."

"Well, I hope that doesn't happen too often."

"My old Mum would've been goin' to pieces if she'd been 'ere. Always said that a bird in the 'ouse, or tryin' to get inside, came with a message from the dead."

"Oh, just what I wanted to hear!"

"Nah, Miss, nothing to worry about. Old wives' tale, it is. Me, well, I can't stand birds. Hate the bloomin' things, ever since the war."

The telephone began to ring, and Billy walked over to Maisie's desk.

"Billy—why since the—" Maisie stopped speaking as Billy picked up the receiver.

"Fitzroy f—" Billy was interrupted while trying to give the telephone number. "Yes, sir. Oh, that is good news, sir. Yes, I'll put her on." Billy cupped his hand over the receiver.

"Who is it, Billy?"

"It's that Detective Inspector Stratton. All pleased with 'imself. They've just arrested the fella who murdered them women."

Maisie took the receiver, greeted Stratton, and listened carefully, punctuating his news with "Really?" and "I see" along with "Very good!" and "But—" before endeavoring to deliver her final comment.

"Well, Inspector, I must offer congratulations, however, I do feel—"

There was an interruption, during which Maisie ran her fingers through tendrils of black hair that had once again escaped the pins securing her tresses in an otherwise neat chignon. Billy leaned over the case map while listening to Maisie's half of the conversation.

"That would be lovely, Inspector. Tomorrow? Yes. All right. Schmidt's at noon. Of course. Yes. I look forward to it."

Maisie replaced the receiver and returned to the table near the window. She took up a pencil, which she tapped on the paper.

"So, good news, eh, Miss?"

"I suppose you could call it that."

"Is there anything wrong?"

Maisie turned to Billy. "Nothing wrong, really."

"Phew. I bet a few women will answer their doors a little easier for that news, don't you?"

"Perhaps, Billy."

"Well, who is it? Anyone we know?"

"They have just arrested Magnus Fisher at his hotel. I only left him just over an hour ago. Stratton could not disclose details of the evidence. And by the way, Billy, keep quiet about this, as news hasn't reached the press yet. Stratton said that there was a witness to Fisher entering the Cheyne Mews house on the evening of his wife's death, and that he'd been having an affair with Philippa Sedgewick." Maisie clasped her hands and rested her lips against her knuckles.

"Whew, would you believe it?" Billy noticed Maisie's furrowed brow. "It sounded like you 'ad a few crossed words with ol' Stratton."

"I wouldn't say 'crossed,' Billy, but I did try to caution him."

"Caution 'im? Why?"

Maisie looked at Billy, her midnight blue eyes piercing through his puzzlement.

"Because, Billy, in my opinion Detective Inspector Stratton has arrested a man who is innocent of the crime of murder."

# CHAPTER FOURTEEN

aisie made her way along Charlotte Street toward
Schmidt's.

The day was once again changeable and brisk,
so she wore her mackintosh over the new black dress. She had changed
three times before leaving the house this morning, considering not
only lunch with Detective Inspector Stratton but the meeting that
afternoon with Joseph Waite. As she dressed she was aware of feeling in
her stomach and legs that she attributed to anxiety. Though she looked
forward to seeing Stratton, she was disappointed at the peremptory way
in which he had brought the case of the murdered women to a close.
She felt that a grave error had been made. Was this the source of the
physical sensations that seemed to render her temporarily dizzy on two
occasions before she left the house?

Now, as she walked along the gray flagstones, heat seemed to rise
up through her body. She felt faint. She quickly turned into a side
street and leaned against a brick wall for support. As she breathed
deeply, her eyes closed, Maisie hoped that no one attempted to
inquire after her health, or to assist her. *I feel as if my foundations have*

*been rocked,* thought Maisie. She opened her eyes and gasped, for it seemed that her surroundings *had* changed, although they remained the same. As she tried to focus her gaze, it was as if she were looking at a picture that had been hung incorrectly, a picture that she could not quite set straight. Up a bit . . . no, down a bit . . . to the left . . . too much, just a hair right . . . And as she continued to look, the picture changed, and now she saw the Groom's Cottage at Chelstone. Then it vanished.

Regaining her composure, Maisie stood away from the wall, keeping one hand outstretched, touching the bricks. As confidence in her stability returned, she walked slowly into Charlotte Street. Maisie brushed off the interlude, telling herself that it served her right for skipping breakfast. Frankie Dobbs would have had something to say about that! "Breakfast, my girl, is the most important meal of the day. You know what they say, Maisie: 'Breakfast like a king, lunch like a lord, and dinner like a pauper.' Key to bein' as fit as a fiddle, is that." But as she saw Stratton in the distance, waiting for her outside Schmidt's, Maisie decided to telephone Chelstone after luncheon. Perhaps the foal had been born by now. Perhaps. . . .

e*M*aisie poked a fork into the rich German sausage, which was served with cabbage and potatoes.

"Miss Dobbs, I'm glad to be away from the Yard this afternoon, if only for an hour," said Stratton. "Since news of the arrest was published in the newspapers, we've been deluged. Of course, I give Caldwell credit for inserting the final piece of the jigsaw puzzle."

Maisie continued to clutch her knife and fork, but she could not eat. "Inspector Stratton, I think you—and Sergeant Caldwell—are mistaken."

Stratton leaned back in his chair. "Miss Dobbs, I know that you have certain skills in this field."

"Thank you, Inspector. It's just that"—Maisie set down her cutlery onto her plate—"I think there has been a rush to judgment."

Stratton straightened his tie. "Look, if you've evidence that I am not aware of . . . ?"

Maisie considered the white linen handkerchief and asked herself whether the delicate items held within could be termed "evidence." But evidence of what? She had made an assessment of Fisher's character based on a single interview, of Philippa Sedgewick's on the word of her husband. The police case against Fisher was based on concrete fact.

"No, Inspector. I have nothing tangible."

Stratton sighed. "I respect your work, Miss. Dobbs. But we are all wrong at times, and this time the evidence points to Fisher. Even if he were not having an affair with the Sedgewick woman, and his communication with her *was* regarding his wife as he claims, he had been seen with her on several occasions. We believe that the Sedgewick woman knew he was after his wife's money so she represented a risk to him. And we know, Miss Dobbs, that the mind of the killer may not be rooted in reality. They think they can get away with it. In Fisher's case he knew what he wanted—ultimately the money—and he thought he could take it once his wife was dead, and then leave the country."

"But the method—"

Stratton raised his right hand before taking up his knife again.

"Fisher has no shortage of tools, in view of his work, which seems to be something between archaeologist, raconteur and inveterate gambler. He was always in debt to someone somewhere, and Mrs. Fisher was an heiress. He stood to inherit the lot at her death."

"Has Spilsbury positively identified the weapon?"

Stratton cut into the thick sausage on his plate and speared a piece on his fork, along with some red cabbage.

"Yes. The bayonet from a short-barrel Lee Enfield rifle. Standard issue in the war. And—surprise, surprise—something that Fisher kept among the tools I just mentioned. Bit of a cheek, considering he was nowhere near the

battlefield. Of course his story is that he has several items that are not usually employed by archaeologists, but he uses them for the *ooh-ahh* effect from
the audience of fearless travelers that accompany him. According to Fisher,
poking around a pile of old bones in the sand with the tip of a bayonet
keeps the intrepid followers happy and gives them something to talk about
at the dinner table when they get back to Britain. The evidence against him
is strong. I'm sure we will have a confession soon."

Maisie, who had barely touched her food, could not face another
bite. "Inspector, I have the impression that you are more than usually
intent on securing a conviction."

Stratton tried not to reveal his exasperation.

"The man killed his wife, Miss Dobbs. And he killed another man's
wife. He is a murderer, and he should hang for it!"

Maisie wondered if he was allowing his personal history to affect the
outcome of this case. After all, Stratton, like John Sedgewick, was a man
who had lost his wife.

Stratton settled the bill.

"Thank you for lunch, Inspector Stratton."

"You are most welcome, Miss Dobbs. Indeed, I hope you are successful, though I do wish you would try to avoid becoming involved in
investigations that should have been referred to the police."

"That is my client's choice. It seems to me that such involvement
would have represented a waste of police time."

Stratton ran his fingers around the brim of his hat before placing it
on his head. "Perhaps we could meet again for lunch, or supper?"

"When we have both completed work on our respective cases,
Inspector, certainly."

Stratton tipped his hat. "Until then, Miss Dobbs."

Maise smiled and inclined her head. "Until then, Inspector." She
made one last effort. "Inspector, I urge you to go back over the evidence that has led to Fisher's arrest. You know better than to be
pressured by the public's wish to see a suspect behind bars. More time
is needed, Inspector."

"We must agree to disagree, Miss Dobbs. Good-bye."

As she made her way back to Fitzroy Square, Maisie admonished herself for alienating Stratton. Then, reconsidering, she drew back her shoulders, and set forth at a brisk clip. No, she thought. He's wrong. They've got the wrong man. And I'll prove it!

As Maisie lifted her head, she saw a flash of gold in the distance, over the heads that bobbed to and fro past her. It was Billy's familiar shock of hair. He was walking—no, running— in her direction.

"Billy," she yelled, "Walk! Don't run! Walk!"

Still he came toward her in an ungainly stumbling lope that was more than a walk but not quite a run, as if one side of his body were intent on speed that the other simply could not match. Maisie in turn ran to him so that those observing the scene might have thought them lovers who had been separated by distance and time.

"Billy, Billy, what is it? Take a deep breath, calm down, calm down."

Billy gasped for breath. "In 'ere, Miss. Let's get off the street." Billy jerked his head to the right, toward a side street.

"Right. A deep breath, Billy, a deep breath."

Billy fought for air, his gas-damaged lungs heaving against his ribcage so that Maisie could see the steep rise and fall of his chest. He brought his chin down as if to retain more of the life-giving air that his body craved. "Miss . . . I thought I'd never find you . . . that you might've gone off with Stratton."

"What's happened, Billy? What's happened?" As she clutched at the cloth of Billy's overcoat, knowledge flooded Maisie. "It's my father, isn't it, Billy? It's Dad?"

"Yes, Miss. Got to get you to Chelstone. 'e's awright, comfortable, apparently."

"What's *happened*?"

"Miss, stop. It's awright, awright. Listen to me. It was an accident, with the 'orse this mornin'. Word just came from Mr. Carter. The mare was 'avin' trouble, so Mr. Dobbs 'ad set up the ropes, you know."

"I know what they do, Billy." Maisie was thinking clearly now, and began to walk into Charlotte Street, Billy limping behind her.

"Well, anyway, something 'appened and 'e slipped, then something else 'appened and he got knocked out cold. Rushed to the 'ospital in Pembury, 'e was, for X-rays. Bad old do at 'is age."

"I want you to telephone the Waite residence. Cancel our appointment."

"Miss, you ain't thinkin' of goin' on yer own, are ya? Not drivin' all that way, bein' as you're not—"

"Not what, Billy?" Maisie stopped, her eyes flashing at Billy. Yet as she looked at him, rivulets of perspiration oozing from his forehead and running across his cheekbones, tears sprang into the corners of her eyes. "I'm sorry. Thank you."

" 'e'll be awright, you'll see. Strong as 'ouses, your dad is, Miss. But I reckon I'd better come with you, Miss."

"No, I haven't the time to wait while you go to Whitechapel, and you can't leave without letting your wife know."

"She'll be awright, Miss. I can get on the dog'n'bone to the shop up the street. They just 'ad one put in. They'll run along to 'er wiv a message."

Maisie shook her head. "I'm going alone. I need you here. There's business to take care of. Have a rest, a cup of tea, and look after my business for me, Billy."

"Yes, Miss."

Maisie started the motor car as he closed the door for her.

"Oh, and Billy, your nose is bleeding again. And I'll tell you now, Billy Beale, that if I ever learn that you are at that stuff again, I will box your ears for you!"

Billy watched Maisie screech into Warren Street on her way to Kent, knowing that she would push the MG to maximum speed whether on a London road or along a country lane.

> Faster than fairies, faster than witches,
> Bridges and houses, hedges and ditches;
> And charging along like troops in a battle . . .

It had been Maisie's favorite poem as a child, when her mother would set the small, dark-haired girl on her knee, then rhythmically recite the verse, tapping her foot so that Maisie felt propelled forward by the momentum of movement, imagining that she really was in a railway carriage.

> All of the sights of the hill and the plain
> Fly as thick as the driving rain . . .

Pressing the MG as fast as it would go, Maisie sped toward Pembury. Rain was now coming down in thick icicle-like slants across the windscreen. As she moved closer to see the road, wiping condensation from the glass with the back of her hand, her heart was beating furiously against her chest. And still the poem echoed in her mind.

> Here is a child who clambers and scrambles,
> All by himself and gathering brambles . . .

And in her mind's eye Maisie saw the small kitchen at the terraced house in Lambeth, where she had spent the years before her mother's passing. She looked again into the kind, sparkling eyes, then over to the stove, where her father leaned against the wall while listening to his wife and his girl laughing together. So long ago; it was so long ago.

> Here is a cart run away in the road
> Lumping along with a man and a load;
> And here is a mill and there is a river;
> Each a glimpse and gone forever!

Her mother was gone forever, Simon was gone forever. What if her father was lost, too? Maisie cried out as she whirled though Tonbridge and on toward her destination.

Swinging in through the broad driveway, Maisie saw the large brick-built hospital in front of her, the tall chimney at the far side belching smoke. She remembered passing the hospital in an earlier time, when her companion had told her that if the chimney was smoking it meant that amputated limbs were being burned. Maisie had rolled her eyes, sure that she was being teased. But now the chimney loomed over the hospital like an evil genie who would grant no wishes. She parked the motor car quickly and ran toward the main building.

"I'm looking for Mr. Francis Dobbs. He was brought in this morning, injured. Where is he?"

The uniformed porter was clearly used to dealing with the emotions of breathless relatives, but at the same time he would not be rushed.

"Let me see." He ran his finger down a list of names. But Maisie could not wait, and snatched the clipboard, scanning the names for her father.

"Ward 2B. Where is that? Where can I find him?"

"Easy up, Miss. Visiting time's over, you know." The porter reclaimed his clipboard.

"Just tell me where to find him!"

"All right, all right. Keep your hair on! Now then, here you go."

The porter stepped from his office and directed Maisie with his hand. She thanked him, then ran toward the staircase.

*They must have made all these hospitals the same.* Maisie recognized the building though she had never set foot within its walls before. The tiled corridors, disinfectant-smelling staircase, long wards and iron-framed beds were all so reminiscent of the London Hospital in Whitechapel, where she had enlisted for VAD service in 1915.

She entered the cloister-like ward, with two lines of beds facing one another, not even one-eighth of an inch out of place. She knew that each day the nurses would go along the ward with a length of string and a yardstick, ensuring that all beds were positioned precisely, so that during her rounds Matron would see a ward that completely adhered to her high standards of order. Not one patient, nurse, bed, or bottle would be anywhere but where Matron expected them to be. Amid this order, as the slowly setting late-afternoon sun glanced off the ward's cream-painted walls, Maisie searched for her father.

"Follow me, Miss Dobbs," instructed the Staff Nurse, who checked the watch pinned to her uniform in the same way that Maisie still consulted her own watch every day. "He's comfortable, though not yet recognizing anyone."

"You mean he's in a coma?"

"Doctor expects him to be much better tomorrow. The other gentleman hasn't left his side. Allowed to stay on doctor's orders." The nurse whispered as they moved along the ward, to a bed set apart from the others, with screens pulled around to ensure privacy so that other patients would not see the man who lay unconscious.

"What other gentleman?"

"The older gentleman. The doctor."

"Ah, I see," replied Maisie, relieved that Maurice Blanche was here.

The nurse pulled back the screens. Tears welled up in Maisie's eyes as she quickly went to her father's bedside and took his hand in hers. She nodded at Maurice, who smiled but did not move toward her.

Leaning over her father's body, which was covered with a sheet and standard-issue green hospital blanket, Maisie rubbed her father's veined hands as if the warmth she generated might cause him to wake. She reached across to touch his forehead, then his cheek. A thick white bandage had been bound around his head, and Maisie could see dried blood where a deep wound had been tended. Looking down at his body, she saw a small frame over his legs. Fracture? Remembering the smoking chimney, she hoped so.

"I'm glad you're here, Maurice. How did you manage to be allowed to stay?"

"I informed the ward sister that I was a doctor, so I was allowed to remain. Apparently, they are a bit short staffed and we both thought it best that your father be attended at all times."

"You must be tired, but thank you, thank you so much." Maisie continued to massage her father's hands.

"Those of us who have reached our more mature years know the value of a nap, Maisie, and we can indulge ourselves without the comfort of pillow or bed."

"Tell me what happened, Maurice."

"The mare was experiencing some difficulty. According to your father, she was presenting incorrectly. Your father instructed Lady Rowan to summon the vet. Of course he was out on a farm somewhere. It's lambing season, as you know. In the meantime your father was following all recognized procedures and had requested a length of rope to maneuver the foal into a better position for the birth. Lady Rowan was there, as were two of the farmworkers. From what I understand, your father lost his footing on hay that had become damp and soiled, and fell awkwardly. His head connected with the stone floor, which is bad enough, but a heavy implement that one of the farmworkers had left standing against the stall fell and struck your father."

"When did this happen?"

"This morning, about half past nine or so. I came as soon as I was summoned, tended his immediate wounds, then deferred to Dr. Miles from the village, who arrived straightaway, followed by the vet. Your father was brought here immediately."

Maisie watched the rise and fall of her father's chest beneath the white and blue stripes of hospital-issue pajamas. She had only ever seen her father in his old corduroy trousers, a collarless shirt, waistcoat, and somewhat flamboyant neckerchief. Though a country groom since the war, on a working day he still looked more like a London costermonger, ready to sell vegetables from his horse and cart. But now he was pale and silent.

"Will he be all right?"

"The doctor thinks that the loss of consciousness is temporary, that he'll be with us soon enough."

"Oh God, I hope he's right." Maisie looked at her hands, now entwined with her father's. Silence seeped into the space between Maisie and her former teacher and mentor. She knew that he was watching her, that he was asking questions silently, questions that no doubt he was waiting to put to her in words.

"Maisie?"

"Yes, Maurice? I think you want to ask me something, don't you?"

"Indeed, yes." Maurice leaned forward. "Tell me, what is at the heart of the division between yourself and your father? You visit rarely, though when you do you are pleased to see him. And though there is conversation between father and daughter, I see none of the old camaraderie, the old 'connection' in your relationship. You were once so very close."

Maisie nodded. "He's always been so strong, never ill. I thought nothing could stop him, ever."

"Not like illness stopped your mother, or injury stopped Simon?"

"Yes." Maisie brought her attention back to her father's hands. "I don't know how it started, but it's not all my fault, you know!"

Blanche looked up intently. "Since our very early days together, when you were barely out of childhood, I can safely say that I do not think I have ever heard you *sound* like a child until now. You sound quite petulant, my dear."

Maisie sighed. "It's Dad, too. He seems to be drawing back from me. I don't know what came first, my work keeping me in London, even at weekends, or my father always finding jobs to do. He's preoccupied with other things when I visit. Of course he loves me, and there's always a warm welcome, but then there's . . . nothing. It's as if seeing me is troublesome to him. As if I'm not part of him anymore."

Maurice said nothing for a while, then asked, "Have you given it much thought?"

"Of course I've thought about it, but then I just put it out of my mind. I suppose I keep hoping that I'm imagining it, that he's just immersed in Lady Rowan's ambition to raise a Derby winner, or that I'm too caught up in a case."

"But if you had to guess, if you brought your intuition into play, what would you say—truly—is causing the change?"

"I . . . I don't really know."

"Oh, Maisie, I think you do know. Come on, my dear, we have worked together for too long, you and I. I have seen you grow, seen you strive, seen you wounded, seen you in love, and I have seen you grieve. I know when you are evading the truth. Tell me what you *think*."

Kneading her father's hands, she spoke quietly. "I think it has to do with my mother. I remind him of her, you see. I have her eyes, her hair—even these." She pulled at a tendril of hair, then pushed it back into the chignon. "In just a few years I'll be the same age as she was when she first became ill, and I look just like her. He adored her, Maurice. I think he only kept going because of me. The fact is that he can't see me without seeing her, though I'm not her. I'm different."

Maurice nodded. "The pain of being reminded is a sharp sword. But there's more, isn't there?"

"Yes. Yes, I suppose there is." Maisie swallowed deeply. "He sent me away, didn't he? To Ebury Place. And I know, I know, it all worked out for the best, and I wouldn't be where I am today if he hadn't, but—"

"But you can't forget."

"No."

"And what of forgiveness?"

"I love my father, Maurice."

"No one is questioning your love. I ask again: What of forgiveness?"

"I suppose . . . yes, I suppose some resentment still lingers. When I think about it, even though we made up and he would do anything for me. I . . . I suppose I am still upset, in a deep part of me, right in here." Maisie placed her hand against her ribs.

Silence filtered into the air around them once again, drowning out the echoes of Maisie's whispered confession until Maurice spoke again.

"May I make a suggestion, Maisie?."

She nodded and replied quietly, "Yes."

"You must speak with your father. Not *to* him, but *with* him. You must create a new path. You do not need me to tell you that, strong as he is, your father is not getting any younger. This accident will have weakened him, though I expect he will enjoy a full recovery. I observed you enter this ward dragging your guilt, regret, and—yes—fear with you, fear that you might have lost your chance. But you haven't lost it at all. Use your training, Maisie, your heart, your intuition and your love for your father to forge a new, even stronger, bond."

Maisie watched Maurice as he spoke.

"I feel so . . . weak, Maurice. I should have known better than to allow the situation to continue."

"*Should* have? *Should*, Maisie? Fortunately you are a human being, and it is recognizing our own fallibility that enables us to do our work." Blanche stood up from his chair and rubbed his back and neck. "Now then, it's getting late."

"Oh I'm sorry. I shouldn't have kept you."

Blanche held up his hand to silence her. "No, I wanted to remain here until you arrived. But now, I must report back to Lady Rowan. I suspect that our patient will improve with your presence."

"Thank you, Maurice."

Blanche inclined his head, and took up his coat and hat, which had been placed on the back of the chair.

"Maurice, I wonder if I might speak with you tomorrow about a case."

"Waite?"

"It's gone a bit further than that, really. I'm now convinced that the Coulsden and Cheyne Mews murders, and perhaps one more, are connected with the Waite case."

"You will need to return to Chelstone later, perhaps after doctor's rounds tomorrow morning, or before if Matron learns that you are here. Come to the Dower House when you are ready."

"Thank you." Maisie looked at her father again, then turned back to Maurice. "You know, it's strange, but I believe the murders have to do with being reminded, and remembering . . . and, now that I think about it, with forgiveness, too."

Blanche smiled and drew back the screen to leave. "I am not at all surprised. As I have said many times, my dear, each case has a way of shining a light on something we need to know about ourselves. Until tomorrow."

Maisie took Maurice's seat at her father's bedside, ready to continue the vigil until he regained consciousness. In the distance she heard a receding footfall as her mentor left the ward. She was alone with her thoughts, and though she held on to her father's hands firmly, and made a commitment to better times together in the future, she was wondering about the murdered women, and about Charlotte.

## CHAPTER FIFTEEN

*M*aisie opened her eyes as dawn was just visible through the tops of rectangular paned windows beyond the screens. How long had she slept? She moved her head to look at her father and sat up carefully so that she would not disturb him.

"Dad! Dad—you're awake!"

Frankie Dobbs forced a smile. "Been awake for a while, love. Just didn't want to unsettle you."

"Oh, Dad, I'm so glad." Maisie leaned across the bed to embrace her father, then sat back.

"And I'm glad you came, love."

"Straightaway, as soon as I heard."

Frankie squeezed his daughter's hand in his own broad palm. "To tell you the truth, for a moment I thought you were your mother. Fair took my breath away, it did, seeing you there. Thought I'd been taken, I did, and was with 'er again."

Maisie checked her father's pulse and touched his forehead with her slender fingers.

"Always checking something, my girl. Always making sure, eh?"

Father and daughter were silent for a while. Maisie knew she must use the door that Maurice had opened, in speaking of her mother.

"We don't seem to talk of Mum any more do we, Dad?"

Frankie tried to move toward Maisie, and grimaced. "No, love, we don't. Kept my memories to myself, and I s'pose you did, too."

"Oh, Dad—"

"And I was thinking, as I was watching you 'ave a kip, that we've let a few things get between us, 'aven't we?"

"I know—"

With a low screech the metal feet of the screen were pulled across the floor, and the nighttime Staff Nurse interrupted their conversation.

"I thought I heard voices. Good to see you awake, Mr. Dobbs. Had us all worried there. Doctor will be along to see you soon, and Matron will have a fit if she finds you here, Miss Dobbs. I'll be going off duty directly doctor has finished, but you'd better be off, Miss."

"Yes, I'd better. Dad, I'll be back later today, during visiting hours." Maisie reached down to kiss her father, then left the enclosure to step out into the ward. Morning sunlight was filtering in, warming patients and nurses alike.

Walking toward the exit, Maisie turned to the nurse.

"What's the prognosis?"

"Well, Miss—"

"I was a nurse myself, so I have some understanding of the situation."

"I'm not supposed to say, but I can tell you this—of course, we'll know more after Doctor sees him this morning—but he sustained a serious concussion, plus he's cracked both tibia. Not complete fractures, but something to watch all the same. I suspect he will need at least two or three months of rest, considering his age, and they will probably advise convalescence where he can receive adequate care."

"I see."

"But we'll be able to say more when you come back this afternoon. Go home, have a nice cup of tea and a good sleep. Your father needs you in tip-top health!"

*As* Maisie drove, she thanked any unseen entity or power that might have had a hand in the events of the past hours, for openings that seemed to have materialized in several directions. It occurred to her that helping out with the horses in her father's absence would be a real job for Billy. He would be close enough to be guided by Maurice, to receive instruction from Gideon Brown, and to be monitored by Andrew Dene. Her father wouldn't rest until he knew the horses were being cared for by someone he knew, and who better than another London man? If her father needed to enter a convalescent home for a month or so, perhaps All Saints' would be a good choice. Dr. Andrew Dene would understand a man who spoke his own language.

Her brain was in top gear as she sped along the country lanes to Chelstone, a list of things to do growing in her mind.

> Faster than fairies, faster than witches,
> Bridges and houses, hedges and ditches;
> And charging along like troops in a battle . . .

But before she did anything, before she bathed, took nourishment, or slept, she must go to Maurice. Maisie leaned sideways toward the passenger seat and, keeping her eyes on the road, reached inside the document case to feel the linen handkerchief into which she had carefully placed the tiny items she had taken from the homes of Lydia Fisher and Philippa Sedgewick. She wanted to share her delicate clues with Maurice. She wanted his counsel.

Maisie slowed as she drove along the gravel carriage sweep leading to Chelstone Manor. As grit began to spit and crackle under the tires, she rubbed her eyes against the onslaught of spring sunshine rising at a low angle into a clearing sky. It would be a bright but cold day. Frost-dusted daffodil heads bobbed in columns along the driveway, interspersed with bluebells and primroses. Yes, it would be a good day. Frankie Dobbs was out of the woods.

The upstairs curtains at the Dower House were still closed; Maurice was not yet up and about. Maisie felt a tinge of frustration, but she checked herself. Perhaps it was fortunate that she would have more time alone to marshal her thoughts and to anticipate questions. She missed working with Maurice, though awareness of the chasm left by his retirement was fading as she grew in skill and confidence. She maneuvered the car into the courtyard behind the manor house, the domain of George, the Comptons' chauffeur.

"Mornin', Miss." George wiped his hands on a clean white cloth and walked across the flagstones toward Maisie. "Blimey O'Reilly, what've you been doin' with that little motor of yours? Racin' 'er at Brooklands? I'd better get the full kit out this mornin'. You'll need oil, a good cleaning under the bonnet, to say nothing of 'er paintwork. And look at them tires!"

"You're the man for the job, George!"

"Actually, Miss, it'll be nice to 'ave something to get me teeth into." George lifted the bonnet, then turned to Maisie again. "How's Mr. Dobbs this mornin'? Better?"

"Much better, thank you. He's awake, though it might be a while before he's up on his feet."

"Fair gave us all a shock, did that. Everyone's waitin' for news."

"I'll see that the household is kept posted. Can I leave Lily with you then? I'll need her by three this afternoon—to be at Pembury by visiting time."

"*Lily*? You give a car like this the name 'Lily'?"

Maisie smiled, then laughed. "By three, thank you, George."

"Right you are, Miss. By the way, I saw 'er Ladyship walking over to the stables a little while ago."

"Oh, good. I'd better give her the latest news."

Lady Rowan was leaning on a fence surrounding the paddock adjacent to the stable where Frankie Dobbs had fallen. She seemed thoughtful as Maisie approached. The older woman's three canine companions, investigating bushes alongside, lifted their heads and greeted her with tails wagging.

"My dear girl, how is your father? I have been beside myself with worry."

"He is better, Lady Rowan, much better, though I will know more this afternoon when I see his doctor."

"Your father, Maisie, may well surprise us all. I think he'll live until he's one hundred years old!" Lady Rowan looked at Maisie with more gravity as she, too, leaned on the fence to watch mare and foal together. "You will not have to worry about convalescence, Maisie. Your father's recovery is in my interests, and the costs of any necessary procedures or care—"

"Thank you, Lady Rowan."

"Good." Lady Rowan turned to the paddock. "So what do you think of him?"

Maisie watched the foal standing under the protective custody of his mother's head and neck. His chestnut coat shone with newborn softness, the tufted promise of a rich, thick mane standing up like a shoebrush on his long and delicate neck. The foal's legs were surprisingly straight, and as the two women watched him, Maisie could swear she detected a certain defiance in his manner.

"He's quite . . . quite the little man, isn't he?"

"Oh yes, he certainly is, and only a day old, mind you." Lady Rowan continued to regard her new project closely. "Thought I'd call him 'Francis Dobbs' Dilemma.' But no, he'll be named Chelstone Dream. Apt, don't you think? I'll call him 'Dreamer' for short."

The foal stared at them intently in return.

"You see that look, Maisie? The way he's standing?"

Maisie nodded. "Yes."

"They call that 'the look of champions,' Maisie. He's the one; he'll do it for me. In four or five years he'll bring home The Derby for me—I know it! Can't you just see Gordon Richards atop Chelstone Dream, flying past the post at Epsom?" Lady Rowan became pensive again. "But in the meantime, what will I do without your father?"

"Ah," said Maisie. "Don't worry. I have a plan."

Lady Rowan laughed, her voice cutting through the morning quiet in such a way that the mare started, and moved her foal to the back of the paddock. "I would have put money on your having a plan, Maisie. What is it?"

"I'll tell you this evening, Lady Rowan, when I've sorted out a few details." She looked at her watch. "But I have to telephone my assistant, then I must see Maurice. May I use the telephone at the manor?"

"Of course. I shall expect to see you for supper this evening, when you can give me news of your father's progress. And I cannot wait to hear your plan!"

Maisie looked back at the foal as she made her way toward the manor house. And she could have sworn that Dreamer, the foal with the look of champions, had watched her every move.

"Billy, I'm glad I've caught you!"

" 'Oldin' the fort, Miss. 'Oldin' the fort. How's Mr. Dobbs?"

"Much better, thank you. Out of the woods. What happened when you canceled our appointment with Waite?"

"Well, at the beginnin', I 'ad to give a message to 'is secretary, who then 'ad to speak to 'im. Poor woman, you'd 've thought I'd asked 'er to tell 'im that 'is shops'd all burned down. Scared of 'im, she is, scared silly."

"Billy—"

"Anyway, she went off; then Waite 'imself comes on the blower, boomin' down the pipe 'e was, boomin' about how 'e was Joseph Waite and that no one does this to 'im."

"Oh dear."

"Then I told 'im what the reason for you not bein' available was, and I must say, 'e wound 'is neck in a bit sharpish. Funny that, innit? Says somethin' about family comin' first, and that it was nice to know that a daughter 'onored 'er father, and all that."

"Can he see me soon?"

"Made an appointment for Friday, sayin' that I just 'ad to let 'im know if there were any difficulties, and that you was to let 'im know if 'e could be of service. Very strange man, Miss. Very odd, that about-turn."

"He's certainly odd where family are concerned, I'll give you that." Maisie paused as she noted the details. "With a bit of luck I'll have good news for Waite. I'm going to Camden Abbey tomorrow, to speak with Charlotte."

"Sounds to me like you've got your plate full."

"My father's not allowed any visitors until late this afternoon, and probably only once a day until the doctor says anything to the contrary, so I'll be able to work on the case while I'm here."

"Right then. Dr. Dene telephoned again."

"Really?"

"Yep. And it's interestin' because 'e wanted to leave a message for you about your visit to see—let me look 'ere. I tell you, Miss, I can't even read me own writin' sometimes—Mrs. Thorpe's housekeeper."

"What was the message?"

"Didn't say, except 'e wanted to pass on a message from 'er, that she'd like to see you again. She remembered something that might be useful."

Maisie wrote notes on an index card as she spoke to Billy, and checked her watch.

"I'll *make* time."

"Awright, Miss. Anythin' else?"

"Actually, there is. You know we spoke about your coming down to Chelstone for a while, perhaps a month or so? And you didn't want to 'sit on your duff,' I think you said?" Without pausing to allow Billy to reply, Maisie said, "Well, I've got something for you to do that's vital to me and to Lady Rowan. Billy, it's to do with Chelstone Dream, the odds-on favorite to win the Derby in 1934."

Before she was able to retreat to the Groom's Cottage, Maisie fielded inquiries about her father's health from Carter and Mrs. Crawford. As she walked into her father's home, Maisie shivered. Never before had she felt a chill in the house, yet today the heavy dew outside seemed to permeate the stone walls and storm windows, creeping into each nook and cranny to claim a place.

*Well, this won't do!* thought Maisie as she looked around the cottage.

Her father had obviously left in a hurry to tend to the mare. An enamel teapot three-quarters filled with old cold tea sat on the table; a loaf of bread, now crusty and hard around the edges, had been roughly cut and not returned to the bread bin. The butter dish and a jar of Mrs. Crawford's homemade three-fruit marmalade were open on the table, with a sticky knife set on a plate. Maisie smiled, imagining her father hurriedly drinking scalding tea, quickly spreading a doorstep-like slice of bread with marmalade, then running out to get to the stable. She set about cleaning the room before seeking the comfort of a hot bath.

She lit the fire and set two large kettles of water on the hotplate, along with a cauldron usually used for soup. She dragged a tin bathtub from a hook in the scullery and placed it on the floor in front of the stove, ready to receive the scalding water, which she would cool to stepping-in temperature with cold water from the tap. She closed the curtains, locked the doors and went to the small box-like bedroom that had once been her own. Opening a wardrobe, she wondered if she would find anything to wear. She touched garments that should have been given to the rag-and-bone man years ago. There were her clothes from university years, the cast-offs from Lady Rowan so expertly fitted for her by Mrs. Crawford's dexterous needlewoman's fingers. There was the blue ball gown given her by Priscilla, her friend at Girton. As she touched the cool blue silk, she thought of Simon, of the party where they had danced the night away. Shaking off the memories, Maisie pulled out a pair of rather baggy brown trousers that had also been given her by Priscilla, at a time when women who wore trousers were considered "fast."

As soon as she had found an old pair of leather walking shoes, Maisie took a clean white collarless shirt from her father's chest of drawers, along with a pair of socks to complete her ensemble for the day. She would find an old corduroy jacket hanging up in the scullery, or she would simply wear her mackintosh while waiting for her clothes to be cleaned up at the manor. She'd not had time to pack a bag before leaving for Kent, but she could make do.

Maisie prepared her bath, opened the door to the fire and settled down to soak before embarking on the rest of her day. She began to soap her body, wondering what Rosamund Thorpe's housekeeper might want to speak to her about. The Old Town in Hastings housed a small community, and Maisie imagined the grieving woman remembering something, some vital piece of information, after her visit. Then, not knowing how she might contact Maisie—for she would not readily have used her former employer's telephone—Mrs. Hicks would have sought out Dr. Andrew Dene hoping that he might pass on a message for Maisie to see her when next in Hastings. But why did she not simply tell Dene what it was that she had remembered? Maisie suspected that the loyal housekeeper probably would consider such a disclosure tantamount to gossip. *And that would never do.* She soaped her shoulders and with a cloth allowed hot water to run across her neck. Rosamund Thorpe, Lydia Fisher and Philippa Sedgewick. Maisie saw each woman in her mind's eye. *What have you in common? Charlotte Waite, why did you run?* Four women. Four women who had known each other years ago. A coterie. A coterie of young girls on the cusp of womanhood. *What did that feel like?* Maisie closed her eyes, plunging her thoughts once again into the past. The library at Ebury Place, Girton, old clothes from Lady Rowan, the blue ball gown, Priscilla laughing as she pressed another cigarette into an ivory holder, the London Hospital . . . *France.* When she had been little more than a girl, she had served almost at the battlefront herself. Still sitting in the cooling water, Maisie allowed her thoughts to wander further. *What did* you *do during the war, you sheltered young women cocooned in your world of privilege, your safe little circle?*

A sharp knock at the door jolted Maisie from her reflections. Unwilling to interrupt her train of thought, she did not move, did not reach for a towel hanging over the back of a chair, did not call out, *Just a minute!* Instead, she silently waited until she heard the rustle of paper being poked under the door, and footsteps receding along the garden path. She settled back into the water for just a few more minutes, the now-blazing fire keeping her warm. *Rosamund, Lydia, Philippa and . . . Charlotte. What did you do in the war? And if Charlotte, too, is in danger, why does someone want you all dead?*

A note had been delivered by Maurice Blanche's housekeeper, inviting Maisie to join him for breakfast. She dressed quickly, pulling on trousers, white shirt and the pair of brown leather walking shoes which, she thought, were set off quite nicely by her father's best Argyll socks. Before leaving the groom's cottage, Maisie took her folded linen handkerchief from the document case and slipped it into the pocket of the old jacket she had found, as predicted, hanging up in the scullery. Instead of drawing her hair back into a tidy chignon, Maisie plaited her long tresses into a loose braid so that, walking toward the manor house with her clothes folded under one arm, she caused Mrs. Crawford—who was on an expedition into the far reaches of the kitchen garden—to exclaim, "Maisie Dobbs, you look five and ten all over again!"

Seeing Maisie approach, Maurice opened the door as she made her way along the path leading from the Groom's Cottage to the Dower House.

"He came round, Maurice, he came round as I was sleeping!"

Maisie ran to his side, and in the same way that Mrs. Crawford was taken aback, so Maurice was reminded of the years when Maisie was his pupil, drinking eagerly from the well of knowledge he provided.

"I am so glad, so very glad. Now he will be on the mend. It's amazing how the body and mind are connected. Even when conscious thought has slipped away, the patient is aware of the healing presence of love."

"If I had that much power, Maurice, he'd walk out of there today. But, listen, there's more. We began to speak . . . together."

Maurice stood aside, holding out his arm to allow Maisie to enter his home.

"It is indeed a wondrous universal alchemy, is it not? When one's heartfelt intentions cause mountains to move."

"Well, whatever it is, I'm glad, very glad. And if it's not too selfish of me, I'd like a mite more alchemy in my work on this case. The conservatory?"

"Yes. There's eggs and bacon, if you like, and some quite delightful fresh rolls. They quite remind me of my childhood in Paris."

Maisie smiled, looking forward to the strong black coffee that Maurice favored.

Teacher and pupil, master and apprentice, Maurice Blanche and Maisie Dobbs sat together in the warm, light-filled conservatory, which commanded a flower-filled view across the garden to the fields beyond, as Maisie gave Maurice a full account of her work on the Charlotte Waite case, and how it had expanded to encompass the murders.

"Yes, your investigation thus far does seem to indicate that the Thorpe woman's death should be looked at more closely." Blanche leaned back in the Lloyd Loom wicker chair, watching a flight of sparrows descend on the bird table freshly laden with breadcrumbs. Maisie waited.

"An overdose for Thorpe? Followed by morphine *and* the bayonet of a Lee Enfield rifle for the other two women, you say?"

She sipped the soothing coffee but hardly touched her crusty roll, despite her realization that she hadn't eaten anything since yesterday's lunch with Detective Inspector Stratton. She was beginning to wish she had a glass of Maurice's elderflower wine clasped in her fingers. Her interrogation was beginning.

"It's as if the murderer was not satisfied with the poison alone, as if a deeper . . . emotion—yes, I think that's the right word, *emotion*—needed to be vented. Vindicated."

"Have you spoken to Mrs. Thorpe's physician regarding her mental well-being? Have you completely ruled out suicide?"

"No . . . not completely. Her physician is the one who issued the death certificate. He'd concluded it was suicide. I spoke to the house-keeper, who knew her very well, and to others in the town."

"I don't doubt your instinct, but intuition must be supported by footwork. Now then, about the Sedgewick woman. You say that Fisher has been arrested based on evidence linking him to Mrs. Sedgewick, suggesting that they were romantically involved?"

"According to John Sedgewick, her husband, Fisher had been in touch regarding his wife's drinking, which was beyond his power to control. He also said that his wife did not want to meet with Fisher, but acquiesced out of some sort of loyalty to her old friend. It's a very different relationship to the one the police have posited. I get the impression, Maurice, that—with the exception of a level of communication between Lydia and Charlotte—these women, who had once been good friends, kept well away from one another."

"And why do you think there was a division among them?"

Maisie allowed her eyes to rest on the bird table, at the flurry of excitement, beaks peck-pecking for a crumb of food, peck-pecking at one another as they pressed tiny, fragile bodies onto the wooden platform.

"What do you *think*, Maisie?"

"I think that *something* happened, years ago." Maisie spoke slowly and deliberately while watching the frenzied feeding at the bird table. "Something . . . I'm not sure, but I feel . . . very much, that it's something of which they want no reminder. And seeing each other, keeping in touch, brings back the . . . *shame*."

Silence enveloped the room. Then Blanche said, "Do you have something to show me."

"Yes, I have." Maisie reached into her pocket, taking out the folded handkerchief and setting it on the table between them. "Shall I get your spectacles, Maurice? I think you'll need them."

Blanche nodded.

"Here you are." Maisie handed the lizard-skin-covered case to Maurice, who opened it so carefully that she could hear the almost imperceptible whine of hinges separating. He took out the wire-rimmed half-moon spectacles, placed them on his nose and leaned forward to watch as Maisie unfolded the handkerchief, his chin tilted upward just slightly to improve his view.

With the tips of the thumb and forefinger of each hand, Maisie spread out the handkerchief to reveal her evidence.

Maurice looked at the opened fine linen square, then back into Maisie's eyes. They had moved into such proximity that they could feel each other's breath.

"Ah, so delicate. Nature is by far the most talented artist."

"Yes, she is, isn't she?"

"And you found one at the Fisher house and the other at the Sedgewick house?"

"I entered Lydia Fisher's house soon after her murder, and was drawn to the first, although it was almost concealed. The one at the Sedgewick house was hidden inside a book."

"Which you just happened to open, no doubt?"

"Yes."

"And the woman in Hastings? Mrs. Thorpe?"

"Many weeks have passed since her death, Maurice, and Mrs. Hicks has ensured that the house is immaculate for a potential buyer. I fear that if there was one, it would have been swept away by now."

"So, Maisie, what are your thoughts? What does this mean?"

"I'm not sure, but I feel that they are significant."

Like marionettes orchestrated by the same puppeteer, Maisie and Maurice reached forward at the same time to touch the delicate perfection that lay before them: two small, white, downy feathers.

## CHAPTER SIXTEEN

fter breakfast Maisie reclaimed the MG from George—
who protested that he had barely started work on
paintwork—and left for Hastings, planning to be there
in plenty of time to allow her to return to her father's side that afternoon. As she came over the hill into the Old Town, the sea sparkled on
the horizon with sunlight reflecting on the water, making it seem as if
diamonds had been sprinkled liberally on the surface. Parking outside
All Saints' Convalescent Hospital, Maisie stopped for a while to admire
the view and to look down at the lilliputian Old Town itself. In the distance she could hear the clinker-built fishing boats being drawn up
onto the pebble beach with heavy winches, and seagulls wheeling
overhead. The morning catch was late coming in.

"That sea air does you the power of good, you know!"

"Oh, Dr. Dene! I didn't see you walking as I drove up the hill."

"No, you wouldn't have, I took a short-cut. The Old Town's full of
nooks, crannies, twittens and secret places that only the locals know
and I'm a fully fledged local now."

Andrew Dene reached to open the door for her. She saw that he had
noticed her informal attire.

"I just have to let the office know I'm here; then let's go to my lair, where we can discuss the two things on your mind." Dene poked his head around the door to the office. She heard his voice, then laughter among the staff before he retracted his head and led Maisie along the corridor to his "lair," which was still just as untidy.

"So: Your father's convalescence and Rosamund Thorpe?"

Maisie removed her gloves. "How do you know about my father?"

Dene raised an eyebrow. "The jungle drums have been a-beating. *And* I had cause to speak with Maurice this morning. I know Dr. Simms at Pembury who attended your father when he was brought in. Good man. All his patients make an excellent recovery. I've worked with him on several cases."

"I see."

As if reading her mind, Dene continued. "We have a first-class accident recuperation record here, Miss Dobbs. I'd be delighted to arrange for your father to be admitted upon his discharge from Pembury. I can start—" Dene leaned toward a pile of folders that wobbled precariously at his touch. Maisie instinctively reached to steady the pile.

"Don't worry, Miss Dobbs, haven't lost a file yet." He pulled a buff-colored folder from the mountain of paperwork. "That'll tell you how much work I have to do. As I was saying, I can start the file right now and contact Dr. Simms to let him know we've spoken."

"Thank you. That will be a weight off my mind."

"Good, good. It's settled, then. We can go over the admitting details with the administrator as you leave." Dene made several notations on a sheet of paper, closed the folder and set it on the desk. "Now to Mrs. Thorpe."

"Yes. I wonder if you could tell me something more about her, especially her demeanor in the days leading up to her death. I know she spent a good deal of time here."

"Frankly I thought she was doing quite well, especially as she was so recently a widow. But she was clearly still in mourning." Dene leaned to one side, moved another pile of folders, and looked out at the sea before turning to Maisie again. "You think she was murdered, don't you?"

Maisie's eyes registered her surprise. She had not expected to hear such speculation from Andrew Dene. "Well, actually—"

"Oh, come on, Miss Dobbs. I know Maurice, remember. I know very well what you do. And Rosamund Thorpe was well liked and respected in the Old Town, even though she was an outsider."

"Do you think she killed herself, Dr. Dene? Wouldn't you recognize the symptoms of the despair that precedes such an action?"

Dene was thoughtful.

"Does your silence mean there is doubt?"

"My thoughtfulness is simply that, Miss Dobbs: Thoughtfulness. You see, though I think it *unlikely* that a woman such as Mrs. Thorpe would take her own life, I noticed her sadness on several occasions, particularly when she was reading to veterans. Now, it's a subjective observation, completely lacking in the protocols of diagnosis, but —her sadness seemed more poignant than anything I observed with respect to other volunteers. You have to understand that among volunteers there are differing emotional responses to what they see. For example, we all know a veteran of the war when we see one on the street, whether he's an amputee, blinded, or disfigured, but when we are close to that person, in a setting like this, filled with others who are equally disabled—it's a reminder, a terrible reminder. I believe it can make people recall events and feelings that they would rather forget. Most quickly get over it and before they know where they are, they're singing 'I Don't Want To Go Into The Army' with the patients at the hospital Christmas party."

"But Mrs. Thorpe?"

"She wasn't like that. Though she had a broad smile for every patient—and she particularly asked to be of assistance to those who were soldiers—she was grieving as she left after each visit. It was as if coming here, doing this volunteer work, was a sort of self-flagellation."

"Do you think she killed herself?"

"Put it like this: Because of what I saw, I think she had it *in* her to reach certain depths of despair, but at the end of the day, I just can't see her actually taking her own life."

"Why?" asked Maisie.

Andrew Dene sighed. "I'm trained as a doctor of medicine. I specialize in accidents and rehabilitation. I deal in the specifics of what is happening to the body, though I am interested in what motivates a person to become well again. I am used to fine lines, but only have a passing familiarity with the type of speculation that is clearly your bailiwick. But if I were to hazard a guess . . ."

"Yes?"

"I would say that she . . ." Andrew Dene faltered. As Maisie said nothing, Dene exhaled, and continued, "I think she felt she had a debt that had not yet been repaid. So coming here was part of that repayment, wasn't it? Don't get me wrong—" For just a moment, Maisie detected Dene's original accent breaking through. "I don't want to stick my neck out and have you take it as fact. It's just my opinion."

"Thank you, Dr. Dene. I appreciate your honesty, which will be kept in absolute confidence. Now, you said that Mrs. Hicks wants to see me again?"

Dene looked at his pocket watch. "She'll be at the house now. I'll telephone her, to tell her you're on your way."

Andrew Dene moved several books and papers to reveal the telephone. He quickly placed a call to the Thorpe house and informed Mrs. Hicks that Miss Maisie Dobbs was just leaving the hospital. Then he set down the receiver and pushed the books and papers back on top of the telephone. Maisie's eyes widened at such disarray.

"Dr. Dene, please forgive me for saying this, but wouldn't it behoove you to invest in a cabinet for your files?"

"Oh no. I'd never find a thing!" he replied with an impish grin. "Look, would you be free for a spot of lunch after you've seen Mrs. Hicks?"

"Well . . . visiting time at Pembury is at four, so . . . as long as I'm on my way again by one-thirtyish. I like to leave plenty of time."

"Yes, I'm sure you do. We can walk along by the net shops and perhaps have some fish and chips. There are no posh restaurants down there, it's all a bit spit and sawdust. But you'll never taste fish like it anywhere else in the world."

As Maisie parked the MG outside Rosamund Thorpe's house on the West Hill, Mrs. Hicks opened the front door to greet her.

"Thank you for getting in touch, Mrs. Hicks, I do appreciate it."

"Oh, Miss Dobbs, I'm only glad to help. I had the feeling that you were acting in Mrs. Thorpe's best interests, so when I remembered, I thought I'd better get in touch. Hope you don't mind me asking Dr. Dene. Such a nice man." She closed the door behind Maisie and led her into the drawing room, where a teapot and two cups were set on a tray with some biscuits.

Maisie took a seat on the settee and once again removed her gloves. Despite extra clothing she still felt the cold, in her hands as much as in her feet.

Mrs. Hicks poured tea for Maisie, passed her cup, then offered biscuits which Maisie declined. She would need to leave space for a hearty helping of fish and chips. "Right. I expect you'll want me to get straight to the point."

"Yes, please. It really is important that I understand why Mrs. Thorpe might have taken her own life or, on the other hand, who might have wanted her dead."

"Well, as you know, I've racked my brains trying to answer the first question, and haven't had much luck with the second. Everyone thought well of Mrs. Thorpe. Then I remembered a visit; years ago, it was, not long after she was married. Probably not long after the war, either. Joseph Waite—"

Maisie set her cup into the saucer with a clatter.

"Is that tea cold, Miss?"

"No . . . no, not at all. Please continue, Mrs. Hicks." Reaching into her document case, she took out an index card and began to make notes.

"Well, anyway, Joseph Waite—he's the father of one of her old friends. Mind you, they hadn't seen each other for years and years, not since the war. Anyway, Mr. Waite came here, big motor car and a chauffeur and all, and asked to see Mrs. Thorpe. Perhaps he didn't know her married name, because he took liberties. What he actually said was, 'I'd like to see Rosie.' It was the first I knew that she used to be called Rosie, and I thought it was a bit of a cheek, calling a respectable married woman by the name of Rosie—in fact, *any* woman, when I come to think of it."

"Go on."

"Well, I showed him into the front parlor, then informed Mrs. Thorpe that she had a caller and who he was. She was shaken, I know that. Didn't like it at all. Said, 'Thank heavens Mr. Thorpe isn't here'; then, 'You will keep this to yourself, won't you, Mrs. Hicks?' And I never told anyone, until now."

"What happened?"

"Well, she goes into the parlor to greet him, like the lady she was, and he was all huffy. Didn't want tea or any refreshment. Just says he wants to speak to her in private, looking across at me. So I was dismissed."

"Do you know what he came to see her about?"

"No, sorry, Miss, I don't. But he was angry, and he got her all upset, he did."

"Did you hear anything?"

Mrs. Hicks sighed and tried to gather her thoughts. "Of course, at my age, you forget things, but him I remember. These houses are built like fortresses, on account of the wind and storms. Built for Admiral Nelson's lieutenants, they were, originally. You can't hear much through these walls. But he upset her, I do know that. And as he was leaving the parlor—he'd opened the door, so I heard everything—he said something . . . well, threatening, I suppose you'd call it."

"What was it?"

"He said 'You'll pay. You'll all pay one day. Mark my words, my girl, you will pay.' Then he left, slamming the front door behind him so hard I thought the house would fall down. Mind you, as it's been here this long, the likes of Joseph Waite won't hurt it now!"

Mrs. Hicks was quiet for a while before speaking again, this time with less forcefulness.

"But you know what was the strangest thing?"

"What was that, Mrs. Hicks?" Maisie's voice was so low it was almost a whisper.

"I came out of the dining room, where I had been arranging some flowers, when I heard the parlor door open. I wanted to be ready to show him out. Well, he held up his hand to me, like this"—Mrs. Hicks held her arm out as a London bobby might when stopping traffic— "when he'd finished speaking, to stop me from coming toward him. Then he turned away quickly. You see, Miss, he was crying. That man had tears streaming down his face. I don't know whether it was anger or sadness, or what it was. But . . . very confusing it was, what with Mrs. Thorpe so upset, too."

That the control-obsessed Joseph Waite had lost his composure did not surprise Maisie, for she knew that when such people cross an emotional boundary, it often leads to a breakdown. She remembered Billy's despair, and those times when she, too, had known such sadness, and as she did so, her heart ached not only for Rosamund but, strangely, for Joseph Waite. Whatever else he might have done, this was a man who had truly known sorrow.

"Did he come here again?"

"Never. And I would have known about it if he had."

"And she never took you into her confidence, about the reason for his visit?"

"No. Seemed to me like he wanted to make her as miserable as he was."

"Hmmm. Mrs. Hicks, I know I've already asked you this, but I must be sure: Do you really think that Mrs. Thorpe's death was caused by someone else?"

The housekeeper hesitated, turning her wedding ring around on her finger repeatedly before replying.

"Yes, I do. There is some wavering in my heart. And I can't be sure because I wasn't here. But to take her own life? I do doubt it very much, very much indeed. She seemed to be on a mission to help people, especially those men who'd been to war, the ones who were just boys, wounded boys."

The clock on the mantelpiece began to strike a quarter to twelve.

"Thank you so much for your time, Mrs. Hicks. You have been very helpful once again."

Mrs Hicks took a handkerchief from her pocket and dabbed her moist eyes.

Maisie stood and placed an arm around the housekeeper's shoulder. "Oh, Mrs. Hicks, you must miss her very much."

"Oh, I do, Miss Dobbs. I do miss her very much. Mrs. Thorpe was a lovely, kind woman, and too young to die. I haven't even had the heart to send her clothes away, like Mr. Thorpe's children told me to do."

Maisie felt a sensation of touch, as if another hand had gently been placed upon her own as it lay on Mrs. Hicks shoulder. A picture of Rosamund had formed in her mind.

"Mrs. Hicks, was Mrs. Thorpe in mourning attire when she died?"

"Well, yes, as a matter of fact, she was. Her nice black dress, very proper, yet fashionable. She wasn't a dowdy one, Mrs. Thorpe, always beautifully turned out."

"Was she buried in—"

"The dress? Oh no, I couldn't allow that, not going into the cold ground in her widow's weeds. No, I made sure she was in her lovely silk dressing gown. Like a sleeping beauty, she was. No, the dress she was wearing is in the wardrobe. I put it away as soon as I'd dressed her. Didn't want strangers putting clothes on her so I dressed her myself. I thought I should throw it out, the black dress, but I couldn't bring myself to."

"May I see the garment, please?"

Mrs Hicks seemed surprised at the request, but nodded. "Well, of course, Miss Dobbs. Through here."

Mrs. Hicks led the way into the bedroom, where she opened a mahogany wardrobe and took out a black low-waisted dress in fine wool with a silk sash that matched silk binding at the neckline and cuffs. There were two elegant patch pockets on the bodice, each rimmed with black silk.

Maisie held up the dress by the hanger, then walked to the bed and laid the garment out in front of her.

"And the dress has not been cleaned since?"

"No, I put it straight in the wardrobe, with mothballs of course."

Maisie nodded and turned to the dress again. As Mrs. Hicks moved to open the window to "let some air in here," Maisie reached into the left pocket and searched inside carefully. Nothing. She leaned over and looked down into the right pocket and again reached inside. Something pricked at the pillowed skin on the underside of her fingertips. Maintaining contact, with her other hand Maisie reached into her own pocket for a clean handkerchief, which she opened before carefully pulling out the object that had so lightly grazed her fingertips. The soft white feather of a fledgling. She inspected her catch briefly before placing it in the waiting handkerchief, which she quickly returned to her jacket pocket.

"Everything all right, Miss Dobbs?"

"Yes, it's lovely. Such a shame to waste a beautiful dress, yet it's tinged with so much grief."

"I thought the same myself. I should've burned it, really I should. Perhaps that's what I'll do."

The dress might be evidence, and must not be lost. Maisie cautioned the housekeeper, careful not to cause alarm. "Oh no, don't do that. Please keep it—look, I think I know someone who could make good use of the dress. Shall I let you know?"

The housekeeper nodded. "Well, it is too good to destroy. I'll keep it until I hear from you."

"Thank you, Mrs. Hicks. You've been most kind, especially as I came unannounced and on short notice."

"Oh, but you weren't unannounced. Dr. Dene said to help you in any way I could. That you were completely trustworthy and acting in Mrs. Thorpe's best interests. You'd better hurry or you'll be late for your lunch."

"How did you know?"

"It was just a good guess, Miss Dobbs. Dr. Dene seemed a bit too sparky when I told him I had some information for you, as if he quite liked the idea of speaking to you again himself. Now, it's none of my business, and it's not how it would have been done in my day, not when Mr. Hicks and I were walking out together. But I thought he might invite you to have a spot of lunch with him today. He had that sound in his voice."

Maisie blushed. "And what sound is that, Mrs. Hicks?"

"Oh, you know. That sound. The one that a gentleman has when he's pleased with himself."

Maisie suppressed a smile and said good-bye to Mrs. Hicks. Though she was looking forward to lunch with Andrew Dene, she was also anxious to be alone, to spread out the index cards that she had made notes on, to assess what this morning's gathering of information meant. The picture was becoming clearer, as if each conversation were a series of brushstrokes adding color and depth to a story that was now unfolding quite rapidly. She had three feathers, evidence that the three deaths were linked, and that Rosamund Thorpe, too, had most definitely been murdered.

She drove down the hill to meet Andrew Dene, by the fishing boats at the place where the old horse turned the winch that brought the boats ashore, wishing she could get back to London, yet feeling guilty for wishing because of her father's need for her. She was anxious to sit with Billy at the incident table with all their clues, suspicions, evidence, hunches, and scribbles laid out in front of them. She wanted to find the key, the answer to her question: What was the connection between three small white feathers, three dead women and their

murderer? And how was Joseph Waite involved? She felt for the handkerchief in her pocket, and patted it.

"Thank you, Rosamund," she said, as she placed her hand on the
steering wheel again.

Maisie parked the car at the bottom of the High Street, to much
attention by passersby. As she walked along the seafront, where seagulls
and pigeons followed pedestrians in the hope that a breadcrumb or two
would be dropped, she made a mental note to ask Billy why he couldn't
stand pigeons.

The weather was crisp, but fine enough for Andrew Dene and
Maisie to walk to the pier after a quick fish-and-chips lunch. The sun
was higher in the sky and had it been warmer, one might have thought
it summer.

"I cannot believe you removed all that lovely batter before eating
the fish!" Andrew Dene teased Maisie.

"I love the fish, but don't really care for batter. Mind you, the chips
were tasty."

"But you fed most of them to the seagulls, and they're fat enough
already!"

They walked in silence. Maisie looked at her watch once again.

"Do you know how many times in one minute you've looked at
your watch? I know you can't find my company *that* tedious. You
should break yourself of the habit."

"I beg your pardon?" Maisie's eyes widened. She had never met a
man of such impertinence. "I was going to say that I ought to be turning around, to get to my motor by—"

"Half past one? Ish? Yes, I haven't forgotten. Have you made any
headway today, Miss Dobbs?"

"I've certainly gleaned more information, Doctor. It's putting the
pieces together in a logical form that's the challenge. Sometimes it's
guesswork all the way."

"Anything more I can do to help?" They were strolling back to the
car, Maisie consciously keeping her hands deep in the pockets of her
raincoat, holding tight to the linen handkerchief that held the third

feather. She would not look at her watch again until she was well away from Andrew Dene.

"No . . . yes, yes there is, actually. Tell me, Dr. Dene, if you were to name one thing that made the difference between those who get well quickly and those who don't, what would it be?"

"Phew. Another simple question from Maisie Dobbs!"

"I'm serious."

"And so am I. It's a tricky one, and one that you are probably more qualified to answer than I. You were a nurse and, more important, you have training in psychological matters."

"I'd like your opinion. Please, take a stab at it." Maisie turned toward him as she walked, challenging Dene to respond.

"Well, if I were to name one thing, it would be acceptance."

"Acceptance? But doesn't that stop the injured or wounded from trying to get better?"

"Ah, now you're playing devil's advocate, aren't you? In my opinion acceptance has to come first. Some people don't accept what has happened. They think, 'Oh, if only I hadn't walked up that street when I did,' or in a case like your father's: 'If only I'd known the ground was that wet and that Fred, or whatever his name was, had left his tools in the way.' They are stuck at the point of the event that caused the injury."

"Yes, I think I know what you mean."

"So, in the case of the soldiers who find it difficult to move on—and of course, some have had terrible injuries that all the therapeutic assistance in the world can't help—but those who find it difficult to accept are stuck in time, they keep thinking back to when it happened. And it's not so much, 'Oh, I wish I'd never enlisted.' In fact most say, 'At least I went,' but instead it's a case of 'If only I'd ducked, jumped when I could have, run a bit faster, gone back for my friend.' And of course, it all gets mixed up with the guilt of actually surviving when their pals didn't."

"So what's the answer?"

Dene stopped as they came alongside the MG, and Maisie leaned on her car, facing the Channel, her face warmed by the sun.

"I wish I had *one*, but, I would say that it's threefold: One is accepting what has happened. Three is having a picture, an idea of what they will do when they are better, or improved. Then in the middle, number two is a path to follow. For example, from what I've heard about your father, he'll make a good recovery: He's accepted that the accident happened, he has a picture of what the future holds for him when he's better—ensuring that the colt is in tip-top condition ready for training at Newmarket—and in the middle he's already aware of the steps that he'll take. At first he'll only be able to stand for a minute or two, then he'll use crutches, move on to walking sticks, and then the casts will come off. Dr. Simms will give him instructions as to what not to do, and the sort of activities that will set him back."

"I see."

"There are gray areas," Maisie resisted the urge to look at her watch again as Andrew Dene went on. "For example, if we take Mr. Beale—oops, you had better get going, hadn't you, Miss Dobbs?" Andrew Dene opened the door of the MG for Maisie.

"Thank you, Dr. Dene. I enjoyed our lunch."

"Yes, I did too. I look forward to seeing your father at All Saints' soon."

" I'll be in touch with the administrator as soon as I can confirm the arrangements."

"Right you are, Miss Dobbs."

*Phew! What a character he is!* Still, Maisie found Dene to be interesting, engaging, challenging—and fun. He was able to laugh at himself. But there was something else about him, something that nagged at her, that she both liked and found confusing at the same time: He seemed to know who *she* was. Not by name. Not by accomplishment or by profession. No. There was more than that to her identity. Andrew Dene understood her roots. Even if he had never been privy to her story, Maisie knew that he understood her.

Following her father's accident, and the talks at the hospital with Maurice and later her father, Maisie had been able to recollect more of the times spent with her mother. She remembered being in the kitchen, a girl of about nine. Her mother had been telling her the story of how she'd met Maisie's father and known straight away that Frankie Dobbs was the one for her. "I set my hat for him there and then, Maisie, there and then." And she'd laughed, wiping the back of her sudsy hand across her forehead to brush back ringlets of black hair that had fallen into her eyes.

Maisie wondered about the business of setting one's hat for a man, and how a woman of her age might go about doing such a thing.

As she drove along, up over the ridge toward Sedlescombe, her thoughts shifted to Joseph Waite and the many tragic events that had befallen him. A father and brother killed in mining accidents, a wife dead in childbirth, a son lost to war, and an estranged daughter whom he tried to control without success. Hadn't Lydia Fisher indicated to Billy that Charlotte had been something of a social butterfly? But as she passed into Kent at the boundary near Hawkhurst, Maisie checked herself, and the certain pity she had begun to feel for Joseph Waite. Yes, she felt pity. But was it pity for a man who had stabbed three women, quite literally, in cold blood?

Perhaps Charlotte Waite had the answer. Tomorrow she would be able to judge Charlotte for herself. Was she, as her father believed, a 'wilting lily'? Or, was she, as Lydia Fisher had intimated to Billy, a habitual bolter? Magnus Fisher's account did not help. But each narrator's story revealed only one perspective, one representation of the person that Charlotte revealed herself to be in their company. Where did the truth lie? Who was Charlotte, really?

# CHAPTER SEVENTEEN

*T*hursday greeted Kent with driving rain and howling winds. Maisie looked out at the weather from the cozy comfort of the Groom's Cottage, shivering but not at all surprised.

"Typical! Bring in the clouds for a drive to the marshes!"

Today she would make her way across Kent again and on through the relentless gray of the marshlands, where people—if she saw any—would be rushing along with heads bent, anxious to get to and fro from work or errands. It was a day when locals tried not to venture outside and even farmworkers found jobs to do in the barn rather than out in the fields. Today she would finally meet Charlotte Waite.

"Ugh," uttered Maisie as she ran to the MG.

George joined her, wearing the sort of foul-weather clothing one usually associated with fishermen.

"Going to catch a trout for tea, George?"

"No, Miss. I'd've thought catching things was more in your line of work."

"I deserved that, George." Maisie laughed as George lifted the bonnet to turn on the petrol pump, the first of five steps to start the MG. "Thank you for coming out."

"Saw you running across in this rain, Miss, and wanted to make sure you got off safely. Pity you've got to go somewhere today, so you mind how you go, Miss. Take them corners nice and easy."

"Don't worry, George."

"Know what time you'll be back? Just so's I know?"

"I won't be back to Chelstone today. After Romney Marsh, I'm off to Pembury to visit Mr. Dobbs, and afterwards straight on to London. I expect to return to Kent as soon as I can to see my father." Maisie waved good-bye to George, who patted the back of the MG with his hand before running into the garage and out of the rain.

Apple orchards that were filled with blossom only yesterday were now sodden and sorry. Tall cherry trees bent over and the branches of roadside elder laden with bloom seemed almost to ache with the task of standing tall. Maisie hoped that the storm would pass, that the trees and land would dry quickly, and that spring, her favorite season in Kent, would be restored to its resplendent richness soon.

As she maneuvered the MG, Maisie reflected upon her visit to see her father the day before. She had entered the ward to see Frankie at the far end of the column of beds, straining forward in his sitting-up position to greet her as she approached.

"How are you, Dad?"

"Better every day, expect to be up and about soon."

"Oh, I don't know about that. I've just spoken to Dr. Simms, and he says that you should have two weeks convalescence by the sea before returning home, and even then, you shouldn't be putting any weight on your right leg at all."

Frankie was about to protest, then looked at his daughter. "You've got a bit more color in your cheeks, my girl, and you're looking more rested."

It was true, even Maisie had noticed that the gray rings usually etched under her eyes had diminished, her hair seemed more lustrous, and she felt much better, though she'd had so much on her mind that she hadn't even noticed feeling below par in the first place. It was Maurice who pinpointed a possible reason for Maisie's fatigue: "You've taken something on, Maisie. You've absorbed something of whatever was held inside the three women. And though being a sponge can aid in your work, it can also hinder, for becoming one with the subjects of your investigation does not necessarily help you."

During her visit more was revealed to Maisie, more wounds were healed, more firm footing added to the ground as father and daughter tentatively made their way forward. As her reflections became illuminated by the light of understanding, so she felt a certain resentment lift, enabling her to look back on the past more kindly, with a little more compassion. And as she made her way toward Camden Abbey, she thought of Lydia, Philippa, and Rosamund, her thoughts coming back time and time again to who might not have been able to forgive them, and what it was they might have done to warrant such deep, unrelenting anger. An anger laced with a passion that led to murder.

She was close to Camden Abbey when the rain seemed to become lighter and for a moment it seemed as if the sun might manage to push its way through leaden clouds scudding across an already purplish gray sky. But that was the way of the marshes. The promise of light made it seem as if the elements were holding their collective breath. Then the observer realized that such a breath was only a minute's respite before it started blowing again even harder, a biting wind with a volley of more stinging rain.

Parking in front of the abbey, Maisie secured the car and ran inside, where she was immersed in silence, broken only by the drip-dripping of water that came from her mackintosh.

"Dame Constance has instructed me to escort you directly to the sitting room, where you can dry off." The young postulant avoided eye contact as she reached out to take Maisie's outer clothing. "Your coat, hat, and gloves will be ready for you by the time you leave."

"Thank you." Maisie inclined her head, and followed her guide, who walked close to the wall as she made her way to the room where Maisie had met with Dame Constance previously.

Once again, a fire crackled in the grate, though this time two wing chairs had been positioned alongside the grille. Maisie sat down, and leaned back with an audible sigh. The door behind the grille slid open to reveal Dame Constance. Her eyes sparkled as she spoke.

"Good morning, Maisie."

"Good Morning, Dame Constance. You have been most kind to encourage Miss Waite to agree to this meeting."

"I know it's important for you, Maisie, and the work you must do. However, my concern is primarily for Miss Waite. We have to consider how we can best be of service in her healing and recovery."

Maisie understood that this preamble to the meeting with Charlotte was important.

"You see, when a young woman makes a petition to join the community . . ." Dame Constance looked at Maisie intently. "You are surprised? Ah, Maisie, I would have thought that you had intuited by now that Miss Waite wishes to remain here, to join us. It is an attractive option for a woman who has found a measure of solace within these walls. However, I should add that there is no instant acceptance. Ever."

Dame Constance waited for a comment from Maisie. Then she went on. "There is a misconception that a religious community is a place of escape, that the refuge offered on a temporary basis can easily become more permanent. But that is not so. Our novices are women who are at peace with the world outside. They have enjoyed society in its broadest sense; they have had the support of loving families and in some cases no shortage of suitors. I have advised Miss Waite that her foundations must be solid before she can commit to a relationship with God. She cannot come out of fear, to hide."

"What do you mean, Dame Constance?"

"Joining a religious order is not a means of escape. It is a positive undertaking. One's foundation is the relationship one has with family, with one's first love, so to speak. Charlotte Waite has had difficulties with familial interactions, especially with her father. Such difficulty represents a crack in the foundation. The house of her future cannot be built if her very foundations are compromised."

Maisie frowned, thinking of her own situation rather than Charlotte's. Was that why she had felt such loneliness? Had it been the rupture in her relationship with Frankie that had prevented her from making other associations, so that she felt that she was always missing the mark in some way? Never quite able to join in, and surprised when she did? Never able to open her heart to another? Perhaps. After all, hadn't she noticed, now she came to think of it, a greater ease in her more personal interactions of late? She thought of Andrew Dene.

"Ah, I see you understand, Maisie."

"Yes, I think I do, Dame Constance."

The nun smiled, then continued. "I believe that Charlotte Waite might reveal to you what is at the heart of discord between her father and herself. I will summon Miss Waite to meet you, but I will remain during your interview, at her request, though she will join you here in the sitting room."

"Thank you, Dame Constance."

The small door closed and Maisie was left alone with her thoughts. She would rather have seen Charlotte alone, but was grateful for any meeting. She had undertaken to urge Charlotte to return to Dulwich, to her father's home. But in so doing, would she be persuading Charlotte to risk her life? Might she be putting the lives of others in harm's way? Was it even possible that Charlotte was now seeking a religious life to expiate the crime of murder?

The sitting room door opened quietly and a woman of average height entered the room at the same time as the sliding door behind the iron grille that separated Dame Constance from visitors opened again with a thud.

Maisie studied Charlotte quickly. She wore a gray skirt, a long woolen cardigan knitted in a fine gauge, a plain white blouse, black shoes and opaque stockings. Her mousy hair, parted in the center and drawn back into a loose bun, seemed to form a pair of curtains framing her face. Her only color came from her bright, pale blue eyes. So presented, she was unremarkable and completely forgettable. And as she opened her mouth to greet Charlotte, Maisie remembered Andrew Dene's remark about Rosamund Thorpe: "It was as if coming here . . . was a sort of self-flagellation."

Maisie rose from her chair. "Good morning, Miss Waite." She held out her hand, quickly trying to take the measure of her subject in the mood and emotions revealed by her stance. "I am so pleased that you agreed to see me," Maisie assured the still figure before her.

Charlotte Waite seemed to be frozen to the spot. Only her eyes gave away a certain dislike of Maisie, based in all likelihood upon her hostility toward the person whom she represented.

"Let's sit down," offered Maisie.

Charlotte moved silently toward the other wing chair set opposite, smoothed the back of her skirt and was seated, her knees together with her legs slanted to one side, as she had been taught at her finishing school in Switzerland.

Maisie cleared her throat. "Charlotte, your father is very worried about you."

Charlotte looked up, then shrugged, giving the impression of a spoiled girl rather than a grown woman.

Maisie persisted. "I realize that there may be some miscommunication between yourself and your father. Please help me to understand what has come between you. Perhaps I can be of service in some way."

Charlotte Waite appeared to consider the question. Eventually she spoke in a voice that seemed to Maisie very much like her father's. It was a strong voice, a voice that didn't belong in the gray-clad, slender, almost frail body.

"Miss Dobbs, I appreciate your efforts. However, Joseph Waite wants only to have what he considers his property collected nicely together with all the rest of his possessions. I am exercising my choice to belong not to him but to myself."

"I understand your position, Miss Waite. But surely this cannot be attained by flight?" Maisie stole a glance at Dame Constance through the grille.

"I have tried to speak to my father. I have lived in his house for a long time. He wants me to be dependent upon him for my every thought, for me to remain in his sight, under his control."

"And what is the reason, in your estimation, for such behavior?"

Maisie knew she must suspend all judgment. But she had begun to dislike and mistrust Charlotte Waite and her rationalizations. Had her earlier feeling of pity for Joseph Waite biased her?

"Well, you're certainly different from the last investigator he sent after me."

"Indeed. But my question remains."

Charlotte Waite took a handkerchief from her pocket and blew her nose. "I've tried, Miss Dobbs, all my life, to make up for the fact that I am not my brother. I am not Joseph the Second. All the things I was good at were so different from all the things that he was good at, and he excelled at being my father's favorite." Charlotte Waite blurted out her words.

Maisie suspected that she had never confided her true thoughts before. "And what were your feelings toward your brother, Miss Waite?"

Charlotte Waite began to cry.

"Speak to me, Charlotte." Maisie deliberately addressed her by her first name.

"I loved Joe. I adored him and looked up to him. He was always there, always. He protected me, but . . ."

"Yes?"

"I was torn, too."

"Torn?"

"Yes, I . . . I was sort of . . . envious of him, especially as I grew older. I wondered why he was the favorite and not me. He could work for my father, while I was treated as if I didn't have a brain at all. I was pushed to one side and ignored."

Maisie was silent. How fortunate, by contrast, she had been in her growing up and in her opportunities, though Charlotte was a rich man's daughter. How very lucky she had been. She took a deep breath.

Maisie wanted to move on, to the day that Charlotte left her father's house. She must balance her undertaking to bring back Joseph Waite's daughter to him with her need to solve the murders of three women. The other members of Charlotte's coterie.

"Miss Waite. Charlotte, if I may. Perhaps you could explain to me the connection between the feelings you describe, and what happened on the day you left your father's house."

Charlotte sniffed, and dabbed at her nose. Maisie watched her carefully, mistrusting the volatility of the other woman's emotional state. *She's on her guard again.*

"Frankly, I was fed up with being in my father's house. I had wanted to leave for years, but he wouldn't support me unless I remained under his roof."

Maisie bristled at Charlotte's words of entitlement. *Remain dispassionate.* Maurice's teaching echoed in her mind. This case was challenging Maisie at every turn.

"Support you, Miss Waite?"

"Well, it would never do, would it? The daughter of Joseph Waite living alone and working."

"Hmmm. Yes," said Maisie, in a manner she hoped would encourage Charlotte to continue. She could feel Dame Constance watching her now, and suspected that she had intuited her thoughts and understood her dilemma.

"Anyway, life had become difficult. Breakfast was the last straw."

"Did you have an argument with your father?"

"No, we didn't say a word to each other, except 'Good morning.' Perhaps it would have been better if we'd argued. At least it would have meant he noticed me."

"Go on, Charlotte."

Charlotte breathed in deeply. "I sat down, opened the newspaper and read that an old friend had . . ."

"Been murdered."

"How did you know?"

"It's my job, Miss Waite."

"You knew that I had been upset by reading of Philippa's death?"

"I suspected it. But why did you leave your father's home? What did you fear?"

Charlotte swallowed. "I hadn't actually seen her for a long time, not since the war. If I had told my father about her death, he would have thought my distress unwarranted."

"Is that all?"

"Yes."

*She's lying,* thought Maisie, who continued to press her subject, as far as she dare. "Was there another reason for your departure? You said that relations between you and your father had been trouble-some for a while."

"All my life!" Charlotte was vehement.

"Yes, I realize that. It must have been very difficult for you. But you seemed to suggest that relations with your father had been more difficult than usual."

Charlotte stared at Maisie, as if trying to guess how much she already knew, then relented. "Another friend had died several weeks earlier. She . . . had taken her own life. We hadn't been in touch since the war either, and I only knew because I read about it in the obituary column of *The Times.* In fact, I didn't know at first that she'd . . . done it herself. I found out later when I telephoned the family to offer my condolences."

"I see. And your father?"

"Wouldn't let me attend the memorial service. Forbade it. Of course, she didn't have a funeral, not a proper one, because the church doesn't permit funerals for suicides."

"And why do you think he forbade you to attend?"

"Oh, probably because I had known her so long ago, and I . . . I get upset."

"Is there anything else, Charlotte? Any other reason?"

"No."

*Too quick. Too quick to answer.*

"How did you first become acquainted with these two friends, Philippa and . . . ?"

"Rosamund." Charlotte picked at a hangnail. "We knew each other ages ago, first at school, then during the war," she replied, dismissively.

Her manner was not lost on Maisie, who pushed for a more concrete answer.

"What did you do during the war, together?"

"I can't remember now. It was so long ago."

Maisie watched as Charlotte Waite rubbed her hands together, in an effort to disguise their shaking.

"So, your father disliked two of your friends. And what did he think of Lydia Fisher."

Charlotte jumped up from her chair. "How do you know Lydia? Oh, my God, you knew all the time, didn't you?"

"Sit down, Miss Waite. Take a deep breath and be calm. I am not here to antagonize you or to harm you. I am simply searching for the truth." Maisie turned briefly to the grille and saw Dame Constance raise an eyebrow. *I'm on shaky ground, but she'll let me press on. For now.*

Charlotte took a seat once again.

"What's Lydia got to do with this?"

"You won't have seen the papers, Charlotte, but Lydia Fisher is dead."

"Oh, no! *No!*" It seemed to be an outcry of genuine surprise.

"And her husband, Magnus, has been arrested for the murders of both Philippa and Lydia."

"Magnus?"

"You seem surprised."

Charlotte Waite's throat muscles were taut. "But he hadn't seen Rosamund since school!"

"Rosamund? I thought she took her own life?"

Charlotte hid her face in her hands. Dame Constance cleared her throat, but Maisie tried for one last answer.

"Charlotte!" The tone of Maisie's voice made her look up. Tears were running down her face. "Charlotte, tell me—why was a white feather left close to each of the victims?"

Charlotte Waite broke down completely.

"Stop! This must stop now!" said Dame Constance, her voice raised. The door to the sitting room opened, and two novices helped Charlotte from the room.

Maisie closed her eyes and breathed deeply to steady her heartbeat.

"So, that is how you work, Maisie Dobbs?"

"When I have to. Yes, it is, Dame Constance."

Dame Constance tapped the desk in front of her and thought for a moment. Then she surprised Maisie.

"She'll get over this interlude," she sighed. "And it is evident even to me that she is withholding information. That, however, is her prerogative."

"But—"

"No buts, Maisie. Your questioning was not what I had expected."

"Perhaps I could have been kinder."

"Yes, perhaps you could." Dame Constance was thoughtful. "However, you might have rendered me a service, not that it excuses your manner with Charlotte." She sighed again and explained. "To rebuild a relationship means first confession, which is best spoken aloud to one who hears. There is a confession to be spoken here and you managed to lead her to the edge of the fire, though Charlotte is clearly afraid of the heat."

"That's one way of putting it, Dame Constance." Maisie thought for a minute. "Look, I know I pushed rather hard, but three women have been murdered, and an innocent man has been arrested. And Charlotte. . . ."

"Holds the key."

"Yes."

"I will advise her to speak with you again, but not before she has recovered. Maisie, I must have your word that you will not conduct your next interview in such a hostile manner. I remain deeply disappointed in you."

"Dame Constance, I would be most grateful if you would urge Miss Waite to speak to me again. I give my word that I will be more considerate of Miss Waite's sensibility when we meet. But . . . time is of the essence."

Dame Constance nodded, and when the sliding door behind the grille closed, Maisie stood to leave.

A postulant entered the room with Maisie's dry mackintosh, hat, and gloves, which she donned before returning to the MG. As the engine stuttered into life, Maisie hit the steering wheel with her hand. "Damn!" she said.

# CHAPTER EIGHTEEN

aisie was already at her desk when Billy arrived on Friday morning. Much work had to be completed on several cases, and two potential new clients who had come to the office during her absence had to be discussed.

"You've been working long hours, Billy."

"Takes my mind off it."

"Leg been bad this week?"

"Just nags away at me all the time now. And I've bin good, Miss. On the straight and narrow."

Billy's eyes seemed to be framed with circles as dark as her own. If only he would go to Chelstone soon.

"Have you given thought to my proposal?"

"Well, Doreen and me 'ave talked about it and all. Of course we're worried about the money."

"I've given you my assurance, Billy."

"I know, I know, Miss. But, I feel sort of, oh, I dunno. . . ."

"Vulnerable?"

"Sounds about right."

"Billy, that's to be expected. I cannot tell you how much your help with my father means to me. Having someone I trust to be with him, and to assist with the horses—he'll make himself ill worrying about them otherwise. And I know your leg bothers you, so one of the farmworkers will take on the really heavy work. Dad's doing very well. He'll be out of the wheelchair by the time he comes back to Chelstone, and we'll set up a bed downstairs at the cottage. You won't have to do any lifting."

"Be like two old peg legs together, won't we?"

"Oh, come on now, you'll see—you'll come back with all fires blazing. I've heard that Maurice's friend, Gideon Brown, is an amazing man and has worked wonders with wounded and injured people. Plus you'll be outdoors, in the fresh air. . . ."

"And well away from temptation, eh, Miss?"

Maisie sighed. "Yes, Billy. That's another thing."

Billy nodded. "Awright, then. Awright, I'll go, but not until this business with Miss Waite and them women is closed. I can't leave work 'alf done."

"Right you are, Billy." Maisie acquiesced. "And is there anything else?"

Billy looked at Maisie in earnest. "Can Doreen and the nippers come down?"

"Of course they can. It isn't prison, you know. In fact, if she wants, I think Doreen could get work from Lady Rowan."

"Oh, she'd like that."

"Yes, apparently Lady Rowan has been so preoccupied with the mare and foal, that she is 'behind'—as she puts it—with preparing for her return to London. She wants to have several gowns altered rather than buy new ones, so I told her about Doreen."

"You should get a job down the labor exchange, Miss. You'd 'ave everyone in work and off them lines in next to no time."

Maisie laughed. "Come on, let's get cracking. I want to see where we are with everything that's happened while I've been away. We should leave here by ten. And we'll continue this afternoon as soon as we're back. Also, I'll need to speak to Detective Inspector Stratton later today."

"T' see whether Fisher has spilled the beans?"

"Yes, in a way. Though I think the only beans Fisher has to spill concern his wife's drinking and his gambling debts. But the newspapers are having a field day with him."

"All over him like a rash, Miss. Feel a bit sorry for him, I do."

"You should. I would bet my business on his innocence."

Quite deliberately, Maisie had not discussed her latest news on the Waite case in detail with Billy. Though she wanted to work on the case map as an artist would an unfinished canvas, she also knew the value of letting facts, thoughts, observations and feelings simmer. In the hours of driving that followed her meeting with Charlotte Waite, Maisie had concluded that the only person who was at risk now was Charlotte. A plan had begun to form in Maisie's mind. Execution of that plan would depend upon Charlotte.

At ten o'clock on the dot, just as they were about to leave for the appointment with Joseph Waite, the telephone rang.

"Always the way, innit?"

"You can say that again." Maisie reached for the receiver and gave the number.

"May I speak to Miss Maisie Dobbs?"

"Speaking."

"Ah, Miss Dobbs. My name is Reverend Sneath, from the village of Lower Camden. I have an important message for you from Dame Constance at Camden Abbey. I visited her earlier today, and she asked me to telephone you as a matter of some urgency as soon as I returned to the vicarage."

"What is the message, Reverend Sneath?" Maisie was filled with dread. Seeing her complexion change, Billy moved closer to the desk.

"I'll read it out to you, so I don't miss a thing."

Maisie bit her lip as she listened to the rustle of paper, the message being unfolded. The reverend cleared his throat. "Dear Maisie. Miss Waite has left Camden Abbey. She went to her cell immediately after your meeting with her yesterday, and did not join us for our meals or for our devotions, as is her practice. I gave instructions for a food tray to be left for her, and when it was discovered untouched this morning we searched the abbey to no avail. I fear that yesterday's distressing events have weighed heavily on her. I have not informed the authorities as Miss Waite is not a member of the community. However, I am concerned for her well-being. Do all that you can to find her, Maisie. I need not remind you that her safety is your responsibility. We will hold you and Miss Waite in our prayers."

"Oh God." Maisie slumped into her chair.

"Yes, quite."

"Thank you. Reverend Sneath. Please destroy the message. And would you be so kind as to get word to Dame Constance that I will be in touch as soon as I have located Miss Waite."

"Of course. Good day to you, Miss Dobbs." The line clicked.

"She's run away again, Billy." Maisie's hand was still on the receiver, as if willing the telephone to ring with news of Charlotte.

"Oh blimey! Now what're we goin' t' tell ol' Waite?"

"Nothing. I don't want to alarm Waite until we've made inquiries. For now we'll carry on as if we know where she is. But we have to find her—and pretty sharpish. Come on, let's get going. We can talk about it in the car."

Maisie and Billy exchanged ideas throughout the journey to Dulwich, until Maisie put a stop to their speculation. "Let's give this problem some air. Now we've speculated back and forth, let's allow some room for inspiration."

"Awright, Miss. Let the ideas come to us instead of chasing them."

"Exactly." Maisie spoke as forcefully as she could but was unable to escape the dread that pulled at her stomach. Where was Charlotte Waite now?

Once again, Maisie was required to park "nose out" at the Waite mansion and, once again, after being most cordially greeted by Harris, the calm was broken by the entrance of Miss Arthur, Joseph Waite's secretary, clutching her files.

"Oh, Miss Dobbs, Miss Dobbs, Miss Dobbs. I tried to telephone you, but your line was engaged, and then when I telephoned a second time, there was no answer. I'm sorry, I'm sorry, I'm sorry." Miss Arthur reminded Maisie of a startled hen, with her arms flapping. Maisie raised her hand, as if to smooth the other woman's ruffled feathers.

"What is wrong, Miss Arthur?"

"It's Mr. Waite." Miss Arthur ushered Maisie and Billy into her wood-paneled office neighboring the entrance hall. "Of course, he sends apologies, many apologies, but he has been . . . called away urgently . . . on a business matter."

Miss Arthur was not a practiced liar, Maisie noted. She frowned. "I see."

"I tried to reach you, but I expect you had already left," the flustered secretary continued.

"Not to worry, Miss Arthur. Of course I have much to report to him."

"Yes, yes, he expected that. He asked me to attend immediately to any interim bills you may wish to submit. For your services."

"That is very kind." Maisie turned to Billy, who handed her a brown envelope, which she in turn handed to Miss Arthur. "Perhaps I can make an appointment for next week?"

"Indeed, Miss Dobbs." Miss Arthur stepped quickly to the other side of her desk, reached into a drawer and pulled out a checkbook and ledger. She glanced briefly at the bill, and commenced writing a check while still speaking to Maisie. "In fact Mr. Waite said to let you know that he's reviewed your previous conversations and he's satisfied with your progress. He trusts that you will be bringing Miss Waite back to the house in the fullness of time."

"A bit of an about-turn, Miss Arthur?" Maisie was suspicious of the fact that both Charlotte *and* her father were eluding further confrontation by her. A coincidence? Or by design?

Miss Arthur did not respond as she continued to sign the check in her small, rounded hand. She slipped the check into an envelope that she passed to Maisie; then she looked down to complete the ledger entry before reaching for a substantial desk diary. "Let me look at his diary. How about next Wednesday? At noon?"

Maisie nodded at Billy, who noted the time on an index card.

"Perhaps you would be so kind as to inform Mr. Waite that I expect to be in a position to make arrangements for Miss Waite's return very soon."

"I understand, Miss Dobbs. We are all very anxious to see her back home."

"Yes." Maisie looked sharply at Miss Arthur, who seemed intent on shuffling the papers on her desk. She had always thought that Miss Arthur, along with the other members of Joseph Waite's household, dreaded Charlotte's return. What was the secretary keeping from her? Was Charlotte already in the house? Had Waite located his daughter and dragged her home? But, if so, why conceal her whereabouts from Maisie?

"I'll summon Harris to show you out."

"Thank you, Miss Arthur."

Maisie and Billy were almost at the door when Maisie turned to the butler. "Is Mrs. Willis available? I just want to see her for a moment."

"She's taken an afternoon off, Miss. Mind you, she may still be in her quarters. Shall I summon her?"

"Oh no, I'll quickly knock on her door, if that's all right. I saw her at the bus stop in Richmond recently, and wanted to offer her the occasional lift." Maisie began to move as she spoke, which she knew would subtly pressure the butler into acquiescing.

"Of course, M'um. Follow me."

"Billy, wait for me in the car, won't you?"

Billy hid his surprise. "Right you are, Miss."

Maisie was escorted along a corridor that led first to a staircase giving access to the lower floor, then, once downstairs, continued to the side of the house. The property's design, though intended to give the impression of an older architectural style, was actually modern. The staircase leading to the kitchens was wide and airy, the apartments for senior staff spacious. This house had been designed to give owner and servants alike a measure of comfort unknown in times past.

Harris knocked on an eggshell-gloss-painted door. "Mrs. Willis? Visitor for you."

Maisie could hear movement inside; then the door opened to reveal the housekeeper, who was patting the sides of her head to calm any stray locks of hair. She wore a light amethyst woolen day dress, with a narrow white collar and cuffs, and was still kneading the leather of one of her black shoes with her heel in an attempt to get it on her foot without having to stoop in front of her visitor.

"Oh, this is a surprise."

"I'm sorry to disturb you, Mrs. Willis." Maisie turned to Harris. "Thank you for showing me the way." He bowed and left, as Maisie turned again to Mrs. Willis.

"May I come in?"

"Of course, of course. I am sorry. I don't get visitors, so do pardon me not being ready to receive a guest." Mrs. Willis beckoned Maisie to follow her into the immaculate sitting room. A small settee and matching armchair were positioned to face the fireplace and a gate-leg table, one flap folded to fit neatly into the limited space, was placed near the wall, the highly polished wood reflecting a vase full of daffodils that stood on a lace doily. A series of photographs sat on the sideboard by the window, which offered a pleasing view to the gardens at the side of the house.

"May I offer you refreshment, Miss Dobbs?"

"No, thank you, Mrs. Willis."

"Do sit down. I expect you've come to make arrangements for Miss Waite coming home."

"Actually, Mrs. Willis, I came to see you."

The woman looked across at Maisie, her eyes wide. "Me, Miss Dobbs?"

"Yes. I hope this isn't a cheek, but I saw you in Richmond last time I visited a dear friend. He's being cared for in the same home as your son."

"Oh, I am sorry, Miss Dobbs. Was he your sweetheart?"

Maisie was a little surprised by the forthright question. But such an observation might be expected, as there were many women of Maisie's age who had remained spinsters, their loved ones lost to war. "Well, yes. Yes, he was, but it was a long time ago, now."

"Hard to forget though, isn't it?" Mrs. Willis sat opposite Maisie.

Maisie cleared her throat. "Yes, sometimes. But look, Mrs. Willis, I just wanted to say that if I can give you a lift, you must let me know."

"That's very kind of you, but—"

"I don't go there every week, but I can telephone first to see if you would like a lift when I am planning to visit, if you like."

"Well, Miss, I can't put you to any trouble. Really I can't."

"It's no trouble at all. And if you should see my motor car outside when you're visiting, do wait for me to bring you home."

"All right, Miss Dobbs. I'll do that." The housekeeper smiled at Maisie.

She won't ask for help. Ever, thought Maisie.

Suddenly, a clatter at the window caused Maisie to gasp. Mrs. Willis stood. "Here they come, after their lunch!"

"What on earth is that noise? It frightened the life out of me."

"It's just the doves, Miss Dobbs. Always after a bit extra, always. It's lunchtime; they know who's a soft touch and where they can get a tid-bit or two." The housekeeper took the lid off a brown-striped earthenware biscuit barrel set on the mantelpiece, selected a biscuit, and walked to the window. Maisie followed, and watched as she leaned over the sideboard and lifted the sash window to reveal a dozen or more doves sitting on the windowsill.

"There you are, you little beggars. Eat up, because that's all you're getting today!" Mrs. Willis crumbled the biscuit onto the windowsill.

Maisie laughed to see the birds jostle for position, pushing and shoving in an effort to get more.

"You watch, they'll try upstairs next."

"Why, who else feeds them?"

"Oh. Mr. Waite. He's a soft one, if ever there was. He pays all the bills for my son's care, you know. His bark is far worse than his bite, as they say."

As if drawn by the unheard signal of a mystical piper, the doves swept up and away from the windowsill, taking to the air in a cloud of wings. Maisie watched as they flew up, while Mrs. Willis closed the window very slowly. And for a moment it seemed to Maisie as if time were faltering yet still moving forward, for in their wake the doves discarded dozens and dozens of tiny, perfect white feathers, each one zigzagging down, borne on a light breeze, until it fell onto the freshly cut lawn, or fluttered against the windowpane like snow.

"Oh dear, are you one of those people who doesn't like birds?" asked Mrs. Willis.

"No, not at all." Maisie turned back into the room, and regained her composure. "Mind you, my assistant doesn't care for them."

"Why ever not? They're so beautiful."

"Yes, they are, aren't they? I don't know why he doesn't like them. I must make a point of asking him." Maisie looked at her watch. "I really should be going now, Mrs. Willis. Don't forget to ask if you need a lift."

"That's very kind of you, Miss Dobbs." Mrs. Willis walked Maisie to the door, which she opened for her. "Will we be seeing Miss Waite home soon?"

"Yes you will. Probably in the next week."

"That's very good news, very good. The sooner she's back home, the better. Let me show you the way."

Maisie allowed Mrs. Willis to escort her to the front door. It would not have been correct for a guest to be left to find her own way out, especially in the mansion of Joseph Waite. At the door, she bade farewell to Mrs. Willis again. Then, as she reached the bottom of the front steps and heard the door closed behind her, Maisie set a course for the corner of the house where the front garden looped around. She heard Billy rushing to catch up.

"Don't run, Billy! For goodness' sake, spare your leg and your lungs!"

Billy came alongside. "What was all that about, Miss? The little chat with Mrs. Willis?"

"Initially just doing a favor. But now I don't know."

"Not followin' ya, Miss."

"I'll explain later." Maisie reached the corner of the house and looked first toward the outer windowsill of Mrs. Willis rooms, then up to the windows above.

"Aw, them bleedin' birds!"

"Don't worry, Billy, they're not interested in you," said Maisie, her attention on the window as she watched a hand reach out to sprinkle more crumbs for the hungry doves. It was a broad hand, a hand that Maisie could easily recognize from the ground, helped by the sun which broke through the clouds at just the right moment to catch the light reflected by a gold ring encrusted with diamonds.

"See anything interestin', Miss?"

"Oh yes, Billy. Very interesting. Very interesting indeed."

Billy seemed relieved to be inside the car again and on his way back into London.

"Shall we talk about Charlotte Waite's possible whereabouts?"

"No. Wait until we get back to the office. We need to get our heads really clear. First, tell me why you don't like doves or pigeons. Does your dislike extend to all birds?" Maisie pulled out into the middle of the road to pass a rag-and-bone man, his horse clip-clopping along as if it knew instinctively that it had been a bad day for business.

"Aw, Miss, it don't make sense, not really. I mean, it ain't the bird's fault, is it?"

"What isn't the bird's fault?"

"Nah, Miss. Can't tell y'. It'll make you think I'm a few coals shy of a load, it will. S' all a bit silly, all a bit in me 'ead, as you would say."

"I don't think I'd say anything of the sort." Maisie pulled over to the side of the road and stopped, allowing the engine to idle as she turned to him. "Spill the beans, Billy. Why do you hate birds?" She had a distinct feeling that, with his "silly" feelings, Billy might have something for her to consider.

He sighed. "S'pose I'm gonna 'ave to tell you, ain't I?"

"I suppose you are."

"And you ain't gonna move this jam jar till I do, are you?"

"Absolutely right."

He sighed again. "Well, it in't all that stupid, now I know a bit more about what goes on up 'ere, from working wiv you." Billy tapped the side of his head. "But . . . I don't like 'em because of the war, and even thinkin' about it makes me leg get bad again." Billy rubbed his leg.

"What's your leg got to go with it?"

"Well, y' see, I didn't enlist straightaway. There was only me and me brother, both workin' for me dad. Not like we came from one of them big families, not like there was ten of us and if one went there was always a few left. Anyway, I was going to join up, but me mum didn't like it, though I thought I should do my bit. But you know what it's like when you keep meanin' t' do something. . . ."

Maisie nodded. *You're rambling, Billy.*

"Then one day, I decided that there was no time like the present, so I went down and got meself enlisted. Me mum, when I told 'er, aw you should've 'eard 'er go on, and on, and on. At least me brother was too young to go, so she'd still 'ave 'im at 'ome. Anyway, I 'ad a few days at 'ome before I 'ad to report for duty, so me and me little brother, fifteen at the time, 'e was, went out for a bit of a laugh one afternoon. I didn't 'ave a uniform yet, in fact, let me tell you, even after I was at the barracks in Colchester, I never 'ad a uniform for three weeks. They were enlistin' so many at once, they'd run out of uniforms. Run out of uniforms? I tell you, it's no wonder we 'ad trouble over there. No wonder."

Billy shook his head, while Maisie waited for his story to unfold.

"Gawd, seems I was like an old man already, but I was only eighteen. Anyway, there we were, walking down the street, when this young lady comes up to us, all smiles. Then she 'ands me and 'im a feather each, and tells us we should be in uniform, and—"

"Oh my God!" Maisie gasped. "It was there all the time, only I couldn't see it!"

Maisie pushed the car into gear, looked over her shoulder, and pulled out onto the road.

"See what, Miss?"

"I'll tell you later, Billy. Keep on with your story."

Billy was silent.

"It's all right, Billy, I'm still listening." Maisie pressed down on the accelerator to gain speed.

"Well, it's them feathers. Sign of cowardice, ain't they? I mean, I was signed on anyway, so it didn't bother me, did it? Water off a duck's back. But not Bobby, oh no, 'e was only a youngster. Couldn't wait to be a man. And o' course, nice young woman comes along, calls 'im a coward, what does 'e do, eh? Goes an' enlists on the sly, just after I left."

Maisie blushed, remembering the lies she told about her age in order to enlist for nursing service, and her father's furious frustration at her actions.

"Me mum does 'er pieces, me father went mad, and all the time, I'm runnin' around takin' orders from 'igher-ups who didn't know much more than I did."

Suddenly, Maisie slowed the car, her speed checked by the cold chill of realization. "What happened to your brother, Billy?" She looked sideways at him, her hands clutching the steering wheel.

Billy looked out of the passenger window.

"Copped it, didn't 'e. Silly little bugger. Sixteen years of age, and pushin' up daisies in a place where 'e couldn't even talk the lingo. All because of a bleedin' feather."

"Why ever didn't you tell me all this?"

"S'long time ago, ain't it, Miss? Mind you, it seems that every time I see a bird, you know, *look* at a bird, well, the stupid animal seems to drop a feather or two, just as they're flappin' their wings t' get away, and every time I see a feather, I see our Bobby with the feather between 'is fingers, runnin' after me, sayin', 'She called me a coward. Did you 'ear that? Eh, Billy? She called me a *coward*! Now everyone'll think I'm not up to it!' But 'e weren't no coward. Sixteen, and gave 'is life."

Billy rubbed at his legs again. Maisie let the silence linger. *I must get him to Chelstone as soon as I can.*

"Billy, Billy, I am so very sorry."

"Named my boy after 'im, I did. Just 'ope there won't be any more wars, in case I lose 'im. My biggest fear, that is, Miss. That there'll be another war, when 'e's enlistin' age."

Maisie nodded, fearfully.

"So what's all this about, then? Y'know, what you couldn't see when it was there all the time."

# CHAPTER NINETEEN

aisie picked up the telephone to place a call to
Scotland Yard as soon as she and Billy returned to
the office.

"My old mum always used to say that the best place to 'ide a thing
was in plain view. She'd say that when I gave up me wage packet of a
Friday night. She'd take the money, stick it in a pot on the table, and
then give me a couple o' bob back for meself. P'raps Miss Waite is 'iding
somewhere in plain view?"

Maisie held up her hand for silence as her call was answered.

"Inspector, I wonder if we might meet to discuss the Sedgewick-
Fisher case? I have some information that might be of interest to you."

Maisie heard an audible sigh.

"Is it regarding Mr. Fisher?"

"Well . . . no, no, not directly."

"Miss Dobbs, we are convinced we have the right man."

Maisie closed her eyes. She must tread carefully. "I've made some
observations that may be useful to you."

Another sigh, augmented by the sound of voices in the background.
Would this telephone call to Stratton be fodder for mirth among the

men of Scotland Yard's Murder Squad? It was a risk she would have to take. She could not withhold evidence from them once she was convinced of its importance. If the police refused to listen, that was quite another matter.

"Look, Miss Dobbs, I am grateful for any and all information. Obviously in my position I can hardly say otherwise, and if your information concerns Fisher, I would be more than delighted to have it. But the point is that we find that investigating many so-called leads wastes valuable time when we already have the killer."

"You've taken an innocent man into custody, and you should hear me out!"

"I say, Miss Dobbs, now just you wait a minute!"

"But Inspector, another perspective might—"

"All right, Miss Dobbs." Stratton sounded exasperated, but Maisie knew she had appealed to his sense of duty. "Meet me at the caffy on the corner of Oxford Street and Tottenham Court Road in—let me see— half-an-hour. "

"Thank you, Inspector Stratton. I know exactly where you mean—diagonally opposite Waite's International Stores."

"That's it. See you in half-an-hour."

"Until then."

Maisie replaced the receiver and blew a gust of breath between lips rounded into an O.

"Bit frosty, was 'e, eh, Miss?"

"More than a bit. And I've got to be careful too. In providing Stratton with information, I risk undermining him or antagonizing him further. After all, if he chooses to listen, he's the one who has to return to The Yard and retract the accusations against Magnus Fisher. I need to keep him as an ally."

"What's wrong wiv 'im, then?"

Maisie took the folded linen handkerchief from her case and walked to the table where the case map had already been unfurled and pinned ready for work. She motioned for Billy to join her.

"He's let two things get in the way, I think: His personal history and his standing in the department. Of course, he has to be careful, because if I were to take a bet on it—"

"And we know you're not the bettin' type." Billy smiled at her.

"No, but if I were, I'd wager that Caldwell is after the Detective Inspector's job, and is making Stratton's life a misery while he's nipping at his heels. So Stratton has to be careful in terms of who he is seen taking information from."

"What's 'is personal history, then?"

Maisie leaned over the map, and unfolded the handkerchief. "Well, he's a widower. His wife died in childbirth about five years ago, leaving him to bring up his son alone."

Billy scrunched up his face, "Aw, blimey, Miss. Tha's terrible. Wish you 'adn't've told me that. Now I'm gonna think about it every time I see the man." He leaned forward. "What've you got there?"

"Feathers. Tiny white feathers. The ones I collected during my investigation. I found one feather for each woman. Two were close to where the victims had been sitting just prior to meeting the murderer. In Rosamund Thorpe's case, the feather was in the pocket of the dress she was wearing when she died."

"Ugh." Billy shuddered.

"They can't hurt you. The women who gave them out in the war are the ones who did the harm."

Billy watched as Maisie placed the feathers on the case map, using a smudge of paste to secure each one to the paper.

"Do you know who the killer is, Miss?"

"No, Billy, I don't"

Billy looked sideways at Maisie and refleced for a moment. "But you've got an idea. I can see it there."

"Yes, yes, I have, Billy. I do have an idea. But it's just an idea. Right now we've got our work cut out for us. We must find Charlotte Waite. Here's what I want you to do—"

Billy flipped open his notebook ready to list his instructions as Maisie closed her eyes and ran though a catalog of possibilities: "An animal will make for its lair if in fear or wounded. Mind you,

Charlotte may have no reason to fear, she may just want to get away, to escape from being Joseph Waite's daughter. We have to consider that she may have fled to Europe, after all, she's familiar with Lucerne and Paris. See if you can check the passenger list for the boat-train. Charlotte might have traveled from Appledore station on the branch line to Ashford, or she may have come to London first. There are one hundred ways she could have traveled. Check with Croydon Aerodrome and Imperial Airways—oh, and there's an aerodrome in Kent, at Lympne. Check as many hotels in London as you can—but don't start with the big ones. Contact the hotels that are neither too posh nor too shabby. Telephone Gerald Bartrup. No, *visit* Bartrup. I want you to look at him when you ask him if he's seen Charlotte in the past twenty-four hours. Pay attention, Billy, with your body as well as your eyes. You'll know if he's lying."

The list was long and Billy would be hard at work until late. Maisie wondered if Charlotte had funds that were known only to her, squirreled away into a private account. Where had she gone? *Where was she now?*

Though their conversation was sometimes strained, Maisie looked forward to her meeting with Detective Inspector Stratton. She knew that he admired her and was taking tentative steps to further their acquaintance. But how prudent would it be to agree to such an outing? Would her work and her reputation be put at risk by a closer friendship?

Stratton stood outside the cafeteria where Maisie joined him after walking down Tottenham Court Road from Fitzroy Square. He lifted his hat and opened the door for Maisie.

"There's a seat over there. This place is definitely more *caff* than *café*, but it's quick. Tea, toast, and jam?"

"Lovely, Inspector Stratton." It was at that point, that Maisie realized that she hadn't eaten since breakfast.

Maisie sat on a bench by a wall decorated with floral wallpaper that was now quite faded and stained in places. She unbuttoned her jacket and looked out of the window while she waited for Stratton, who was at the counter placing cups of tea and a plate of toast and jam on a tray. She craned her neck to watch customers going in and out of Joseph Waite's double-fronted grocery shop across the road. *And they say there's no money about!*

"Here we are." Stratton set the tray down on the table, pulled out the chair opposite Maisie, and sat down. "You could stand a spoon up in that tea. They make it strong here."

"Stewed tea, fresh from the urn—nothing like it, Inspector. It's what kept us going over in France."

"Yes, and there's been many a time when a flask of that stuff has sustained me when I've had to work all night, I can tell you. Let's get down to business. I didn't come here to discuss the tea. What have you come across, Miss Dobbs? I know you did some snooping around when you found Lydia Fisher's body."

"Lydia was a friend of Charlotte Waite. I had been asked by Joseph Waite to locate his daughter, who had left her father's home temporarily. He is my client." Maisie reached for a triangular wedge of toast. She was ravenous and quickly took a bite, then dabbed at the sides of her mouth with a handkerchief. This was not the kind of establishment where table napkins were supplied.

Stratton raised an eyebrow. "Not much to get your teeth into, a missing debutante, if you don't mind me saying so, Miss. Dobbs." Stratton reached for a slice of toast.

"But enough to pay for my own office, an assistant, and a nippy little motor car, Inspector," replied Maisie, her eyes flashing.

Stratton smiled. "I deserved that one, didn't I?"

Maisie inclined her head.

"So, let's get down to brass tacks. What have you got to tell me?"

"Lydia Fisher and Philippa Sedgewick were friends."

"I know that!"

"As was Rosamund Thorpe, of Hastings."

"Who is?"

"Dead. She is thought to have committed suicide some weeks before Mrs. Sedgewick was murdered."

"And this has . . . what to do with your investigation or our murder inquiry?"

"They were all friends once, the three dead women and Charlotte Waite. A coterie, if you like."

"So?"

Maisie appraised Stratton before speaking again. *He's being deliberately obtuse.*

"Detective Inspector Stratton, people who knew Rosamund Thorpe cannot believe she took her own life. Also, the four former friends seemed to have made a point of avoiding one another. I think they were kept apart by shame. During the war, I believe they distributed white feathers to men who were not in uniform."

"Oh, those terrible women!"

"And . . ." Maisie halted. *Shall I tell him about the feathers I found? Will I be mocked?* "And . . . I believe that Magnus Fisher did not kill his wife or Philippa Sedgewick. The person you seek is someone—"

"We have our man!"

"Inspector, why are you so . . . so . . . quick to send Fisher down?"

"I'm not at liberty to say."

"The public wants a murderer behind bars, and you—you and Caldwell—have decided to give them one."

Stratton sighed. "And we are right. It's an open-and-shut case."

Maisie clenched her fists in frustration. "And you can't stand a man who abandoned his wife, and whom you believe deprived a loving husband of his."

"Look here, Miss Dobbs, leave this sort of work to the professionals. I know you've had some luck in the past. You've helped us before when you worked for a man of some stature, but . . . do not interfere!" Stratton stood up. "I hope we can meet again under less strained circumstances."

As much as she wanted to have a last word, Maisie knew that she must not allow them to part with rancor. "Yes, indeed, Inspector. I am sorry if I have offended you. However, do expect to hear from me again soon."

Stratton left the cafeteria, as Maisie took her seat once again. *I should have known better. I shouldn't have lost control. I could see by the way he moved, the way he sat and the manner in which he spoke, that he was obdurate. I've told the police as much as they would hear. Should I have mentioned the feathers? No, he would have laughed.*

Maisie gathered her belongings and followed Stratton out.

She was ready to turn the corner into Tottenham Court Road, when she stopped to look back at the blue and gold-fronted Waite's International Stores. She changed direction and walked instead toward the entrance of Joseph Waite's most prominently situated grocery store.

Once again, when Maisie entered the hubbub of the shop, she watched as assistants reached forward to point to a cheese and nod, or hold up a cut of meat for inspection. Dried fruits were weighed, biscuits counted, and all the time money passed back and forth and shop assistants constantly washed their hands. Maisie stood in the center of the floor, near the round table with a display of the latest foods imported from overseas. Yes, there was money about, despite long lines at soup kitchens in other parts of London.

Maisie watched the busyness of business in Joseph Waite's domain. *Why have I come back? There is something here for me. What is it? What did I not see last time?* She looked up at the walls, at the intricate mosaics that must have cost a fortune. Then down at the polished wood floor and across at the boy whose job it was to walk back and forth with a broom, ensuring that Waite's customers never noticed so much as a crumb underfoot.

No one paid attention to the young, well-dressed woman who stood without a shopping bag, making no move toward a counter, and displaying no intention to purchase. Both shop assistants and customers were too preoccupied with their tasks and errands to see her close her eyes and place her hand where she could feel the beating of her heart. Just for a second, just for fleeting moment, Maisie gave herself over to her inner guidance in this most public place. Then, as if responding to a command that only she could hear, she opened her eyes and looked up at the place above the door, at the tiled memorial to the employees of Waite's International Stores. She allowed her eyes to rest on the tile dedicated to Waite's son, Joseph, beloved heir of a self-made man. A man known to be as hard as rock but at times also a man of compassion. A man of extremes. *Don't stop,* said a voice in her head. And Maisie obeyed. She read each name, starting from the beginning: Avery . . . Denman . . . Farnwell . . . Marchant . . . Nicholls . . . Peters . . . so many, oh, so *many* . . . Richards, Roberts . . . Simms, Simpson . . . Timmins . . . Unsworth . . . every letter in the alphabet was represented as she silently mouthed the names, like a teacher reviewing the class register. Then Maisie stopped reading. *Ah.* She closed her eyes. *Ah. Yes. Of course.*

Opening her eyes again, Maisie looked at each food counter until she saw one of the older members of staff. "Excuse me. I wonder if you could help me?"

"Yes, Madam, Of course. The sausages are fresh made this morning, by our very own butchers. Personally trained by Mr. Waite, they are. These are the best sausages in London."

"Oh, lovely, I'm sure. But could you tell me where I can find someone who worked for Waite's during the war? Someone who might have known the boys up there?" Maisie pointed to the memorial.

"But, Miss, there's names up there from all over. Mind you, old Mr. Jempson in the warehouse knew just about all of the London boys. Joined up together you know, as pals. Most of the boys who enlisted came from the warehouse; it's where the apprentices start, and where the butchering is done before the carcasses go out to the shops. Waite's delivers to its own shops with special ice-packed lorries, you know."

"Could you tell me where the warehouse is?"

"Across the water. In Rotherhithe, the 'Larder of London,' where all the warehouses are. Let me get a piece of paper and write down the directions for you. It's easy to find, close to St. Saviour's Docks, Madam. Relative, are you?"

"A friend."

"I see. Mr. Waite's own son was down at the warehouse, before he went over there. Started him at the bottom, did Mr. Waite. Said he had to work his way up like anyone else." The assistant left the counter and returned with a folded piece of paper, which she handed to Maisie. "There you are, Madam. Now then, what about some sausages for your supper?"

Maisie was about to decline, then thought otherwise. Smiling at the assistant, she gave her order. "Lovely. A pound, please."

"Right you are." And with a flourish copied directly from Joseph Waite, the assistant swept up a string of bulbous pork sausages, and laid them on the scale. The Beale family would eat well tonight.

"Stratton any easier to talk to this afternoon, Miss?"

"I wish I could say yes, Billy. It started out well enough, then became rather difficult."

"Funny, that. 'e always seemed such a reasonable bloke."

Maisie took off her mackintosh, hat, and gloves, and laid her document case and a brown carrier bag on her desk. "It'll settle down and we'll all be talking again after this case is closed, Billy. Men in Stratton's position can't close too many doors, especially those leading to people they've consulted with in the past. No, there are two struggles going on there: One in the department and one inside Stratton. As long as we are *seen* to be doing our part, I'm not going to worry." Maisie looked at her watch. "Oh, look at the time, Billy! It's almost half past four. Let's just go over some details on the Waite case and make plans for Monday. I'm driving down to Chelstone tomorrow morning first thing, and I must also visit my fath—"

Maisie was interrupted by the telephone.

"Fitzroy five —Miss Waite. Where are you. Are you all right?"

"Yes." The line crackled.

"Miss Waite? Miss Waite you may be in danger. Tell me where you are."

Silence.

"Miss Waite? Are you still there?"

"Yes, yes, I'm here."

"Well, can you speak up a bit, please? This is a terrible line."

"I'm in a telephone kiosk." Charlotte's voice was slightly louder.

"Why have you called me, Miss Waite?"

"I . . . I . . . need to speak to you."

"About what?" Maisie held her breath as she pushed Charlotte just a little.

"There's more to tell you. I didn't tell you . . . everything."

"Can you tell me now?"

Silence.

"Miss Waite?"

"I have to speak to you privately, in person."

"Where are you? I'll come right away."

Maisie thought she heard Charlotte crying; then there was silence but for the crackling telephone line.

"Miss Waite? Are we still connected?"

"Oh, it's no use. It's no use—"

There was a click and the line was dead. Maisie replaced the receiver. "Damn!"

Billy's eyes widened. "What was all that about, eh, Miss?"

"Charlotte Waite. She said she wanted to talk to me, then hung up the receiver saying it was 'no use.'"

"Lost 'er bottle, did she?"

"She certainly did. It was a bad line. She could have been anywhere. Mind you, there was noise in the background." Maisie closed her eyes as if to hear the entire call again. "What was that sound?"

"D'you still want me to do all this?" Billy held up the list.

"Yes. She could have been in Paris for all I know. Or outside an hotel on the Edgeware Road. But at least we know she's still alive. It's getting late, but you can make a start, and then get on with it again tomorrow morning."

"Right you are, Miss."

"I'll need to speak to Lady Rowan at Chelstone before I see my father, then I'll come back to London to continue the search for Charlotte Waite."

"How can 'er Ladyship help?"

Maisie turned to Billy. "She was involved in the suffrage movement before the war, and knows a lot about what different women's associations did. I could use more color on the page."

"I know, Miss."

Maisie looked up at Billy, walked over to her desk, and sighed. "Billy, give it another half an hour or so and then get on your way. It's been a long day—in fact, it's been a long week, and you'll have to put in quite a few hours tomorrow."

"Aw, thanks, Miss. I want to see the nippers before they go to bed."

"Oh, and Billy—here's something for you." Maisie held out the brown paper carrier bag.

"What's all this, Miss?"

"A pound of Waite's sausages. Best in London, they say."

*Shortly* after Billy began his evening journey back to Whitechapel, Maisie climbed into the MG, started the engine, and pulled out of Fitzroy Square. A telephone call had confirmed that Waite's warehouse in Rotherhithe remained open until late in the evening, while lorries bound for the shops were packed with the next day's deliveries. Mr. Jempson, the warehouse manager, was available and had kindly agreed to see Maisie as soon as she arrived.

Fog horns bellowed along the Thames as carriage drivers, motorists and barge captains alike made their way through the murky smog that once again began to shroud London. Maisie negotiated the MG along narrow roads that were almost lanes, byways that led from the docks to riverside warehouses. Following directions carefully, she eventually turned into a cobbled side street and drew up in front of a pair of open gates with a sign above in blue-and-gold lettering: WAITE'S INTERNATIONAL STORES. SOUTH-EASTERN WAREHOUSE. A guard in a blue-and-gold uniform waved from the gatehouse and came out to greet Maisie, a clipboard under his arm.

"Evening, Miss." He touched the peak of his blue cap. "Expected, are you?"

"Yes, I'm here to see Mr. Jempson, in the offices."

"Ah, of course, he telephoned through to put you on the list not long ago." The guard leaned down toward Maisie and pointed ahead, to an extensive courtyard illuminated by a lamp in each corner. "Don't park by the lorries, otherwise you'll have them drivers givin' me a row. Go over to where it says 'Visitors' and put the motor there. And, Miss, park nose out, if you don't mind."

*Nose out at the warehouse, too?* Maisie's countenance revealed her thoughts.

"It's the way Mr. Waite likes it, Miss." He smiled at Maisie. "You see that door there, the big wooden one? You go through there, up the stairs, and one of the clerks will be there at the top to meet you. I'll telephone to let them know you're on your way."

Maisie thanked the guard, noting that no expense seemed to have been spared even in equipping the warehouse. Having parked the MG following the guard's instructions to the letter, Maisie entered the granite building through the wooden door and was greeted at the top of the stairs by a young man in dark gray trousers, polished brogues, a crisp white shirt, and black tie, with armbands to keep his sleeves drawn away from his wrists. A freshly sharpened pencil protruded from behind his right ear.

"Evening, Miss Dobbs. My name's Smithers. Come this way to Mr. Jempson's office."

"Thank you."

Maisie was led to an office surrounded by windows that looked down onto the warehouse floor, the rich cherrywood frames and paneling gleaming under the glow of several lamps that illuminated the room.

"Thank you, Mr. Smithers."

Jempson held out his hand for Maisie to take a seat in the leather chair on the opposite side of the desk. It was obviously reserved for guests. A rather less comfortable chair was situated alongside.

"I am most grateful for your time, Mr. Jempson."

"How may I be of service to you?"

Maisie had to tread carefully. She already knew that Mr. Jempson's employer was held in great esteem by his staff

"I wonder if you could help me with a most delicate matter."

"I'll try." Jempson, a tall, thin man wearing an ensemble almost identical to his assistant's, looked over half-moon glasses at Maisie, on his guard.

Maisie relaxed into her chair, an adjustment that was mirrored by Jempson. *Good.* Sensing that the conversation might now proceed, Maisie envisioned the tiled memorial of names in Waite's International Stores, and began to ask the questions that had plagued her since the visit to Dulwich this morning.

Maisie took her leave from the warehouse an hour later. Mr. Jempson had indeed been most helpful. In fact, as he confessed while escorting her to the MG, "It's done me good to talk about it all. I saw them all go, and most of them never came back. Broke the boss's heart, it did. Couldn't do enough for the families either. Must be terrible for him. To be reminded of it every day, every day when you look into the eyes of your own daughter. It's a wonder he wants her back, if you ask me. Mind you, like I said upstairs, he had to keep her at home, after all that business with the windows being broken when he got her that flat on her own, after the war. Everyone loved Mr. Waite, but there's no love lost on his daughter or them harpies she was with. I wouldn't blame anyone who, you know, had lost someone. . . ."

Maisie placed a hand on his arm. "Thank you again, Mr. Jempson. Take good care, and don't worry, this conversation is in absolute confidence."

The man touched his forehead as Maisie left him to drive away into the thick darkness pierced by foghorns. Maisie did not go far. Parking close to the water, she remained in the motor car for some moments to review her plans. She would telephone Lady Rowan that evening, to ask if she might join her for a walk before breakfast. She knew that the older woman would have valuable insights to add to the evidence Maisie now had to hand. Her absolute priority was to find Charlotte. Was she ready to make a confession? Or was she in immediate danger?

Maisie shook her head, pulled her collar up, and stepped from the car. She walked along Bermondsey Wall and stopped to watch the thick smog which seemed to curdle above the water. A wall had originally been built to keep out floodwaters in the Middle Ages; as people walked on the wall to avoid the muddy ground, the wall became a road, but the name was never lost. Maisie stood in silence feeling as if she were caught in the mud, unable to move. Charlotte was lost, and it was her fault. The chain of foghorns up and down the Thames began their round of blasts again, and as they did so, Maisie closed her eyes. *Of course!* What was it that Billy had said to her? Just after she'd received the call from Reverend Sneath? Something about being hidden in plain view? While listening to Charlotte speaking from the telephone kiosk, she'd heard the foghorns from south of the river. Charlotte was somewhere right under her father's nose. She was close to the warehouse. But where?

The area was always teeming with people. It would be like finding a pebble lost on the beach. Sarson's Vinegar, Courage's Brewery, Crosse & Blackwell's tinned foods, the leatherworks, Peek Freans biscuit factory, the docks, warehouses receiving foods from all over the world—she could be anywhere in Bermondsey. Maisie knew that the journey to Kent could not be delayed, but she would return to London quickly. Charlotte might have chosen to call from an identifiable area deliberately to send them in the wrong direction. She needed a source of information in Bermondsey. Maisie smiled. *A Bermondsey boy. That's what I need.*

# CHAPTER TWENTY

*L*eaving London at the crack of dawn, Maisie arrived at
Chelstone early. The interior of the small cottage was cold
and not at all welcoming as it would have been if Frankie
Dobbs were at home. Maisie began opening curtains and windows to
let in shafts of early morning sunshine, and a breath of fresh air. The
rooms were neat and tidy, revealing regular attention from staff up at
the manor house. Frankie Dobbs was much loved at Chelstone. His
house had been well kept in anticipation of his return, but it lacked the
life that Frankie brought to his simple dwelling.

Maisie moved around the cottage, running her fingers across her
father's belongings, as if touching the leather traces kept in the
scullery awaiting repair, or his tools and brushes, brought him closer.
She made a list of things that required attention. A bed must be moved
into the small sitting room so that Frankie would not have to negotiate the stairs. A room must be prepared for Billy upstairs. She must
speak again with Maurice about plans for Billy's rehabilitation, in body,
mind, and soul. She knew her father's contribution to this part of Billy's
recovery was just as important, for Frankie was above all else a father,

and Billy would gain as much from him as he would from Maurice, Gideon Brown, or Dr. Andrew Dene.

Her task complete, she left the cottage to join Lady Rowan, who was in the distance striding as purposefully as she could across the lawns at the front of the manor.

Lady Rowan waved to Maisie with her walking stick and called out. "Good morning, Maisie," followed by, "Nutmeg, drop it! Drop it now and come here!"

Maisie laughed to see the dog come to his owner, tail between his legs, head down, and filled with remorse.

"This dog will eat anything, absolutely anything. How lovely to see you, my dear." Lady Rowan reached out and squeezed Maisie's upper arm. Though she held Maisie in great affection, Lady Rowan, restrained by considerations of position and place, had only once demonstrated her feelings. When Maisie returned from France, Lady Rowan had taken her in her arms and said, "I am so relieved, so very relieved that you are home." On that occasion Maisie was silent in her embrace, not knowing quite what to say.

"And it's lovely to see you, too, Lady Rowan," replied Maisie, placing her hand on top of Lady Rowan's for just a second.

"Now then, before we get down to business"—she glanced at Maisie as they began to walk together across the lawn—"because I know you're here on business, Maisie, what's the news about your dear father and the young man you're sending to help."

"Well, I'll see my father later, before I return to London. I've spoken to Dr. Simms, who thinks it'll be another week before he's transferred to the convalescent hospital. I think he'll be there for about three or four weeks, according to Dr. Dene, who says it might have been longer, but he's spoken to the doctors at Pembury, and my father is making excellent progress, even at this early stage. During that time Mr. Beale will look after the horses. Then, when Dad comes home to Chelstone, Mr. Beale will stay on at the cottage and work under his supervision."

"Which as we both know means that your father will be hobbling over to the stables each day even though he shouldn't."

"Probably, though I've told Mr. Beale to keep an eye on him."

Lady Rowan nodded. "I'll be so relieved when he's back in charge. Then I'll feel I can leave for Town."

"Yes, of course. Thank you, L—"

Lady Rowan held up her hand to silence Maisie, as they leaned toward each other to avoid the low branch of a majestic beech tree.

"What can *I* do for you, Maisie Dobbs?" Lady Rowan smiled at Maisie, a gleam in her eye.

"I want you to tell me what you know about the different women's affiliations in the war. I'm particularly interested in those women who handed out white feathers."

Lady Rowan blinked rapidly, the sparkle vanishing instantly. "Oh, those harpies!"

"Harpies." It was the second time in two days that Maisie had heard the term in connection with the women. And in her mind's eye she saw the illustrated flyleaf of a book that Maurice had given her to read, years ago. A short note had accompanied her assignment: "In learning about the myths and legends of old, we learn something of ourselves. Stories, Maisie, are never just stories. They contain fundamental truths about the human condition." The black-and-white charcoal drawing depicted birds with women's faces, birds carrying humans in their beaks as they flew away into the darkness. Maisie was jolted back to the present by Lady Rowan.

"Of course, you were either engrossed in your studies at Girton or away overseas doing something worthwhile, so you would have missed the Order of the White Feather." Lady Rowan slowed her pace, as if to allow memories to catch up with the present. "This was before conscription, and it was all started by that man, Admiral Charles Fitzgerald. After the the initial rush to enlist had fallen off, they needed more men at the front, so he obviously thought the way to get them there was through the women. I remember seeing the handbills starting to pop up all over the place." Lady Rowan mimicked a stern masculine voice: "Is your best boy in uniform yet?"

"Oh yes, I think I saw one at a railway station before I went into nursing."

"The plan was to get young women to go around giving the white feather—a sign of cowardice—to young men not in uniform. And—" she raised a pointed finger in emphasis. "And those two women—the *Scarlet Pimpernel* woman—what was her name? Oh yes, Orczy, the Hungarian baroness, well, she was a great supporter of Fitzgerald, and so was Mary Ward—Mrs. Humphrey Ward."

"You didn't care for her, did you?"

Lady Rowan pursed her lips. Maisie realized that she was so intent upon Lady Rowan's words that she had been ignoring the vista of the Weald of Kent around her. They had reached a gate and stile. If she had been alone, Maisie would have clambered over the stile with the same energy as the three dogs before her. Instead, she pulled back the rusty iron gate lock, and allowed Lady Rowan to walk through first.

"Frankly, no, I didn't." Lady Rowan continued. "She did a lot of very commendable work in bringing education to those who might not otherwise have had the opportunity, organizing children's play groups for working women, that sort of thing. But she was an anti-suffragist, so we were like oil and water. Of course she's long gone now, but she supported recruiting men for the trenches by this most horrible means, through the accusations of women. And as for the women themselves—"

"Yes, I'm interested in the women, the ones who gave out the white feathers."

"Ah yes." She sighed. "You know, I wondered about them at the time. What made them do it? What made young women say, 'Oh, yes, I'll do that. I'll walk the streets with my bag of white feathers, and I'll give one to each boy I see not in uniform, even though I don't know one jot about him!'"

"And what do you think, now that time has passed?"

Lady Rowan sighed and stopped to lean on her walking stick.

"Maisie, that question is more up your alley than mine, really. You know, the business of discovering why people do what they do."

"But?" Maisie encouraged Lady Rowan to speak her mind.

"When I think back, it's alarming, some of the things that came to pass. One minute the suffrage movement was seen as a tribe of marauding pariahs by the government, then, as soon as war was declared there was a division in our ranks. One lot became the darlings of Lloyd George, who persuaded women to release men to the battlefield by taking up their work until they returned home. The other half of our number went all out for peace, joining with women throughout Europe. Frankly, on an individual level, I think women needed to take part. We're all Boadiceas really." Lady Rowan's smile was sad. "But some women, some young women who perhaps didn't have a cause, found some level of belonging, of worthiness—possibly even of some sort of connection—in joining together to force young men to join the army. I wonder if they saw it as a game, one in which they scored points for each man intimidated into joining up."

The two women turned simultaneously and began to make their way back toward Chelstone Manor. They walked together in silence for some moments, until Lady Rowan spoke again.

"Aren't you going to tell me why you've come to me with these questions? Why the curiosity about the Order of the White Feather?"

Maisie took a deep breath. "I have reason to believe that the recent deaths of three young women are connected to the white feather movement." Maisie checked her watch.

Lady Rowan nodded, seeming somewhat weary now that the early walk was coming to an end. "That's one more thing that I detest about war. It's not over when it ends. Of course, it seems as if everyone's pally again, what with agreements, the international accords, and contracts and so on. But it still lives inside the living, doesn't it?" She turned to Maisie. "Heavens, I sound like Maurice now!"

They followed the path back to the manicured lawns of Chelstone Manor.

"Will you join me for breakfast, Maisie?"

"No, I'd better be on my way. Before I go, may I use your telephone?"

"You've no need to ask. Go on." Lady Rowan waved Maisie on her way. "And take good care, won't you? We expect to see your Mr. Beale here by the end of the month!"

*Only if I close this case quickly,* thought Maisie, as she ran toward the manor.

<br>

&#9642;

<br>

"*M*iss Dobbs. Delightful to hear from you. I've had another word with Dr.—"

"This isn't about my father, Dr. Dene. Look, I must hurry. I wonder if you can help me. Do you still know Bermondsey well?"

"Of course. In fact, once a fortnight I work at Maurice's clinic for a day or two on a Saturday or Sunday."

"Oh, I see." Maisie was surprised that she didn't already know about Dene's continued connection with Maurice's work. "I need to find a person who may be hiding in Bermondsey. She may be in danger, and I have to locate her soon. Very soon. Do you know anyone who might be able to help me."

Dene laughed. "All very cloak-and-dagger isn't it, Miss Dobbs?"

"I am absolutely serious." Maisie felt herself become impatient with him. "If you can't help, then say so."

Dene's voice changed. "I'm sorry. Yes, I do know someone. He's called Smiley Rackham and he can usually be found outside The Bow & Arrow; it's just off Southwark Park Road, where they have the market. Just make your way along the market until you see a pie 'n' mash shop on the corner, turn on that side street and you'll see The Bow. Can't miss it. Smiley sells matches and you'll recognise him by the scar that runs from his mouth to his ear. It makes him look as if he's pulling a huge grin."

"Oh. Was he wounded in the war?"

"If he was ever in a war, it was probably the Crimean. No, Smiley worked on the barges as a boy. Got an unloading hook caught in the side of his mouth." He laughed, "Knowing Smiley, it was open too wide at the time. Anyway, even though there are lots of new people in Bermondsey now, he doesn't miss a trick. He's a good place to start. He'll cost you a bob or two though."

"Thank you, Dr Dene."

"Miss Dobbs—"

Maisie had already replaced the receiver. She had just enough time to drive to Pembury for morning visiting hours.

***

Maisie was filled with guilt from the time she left Pembury Hospital until she parked the car in Bermondsey. The conversation with her father had been stilted and halting, each searching for a subject that would engage the other, each trying to move beyond a series of questions. Maisie was too preoccupied to speak of her mother. Finally, sensing her discomfort, Frankie had said, "Your mind's on your work isn't it, love?" He insisted that she need not remain and, gratefully, she left the ward, promising that she'd stay longer next time. Next time . . . *He's not getting any younger.* With Maurice's words pounding in her head, Maisie sped toward London. Now she had to locate Smiley Rackham.

The market was a writhing mass of humanity by the time she arrived, and would be alive with people until late at night. Even the women stallholders were dressed like men, with flat caps, worn jackets, and pinafores made from old sacks. They called to one another, shouted out prices, and kept the throng noisy and moving. Maisie finally found The Bow & Arrow. Smiley Rackham was outside, just as Dene had predicted.

"Mr. Rackham?"

Maisie leaned down to speak to the old man. Smiley's clothes, though dapper, as if they had once belonged to a gentleman, had seen much better days. His eyes sparkled below a flat cap, and his stubbled chin dimpled as he smiled. It was a broad smile that accentuated the livid scar so well described by Dene.

"And who wants 'im?"

"My name's Maisie Dobbs," Maisie continued, deliberately slipping into the south London dialect of her childhood. "Andrew Dene said you'd 'elp me."

"Old Andeeee said to see me, eh?"

"Yes. *Andy* said you knew everyone hereabouts."

"Gettin' tricky, what wiv all these Oxford and Cambridge do-gooders comin' in."

Had the situation not been so urgent, Maisie might have grinned. Now she wanted to get down to business. She took out the photograph of Charlotte Waite and handed it to Rackham.

"Course, me old eyes ain't what they were. Probably need to get some glasses." He squinted at Maisie. "Mind you, cost of glasses today—"

She reached into her purse and handed Smiley a shining half-crown.

"Very nice pair of glasses, too. Now then let me see." Smiley tapped the side of his head. "This is where I've got to rack 'em, you know, the old brain cells." He looked at the photograph, brought it closer to his eyes, and squinted again. "Never forget a dial. Got a photographic memory, I've been told. Now then"—Smiley paused—"she looks a bit different nah, don't she?"

"You've seen her?"

"I'm not one 'undred percent. It's me eyes again."

Maisie handed him a florin.

"Yeah. Dahn the soup kitchen. Only been there a coupl'a days, but I've seen 'er comin' and goin'. She weren't all dolled up like this though."

"Which soup kitchen? Where?"

"Not the one run by the Quakers, the other one, on Tanner Street, just along from the old workhouse—" Smiley gave directions.

"Thank you, Mr. Rackham."

Smiley's eye's sparkled. "O' course my name ain't Rackham."

"It isn't?"

"Nah! My surname's Pointer. They call me Smiley Rack'em cos that's what I do." He tapped the side of his head. "But now I won't 'ave to do anythin' for a day or two, thanks to you, Miss Dobbs." Smiley rattled the coins as Maisie waved and went on her way.

She stood for a while just inside the door of the soup kitchen, in the shadows, where she would be able to observe without being seen. There was one large room lined with trestle tables, all covered with clean white cloths. The staff were working hard to maintain the dignity of people who had lost so much in a depression that was affecting every stratum of life. And at the lowest end there was little or no comfort. Men, women, and children queued for a bowl of soup and a crust of bread, then filed to the tables to find a place among known faces, perhaps calling out to a friend, "Awright, then?" or making a joke, even starting a song going for others to join in. Maisie saw that there was something here that money could not buy: Spirit. As she watched, one man at the front of the line began to shuffle his feet in a dance, then clapped out a tune. Everyone started to sing as they waited, so that even in her anxiety to find Charlotte, Maisie smiled.

> Boiled beef and carrots,
> Boiled beef and carrots,
> That's the stuff for your Darby Kel,
> Makes you fat and it keeps you well.
> Don't live like vegetarians,
> On food they give to parrots,
> From morn till night blow out your kite
> On boiled beef and carrots.

Then she saw Charlotte.

It was a different woman whom Maisie watched moving back and forth between the kitchen and the tables, talking to other workers, smiling at the children, leaning over to tousle the hair of a mischievous boy or stop a fight over a toy. Two days. She's been here only two days and people are looking up to her. Maisie shook her head as she watched Charlotte help another worker. *And no one knows who she is.* There was something in the way that Charlotte moved and spoke with the people that reminded Maisie of someone. *A natural and decisive leader.* Charlotte Waite was her father's daughter.

Maisie made her move. "Miss Waite." She touched Charlotte's sleeve as she was returning to the kitchen with an empty cauldron.

"Oh!"

Maisie reached for the pot just in time, and together they placed it safely on a table.

"How did you find me here?"

"That's not important. You wanted to speak to me?"

"Look—" Charlotte glanced around her. "I can't talk here, you know. Meet me when I've finished. I'm on duty until seven, then I go back to my digs."

Maisie shook her head. "No, Miss Waite. I'm not letting you out of my sight. I'll stay here until you finish. Find me an apron, and I'll help out."

Charlotte's eyes grew wider.

"Oh, for goodness' sake, Miss Waite, I'm no stranger to a bit of elbow grease!"

Charlotte took Maisie's coat, and when she returned they began to work together while another refrain from the hungry Londoners echoed up into the rafters.

> I like pickled onions,
> I like piccalilli.
> Pickled cabbage is all right
> With a bit of cold meat on Sunday night.
> I can go termartoes,
> But what I do prefer,
> Is a little bit of cu-cum-cu-cum-cu-cum,
> A little bit of cucumber.

The women left the soup kitchen together at half past seven. Charlotte led the way through dusky streets to a decrepit three-storey house that was probably once the home of a wealthy merchant, but now, a couple of centuries on, had been divided into flats and bed-sitting rooms. Charlotte's room on the top floor was small, with angled ceilings so that both women had to stoop to avoid collision with the beams. Despite being confident in her soup kitchen role, Charlotte was now nervous and immediately excused herself to use the lavatory at the end of a damp and dreary landing. Maisie so mistrusted her charge that she waited on the landing, watching the lavatory door. In those few moments alone she prepared her mind for the conversation with Charlotte. She breathed deeply, and with eyes still closed she visualized a white light shining down on her head, flooding her body with compassion, with understanding, and with spoken words that would support Charlotte as she struggled to unburden herself. *May I not sit in judgment. May I be open to hearing and accepting the truth of what I am told. May my decisions be for the good of all concerned. May my work bring peace. . . .*

Charlotte returned and, stooping, they entered her room again. It was then that Maisie saw a framed prayer on the wall, most probably brought from Camden Abbey to her Bermondsey refuge.

> In your mercy, Lord, give them rest.
> When you come to judge the living and the
> dead, give them rest.
> Eternal rest grant to them, O Lord,
> And let perpetual light shine upon them; in
> your mercy, Lord.
> Give them rest.

Had Charlotte found any rest at Camden Abbey? Were Rosamund, Lydia, and Philippa now at rest? And the killer? Would there ever be rest for all of them?

Charlotte pulled up two ladderback chairs in front of a meager gas fire, and they sat down, neither taking off her coat as the room was far too cold. They were silent for some minutes before Charlotte began to speak.

"I don't know where to begin, really. . . ."

Maisie reached across with her now-warm hands and, taking Charlotte's hands in her own, spoke gently. "Start anywhere; we can go back and forth as we need."

Charlotte swallowed and pursed her lips before speaking.

"I . . . I think the beginning is when I first realized how much my father loved my brother, Joe. It wasn't that he didn't love me. No, it was just that he loved Joe so much more. I think I was quite young. Of course, my mother wasn't there very often. They weren't at all suited, I expect you know that already." Charlotte sat in silence for a few moments, her eyes closed, her hands trembling. Maisie noticed how her eyelids moved, as if conjuring up the past caused her pain.

"It wasn't obvious, it was little things, really. He'd come home from work and, as soon as he saw Joe, his eyes would light up. He'd ruffle his hair, that sort of thing. Then he'd see me. The smile he gave me wasn't so . . . so *alive.*"

"Did you get along with your brother?" asked Maisie.

"Oh, yes, yes. Joe was my hero! He *knew*, I know he knew how I felt. He'd always think up a special game for us to play, or if my father wanted to play cricket with him or whatever, Joe would always say, 'Charlie has to come, too.' That's what he called me: Charlie."

Maisie was silent, then touched Charlotte's hand again for her to continue.

"I don't know when it started to *annoy* me. I think it was when I reached twelve or thirteen. I felt as if I were running a race I could never win and I was out of breath with trying. Of course my mother was firmly ensconced in Yorkshire by then, kept out of the way by my father, who was doing very well in business. New shops were opening, and Joe was always there with him. Joe was seven years older than I and being groomed to take over the business eventually. I remember at breakfast one day, I announced that I wanted to do what Joe was doing, start working for the business, at the bottom, like all the other apprentices. But my father simply laughed. Said that I wasn't cut out for hard work—graft he called it. Not got the 'ands for a bit o' 'ard graft.'" Charlotte mimicked her father's broad native accent perfectly.

"Then he sent me off to Switzerland, to school. It was horrible. I missed Joe, my best friend. And I missed home. But . . . but something happened to me. I've thought about it a lot." She looked directly at Maisie for the first time. "I've really considered what might have happened. I became . . . very detached. I had been pushed away for so long, you see." Charlotte began to stutter. "It *seemed* the best thing to do, to be. If I was going to be the one pushed to the outside, I might as well stay there. Do you understand?"

Maisie nodded. Yes, she understood.

"I made some friends, other girls from the school. Rosamund, Lydia, and Philippa. It was the sort of school where girls were 'finished' rather than educated. I felt humiliated, as if he thought me only good for arranging flowers, buying clothes and knowing how to correctly address servants. Then, when war was declared, we all came home to England. Of course, my father, the great man of commerce"—Maisie noticed the sarcasm in Charlotte's voice—"had already secured government contracts to supply army rations." Charlotte looked up thoughtfully. "It's amazing, when you think of it, the people who do well out of war. My clothing allowance came courtesy of soldiers being fed by Joseph Waite." She looked away and for a while they sat in silence until Charlotte was ready to take up her story again.

"After we'd returned home, the four of us were pretty much at a loose end. We tried knitting scarves, socks, that sort of thing. Rolling bandages. Joseph was working at the warehouse. He'd started off at the lowest rung and at that time was a clerk in receivables. Mind you, he had apprenticed with the butchers, taken the deliveries out, and he was the blue-eyed boy of the whole business. Everybody loved 'Young Joe.'" She mimicked a south London accent, which made Maisie look up suddenly.

"How did you get along with Joe after your return?"

"Very well, actually. When I asked to work for the business and my father refused, Joe stuck up for me, said it would be a good idea, a good example." Once again, she looked into the distance. "He was a wonderful young man, Joe."

Maisie said nothing while Charlotte paused to gather her thoughts.

"So, there we were, young girls with few skills, time on our hands and—for my part—nowhere I seemed to . . . to . . . *belong.*" Charlotte exhaled deeply. "Then I found out about the Order of the White Feather. I saw a bill posted. So I persuaded the others. It didn't take much. We went along to a meeting." Charlotte held out her upturned hands helplessly. "And that was the beginning."

Maisie watched Charlotte. *A natural and decisive leader.*

"Then the game went on, and we were more than willing players. Each day we would venture forth with our little bags of white feathers, and we'd hand them out to young men not in uniform. We each took out an equal number of feathers and when we saw one another later, we'd see if all the feathers were gone. Of course, we thought we were doing the right thing. Sometimes . . . sometimes, I'd walk past an enlistment office and I'd see a young man standing there, or two together, still holding the feathers I'd given them. And I thought, *Oh, good.*"

"No one at home knew what I was up to. My father was busy, always so busy, and Joe was working hard at the warehouse. No one wondered what I might be doing. Joe always asked for me as soon as he came home. I think he knew that I was unraveling. But inside me . . ." —she touched the plain belt buckle of her dress with the flat of her hand— "inside me, I was resentful toward Joe. It was as if I didn't know where to put all the *horribleness* that was festering inside me. It was like a disease, a lump." A single tear slid down her cheek. "Then, one day, I thought of a way to get back at him—my father—and to get Joe out of the way for a while. The trouble was, I didn't *think.* I didn't think that it would be forever."

Silence descended. Maisie rubbed her upper arms with hands that had become cold once again. *May I not sit in judgment.*

"Go on, Charlotte."

Charlotte Waite looked at her. Some might have thought the woman's posture arrogant, Maisie knew that she was searching for strength.

"I suggested to the girls, to Rosamund, Lydia, and Philippa, that we should try to place feathers in the hands of as many young men as we could. And I also suggested a means of accomplishing the task. The warehouse, which employed so many young men—the runners, the drivers, the packers, the butchers, clerks . . . an army, in fact—was run in shifts, with a bell sounding for the change between each shift. It was my plan for the four of us to wait outside the gates when the shifts changed, to hand out feathers." Charlotte put her hand to her lips together, then plunged on. "We handed a feather to each and every man who walked from the warehouse, regardless of age or job. And when we had done that, we went to the main shops, as many as we could get to in a day, and did the same thing. By the time my father found us, I'd handed out all but one of my feathers." Charlotte's chin dipped. "He drew alongside us in the motor car, with another motor following. The door opened, and he was furious. He instructed the chauffeur in the other car to take Rosamund, Lydia, and Philippa to their homes, and he grabbed me by the arm and almost threw me into the motor." Opening her eyes, Charlotte looked again at Maisie. "You are no doubt familiar, Miss Dobbs, with the wartime practice of men enlisting as 'pals'—men who lived on the same street, worked with one another, that sort of thing?"

Maisie nodded.

"Well, Waite's lost a good three-quarters of its workforce when the men joined up as pals within a week of our handing out the feathers. Waite's Boys, they called themselves. Joe was one of them."

Maisie's attention was drawn to Charlotte's hands. The nails of one had dug into the soft flesh of the other. Her hand was bleeding. Charlotte covered the wound and began speaking again.

"My father is a quick thinker. He saw to it that the families knew that the men's jobs would be there for them upon their return. He offered wives and daughters jobs, with the promise that they would be paid a man's wages and he saw to it that each man who enlisted was sent a regular parcel from Waite's. He's good at taking care of the families, my father. The trouble is, none of that compassion extended to me. The workers thought he was marvelous, a real patriarch. There were always parties for the children, bonuses at Christmas. And all through the war, Waite's kept going, doing very well."

Without thinking, Charlotte inspected her bloody hand and wiped it along the side of her coat. "And they were all lost. Oh, a few came home, wounded, but most of them were killed in action. Joe died. He's buried over there." She looked into Maisie's eyes again. "So, you see, we—I—killed them. Oh, I know, you might say that they would have been conscripted sooner or later, but really, I know that we sent them off to their deaths. Counting the parents, the sweethearts, the widows, and the children, there must be a legion of people who would like to see the four of us dead."

In the silence that followed, Maisie took a fresh handkerchief from the pocket of her tweed jacket. She held it between Charlotte's hand and her own, pressed their palms together, and closed her eyes. *May I not sit in judgment. May my decisions be for the good of all concerned. May my work bring peace.*

aisie insisted that Charlotte accompany her back to Ebury Place. It was too dangerous for her to be left alone in Bermondsey. They said little on the drive across London, which included a detour to Whitechapel where Charlotte remained in the MG while Maisie called upon Billy briefly to ask him to meet her at the office the next morning. Sunday was to be another working day, and an important one.

Confident that Charlotte would not abscond now, Maisie settled her into a guest suite on the same floor as her own rooms, before finally finally taking rest. It had been a very long day and would be a long night as her plan, which must be executed soon, took shape. It was past ten o'clock when she went to the library to telephone Maurice Blanche. She heard only one ring before her call was answered.

"Maisie!" Maurice greeted her without waiting to hear her voice. "I have expected your call."

Maisie smiled. "I thought you might."

They both knew that Maisie needed to speak with her mentor when a case was nearing closure. As if drawn by invisible threads, they each leaned closer to their respective telephone receivers.

"I was speaking with Andrew Dene this morning." Maurice continued.

"Oh—did he telephone to talk about my father?"

"No, actually, he came here this morning."

"Oh?" Maisie was startled.

Maurice grinned. "You are not the only pupil who comes to my house, Maisie."

"Well, yes, of course." Maisie was glad that Maurice could not see the blood rising to her cheeks.

"Anyway, Andrew came to see me about several things, including Mr. Beale."

"And?"

"Nothing of great concern, simply a discussion of how we may best help the man."

"I see."

"I expect he'll be here shortly, in the next day or so?"

"Yes. When this case is closed."

"So, Maisie, I sense that as far as your assignment is concerned, the case is already closed. You have found Charlotte Waite?"

"Yes. Though Mr. Waite insisted that her return to his home in Dulwich would be the point at which he would consider our work complete."

"And when will that be?"

"I will be meeting Billy at the office tomorrow morning. The three of us will take a taxi-cab to Dulwich."

"You have another plan, don't you, Maisie?"

"Yes. Yes, I do"

Maisie heard Maurice tap out his pipe and the rustle of a packet of sweet Old Holborn tobacco. Maisie closed her eyes and envisaged him preparing the bowl, pressing tobacco down, then striking a match, holding it to the tobacco and drawing on the stem to light the fragrant leaf. Maisie breathed in deeply, imagining the aroma. In that moment she was a girl again, sitting at the table in the library at Ebury Place, reading aloud from her notes while her teacher paced back and forth, back and forth, then, holding the bowl of the pipe in his right hand, pointed at her and asked out loud, "Tell me what evidence you have, upon which to base such conclusions."

"So, what else have to to tell me? And where, if I may ask, are the police?" asked Maurice.

"Charlotte has confessed her part in bringing about the enlistment of a good number of her father's employees, including her older half-brother, Joe, who was the apple of her father's eye." Maisie drew breath deeply and told Maurice the story that she had first heard from the warehouse manager and then from Charlotte. "She believes herself guilty of a crime."

"I take it that you do not consider Charlotte capable of murder."

"I am sure she is not the killer, though she may be the next victim."

"And the man in custody, the man the police believe to be the murderer?"

"I believe him to be innocent of the crime of murder. He may not be a good man . . . but he did not kill Rosamund, Philippa, and Lydia."

"Stratton seemed a fair man in the past. Has he not heard your protests?"

As they spoke, Maisie felt, not for the first time, a sensation of oneness with the mind of her teacher, an intimacy of intellect and understanding, even as he quizzed her. "Detective Inspector Stratton has brought his prejudices to the case. He lost his wife in childbirth and was left with a son. His inner turmoil has clouded his usual sound judgment. The man he believes to be the killer—Magnus Fisher—is an unlikable character, one who has not treated women fairly. Indeed, he admits that he married Lydia Fisher for her money."

"Ah, I see."

"I've tried to communicate my suspicions to him on several occasions, to no avail. Stratton will not believe that Fisher is not the guilty man until I hand him the real murderer on a plate."

"Yes, yes indeed." Maurice drew deeply on his pipe. "And you plan to trap the killer, do you not?"

Maisie nodded. "Yes, I do."

Maurice began to speak once more. "Tell me about the means of death again, Maisie."

"Sir Bernard Spilsbury has concluded that poison was administered, which Cuthbert has identified as morphine. In two of the cases the victim's death was followed by a brutal stabbing."

"The weapon?"

"The bayonet from a short-barrel Lee Enfield rifle."

Maurice nodded. "The killer venting his fury after the death of his victim."

"Yes."

"Interesting."

"Anger, pain, suffering . . . loneliness," said Maisie. "There's quite a cocktail of motives there to be going on with."

"Charlotte is right, Maisie. It could be any one of a hundred people."

"One hundred people might have reason for vengeance, but not every one of those people would seek revenge in such a way. The killer is a person tormented day in and day out, one for whom there is no respite, not for one minute in twenty-four hours. And that person has discovered, tragically, that in meting out punishment, there has been no escape from the terrible ache of loss. The killer isn't just anyone in that mass of grieving relatives, Maurice. No, it's one person in particular."

Maurice nodded. "And you know who it is, don't you?"

"Yes. I believe I do."

"You will take all necessary precautions, Maisie."

"Of course."

"Good."

They were silent for a moment, then Maurice spoke quietly. "Be wary of compassion, Maisie. Do not let it blind you to dangers. Never let pity gain the upper hand. I know this killer must be stopped, that he may not feel that his pain is assuaged even if he kills Charlotte. He may go on killing thereafter. We have together faced great dangers,

Maisie. Remember all that you have learned. Now then—go. You must prepare for tomorrrow. It will be a long day."

Maisie nodded. "I'll be in touch as soon as it's over, Maurice."

Before finally seeking the comfort of her bed, Maisie once again put on her coat and hat and slipped out of the house, remembering her mentor's counsel when they first worked together: "When we walk, and when we look out at a view other than one we are used to every day, we are challenging ourselves to move freely in our work and to look at our conclusions from another perspective. Move the body, Maisie, and you will move the mind." As she walked the quiet night-time streets of Belgravia, Maisie realized that in his final words to her, Maurice had made an assumption, an assumption that was quite wrong.

$\mathcal{S}$he had spent hours in silent meditation and was now ready for what the next twenty-four hours might hold. Before taking a light breakfast in the kitchen, where Sandra confirmed that she had personally served breakfast on a tray to Miss Waite in the guest suite and had run a bath for her, Maisie placed a telephone call to the Waite residence. In the kitchen, she went over her other arrangements before knocking on the door of Charlotte's room.

"Good morning." Charlotte answered the door.

"Are you ready, Miss Waite?"

"Yes."

"Well, let's get on then, shall we? It's time we left. I will meet you by the front door in twenty minutes."

It was ten o'clock when they arrived at the Fitzroy Square, which was Sunday quiet. As they drew up alongside the Georgian building that housed Maisie's office, Billy crossed the square.

"Oh, good timing," said Maisie. "My assistant has arrived. He is part of my plan, and will be going with us to Dulwich."

Maisie formally introduced them and, once in the office, Billy reached out to take Charlotte Waite's coat. Maisie removed her jacket and hung it on the back of the door.

"Let's get down to business. We should leave by one. That should give us enough time to be absolutely sure of each step." Maisie beckoned Charlotte to join her and Billy at the incident table. A large sheet of paper had been placed where a case map would usually have been unfurled and pinned. "Here's what we're going to do." Maisie took up a pen, and began to explain.

During the conversation that followed, Charlotte excused herself twice and each time Billy stood outside the office door until she returned, to ensure that she did not leave the building. These were the only interruptions until Maisie pushed back her chair and walked over to the telephone on her desk. She dialed the Waite residence in Dulwich.

"Hello. Maisie Dobbs here. I want to confirm that all necessary arrangements have been made for Miss Waite's arrival home this afternoon." Charlotte and Billy looked on as Maisie listened. "Indeed, yes, I spoke with Mr. Waite early this morning and I know that he was just about to leave for Yorkshire. Back on Tuesday, isn't he? Yes, good. Do remember, though, Miss Waite does not wish to see anyone and no one must be informed of her arrival. Yes, she'll go straight to her rooms and I will remain there with her until she is settled. Quite. Yes. No, absolutely no one. Good. Right you are. Thank you." Maisie replaced the receiver and turned to Billy.

"Time to get us a taxi cab, Billy."

Billy reached for his coat. "Back in two shakes of a lamb's tail, Miss."

As Billy closed the door behind him, Maisie turned to Charlotte. "Now then, you are clear on what you are to do?"

"Of course. It's simple, really. You're the one taking all the risks."

"As long as you know that when you do your part, you must not be recognized. It's imperative."

"And you think it'll—you know—all be over in a few hours?"

"I believe the murderer will strike again quickly."

Billy returned, flushed with exertion.

"Billy, I've told you not to run!"

"Miss, the taxi cab's outside. Better get going."

They climbed into the taxi cab but were silent throughout the journey, each mentally reviewing the part to be played as the evening unfolded. Upon arrival at Waite's Dulwich mansion, Billy took Charlotte's bag.

"All right?" Maisie put her arm around Charlotte's shoulders and led her toward the house. Charlotte's head was lowered, with only a few strands of hair visible beneath her close-fitting gray hat.

"Yes. I won't let you down."

"I know."

The door opened before they reached the bottom step leading up to the front door, and Maisie nodded acknowledgment to Harris as she hurried Charlotte inside.

"Thank you. We'll go straight to Miss Waite's rooms."

The butler bowed, inclined his head to Billy as he came though the doorway with Charlotte's bag, then followed the two women upstairs.

"Billy, wait outside this door until I come for you."

"Right you are, Miss." The door to Charlotte's rooms closed behind him as Billy took up his place.

Maisie took off her coat, then her hat, followed by her blouse. "Hurry, I want you to leave as soon as possible."

Charlotte began to undress. "I . . . I'm not used to . . ."

Maisie pointed to the bathroom. "Go in there, undress, leave your clothes behind and use your dressing gown."

Charlotte scurried into the bathroom, while Maisie removed the rest of her clothing. After several moments, Charlotte opened the door and came into her small sitting room again. Maisie pointed to the pile of clothes on the chair.

"Now, put those on and pull some strands of hair free. I'll be out in a minute."

She dressed as swiftly as she could. Her hands were cold and she found it hard to work the buttons at the front of Charlotte's dress. Perhaps she didn't really need to wear Charlotte's clothes, but in case someone looked up at the sitting room from the garden, she must be prepared. It would be Billy who had to take care not to be seen.

Returning to the sitting room, Maisie gasped. "Oh, my . . . if I didn't know better"

"Your clothes fit me very well, Miss Dobbs."

"And the hat seems to be a good size for you, too."

Charlotte smiled. "I . . . I should thank you—"

Maisie held up her hand. "Don't say anything . . . not yet, anyway. This day is far from over. You know what to do next?"

"Yes. I have to return directly to Number 15 Ebury Place. Sandra is expecting me and will remain with me at all times until you return."

"And you must not leave your room. Is that understood? You must stay with Sandra!" Maisie spoke quietly but urgently.

"I understand, Miss Dobbs. But what about my father?"

"One step at a time. One step at a time. Right, are you ready?"

Charlotte nodded.

"Good." Maisie opened the door and beckoned Billy into the room.

Billy looked from Maisie to Charlotte Waite and back again. "So, this is it, then?"

"Ready, Billy?"

"I'm ready." Billy reached for the door handle. "You know, there's one question I've been meaning to ask you, Miss Waite?"

Charlotte looked first at Maisie, then back at Billy. "Yes, Mr. Beale?"

"Did you 'ave two address books, you know, one what was old with all your addresses in, and another what you left behind?"

"Why . . . yes, yes I did. I took the old one with me, because I never did get used to the new one. It was so empty, it made me feel as if I didn't really know anyone."

"Thought so. We'd better be on our way now." He turned to Maisie. "Take care, Miss."

The light was beginning to fade. Maisie watched from the window of Charlotte's sitting room as they left, noticing how Charlotte had straightened her spine. The small rear lights of the taxi-cab were extinguished as it drove toward the gatehouse. She knew that she had taken a chance with Billy; his weak leg rendered him a questionable asset. But she was forced to ask him to return surreptitiously to the Waite mansion. She needed a witness, someone on her side, and did not know how far the household could be trusted. If only Stratton had been open to another view—but he had not.

Maisie's eyes were drawn to the dove-cote, where it seemed for just a second that she saw movement in the evening shadow. Something stirred again, and a few doves flew up. Maisie watched the ghost-like flapping of wings in the twilight sky as the doves circled before swooping down to return to their home for the night. When she looked at the dove-cote again, the shadow was gone. She knew that, disguised as Charlotte Waite, she had cause to fear. Entering the bedroom, Maisie closed the curtains then walked across to the bed. Drawing back the counterpane and bed linens, she pulled off the pillows and repositioned the long bolster so that it seemed as if the bed were occupied.

*The oldest trick in the book—let's hope it works.* She turned on the dressing-table lamp and scanned the room before reopening the curtains; then she surveyed her handiwork from the door. *Yes. Very good.*

In the sitting room, Maisie was reaching for the curtains when she heard a soft knock at the door. She did not answer. There was another gentle knock, then a woman's voice.

"Miss Waite? Miss Waite? I thought I'd come to see if you'd like a cup of tea. Miss Waite?"

Maisie breathed a sigh of relief. She sat in silence. A minute passed before she heard steps receding along the hallway. She checked her watch, the one accessory she had not relinquished. Billy should be back soon. She sat in the same chair she had occupied on her initial visit to the rooms, when she had first felt Charlotte's lingering fear and sorrow. And she waited.

Another knock at the door. She listened carefully, for if all had gone well, Billy should have returned by now.

"Miss Waite? Miss Waite? Can you hear me? What about a bowl of thick chicken-and-dumpling soup? You need to keep up your strength, Miss Waite."

Maisie was silent, listening. When at last footsteps receded along the hallway for a second time, Maisie realized that she was indeed in need of sustenance. Opening Charlotte's bag, she took out a bottle of lemonade and a sandwich. To maintain absolute silence, she went into the tiled bathroom to eat and take a few sips of lemonade.

It was now completely dark outside. Had she been wrong to anticipate that the murderer would strike again quickly? Time passed slowly.

Ten o'clock. Another knock. Maisie tensed.

"Miss Waite? Miss Waite? You must be gasping for a nice cup of tea and something to eat by now. As you don't want to see anyone, I'm leaving a tray outside the door. There's a pot of tea and some macaroons. They're fresh from the oven, I made them especially for you."

The tray was set down. Retreating footsteps indicated that the corridor was now empty. Very slowly Maisie turned the key and handle and pulled the tray inside. She closed and locked the door behind her, then set the tray down on the table next to the wing chair.

Maisie lifted the lid of the teapot and sniffed the Earl Grey, strong with the smell of bergamot. *Yes.* Then she crumbled the fresh macaroon, still warm and filled with the aroma of almonds. Simple attempts to disguise a toxic feast. Taking up the pot, she poured a cup of tea, added milk and sugar, swirled the liquid around then went to the bathroom to pour all but a few dregs into the sink. She poured away half of the tea in the pot, so that the provider would think she had taken two or three cups. Then, leaving the door to the bedroom ajar, she dropped the cup and saucer to the floor, spilling what poison-laced tea was left across the carpet. She was so close to the window that her silhouette could be seen from the gardens so, knowing that there was an observer, she half-staggered across the bedroom and fell onto the bed. Once there, Maisie rolled sideways onto the floor and crawled to the corner, where she took up her hiding place behind the wardrobe. From this vantage point she could see the doorway and the bed. Her only concern now was for Billy's arrival.

She waited.

Just at the point when she thought a leg cramp was becoming unendurable, a key turned in the lock of the main door to Charlotte Waite's suite of rooms. Maisie held her breath. A light footfall stopped at the chair; then came a clinking sound as the intruder reached for the fallen china and set it on the tray. She heard the lid being taken off the teapot, then replaced. Another moment passed, footsteps came closer and Maisie crouched lower as a long shadow unfolded across the floor when the door opened wide.

She swallowed and, in the tension of the moment, feared that the person who had come to kill Charlotte Waite might have heard her. Once again she held her breath and watched as a hand was held high with blade ready. The killer moved toward the bed, then lost all control and screamed to the heavens. Doubling over, she keened so deeply and with such passion, that even her shadow seemed to emit a deep guttural cry. She sobbed as only a mother can, her whole body given over to the grief and rage of one who has lost her children. Again and again she rammed the bayonet home into what she believed to be the already cold body of Charlotte Waite.

The killer slumped to the floor, her chest heaving, her lungs gasping for air. Maisie moved to her side, knelt and pulled the woman to her, holding her close while taking the bayonet from her limp, unresisting grasp.

"It's all over now, Mrs. Willis. It's all over. It's over,"

# CHAPTER TWENTY-TWO

"Miss!" Billy snapped on the light, kneeling awkwardly beside Maisie. He pulled a handkerchief from his pocket and carefully removed the bayonet from her hand.

"Miss, I couldn't get back in again. I tried, but there was too—"

"Never mind, Billy. Summon Stratton immediately. Go now, but first make sure that bayonet is somewhere safe!"

When Billy returned, Maisie had already helped Mrs. Willis into the sitting room, seating her in Charlotte Waite's wing chair. She was calm, but her eyes were dull as she stared in front of her.

"He's coming right over. They telephoned 'im at is 'ome, Miss, and 'e's on 'is way."

There was time to sit with the woman who had taken three lives and would have taken a fourth. Billy stood by the door, Maisie kneeling beside Mrs. Willis, who sat gazing into the fire Maisie had lit for her comfort. The scene might have reflected a young woman visiting a favorite aunt.

"I'll hang, won't I, Miss Dobbs?"

Maisie looked into the glazed eyes of the woman leaning forward in Charlotte's wing chair

"I cannot second-guess a jury, Mrs. Willis. When the whole story is told, they may find grounds for mercy. You may not even be considered fit to stand trial."

"Then they'll send me away."

"Yes. You will lose your freedom."

Mrs. Willis nodded, her lips forming a crooked smile. She gazed into the flames. "I lost my freedom a long time ago, Miss Dobbs."

Maisie remained still. "I know."

"They *killed* my whole family. All except my youngest, and he's as good as lost to me."

"Yes." Maisie knew that now was not the time to raise the issue of nuances, of what might have happened anyway, after conscription.

"It seems if it were yesterday." Mrs. Willis looked up at Maisie. Billy came a little closer so that he, too, could hear.

"My Frederick was a master butcher. Had worked for Waite's for years. We were young when we got married. I fell for our eldest straight away; honeymoon baby, that's what they called him. Our Anthony. Oh, he was a love. Soft, was Tony. If that boy saw a bird in the street that couldn't fly, well, it would be in the kitchen with a saucer of bread and milk before you knew it. Then a year later came Ernest. Different kettle of fish altogether, that Ernest. . . ." Mrs. Willis smiled as she looked into the past.

"Ernest was a little tyke. If there was mischief, then you could bet Ernest was in the middle of it. But Tony was there to put him right, and as much as they were chalk and cheese, they were always together. Always. Then came Wilfred, Will, our youngest. Loved books, loved to read. And so thoughtful, you'd have supposed he was in a dream half the time. The neighbors said I was lucky, to have three boys who got on so well. Of course there were times that they had a bit of a dustup. Like puppies, tumbling all over each other until Frederick had to go out and take each of them by the scruff of the neck. He was a big man, my Frederick. He'd end up there with them, wrestling in the garden with them all over him. People said I was born under a lucky star, with my boys."

Billy had moved even closer. In the distance, Maisie heard the main gate open, and the crunch of tires as Stratton's Invicta motor car made its way to the front of the house. Another vehicle followed, presumably the van that would transport Mrs. Willis. She motioned to Billy to stand by the door, ready to prevent a noisy entrance by the police

"Well, first Tony went to work at Waite's, then Ernie went, and Will last." Mrs. Willis brought her gaze back to Maisie. "Mr. Waite liked having families work for the company, said it was good for morale for sons to learn from their fathers. He was doing the same thing, with young Joseph." She stared silently

"Go on." Maisie could hear voices in the corridor, which then subsided as Billy met the police. When Billy, Stratton, and a newly-minted woman police constable stepped into the room, Maisie raised her hand to stop them. Mrs. Willis continued her story, oblivious to the new arrivals.

"Then one day Tony came off his shift, very down at heart. Not like himself. Ernie and Will came home, didn't say much. Went straight upstairs. I could hear the three of them talking, but I thought something had happened in the warehouse, you know, a bit of trouble, something like that. Frederick wasn't there that day, he'd gone to the abattoir. Mr. Waite liked one of his master butchers to go there, to check up, to make sure work was being done to the highest standards."

Mrs. Willis paused. Maisie's eyes met Stratton's. He was prepared to wait.

"You know, I can't say as I know quite what happened next. It was as if one minute there we were, going along nicely, this lovely little family. We weren't well-off, not by any means, but we got by with a bit of room to spare, 'specially now that the boys were bringing something home. Then it all changed. Tony and Ernie came home the next day—they'd been very quiet—and they'd joined up. Enlisted! Their father and me, we just couldn't believe it. Everything crumbled, my house crumbled. Frederick said that he couldn't have his boys joining up without him to look after them. He was still a young man, really. Not even forty. He was too old on paper, but the enlisting office wasn't that picky, as long as you were a fit man. Joined up with them, he did, and of course, they were together with all the other men and boys who'd enlisted from Waite's." Mrs. Willis looked up into Maisie's eyes again. "And do you know, the thing was that I still didn't know then what had caused it all, what had made them run off and do it. Frederick said it was that being a soldier made them feel big, that they were still so wet behind the ears, they didn't know what it was really all about. I don't think any of us did."

Mrs. Willis fell silent. The WPC moved toward Mrs. Willis, but Stratton placed a hand on her arm.

"It was Will that told us. Mind you, word had already started to go around, about the Waite girl and those friends of hers with their little white feathers. Stupid, stupid, stupid girls." She balled her fists and pounded her knees. Tears began to flow again as she spoke. "Frederick told Will—I can see him now, standing in the doorway on the day they left, all in uniform, a little family army marching off to war—'You look after your mother, my boy. You stay here and do the work for me and your brothers.'" She placed a hand on her chest. "But the silly little beggar wouldn't listen. Too young by half, he was, too young by half. He had to go and join up, didn't he? Said that no one called the Willis men cowards, that if his dad and brothers were over there, then he'd go too. Oh, I wish his father had been there to stop him. 'You'll be all right, Mum, Mr. Waite will look after you, all the families will be all right. Then we'll all be home again before you know it.' But they weren't. Even Will, he might have come home in body, but he never came home to me again, not as my Will." Mrs. Willis slumped forward, crying into her hands. Maisie moved to her side. "I lost them all, I lost them because of those wicked, wicked girls. And . . . and . . . I just couldn't bear it anymore. I just couldn't bear the . . . the . . . ache. . . ."

Maisie was aware of the silence of the group watching, but did not look back. She placed a comforting arm around Mrs. Willis.

"It was like a knife through my heart," the woman sobbed. "The man came with the telegram, and at first I couldn't do a thing. I couldn't hear, couldn't even breathe. I just stood there like I'd been frozen." Mrs. Willis pressed her hand to her heart. "The man said, 'I'm sorry, love' and there I was, completely alone. I was in a daze, a terrible daze, with this flimsy piece of paper in my hand, wondering, Which one? *Which one?* Then the knife went in, right there. And it happened three times; three times I was stabbed, and then again when I saw the state Will was brought home in. And the pain hasn't stopped since . . . right here, right here. . . ." The woman pounded her chest and struggled for breath.

Maisie closed her eyes and remembered the last three names commemorated in hand-made tiles above the door of Joseph Waite's shop on Oxford Street: Frederick Willis, Anthony Frederick Willis, Ernest James Willis. She spoke softly, yet took care to ensure that Stratton could hear all that was said.

"Is that why an overdose of morphine wasn't enough?"

Mrs. Willis nodded. "I drugged them first. I wanted them to hear, before they died. I didn't want them to walk away or ask me to leave. I wanted them to die as they listened to me tell them about my boys. I wanted them to know *why*, and I wanted it to be the last thing they heard on this earth. God only knows what my boys heard."

"And then you left the white feathers behind?"

"Yes. I left them behind. If their spirits lingered, I wanted them to linger in torment. I wanted them to be reminded. I wanted them to suffer as my boys suffered, as all those boys suffered, and as their people at home suffered. I wanted them to be between this world and the next, never at peace. Never, ever at rest." Exhausted, Mrs. Willis leaned into Maisie's arms and wept.

As Maisie held the grieving woman to her, she lifted her head and motioned for Stratton and the WPC. Passing the weight as gently as one would hand a new baby back to its mother, Maisie allowed the WPC and Stratton to help Mrs. Willis to her feet. As Maisie joined Billy, she noticed moisture in his eyes. She touched his arm.

"S'awright, Miss. I'm awright."

Mrs. Willis mustered the strength to stand tall while Stratton formally cautioned her and as the three moved toward the door, she stopped in front of Maisie.

"Would you look in on my Will, Miss Dobbs? He won't even know I'm not there. I think my visiting is just for my sake, really. But I'd like to know that someone is looking out for him every now and again."

"Yes, of course, I'll visit, Mrs. Willis."

"Me, too. I'll go, too," added Billy.

Two constables stationed outside the door accompanied Mrs. Willis and the WPC to the idling vehicles. At the far end of the corridor, a cadre of staff waited, all of whom reached out to touch Mrs. Willis as she passed. Two more constables waited for orders to secure the crime scene.

"I owe you an apology, Miss Dobbs," said Stratton.

"I think the apology must go to Magnus Fisher. And perhaps to John Sedgewick." Stratton nodded, and for a moment neither knew quite what to say.

"And once again, I must offer my congratulations. I'll also have to ask you to come down to the Yard to make a formal statement."

"Of course."

"And you, too, Mr. Beale."

"Right you are, Detective Inspector. Oh, and by the way . . ." Billy reached over to the fire irons and took out the bayonet. "Couldn't think of where else to put it. But like I mentioned to you before, Miss, my old mum always said that it was 'ardest to find something 'idden in plain view."

# CHAPTER TWENTY-THREE

*B*illy was loath to leave his family, and Maisie despaired of ever getting him to Chelstone. But he finally acquiesced, and on the first Monday in May, Maisie parked the MG at Charing Cross station and accompanied him to the platform.

"Thanks for bringing me to the station, Miss. Don't think I would have left Doreen and the nippers if you 'adn't."

"It won't be long until you see them again, Billy. And it's for the best."

Billy pulled change from his pocket to buy a newspaper. "Look at this, Miss." Billy pointed to the front page, "I dunno, there's this young lady, Amy Johnson, flying off to Australia on 'er own—twenty-six she is—and goin' in a little aeroplane, if you please. And here I am, scared of going down to Kent on the train."

Maisie placed her hand on Billy's shoulder. "Never judge a journey by the distance, Billy. Your journey, from the time you went over to France, has demanded bravery of a different kind—and I admire you for it."

*M*aisie drove to Joseph Waite's house in Dulwich after seeing Billy off. It was a fine day, one that was welcome after the fiercely cold Easter. It seemed to presage another long hot summer, perhaps to rival the previous one. Maisie had dressed in summer clothes for the first time that year, and wore a new pale gray suit, with a hip-length jacket and mid-calf skirt with two small kick pleats at the front and back. Simple black shoes matched a new black hat made of tightly woven straw with a gray ribbon joined in a flat rosette at the side—at two guineas the hat had been an extravagant purchase from Harvey Nichols. The jacket had a shawl collar, a style that Maisie favored, even though it had been more fashionable several seasons earlier.

She parked according to the usual instructions, and smiled as the door opened and Harris inclined his head in greeting.

"Good morning, Miss Dobbs. I trust that you are well?"

"Yes, very well, thank you very much, Harris."

The butler smiled and a moment passed when neither knew quite what to say next. Maisie took the lead.

"Have you seen Will this week?"

"Oh yes, Miss Dobbs. Two of the maids went on Sunday afternoon, and I expect to go on Thursday, my afternoon off."

"How is he?"

"The usual, Miss. The usual. He seemed a little confused when new people turned up to take him into the gardens, but settled down again quickly. We can let his mother know that he's not been forgotten."

"Yes, of course."

"Will you visit him, Miss Dobbs?"

"I promised Mrs. Willis that I would, so I'll see him when I next visit my . . ." Maisie stopped speaking for a second as an image of Simon came to her, not as he was now, but as a young man. "When I next visit my friend."

The butler indicated the library's open door.

"Mr. Waite will be with you shortly."

"Thank you."

Maisie walked over to the library window, which commanded a broad view of the gardens and the dove-cote. The white birds flew to and from their home, cooing as they settled again, perched among their kind.

"Good morning, Miss Dobbs." Joseph Waite closed the door behind him and offered her one of the chairs by the fireplace. He waited until Maisie was seated, then settled into his own chair.

"How are you, Miss Dobbs?" he asked.

"I'm well, thank you. Is Charlotte settling in comfortably?"

"Yes, she seems to be."

"Have you spent much time with her, Mr. Waite?"

Joseph Waite shifted uncomfortably in his chair.

"I know this is a difficult time for you, Mr. Waite—"

"You think this is difficult? I lost my son, you know."

Maisie allowed a moment for Joseph Waite's still pent-up anger to settle, and watched as the tension he felt coursed through him. Unmoved, she was determined to continue.

"Mr. Waite, why did you instruct your staff to tell me you were not at home when I came here for our previous appointment?"

Joseph Waite twisted the diamond ring on his little finger, the ring that had caught the sun so easily as he reached out to feed doves at his windowsill.

"I . . . I don't know what you're talking about."

Maisie settled into the chair, a move that caused Joseph Waite to look up.

"Yes, Mr. Waite, you know very well what I'm talking about. So please answer my question."

"I don't have to take this! Just give me your account and—"

"With respect, Mr. Waite, I risked my life in this house, so I will be heard."

Waite was silent, his face flushed.

"The truth is that you kept your daughter in this house because you feared for her life. Your grief and anger over what she had done when she was but a foolish young girl festered, but your love for her caused you to keep her close."

"*Hmmmph!.*" Waite looked away.

"You thought that if she lived alone, she would be in danger." Maisie paused. "So you insisted that she, a grown woman, live at home. You didn't even trust a potential husband to keep her safe, did you? Yet, though she was under your roof, you could not forgive her."

Waite was restless and again fidgeted in his chair. "You don't know what you're talking about. You have no idea what it's like—"

"You gave Mrs. Willis a job as soon as her family went to war. You felt her predicament so keenly that you asked her to come to your home to work as your housekeeper. You paid for Will's care, so that she would never have to worry. And you watched her bitterness grow. But you thought that as long as she, too, was under your roof, you would be in control. When Rosamund and Philippa were murdered, you suspected Mrs. Willis, but you didn't do anything about it. Was it because you felt as angry and aggrieved toward them as she did?"

Waite placed his head in his hands, but still he did not speak. Maisie continued.

"When Charlotte disappeared you wanted her back, for you believed that Mrs. Willis would not strike at her in your home. It was only close to the end that you became unsure. Though the three deaths were terrible, you did not grieve for those families. Your all-consuming rage at what the women had done was still as sharp as a knife in your side. But if Charlotte was taken from you, too . . ."

Waite shook his head. "I couldn't go to the police. I had no evidence. How could I point the finger at a woman who was broken already, whose family had given their all for my business and for their country."

"That decision, Mr. Waite, is subject to debate. You'd visited each woman a few years after the war, to give them a piece of your mind. But it didn't afford you much relief. Anger still gnawed at you, along with the terrible grief at losing Joe."

"Your final account please, Miss Dobbs. Then leave."

Maisie did not move. "What are you going to do about Charlotte, Mr. Waite?"

"It'll all work out."

"It hasn't worked out in fifteen years, and it won't work out now unless both you—particularly you—and Charlotte embrace a different idea of what is possible."

"What do you mean? You come here with your fancy ideas—"

"What I mean is this: Resentment must give way to possibility, anger to acceptance, grief to compassion, disdain to respect—on both sides. I mean change, Mr. Waite. Change. You've remained a successful business-man by embracing change, by mastering it, even when circumstances were against you. You should know exactly what I mean."

Waite opened his mouth as if to argue, but then fell silent, staring into the coals. Several minutes passed before he spoke again. "I respect you, Miss Dobbs, that's why I came to you. I don't believe in buying a dog and barking myself. I pay for the best, and I expect the best. So say your piece."

Maisie nodded and leaned forward, forcing Waite to look at her. "Talk *with* Charlotte, not *at* her. Ask her how *she* sees the past, how she feels about losing Joe. Tell her how you feel, not only about your son, but about her. Don't expect to do it all at once. Go for a walk every day in that big garden of yours where the grass is never disturbed by a footprint, talk a little every day, and be honest with each other."

"I don't know about all this talking business."

"That's quite evident, Mr. Waite." Maisie continued while she had his ear, "And give her a job. Ask Charlotte to work for you. She needs a purpose, Mr. Waite. She needs to stand tall, to do something, to gain some self-respect."

"What can she do? She's never done—"

"She's never had the chance. Which is why neither of you know what she is capable of accomplishing, of becoming. The truth is that from the time she was a girl you knew which of your two children had it in them to succeed you, didn't you? Joe was a lovely young man, as everyone who knew him agrees, but he didn't quite have what it takes to be the leader your company needs, did he? And though you love Charlotte, you wanted Joe to be the leader so much that you stifled her spirit and she floundered."

"I don't know . . ." Waite struggled. "It's too late now."

"No, it isn't. Experiment, Mr. Waite. If one of your grocery items doesn't sell in the front of the shop, you put it in another place, don't you? Try that with Charlotte. Try her in the offices, try her out on the shop floor, have her check quality. Start her at the bottom, where she can show her worth to the staff as much as to you—and to herself."

"I suppose I could."

"But if you really want to blaze a trail, Mr. Waite, you'll put her where she can do some good."

"Whatever do you mean?"

"Joseph Waite is known for philanthropy. You give away surplus food to the poor, so why not put Charlotte to work on distribution? Make your contributions into a job and allow her work her way up. Let her prove her mettle, and give her a means to earn respect."

Joseph Waite nodded his head thoughtfully, and Maisie knew that the canny businessman was three steps ahead already, was envisioning capitalizing on her advice in ways that even she could not imagine. She fell silent. Joseph Waite looked at her directly. "Thank you for bringing Charlotte home. And for being frank. We might not always like what we hear but, where I'm from, folk value honest talk, plainly spoken."

"Good." Maisie stood up, reached into her document case and pulled out a manila envelope. "My final account, Mr. Waite."

Over the summer months, Maisie traveled to Chelstone each weekend, to spend time with Frankie and to see how Billy had progressed. A generous bonus from Joseph Waite allowed her the financial leeway to enjoy her father's company for longer periods of time. In addition, Waite retained Maisie's services for her continuing counsel in rebuilding the relationship between Charlotte and himself.

For his part, Billy regained strength and movement in both legs, each week meeting with the practitioner who instructed him in exercises and movements to counteract the lingering effects of battlefield injury.

"What 'e says, Miss, is that I'm increasing my core."

"Your core?" Maisie watched Billy brush out the mane of Lady Rowan's latest purchase, a bay mare with an enviable track record, now out to grass and ready for breeding.

"Yep, me core. Makes me sound like a Cox's Orange Pippin, don't it?" Billy curried the horse's mane, continuing with his work as he spoke. "There are all these different exercises, some to stretch me legs, some me arms, and me middle, and some of 'em are really small movements right 'ere." Billy pointed to his stomach with the curry comb. "Which is me core."

"Well, it seems to be doing you a lot of good. I saw you walk across the stable yard with barely a limp."

"The main thing is that the pain ain't what it was. Of course I 'ave to go over for these little chats with Dr. Blanche, and then there's Dr. Dene, who comes up to see me every now and again, you know. And of course, 'e sees yer dad as well."

Maisie felt her face flush, and she looked at the ground. "I would have thought that Dad didn't need any more checkups from Dr. Dene, not with the doctor coming up from the village."

Billy secured a lead rein to the mare's halter, and they walked outside into the sunshine.

"I think Dr. Dene likes to see Dr. Blanche, so 'e drops in on yer dad. Asks about you every now and again, 'e does."

"Asks about me?" Maisie shielded her eyes.

Billy grinned, then looked around as tires crunched on the gravel and a new Austin Swallow came to an abrupt halt at the far end of the courtyard, close to the Groom's Cottage.

"Well, talk of the devil, there's Dr. Dene now."

"Oh!"

"Miss Dobbs. How very nice to see you here. And Mr. Beale, still making good progress, I see."

"Yep, doing very nicely, thank you, Dr. Dene. Wasn't expecting to see you today."

"No, I'm on a flying visit to see Maurice." He turned to Maisie. "Stroke of luck meeting you, Miss Dobbs. I've to come up to London soon, for a meeting at St. Thomas's. I wondered if you would join me for supper, perhaps a visit to the theater."

Maisie blushed again. "Um, yes, perhaps."

"Righty-o, I'll get on the dog-and-bone when I'm up there." Andrew Dene shook hands with Billy again, executed a short bow in front of Maisie, then turned and sprinted in the direction of the Dower House.

"Don't mind me sayin' so, Miss, but 'e's a bit of a cheeky one, ain't 'e, what with the old rhymin' slang and all. Where did 'e learn that then?"

Maisie laughed. "Bermondsey, Billy. Dr. Dene's a Bermondsey boy."

Now that her father was well on the way to a full recovery, and Billy's sojourn in Kent almost at an end, it was time for Maisie to complete the ritual of bringing a major case to a close in the way that she had learned from Maurice. In visiting places and people pertinent to the case, she was honoring her teacher's practice of a "full accounting" so that work could move on with renewed energy and understanding. First she visited Hastings again, spending time with Rosamund Thorpe's housekeeper, who was busy packing belongings now that the house had been sold.

"I've found a very nice little cottage in Sedlescombe," said Mrs. Hicks. Maisie had declined to come into the house, respectful of the task of packing up to begin a new life. Now she strained to hear the woman's soft voice which was drowned by the seagulls wheeling overhead. "Of course, I'll miss the sea, people always do when they leave the Old Town, not that many do."

Maisie smiled and turned to leave, but Mrs. Hicks reached out to her.

"Thank you, Miss Dobbs. Thank you for what you did."

"Oh, please, don't—"

"You know, I always thought that I'd see Mrs. Thorpe's killer hang and not feel a shred of pity about it. But, I feel terrible for that woman. Terrible. They say she probably won't hang, that they'll send her away. Mind you, if it was me, I'd *want* to be dead. I'd want to be with my family."

*L*ater, when Maisie pulled up outside the Bluebell Avenue house in Coulsden, which John Sedgewick had shared with his wife, Philippa, a 'For Sale' sign was flapping back and forth in the breeze, and Sedgewick was working in the garden. He brushed off his hands and came to greet Maisie as soon as he saw her opening the gate.

"Miss Dobbs, I am so glad to see you!"

"Mr. Sedgewick." Maisie held out her hand, which Sedgewick took in both of his.

"How can I ever thank you?"

"Please, there's no need."

"Well, thank you for finding out the truth." Sedgewick placed his hands in his pockets. "I know that what Pippin did was wrong, but I also know that she was a good person. She tried to make up for it."

"Of course she did, Mr. Sedgewick. I see you're moving."

"Oh, yes. Time for a complete change, a very complete change. I've accepted a position in New Zealand. There's a lot of building going on there, so chaps like me are rather welcome."

"Congratulations. It's a long way, though."

"Yes, it is. But I had to do it, make a clean break. It's time to go, no good staying here and moping. In any case, this is a street for families, not widowers. They say that change is good for you."

"Good luck, Mr. Sedgewick. I'm sure you'll find happiness again."

"I hope so, Miss Dobbs. I do hope so."

*T*hough she walked by the mews house owned by Lydia Fisher, she did not ring the bell. The upper windows were open, and she could hear a gramophone playing at a volume that showed no consideration for neighbors. A woman laughed aloud, and even from the street below Maisie could hear the clink of glasses. She thought of the vaporous loneliness that had seeped into every piece of furniture, every fabric in Lydia Fisher's home, and whispered, "May she rest in peace."

*T*he red brick of Camden Abbey seemed almost aflame against a seldom-seen blue sky that graced the Romney Marshes, but a chill breeze whipped across the flat land to remind all who came that this was pasture reclaimed from the sea. Once again Maisie was led to the visitor's sitting room where, instead of tea, a small glass flagon had been placed on a tray with some milky white cheddar and warm bread. Dame Constance was waiting for her, smiling through the grille as she entered.

"Good afternoon, Maisie. It's lunchtime, so I thought a little of our blackberry wine with homemade bread and cheese might go down well."

Maisie sat down opposite. "I don't know about wine, not when I have to get behind the wheel again soon. I think I should beware of your Camden Abbey brews."

"In my day, Maisie—"

Maisie raised a hand. "Dame Constance, I confess I wonder how they ever let you in, what with the things you did in your day."

The nun laughed. "Now you know the secret of the cloister, Maisie, we only take people who know the world. Now then, tell me how you are. We are not so isolated that we know nothing of the news here, you know. I understand that your investigations met with success."

Maisie reached toward the flagon and poured a small measure of translucent deep red wine. "I find the word 'success' difficult to apply to this case, Dame Constance. Yes, the murderer has been brought to justice, but many questions linger."

Dame Constance nodded. "People assume that we have a head start on wisdom in a place such as this, where women gather in a life of contemplation, a life of prayer. But it isn't quite like that. Wisdom comes when we acknowledge what we can never know."

Maisie sipped her wine.

"I have come to wonder, Maisie, if our work really *is* so different. We are both concerned with questions, are we not? Investigation is part of both our lives, and we are witnesses to confession."

"When you put it like that, Dame Constance—"

"We both have to avoid making personal judgments and we are both faced with the challenge of doing and saying what is right when the burden of truth has been placed on our shoulders."

"My job is to look hard for the clues that evade me."

"And you have learned the lesson, no doubt, that while looking hard for clues in your work, you may be blind to the unanswered question in your own life. Or you may be providing yourself with a convenient distraction from them."

Maisie smiled in acknowledgment as she sipped again from the glass.

Stratton was restrained as usual during their long-postponed lunch at Bertorelli's. He did not repeat his regret at failing to listen to her theory, though they could not help but discuss the case.

"Has Mrs. Willis told you yet where she obtained the morphine?" asked Maisie.

Stratton rested his right forearm on the table and ran a finger around the rim of his water glass. "Various sources. There was an attempt to procure some from the hospital in Richmond, but she was disturbed"

a nurse just as she was entering the nurses' office. Of course they couldn't prove anything, but they became rather more vigilant regarding the security of medicines. Some of her supply came from—you will never believe this—the belongings of a maiden aunt who had passed away earlier this year. Mrs. Willis found several of those tins of morphine in phials that were once so fashionable among the ladies, and easily purchased. Though old, the substance had lost none of its strength. She bought some from a chemist, and also used the deceased Mr. Thorpe's supply. Morphine can take a long time to do its work, but she was lucky—if you can call it that—in rendering her victims helpless enough to hear what she had to say before administering a fatal dose."

"And the bayonet."

"Street market."

Maisie shook her head.

They were quiet, and for a time Maisie wondered whether Stratton might talk about his son, but when he spoke again it was of a business matter, an offer that rather surprised her.

"Miss Dobbs. You must have read the news, in the papers about two weeks ago, that there's a new Staff Officer in charge of the Women's Section at the Yard."

"Yes, of course. Dorothy Peto."

"Yes. Well, she's suggesting all sorts of changes, including women being posted to the Criminal Investigation Department. I was wondering if you might be interested. You know, I could put in a word—"

Maisie held up a hand. "Oh no, Inspector. Thank you all the same, but I prefer to work alone, with only Mr. Beale to assist me."

Stratton smiled. "Just as I thought."

Conversation idled as lunch came to a close, though Stratton's demeanor had changed, becoming warmer.

"I wonder," he said, "If you would care to join me for supper, perhaps. I was thinking of next Wednesday evening, or Thursday."

Very clever, thought Maisie. Wednesday didn't have the significance of Friday, not when it came to a man asking a woman out to dine. "Thank you for the invitation, but I . . . I'll let you know. My assistant

returns to work next week. He's been taking time for a special course of therapy to ease a troublesome war wound. I have much to do before he comes back."

Stratton rallied quickly. "Then may I telephone you on Tuesday afternoon?"

"Of course. I'll expect to hear from you, then."

Maisie heard the telephone in her office ringing even before she opened the front door, and hurried up the stairs before the caller lost patience.

"Fitzroy five—"

"Is that Miss Maisie Dobbs?"

"Speaking."

"Andrew Dene here."

"Good afternoon, Dr. Dene."

"So glad to have reached you. I'll be up in London early next week. That meeting at St. Thomas's? It was postponed, but now it's on again. Look, I wonder, would you care to have supper with me, say, Wednesday or Thursday?"

Maisie quickly ruffled some papers on her desk. "Let me see . . . I'm really quite busy at the moment. Could you give me a ring on, oh, Tuesday afternoon?"

"Right you are, Miss Dobbs. I'll telephone you on Tuesday. Until then."

"Yes, until then."

She replaced the receiver.

*M*aisie stood by the window on Wednesday morning waiting for Billy Beale to return to work. She rubbed the back of her neck and paced to the mirror, checked her appearance for the one hundredth time since her visit to Bond Street the previous afternoon. Time for a change. She thought of Simon. Yes, though she would continue to visit, probably forever, it was time to move on, to set her cap for . . . whatever fate might bring her way.

Turning to the window again, she saw Billy round the corner, walking briskly. *Yes.* With a spring in his step and barely any sign of a limp, Billy Beale made his way across Fitzroy Square, tipping his cap at a woman walking with her children, and—she was sure of this—whistling as he walked. *Yes.* He was the old Billy again. *Good.* Just before he reached the front door, Billy stopped in front of a flight of pigeons that had gathered to pick at the flagstones. He shook his head, then carefully made his way around the birds before running up the steps and polishing the brass nameplate with the underside of his sleeve before entering.

Maisie listened. The door closed with a loud thump and Billy whistled his way up the stairs. She rubbed at her neck again as the door swung open.

"Mornin' Miss, and ain't it a lovely—blimey!"

"Good morning, Billy. It's good to have you back, even though you've brought some rich language with you."

"You've . . . you've changed."

"Thank you for being so observant, Billy. That's what you're paid for." Maisie touched her hair.

"I mean, Miss, well, it's a bit of a shock, innit? But it suits you, really it does."

Maisie looked at him anxiously. "Are you sure? You're not just saying that, are you, Billy?"

"No, Miss. Even though my Dad always said that a woman's 'air is 'er crownin' glory. It suits you, makes you seem more . . . sort of modern."

Maisie walked to the mirror again, still surprised to see her reflection, with her hair cut into a sharp bob.

"I just couldn't stand all that hair any more, especially the bits that always flew out at the sides. I wanted a change."

Billy hung his coat on the hook at the back of the door and turned back to Maisie. "Now all you need is somewhere nice to go."

"Well, I *am* going out for supper tonight."

"Supper?" said Billy with a mischievous grin. "Now, Miss, I thought you said you didn't dine out in the evenings because supper meant something more than lunch."

Maisie laughed. "I changed my mind."

"I 'spect it's with Dr. Dene. 'e's up here this week for 'is meetins, ain't 'e?"

"Yes, I believe he is."

"Or is it the Detective Inspector?"

"Now then, Billy."

"Go on, Miss, you can tell me."

"No, Billy, I can't. Let's just say that it's something for me to know and you to deduce. And talking of powers of deduction, I've just taken on an interesting new case."

# ACKNOWLEDGMENTS

My friend and writing buddy, Holly Rose, was the first to read *Birds of a Feather* and I am ever-grateful for her support, honesty, insight and enthusiasm. My agent, Amy Rennert is a powerful blend of friend, mentor and coach—and is the best. Thanks must also go to my editor Laura Hruska and to everyone at Soho Press—a terrific publishing team.

I am indebted to my Cheef Resurcher (who knows who he is) for the hours spent among dusty old copies of *The Times* and for his invaluable counsel on the history of the inner workings of "The Yard." Any wide turns with fact and procedure may be attributed to the author who will gladly repay his hard work with a few bottles of the peaty stuff.

My parents, Albert and Joyce Winspear, have once again been wonderful resources regarding "old London" and have also entertained me with their renditions of Cockney ballads via long-distance 'phone calls.

Kenneth Leach, to whom this book is dedicated, was the foundation-stone of my education. It was in his classroom, when I was ten, that I first heard the Great War story that inspired *Birds of a Feather*. He was a great teacher and a very dear person.

To my husband, John Morell: Thank you for being my numero uno fan—and for scouring used bookstores for even more sources for me to draw upon in my quest to bring color and depth to the life of Maisie Dobbs.

Every writer should have a dog and I have Sally, my constant companion while I'm working, along with her friend, Delderfield, a completely idle cat.